# SISTER, MAIDEN, MONSTER

# SISTER, MAIDEN, MONSTER

## LUCY A. SNYDER

NIGHTFIRE

TOR PUBLISHING GROUP
NEW YORK

SISTER, MAIDEN, MONSTER

Copyright © 2023 by Lucy A. Snyder

All rights reserved.

A Nightfire Book
Published by Tom Doherty Associates / Tor Publishing Group
120 Broadway
New York, NY 10271

www.tornightfire.com

Nightfire™ is a trademark of Macmillan Publishing Group, LLC.

Library of Congress Cataloging-in-Publication Data

Names: Snyder, Lucy A., 1971– author.
Title: Sister, maiden, monster / Lucy A. Snyder.
Description: First Edition. | New York : Nightfire, 2023. |
"A Tom Doherty Associates Book."
Identifiers: LCCN 2022040601 (print) | LCCN 2022040602 (ebook) |
ISBN 9781250825650 (trade paperback) | ISBN 9781250825667 (ebook)
Subjects: LCGFT: Novels.
Classification: LCC PS3619.N936 S57 2023 (print) |
LCC PS3619.N936 (ebook) | DDC 813/.6—dc23/eng/20220829
LC record available at https://lccn.loc.gov/2022040601
LC ebook record available at https://lccn.loc.gov/2022040602

Our books may be purchased in bulk for promotional,
educational, or business use. Please contact your local bookseller
or the Macmillan Corporate and Premium Sales Department
at 1-800-221-7945, extension 5442, or by email at
MacmillanSpecialMarkets@macmillan.com.

First Edition: 2023

Printed in the United States of America

0  9  8  7  6  5  4  3  2  1

*For Erica M., Jaymie W., and Carol S.*
*Here's a toast to surviving our own personal apocalypses*

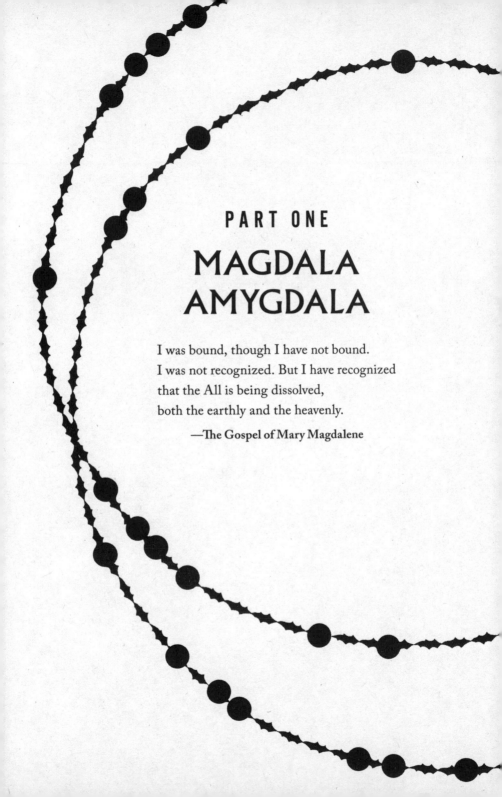

# PART ONE

# MAGDALA AMYGDALA

I was bound, though I have not bound.
I was not recognized. But I have recognized
that the All is being dissolved,
both the earthly and the heavenly.

—The Gospel of Mary Magdalene

# CHAPTER 0

It was only Tuesday evening, and I was already bone-tired. Wrung out. I stepped through the front door of our apartment, peeled off my white disposable KN95 filter mask. Dropped it in the small beige plastic trash bin my boyfriend, Gregory, had mounted on the wall. Squirted hand sanitizer into my palms and rubbed the stinging gel all over my hands and wrists. The alcohol burned inside my nose. I rolled my neck and shoulders to work some of the stiffness out. Unbuttoned my green wool peacoat and hung it and my purse on the coatrack.

I blamed my exhaustion on stress and anxiety. Last week, the world had gotten the worst Valentine's Day present ever: a new pandemic called PVG. Polymorphic viral gastroencephalitis. It had popped up in London, Tokyo, Hong Kong, Toronto, Honolulu, Los Angeles, Seattle, New York City, and Mexico City at roughly the same time, which made finding Patient Zero (if he or she existed) a challenge. Nobody knew yet where it had come from, exactly how it spread, or what it was likely to do in the long run. All anyone knew for sure was that it was landing people in the hospital with scary symptoms.

Someone on CNN described it as "the stomach flu on nightmare mode," but apparently it wasn't an influenza virus. Or a rotavirus or a norovirus, everyone's favorite cruise ship plagues. It was something new and strange. Our governor hadn't declared a mask mandate yet, but many of us instinctively fell back on the protective measures we'd learned during the coronavirus years.

It was a relief to be home. Home felt safe. The outside world? Not so much. Even though Gregory and I had built a pretty cozy space for ourselves, I hated the idea that we might be in for months of depressing isolation and shitty delivery food. Months of mostly only getting to see the world secondhand, through screens. I silently prayed that the disease would burn itself out quickly.

"Erin, is that you?" It sounded like he was in the dining room.

"Nope, I'm a burglar." I hung my keys on one of the brass hooks below our coupon-plastered corkboard. "I'm here to steal your Funko Pops."

"You're early! I was expecting the robbery around six thirty." His tone was cheerful but held an anxious edge.

"Yeah, there wasn't much traffic this evening." It occurred to me that I'd just touched my keys, which I'd previously handled with possibly contaminated hands . . . so I gave myself another sanitizer squirt. We were probably going to have to buy the stuff by the gallon before this was over. Hopefully there hadn't been a huge run on the stock at Costco yet.

I continued: "It looks like most of the other companies on the West Side have already shifted to work from home."

My company was headed that direction, too, but it would be another week at least. Universal Corporate Computing had a huge, stegosaurian bureaucracy; change came slowly, when it came at all.

"That's cool . . . but don't come in here yet!" I could hear the scrape and clack of him shuffling china plates. "And don't look down the hall! Just, uh, look at your feet or something."

"Okay . . ." I stared down at my black Chuck Taylors and shucked them off with my toes.

A bright pink business card on the floor below the trash bin caught my eye. I picked it up. The card had an all-over design of fuchsia roses on a light pink background. It bore only a name— Savannah—and a local phone number. No business name, no address.

I didn't have much time to wonder about the card, or to think to apply yet more hand sanitizer, because Gregory gave a triumphant "Ha! Done!" and rushed into the foyer, his white shirt-sleeves rolled up and his shirttails half out over the belt of his khakis. A brown substance I hoped was chocolate was smeared on his breast pocket.

"Don't look!" He blocked my view of the dining room, waving his arms like he was playing defense in a pickup basketball game. "Cover your eyes, please."

"Uh, sure." The alcoholic goo hadn't quite dried on my hands, so I tucked my upper face into the crook of my arm. Pandemic dabbing.

He took me by the elbow and led me down the hall. As I stepped from carpet to the vinyl planks of our dining room, I smelled soy sauce and burning candles.

"Okay, open!" he declared proudly.

I dropped my arm and beheld our small dining room table decked out in fresh red roses and pink carnations, gold-and-silver streamers, and candles. A glittery gold HAPPY 5TH ANNIVERSARY! banner hung from the wall. Amidst the table decorations was a big platter of fresh sushi decorated with edible blossoms, two place settings from the good china set he'd inherited from his grandmother, lacquered red chopsticks, tall wine flutes, and a dewy green bottle of Riesling from Schaff's Winery. Their vineyards were south of the city, and we'd gone on a tour there the first weekend we spent together, when we first started dating.

"Ta-da!" He spread his arms wide. "Are you surprised?"

I stared at the table, confused. "But our anniversary isn't until next week."

Then panic surged in my throat. Oh God. Had I gotten the dates mixed up? I'd ordered him a new tablet, but it wouldn't arrive for a bit. "It's not our anniversary *today*, is it?"

He laughed and said reassuringly, "No, our anniversary is next week. You're fine. But it wouldn't have been much of a surprise if I threw this the day of, would it?"

"No, I guess not." I stared at the table, feeling a little stunned. And deeply touched. None of my previous boyfriends had ever done anything like this. Not even my family had thrown me a big party like this for my birthdays, not since I'd turned ten. Part of me was thrilled, but another part awkwardly wondered if all this was really for me or if I'd suddenly crossed over into the life of some other, more fortunate woman. "Wow, you went all out."

"Ope!" He'd noticed his shirttail was flopping loose, so he quickly tucked it in, smoothed his short brown hair, and then pulled my chair out for me.

I sat down, absently setting the rosy business card on the table by my plate. "The sushi looks great." There had to be at least ninety dollars' worth of artfully sliced rolls and sashimi on the platter. Mostly salmon, tuna, and barbecued eel. My favorites.

"I got it at a new place called Oiwai Sushi." He smiled. "My boss took our team there for lunch last week. I was really impressed with their tako sashimi. It was nice and firm and fresh. Not watery and limp." He made a face. "The last time I got it at Hibachichan, it was really disappointing. Like it had been frozen and thawed a couple of times."

"Yeah, they seem to have gone downhill since their chef quit."

"Well, you know me . . . I like to support good places. Especially when it looks like they might be in for a rough ride."

"Yeah." I used my chopsticks to grab a couple of pieces of salmon sashimi for my plate. Perfect glossy rectangles of orange fish secured to plump mounds of rice with savory seaweed bands. My mouth was watering in anticipation. "So many good restaurants went under last time . . . I hope that doesn't happen again."

"Your words to God's ears," he said. "Anyhow, let's talk about something more cheerful. How was your day?"

"Pretty good, all things considered. I ran into Mareva Buduci in the lunchroom today and we got to chat about the new Spider-Man movie for a bit before I had to get back. That was fun."

"She the one you hit it off with at the Christmas party?"

I nodded. Mareva and I had bonded over the new megacephalopod species scientists had recently discovered in the Pacific, when she overheard me geeking out about it. She had a life sciences degree, too, but had gone further and started her Ph.D. I envied her a little for that, even though she'd had to quit for health reasons. "Yep. Nerds of a feather!"

He poured me some wine. "You gonna ask her to hang out after work sometime?"

"Maybe." I took a sip. It was just as sweet and crisp as I remembered. "Right now, it seems like a bad idea to make any social plans."

He nodded slightly, looking pensive. "It's hard to know how careful everyone is, or where they've been."

The cryptic pink business card on the table caught my eye again.

"Speaking of going places . . ." I picked up the card and flashed it at Gregory. "Where the heck is this from?"

He stared at the card for a moment, his expression unreadable. Then he rolled his eyes and smiled sheepishly. "Oh, that. That's just trash. I was thinking of getting you a massage, and went around to a half dozen places to check them out. After the virus news broke, I tossed all the business cards I picked up. Must have missed the bag with that one."

"A massage would have been nice." I smiled and put the card down. "But honestly, I'm just as happy with wine and sushi."

"Well, this isn't *all* of your present. Though the rest isn't exactly a present. I mean, there's cake for dessert. But the other thing. I mean. Wait. I'm babbling, aren't I? Sorry." He rubbed his palms on his khakis as if to wipe sweat off them, looking nervous and excited.

I nodded, confused. "It's okay, honey. But what do you mean?"

He cleared his throat, stood up, and smoothed the front of his shirt. Took a deep breath, stuck his hand in his pocket, and strode around the table to me.

"What are you—" I began.

He pulled a red velvet box out of his pocket and got down on one knee beside me.

"Will you marry me?" He opened the box to reveal a glittering, expensive-looking engagement ring. A large, sparkling square diamond flanked by two smaller diamonds on a burnished gold band. At least, I figured they were diamonds. The way they caught the light was mesmerizing.

I was stunned into absolute silence for a moment. Sure, I'd assumed that after five good years, Gregory and I were in it for the long haul, but we'd never really talked about formalizing things. After having spent my teens and college years dating casually indifferent boys and men who mostly all thought a fancy date meant going to Olive Garden, I'd never expected to be the recipient of a grand, romantic proposal like this. I hadn't imagined it, not once. My brain just didn't know how to process what was happening.

"Wow," I finally said, still staring at the expensive-looking ring.

His face fell a little. "If you don't like it, I can exchange it. We can go look at rings together. I know I should have had you pick out something you like, but it was hard to do that and make this a surprise—"

"No, it's great," I assured him. I'd never been especially girly, and since I seldom wore jewelry, I knew close to nothing about it. The ring was pretty, and it wasn't ostentatious. "It's *perfect*."

He beamed up at me. I scooted my chair around, took his face in my hands, and kissed him deeply.

When we both came up for air, I said, "But."

He looked nervous again. "But what?"

"But . . . what brought this on? I mean, we haven't talked about marriage. Don't get me wrong, I'm not opposed! I just . . . want to know what's happened to change your mind."

He took a deep breath. "First, I love you, and I want the whole world to know. But the other thing is . . . the pandemic could last years, like it did before."

"We don't know that for sure." I definitely wasn't connecting the dots on what he was telling me yet.

"I know. But hear me out. During those years, one of the worst parts—for me, anyway—was feeling like I couldn't make any plans. Like I didn't have anything to look forward to. And I want us both to have that. I want us to plan a cool wedding together, and an even cooler honeymoon. I want us to get a house together. A house with a real yard, where you can have an amazing garden. We could have a kid. Maybe a couple of kids. If you want! We could start with a puppy or kitten first. Probably should, in fact."

He paused anxiously. Tears welled in his eyes. "I mean, if you want all that with me."

My heart seemed to melt into warm, pink, sugary goo in my chest. "I do want that with you."

"So you'll marry me?"

"I will."

"So, try the ring on! Try it on!" He was adorably excited.

"Okay," I laughed. "Put it on me, then."

He carefully extracted the ring from the white satin crease and tried to slip it on my finger. It wouldn't go past my second knuckle. "Uh-oh. I guess I should have picked a size eight."

I laughed again. "It's fine. We can go out this weekend to exchange it, right? I promise you, it's the thought that counts."

— • • —

After we finished our wine and sushi, we went to the bedroom to fool around for a while, then put on our robes and came back out to have dessert. Gregory had gotten an amazing red velvet cake layered with vanilla cream and covered in chocolate ganache. We both had two huge slices, and afterward I was glad we'd gotten busy before dessert, because I was nearly too stuffed to move.

"Oof," I said. "That cake feels a lot bigger than it looked."

Gregory surveyed the tableau of dirty plates. "Well, I should attempt to clean this up before my sugar coma hits."

I started to get up. "I can help you."

He waved me off. "This was my gift to you. Not much of a gift if you have to do dishes at the end, right? And besides, it won't take long."

"Do you mind if I call my family to tell them the news?" I asked.

"I don't mind at all." He smiled at me. "Like I said, I want the whole world to know I love you."

I got up, planted a kiss on the top of his head, and went to get my phone from my purse. On my way into the foyer, I realized that an itchy, stabby pain was building behind my eyes. I felt a little warm, too. Probably I'd had too much wine and the wine had too many sulfites in it. Oh, well. I took a couple of ibuprofen in the kitchen, then went into the bedroom to make my calls.

I had a moment of indecision. Who should I call first, my father or my sister? I didn't have any other family left to tell. My long-gone grandparents were all only children, and so were my parents.

My mother died of pulmonary fibrosis when I was a junior at Northwestern and Claire was working on her MFA in fine arts at RIT. A long-haul complication of a stupid, random flu infection that just kept getting worse every year. Mom fronted that everything was fine, pretended that the steroids were working and she wasn't slowly suffocating. My parents' logic for hiding how sick she'd gotten? We kids needed to focus on college. Her dying was so *distracting*. They didn't want me doing something that might endanger my future, like abandoning my classes in the middle of the semester so I could come home to be with her during her final weeks. And I'm sure it was also a matter of their own denial: If they admitted to us that she wasn't long for the world . . . well, by default they had to admit it to themselves, didn't they?

Claire and I both took her death pretty hard, and instead of pulling us together as a family, like you'd see in some heart-warming Hallmark Christmas movie, it created uncomfortable distances. We were upset with Dad that he'd kept the truth from us, and we both collapsed into depression and withdrew from each other. Claire buried herself in her art and anger and made some brilliant pieces, but I mostly hid under the covers. Nearly flunked out.

The three of us still loved and cared about one another, but Mom's death hurt us all too much, I supposed, even after a decade. Time just hadn't done a very good job of healing the wounds. I hoped that maybe someday we'd all get back to a better place as a family.

Claire frequently opined that men all low-key suck as romantic partners and I should date women instead. But she seemed to like Gregory well enough anyway. So I decided to call her first.

But the phone went to her voice mail: *"Hey, this is Claire. I'm probably in the garage blowing glass, or Liz and I are out gardening. Leave a message."* In the background of the recording, I could hear one of her Yorkshire terriers yapping for attention.

"Hey, it's me," I said. "Got some great news . . . Gregory and I are going to get married whenever it's safe to have a ceremony. I hope you'd like to be in the wedding. Matron of honor? No pressure. But let's talk about it. Please call me back!"

I ended the call. Pain spiked behind my left eye, and my stomach churned sourly. Ugh, the sushi, wine, and cake were *not* sitting well. I got a bottle of Pepto from the linen closet, took a disgusting thick pink shot, and dialed my father in Leander, Texas. He still lived in the house Claire and I had grown up in. The house our mother died in.

"Hello, young'un!" It sounded like he was on the old landline in the kitchen; I could hear the white noise of the vent fan and the pop and crackle of something frying. "What's new with you?"

"Hey, Dad." I sat down on the bed. "I just wanted to tell you that Gregory and I are going to get married. He proposed this evening!"

"Well, that's fine news! I'm so pleased to—"

Whatever he was about to say was cut off by the panicky beeping of his smoke alarm. The screechy noise made my skull throb.

"Grease fire! Gotta go!" His shout felt like an ax in my forehead.

"Call Saturday?" I gasped.

"Yup. Love ya!" He hung up.

A sharp cramp hit me like a baseball bat in the gut.

"Shit!" I curled up on my side on the bed, hugging my knees, hoping the cramp would pass. It did not. The increasing pain made my eyes water. It felt like a glob of lava boiling in my stomach. The heat of it spread up my neck into my skull, making the pounding behind my eyes ten times worse. Tears rolled down my cheeks. My whole body broke out in a sweat and I started to shiver. Magma leaked out of my stomach, into my intestines. A searing bolus snaked through my gurgling bowels.

Oh Jesus. Bad fish? The sushi had seemed so fresh. Damn it. I sat up, shrugged out of my fluffy purple robe—no good in getting vomit or diarrhea all over it—and stumbled into the bathroom.

I flinched when I turned on the light and saw myself in the mirror. My face and chest had turned a bright, fevered red. My eyes were glassy, the whites deeply bloodshot, like I'd just smoked an entire bowl of Purple Haze. My blue irises had gone nearly white.

Another cramp made me double over and curse in pain. A tear dripped off my nose, onto the white tiles, and splattered red between my feet. Blood. I was crying *blood*. What the hell?

*This isn't food poisoning,* a little voice warned in the back of my head. But I quickly pushed the thought away. No. I'd been so *careful*. It couldn't be PVG.

Vomit rose in my throat. I barely had time to lunge for the

toilet and fling the lid up before I hurled. Pepto-pink chunks splattered into the bowl as I gagged. Acidic rice stuck in my sinuses, burned. I broke out in a sweat again, and my trembling muscles felt like they were turning to overcooked noodles.

I groaned, swore, and barfed again. This time it was dark red. The cake, I guessed.

My vision was starting to blur, and it felt like all I could do to cling to the toilet. Shivering. Thank God we'd cleaned the bathroom a couple of days before so I wasn't sitting naked in pee splatter and hair. And I hadn't shit myself yet. Small mercies.

I heard Gregory step into the bathroom and cross the tiles.

"Honey, are you okay in here?" It sounded like he was a few feet behind me. "Oh, you poor thing! Do you want me to hold your hair?"

I nodded, moaning. He knelt beside me, gently gathered my sweaty brown hair at the nape of my neck, and pulled sticky strands away from my face.

"Thank you," I tried to say, but instead I vomited copiously into the bowl. Red. So much red. As scarlet as the anniversary roses on the dining room table. I didn't eat *that* much cake, did I?

Then I realized I was smelling iron.

Gregory froze beside me. "I think that's blood. I think that's a *lot* of blood."

He dropped my hair, stood up. Backed away. "I—I'm going to get you some help."

*Please don't go I'm so scared,* I wanted to say, but I was throwing up again, purging the remains of the expensive anniversary dinner. Painfully bleeding out through my throat. Dying. I was sure of it.

The bathroom seemed to be spinning, and my vision was going dark at the edges. I was distantly aware of the hiss of a spray can, the medicinal smell of Lysol. Gregory urgently pleading with the 911 operator.

I lost consciousness right as I lost control of my bowels. So I have no idea what it was like, lying there helplessly in my congealing blood and sour filth on the cold tiles while my fiancé paced in the living room, waiting for the emergency squad.

It was the last mercy the universe would grant me for quite a while.

# CHAPTER 1

"So how are you feeling today, Erin?" Dr. Shapiro's pencil hovers over the CDC risk evaluation form clamped to her clipboard. Her expression is unreadable behind her disposable blue mask.

I fiddle with the elastic ear loops of the mask in my lap. "Pretty good, I guess."

When I talk, I make sure my tongue stays tucked out of sight; I've learned to speak around it reasonably well. At least I no longer slur my words like I'm drunk. I smile at her in a way that I hope looks friendly and not like I'm baring my teeth. The exam room mirror reflects the back of the good doctor's head. Part of me wishes the silvered glass were angled so I could check my expression; the rest of me is relieved that I can't see myself.

Nothing existed before this. The present and recent past keep blurring together in my mind. Days and months both somehow seem like weeks in my memory. I've learned to take a moment before I reply to questions, speak a little more slowly to give myself the chance to sort things out before I utter something that might sound abnormal. My waking world seems to have been taken apart and put back together so that everything is just slightly off, the geometries of reality deranged.

"Are you able to sleep?" Dr. Shapiro shines a penlight in my eyes and nostrils and marks off a couple of boxes. Thankfully, she doesn't ask to see my tongue. Bad enough I have to glimpse the thing in my bathroom mirror when I'm brushing my teeth. Revulsion and shame burn deep in my chest if I have to show it to anyone else. Even when it's for strictly medical reasons, in front of someone who's probably seen fifteen far more grotesque things just that morning.

I got a brutal case of genital warts after I slept with Gregory for the first time. He was absolutely mortified, but there was nothing he could do. (Not-so-fun fact: There's still no routine human papillomavirus test for men. A guy can be collecting strains like they're Pokémons and have no idea he's about to give his new girlfriend warts or cancer or both.) One wart was this dime-size prickly thing that looked like a pink and gray table saw blade embedded in the opening of my vagina. Obviously I had to get the nasty thing cut out, but my company's new health plan didn't cover the gynecologist I'd been seeing for years. Going into the new doctor's office, which was entirely decorated with photos of adorable infants, felt like the worst, most embarrassing walk of shame I'd ever done in my life. That it cost $900 after insurance was just the cherry on the shit sundae.

My tongue is so much worse than that damned growth in every way . . . it's hard to even compare the two. (Although, yes, the tiny circular teeth growing inside its weird pores do remind me of the wart's spines.) And it's not going away, no matter how much green tea I drink or how conscientious I am about seeing my physician.

Dr. Shapiro asks me the same set of questions every week, straight off the CDC checklist. Surely, she's certainly got them all memorized by now, but she keeps her eyes on her clipboard unless I ask her a question. I'd have to be pretty far gone to answer badly and get myself sent back to the Greenlawn facility. The endless doctor visits wear down other Type Threes. Bleeding into a million vials. Peeing into thousands of cups. Pooping into hundreds of boxes. Dignity a thing of the past. But I hang on to the belief that someday there might be actual help for me here.

So I nod and tell her, "Yes. Sleep's not a problem. I have blackout curtains."

This is a desperate lie. Sleep is *always* a problem. Sometimes

I lie awake the whole day in my bed, too exhausted to get up and actually do anything but still aware of every dog barking and door slamming on my apartment block. *Especially* aware of every baby crying. My bedroom walls might as well be cardboard. I covered them in sound-dampening felt squares, but those only do so much. Part of my brain is always alert and restless no matter what I do. Hungry-predator gray matter I can't leash or satisfy.

I can't remember the last time I felt fully, authentically rested. But if I tell her this, she'll feel obligated to prescribe me yet another new drug that has yet another set of side effects. Anything that puts me down for the day is likely to make me oversleep my alarm. And even though I'm chronically ill, and chronically a danger to my community and myself, the world still expects people like me to make it to work on time. My rent, student loans, and medical bills won't pay themselves. Company shareholders need their European vacations. Be a productive member of the economy or die; it's the American way.

"So is the new job going well?" Dr. Shapiro asks.

"It's fine, too . . . They seem pretty happy with my work."

This, at least, isn't a *complete* lie. My most recent review was good. But it's certainly an enormous oversimplification. How can any supervisor be truly, authentically happy with the work of an employee they're afraid will infect them with a deadly disease? Or go on a murder rampage someday?

Human resources moved me off desktop support and put me on the graveyard shift in the company's cold network operations center. These nights, I'm mostly raising processes from the dead, watching endless scrolling green text on cryptic black screens. I'm pretty sure the company discreetly advised my coworkers Mareva and Jorge to carry Tasers and Mace just in case.

I'm positive that in any other scenario, they'd have terminated me while I was still in the hospital. Shipped my belongings to my apartment. But UCC lost a huge chunk of its workforce in the first waves of the pandemic. Especially in Bangalore and Hyderabad.

Eighty percent of the world's e-commerce travels through the web servers and mainframes in our data center. Tens of millions of dollars a day, billions a week. It's the fluorescent, buzzing carotid artery of the whole country's economy. They need people in that center monitoring, administering, and fixing systems 24/7/365, without fail. Thanks to the handful of IT certifications I got after I couldn't find a decent job with my environmental science degree, I'm one of the relative few qualified to keep the supply chains running and the currency flowing.

And I've convinced myself that it's good to be needed so badly that UCC is willing to overlook my many, many flaws as a white-collar employee.

One major flaw? My glitchy, slow memory. Thank God for operations manuals.

Most of my memories before the virus are as insubstantial as dreams; the strongest of them feel like borrowed clothing. The sweet snap of peas fresh from my garden. The crush of hot perfumed bodies against mine at the club and the thud of the bass from the huge speakers. The pleasant twin burns of the sun on my shoulders and the exertion in my legs as I pedal my bike up a mountainside.

The life I had in those memories is gone forever. I don't know why this is happening to humanity. To me. I'd like to think there's some greater purpose behind this disaster, some cosmic meaning in all this, but God help me, I just can't see it.

The worst memories? The bits and pieces I can recall of being desperately sick in the hospital. Puking up blood and wormlike bits of my stomach lining into a plastic emesis basin while ICU nurses watched from behind the clear plastic curtains they'd strung around my bed. My throat raw from acid. The unrelenting twisting agony in my guts. Cold sweats and aching muscles. Head pounding, everything in my vision warped with migraine auras. Unless I was coding, nobody was willing to come close enough to me to do so much as give me an encouraging pat on the shoulder or hold back my hair.

Delirium set in. After that, it's hard to know which of my memories are real and which were figments of my fevered brain. Some things were obvious nightmares. But they were so vivid, I recall them with the same clarity as I do anything else that happened in that time.

One recurring dream started out with me sitting in the beige waiting room of some doctor's office. Across from me sat my UCC acquaintance Mareva. She was wearing her typical outfit of jeans and a T-shirt under the tan cardigan she kept in the network ops center to ward off the air-conditioned cold. She wasn't wearing any makeup—I never saw her wear makeup in real life—and her brown hair was up in a messy bun. Beside her sat an attractive blonde woman in painful-looking stiletto heels, fishnets, and a strappy red nightclub dress that showcased her legs and cleavage. Her makeup was so stylized she almost looked like a drag queen. Within the dream, I'd known the blonde for a very long time but couldn't remember her name.

They both smiled at me, then gave each other knowing glances. The blonde took Mareva's hand in hers, holding it protectively on her lap.

"Are you two dating?" I asked.

"We're *expecting*," Mareva replied solemnly.

"Oh." Somehow this news didn't surprise me, even though I knew Mareva had a complicated uterine tumor when she was younger and had to get a hysterectomy. "Is it a boy or a girl?"

"It's a brand-new epoch," the blonde replied. "A new period, a new era. A new eon, probably. But we haven't any idea what we'll name it."

Mareva uttered a word in a language that sounded like black dwarf stars exploding before the heat death of the universe. Hearing it made me feel as if my brain was boiling inside my skull.

In the dream, the door from the waiting room opened into the exam area and I saw the blurry silhouette of a woman. "They say they're ready for the next patient."

"You go first," said the blonde.

I lurched up from my chair and staggered toward the door. But the dark floor wasn't carpet or vinyl planks but some kind of thick, sticky liquid. A tar pit trap. I was sinking.

I flailed, panicking. "Help me!"

The woman in the doorway stepped forward and grabbed my hand, pulling me free with her surprising strength.

I stood up on the now solid floor. We were no longer in a waiting room but were standing in the foyer of a dim motel room with cheap, thin carpeting. The blackout drapes at the other end of the room were drawn. Harsh sunlight leaked in around the edges.

The dark-eyed woman, who still gripped my hand, was in her late twenties. A little younger than me. Her thick chestnut hair was side shaved and tumbled over her left shoulder. She seemed familiar, but I couldn't place her.

"Do I know you?" I asked.

She shook her head. "You're not allowed to know me."

"What am I doing here?"

"You're leaving." She turned me around and pushed me toward the door, which was open to the empty sidewalk and sunlit parking lot beyond. "You're late for your appointment."

As I crossed the threshold, the concrete and pavement fell away. I plunged forward into a bright pale nothingness.

I plummeted, screaming . . . but then just as suddenly I sprouted wings that caught an updraft.

I was a raptor flying high above the heart of the city. The sun was dim behind brown smog clouds. The streets below me were abandoned, the blacktop thickly vined by strange twisted weeds and lovely crimson flowers. The blossoms resembled poppies, but I knew they were not of this earth. Sometimes, I spotted pregnant Mareva and the blonde down among the flowers, tending to them with watering cans. They'd see me in the sky and wave.

The air rushing over my face and wings stank of rotten meat and gasoline, and it took me a few wingbeats before I realized that the lawn of the downtown park was piled high with corpses. Someone had tried to burn them, but cremating tons of human flesh took far more fuel than a few cans of gas. I circled over the corpses, and the bodies I saw were strange, faces distorted with tumors. Some people had grown extra arms or legs before they died. One bloated corpse looked more like a centipede.

I had variations of that dream at least six times, each version a little longer and more detailed than the last. They weren't nightmares while I was in them. I was soaring, my body painless and free, and the stink of festering flesh was no more disturbing than the delicate scent of cherry blossoms during a springtime stroll. The twisted, diseased bodies of the people who had died in abject misery were as pleasant to behold as nodding sunflower heads.

It was only after I awoke that the full horror of the dream hit me, and I wanted to scream and scream to purge the terrible images from my mind. But my acid-scorched vocal cords could only manage a strangled, thin wail. I'd end up grabbing blindly for the basin and dry heaving into it.

In my rare lucid moments during those awful weeks, I held on to the idea that if I could just survive, I could get well and go back to my regular life. Back to my cozy apartment and Gregory. Back to our plans to get married, find a house with a good space for a garden, and start a family. Back to having a future to look forward to.

I held on to that idea like it was a precious, magical, wish-granting coin I'd found in a pirate's treasure chest in a dream, only to find my fist empty when I awoke alone in a cold bed.

# CHAPTER 2

"Are your hospitalization nightmares improving?" Dr. Shapiro asks.

"Maybe a little?" I'm momentarily relieved to not have to tell another lie. "They're probably about the same, though."

Everyone who's been through what I've been through has nightmares about being in the hospital. You don't survive all that without getting a case of PTSD. It's funny, though, how she always asks how I'm dealing with my memories of the hospital but never about the high-security convalescent facility.

I don't really remember being transported from the hospital to Greenlawn, which is actually a recommissioned insane asylum. I mean, nobody would call it that *now*, but that's how city residents referred to it when it was built in 1908 on a few rolling acres outside the city. The official, original name was the Greenlawn Sanatorium and Asylum. Designed by an eccentric local architect named Lewis Castaigne, it was a huge old square brick building with barred windows that the city gradually swallowed. The asylum started to decline after World War II and was finally shut down in the early eighties. It stood empty for a while, became some kind of army training facility for a few years, and then was abandoned again.

Once the neighborhoods surrounding the maple-dotted hospital grounds had cycled through slums into gentrification, a revolving door of real estate investors hatched various plans to turn it into high-end lofts for investment bankers and cryptocurrency bros who wanted an edgier address. The latest owners had gotten so far as to modernize the HVAC system and deal with all the asbestos tile, lead plumbing, and black mold poisoning the place. But then the pandemic landed and the need for secure recovery space was obvious. So the state declared eminent domain and took it. After some new coats of paint, new vinyl flooring, new medical equipment, and new heavy doors with electronic locks on the rooms, it was ready for the flood of patients.

The facility had been open for maybe a month (and I'd been there about a week) when my fever finally broke and I regained lucidity.

I remembered waking up slowly, groggily wondering why I couldn't move, why I couldn't reach up to rub the itchy crusts out of my eyes. My guts and head hurt, but *that* seemed perfectly normal. The longer my immobility lasted, the more frightened I was that I'd had a stroke. But I finally blinked my vision clear enough to see that white padded leather cuffs bound my wrists and ankles to the rails of a hospital bed. An IV dripped clear liquid into a needle in the crook of my left arm, and the clear tube of a Foley catheter trailed from beneath my white hospital gown, across my bare knee, down to a bag somewhere on the floor. My pee was the color of a slight sunburn. Probably not the healthiest shade, but I couldn't summon any fresh panic over it.

A few more blinks and my vision cleared further. The LED can lights above me were dimmed but still hurt my eyes. I craned my neck around to take in the thick, old-fashioned bars covering the safety glass windows, the heavy steel door, the bolted-down chair, the intercom speaker above the door. My relief at not being paralyzed evaporated as I realized I was more a prisoner than a patient. At least there was a Plexiglas-shielded flat-screen TV bolted way up in the corner of the room, although it had been turned off. People in jail didn't get their own TVs, did they?

There wasn't a nurse call button or TV remote, at least not where I could see. Certainly not anywhere I could reach.

"Hello?" I croaked. It was difficult to speak; my tongue felt swollen and stiff. The inside of my mouth was dry and sour, and my teeth were fuzzy-slimy. I did *not* love the smell of my own breath inside my papery mask. Frankly, it stank like rats had died in my tonsils.

After a few minutes, it was clear that nobody had heard me, so I tried again, more loudly: "Hello? Is anyone there?"

The effort made my parched throat ache. But a moment later, the door lock buzzed and a young, cheerful nurse in royal blue scrubs, her glossy black-brown hair done in elegant short finger waves, came through the door. She wore a clear full-face shield and carried a tablet in a rugged black silicone case. I spotted the huge hornet-colored Taser clipped to a belt beneath the hem of her shirt before I noticed her name tag: A. TESFAYE, PMHN. Psychiatric mental health nurse.

"My name is Allegra, and I'm your nurse during the day shift this week." She had a faint, lilting Caribbean accent. "So, how are we feeling today?"

"Okay?" I replied hoarsely. "Confused. Did I . . . do something wrong?"

I wiggled my hands in their restraints.

She smiled broadly, cautiously. Her teeth were very white, and I felt more self-conscious about mine. They were probably green. Mossy and gross. At least she couldn't see them.

"Oh, not at all," she said lightly. "All this is, you know, just precautions. Some people wake up, don't know where they are, throw a punch or two. Agitated, you know? It just gets ugly, and nobody wants that to happen."

I couldn't help but notice that she was making no move whatsoever to undo my cuffs.

So I wiggled my fingers at her again. "How can I get out of these?"

"Well." She stood at the foot of my bed and logged in to her tablet. "First, we need to make sure that you won't get agitated. Do you know what your name is?"

"My name? Erin Holdaway."

Nurse Tesfaye made an encouraging "Mm-hmm" and then proceeded to ask me where I lived, what year it was, who was president. I passed those with flying colors, apparently.

"Do you know where you are?" she asked.

"Not exactly," I admitted. "If anyone told me, I don't remember. This seems to be a hospital? But not the one I remember being in before."

She nodded and marked something on her tablet. "It's not the same. This is Greenlawn. The hospitals in the city are at full capacity, so we needed to find a place for people who are relatively stable, and the regular skilled nursing facilities aren't equipped to properly care for patients like you. We are."

My brain felt like it was stuck in mud. Every individual word she said to me made sense, but all together? Just a jumble of sounds. No connection to each other, no coherent meaning.

"Do you need me to repeat any of that?" she asked, not unkindly or impatiently.

"I got PVG?" I said, blinking, still trying to make sense of everything. But at least I'd grabbed hold of the most important detail. "No wonder I got so sick."

I paused, dimly remembering the night I went to the ER. Gregory. Oh, no. What if he'd gotten sick, too? I shivered as I pictured him lying unconscious on the bathroom floor, too weak to crawl to his cell phone on the nightstand. Slowly bleeding to death with nobody to check on him.

"Gregory . . . my boyfr—fiancé . . . is he alright?"

"Yes, he's just fine. I spoke with him this morning."

"Oh, thank God."

"He calls every day for updates on your condition. He'll certainly be glad to know that you're awake, because that means you'll be going home to him soon."

I wanted to call him right away, but I couldn't remember

whether my cell was with me when I went to the hospital. It wasn't on the orange plastic seat of the bolted-down chair, and I didn't see any other furniture where it could be sitting. "Where's my phone?"

"It's in a locker downstairs with your other personal items . . . Don't worry, we'll bring it to you soon."

I felt an unexpected, sharp spike of panic at not being able to talk to him. "When is soon?"

She smiled at me sympathetically. "I know you want to talk to your man, but Dr. Sallow thinks it's important that patients not have their phones for a while. Too easy to doom scroll, you know? Too easy to read some nonsense some hateful person wrote and let it poison your head."

"I guess that makes sense. Can't really hold up my end of a conversation right now, anyway." I felt helpless and out of touch without a screen and the internet to check on the world whenever I wanted. In the dim light, I suddenly felt a strong sense of disconnection, as if I'd shifted out of time and space into some strange bubble universe. "How long have I been out of it?"

"Well." She scrolled through whatever was open on her tablet. "It looks like you were in Cary Hospital for nine days total, and you've been here for seven days. So about sixteen days? You're doing better than many; some people been here since we opened and they still aren't scoring more than six points on the Glasgow Coma Scale."

I didn't really know what that meant, but I imagined it wasn't good. "I guess I'm lucky to be alive?"

The nurse gave me another wide, cautious smile. "Alive is always a good patient outcome!"

She cleared her throat. "So, I know that your stomach probably still hurts, but do you think you could try to eat some soft foods? It's part of the assessments we need to give you to figure out your future treatment plan."

The burst of words momentarily stunned my brain, but I

sensed that agreeing was key to my getting untied. "Food? I mean . . . I might throw up again . . . but I guess I could try?"

"Wonderful! I'll have the kitchen make a tray. But before I do that, I need to know if you have any known food allergies, intolerances, or restrictions? Like religious prohibitions against eating certain things?"

Too many words again, but "allergies or restrictions" stuck. "No, I don't."

"Great. Because you're conscious now, I need to get you to sign some consent forms before we can proceed with any assessments or do any further treatments."

I wiggled my fingers helplessly. "How am I supposed to—"

"Oh, the forms are all here on my tablet. I can hold it up so you can read, scroll it for you, and then you can sign with your finger."

She brought up the first form and held her tablet a few inches in front of my face. Her hands were steady enough, but the tiny pixelated letters blurred in and out of focus.

"Let me know when you're ready for me to scroll down," she said cheerfully.

There was no way I could read any of this. And if I could read it, I wasn't sure I could comprehend it. And even if I comprehended it now, would I remember what I'd read tomorrow? But if I didn't sign, was I just going to be stuck in these cuffs forever?

"Okay, scroll, please," I replied weakly.

She had me sign five different electronic forms and I hadn't the slightest idea what was really on any of them.

"Looks like we're all set." She paged through the forms on her tablet, nodded to herself, and then gave me a bright smile. "I'll be back soon with some food."

She turned and left the room, the door thudding closed behind her. It certainly sounded like a prison door. My nose itched under my mask, and I vainly tried to scratch it by rubbing the side of my face on the thin pillow. The room was silent except for the cells of the pneumatic mattress periodically inflating or deflating to keep me from getting bedsores.

In the quiet, my mind started to focus.

•  •  •

The nurse returned with a whole entourage of people behind her. First, a young woman in pink scrubs pushed a meal cart into the room. She was twenty at most and wore her dishwater blonde hair up in a ponytail. Her scrunchie and Crocs matched her scrubs. A moment later, a huge bald orderly in orange scrubs, who looked like he could have worked as Jason Momoa's stunt double (with the aid of a wig and beard, anyway), opened the door and held it wide. A slightly built fiftysomething doctor in a white lab coat over black pants stepped through. My eyes were too blurry to read his name tag. Everyone but Tesfaye was wearing masks under their face shields, so I couldn't completely read their expressions. Pink scrubs's eyes were wide with worry, though.

"So I know this is a lot of people all at once," Nurse Tesfaye said, gesturing to the others broadly, then pointing individually. "This is Dr. Sallow, from pathology. He's here to speak with you about your diagnosis. This is Lisa, our nursing student. And this is Darius."

She didn't say anything more about why the huge man was there, but on the other hand, she didn't really need to.

"Okay," I said. Clearly, all this was going to happen whether I wanted it to or not.

Nurse Tesfaye came over to the left side of my bed and moved my IV pole back against the wall.

"I need to remove your IV," she said. "It might sting a bit when I take the tape off."

"Okay," I replied.

While she worked, Darius stepped up to the foot of my bed.

"Alright, Miss Holdaway, after she's done, I'm going to undo your cuffs, starting with your legs."

"Looks like you're bleeding a little bit," Nurse Tesfaye said, after she pulled the plastic IV line out of my arm. She pressed a square of gauze against the tiny wound in the crook of my arm. It rapidly darkened with a dime-size spot of blood.

"Lisa, I need an extra hand," she called over her shoulder.

The young woman hesitated, her wary eyes shifting from me to the nurse.

"Lisa, *now*, please. And put on gloves."

The young woman darted to the PPE dispenser by the door, grabbed a pair, then approached me, nervously pulling on the purple nitrile gloves.

"Just put your finger here and apply pressure while I get a Band-Aid, okay?" Nurse Tesfaye said. "Her blood can't infect you if it's not airborne—and if you remember to take your gloves off the way we taught you."

Lisa stopped several feet away, reaching out as far as she could, on tiptoe, to do as she'd been told, pressing her index finger gingerly against the gauze. Nurse Tesfaye rolled her eyes, quickly unwrapped a sterile bandage strip, and applied it across my IV puncture.

"You might get scared," Darius told me as he moved over to my right foot. "Sometimes people see or feel things that ain't there. But I need you to stay calm and not move while I'm doing this, okay?"

Although he spoke softly, his deep voice still bore a threatening edge. This man would not hesitate to use force against me if he thought it was necessary.

"Yes, sir." I lay limp as a rag doll as he methodically unbuckled the straps and cuffs and tucked the restraints somewhere under the mattress.

Once he was done, Nurse Tesfaye bent down behind the foot of the bed and came up with a wired controller.

"I'm going to raise the head of the bed so you can sit up to eat," she said. "Just let me know if this gets uncomfortable, okay?"

"Okay." I nodded.

The electric motor whined like mosquitoes as the bed slowly eased me up into a sitting position.

Dr. Sallow suddenly spoke to me in his brassy New Jersey accent: "Miss Holdaway, do you remember the night you went to the ER? If so, can you tell us about it?"

I blinked at him. "I think I remember most of it? My boyfriend Gregory got us sushi and a bottle of wine. Riesling. We were celebrating our fifth anniversary. He . . . he proposed to me. Got down on one knee and everything."

Sadness suddenly overwhelmed me, and I had to blink back tears.

"Take your time if you need to." Dr. Sallow glanced down at his smartwatch.

Nurse Tesfaye handed me a tissue.

Feeling embarrassed, I wiped my face and continued. "My head started to hurt after we had dessert. I took medicine, but it didn't help. Then I started feeling hot, and I got sick. *Really* sick. It was all red. It just didn't stop."

I paused, remembering Gregory's panic, how he dropped my hair and ran out of the bathroom. How alone and scared and abandoned I felt.

"What happened after that?" Dr. Sallow prompted.

"I'm not sure," I lied. I didn't want to talk about how one of the best evenings of my life had turned into the absolute worst night. "My memory's kind of weird and mixed up after that."

Dr. Sallow glanced down at his tablet and nodded. "You've been describing sudden-onset symptoms . . . Do you recall feeling ill in the days before?"

I shook my head. "Not really? But maybe a little? Could I have gotten infected by our dinner? Maybe by someone who handled our takeout?"

"No," he replied. "Nobody's seen any cases that had less than a twenty-four-hour incubation period. Most are in the forty-eight-to-seventy-two-hour range."

Dr. Sallow glanced at the student nurse. "Let's begin the diagnostic procedure. Go ahead and serve her lunch."

Lisa pushed the lunch tray in place across my bed and lifted the beige plastic cloche covering it, revealing a bento of mushy hospital foods and liquids in Styrofoam containers. There were four-ounce cups of a clear soda over ice, plain water, apple juice, and something red that I figured might be beet juice. My entrée items, such as they were, looked to be little bowls of applesauce, vanilla pudding, and a warm, grayish, lumpy mush that I assumed might be scrambled egg whites. They didn't smell like egg whites, though. I don't really like eggs, and it looked terrible, but the savory scent of it made my mouth water.

"Try the beverages first," Nurse Tesfaye said. "Go easy and let your body get used to the idea of drinking and eating again."

"And let us know how consuming the items make you feel," Dr. Sallow added. "Taste, appeal, emotional response . . . really, any reaction you feel at all."

I felt as though I'd been dropped into a focus group study for some new line of hospital cuisine. "Okay, if that's what you want?"

"It is," Dr. Sallow assured me. "I know it all seems strange, but these details are critical in determining your long-term prognosis. We can't determine your best course of treatment otherwise. So please be absolutely honest with us. We're not here to judge you in any way."

Why would I be judged for reacting to hospital food? Clearly, I was missing something, and that made me nervous. But all four of them were staring at me expectantly, so I reached out for the cup of water and took a sip. My hand and arm felt appallingly weak and shaky. I swished the sip of water around to rinse some of the sourness out of my mouth and swallowed. Waited a beat to see if my stomach would violently reject it, but aside from a slight cramp it felt okay.

"That seemed fine," I said. "Tepid. A little chlorine-y. Could use some ice."

I moved on to the clear soda. "7 Up? Sprite? Nice. Refreshing. Kind of a sickly aftertaste, but that could just be me."

The nurse tapped something into her tablet, and I drank the apple juice. "Tarter than I expected. Sweet. Maybe too sweet."

I reached for the cup of beet juice and lifted it to my lips. Instead of a sweet, earthy flavor, my taste buds were met with salt and iron. The taste of raw meat. Surprised, I spat the sip back into the cup.

"What the hell is this?" I demanded.

"How do you feel?" Dr. Sallow's voice was absolutely calm.

"Is . . . is this blood?" I stared down into the cup of crimson in my hands, recognition dawning as I spoke. "Did y'all serve me *blood*?"

I looked from the impassive doctor to Nurse Tesfaye, who gave me an apologetic nod and shrug.

"It's pasteurized, and it's part of the assessment," she said calmly. "It can't hurt you, and it's necessary. Please try to trust the process."

"Blood. Jesus Christ." I set the cup back on the tray with a quivering hand, then leaned back into my pillow, giving them all a hard look.

Dr. Sallow blinked at me slowly, like a large cat. "Can you tell us how you feel?"

"Appalled? Grossed out? What do you want me to say?" I snapped, reaching for the water so I could rinse the gory residue off my tongue.

"Do you feel any different physically?" he asked.

"I feel creeped out."

"Anything else?"

"No. I mean, what else am I supposed to feel about drinking blood?"

"You're not necessarily supposed to feel anything at all," he replied. "Please continue with the solid food."

I stared down at the bowls in front of me. Especially at the mystery mush. And shook my head. "I do *not* trust y'all."

"Miss Holdaway, please continue," Nurse Tesfaye said. "I promise you on my mother's name that nothing on that tray is physically or morally harmful. It's all ethically sourced. I *promise.*"

"We really can't leave until you do the thing," Darius said, with sympathetic menace.

Later, as I tried to sleep that night, I would realize that her reference to ethical sourcing meant the blood was from a human volunteer. Much later, I'd wonder what the hell they gave vegans during the test.

But in that moment, I glared at everyone and said, "Fine. Whatever."

Might as well get the most suspect thing on the tray over with, right? I picked up the plastic spoon and plunged it into the mystery mush. Angrily put the scoop of *whatever* into my mouth.

Its gelatinous, eggy texture sent little frissons of disgust down my spine. The flavor, though . . . I can't say that I objectively thought it was *good*. Savory, yes, but bitter. Imagine tofu that had transformed itself into meat without bothering to become muscle. I liked it, though. I liked it *a whole lot*. I liked it the way a person dying of thirst in the desert likes a cool bottle of water.

Before I realized what I was doing, I'd dropped the spoon, lifted the bowl to my lips and was slurping the mush out of it like a hungry dog. My heart was pounding like I was making a run for it across the hospital grounds.

"Ope, back up, fam," Darius drawled. "Looks like we got a Type Three up in here."

His remark didn't really register. Days later, I would have questions, and I wouldn't like the answers.

Dr. Sallow stayed perfectly still. "What do you think, Miss Holdaway?"

"I think this would be better raw." My stomach was growling with hunger, my arms shaking with adrenaline. "I think this would be better if there was *more*."

The bowl was empty. I'd licked it clean. I did want more, I wanted a *lot* more, and there wasn't any. Rage at its absence rose inside me like a wave.

I glared at Lisa, who flinched. "Give me another bowl. *Two* bowls."

"Unfortunately, she can't bring you more." Dr. Sallow's voice was very even, but I caught just a hint of a fearful tremor.

I looked up at him, really *looked* at him. His pupils were constricted to small, dark points. A single bead of sweat trickled from his tidy gray hairline down his golf-tanned forehead. He was *afraid*. I knew it deep in my bones. A man is only afraid of a woman if she has *power*.

I slid my gaze to Darius. His face was an impassive mask behind his mask, but his fists were clenched at his sides. He was afraid, too.

And that realization made me feel absolutely exhilarated.

"One serving per day is all we can give each patient," Dr. Sallow said. "But you can have as much pudding and applesauce as you like."

"I don't fucking *want* pudding or applesauce." I stared at the good doctor's head. His skull beneath that tidy professional haircut looked like a bowl. A bowl full of the mush my body and soul craved.

They only *thought* I was sick. They only *thought* I was weak. I imagined myself springing out of the bed, fast as a striking rattlesnake. I'd bash his skull against the steel doorframe and get to that creamy, expensively educated goodness inside. Get my licks in before Darius could put his thick hands on me. And then I'd do Darius, too.

"How about you give me what I want," I growled, "or I'll crack you open like a goddamned coconut, you smug motherfucker."

I heard the swish of metal and plastic across fabric.

Nurse Tesfaye had drawn her Taser and leveled it at my chest. "Miss Holdaway, I think you're getting agitated. I think you need to try to calm down."

"What if I don't *want* to calm down?" I stared at the shiny prongs of the Taser, trying to figure out if it would stop me or not.

"If you're like some of our other patients, you probably feel like you can take on the whole world right now," she said gently. "You're probably feeling some urges. But I need you to realize that *this isn't you. This* isn't what you want to be, right?"

"I . . . I don't know." In the few seconds she'd been speaking, my desire to kill Dr. Sallow and Darius had ebbed, and in its wake I felt confused and shaky.

"I know you want to get back to your man Gregory," she said. "He cares so much about you; I can hear it in his voice. He wants you to come home to him. But you can't go home if you're going to be agitated like this. And if you make me use this thing, it *will* hurt you. I know you don't think so, but it will. If I have to use this thing, your recovery will be set back, maybe by a week, maybe longer."

"That'd be bad, yeah." The adrenaline rush had really taken a toll. I felt completely wrung out. Weaker than when I'd awakened. "What . . . what the hell was in that bowl? Drugs?"

"No drugs," Dr. Sallow said evenly. "Just brains."

"Brains?" I stared at him, a cold knot of horror forming in my belly. "Like . . . cow brains, right? Pork brains?"

He inclined his head, his eyes unreadable behind his face shield. "You received a diagnostic mixture of ninety percent bovine brain matter and ten percent tissue from harvested human cerebrums."

"H-human?" I stammered. "Y'all turned me into a fucking *cannibal*? What kind of mad scientist bullshit are y'all into here?"

I must have looked like I was about to choose violence, because Nurse Tesfaye took a step closer with the Taser.

"Miss Erin, it's not helpful to think that way," she warned. "You have a condition that requires a special diet. That's all this is."

"But did you have to give me *human* brains?" My voice shook.

"We absolutely did," she replied firmly. "It was the only way to know your Type for sure. The only way to know how to treat you from here on out."

Sudden regret and existential misery flooded me. I started to weep, tears streaming hot down my face. "I wanna go home."

"And we want to get you home," she said. "All of us, we just want to see you get well. So will you trust us, and work with us? Be a good patient?"

"Yeah." I sank back on the bed. "Yeah."

And in the back of my diseased mind, a perversion of a children's song echoed:

*Brains, brains, the magical meat.*
*The worse you feel, the more you eat.*
*The more you eat, the more vicious you get.*
*Brain eaters are the worst kind of threat!*

# CHAPTER 3

"Are you having trouble staying awake during the day?" Dr. Shapiro asks.

"Not since I left Greenlawn."

— • • • —

A few hours after my food test, Darius came into my room to take me outside for some fresh air while the janitorial team changed my linens and disinfected everything. My legs were still pretty weak, so he helped me into a transport chair, bundled me under a blanket, and wheeled me down the hall to the courtyard door.

"You feeling any better?" he asked as he backed my chair over the threshold. A cold March breeze ruffled my hair and blew down my neck. The hazy crescent moon was barely visible through scudding clouds.

"A little," I replied.

He pivoted my chair around. The courtyard was square, maybe half the size of an Olympic pool, paved with dark slate and yellow ceramic tiles. There were just a few round, shaggy boxwoods in strips of dirt by the building's walls and a pair of stone benches flanking a bone-dry concrete fountain. The basin and two tiers were shaped like stars.

The decorative paving stone pattern was . . . strange. Three large yellow arms arced and wound out from the fountain. The arms were too irregular, too dissimilar to be intended as decoration. I got the impression that if you looked at the pattern from the roof, it would form some type of symbol. Maybe an Arabic character, or two characters joined as a glyph?

Whatever it was, something about the pattern made me uneasy.

Darius said, "Dr. Sallow wants me to get you used to walking a bit."

He started to push me toward one of the benches, but suddenly a high-pitched alarm went off. A computerized female voice sounded through speakers I couldn't see: "Staff alert. Code gray. Staff alert. Code gray."

"Well, crap." Darius scanned the windows that overlooked the courtyard, frowning. I was sitting too low to see whatever he spotted. "I hafta go help with that. Can you just chill here for a minute or three? Don't try to get up, though. They'll have my ass for breakfast if you fall and I ain't here."

I nodded. "I'll stay put."

"Thanks." He jogged back to the door and went through. I heard the lock latch when it closed behind him.

I shivered and drew the blanket tighter around my shoulders. Spread it out a bit across my thighs. It felt like it was freezing out here, but my breath wasn't even steaming. So it wasn't any lower than 46 degrees. Of course, I'd lost most of my insulation in the hospital.

The strange yellow paving stone design caught my eye again. What could it possibly represent?

As I studied the curves and angles, my shivering intensified, and my vision began to blur. I felt myself pitch backward, into darkness. I flailed blindly for a heart-stopping moment, but then wind caught my arms. Not arms. Wings.

Once again, I was a raptor soaring high in the afternoon sky somewhere to the northwest, skimming over the rocky hills that overlooked the valley-nestled city. I saw an old, stately manor set back on a gray limestone cliff. The house had a black slate roof and a crenellated stone tower that reminded me of a medieval castle. Lovely gardens and twin hedge mazes spread on either side of it. Far behind the building was a broad red barn, and beyond it on a gentle slope, a glittering field of dark glass solar panels.

I'd never seen the manor before, but I knew it was filled with priceless rarities. Far more than mere money could acquire. A keep fit for a king. Or a living god.

Suddenly, an invisible chain yanked me straight down out of the sky, and I was plummeting—

I jerked awake in the chilly transport chair. Darius looming over me, his panicked scowl melting into an expression of relief.

"Oh, thank the Man Upstairs, for a sec I thought I lost you." He straightened up and ran his huge hands over his shaved scalp.

"Lost me?" I blinked at him in confusion.

"I came back out . . . you was slumped over. Lookin' real dead. I know I'm not supposed to say so, but I seen dead people before, and . . . yeah." He swallowed. "I couldn't find your pulse. I thought you stroked out or had a heart attack or somethin'. I was 'bout ready to put you on the ground and bust out the paddles."

He nodded to the white emergency defibrillator kit bolted to the wall by the door.

"I feel okay," I offered. "I mean, I *think* I do. I just . . . had a dream, I guess?"

He frowned down at me, concerned. "Like a nightmare? Scary?"

"No, it was nice." I paused. Already the details were fading away. "I was flying."

"See, I *swear* you did not look asleep. I guess it could've been a seizure? Sometimes people stop breathing and they see things." He grimaced, looking over his shoulder at the strange tile design. "This place creeps me out. That weird yellow thing and shit. I do *not* know why the doc wanted me to take you out here and not out front where there's grass. It'd be safer there."

"Yeah, what's up with that symbol? Do you know?"

He shrugged. "I guess the architect had it put in. Some dude named Castle or Stayne or something. Dunno why. But I guess he was famous back then, and they let him do what he wanted. And now it's so old it's historical, so nobody will paint it over or tear it out. Oh well." He moved behind my chair and wheeled me around. "Let's get you back inside. I'll get the night resident to give you a good look-over to make sure your heart's not about to pop."

"Much appreciated, thanks."

# CHAPTER 4

"Is the daily health app on your phone still working well for you?" Dr. Shapiro asks.

"As well as ever," I reply. Not a lie, but I also know she won't interpret my words in the spirit they're intended.

• • •

My heart was fine. I finally got my phone back for limited use, three long days after that damnable food test. By then they'd taken out my catheter and given me a commode chair, a recliner, and some old magazines to read, along with the TV remote, although the only channels I got were the weather and Bob Ross reruns. I got better clothes, too, after Gregory made a late-night delivery downstairs: my own pajamas, underwear, and socks instead of the flimsy hospital gown and papery disposable panties.

Nurse Tesfaye and Lisa wheeled my lunch tray in, and my mood soared when I saw my iPhone lying on the paper napkin.

"I made sure to charge it up to one hundred percent for you." Nurse Tesfaye beamed at me.

"Thanks." I picked up the phone . . . and realized it was unlocked. I *always* lock my phone. Years at UCC had drilled data security into my head, and I was careful with my personal devices.

I looked at Nurse Tesfaye. "This didn't ask for my passcode. It should have."

Her smile faded. "Right."

She paused, seeming to consider whether to tell me the truth or not. "We . . . we have to turn patients' phones over to Home-land Security."

Lisa took that as her cue to quietly abandon the lunch cart and leave the room. Nurse Tesfaye didn't call her back.

"Homeland Security?" When did Homeland Security get involved in the pandemic? I suddenly felt sick to my stomach. Anxious and furious. I wanted to let loose a whole string of curses, but I knew that acting *agitated* would land me more time in the facility.

So I took a deep breath and held it for three beats before I replied. "I'm sorry, but I didn't consent to a digital search. Why were they in my phone?"

She looked deeply uncomfortable. "While you were in the hospital, Congress passed an emergency law that affects people infected, or thought to be infected, with PVG. The Pandemic Security Act. It suspends HIPAA requirements when it comes to state and local authorities managing infection threats, contact tracing and notifications, and things like that."

My brain churned. It took me a moment to remember exactly why what she'd said didn't sound right. "But unwarranted digital searches aren't prevented by HIPAA. That's a Fourth Amend-ment protection."

I only knew that because I'd had a coworker who was a dig-ital rights activist and a chatterbox. A law school washout with ADHD. He hadn't lasted that long at UCC because he started trying to get us to unionize. But while he was there, I learned a surprising amount from him, and the vast majority of it was even accurate.

Nurse Tesfaye put her hand over her heart. "Look, I'm not an expert on that-all. I never touched your phone except to charge it for you. You'll learn all about how the new law affects you on your discharge day."

My heart was pounding loud in my ears. She hadn't said so, but it sounded like some enterprising political cabal had used panic over the pandemic as an opportunity to turn civil rights into civil privileges . . . and I had lost some of mine.

"But why were they looking at my phone?"

She winced. "I don't really know? Contact tracing is what they said."

"Uh-huh." Homeland Security could have simply demanded my phone's location data from my cell carrier. They only needed my phone if they wanted to dig around in my data . . . or plant software of their own.

I brought up my home screen, and sure enough . . . right there at the top of my apps was a new HEALTH CHECK-IN icon in cheerful, patriotic red, white, and blue.

"What's this?" I held my screen toward her and pointed at the app.

She looked utterly unsurprised. "Right. That. You'll learn more on your D-Day, but . . . that's for logging your daily symptoms. It's so your care team can quickly identify if you're in crisis. They installed it as a convenience for you."

"A convenience." I tried not to show the incandescent rage I felt. I'd saved up for months for my shiny, brand-new iPhone. It was the first really nice thing I'd owned in a long time. An electronic treat of the highest order, and nobody but me had ever owned it. I'd loved it as much as my sister, Claire, loved her tiny yappy dogs.

And now it was tainted. Unsafe. I wondered how Nurse Tesfaye would feel if some creepy man came into her home while she slept and groped through all her underthings. Sniffed the fabric that had touched her most personal parts. Rearranged her lingerie as a "convenience." But I knew that if I asked her that, she'd think I sounded *agitated*.

"That's *great*," I told her.

I knew that, from then on, I'd have to treat my phone as my own personal digital spy. Not that it hadn't been before. Maybe I should have been more worried, but it always seemed to me that Corporate America's attempts to get me to be a good little consumer were straightforward. They weren't there to judge anyone for their needs or desires. They just wanted people to buy their stuff. Probably it was junk you didn't need, probably it was plastic crap that was slowly destroying the planet. And yeah, they'd prey on your personal insecurities to do it . . . but even the friendly neighborhood Avon ladies back in my great-grandmother's day did that, too.

This new invasion of privacy, though? It felt a whole lot more personal. The stakes might be *much* higher than me getting myself into debt—more than college and my hospital stay already had, anyway—and ruining my credit score. Who the hell knew what was in store for me if my "care team" decided I was having a crisis?

I must have had quite a dismayed look on my face, because Nurse Tesfaye said apologetically, "I know this all seems sneaky, but it's for your own safety. The law says they have to treat all the patients the same at first, and some folk leave here not knowing how to tie their shoes. Expecting them to go through all the steps of downloading a new app is just too much. It's easier on everyone this way."

I tried not to argue, but I couldn't quite stop myself. "If they don't remember how to tie their shoes, how do you expect them to follow directions?"

"If you don't respond to the on-screen prompts, it switches to voice prompts and records what you say to it. It also prompts you automatically if you haven't checked in that day."

"Voice recordings . . . that's a *lot* of data. More than some people can afford. And what about patients who don't have a smartphone?"

"They'll go over that on your D-Day." She looked and sounded exhausted, as if this whole conversation was draining away her will to live. I almost felt sorry for her.

"But the short of it is," she continued, "any patient who can't afford the tech gets it for free. But you have a good job still waiting for you, I think?"

"Yes. As far as I know." I glanced down at the phone in my hand and suppressed the urge to hurl it against the whitewashed cinder-block wall. It might be a spy, but I still needed it. It was my only connection to the outside world.

"I guess I should eat lunch, and then call my boyfriend."

She looked profoundly relieved that an escape hatch had finally opened in the conversation. "Right. I'll step out for a bit and give you some privacy."

*Privacy.* I'm still proud of myself that I didn't break into bitter hyena laughter when she said that. "Thanks. You're the best."

# CHAPTER 5

"How are things going with your boyfriend? Gregory? Or is it Greg?" Dr. Shapiro asks.

Her question hits me like a stomach cramp, and it's hard to reply. I should have expected it. And it's a bit of a trick: she already knows his name is Gregory. He never liked people shortening it, because his jerk cousin was named Greg. She's testing my memory.

"Gregory. And it's . . . going . . . as well as it can?" I can't keep a stressed quiver out of my voice. "Long-distance relationships are hard."

She nods sympathetically. "They are."

• • •

I ate my lunch—taking time to savor my too-small bowl of what I'd come to learn were lightly poached cow brains—and then I texted Gregory.

> I just got my phone back! You have time to
> video chat? I miss yr face.

Three promising dots appeared and pulsed for a few seconds.

> Honey! Im so glad. I can take a break. Call u in
> 5 minutes?

Sure, I typed back.

I spent the next few minutes using the selfie camera on the

phone as a mirror, attempting to make myself somewhat pre-
sentable. I had a bad case of bedhead and only a rubber comb to
deal with it. No makeup to cover the deep circles under my eyes.
There's fashionably thin and then there's hospital gaunt. I was
gaunt. My complexion wasn't close to rosy. But I did my best.

The video call came through, and I touched the green camera
icon to accept it.

"Sweetie!" Gregory exclaimed. Smiling, sun on his face. I could
see he was sitting outside under a tree. Probably in the company
courtyard, where there was still a decent wireless signal. He didn't
like burning his cell data if he didn't have to. "It's so great to see
you. How are you feeling?"

Boy, that was a loaded question, wasn't it?

"I'm doing okay," I replied. "My fever's gone, but I still get
headaches. You can probably see I lost a ton of weight. There
have been some other . . . changes, you could say."

He nodded, his smile fading. "Your nurse said you're on a
pretty restricted diet. I guess you'll be on it awhile?"

"Yeah." I sighed. "The virus wrecked my guts. If I'm lucky,
it'll get better over time. Nobody knows how long it might be,
though."

"She said you can eat bland foods like bananas, rice, applesauce, tapioca, saltines?"

"Yeah. I got lucky compared to some. I can still handle a little
bit of dairy and egg whites, too. But my stomach can't deal with
muscle meat anymore, apparently. Or anything with a lot of fiber
or acid. An orange and a roast beef sandwich would make me
barf for days. And I guess my body isn't making certain proteins
anymore. I need special easy-to-digest supplements now."

Gregory's face shifted to the very neutral expression he puts
on when he's freaked out but doesn't want to show it.

"What kind of supplements?" he asked. "Did they tell you
yet?"

I didn't want to mention my daily bowl of brains. It's a hell of a thing to have to eat every day. But I wasn't surprised when I found out they were my new favorite food. I knew exactly what I wanted the moment I started thinking about attacking Dr. Sallow and Darius.

"I mean, not really?" I hedged. "I guess they're letting me know things a little at a time so I don't get overwhelmed. Glycine and proline for sure, though. The nurse told me they put that in the pudding."

"Yeah." He bit his lip uncertainly. "Your nurse told me that I shouldn't discuss anything that they haven't covered with you yet. But it's hard to know what you don't know."

"And it's not like this frustrates *me* at all," I replied, unable to keep a bitter edge out of my voice. "This whole thing of not knowing basic facts about myself when my entire career has centered on knowledge."

"I know. It would drive me crazy, too." He sounded sympathetic, and looked worried. "I've been reading up on the virus a whole lot the past two weeks. Kinda obsessively, if I'm honest. I *want* to fill you in. There's a lot of logistical stuff we need to talk about. But your nurse . . . she was very clear and very firm that I not do that. I guess we have to just trust the process, right?"

"I guess so." I paused. "So how have you been?"

"Me? I'm fine. They gave me a fast antigen test at the ER after I followed the squad there, and I got another test ten days later. Both came back negative. I didn't catch the virus from you. I'm clean."

His comment made me unreasonably angry and I tried hard to tamp down my sudden rage. But I didn't succeed. "Clean. Like how you told me you tested clean of sexually transmitted diseases, except, *whoops*, you totally weren't?"

He looked shocked. "Whoa, whoa, this isn't like that—"

"Why not?" I shot back. "Viruses are viruses. Tests are fallible. For all either of us really knows, *I* caught this virus from *you*.

Remember all those asymptomatic carriers during the coronavirus years? We don't know that's not you."

His face blanched, and he set his lips in a thin, determined line. "No. I *don't* have it. They were clear on that. I didn't make this terrible thing happen to you."

"That's great. That's wonderful." I took a deep breath, trying to calm myself down. He and I shared everything: kisses, glasses, towels, passwords. Regardless of how the virus was transmitted, it seemed impossible that I could be infected and he wasn't. But on the other hand, that didn't really matter, did it?

"Look, honey, I'm sorry I snapped at you," I said. "I haven't . . . I haven't been myself lately."

His expression relaxed. "I know. I'm sorry, too. I know you've been through a whole lot. More than I can really imagine. And I want you to know that I love you, and I've got your back. I called UCC's HR department and made sure that your short-term disability was all set. You don't have to worry about that. They said to just focus on getting well and they'll have a place for you when you're ready. I've been taking care of business while you've been gone. Cleaned up your garden, too."

"Thank you," I replied. "I appreciate it. I appreciate *you*. I love you."

He smiled at me, but then his face clouded. "There's . . . there's something else I need to tell you. I don't know that now's a good time, but there probably isn't gonna be a really good time for it. And you deserve to know."

My stomach dropped. "What's happened?"

"I talked to your sister the morning after you went to the ER and let her know what was going on. I phoned her back every few days to give her updates, but then my calls started going straight to voice mail. A few days ago, I got a call from Liz. She told me your father and your sister have both passed on."

He'd phrased everything so euphemistically and buried the

lede so thoroughly that the meaning of his words didn't register right away. "Passed on? As in *dead*?"

He nodded uncomfortably. "Yes. I'm so sorry."

"What happened?" My brain jumped to the obvious conclusion. "Was it the virus?"

"Your sister got sick, yeah. Your father had an accident like two days after you landed in the ER. Broke his neck falling off his roof. Looked like he was cleaning his gutters. Claire went down to deal with his cremation and the estate, and I guess she got infected on the trip. Liz said it just took her apart at the seams. She bled out in the ICU forty-eight hours after they admitted her."

"Jesus." My family was dead. *Gone.* Everyone I loved was gone. Everyone but Gregory. He was the only person left in the world who gave a damn whether I lived or died.

And I was pretty sure I hadn't told my dad or Claire that I loved them when I spoke to them last. God, I was such a jerk.

Before I knew it, I was sobbing.

"I'm so sorry, honey," Gregory said. "I wish I could be there to give you a hug."

"I wish I could hug you, too," I wept. "But I'm glad you're not here. This place really sucks."

"I'm so sorry," he repeated.

"Me, too."

·  ·  ·

I thought, afterward, that my next conversation with Gregory would *have* to be a whole lot cheerier. I'd be coming home. We'd be making big plans to get on with our lives.

But the following day, Dr. Sallow decided I was recovered enough—meaning mentally stable enough—to get tied to the tracks of the hard facts freight train. And he filled in all those frustrating gaps in my knowledge like Montresor relentlessly stacking bricks in Fortunato's wall. Afterward, Nurse Tesfaye offered to let me call Gregory, but I opted to sit there watching

Bob Ross paint soothing landscapes and talk about happy accidents for six hours instead.

The next morning, I pulled on my big girl pants and asked her for my phone.

- - -

"Hey, honey." Gregory's expression was somber. "How are you feeling?"

"Okay, physically. Lousy otherwise." I paused, wondering if I should just rip off the proverbial Band-Aid. "I guess you probably talked to Dr. Sallow?"

"Some, yeah. He said you'll be well enough to leave next week, which is good . . ." He trailed off.

"But I guess he told you about my blood test?" My most recent virus titer showed that viral activity in my bloodstream was *increasing*, not decreasing, meaning I was still significantly contagious and more likely to experience chronic problems because of my infection.

"Yeah." Gregory looked grim. "He told me. I already bought some blackout curtains, and I'll get those hung up before you come home."

Most people weren't in my situation. They got the virus, and maybe it gave them a bit of a headache and some nausea, but after a few days' bed rest they were going out for Thai again. They never went to see their doctor, much less an ER. Congratulations to them! They're Type Ones, and unless they need to get tested, they probably don't even know it.

But some were like me. Their headache turned into the worst they'd ever had, and they started vomiting up blood and then their stomach lining. The least unfortunate ones were able to get to an ER for lifesaving treatment. But if they left the hospital in anything other than a body bag, many of them had lost the ability to digest most foods and to make certain proteins.

And in the absence of those proteins, Dr. Sallow had

explained, my body would have trouble healing itself. If I were still a kid, normal growth would be a problem. Even worse, the enzymes my DNA uses to repair itself didn't work very well anymore.

Sunlight was no longer my friend. Which explained why they'd never taken me outside during the day for any recreational activities. X-rays were trouble, too, so trips to the dentist were going to get tricky.

I wasn't a smoker or much of a drinker, which meant I was less likely to suffer from DNA damage. But even if I quit eating junky, carcinogen-laden processed foods and covered up like I was trekking across the Andes, I could look forward to my skin cracking and my body sprouting tumors. If I was particularly unlucky, I'd turn into a total cancer farm by my thirty-fifth birthday.

As for our plan to start a family? Pregnancy was off the table. My chance of giving birth to a healthy baby with ten fingers and ten toes was almost nonexistent. The luckiest women who got infected during or before their pregnancies miscarried early.

And there was my brain. Sooner or later, malfunctioning DNA repair meant my brain would degenerate. I was already extremely worried about that.

"So, are you a Type Two?" Dread and hope were both clear in Gregory's expression.

Even that early in the pandemic, doctors had discovered that if a patient survived all that pain and vomiting, the symptoms of their chronic disease *could* be controlled, if they were given daily supplements of certain vitamins and amino acids.

If your best natural source for all that is fresh human blood, congratulations! You are a Type Two! It's ghoulish and expensive, but fortunately fresh animal blood is nearly as good as human juice. Pasteurized animal blood? Much safer, less effective, but still works well enough to keep you calm and alert enough to work an average white-collar job.

If, however, the best source for you is a nice fresh bowl of raw brains . . . you are a Type Three. Much more ghoulish, much more expensive. And you are *much* more prone to rages and violent psychotic episodes if you don't get what you need.

"I'm a Type Three," I told Gregory.

His face went utterly slack for a moment as the bad news settled in his mind. Nobody was going to let a Type Three spend time around a young child unless they were not so secretly hoping the child would die. So adoption and fostering were off the table, too. Even owning dogs was probably a terrible idea. Our plan for a family was thoroughly, absolutely shot.

"Oh, shit," he finally said.

"I'm a *contagious* Type Three. They might be able to fix the contagious part in a few months with antivirals. Or maybe we'll get lucky with one of the RNA vaccines they've fast-tracked. But the rest? Yeah. *Oh, shit.*"

I paused, inhaling deeply. Gregory had read much more than I'd been told, so he probably knew in far more detail how disastrous the situation was. He surely knew what needed to happen next, and I didn't want to make him feel like the bad guy by his having to be the one to say it out loud.

"We can't live together after this," I blurted. "It's not safe for you. I don't know how I can afford my own place, or who would rent to me, but I'll have to find something fast—"

"Please, keep the apartment. You're not well enough to deal with a move. I'm pretty sure the landlord will be cool with it. I'll make sure he's cool with it. We're on a two-year lease anyhow and I don't think he can break it without cause. As for me . . . I can just stay with my brother for a while."

"Move in with Joey?" I was legitimately shocked at his suggestion. "But he's such a . . . a *slob*."

I was being polite. Joey was more than a slob. He was a *pig*. Boorish, chauvinistic, more than a little sadistic. He was intelligent—he had a lucrative job as a senior programmer—and could be incredibly charming and put-together when it suited him. I'm sure all his bosses were impressed with him and thought he was a stand-up guy. He *knew* how to clean up and behave. But he loved being a bully. His abusive behavior had cost him his marriage, but the expensive divorce hadn't been the wake-up call Gregory hoped it would be.

I absolutely cringed at the thought of *anyone* living with Joey, much less someone I loved and cared about.

"I know it's not ideal," he replied. "But he's got a huge place in Upper Darington, and since his wife and kids moved out, I know he has plenty of room."

"I guess if the house is big enough, you won't have to deal with him and his mess that much?"

He laughed nervously. "Better the devil you know, right? I spent sixteen years living with the guy . . . what's a couple more months? Let's keep a good thought: If things go well, this is just temporary. I'll be able to move back in after they have vaccines and better treatments. I mean, so many people are affected, they *have* to come up with that stuff, right?"

"Sure," I said. "Let's keep a good thought."

# CHAPTER 6

Dr. Shapiro turns to her computer and scrolls through my file. "I see that during your discharge from Greenlawn, the counselor recommended you for an IUD. But you haven't gotten one yet?"

I shift uncomfortably on the exam table. I'd really hoped this topic wouldn't come up. "No, I don't have one. Could . . . could we put that off? I mean . . . it's not like I see anyone. Gregory can't get me pregnant when he's fifteen miles away."

"I don't honestly see a medical need for one," she says. "So, yes, I think we can put that off if that's your choice."

"It is," I say. "Thanks."

• • •

On my discharge day—my D-Day—Nurse Tesfaye brought me my street clothes and a bag of my things she'd kept in my downstairs locker. Shortly after I got dressed in jeans and a T-shirt that hung huge on my body, a short redheaded counselor from Homeland Security came to my room, decked out with a face shield, black N95 mask, black nitrile gloves, and a Taser. She was there to tell me what my new normal was going to look like in the wake of the Pandemic Security Act. I didn't have much experience dealing with counselors or cops, but it seemed to me that she carried herself more like a cop. She certainly dressed more like one.

"My name is Candy Kleypas and I am here to be very honest with you about your situation." She pronounced it *sitch-ee-AY-shun.* A southerner. Maybe from somewhere near Atlanta? My ears were pretty blunt from years of living in the Midwest.

She tugged down the hem of her black polo shirt under her bulletproof HOMELAND SECURITY tactical vest. "You have been diagnosed with Type Three Post-PVG Syndrome and that is *not* a good thing. It ain't good for you, it ain't good for your neighbors, it ain't good for your family."

I wanted to make a darkly sarcastic remark about not having any family left to endanger, but I figured that smarting off wouldn't help my cause much. So I just nodded.

"The news—which I know you probably ain't seen in a while—has widely publicized incidents in which other Type Threes have committed murder, assault, and even acts of cannibalism. One woman ate her dang baby on national TV. As far as the public is concerned, all y'all are a bunch of menaces. Our statistics back that up. The average Type Three has a fifteen percent chance of committing a violent criminal act after release."

*Fifteen percent?* I thought. *That's your idea of backing it up?*

In college, I'd volunteered as a shuttle driver to help female students reach their dorms safely after dark. As part of that job, I'd learned a lot about both sexual assault and domestic violence. The average woman has about a 29 percent chance of being beaten, burned, strangled, or sexually assaulted by an intimate partner sometime during her lifetime. And the situation is even worse on college campuses: 43 percent of women students have had violent or abusive partners.

As much as I dearly wanted to remind her of the statistics and ask her if the average Type Three was *actually* proven to be more inherently dangerous than a frat boy with rage, alcohol, and entitlement issues, I did want to leave Greenlawn that day. I wanted that *way* more than I wanted her to acknowledge how messed up the situation looked from my perspective.

So I simply nodded again.

"Those violent, often unspeakable criminal acts are what drove our lawmakers to create the Pandemic Security Act." That line sounded like part of a practiced speech; even her accent had shifted to something more Middle American.

She handed me a thick folder of papers. "Here's a copy of all the new regulations."

"Thanks." I tried to keep my voice neutral.

"But the first thing is that because you're contagious, you need to drastically limit your contact with other people. The virus is in your blood, saliva, urine, sweat, and other bodily fluids, and it can stay active awhile on surfaces. Be mindful of that."

I nodded. "Dr. Sallow and Nurse Tesfaye already told me how I can accidentally infect people."

"Good. The second thing is, we cain't do this by the honor system. This isn't like the flu or coronavirus or something." Her tone made me think that she was one of the people who thought COVID-19 had been overblown. "This is *serious*. Every Type Two or Type Three must stay in contact with their care teams. In many states, Twos and Threes must get ankle monitors from SCRAM Systems within twenty-four hours of being released from a care facility. Here, that only happens after a citation for noncompliance."

Ankle monitors? They sure were doubling down on making the chronically ill feel like criminals. At least I wouldn't have to wear one unless I got myself in trouble.

She continued: "You *are* required to have our Health Check-In app running at all possible times. Dr. Sallow says our techs have already installed the app?"

"Yes." I pulled my iPhone out of my jeans pocket to show her.

She nodded approvingly. "Check in to report your symptoms each day. Your phone will prompt you. If it's been more than twenty-four hours, you'll hear an alarm. If your phone is off the network for more than four hours, or if it's been more than thirty-six hours since you checked in, your care team will call an agent to check on your welfare."

"What if I need to go someplace where there isn't any cell coverage?"

"We discourage that," she replied. "But if it's absolutely necessary, let your care team know in advance."

"What if my battery dies?"

"Then you best get it charged up again." Her expression hadn't changed, but she sounded impatient. "Get an external battery and an extra charging cable and keep it in your car. Any questions about that?"

"No, ma'am."

"Use your phone as normal." Her voice had shifted again; I suspected this was more of the canned speech she gave everyone. "We will monitor your use of dating apps and social media. Meeting strangers for sex is a high-risk activity and is prohibited. You can continue preexisting relationships, but your partners will be subject to testing and quarantine under the PSA. You are absolutely forbidden from having *any* sort of close physical contact with Type Twos or other Type Threes."

I blinked at her. "But why? If we're already all infected, what's the problem?"

"There's concern about mutations. The virus is doing some real weird things and we don't want that bear poked."

"Okay . . ." That didn't sound like anything based in real science, but what did I know? I could look it up later.

"As the final and most important part of thing two, you will need to meet with your care team physician on a monthly basis. There is no cost to you for these appointments. If you are too ill to get to the doctor's office, do a telehealth visit through our app instead."

Kleypas reached into a pocket of her vest and pulled out a white business card. "You've been assigned to see Dr. Astrid Shapiro. She's your care team lead. You can contact her by phone or through the app."

I took the card and read it. The doctor's office was very close to our apartment; I could walk there if I needed to. At least that was something.

"Y'all are *not* allowed to go out in crowded public areas. If you can look around and see more than ten people? You ain't supposed to be there. Gyms are off-limits regardless, because nobody wants to touch your sweat. You are not allowed to go within a thousand feet of occupied playgrounds, day care centers, K12 schools. Cain't go to churches, neither. Which, if you ask me, is a real shame, 'cause all y'all need Jesus."

I bit my lip. While I wanted to make the sarcastic remark that what we actually needed was a freakin' vaccine, I was also thinking, *Wouldn't Jesus be* nice, *though?*

Wouldn't it be great to be absolutely certain that Jesus—or someone like him—was real? To pray and know, deep in your heart, that you were forging an eternal, intimate relationship with the endlessly loving, endlessly forgiving, tender and merciful son of God? To know that if you repented your earthly mistakes and took him into your heart, he would make sure that everything worked out okay in the end? That even if you suffered and died, he would take you into his strong, gentle arms and you would live on and on in his love and understanding? That you were a part of a great and wonderful thing, and your life on this earth among billions of other souls served a unique, divine purpose?

Wouldn't that kind of faith, that kind of certainty, be such an incredible comfort to someone in my situation? Wouldn't it be such a *relief* to just let Jesus take the wheel?

It sounded really, really great. But I knew that, like all other things that seemed far too good to be true, Jesus was mostly a comforting myth. That whole "God works in mysterious ways" thing felt like a bunch of hand waving.

I wasn't an atheist, though. What did I know about souls? There *could* be a god out there, somewhere. Maybe more than one! I figured the modern Jesus was based on a real man: a charismatic, rebellious mortal with some forward-thinking ideas and a really effective street team. But no supernatural powers until storytellers gave him some. I hadn't seen any evidence of the supernatural, so I also hadn't seen evidence that gods really exist, at least not in the way most churches claim.

When I met Gregory, he described himself as a recovering Catholic. We didn't talk about religion a whole lot. It only really came up the first time he took off his shirt and I saw his colorful tattoo of Saint Michael the Archangel slaying Satan in the form of a dragon. It's on his left pectoral. I figured if he was extremely religious, our relationship probably wouldn't work out over the long haul. Too many differences, you know? But he said that he'd mostly lost his faith because of bad experiences growing up in the Church. He still appreciated the ritual and symbolism, though. His family attended St. Mary's Catholic Church in Belding, Michigan, and he was quite taken with its stained glass window depicting Saint Michael's battle. He got the tattoo to remind himself that good could triumph over evil.

Gregory said he believed in Jesus and the angels as symbolic figures but not as literal divine beings. He said he didn't really believe in them so much as he liked the idea of them. And that seemed reasonable to me.

Sometimes I envied people who believed in Jesus, heart and soul. I envied their faith that they had been born with a clear spiritual purpose in the world. That they were part of something bigger than themselves. Sometimes I envied them really, really hard.

I knew I wasn't capable of that kind of faith, though; my critical thinking kept getting in the way.

Kleypas was oblivious to the swirl of thoughts she'd set off inside my head, and she'd moved on to my *practical* purpose in the world.

"Obviously, you're allowed to go to work. All employers have been advised of current laws and guidelines."

"Okay." *All of them?* I wondered. It seemed implausible that they'd gotten the word out to tiny under-the-table businesses, family farms that used migrant labor, or every wealthy home-owner who was paying a housekeeper in cash. Of course, any employer who wasn't paying payroll taxes probably didn't care about PSA regulations, either.

"When you're at work, or out in public—and we recommend staying home unless it's absolutely necessary to go out—you need to wear a mask. *Always*. And you need to make sure it's over your dang nose! You *will* face consequences for noncompliance. Do you understand?"

"Yes, ma'am." From what Dr. Sallow had told me, there was still argument about whether the PVG virus was too big to be carried far in the air or not, but sneezes and spit droplets were clearly a problem.

"Good. Because if you don't follow the rules, you'll end up someplace that ain't nearly as nice as Greenlawn."

"Where would I end up, exactly?" My heart beat loud in my ears. It felt unsafe to ask that, but it *was* a fair question.

She eyed me from behind her clear face shield. "Well, obviously, y'all cain't go in with the general population. They've designated certain prisons and county jails as PVG facilities. They're moving all the healthy inmates out of the supermax in Elderville to keep that place open for PVGs who are particularly violent. I assure you, none of those are places you want to go."

"Noted."

Clearly, something in my tone displeased her, but she didn't remark on it. Instead, she asked, "You got kids, Miss Erin?"

I shook my head, a sudden lump rising in my throat. "No."

"Good. That makes everything a lot simpler. Do you have an IUD?"

My stomach clenched and I couldn't help twitching. I had to work hard to keep my face neutral. "Yeah, no, Gregory and I were using condoms."

"You need to make an appointment to get an IUD," she replied briskly. "ASAP."

*Oh hell no,* I thought.

I'd talked to women who thought their IUDs were the best thing since ice cream. Sure I had. And all respect to them.

But I'd also taken my college roommate Kayleigh to get an IUD when she got her very first boyfriend our freshman year. I held her hand and watched as the nurse laid out an array of plastic and surgical steel tools. And when the doctor put those tools up inside her, each of which came out covered in her blood, I tried to distract her by asking her about her favorite animals. That didn't work for very long. She was in extreme, jaw-clenching pain, and then she straight-up went into shock. Her face had lost all color, her lips had gone gray, she was sweating profusely. Her skin had turned cold and clammy. If the procedure had gone on any longer, I think she would have been in a seriously bad way.

The nurse was lightning quick to give her an ice pack and a juice box afterward. Which seemed like good, proper care at the time. But I thought about it later . . . and I realized that they'd *clearly expected* some portion of their patients to go into shock during the procedure. Had they warned Kayleigh about that, or about the level of pain she'd experience? No. All they'd done was suggest she take some Tylenol before her appointment. Which she had done, and which was not nearly enough to blunt the torture of *unanesthetized surgery*.

Afterward, I wished her boyfriend could have been there. It wasn't that I minded taking her and holding her hand. But *he* needed to witness her pain. *He* needed to see with his own two eyes what the basic, up-front cost of sex was for her. Then maybe neither she nor I would have heard a single whining complaint from him about how condoms were so uncomfortable.

But the worst part? The gynecologist acted like Kayleigh's pain and shock were some puzzling inconvenience to him, like it was all just in her head. Grade A medical gaslighting. Even before I had a chance to really think about what happened, I wanted to punch him in his nuts and then innocently ask him why he was on the floor, groaning. But obviously, I didn't want to go to jail for assault, either.

So, no thank you. I did *not* want an IUD. Not when I hadn't had a kid to stretch out my uterus first. And that was not going to happen.

"My boyfriend moved out," I told Kleypas. "I'm going to be by myself. And you just told me I can't have new sex partners. So I don't see why I need one."

"Bless your heart." She gave me a hard look. "Are you new to bein' a woman? The world is just bursting with psychos. Some maniac could break into your apartment and rape you. A pregnancy would be a hell of a complication. I hear the virus is turnin' embryos into cancers. Gettin' an IUD is just common sense, honey."

I felt sick. "Couldn't I get an abortion?"

"That's still illegal in this state. PVG didn't change that."

"Seriously? They're not making an exception?"

The counselor shrugged, and gave me a sympathetic, apologetic look. "I think your doctor can still get you Plan B. I *think* morning-after pills are still legal here."

"Well, that's something." I took a deep breath. "I guess you're advising the men to get vasectomies?"

She blinked at me. "Why would we do that?"

# CHAPTER 7

"Have you made any new friends lately?" Dr. Shapiro asks.

"There are some new people I chat with. Type Twos and other Type Threes. I met them in online support groups. They're nice. We've had some movie watch parties online. I guess they count as friends?"

She nods. "Have you met with any of your new friends in person?"

"Of course not," I lie. "That would be illegal, wouldn't it?"

She nods again. "It would."

• • •

Dr. Sallow had scheduled my release for 8:45 p.m. so that the sun would be down by the time I had to go outside. Gregory was supposed to pick me up from Greenlawn. We figured that if I sat in the back row of his SUV and we both wore masks and kept the windows partway down, that would be enough air circulation and social distancing to keep his risk of infection low. But we'd have the chance to see each other in person, chat a bit on the drive to the apartment. At least share an elbow bump before he left, even if we couldn't hug or kiss. It would be better than nothing, right?

But after Kleypas left me with my folder of paper and deep misgivings, I checked my iPhone and discovered that Gregory had texted me.

Im so so sorry honey but work is blowing up.
they called me back in. legit emergency here.

gonna have to work late into the nite. Found
a service called DocRyde and called u a car.
driver's name is Betty. ETA 9:00.

I started crying well before any coherent thoughts formed in my head. Getting to see Gregory was practically the only thing I'd really been looking forward to that week. I'd already tried to practice radical acceptance about the situation. About not being able to sink into his arms, not being able to fall asleep on the tattoo of Saint Michael on his chest. I'd tried to get my head and heart right about all those things, and I thought I'd done an okay job.

But to not be able to see him at all that day? I wasn't just disappointed. I felt utterly abandoned, discarded, even if logically I knew he was still doing his best to see that I was taken care of. My head couldn't convince my heart that everything would be okay.

When can i see you? I texted back.

Video chat 2nite? i can come by this wknd?

The weekend felt like it was years away. What would I do to distract myself until then? But I typed back, ok. love u.

love u too.

I swiped the chat app away and cried for a few more minutes. Then dried my face, got my stuff together, and let Nurse Tesfaye know I was ready to go downstairs.

• • •

Darius escorted me out to the front parking circle and we waited for my ride. It was the first time I'd been outside in weeks. I breathed deeply, smelling honeysuckle and lilac on the warm spring air. The air felt real. But when I looked around me, part of my brain was convinced that this was all a clever illusion, that I'd walked out onto a Hollywood set and not into the real world. Dr. Sallow mentioned I might get this feeling sometimes. *Derealization,* he said it was.

"You got anything fun planned after this?" Darius asked.

I laughed bitterly. "What am I gonna do that's fun? Can't go to the bar, can't go to the beach, can't go to the movies, can't get laid."

It felt taboo to mention sex around Darius. Which I guess is why I said it.

He, of course, was utterly unperturbed. "There's always video games. The new *Far Cry* is pretty sick."

"That's true. I could try games." The idea didn't really fill me with much enthusiasm.

I saw the headlights of an electric car coming up the long, oak-shaded drive well before I heard its artificial engine noise or the rumble of its tires across the uneven blacktop.

"Looks like your ride's here," Darius said.

A green Toyota Sienna with DOCRYDE stenciled on the side in white lettering pulled into the circle. A young woman in a blue paper mask slid out of the driver's seat and came around the side with a small tablet in a purple case.

"Erin Holdaway?" She used one hand to absently flip her long chestnut hair away from her side-shave.

I stood frozen, staring at her hair. Flashing back on the recurring nightmare I'd had in the hospital. This woman was a stranger, but . . . I was sure she looked just like the woman in the dream who'd pulled me free of the tar pit. The one who'd pushed me through the motel door.

"Miss Holdaway?" Darius touched my shoulder. "You still with us?"

"What? Yeah." My cheeks flushed warm, and I looked from him to her. "Yes, I'm Erin Holdaway. Sorry."

The young woman didn't seem fazed. "My name is Betty, and I'm here from DocRyde. Gregory Watkins contacted us to give you a ride to your apartment. Does that sound right?"

"Yeah, that's right," I said.

"And is this your address?" She showed me her screen.

"Yeah."

"Great!" She opened the rear door of the van and let me climb inside with my plastic bag of stuff. The air inside the vehicle smelled strongly of disinfectant. The van was equipped with a wheelchair lift, and one row of seats had been taken out. A sturdy floor-to-ceiling Plexiglas panel separated the front seats from the passenger section. I settled in the back right as Betty got into the driver's seat.

"All belted in?" she asked over her shoulder.

"Yep."

"Super. Gotta follow all the rules." She put the van into gear and slowly circled back to the long driveway.

"Yeah. Lots of rules to follow now, I guess." I couldn't stop staring at her side-shave. And I wanted to tell her about the dream I'd had about her before I'd even met her, but there was no way that wouldn't make me seem like I'd absolutely lost my mind. No way that wouldn't seem creepy.

"So, uh, I've never heard of DocRyde before," I said, desperately casting about for a safe topic of conversation.

I didn't want to just sit there in silence, because then I wouldn't be able to stop myself from thinking about the dream. I couldn't *really* have dreamed about her, could I? It had to be my mind playing tricks on me. Editing my memory to make it *seem* like she'd been the one I'd dreamed of. She'd been blurry in most of it, anyhow, and young women with chestnut hair and side-shaves had to be pretty common, right? It *had* to be just a strange memory thing.

I was fine. I wasn't losing my mind. Everything would be fine.

"Yeah, it's a pretty new service," she said. "I guess they launched sometime last year, but business really picked up for them during the pandemic."

"Have you been driving for them very long?" I was starting to realize that, even with the barrier up, I could smell Betty. Not her perfume. *Her.* And she smelled fucking delicious.

I didn't know whether I wanted to make out with her in the back of the van or crack her skull open. Maybe both. Jesus Christ. What was wrong with me?

"Just a couple of weeks," she replied, oblivious to the state I was in, thank God. "I had to go to the hospital, and afterward the restaurant laid me off. They didn't have a choice. Can't have me sweating and breathing on the duck à l'orange, you know? But after that, I still needed a job. DocRyde needed people who didn't mind driving PVG patients around at night. So here I am."

My physical reaction to her was making it hard to focus on what she was saying. "You . . . you caught PVG, too?"

Why hadn't I reacted to any of the hospital staff like this? I'd occasionally wanted to kill them for their brains, sure. Just a passing urge. But I'd never been viscerally attracted to any of them like this. And it wasn't because I found them unattractive: Dr. Sallow had a silver fox thing going on, Darius had an amazing body, and Nurse Tesfaye was a damn pretty woman. I never felt like I'd seriously lose control around any of them. At least not for more than a few seconds.

I'd been in the van for more than a few seconds, and my body was convinced that Betty was an absolute, entire snack.

"Yup," Betty said. "Type Two, if you're curious. And no, we're not breaking any rules being in this van together." She rapped the Plexiglas barrier with the back of her right hand. "This is business. Precautions taken and all."

Was I reacting to her like this because she was a Two? Was *this* the reason we were forbidden from getting with other Types? Maybe it wasn't about mutations so much as the possibility of horrifying bloodbath orgies? Couldn't really blame Homeland Security for wanting to nip that in the bud.

"What did you do before?" I asked, praying that she had a Taser tucked away someplace, in case I did something really, really stupid. Thinking about Homeland Security was helping me calm down. A little, anyway.

"I was sous chef at Le Pamplemousse." She sighed. "Working in a kitchen is a tough job. Long hours on your feet, you know? Burns . . . cuts . . . the chef losing his mind and screaming at everyone. Crazy stress. Driving is a whole lot easier. But I miss the restaurant so much sometimes. The energy, the camaraderie we all had."

"I bet." I took a deep breath, trying to focus on what she'd said. Trying to imagine what being a sous chef was like. I'd never worked in food service, but the cooking shows certainly made it seem like a high-pressure environment. "HR says I still have a job, but I don't know that it will be the same one. It probably *can't* be, since I can't be out in the daytime much. I have no clue what they'll do with me."

"It's good you still have a job, though. A lot of us have been fired. What did you do before?"

"Desktop support," I said. "It's fun. I get to help people with their computers at UCC. *Got* to, anyhow."

"Hey." She adjusted the rearview mirror so she could look at me. Meeting her gaze absolutely thrilled me. "This is going to sound like some dumb pickup line—and I promise you it isn't—but. Haven't I seen you around before?"

My heart beat faster in my chest. I started sweating. *Don't tell her about the stupid dream. Don't.*

"No, I'm pretty sure we haven't met before this. I've . . . I've never been to Le Pamplemousse."

"What about Hot Chicken Domination? The Sassy Gal Saloon? The swing dance club in University North?"

I shook my head. "No. I haven't been to any of those places."

"Huh. Weird! It's just that you seem *super* familiar. Anyhow, those are all amazing spots and you should totally go." She winced behind her mask. "I mean, whenever we're allowed to go anywhere again."

• • •

When I got back into the apartment, I turned on our bedroom TV to drown out the awful silence. Gregory had left it tuned to CNN. The screen showed shaky aerial video of a large square concrete building engulfed in smoke and flame. My stomach dropped. This did not look good.

"PVG vaccine production efforts suffered a major setback this afternoon," a woman announced over the video. "Multiple manufacturing sites across the US were targeted in a coordinated fire bombing attack. Thirty people are dead and hundreds are missing or injured. The neo-Nazi antivax group Blood Pure has claimed responsibility."

The screen switched to a feed of a man in a white balaclava, sunglasses, and gray combat fatigues standing in what looked like a concrete bunker. An AR-15 was slung across his chest. "Today, we have struck a blow—"

"Not today, Satan." I flipped over to my music streaming service and cued up some chillwave. "I can't stop you, but at least I don't have to listen to your violent bullshit."

I opened a spa basket I'd been saving for a romantic getaway and decided to bath bomb my senses into oblivion. If a nice soak didn't help me sleep that night, well, at least it would get the stink of Greenlawn out of my pores.

My iPhone pinged as I was toweling off.

Gregory had texted me: got time 4 a video chat? Use ur cmpter. . . . i wanna screen share something.

Sure. Give me a sec, I replied.

I put on my fluffy purple robe and went into the bedroom to

boot up my laptop. A few moments later, I logged in to my video chat program and connected.

"Hi, sweetie." Gregory grinned and waved at me. He was in black boxers and a plain white T-shirt, sitting cross-legged on a bed, his back against a blank beige wall. "Did your ride home go okay?"

"Yeah, it was fine. No problems."

"That's good." He looked a little ashamed. "I'm so, so sorry that I couldn't be there myself."

"It's okay. Honest. I know you're doing your best. I really appreciate that you cleaned the place up for me."

"The least I could do, considering."

"How have you been? Did things calm down at work?"

"Yes, *finally*." He rolled his eyes, looking exasperated. "But that's not what I wanted to talk about."

"Oh?"

"Yeah!" His expression brightened. "Lemme share my screen . . ."

My view switched from Gregory to a gallery of computer-rendered garden images: rows of bright tulips and willow-shaded hostas. A carpet of pink and purple phlox around a calm koi pond with a wooden footbridge. They looked like high-end landscaping designs.

"Those are nice," I said. "What are they for?"

"So there's this place up in the hills outside town." He switched the view back to his face. "I'd never heard of it until the other day, when Mark Mayne came to the office and a couple of us started chatting with him."

Gregory paused, looking pleased and expectant. Like he figured I'd be impressed.

So I had to wince and say, "I'm sorry, honey. I don't know who that is."

"Oh." His face fell. "He's been all over the local news . . ."

"Remember that whole hospital thing?"

"Ope." He blushed in embarrassment. "Yeah. Sorry. Anyhow, he's the CEO of Mayne Sequence Solar, which just had their IPO. Investors went *nuts* for it. Mayne Sequence is like the only big local company that isn't floundering around like a dinosaur in a tar pit right now. Good news is hard to come by, so he's getting a lot of press."

"Gotcha. So, what does he have to do with the photos?"

"Right. The place up in the hills was the family mansion in the nineteenth century. His great-whatevs Charles Castaigne had it built in 1855. Gothic revival, looks like a castle. Had *amazing* gardens. People came from all over to see them. But the family hit hard times after the 1929 stock market crash and they lost the house to the bank, which sold it to another bank, et cetera. It stood empty and nearly abandoned for nearly a century."

Gregory made a sad trombone noise. "But, a few years ago, Mark—he told me to call him Mark—got the money together to buy back Castaigne Manor and the grounds. He's planning to bring the gardens back even bigger and fancier than they were. He's going to open them up for tours, weddings, corporate events."

He paused, grinning. I sensed that a serious bro crush had taken hold.

"I really hit it off with Mark, and he offered me a special no-deposit deal on a reservation. It's good for two years after they open. We're gonna have such a rad wedding there! We'll have all this space, and it'll be absolutely gorgeous . . . Seriously, look at this!"

His window switched to an image of a white gazebo surrounded by blossoming cherry and pear trees. Behind it rose a gothic manor with a crenellated tower.

My vision blurred and my heart began to beat fast. Details of the strange dream I'd had in the Greenlawn courtyard started flooding back. Details I thought I'd forgotten.

Or had I forgotten anything? Maybe my brain was just editing my memory to make me think that the castle manor in the landscaping mock-up was the same one I'd dreamed about. I couldn't know for sure.

"Are you okay?" Gregory looked concerned.

"Yeah. I . . . I blank out a little sometimes, still. The doctor said it's a side effect of the fever. Hopefully it'll go away soon."

"Do you need to go to bed? Get some rest?"

"Yeah, I probably should. I love you."

"Love you, too."

After we signed off, I put on my pajamas but didn't go to bed right away. Just puttered around in the kitchen, trying to shake off the lingering creepy feeling I had, trying to figure out what I needed to get from the grocery store.

Shortly before midnight, there was a soft knocking at my front door. Three gentle raps and then silence. I thought it could be a noise from the apartment upstairs, or maybe air in a pipe. It was far too late for anyone to come for a visit. But I went to the door to check, just in case.

On my doormat was a brown padded mailing envelope with "For Erin" written in blue ballpoint on the front. Neat block lettering. I glanced around; nobody was in the breezeway. I picked up the envelope and ducked back inside my apartment, latching the door behind me.

I stared at the envelope. Who could have left this? Should I open it? Whatever was inside was hard, rectangular. Solid. Definitely not a dead rat. And it was the wrong shape to be a vial of poison.

So I decided to stop wondering and tore open the adhesive flap.

And pulled out the compact, shiny black slab of an Android

phone. An inexpensive prepaid LG model. I clicked the side button to wake it up. It was unlocked. On the home screen, a digital note was open.

Text me sometime. This = 1K texts, no voice,
no data.
I really hope I hear from you.♥—B.

# CHAPTER 8

"Have you been able to engage in rewarding personal hobbies and other activities?" Dr. Shapiro asks.

"Yes, I've been keeping myself busy when I'm not at work," I reply. "I'm not bored."

She checks off another box. "That's good to hear."

◆ ◆ ◆

I spent hours poring over the prepaid burner phone Betty had left me. Searching every folder for spyware and malware. Carefully taking the case off and checking it for mysterious chips or bugs. Aside from the note and putting a number in the address book, it looked like she hadn't tampered with it. She hadn't even applied OS updates. It certainly didn't have the hateful Homeland Security app on it.

So I was pretty sure it was clean. *Pretty* sure. But I've never been a genuine phone expert. And obviously I wasn't going to do a whole lot of web searching on the subject on my iPhone. Or my laptop. My PowerBook didn't seem to have been tampered with, but who knew what had gone on at the apartment while I was away?

I already knew Gregory wouldn't tell me things if people he saw as health authorities had told him not to reveal them. He'd probably tell me if he wasn't telling me something . . . but there was the possibility he didn't know, either. I hadn't even started on the thick folder Kleypas had given me. For all I knew, the new law empowered Homeland Security to make the landlord quietly let them into our apartment to plant surveillance equipment.

*Calm down,* I thought. *How likely is that, really?*

Surveillance took time, equipment, and staff. All that took *money.* It was one thing for politicians to beat their chests about national security and public safety, but it was another thing for them to actually spend the necessary funds on it all. They hadn't bothered to give me an ankle monitor. So the simplest probability was also the likeliest: they were mostly using the software they'd installed on my iPhone to monitor me. Just like they told me to my face.

But. It was possible that someone had the bright idea to really ramp up the for-profit prisons in this state. Want to get hundreds if not thousands of fresh bodies into prison call centers and garment factories? Inflict a bunch of draconian, difficult-to-abide-by laws on a newly Othered group that's been stripped of its civil rights. The profits could be tremendous.

And in that light . . . this phone was an obvious honeypot. A trap that would ultimately land me in the supermax in Elderville. Or someplace just as awful.

On the other hand, we Types 2 and 3 were a sickly bunch. The state might stand to spend at least as much on health care as it would make on telesales or athletic jerseys.

So I was back on the simplest probability: my iPhone was my personal spy. And if that was the situation, then Betty giving me a burner phone for texting her was the most logical way to get around it. My iPhone could pick up my conversations, but it wouldn't record me texting on another device, particularly if they weren't on the same network.

And, frankly? I was impressed by Betty's casual power move. The phone in my hands represented cleverness, dedication, and follow-through. I found all those things quite alluring.

*Jesus, what are you doing?* I thought. *You're seriously thinking of cheating on Gregory with a woman you just met? You don't even really know if she's into you. You know nothing about her.*

I wanted to know all about her, though. I wanted that pretty badly. I wanted it nearly as much as I'd wanted to eat Dr. Sallow's brain during the test in Greenlawn.

But I didn't want to hurt Gregory. I *never* wanted to hurt Gregory. That's why I was alone in the apartment—so I couldn't hurt him by infecting him or assaulting him.

Our relationship was too important to destroy. What else did I have left in my life now? Maybe our bond was going to fracture anyhow under the stress of it suddenly becoming a long-distance thing, even though we were still in the same city. But I couldn't deliberately do something I knew would jeopardize what we'd built during our five years together. Not over what so far only amounted to lust and fantasy. At best. What kind of monster would I have to be to do that?

Gregory was a good man. He was someone I could count on, no questions. He treated me with respect. Sure, our sex life was a little vanilla, a little routine, but so what? It was fine. He was the kind of guy millions of women would be perfectly happy to settle down with.

But . . . Gregory was also the reason I had met Betty. Caught between commitments to me and to his work, he'd chosen work, like a good American. I couldn't blame him for that. But there were consequences for every decision. Only, I guess a counselor from Homeland Security didn't show up at the apartment to warn him first.

I sighed to myself, staring at my distorted reflection in the glass of the burner's dark screen. Whatever I ultimately decided to do, I needed to talk to Gregory first.

•   •   •

I splurged on a half pound of pork brains from a little mercado a few miles away. The butcher paper–wrapped package was thirty dollars. The masked delivery guy dropped it on my doormat and scampered away like he'd just completed a heroin deal. But I'd been lucky to find any at all; Kroger and the other supermarkets were completely out. And the supply chain situation was only going to get worse as more people got infected and survived. The pandemic had turned an unpopular offal item into gourmet unobtainium.

I didn't know what I would do when I couldn't get brains at all and had to rely solely on my prescription supplement, bovellum. It's what I and every other upstanding, gainfully employed, fully insured Type Three citizen in America gets: a meager allotment of refrigerated capsules containing an unappetizing gray paste. Mostly it's cow brains fortified with glutamate, GABA, choline, amino acids, antioxidant vitamins, a few fatty acids, and just the barest hint of pureed cadaver white matter. It's enough to keep your skin and brains from ulcerating. It's enough to keep your nose from rotting off. It's enough to help you think clearly enough to function at your average white-collar job.

It is not enough to keep you from constantly wishing you could taste the real thing. Lightly poached pork brains bulked out with egg whites weren't really the real thing, either, but they were more satisfying than bovellum capsules. The ultimate in comfort food, at least for the new me.

I needed a custard bowl of it in my hands before I had The Talk with my fiancé Friday night.

"Howdy, stranger." I waved at Gregory through my laptop's webcam.

"Hey, night owl!" He grinned at me. It looked like he was out on his brother's backyard deck; the last pink streaks of the sunset were just visible over the dark maples silhouetted behind him. "How are things going at the apartment?"

"They're going okay. The blackout curtains are working out really well—thanks for putting those up."

"It was the least I could do for my sweetie! You all fixed for supplies?"

I nodded. "I got grocery and prescription deliveries set up, and I'm getting used to the third-shift schedule."

"Where did they put you?"

"Network ops. I was sort of hoping for a remote, flex-hours kind of gig, maybe as a coder, but apparently they desperately needed a new warm body to babysit the mainframes and server farm."

Gregory raised his eyebrows. "That's unexpected. They know you're still contagious, right?"

"They know!" I shrugged at him. "Apparently I get a socially distanced workstation, and I get the single-seat handicapped restroom down the hall all to myself. And Mareva works the same shift I'll be on. She'll be good to chat with, even if it has to be at a distance."

"It's really nice that you already know someone there."

"It is. Honestly, the situation could be a lot worse," I said. "Speaking of . . . How are things going with your brother?"

His expression clouded. "It's okay. Not great, not terrible. We had a bit of a fight over dishes a little while ago. It's like he expects me to do them all the time, and it's just so tedious . . . but if I don't do them, they pile up forever and we get ants."

"Dishes and laundry, the never-ending chores." I paused to eat a nice big spoonful of brains. Steeling myself. "Hey. I wanted to talk to you about something. It's . . . awkward, I guess."

He frowned, looking concerned. "What's going on?"

"Nothing bad!" I assured him. "It's just . . . I've been thinking about how we can't be close to each other anymore, and about how that's, you know, going to cause stress . . ."

He looked cautious, and a little confused. "Yeah . . . ?"

Another spoonful of brains. I desperately wanted to tell him the truth. I'd left my iPhone in the bathroom with the fan on, and closed the door, but I couldn't be sure that nobody was listening in on my laptop as well.

"It's . . . not fair to you that you can't get physical comfort," I finally said. "It's not fair that you can't have that. And I don't want us cheating on each other. Cheating is lying. And lying eats away at a relationship."

Christ. I was telling him all these perfectly true things and they were still all lies by omission. Lies and meta-lies.

Meanwhile, Gregory's expression had turned to something close to fawn-in-the-headlights terror. "What . . . what are you saying?"

I took a deep breath, squinching my eyes shut. "I'm saying it's okay with me if you see other women right now. I love you and I don't want to break up with you, but I think it would be better under the circumstances if we had an open relationship. For now. I . . . I mean, obviously *I* can't see anyone. That wouldn't be legal. Obviously."

I felt like I'd started babbling, so I stopped talking and opened my eyes.

Gregory was staring at me, white-faced. If I didn't know better, I'd almost think he looked guilty.

"An open relationship?" He sounded stunned.

"I mean, for now. And . . . and you don't have to tell your friends, or anyone in your family. *Please* don't tell your brother or he's gonna try to drag you to some nasty brothel."

I gave a nervous little laugh to show I was mostly joking. I couldn't really picture him going to a brothel. The first time he and I had sex, I'd had to coax him like I was trying to get a baby rabbit to eat from my hand. He'd been too embarrassed to let me see him fully naked for months afterward.

Gregory looked stricken. His mouth worked, but no words came out. Oh God. I'd shocked him. Horrified him. Mortally offended him, maybe.

"Are you okay?" I asked. "Please say something."

"But . . ." He gaped like a goldfish out of water. "But how would me seeing other women be fair to you? How could that not hurt you?"

"I mean, you wouldn't have to, like, give me a play-by-play after you went on a date or anything."

"But what if I fell in love? What then?"

I took another deep breath. I'd expected him to ask this, and had carefully thought out my answer. But I ate another spoonful of brains before I answered, just the same. "Okay, this is a huge *if,* but, hypothetically . . . if I can get well again, do you still want to have kids with me someday?"

"Of course I do."

"And if I had a baby boy, you'd love him?"

"Of course! Absolutely!"

"And if, two or three years later, I had a baby girl, you'd love her, too, right?"

"Naturally, yes."

"Would loving your baby daughter make you stop loving your son?"

He looked deeply hurt. "Of course not! I'd love both my kids!"

"Okay, so if you can love more than one child at a time, why can't you love more than one woman at a time? Why does romantic love have to be different than the love you have for family?" I asked. "Is romantic love like a birthday cake, where you hand it out and then there's none left for anyone else?"

His mouth went a bit slack, his eyes widening. I figured I'd just blown his mind.

"No . . . no, I guess it's not like a cake," he finally said.

"All I ask is that you be safe, you know? Don't catch PVG or HIV or anything else with initials. And be up front with whoever you see. Make sure she knows that you have a fiancée. Make sure she's a person who learned about sharing in kindergarten. I can't say I'd be *thrilled* if you fell in love with someone else, but . . . it's not like I can demand that you not love someone. That's a horrible thing to ask. And it's not like you can just flip a switch and decide you're not going to fall for someone."

At least, *I* couldn't.

He nodded cautiously. "That . . . seems reasonable, I suppose."

"And . . . I might never get healthy again." The admission made my whole body sag in my seat. "If you fall in love with someone else, and you really like her better, then maybe that's just fate. I want to be part of your happiness; I don't want to be the thing that keeps you from being happy."

I paused. "So . . . are you okay with trying an open relationship?"

"Are *you* sure you're okay with it?" he asked.

"Yes. And if I get mad later, please just remind me that this was all my idea."

"If you're sure," he said. "Then yes, I'm okay with it."

"Okay. I'm glad. I think it's for the best. Look, it's getting late and I should probably let you go. I love you."

"I love you, too, sweetie."

"Good-bye."

I logged off and finished the bits of brains left in the little bowl. Scooped the crumbs up with my finger and licked them off. This was the best conversation I'd had with Gregory in weeks, and I felt like an absolute monster.

# CHAPTER 9

"Are you exercising regularly?" Dr. Shapiro asks.

"I'm trying to," I reply. "I work out at home, and sometimes I go for walks at dusk or in the early morning, when it's still twilight."

"I suppose it's not safe to go walking late at night, is it?" she commented.

"No, it's not very safe at all."

• • •

A few nights before I started back at UCC, I decided to do a test run of my nightly commute. Partly because I had no idea what traffic was like at that hour and partly because I wanted to make sure my Honda and my driving skills were okay. Gregory had taken my car out once every week or so to make sure the tires didn't get flat spots, but other than that it had pretty much just been sitting.

After I got on the freeway, I decided I should go ahead and gas up, so I pulled off at an exit that had a handy Speedway. I was approaching the back of the convenience store, so I couldn't see the front doors as I drove up. The fuel canopy lights were on, but there didn't seem to be any customers. I pulled up to one of the pumps and got out to unscrew my gas cap.

And I nearly peed myself when a man off to my right screamed, "Freeze! Put your hands up where I can see them."

My hands shot up automatically and I turned slightly to see who was shouting at me. A SWAT cop in full urban battle gear. And he was pointing a riot shotgun at my head.

"I said *freeze!*" he screamed. With his protective goggles on, he reminded me of some black predatory beetle. Even though I knew how many cops had behaved during the coronavirus years, I was still surprised that he wasn't wearing a mask.

"Yes, sir. Sorry, sir," I stammered.

"Are you with those freaks? Driving getaway?" he demanded.

"I—I don't understand. I'm just here for gas."

I finally looked past him, and saw the bloody carnage in the doorway of the convenience store. There were four bodies that I could see, lying on the sidewalk or holding the sliding doors open. Three were missing huge chunks of their skulls, I figured from shotgun blasts, and their hands were caked in gore. Jesus Christ.

The fourth corpse might have been the store clerk. She'd been torn wide open at the neck and wrists. Bled nearly dry.

"I came up the back way." My voice shook. "I couldn't see."

"You expect me to believe that? You're a freak like them. You got freak eyes."

"If . . . if I were a getaway driver, wouldn't I drive up to the front of the store? Not over here to the pumps?"

He didn't say anything. Didn't lower the shotgun. His eyes flickered down to my Honda, then at the credit card clutched in my hand.

"I have a disease." *Oh God I'm going to die here.* "If . . . if you shoot me, you'll breathe it in."

"Fuck me," he growled, lowering the shotgun maybe an inch. "You got any gas in your tank?"

Hope soared inside me. "A couple gallons?"

"Then get the fuck out of here. Right the fuck *now.*"

"Yes, sir. Thank you, sir."

●　●　●

I was still completely high on adrenaline when I got back to my apartment, and that gave me the courage to finally text Betty.

New phone, who dis?

The three dots pulsed. A moment later: LOL. Plz tell me where we met w/o IDing me.

Green Toyota van, I keyed in. You gave me a ride home.

And u were wearing jeans and tee shirt.

What was I wearing?

Crap. I had to be honest in my reply: I wasn't looking at ur clothes, sorry. But u wore vanilla perfume. U had purple tablet case. Chestnut hair w/side shave.

LOL ok, she typed back. You pass the test. U want to meet up somewhere for drinks and chat?

Yes, definitely.

• • •

We agreed to meet up at 10 p.m. in an industrial area a couple of miles from me, the following Friday. Our rendezvous wasn't in the best neighborhood, and that worried me plenty, but she promised it would be worth it. I could have driven there, to be physically safer, but my Honda had built-in GPS. Even if that was secure, I couldn't be sure that someone hadn't planted a tracker. I decided I'd just walk there, carry pepper spray, and take my chances.

The four days between our text chat and the actual date were agonizing. My nerves were keyed up so much I had a much harder time than usual sleeping during the day. Had I just agreed to meet a Homeland Security agent posing as Betty? Was I going to end up in prison?

Or was it really Betty on the other burner—but the virus had turned her into one of the crazed, bloodthirsty murderers I heard about on the news? Or maybe she was working with a group of

Twos and she'd agreed to be the bait. Was I going to end up in a shallow unmarked grave?

Or was I just being paranoid and this was nothing more than the most normal first date that we could manage under deeply abnormal circumstances?

Honestly? Most of the first dates I'd been on involved possible serial killer scenarios floating around in the back of my head. And while the idea that I might end up raped or dead had been relatively easy to push away, I always took the usual precautions with men I didn't really know. Meet in a well-lit, public spot I was familiar with. Know where the exits are. Keep an eagle eye on my food and drinks. Tell a friend where I was going and who I'd be with.

But now, my status as a Type Three meant all those simple, routine precautions were impossible. Staying safe from the law meant engaging in wildly unsafe behavior. My situation was ironic and terrifying.

I could ghost her. Of course I could. I could absolutely chicken out and stay in my apartment behind my blackout drapes. I'd be safe from the world and the world would be safe from me.

But if I did that, how was I ever going to live any kind of life now? I'd just be existing. My life would be work and sleep, meds and walking, bland food and TV, and that would be it. I'd want to hang myself before the year was over.

So, despite my buzzing nerves and aching stomach, I decided to go through with it.

I'd established a pattern of watching shows or movies for a few hours every night, so around 9 p.m. I left my iPhone sitting on the couch with the TV on and tuned to HBO. Pocketed the burner and my spray, put on my mask, and headed out, closing and locking the door behind me as quietly as I could.

• • •

I don't mind walking. My body is so thin now, so light, it feels like almost no effort. Even when I'm too stupid to do anything else, I can walk. Lots of things hurt pretty much all the time, my guts and my head especially. But my feet and legs are fine. And walking until I'm so exhausted that I just want to sleep is the only thing that reliably takes the edge off my hunger when *that* gets bad.

I can walk for miles and miles. It takes me a while. I'm not fast. But I can get almost anywhere in the city if I have the time.

Problem is, I don't have nearly enough time, and I know it.

• • •

I caught Betty's scent before I saw her. Just as snacktastic and delicious as she had smelled in the van. She was waiting for me under a streetlamp by a tall wooden fence, her face shadowed under the lightweight black hoodie she wore despite the damp heat of the evening. Beneath the hoodie, she was wearing a long, satiny black dress and witchy black ankle boots. I'd worn my best jeans, a nice floral tank top, and sturdy shoes I could run in if I had to. It was warm enough that I couldn't stand anything on my arms. Now I felt awkwardly underdressed.

"Aren't you hot in that?" I said. "Temperature-wise. Because, I mean, you're *definitely* hot in that."

Joking lightly. Trying to make a good impression. Trying desperately not to show how badly I wanted to throw her against the fence and do a terrible thing.

My anxiety eased a fraction when she laughed. "Thank you. I'm fine in this. I've felt cold all the time since I got sick."

"Right. I guess that happens a lot for Type Twos?" I winced under my mask. *Way to be a smooth talker, Erin.*

I'd nervously and optimistically shaved my bikini line and put on a lacy red bra and matching thong that night. An expensive pair I'd ordered online one night when I was feeling particularly pent up. Which practically guaranteed we weren't going to fool around. Sex on a first date only seemed to happen when I was unshaven and wearing ratty, embarrassing underwear. Those instances had been with guys, who largely didn't seem to notice my body hair or what underwear I had on anyhow. Too busy getting to the goodies. But not knowing Betty, I worried I'd be more subject to scrutiny. To critique.

"At least half of us have trouble staying warm," she replied. "You look cute, too, by the way."

She was wearing a paper mask, same as me, so I couldn't tell if she was smiling or not. I looked up and down the street; we were standing under the only significant illumination for three blocks in either direction. I didn't see any bars or restaurants or anything that looked like a possible hangout spot.

"So, what's here?" I asked. "What did you want to show me?"

Her eyes crinkled; she was definitely smiling now. "Follow me."

Betty led me down the sidewalk a few yards until we reached a gap in the boards.

"This way." She ducked through the gap, and I uncertainly followed. Maybe we were going to a hidden patio?

My mood dropped. We were in a junkyard full of old and wrecked cars. Maybe a pick-and-pull kind of place where budget auto mechanics went searching for spare parts. Certainly not a setting I'd imagined for a first date. Unease formed a hard lump in the pit of my stomach.

"You're not a serial killer, are you?" I joked. *Ha-ha, only serious.*

She took her mask off so I could see her face in the dimness. Her lipstick was a very dark purple. "You're perfectly safe here. Have some faith. It's just a little further."

Despite my profound misgivings, I followed her through the maze of scrapped cars, deeper into the junkyard. "How do you know this place?"

"The third-shift fleet mechanic at DocRyde goes here a lot to get parts. I come with him to help out sometimes. He gets nervous being alone here after dark." She paused, craning her neck. "Ah, it's over here."

She gestured for me to keep following her. Soon we came to a clearing, and in the middle, gleaming ghostly in the moonlight, was a white Nissan Leaf stretch limousine. Betty pulled a key fob out of her hoodie pocket and pressed a button. The limousine's interior light came on—the passenger windows were deeply tinted, so I mostly saw the illumination through the front windows—and I heard the click of locks releasing.

"Come on in." Betty opened the back door. Soft yellow light streamed into the junkyard. I glimpsed smooth white leather seats and dark wood panel accents. Two bench seats faced each other, and in the middle of the gray carpeted floor was a small stainless steel cooler. Nobody else was in the limo. No gang of Twos waiting to pounce.

So I followed her inside, settling myself on the bench opposite her, the cooler between us. I pulled the door shut.

*Oh God, oh God* we were really doing this. I started to sweat.

"How . . . um, how did you find this limo?" I asked, glancing around. It even still had that new car smell to it.

"I was here when the DoubleTree hotel had it hauled in on a flatbed." She looked extremely pleased with herself. "Somehow their shuttle driver broke the axle. Had to be an absolute monster pothole. They could have fixed it, but I guess it was better as a tax write-off or something. It's perfectly fine apart from the busted shaft."

She pressed another button on the fob to start the electric engine. I heard the hiss of the air conditioner coming on. King Princess's "Ohio" started playing softly through the speakers. Betty unzipped her black hoodie and shrugged out of it. The dress beneath had thin spaghetti straps, a fitted bodice, and a plunging neckline. And, damn, she looked good in it. I wanted to bury my face in her cleavage. I'm sure she had probably lost weight, but as opposed to me, she actually looked *healthy*.

I was pinioned between desire and insecurity. "I, uh, I really like your dress."

"Thank you." She leaned over to open the cooler. I probably should have been enjoying the very nice view of her breasts, but I found myself staring at the top of her head instead.

Crap. I didn't know what to say next. "So, um, were you a goth before? Or are you just, you know, embracing the *Children of the Night* vibe and all?"

She laughed and handed me a cold can of soda water. "Some of column A, some of column B. I like dancing. Me and my girl-friend ended up at the goth club sometimes. Helps to look like you belong there, you know? So I had a few outfits, and . . . well, black's just a very practical color for me these days. Sexy and it doesn't show stains. And it's harder for the cops to see you at night if you don't wanna be seen."

"That's true." I opened my can. Took off my mask and set it aside so I could drink. The act of removing it felt taboo and made me feel incredibly exposed. "You, uh, have a girlfriend?"

"Had." She shrugged sadly and pulled another dripping can from the cooler. "Louise was scared of catching the virus, so she broke up with me right after I got out of the hospital. We'd been together about a year. Maybe it wouldn't have lasted anyway, but it sucked for it to end like that."

"I'm really sorry to hear it. My boyfriend moved out before I got home," I said. "I mean, we agreed that was best. We haven't broken up, but . . . we agreed to open up the relationship. I . . . I don't like the idea of cheating. But I haven't told him about you."

"And *that's* probably for the best." She sipped her soda water. "I know all the cloak-and-dagger stuff with the phones probably seemed like an overreaction, but . . ."

"It didn't seem that way," I replied. "It's just hard to know how closely anyone's watching us."

Betty nodded. "I mean, they're straight-up merking Types who lose their shit in public. Even if all that blood just creates another biohazard."

My stomach dropped; this was the first I'd heard of it. "What?"

"They got snipers posted on all the buildings downtown now, and undercover officers at all the big shopping centers. They're keeping the media from covering the killings, so most people don't know yet."

"Is . . . is that legal?"

She shrugged. "Well, they're doing it. You been watching *Dr. Kaz Chats*?"

I shook my head. "Is that a network show? Streaming?"

"It's on YouTube. Dr. Alexandria Kasabian is a virologist at the university. She's had the channel a couple of years, but ever since the pandemic, she's been focusing on PVG. And it's not just medicine and science; she's been bringing in legal experts, local activists. It's been really accurate. Good stuff."

"I'll make sure to check it out."

Betty took another drink from her soda water and then fixed me in a direct, speculative gaze that made me nervous. "So, you mentioned a boyfriend. Have you been with a woman before?"

"Yes." I shifted on my seat. "Not since college, though."

She absently ran her finger over the lip of her can. "Was it a drunk-in-the-dorm thing or deliberate?"

I felt myself blush. My heart hammered. "It was pretty deliberate." Then I paused as I remembered the night my roommate Kayleigh and I kissed in bed after we went partying. She'd just broken up with her whiny boyfriend. I was crushed afterward when she acted like our make-out session hadn't happened. But I was a big girl and didn't make a thing of it. "*Mostly* deliberate."

"Interesting." Betty got up and sat beside me. The sudden rush of her scent made me dizzy. In the background, King Princess was singing about being chill. "Let me see your hands."

I showed her. She gently rubbed my fingers and palms, sending frissons through my whole body.

"These fingernails are *not* regulation, young lady," she sternly teased.

Crap. I'd forgotten to trim them. An apology died in my

throat and became a moan when she put my fingers in her mouth and started sucking on them. But a tiny voice way in the back of my head was screaming, *Ack! You do not know where my hands have been!*

"I'll be honest." She whispered in my ear like we were in the middle of a crowded bar and not alone in the back of the limo. "I've wanted to do you since I laid eyes on you."

"I wanted that, too," I breathed.

And then she was kissing me. Deep-throating me with her cool tongue. I was losing my mind at the smell of her, the taste of her. But I was paralyzed, afraid to do anything lest I lose control.

Betty pushed me back against the seat and started kissing my neck. Lightly biting my skin.

"No marks!" I gasped. "Not where the doctor could see!"

"Have some faith," she whispered. "You due for a mammogram anytime soon?"

"No." Her question derailed me for a moment. Was I supposed to get a mammogram? "I'm only thirty."

"Then no worries about the doctor."

Betty slowly pushed my tank top up and ran her fingertips over the red lace of my bra. "Very nice."

She unsnapped the front clip with two fingers and the fabric cups fell away. My nipples hardened in the cooled air. Goose bumps shivered down my spine.

"Even nicer," she whispered.

There was a long pause, and I looked down at her upturned face.

"So I'm going to have my way with you now." Her eyes were bright, hungry. "Your safe word is *red*. Use it and I'll stop. I *promise*. Now, pillow princess time. Just close your eyes . . ."

I did as she asked. Her lips moved to my right nipple. Licking me, gently sucking me while she caressed my breasts with her soft fingers. Oh God, it felt so good. I hadn't been touched in months, and maybe not quite like this in years. Gregory tried, he really did, but he either used too much pressure and hurt me or used too little and tickled me. This was Goldilocks-grade just right.

Then she started licking the curve beneath my breast and it was the perfect thing.

Suddenly, a sharp, jarring pain. A razored cut, an inch below my areola. Betty latched onto the wound, sucking hard.

"What are you—" I began, but her hand was in my pants, her fingers sliding deep into my wet flesh, and just as suddenly the pain was wonderful, oh God, it was amazing.

I gripped the leather seat, arching my back, squeezing my eyes shut tighter. Light bloomed behind my lids. "Oh God, please don't stop."

She didn't stop. I was an instrument under her mastery. It was as if Betty had tapped into my own nervous system, and she knew exactly what effect her slightest finger twitch had on my keening nerves. It wasn't until the fourth time that an orgasm slipped away like a dark fish in the water that I realized she was edging me on purpose.

"Please just let me come," I begged.

Her finger slid to the sweetest of my sweet spots and circled. I rocketed straight into outer space. Wave after wave of pleasure, and at some point I fainted.

When I came to, I was lying limp and sweaty on the bench seat. Betty was carefully patting a medicated adhesive bandage in place on my breast. Her cheeks were rosy. When she realized I was awake, she gave me a pleased, bloody Cheshire Cat grin.

We hadn't gotten a single drop on the creamy leather seats.

* * *

My breast was okay. Sore, but okay. The cut she had made with a razor blade got a little inflamed, but it wasn't anything Neosporin couldn't handle.

Two days after Betty sucked me senseless, my tongue began

its gradual transformation. At first I thought the raw pits on my tongue were strange canker sores. But when the tiny teeth started growing in, I knew something much more profound was happening.

—•—•—•—

Early on, I'd thought that my meeting Betty was Gregory's fault. Karma. I thought that with bitter certainty at first.

But later, I decided our meeting was just a coincidence. So was everything that followed. Random coincidences that just somehow counteracted the entropy of the universe and set enormity in motion. Sort of like a freight train assembling itself on the tracks after another train full of parts exploded. Not *completely* impossible, but very, very improbable. At least as improbable as modern Jesus.

But now? I accept that meeting Betty was predestined. A cosmic inevitability. It was my first proof that gods do exist. My first proof that those gods do have a plan for us all, even if the Bible-wielding men Gregory escaped had it all wrong.

And that proof? It disrupted all the patterns.

# CHAPTER 10

I'm striding up the street to Dr. Shapiro's office, my head shrouded under my hoodie and mask, squinting behind sunglasses, when suddenly I hear a man in the park across the street shouting violent nonsense.

Or he used to be a man, anyhow. He's wearing construction boots, ragged Carhartt work overalls, and a dirty gray T-shirt, all freshly spattered with the blood of the woman whose head he is enthusiastically cracking open against the curb. He howls at the sky, and I can see he's missing some teeth. Probably whatever he did for a living didn't pay him enough to see a dentist. But his skin looks flush and smooth, so much healthier than mine, and for a moment I envy him.

He stops howling and meets my shadowed stare, breaking into a gory, gap-toothed smile. The kind of grin you give an old, dear friend. I've never laid eyes on this wreck before, and the woman beneath him is beyond anyone's help. They both are. I don't want to be outed, not here, not like this, so I pretend I don't even see him and stride on.

A few seconds later, I hear the spat of rifle fire and the thud of a meaty body hitting the pavement and I know that the SWAT team just took out Ragged Carhartts. They're never far away, not in this part of town. And once they've taken out one Type Three, they don't need much excuse to kill another, even if you're just trying to see your doctor like a good citizen.

"Oh God," a lady says. She and another fortyish woman are standing in the doorway of an art gallery, staring horrified at the scene behind me. They're both wearing batik dresses with matching homemade masks and lots of chunky handmade jewelry. "That's the third one this month."

"If this keeps up, we'll have to close." The other woman shakes her head, looking gray-faced. "Nobody will want to come here. The whole downtown will die. Not just us. The theaters, the museums, churches—everything."

"I heard something on NPR about a new kind of gel to keep the virus from spreading," the first woman replies, sounding hopeful.

I keep moving. Her voice fades away. People still talk about contagion control as if it matters, as if masks and gloves and sanitizers and prayers can stop the future.

Experts said from the beginning that close physical contact and bodily fluids are the main modes of transmission. Fomites, sweat, saliva droplets. They say that the airborne risk is low, but I don't know if I believe that. If it's true, then how did *I* get it? Gregory still seems fine, and he was the only person I'd had that kind of contact with for weeks before I got sick. He still insists he's got no signs of the virus in his blood. The pieces just don't fit together.

I think the sneaky truth is, unless you've been living in some isolated Tibetan monastery, you've already been exposed to PVG, one way or another. Sooner or later, you will develop lesions on your frontal lobes, temporal lobes, and hippocampus. Those will cause a variety of antisocial behaviors, which will lead to your friendly neighborhood SWAT team putting a .308 bullet through your skull.

• • •

I wake up at 8 p.m., hours before I'm supposed to go to work, and can't get back to sleep. So I shuffle into the living room, bring up YouTube on my TV, and start watching the latest *Dr. Kaz Chats* video while I fix myself some cream of rice. She's having a split-screen conversation with Dr. Amit Reddy, another virologist, from a lab in California.

"So, I know you've been studying the interaction of PVG with other viral infections," Dr. Kaz says. "Can you tell us more about what you've been finding?"

"We've found some concerning interactions in patients who had existing oncovirus infections, active or latent," Dr. Reddy replies.

"And by oncoviruses, you mean viruses that can cause tumors or cancers, right?"

The mention of cancer makes my stomach turn.

"Exactly," nods Dr. Reddy.

"Which viruses are we talking about?"

"My lab has been looking at the interactions of PVG with human papillomavirus infections, or HPV, and the Epstein-Barr virus, or EBV. We're most concerned about those infections because they are still extremely common, even though vaccines exist for the most dangerous strains of HPV."

*HPV?* I settle on the sofa with my meager breakfast to pay closer attention to the video.

"And there are well over one hundred fifty strains of HPV," Dr. Kaz remarks.

"Yes. So that makes creating vaccines a challenge."

I should have gotten my HPV vaccine when I was a teenager, but my parents were weird about me getting it and kept putting it off. I guess they had trouble with the idea that I was rapidly reaching an age when I'd be having sex. Getting me the shot meant acknowledging that. When I was old enough to arrange it on my own, I was busy with college and jobs and just didn't think about it. Right until it didn't matter anymore.

"So, I'm going to pause here," Dr. Kaz says to the camera. "The next little bit of the conversation might be a bit basic for my longtime viewers. But I know from people's comments that a lot of my newer viewers are watching to try to understand how PVG affects them, and they aren't necessarily science or med students."

She turns back to Dr. Reddy. "Would you like to give our viewers a quick PVG 101 from a functional perspective?"

Dr. Reddy nods. "Sure, I'd be happy to cover that. So, the thing about viruses is that they aren't real cells. They don't have a lot of the parts that real cells have, such as a nucleus or organelles. They don't have a metabolism—they don't eat—so they're not properly alive. They're basically these tiny genetic replication machines. They have a core of nucleic acid, which can be RNA or DNA . . . but if you don't know what that is, you can think of it as a genetic payload. A virus, any virus, injects its genetic payload into a cell. It takes over that cell's machinery, reprograms it so that it stops doing normal cell things and is just focused on making copies of the virus. And because infected cells stop doing what they're supposed to do in your body, that makes you sick."

This is all bringing back dimly remembered biology lectures from college.

"And sometimes cells partly fight off the infection, but the virus alters their genetic structure, and these cells can malfunction and turn into cancer later on," Dr. Kaz adds.

"Exactly."

"Can you talk about PVG from a structural perspective? For instance, why is it called 'polymorphic'?"

"Oh, structure is one of the things that makes this virus so interesting, and so dangerous. It's an unusually large, complex double-stranded DNA virus. Taxonomists have tentatively put it in the Pandoraviridae family, mostly because of its size and structure. It's the first pandoravirus known to infect humans. It carries a payload much, much bigger than it needs to for simple viral replication. We're still trying to understand why these viruses are carrying so much genetic information, what all that information codes for, and what it means for people who get infected."

Dr. Kaz nods. "That part is a mystery for sure! But I was hoping you could talk a little about the envelope?"

"Oh, right. That's definitely worth discussion! Some viruses, including PVG, are covered in an envelope that's made of fat with little spikes of protein coming off it. These spikes make it easier for viruses to attach to and attack cells. Cells communicate with each other through their antigen receptors, and the viral proteins mimic those antigens. You can think of the proteins like the lockpicks that a burglar uses to break into a house. The thing about PVG is that the different strains that were first identified had envelopes that looked very, very different from one another. Just, very different envelope and spike protein configurations."

"Yes," says Dr. Kaz. "And that's why researchers have needed more time to develop a vaccine than was the case with COVID-19. With COVID, they were able to make messenger RNA vaccines that told cells how to recognize the virus's spike proteins and stage a faster, stronger immune response. But with PVG, there are so many different spike proteins in play that it's much more difficult to come up with a vaccine effective against all the strains."

"For sure," says Dr. Reddy. "When people started getting sick, we thought these were completely different viruses, but people started having the same symptoms, and once we opened up the different strains, we realized that the big genetic payloads inside were mostly the same, apart from the bits that code for the spike proteins. So we realized that we were looking at a highly adaptable virus that came in lots of different shapes. *Poly* is Greek for 'many,' and *morphic* is from *morph*, which is Greek for 'shape.'"

"I might be weird," Dr. Kaz says, "but I think of it like kids from the same family who all put on very different Halloween costumes to see who gets the most candy."

Dr. Reddy laughs. "That's an interesting metaphor!"

My iPhone rings, startling me.

I pause the video and pick up my phone. It's Gregory. I press the green button to accept his video call.

He's out someplace dark, his face lit blue and spooky by his phone screen. His sunken eyes are red and tears are streaming down his face.

And I immediately think, *Oh God, he found out about Betty.*

"What's wrong, honey?" I ask aloud.

"Everything's fucked up," he weeps. His voice is slurred. Either he's been drinking or he's had a stroke. Gregory's never been much of a drinker, but he's much too young for a stroke. I immediately assume that whatever's happening, it's probably Joey's fault.

"What happened?" I ask.

"I—I l-lost my job." He shakes his head violently, as if he can shake off reality. He's clearly furious with himself. "I lost my cool with a client. He was such an *asshole*. I just couldn't smile and pretend anymore. I *couldn't.*"

He lost his job? Last I heard, his performance reviews were great and everybody loved him. How could he get fired over just one mistake? Unless this wasn't the first and he just didn't tell me about the others.

But I know that now's not the time to push for details. "I'm so sorry, honey."

My fiancé doesn't even seem to hear me. "I've tried so hard to be what everyone wants me to be, and I just can't anymore. I prayed for the strength to do it, and I can't."

He stops for a second, breaking down into sobbing laughter. "Joey keeps saying I'm not a man, just because I won't do the vile shit he does. If he's a real man and I'm not, well . . . I don't want any goddamned part of being a man anymore. I just don't. And I don't care if God thinks that's wrong."

"What's going on over there?" I'm studying his face as closely as I can. It's difficult to see him in the poor light. But Gregory looks thin. Unwell. That could be stress, but it could be he's gotten sick.

"It's . . . it's complicated," he says. "I haven't been honest with you. I wish I had been, but I was so ashamed. I'm so sorry. It feels like everything's been a lie."

I don't have a clue what he's talking about. This feels more serious than him trying to haltingly explain that he's been cheating on me. I already absolved him of that anyhow. Whatever this is, it cuts him to his very soul. "What's happened? You can tell me. I won't be mad, I promise."

"I . . . I can't." He starts sobbing harder and mumbles something I can't understand.

I can't sit on my worries any longer. "Honey, have you seen a doctor? Have you been tested for PVG recently?"

"I don't fucking have it!" he screams. "I don't!"

And then he throws his phone, or at least it seems like he has, because the image on the screen becomes a bouncing whirl of distant lights. And then the call abruptly cuts off.

I try calling him back right away, but he doesn't pick up. Then I text him. Wait a few minutes. No reply. Of course, if he's just busted his phone against a wall, I might not be getting a reply for days.

Gregory needs help. I check the Homeland Security health app, but there's no feature for summoning help for someone else. Figures.

Then I think about dialing 911. But that might summon the police just as likely as it would an ambulance. The police might just decide to shoot him if he's too upset to follow their orders. I'd never forgive myself if I got Gregory killed.

His parents are local. We're cordial, but not close. Always got the vibe that they think I'm not good enough for their baby boy. His mom has been a bit judgmental because I'm not much into cooking and makeup and other traditional womanly activities. And somehow they believe I'm the reason Gregory stopped going to Mass. He seems to dread visiting with them, but he does it out of obligation.

Still. Maybe they can do something? It's late for them, but I call his mother. She doesn't pick up, so I leave a voice mail.

"Hey, this is Erin. I just spoke to Gregory and I'm really worried about him. You might want to check on him. Hope everyone there is good. Bye."

I end the call and sit there, thinking hard. Leaving a message for his mom doesn't feel like nearly enough. Gregory's always had my back. I need to have his.

There's a route to UCC that goes within a couple of miles of Joey's house. I can swing by without making myself late. Probably. A socially distanced welfare check can't really be against the rules, can it?

So I quickly get dressed, take my medicine, mask up, and head out the door.

● ● ●

I get to Joey's house at 10 p.m.; I'm supposed to clock in at 10:30. I park my car at the curb and hurry up the front steps to the big old midcentury. The porch light is off, and the house looks dark, but I go up anyhow and give the door a hard, loud cop knock.

Joey opens the door. He's wearing a ratty maroon bathrobe. No mask, so I step back a few feet to be polite. Charmer that he is, he frowns at me and says, "What the hell are you doing here?"

"Is Gregory here? We had kind of a weird conversation a little while ago. I'm worried about him."

Joey doesn't smell very good to me. He's got an expired lunch meat sourness to him along with the stink of cigarettes and dirty socks. I absolutely do *not* want to eat his brain. This almost certainly means something, but I don't know what.

Joey looks me up and down, grunts, and then turns back into the house to bellow, "*Gregory!*"

"You're not welcome inside my home," Joey warns me over his shoulder. "Keep your goddamned plague outside."

Then he abruptly walks back into the house and heads upstairs, leaving the door open.

*What the hell?* I wonder.

I stand there nervously for a few moments, and then call, "Gregory? Are you there?"

He slowly emerges from the gloom of the hallway to the kitchen. Stumbles to the door, looking pale and dazed. I can smell the whiskey he's been drinking. He's barefoot, wearing basketball shorts and an old Skillet band shirt. The shirt is an absolute tent on him; he has *definitely* lost weight.

"Oh, hey, Erin." He scratches his face. There's a red, blistery rash along his left cheek and jaw. I wonder if he got into poison ivy or if this is a sign of something worse. "I guess I broke my phone."

"I'm worried about you." Gregory doesn't smell very good to me, either. My nose is picking up a spoiled bologna note under the overwhelming miasma of alcohol and sweat. I relax a little, realizing he's safe being this close to me.

"Joey's mad," he replies. "You shouldn't be here. I didn't ask you to come here. I didn't invite you."

He doesn't look or sound angry. He sounds almost absentminded, like these are thoughts that have just distantly occurred to him.

I feel like I'm having a conversation with a sleepwalker. I want to hug him, slap him, do *something* to shake him out of whatever this is, but I know I shouldn't touch him. "You were very upset. What else was I supposed to do?"

"You could have left me alone," he replies blankly. "I think maybe you should just leave me alone for a while. I prayed to God and He said we shouldn't be together anymore."

"You what?" I pause, the meaning of his words sinking in. He's praying again, and he really thinks he's been talking to God? I feel sick. "Are . . . are you breaking up with me?"

"Yeah, I guess so." He scratches his face again and squints out at the dark sky. "It's late. You gotta be at work, right? You should go now. Don't be late for work."

"Gregory, this is really weird—"

"Go to work!" he snarls.

Then, just as abruptly, his face crumples into abject grief and he starts weeping again. "I'm so sorry. But you need to go. I'm setting a boundary, okay? You need to go."

I don't know what to do but back up slowly. Something is clearly, desperately wrong with Gregory. I know PVG can affect different people in different ways. Sometimes it's purely a brain infection. Dr. Kaz says that's been happening more and more because newer PVG strains snagged genes from varicella-zoster, the chickenpox virus, and they can much more easily infect the spinal cord and use it as an escalator into the brain. It's been happening so much that epidemiologists are talking about a whole new Type. The virus is learning more new tricks all the time.

Maybe something bad is happening to the parts of Gregory's brain that control emotional regulation. But I'm no doctor. I can't tell what's really happening with him.

Can our five years together really just end like this?

Not with a bang, not with a whimper, but just a drunk, absentminded *meh*?

No. This isn't the way things were supposed to go. This isn't how I imagined our story would end. We were supposed to get a house. Start a family. We were supposed to grow old together. Die together as gnarled octogenarians, holding hands in the same deathbed while our loving grandkids and great-grandkids sit around us, weeping.

My mind is full of supposed-tos. Obligations. Expectations. Deep down, did I ever genuinely want any of the future I imagined with him? Or was it all simply what I thought I was supposed to strive for as an American woman?

Did I even ever really want kids? Did I, honestly? Even if it was possible or prudent after PVG's ravages, did I want to destroy my damaged body even more in pregnancy for the sake of small strangers I'd be responsible for? Responsible for literally decades? An endlessly stressful responsibility that, if I failed to do it well, would result in exactly the same kind of distant relationship I'd had with my own family, so that I'd inevitably die alone and dissatisfied, no matter what future I'd envisioned?

Do I—whoever I am *now*, not who I was before everything changed—really want this indifferent, inebriated man more than I want Betty? Even if what she and I have is probably doomed to end in blood?

I feel a guts-deep compulsion to stay and fight . . . but what would I be fighting for now? What am I fighting against? And why does it fall to *me* to be the one to fight for our relationship and not him?

The two men here have told me in plain language that my presence isn't wanted. Could continuing to stand here arguing with Gregory be even remotely helpful? Or will Joey just call the cops if I push things too far?

"Okay," I finally reply. I feel utterly defeated. Confused. Worried. Heartbroken. "If that's really what you want, I'll go. I respect your boundaries. But if you change your mind, I'm here for you. Call me later if you can. Please."

"Okay. Bye." Eyes unfocused and downcast, he shuts the door.

I take a deep breath. Hopefully he'll realize what he's done. And maybe he'll come around. All I can do now is go back to my car and try to focus on my shift at work.

# CHAPTER 11

"Do you find yourself having any unwanted thoughts or violent fantasies?" Dr. Shapiro asks.

"Of course not." I try to sound mildly indignant.

• • •

Something terrible and amazing happened a few days after Betty and I had our third date. I don't know if my memories of the event are accurate; they have the unreal sheen of dream. Of savage fantasy. The only things I know that are absolutely, incontrovertibly real are the texts I got from Betty. They're still in the burner phone:

> You're right, the situation isn't fair. I want things
> to be better 4 us. I made an appointment.
> Please come with me? It's gonna hurt. I need
> someone 2 hold my hand.

Ok, yes I will hold your hand, I texted her back.

She replied with an address, a date, and a time after dark.

I arrived at the correct place at the right time. I don't really remember how. She'd gotten her third-shift mechanic friend to drop by and give my car a thorough search and he'd declared it free of tracking devices. So I feel safer driving to our dates. It's plausible I drove, parked a few blocks away, and walked. But no matter how I rack my memory, I just don't know.

The first thing I remember is meeting her outside . . . what?

A club? A tattoo parlor? It must be downtown. Maybe the old warehouse district. There is loud, bass-heavy dance music that rattles my bones. I don't recognize it. People in masks and dark clothes mill on the sidewalk under neon lights. Too many people. Much too close to each other. I can't keep my distance. My nerves are frayed to sparking threads just being there.

But I find Betty, more by smell than sight. I didn't recognize her at first because she's buzzed her hair very short. Everyone here seems to be wearing black.

Conversation is impossible over the music. She smiles at me and leads me through the crowd into the dark passage between the tall brick buildings. Paved, but too narrow to be a proper alley. Twenty steps in, there is a steel staircase leading to a battered basement door in a square concrete well. It's just barely big enough for both of us. Smells like piss and garbage. The door is maroon, the old paint chipped and rust-bubbled off the steel. In a couple of places, I can see that in years past it was painted dumpster green. Otherwise it is blank. No words or numbers, nor any remainders of markings.

Betty raps a complicated rhythm on the door.

A large bald man in black jeans and a black tee over thick arms entirely blue with tattoos, clearly a bouncer, opens it just a crack. "Yeah?"

"I'm the 11 p.m.," Betty says.

"Password?" he grunts.

"Cabeza."

The bouncer opens the door wide and Betty pulls me in after her. We are in a brutalist space, a bare concrete corridor lit by stark halogen bulbs in caged metal shades bolted to the ceiling. The harsh odor of chlorine bleach burns in my nose.

"This way," the bouncer says, gesturing toward another steel door. "I think the doctor's ready for you."

Inside the room, three gaunt women in green surgical masks,

full-face shields, and green scrubs stand under bright surgical suite lighting. Their hair is tucked up under disposable paper caps. They're arrayed on both sides of what looks like a cross between a dentist's chair and an old-fashioned electric chair. Beside it are a rolling steel surgical cart with instruments laid out on a shining tray and an IV stand loaded with a fresh clear bag of some kind of intravenous liquid. The chair is padded blue vinyl, but it's upright and has sturdy leather straps. Behind it is a machine with a pressure gauge and a lot of clear plastic tubing wound around it. I'm guessing it's for oxygen or suction or something like that. There's another chair in the corner, in front of a hairdresser's sink. On the opposite wall is a white counter with a stainless steel sink—the kind I'm used to seeing in doctors' offices—with white cabinets above and below. There's a red mini fridge under part of the counter, with a biohazard symbol on it.

The walls and ceiling are gray ceramic tile, and it looks pretty new. The floor is glossy gray concrete. I'm guessing it's coated in urethane for easier cleanup. About every square yard on the floor, they've bolted large, sturdy steel D-rings in recessed plates. The air smells like disinfectant.

"Are you Betty?" asks the shortest of the three women. She's standing in the middle.

"Yes, that's me," Betty replies.

"I'm Dr. LaVoie," says the woman. "I was a licensed neurosurgeon at Cary Hospital for ten years. I hold a joint MD and Ph.D. in neuroscience from Vanderbilt University. I lost my position and my medical license as a result of my PVG diagnosis two months ago."

She gestures to the woman at her right. "This is my anesthesiologist, Dr. Gutierrez. She worked closely with me at Cary, and she became infected in the same incident that I was."

Dr. Gutierrez waves at us nervously.

"And this is our assistant, Darnelle. She was a registered nurse, and she was with us at Cary as well."

"Hey." Darnelle gives us an up-nod.

*That must have been one hell of an incident,* I think, imagining someone screaming and thrashing in seizures on an operating table, horrifically bleeding out all over everyone in the room.

"Due to our PVG infection status," Dr. LaVoie says, "we are not legally allowed to perform any sort of medical procedures or body modifications. Therefore, we are not standing here in this room with you. If the authorities talk to us later, we will declare we were not here, and we all have alibis in place. But it would be much better if our names never came up at all. Do you understand?"

Betty nods. "I do."

"That said," Dr. LaVoie continues, "prior to our respective loss of licenses, we all had excellent reviews from supervisors, colleagues, and patients."

"I know of your work," Betty says. "I'm good."

Dr. LaVoie turns slightly toward me. I can't read her expression because of the glare of the light on her face shield. "I see you've brought a friend. Who appears to be a Type Three?"

"Yes, I'm her friend," I reply. "And I'm . . . the other thing, too."

"While we encourage each patient to bring a friend or loved one for moral support," Dr. LaVoie says, "due to the nature of the procedure, we discourage the presence of Type Threes. *Highly* discourage it."

"Well, she's my plus-one," Betty says, tightening her grip on my hand. "She's who I want with me."

"What can we do to make this safer for her?" I ask.

"You'll need to be restrained. Do you consent to that?"

This makes me incredibly uneasy, and I want to say no, but I look at Betty and it's clear she wants me to agree so we can all get on with whatever this is. "Sure, uh, yeah."

Dr. LaVoie steps on a foot pedal that apparently opens up the intercom. "Paul, would you please bring a chair and restraints for my appointment's companion?"

"Will do," he replies over the speakers. "Be there shortly."

"Darnelle, would you please prepare Betty?" the doctor asks.

"Yes, ma'am."

Darnelle leads Betty away from me and takes her to the hair-dresser's sink. Pulls electric clippers out of the drawer and starts shaving Betty's close-cropped hair down to the scalp.

At that moment, Paul the bouncer comes into the room with a padded white plastic folding chair, a coil of strong galvanized chain, and a rig that looks like a straitjacket and a BDSM harness had a baby. My stomach flutters.

Paul unfolds the chair and sets it on the floor about a yard from the blue vinyl chair. "Miss, I'm going to need you to sit down here."

I do as he asks.

"You gonna hold her hand?" He sets the heavy chain on the floor.

I nod.

"Righty or lefty?" He shakes the kinks out of the rig and straightens the brown leather straps.

"I'm right-handed."

"Cool." He puts the harness on me. The straps crisscross my chest and shoulders and buckle somewhere on my back. He cuffs my left hand behind my back but leaves my right hand free. Then he cuffs my ankles to the legs of the chair. I hear and feel him attach a chain to the back of my harness and padlock it tightly to a D-ring somewhere on the floor behind me.

"You able to breathe okay?" he asks.

"Yes, I think so." I try shifting around and can't really move anything besides my right arm. The buckles are unreachable. I absolutely hate being this helpless.

"Cool, cool." He gives me a chummy pat on the shoulder and leaves the room.

Meanwhile, Darnelle has finished with Betty, whose scalp is

bare and wet. It smells like Darnelle washed her head with some kind of strong antibacterial soap.

They sit Betty down in the chair. Dr. LaVoie starts hooking Betty up to an IV in the crook of her right arm while Dr. Gutierrez goes to the mini fridge and pulls out a liter-size Nalgene bottle that is mostly filled with what looks like blood.

"What's in the drip?" Betty eyes the bag full of clear liquid uncertainly.

"Saline solution, a sedative, and a painkiller," LaVoie replies.

"What's in the bottle?"

"O negative from a Type Three along with a different analgesic and an antibiotic," Dr. Gutierrez says. "This looks like a lot, but we're going to need you to drink the whole thing. If it's any consolation, this is going to get you very, very high."

Betty chugs the bottle. When she finishes, her eyes are so dilated they're nearly black, and she's practically vibrating. Darnelle secures her into the chair, strapping down her arms and legs, her torso. I can just barely reach out and hold her left hand.

They put a neck brace on her to immobilize her head, and Dr. Gutierrez clamps a steel band around her cranium, just above her eyebrows. She bolts the brace to a plate on the headrest of the chair. The neck brace has a dip beneath her jaw, I'm guessing so she can still speak without moving the rest of her skull.

"This might feel weird. Might sting a bit at first." Dr. Gutierrez starts swabbing a clear gel all around her head, just above the band. It's got a strong alcohol and chemical odor that makes me afraid I might sneeze inside my mask. As the anesthesiologist works, Betty squeezes my hand hard, looking scared.

I'm starting to figure out what's happening here, and I don't know how I feel about it. Am I touched that she's taking a major step in our relationship? Am I heartened that she's making this sacrifice as a commitment to me? Or am I horrified that my desire, my hunger, carries this dreadful, bloody cost for her?

"Hey," I say to her. "What's your favorite animal?"

"Siberian tiger," she replies, her voice a little thick.

"What can you tell me about tigers?" I ask.

"They're the biggest of the big cats, except for ligers. Absolute units. They're endangered outside zoos. There's only, like, five hundred or so left in the wild." Her voice slurs more and more as she speaks, and her eyes start to flutter a bit.

"Can you feel this?" Dr. Gutierrez raps on a section of Betty's gelled scalp with a little silver hammer. It reminds me of a meat tenderizer.

"Feel what?" Betty's eyes are still hugely dilated, but now seem completely unfocused.

"She's ready," Dr. Gutierrez says to Dr. LaVoie.

Dr. LaVoie nods and adjusts the bright overhead light to shine directly on Betty's skull. "Get the suction online, and then please assemble the Gigli saw."

Oh shit, this is really happening. "Is . . . is she still supposed to be awake?"

"Yes, we need people awake for this." Dr. LaVoie pulls on a fresh pair of purple nitrile gloves as Dr. Gutierrez taps a pedal on the floor to start the suction machine. "I need to make sure I'm not going in too deep, and if I do, we need to rapidly diagnose the damage situation."

Dr. Gutierrez carefully pulls a burred steel cord out of a plastic wrapper. It's maybe a foot long. The burrs gleam in the light, sharper than razors. She attaches each end to T-shaped metal handles that remind me of wine openers, except each has a slim hook at the end instead of a corkscrew.

She offers the assembled surgical implement to Dr. LaVoie, who takes it and begins to calmly and expertly saw into Betty's head using the steel band as a cutting guide. Quick shoe-shining motions that neatly sever flesh and bone. Dr. Gutierrez deftly suctions away the blood and bits of tissue. I notice for the first time that the suction tube deposits the gore into a clear plastic jar on the floor. They're not about to waste those precious, infectious fluids.

Dr. LaVoie breaks through into the brain cavity. Pale cerebrospinal fluid washes out along with the blood. Dr. Gutierrez gets it all.

My heart is pounding. The smell of Betty's brain is heavy in the air. Not even a smell, exactly, but a feeling. Electricity. Magnetism. It draws me. I strain against my harness, but it is good and tight.

I am bound, and I must watch. I must witness this. This is for me. Because of me. This is my present. This is my future. This is my fault.

Betty's eyes roll up and I can see she's shivering. Shuddering.

She opens her mouth and moans. Her moans babble to words in some alien language, guttural coughs and groans and rasping, and I cannot understand the syllables but I can feel the message deep in my core and it's bending my mind, crushing my consciousness, as if this cursed prayer she's uttering has cast us both into the event horizon of the star-devouring monster at the core of a distant galaxy.

It is wonderful. It is horrible. I start laughing and laughing and can't stop myself, and soon I know no more.

# CHAPTER 12

"I was wondering about something," I say, as Dr. Shapiro begins to copy the contents of her survey into the exam room computer.

She stops typing and gives me a wary look. "Yes, what is it?"

"My prescription supplement. I feel okay, you know? But my memory's . . . not what it should be. I've been forgetting dumb stuff at work. I think I should be thinking better. I think I would, if I could have a little more?" I'm choosing my words as carefully as possible. My tongue feels thick, twitchy.

I don't want to tell her how badly my memory is slipping. I can't talk about the cravings I'm feeling. I especially can't mention wanting more energy, because nobody in charge wants someone like me feeling energetic.

I wonder if there's a sniper watching from behind the mirror on the wall. Has he tightened his grip on his rifle? Are gas canisters waiting to blow in the air-conditioning vent above me? My skin itches in dread anticipation.

Dr. Shapiro hedges. "Well, I know there's been a shortage of raw materials these days."

I swallow down my impatience and worry. The capsules are 98 percent cow brains, for God's sake. Probably they can squeeze a single human brain for thousands of doses. And there are so many miscarriages these days. I can't imagine the pharmaceutical companies are actually running short of anything.

"Could you check, just the same? Could you ask for me?" I sound meek. Pathetic. The opposite of hostile. That's good.

She gives me a pitying look and sighs. The mirror doesn't explode in gunfire. Gas doesn't burst from the vents.

"I'll see what I can do," my doctor says. "But I'll probably need to rerun your metabolome analysis to justify any increase."

Ugh. That means yet another blood draw and pee test. Worse, it means having to awkwardly poop in a box in front of the nurse. I can only hope that my fluids and excrement reflect a real biochemical need.

I try to believe she'll come through for me.

• • •

I go home. I take my bovellum capsules with some Mott's apple juice. I rinse my mouth out with peroxide and don't look at my tongue. I rub salve on the places my clothes have rubbed raw, and I climb naked into my bed. Sometime later, the alarm goes off, and I rise, shower, dress, and drive to work in darkness.

My shift is dull clockwork, until just after gray drizzling dawn, when one of the new tech leads comes in to talk to my coworker Jorge about some of the emergency server protocols. I haven't seen this young man before; he's wearing snug jeans, and the sleeves of his black polo shirt are tight over biceps tattooed with angels and devils. His sandy hair is cut close over a smooth, high-browed skull. He starts talking about database errors, but he's thinking about a gig he has with his band on Friday night, and it suddenly hits me not just that *I know what he's thinking* but also that I know because I can smell the sweet chemicals shifting inside his brain. The chemicals tell me his name is Devin.

I am filled with Want in the marrow of my bones. I am filled with Need from eyeballs to soles. I excuse myself and hurry out into the mutagenic morning and text Betty on the burner.

It's early for her. But she answers me right away. We agree to meet that night. It's been a while, but it's her turn to host.

• • •

I sleep fitfully. When my alarm goes off, I call in sick, shower, dress, and check the burner. Betty's texted a cryptic string of letters and numbers for my directions. And so I drive out to a hotel we've never visited before, drinking Aquafinas the whole way. It's a dark old place, once grand, now crumbling away in a forgotten corner of downtown. I wonder if she's running short of money or if the extra anonymity of the place was crucial to her.

Still, as I get out of my car and double-check my locks in the pouring rain, I can't help but peer out into the oppressive black spaces in the parking lot, trying to figure out if any of the shadows between the other vehicles could be lurking cops or Homeland Security agents. The darkness doesn't move, so I hurry to the front door, head down, hands jammed in my raincoat pockets, my stomach roiling with worry and anticipation. I avoid making eye contact with any of the damp, tired-looking sex workers smoking outside the hotel's front doors. None of them pay any attention to me.

My phone chimes as Betty texts me the room number. I take the creaking, urine-stinking elevator up four floors. My pace slows as I walk down the stained hallway carpet, and I pause for a moment before I knock on the door of room 512. What if the watchers tapped Betty's phone? What if she's not here at all? My poised hand quivers as my heart seems to pound out *A trap—a trap—a trap*.

I swallow. Knock twice. Step back. A moment later, Betty answers the door, wearing her Audrey Hepburn wig and a black cocktail dress that hangs limply from her skeletal shoulders. It's appalling how much weight she's lost; her eyes have turned entirely black, the whites permanently stained by repeated hemorrhages.

But she smiles at me and I find myself smiling back, warmed by this spark of real human feeling. I have to believe that we're still human. I *have* to.

In the background, a Savages track is playing on her phone. Jehnny Beth is singing about adoring life while Ayse Hassan's bass line strolls seductive and menacing. I'd forgotten how much I love this album.

"You ready?" Betty's question creaks like the hinge of a forgotten gate.

"Absolutely." My own voice is the dry fluttering of moth wings.

She locks the door behind me. "I'm sorry this place is such a pit, but the guy at the Holiday Inn started asking all kinds of questions, and this was the best I could do on short notice."

"It's okay." The room isn't as seedy as the lobby and exterior led me to expect it to be, and it's got a couch in addition to the queen-size bed. Betty has already covered the couch and the carpet in front of it with a green plastic tarpaulin. Her stainless steel spritzer bottle leans against a couch arm.

"Want some wine?" She gestures toward an unopened bottle of Yellow Tail Shiraz on the dresser.

"Thanks, but no . . . I couldn't drink it right now. Maybe after."

She nods. "There's a really good Italian restaurant around the corner. Kind of a *Goodfellas* hangout, but everything's home-made. Great garlic bread."

Betty pulls off the wig. Before she got the virus, she apparently could grow her thick chestnut hair clear down to her waist. I've never seen hair that long except in pictures. Her bare scalp gleams pale in the yellow light from the chandelier.

The scar circumscribing her skull looks red, inflamed. I wonder if she's been seeing other Type Threes. I quickly tamp down my pang of jealousy. We never agreed to an exclusive arrangement. And maybe she just had to go to the hospital instead; she told me she's got some kind of massive tumor on her pituitary.

She looks so frail. I can't possibly begrudge her what comfort she can get. I should just be grateful that she agrees to see me when I need her.

And, oh sweet lord, do I need her tonight.

Betty pulls me down for a kiss. Her hands are icy but her lips are warm. She slips her tongue into my mouth, and I can taste sweet cerebrospinal fluid mingled with her saliva. The tumor must have cracked the bony barriers in her skull. Before I have a chance to try to pull away, my own tongue is swelling, toothed pores opening and nipping at her slippery flesh.

She squeaks in pain and we separate.

"Sorry," I try to whisper. But my tongue is continuing to engorge and lengthen, curling back on itself and slithering down my own throat. I can feel the tiny maws rasping against my adenoids.

"It's okay." Her wan smile is smeared with blood. "We better get started."

She kisses the palm of my hand and begins to take my clothes off. I stare up at the tawdry chandelier, watching a fly buzz among the dusty baubles and bulbs. When I'm naked, she slips off her cocktail dress and leads me to the tarp-covered couch.

"Be gentle." She presses a short oyster knife into my hand and sits me down, the plastic crackling beneath me. I nod, barely keeping my lips closed over my shuddering tongue, and spread my legs.

With a slow exhalation, Betty settles between my thighs, her back to me. She's a tiny woman, her head barely clearing my chin when we're seated, so this position works best. Her skin is already covered in goose bumps. The anticipation is killing both of us.

I carefully run the tip of the sharp oyster knife through the red scar around her skull; there's relatively little blood as I cut through the tissue. Betty gives a little gasp and grips my knees, her whole body tense. The bone has only stitched back together in a few places; I use the side-to-side motion she showed me to gently pry the lid of her skull free.

She moans when I expose her brain. It's the most beautiful thing I could hope to see. Her dura mater glistens with a half-inch slick of golden jelly. Brain honey. When I breathe in the smell of her, I feel my blood pressure rise hard and fast.

I set the bowl of skin and bone aside and present the knife to her in my outstretched left hand. With a flick of her wrist, she slits the vein in the crook of my arm and presses her mouth against my bleeding flesh. I wrap my cut arm around her head and pull her tight to my breast.

I open my mouth and let my tongue unwind like an eel into her brainpan. It wriggles there, purple and gnarled, the tiny maw sucking down her golden jelly. It's delicious, better than caviar, better than ice cream, better than anything I've had in my mouth before. Sweet and salty and tangy and perfect.

The jelly gives me flashes of her memories and dreams: She's been with other Type Threes. She's helped them murder people. I don't care. I keep drinking her in, my tongue probing all the corners of her skull and sheathed wrinkles of her brain to get every last gooey drop.

I can control my tongue, but just barely. It's hard to keep it from doing the one thing I'd dearly love, which is to drive it through her membrane, deep between her slippery lobes. But that would be the end of her. The end of us. No more, all over, bye-bye.

A little of what my body and soul craves is better than nothing at all. Isn't it?

My arm aches, and I'm starting to feel light-headed on top of the high. We're both running dry. I release her, spritz her brain with saline, and carefully put the top of her head back into place. She's full of my blood, and already her scalp is sealing back together. We've done well; we spilled hardly anything on the tarp this time. But my face feels sticky, and I've probably even gotten her in my hair.

She daintily wipes my blood from the corners of her mouth and smiles at me. Her skin is pink and practically glowing, and her boniness seems chic rather than diseased. "Want to get takeout from that Italian place after we get cleaned up?"

"Sure." I'm probably glowing, too. My stomach feels strong enough for pepperoncinis.

I head to the bathroom to wash my face, but when I push open the door—

I find myself in Dr. Shapiro's office. She's staring down at an MRI scan of somebody's chest. The monochrome bones look strange, distorted.

"There's definitely an organized mass above your ribs and spine. It's growing fast, but I can't definitely say it's cancer."

I'm dizzy with terror. How did I get here? What mass? How long have I had a mass?

"What should we do?" I stammer.

She looks up at me with eyes as solidly black as Betty's. "I think we should wait and see."

I back away, turn, push through her office door—

And I'm back in a rented room. But not the downtown dive with the dusty chandelier. It's a suburban motel someplace. Have I been here before?

The green tarp on the king-size bed is covered in blood and bits of skull. There's a body wrapped in black trash bags, stuffed between the bed and the writing desk. Did I do that? What have I done?

*Oh God, please make this stop.* I have to lean against the wall to keep myself from tumbling backward.

Betty comes out of the bathroom, dressed in a spattered silk negligee. I think it used to be white. There's gore in her wig. Her eyes go wide.

"I told you not to come here!" She grabs me by my arm, surprising me with her strength. In the distance, I can hear sirens. "They'll be here any minute—get away from here, fast as you can!"

She presses a set of rental car keys into my palm, hauls me to the door, and pushes me out into the hallway—

And I'm stepping into the elevator at work.

Handsome blond Devin is in there. A look of surprised fear

crosses his eyes, and I know the very sight of me repels him. His hand goes to his jeans pocket. I see the outline of something that's probably a canister of pepper spray. It's too small to be a Taser.

But then he pauses, smiles at me. "Hey, you going up to that training class?"

I nod mechanically, and try to say, "Sure," but my lungs spasm and suddenly I'm doubled over, coughing into my mask. When did simply breathing start hurting this much?

"You okay?" Devin asks.

I try to nod, but there's bright blood dripping from my mask to the floor. A long-forgotten Bible verse surfaces in the swamp of my memory: *Behold, I am vile; what shall I answer thee? I will lay mine hand upon my mouth.*

I look up and see my reflection in the chromed elevator walls—my face is gaunt, but my body is grotesquely swollen. My knit blouse is stretched tight over a huge curving lump that takes up most of my back. It itches. I don't even recognize the clothes I'm wearing. I must have bought them to accommodate this huge, strange mass, but I don't remember buying them. I've turned into some kind of hunchback. How long have I had this mass?

Instead of the pepper spray, Devin's pulled his cell phone out. I can smell his mind. He's torn between wanting to run away and wanting to help.

"Should I call someone?" he asks. "Should I call nine one one?"

The elevator is filled with the scent of him. Despite my pain and sickness, the Want returns with a vengeance. Adrenaline rises along with my blood pressure. My tongue is twitching, and something in the enormous hump on my back, too. I can feel it tearing my ribs away from my spine. It hurts more than I can remember anything ever hurting. Maybe childbirth would be like this.

Betty. I need Betty. How long has it been since I've seen her? Oh God.

"Call nine one one," I try to say, but I can't take a breath, can't speak around the tongue writhing backward down my throat.

"What can I do?" Devin touches my shoulder.

And the feel of his hand against my bony flesh is far too much for me to bear.

I rip off my mask. Rise up under him, yank his mask down. Grab him by the sides of his head. Kiss him. My tongue goes straight down his throat, choking him. He hits me, trying to shake me off, but as strong as he is, my Want is stronger.

When he's unconscious, I let him fall and then hit the emergency stop button. The Want has me wrapped tightly in its ardor, burning away all my human qualms. The alarm is an annoyance, and I know I don't have as much time as I want. Still. As I lift his left eyelid, I take a moment to admire his perfect chocolate iris.

And then I plunge my tongue into his eye. The ball squirts off to the side as my organ drills deeper, the tiny mouths rasping through the thin socket bone into his sweet frontal lobe. After the first wash of cerebral fluid I'm into the creamy white meat of him, and—

Oh God. This is more beautiful than I imagined.

I'm devouring his will. Devouring his memories. Living him, through and through. His first taste of wine. His first taste of a woman. The first time he stood onstage. He's at the prime of his life, and oh, it's been a wonderful life, and I am memorizing every second of it as I swallow down the contents of his lovely skull.

When he's empty, I rise from his shell and feel my new wings break free from the cage of my back. It's agony, but it's also a pleasure, like finally being able to scratch a nagging itch. As I spread the membranous, fluid-dripping wings wide in the elevator, I realize I can hear the old gods whispering to me from their thrones in the dark spaces between the stars.

And . . . something else. I hear a faint, insistent whisper in the castle manor. My masters in the voids of the cosmos wouldn't approve of me listening to this other, barely audible voice . . . but they don't know about it. Only I can hear it. My special secret. It wouldn't hurt to see what it's about sometime, would it?

I grin at myself in the distorted chrome walls. Everything is clear to me now. I have been chosen. I have a purpose. Through the virus, the old gods tested me and deemed me worthy of this holiest of duties. There are others like me; I can hear them gathering in the caves outside the city. Some died, yes, like the ragged man who must have recognized me as a fellow Archivist on sight. But my Becoming is almost complete. Nothing as simple as a bullet will stop me then.

Earth is ripe, human civilization at its peak. The other Archivists and I will preserve the memories of the best and brightest as we devour them. We will use the blood of this world to write dark, beautiful poetry across the walls of the universe.

For the first time in my life, I don't need faith. I know what I am supposed to do in every atom in every cell of my body. I will record thousands of souls before my masters allow me to join them in the star shadows, and I will love every moment of my mission.

I can hear the SWAT team rush into the foyer three stories below. Angry ants. I can hear Betty and the others calling to me from the hollow hills beyond the city. Smiling, I open the hatch in the top of the elevator and prepare to fly.

# PART TWO

# DOLORE STIMULATUS

The first form is darkness,
the second desire,
the third ignorance,
the fourth is the excitement of death,
the fifth is the kingdom of the flesh,
the sixth is the foolish wisdom of flesh,
the seventh is the wrathful wisdom.
These are the seven powers of wrath.
They asked the soul,
Whence do you come, slayer of men . . .
Where are you going, conqueror of space?

—The Gospel of Mary Magdalene

# CHAPTER 13

According to the textbook we're using this term in Psychology 450 (*The Future Therapist's Guide: Theory and Practice* by Garza-Fieldman), the most important thing you can do to ensure a solid working relationship with your clients—beyond, you know, staying current on research and therapeutic techniques and making sure you don't stink when you go in the room—is to *know yourself*. And at first blush, that sounds like a straight-up platitude, like the LIVE, LAUGH, LOVE canvas on the greige living room wall of your cousin Becky's suburban condo.

But knowing yourself matters. It matters if someone is pouring their black little heart out to you in a session and something they say disgusts you, or irritates you, and that negative emotion catches you by surprise, and in your surprise you let your true feelings show on your face. Because then they see your frown or narrowed eyes and they withdraw or shut down. And congratulations, you've just undone weeks or possibly months of work. So you're back to the Sisyphean task of building trust and rapport all over again, just because for one second you flinched when your client admitted that when he was thirteen he liked to fuck the goats on his mom's Ann Arbor farm.

While I am not a psychologist or a social worker, my clients still have a host of mental illnesses and neurodiversities. And so I have tried my level best to stare my own shames, bigotries, kinks, and squicks square in their beady little eyes so I can maintain my professionalism and not inadvertently destroy the positive feelings my clients have about paying their hard-earned cash to see me.

And yeah, I get that people refuse to understand that I am in fact a professional, even though I'm a top earner at one of the most exclusive, expensive, progressive houses in the world. My parents would not understand it. Everyone eventually asks what my father thinks of what I do for a living. As if anyone's father is supposed to have veto power over a grown woman's life when her teens are a full decade past, a vanishing dark spot in her rearview mirror. When they ask—assuming they're not clients, of course—I just smile sweetly and say, "Aw, honey, does your daddy still run *your* life?," and that usually shuts them up right quick.

Some people press on. They want to know how I can look my own family in the eye. How I can *justify* this lucrative, completely legal job to them.

And so I tell them the truth: my immediate family lost any care about what I do with my life when I was a sophomore in high school. I was away from home at regional band tryouts. My father decided to pick up a gun during a fight with my mother he'd started because he was sure she was cheating on him. (She wasn't.) He shot her between the eyes, then went upstairs and murdered my little sister and little brother because he believed they weren't really his biological children. (They were.) While their corpses cooled, he spent the next hour writing up an aggrieved, entitled, chest-thumping suicide note detailing why he had no possible choice but to slaughter his own family. And then, as is statistically typical of men like him, he blew his own brains out.

I tell the people who question my life choices that my father would have murdered me, too, had I been home. But I wasn't, because I'd chosen to play saxophone in marching band to have a reason to be gone on Friday nights when Dad drank. All the neighbors and his coworkers said my father was so nice and considerate and they were just *shocked* at what happened . . . but I know my mother and my siblings did not die surprised, because violence was *always* on the table behind closed doors. I had worked hard to build an alternate life at school, and so I was safe a hundred miles away when Dad finally made good on the threats Mom had willfully ignored for years because, she always insisted, "Your father means well." (He didn't.)

That's my story of why I survived: because of my individual choices and my hard work. And it's fine to be skeptical about that. So let's take a deep dive there. Maybe there's no justice in this universe and my being alive today is just dumb shithouse luck. And if that's the case, then there's no point in moralizing over anyone's life choices, is there?

My father's choice to murder my family resulted in me having to spend the next two years in the home of my uncle Robert, who is a pastor at a Baptist church. And he loves Christian moralizing in exactly the same way my father loved Scotch. They were both narcissists cut from the same rotten wood. It surely comes as no shock that he disrespects women and women's work in equal measure, nor that I got the hell out of there as fast as I could.

If anyone asks, I tell them that my uncle's opinion matters less to me than a skeet-soaked rag dropped by a client.

And that leads back to this: Most people insist that what I do, despite it being the very oldest profession, is in no way professional. To them, my job is just lying on my back and taking a whole lot of cock.

First, it's not just cock. Okay, yes, when I started out, it was cock all day, every day. Most straight cis guys, when they pay to see a courtesan, they want to have sex as many times as possible during the time they've paid for. And, fine, that's to be expected. *Occasionally* I would get a married couple who were looking for a rental unicorn for a threesome.

But I got a little bored with all that, so I talked with our madam, Em. She helped me make some key contacts at lesbian bars and such. Women are certainly an underserved population at traditional brothels, so she was keen to see if we could attract them. My first couple of female clients had a great time, and word spread. We also did some online advertising targeted at bi women, and that worked out pretty well.

So now a good portion of my clients are lesbians or bi women who need that itch scratched. I can butch down or femme up, depending on what my client's into. Sometimes women come to me because they're still figuring out their sexuality. They just don't know how to seduce or be seduced by another woman—and hell yes I help them with that if they ask. Some of my bi clients tried on their own but got shut down by local lesbians who're shitty with women who still sleep with men. Others are on the autistic spectrum, and they find dating confusing and frustrating. I've even had a few straight-identifying women come to me because they'd been watching girl–girl porn and got curious . . . and they figured I was safer than a hookup at a lesbian bar. And of course, I'm a sure thing. Those ladies are fun, but a little exhausting, because they want to try All The Things.

What just a few of my clients want most is to have someone to talk to. They come in thinking it's sex that they want, but it's intimacy they're starved for. Or they've got uncomfortable thoughts rattling around in their heads and they just need to get them out in front of a sympathetic ear.

A paid-for friend isn't ideal, but it's better than what a whole lot of people in this city have. And if you don't have insurance, I'm *way* less expensive than a psychiatrist. It helps that Em is a pretty damn cool boss and—shockingly, I know!—she actually values us for our individual interests, educations, and skill sets. (It also helps that the guy who owns the brothel is a rich eccentric who took a shine to Em's ideas and lets her run things the way she likes.)

About a year before the pandemic, the state blew up politically over human trafficking. Voters finally decided to legalize sex work so women and children being held in slavery wouldn't have to be afraid of getting locked up if they went to the police. That's the story, anyhow. I'd been working awhile on the down-low as a dominatrix and cam girl and was skeptical that trafficking was really as bad as some people were saying. Em went to local BDSM munches and play parties to recruit me and all the other girls I knew at the brothel, so none of us had typical sex worker backgrounds.

But my apartment neighbor, Allegra, is a psychiatric mental health nurse, and she very politely ripped me a new one when she overheard me scoffing about the whole thing in the laundry room to another neighbor after the election.

"If you don't know anyone who's been trafficked, then all that means is you and your friends have been lucky. Sheltered. And you should thank God for that," Nurse Tesfaye scolded me. "When I worked downtown, the police called us in after they raided a warehouse. Twenty women, men, and children. Naked, chained to the floor. Starved, tortured, drugged. Raped and sodomized repeatedly. Every day, I work with people who've been sold over and over, and they are going to struggle with that physical and psychological trauma the rest of their lives."

I was a little pissed off when she called me "sheltered." Wanted to be all "Hey, lady, my father mass murdered my family, so don't lecture *me* about trauma." But I also decided in the moment that it wasn't really about me, anyhow, so I kept my mouth shut.

The Pink Rose and the rest of the first legal brothels to go online have been extra careful to prove that their employees are 100 percent there of their own free will and are safe for customers. So, unlike our counterparts in Nevada, we do get full medical and dental after we've worked at the house for three months. (Due to new laws, we're employed as hourly or salaried workers and not independent contractors. Base pay can be pretty low, but we also get tips and bonuses. My base pay is not low.)

Considering how many people have come down with polymorphic viral gastroencephalitis and how easily PVG can spread through body fluids, having us work as independent contractors without health coverage would have been criminal negligence. At *least.* People get charged with murder for spreading that shit. The moment the FDA approved an emergency vaccine, Em brought in a nurse practitioner and lined us all up to get our shots. It wasn't so bad. Some of us got a little feverish and light-headed, and our arms ached for a couple of days, but that was about it.

Legalized prostitution is hot like Kīlauea, so reporters are dying to get dirt on the brothels. Just one disgruntled courtesan could bring down one hell of a sticky load of bad press. So it makes sense that Em puts effort into ensuring we're happy with who and what we're doing. We're even allowed to keep guns and Tasers hidden in our playrooms in case a client decides to go all Jack the Ripper on one of us. I never wanted a gun for reasons that should be painfully obvious, but it's good we were given that choice.

I fully agree this is a news honeymoon. The brothels will be passé back-page stuff soon enough. As boring as adult trafficking victims were ten years ago. As boring as my family's murder was a month after they were cremated. It'll all be downhill from here.

I mean, this is still capitalism, right? Filthy lucre fucks up everyone's best intentions. But for now, this is by far the best customer service job I've ever had. Even when I agreed to let an aging B-movie star piss on me in the shower, it was still way better than phone tech support. (And I even got my Blu-ray of *Chainsaw Hobos from Mars* autographed without having to wait in line at Comic Con!)

So I'm always trying to use my education in my work, and always trying to know myself better. Most of the time, that's been a rewarding journey.

But three weeks ago, I learned some things I wish I hadn't. Everyone in this whole damn brothel would wish that, too, if they knew.

# CHAPTER 14

Gregory wasn't a steady regular, but he'd seen me a few times before and had behaved himself perfectly well. And he'd passed our background check with a gleaming gold star. He was shy, polite. Wrestling with gender dysphoria. After a couple of sessions, it was clear he hated existing in a male body. He'd been fronting hard to be who he thought people expected him to be, and it was taking an incredible toll on him emotionally and psychologically. But because his family is (in their own special suburban ways) just as shitty and regressive as my uncle Robert, the notion of identifying as someone other than a man made him straight-up panicky. I got the impression he had a steady girlfriend, but when I asked about her, he clammed up hard.

He mostly wanted me to peg him. Mostly. I kept condoms handy just in case.

Because he seemed scared to death that someone might photograph him, I set things up so he could use the online system to schedule and pay for sessions, rather than having to arrive in person to negotiate scenes. And, more to the point, he could use the secret biometrics-equipped side door that's actually a block away and goes underground. Because of all the news vans camping in the parking lot across the street, the owners wanted to make sure that celebrities could come and go without harassment. But ordinary people stand to lose, too, if the flocking paparazzi stick cameras in their faces, so we offer back passage as a courtesy to good returning clients.

If Em or the receptionist had seen Gregory walk through the front door, or if the security guard hadn't been half asleep when he let Gregory go inside . . . well, none of this would have happened.

I thought I knew all about PVG. The CDC agreed to work closely with brothels in our state to limit the possibility of on-site transmission—thus our swift vaccinations. They'd been sending us weekly informational videos and pamphlets. Big nerd that I am, I read it all, and more.

Viruses have always fascinated me. I mean, think about it: They work by giving an unsuspecting cell new assembly instructions. It's just . . . new information. That doesn't seem so bad, does it? And yet it can be a complete horror show.

This is what I knew about PVG: Within a week of transmission, an infected person typically gets a mild to moderate headache and some nausea. Maybe some diarrhea. For some people, that's all that happens. After a few days of taking it easy, they're back to normal. For a few others, the infection takes root in their brain instead of their guts. They suffer delusions and mood changes that may or may not attract the attention of medical professionals or law enforcement. (Trust me, our society tends to assume that dangerously psychotic white men are just having a bad day until they make it a bad day for the whole house, too.)

But for others the headache turns into the most awful vise-grip migraine they've ever had. Thirty minutes to a day after that, they start puking up blood, then their stomach mucosa. Most everyone who gets that sick ends up in the hospital.

When a PVG patient gets out—*if* they get out and don't straight-up die—their digestive system is fucked all to hell. They can't eat most foods. Their body has trouble growing and healing. The enzymes their DNA uses to repair itself quit working like a tech bro after a four-whiskey lunch.

Sunlight, X-rays, cigarettes, liquor, food preservatives, cosmic rays . . . anything that can even slightly damage your DNA becomes a real problem. Patients' skin breaks down and their bodies sprout tumors. Their brains begin to degenerate. Sooner or later, they develop lesions on their frontal lobes, temporal lobes, amygdala, and hippocampus. Without daily medication, those lesions inevitably lead to a variety of hallucinations, delusions, and antisocial behaviors. And that's when police snipers tend to get involved.

PVG patients are identified by type. And some people get really hung up on that, you know? They don't understand that the type taxonomy is just a way for the medical community to try to make sense of what they're seeing. It's not like Dr. Moses went up the mountain and came down with tablets inscribed by God. It's all descriptive, not prescriptive. The virus is changing all the time and it doesn't give a shit about categories.

But anyway, Type Zeros—who seem to be more theoretical than real right now—are completely asymptomatic carriers. Type Ones are the folks who get sick but just need over-the-counter drugs and a little rest and are fine. They're maybe-probably still contagious if the stars are right. Twos may or may not be contagious, but they definitely need supplements containing the proteins found in fresh human blood. Same thing for Type Threes, but they need the proteins found in fresh brains. Type Fours— that category is pretty new—are the ones who mainly get brain infections and end up needing antipsychotics or antiepileptics. It's all pretty gruesome, but honestly not really that much more scary than a disease like Ebola, or even drug-resistant syphilis.

The CDC's overall message was "This is an incurable, complex, life-changing infection, but it can be managed just like HIV," so most of us in the brothels figured we could get our shots and just roll with it.

The brothels closed for a while at the beginning of the pandemic, but as everyone got restless (and as the CDC decided the quick-prick rapid antigen tests were reliable), the state let us take customers again. But obviously we aren't supposed to service anyone who's infected with PVG. Our vaccinations are insurance against being infected through random sneezes and handshakes on the street; there is no approved protocol for preventing transmission during physical intimacy. People have to pass a PCR antigen test and carry documentation proving it or the front door staff will turn them away. It's not just on the honor system; every prospective client has to pass a test. If someone claims our test generated a false positive—and, to be fair, Type Zeros and a lot of Type Ones don't even know they are infected—the staff smiles and tells them to come back with test results from their doctor.

I didn't even realize until later that Gregory was infected, even though I knew right away that something was seriously wrong with him.

Our playrooms are set up basically like a hotel room, except with a door in the front and the back. We courtesans come in through the front door, which locks and has a foyer beyond with a sink, mirror, etc., so we can do last-minute checks of our costumes and makeup. In the main part of the room, there's a bed and sofa—both have waterproof covers that are easy to disinfect—and *maybe* a bondage chair or frame. BDSM is tricky and we charge a lot more for it; the extra disinfection protocols are a huge pain. Because of the risk of someone getting a cut or bleeding welt, we're supposed to stick to light-impact play, light bondage, etc. Watersports and blood play are forbidden, obviously. Whatever dildos or other toys we use have to get wiped down with alcohol and go in the autoclave afterward. Silicone is our friend.

The back entrance is for our clients, and it opens into a tiled dressing area with toilet facilities and a shower with sturdy handholds. The CDC says that washing with soap and water helps prevent PVG transmission, so clients have to clean up before they play. A lot of them like sexytimes in the shower, and none of us enjoy blowing a dude with swamp ass, so everyone wins.

I wasn't surprised to hear the water running and to find the room filling with steam when I got down to the room for Gregory's session. I slipped off my green silk robe, draped it over the arm of the sofa, and sashayed over to the shower.

"Hey, Gregory, how's it going?" I called, hoping to not startle him.

He didn't answer. I figured he just couldn't hear, so I rounded the corner to the stall door, ready to knock on the shatterproof glass.

And stopped dead.

The glass was fogged up, so I could only glimpse him as a blurry beige shape against the white tiles . . . but something was Definitely Not Right. My mind split in two as instinct raised my pulse and screamed *Get away!* while the rational parts tried to stay calm and make sense of what I was seeing. Had he come here with a little person who was riding him piggyback as he showered? No, that wasn't one of his kinks—bringing someone else to a solo session wasn't allowed, anyway—and the asymmetrical hump I saw rising from his upper back wasn't really shaped like a clinging person.

I took a deep breath and tried again. "Gregory, you okay in there?"

No response. He was in the corner of the shower, pressing his face and chest against the tiles and swaying back and forth. Moaning faintly.

I gripped the handle and eased the door open just the tiniest bit so I could get a clearer look at him. Assess the situation. Use my brain and my education and not jump to any damn conclusions.

My next thought was that he had some kind of massive infection under his skin, like the epically pus-filled humps that Dr. Pimple Popper airs. But my eyes focused a bit more and I saw that his skin was stretched tight over distorted shoulder blades and bulging ribs that looked like they had separated from his spine in places. Good Christ, how could he stand up and walk with that going on? Whatever was causing this ugly hump was pushing out from far inside him.

Cancer? It had to be cancer. How could it have gotten so bad so quick? It had been only six weeks since I'd seen him last, and he'd been perfectly fine then. What kind of tumor grows that fast?

I stepped away from the shower. Turned to the pile of street clothes he'd haphazardly dumped on the dressing room chair. Looking for clues, like maybe a bottle of prescription medications or a clinic wristband or *something*.

The "something" I found was a boxy black pistol in a green nylon shoulder holster.

"God damn it," I whispered. This is a concealed carry state, but clients are forbidden to bring firearms into a brothel. Gregory *knew* that. What was he thinking?

I carefully pulled the pistol free of its holster, holding it gingerly as if it were a dead rat. Just because I hate guns doesn't mean I haven't taken time to learn the basics, like whether the safety is on and whether the thing is loaded. Enough of the other girls brought in firearms for self-defense that I figured it would be stupid not to learn enough to protect myself.

It was a Glock nine-millimeter. The safety was on and the magazine was full.

*God damn it.*

I went back to the shower door and slapped the glass with my hand. "Gregory!"

He jerked in surprise and turned away from the corner.

"Savannah, help me," he moaned.

I backed up as he pushed the stall door open and stumbled out. And couldn't help gasping because, Jesus Christ, I wouldn't have recognized him except for the colorful Saint Michael tattoo on his left pec. His face, chest, and arms were painfully gaunt, like he was a day or two from starving to death. And his eyes were both mottled black and red from eight-ball hemorrhages.

"What . . . what's happened to you?" I stammered.

His face contorted in grief. "This is not my body! This is not the Becoming that God promised me!" He started weeping.

"The other angels are massing in the hills. I . . . I can hear them all. I am called to my mission, but I don't want it!"

*Ah, shit,* I thought. He'd had some kind of break from reality, or was delirious, or both. People knew I was running BDSM scenes in here; screams wouldn't raise any eyebrows. My panic button was over on the side of the bed. If I hit it, two very large men with Tasers and Mace would be down here in less than a minute. But Gregory looked fragile. An electric shock might kill him.

More to the point, he stood between me and my panic button. Was I more likely to be able to dodge past him, or was it better to stay very still and use what I'd learned in class to try to deescalate the situation? In that moment, my mind absolutely refused to consider using his gun. No. I would *not* do that.

I decided it was better to try to calm him down first, and then phone for help.

"Gregory, deep breaths, buddy. Can you tell me what's happened?"

His expression twisted into a rictus of agony and he went into a half-crouch as though he were having a back spasm. "Oh God! It's happening. Savannah, I didn't know where else to go. Help me. I brought a gun . . . Please kill me!"

*Fucking hell.* "What? No—"

He started screaming and fell to his hands and knees.

That huge, twisted hump on his back was spasming, shuddering. Then the skin above his right scapula split with a spurt of dark blood and something amber and watery, and I realized *something was breaking free and clawing out of him.*

"Savannah, please . . ." He sounded like he could barely breathe.

I couldn't move, couldn't speak. Frozen like a rabbit. A leathery blade sliced up through the split in his skin, followed by a long finger of bone and a fringe of pale tissue. Then another blade sliced out through the skin on the left side of his back. The sound of bones crunching and skin ripping made bile rise in my throat.

"The gun. Please. I won't be able to stop . . ." His voice was changing as he spoke. Deeper. Stronger.

I stopped focusing on the gory confusion of his back and realized that his whole body was altering itself. Bloody teeth drooling out of his gasping mouth. His face rearranging itself into something that didn't look exactly human anymore. Bones lengthening. Muscles and sinews stretching.

He screamed like a raptor as his wings broke free. Wings. Holy fuck. They spread seven or eight feet wide, tough membranes stretched tight over thin bones that looked strong as titanium. The air stank of blood and amniotic fluid.

I stumbled backward into the rattling locker as the winged creature Gregory had become rose and towered over me.

"I was bound, though I have not bound," he intoned, his mouth full of long, jagged teeth like you'd see on a deep-sea anglerfish. "I was not recognized. But I have recognized that the All is being dissolved, both the earthly and the heavenly. When a soul has overcome the third power, it goes upward and sees the fourth power, which takes seven forms. The first form is darkness, the second desire, the third ignorance, the fourth is the excitement of death, the fifth is the kingdom of the flesh, the sixth is the foolish wisdom of the flesh, the seventh is the wrathful wisdom. These are the seven powers of wrath. And so I ask the chosen soul, *Whence do you come, slayer of men?*"

"Gregory, I—I don't understand." I was suddenly remembering passages about angels in the Bible. They weren't hot dudes with halos, like you see in Renaissance paintings. They always had to tell mortals "Fear not!" because they were *fucking terrifying*.

"Whence do you come, slayer of men?" He stepped toward me on long legs lightened for flight. "Wilt thou take thine sword? Or wilt thou shirk thy duty?"

The chair with his clothes and the pistol was just a few feet out of reach to my right. "I . . . I don't—"

He reached out and touched my forehead with taloned fingers.

Instantly, my mind filled with images of winged, predatory beings like Gregory falling like a curse from God upon men, women, and children across the world. Ripping their necks out and drinking their blood. Tearing their skulls open with talons or drilling into their eye sockets with grotesque burred tongues. Devouring their brains, their memories, their very souls.

And in this vision I turned my face to the heavens, and suddenly I could hear the old gods whispering to me from their thrones in the dark spaces between the stars: *Follow thy nature, and thou shalt be rewarded.*

"We Archivists shall preserve the worthiest souls," Gregory told me, pulling my mind back to the playroom. "We shall use the blood of this world to write triumphant praises to our ancient lords. Thy duty is to cull the unworthy so that those inferior souls shall not distract us from *our* duty."

The vision had shaken me to my very core. I'd seen the wholesale slaughter of the entire human race. Was it happening now? Or was what I'd seen some glimpse of the future? Part of me had accepted that the vision was an absolute truth right up there with rain being wet and the sky being blue. But the rest of me was resisting the inevitable and thinking, *Oh hell no.*

So I lunged sideways for the gun, flicked the safety off, and unloaded the entire ten-round magazine into Gregory's chest. It would have taken a very special talent to miss him at that distance. (I didn't.)

Every bullet I fired into his flesh was nothing short of exhilarating. And when I saw his body crash lifeless to the tiled floor, I came so hard I lost consciousness.

# CHAPTER 15

I woke in the quarantine wing of a place called Greenlawn. Something between a hospital and a jail. Not much fun. Taser-toting guys in hazmat suits from Homeland Security and the CDC interrogated me about what had happened, and what I remembered. I've done enough research on traumatic memory loss to fake it like a champ. After a few hours, I had them convinced that I didn't remember anything other than sickly-looking Gregory lunging at me when he came out of the shower.

The suits left, and then it was just a matter of waiting out ten days of quarantine in my cell.

It turns out my neighbor Nurse Tesfaye works there now. Apparently her Greenlawn salary was a lot nicer than it had been at the downtown mental health hospital. She came by every once in a while to chat for a bit. Say hi and all. Sometimes bring me a pudding or juice box. Nice of her. I got the impression that they were keeping her pretty busy, so she was deliberately taking time out to sit with me for a few minutes.

I never did come down with any PVG symptoms despite inhaling a fine mist of Gregory's blood. Clearly I *had* to have gotten infected, but their tests told them over and over that I wasn't. Once the week-plus had passed with no symptoms and no change in my viral titer, Greenlawn released me. Em gave me another week off with pay, which was a clear sign she was eager to keep me from quitting.

She told me that Slade, the security guard, insisted he never saw Gregory. Even after they showed Slade the camera footage of him clearly buzzing Gregory through, he stuck to his story and seemed genuinely confused and distraught about it. Slade tested negative for drugs, passed a polygraph, and there was no evidence he'd been bribed, so Em speculated that maybe he had some sort of brain seizure. She did fire him, obviously.

Neither she nor anyone else batted an eye when I told them I was thinking of buying a pistol of my own and bringing it to work. Everyone is very sympathetic and understanding. Some of the girls are telling me to buy three or four. You know, keep one hidden in the playroom, one in my car, one at home, etc.

I'm still not sold on firearms. They're certainly effective. But if I got one, it wouldn't be for self-defense. I don't have anything to fear from those who have Become. As far as they're all concerned, I'm one of the Chosen, too; they won't touch me.

I am a Type Five, and I am not alone. We all received our apocalypse assembly instructions without any headaches at all.

Which isn't to say that all this has been free of unpleasant effects. Ever since I woke up in the hospital, it's been hard to make myself come. And I've tried everything: my hands, my Hitachi, dildos, clients, a random hookup with a guy I met on Tinder. And yeah, Tinder guy did make me come, eventually . . . but only when I slit his throat with a razor after *he'd* come and was snoring away in the back of his camper van.

It was just as glorious as it was with Gregory. The kind of white-light, ascending-to-the-heavens ecstasy the saints used to sing about. Came so hard I sprained my back. And when I woke up, I thought, *Yeah: blades are more my style.*

Fortunately, Tinder guy won't be missed. And yeah, I know that for sure. I can glance at someone and know whether they'll Become or if I must save them for Archiving or if they're just a big ol' waste of time and oxygen for everyone except the *slayers of men* like me.

The biggest revelation from all this, at least for me personally, isn't knowing how and why the world will end, and that it will end in another three years at most.

It's knowing why my father killed himself.

I mean, I thought I knew his reason before. Having read his suicide letter, I knew it wasn't because he was sorry he'd just slaughtered his own family, because there is not a single shadow of regret in those three pages. I figured that he was too chickenshit to face the cops, the trial, and prison. Death was the easy way out.

But if murder is the purest joy I can find in this world, and if murder is just me following my nature like the old gods say . . . well, I surely inherited my nature just like I inherited my blonde hair.

So now I know, deep in my bones, that when my father shot my mother between the eyes, he came harder than he ever had when he'd been balls-deep in her pussy. He'd come harder than he ever had with a prostitute or with his own left hand. And when he murdered my little brother and sister . . . maybe he came even harder.

He killed himself because he realized that the neighbors had already heard gunshots and called the cops, and once he was in custody, he'd probably never be able to experience that kind of existence-affirming ecstasy ever again. Thus the angry, embittered tone of his letter.

I could be wrong about that. But it *feels* right. It's just more satisfying to think that he died out of a deep, soul-wrenching despair instead of garden-variety cowardice.

•   •   •

I saw another Type Five at the grocery store the other day. Nice-looking middle-aged lady. Real grandmotherly type. But we both knew who we really were from the gleams in our eyes. We gave each other a little nod and smile and went on with our shopping.

The old gods still whisper to me in my dreams, but honestly they can all go pound salt. I'm not doing this for them. But if humanity's doomed, and I know it is, I'm gonna get it while I can.

# CHAPTER 16

I killed a Catholic monk, can you believe it? I didn't even know we had any living in this city. He and I connected on one of the dozen hookup sites I'm catfishing on. I agreed to meet him a block from his monastery. Which I would have never even known was there, otherwise, even though I've driven past the side street it's on a thousand times. I had this idea that monasteries are all away from cities, like in isolated vineyards or deep in the woods or on picturesque mountaintops. But nope. His is in Wexney, east of downtown, where the old money lives. If those monks ever have to pay property taxes, they won't be able to afford to stay in the neighborhood.

His name was Michael. Thirtysomething, not bad looking. Bald on top, the rest of his sparse brown hair cut close to his scalp. Skinny. Quiet and intense. Smelled like castile soap and incense. Nervous. I got the impression he didn't do this much. I figured we'd head to one of the fleabag motels a couple miles away . . . but he actually snuck me inside the monastery and took me back to his cell! That's some serious brass.

So, I mean, I *had* to let him fuck me. Seems only fair to reward that kind of bravery, right? A lot of religious guys, they think they're kinky, but really they're so vanilla you just want to pinch their little horndoggy cheeks and tell them how adorable they are. Michael was a legitimate freak, though.

For the appetizer, he wanted to watch me strip and then ritualistically defile his religious objects. I hadn't ever fucked myself with a crucifix before, frotted on the spine of an eighteenth-century leather-bound Latin Bible, or used a rosary as anal beads, but there's a first time for everything. I got the feeling that he was going through a bit of a *thing* with his religion, psychologically speaking. Perhaps experiencing some catastrophic rupture of faith. But it wasn't my job to counsel him.

Then, for the main course, he wanted to fuck me in the ass while I was on my hands and knees on the hard wooden floor whispering the Lord's Prayer. Because of course he did. And we'd negotiated ass play ahead of time. He spent a while rimming me first, reaming my starfish with his soft tongue. And that was fun.

But when he undid the fly of his cassock and levered his dick out, I had me a *concern*. Dude was hung. Hung like *damn*. Thick as my wrist, long as my forearm. The shape of it reminded me of a megamouth shark minus the fins. He had seriously missed out on a career as a porn star.

When we were messaging each other, Michael had refused to send any dick pics, and I'd assumed that meant he was embarrassed because he thought it was too small. As usual, I'd brought an assortment of really good lubed condoms, so I had something to fit him. And it's not like I don't keep myself in shape for accommodating large clients. Still. He was a lot bigger than I was expecting.

And he didn't go nearly as slow as I'd asked him to. Just grabbed me by the hips and shoved right in. For a hot second there, I worried I might have to make an awkward, limping visit to the ER later. Rectal tears aren't anything to fuck around and find out about; you don't want to go septic down there.

Fortunately, having a real, live woman to rut into was so exciting that he came pretty quickly. So I didn't have to bite the proverbial pillow for very long. Only got through the prayer twice before he let out a low, stifled moan and his latex-sheathed cock spasmed and spat inside me.

He got up, stumbled backward onto his cot, and passed right out afterward. So I got my straight razor out of my overnight adventure bag and had my dessert. Made quite a mess but didn't make any noise, which was key. And then I put on some rubber gloves, checked the cell for hidden cameras. Discovered he wasn't that kind of perv. Kind of a shame; I would've liked a video souvenir for later. Yanked the stained bottom sheet out from under his corpse and pulled it off the bed. Gathered up the used condom and uncleanable rosary, tidied up my DNA and fingerprints from everything else with some bleach wipes. Black-bagged the most incriminating stuff for disposal elsewhere. And then I was gone.

I felt a little guilty about killing Michael. He'd been all over the world, studied at the Vatican. Definitely an Archival-quality mind. Definitely would be missed by his order. He wasn't the kind of person I was supposed to be getting out of the way.

I'd broken the rules. Broken them pretty hard, to be honest.

But getting freaky in a monastery? Getting plowed by his *kaiju* of a cock, even though it hurt like a motherfucker? It got me going something awful. It wasn't just Michael's blood I got on the sheet; I'd smeared pussy juice all over it first. Dripped a glistening puddle of girl goo on the unforgiving floor I had to wipe up.

After all that, I wanted to come, damn it. I'd earned my nut. And if I didn't kill him for it, I would've had to do someone else that night, so it might as well be him.

• • •

But tonight, Michael comes to me in a dream. I'm standing in a barren field and he floats in the air above me in a Jesus pose, his arms outspread to the gray, storm-threatening sky above us. Barefoot in his cassock, the gash in his neck gaping like an aroused vagina. Spent, cum-crusted dick flopping through his fly like a hound's lolling tongue. Just as I'd left him.

"Thou hath transgressed." He stares down at me with filmy, dead eyes.

"I have." I know it won't do me any good to pretend otherwise. We both know what I've done.

"Thou must do penance," he tells me. "The old gods demand it."

"How?"

"Thou must turn thine knife to a new task."

The monk is wreathed in fire now, as if he is a holy sign and I am an Old Testament prophet witnessing him. "Thou must protect She who is most precious to the future."

"Who is She?" I squint against the light of his blazing corona. "How will I know?"

"Thou shalt recognize Her as the worthiest of the worthy," he replied. "And thou shalt guard Her as you would guard a chest of gold. And thou shalt care for Her and mend Her as you would thine own flesh."

# CHAPTER 17

When I wake up after the dream, my first thought is, *Mending flesh? I need to learn a lot more medical stuff.*

Second thought: *Right, like I have time to add online nursing courses to my lively psychology class, murder, and fucking schedule.*

But then it hits me. It's so obvious, it's beautiful. Archivists don't have to read books or watch YouTube or go to school to gather other people's thoughts. They have a far more direct, effective method. While I'm not their Type, I'm still one of them. I've been transformed and selected by the gods the same as them. So why can't I borrow their techniques if it's in service to my mission?

My new instinct tells me that I absolutely can.

• • •

I go to the hardware store as soon as it opens and buy a handheld circular saw with a three-inch blade. The unit is small enough to stash in my adventure bag, which is a nice leather diaper bag I Scotchgarded the hell out of. Most of the time it just looks like a big shoulder purse to other people. Nothing to worry about.

When I get back to the apartment complex parking lot, I put on my mask and clip a double-edged boot dagger inside my jeans, at the small of my back, under my shirt. Put a thumbtack inside my left shoe, under my arch. Foot pain reliably makes me cry; I'm a big ol' baby when it comes to bastinado and falanga.

I'm weeping and probably nicely red-eyed by the time I get up the stairs to the second floor.

Nurse Tesfaye answers the door on the third knock. I knew

she wasn't working today; she mentioned she has Thursdays and Fridays off when we chatted in Greenlawn. But I've still gotten a little bit lucky that she's home.

She opens the door a couple of inches and looks at me warily over her mask. Her security chain is on. This lady certainly isn't stupid. The air from her apartment is wonderfully fragrant with fresh, hot coffee.

"What's up, Savannah?" She pulls her pink terry cloth robe closed over her purple satin nightgown.

I put on my best anguished face.

"I . . . I need to talk to you about Dr. Sallow." I'm stammering like I'm embarrassed and freaked out. "He . . . he, um. He found out I work at the Pink Rose and he came to my place last night. Forced me to do things. He said he'd say I failed my virus test and get me fired if I didn't do what he told me. I'm . . . I'm scared he's going to come back, and I don't know what to do."

It's all lies, but her eyes go wide. Bingo. I *knew* this was a push button for her. Sallow was always professional with me, but he stared at my tits a little too long. Exuded just enough of a secret-creeper stink that my gut said accusing him would seem plausible to her. She had told me that she's a mandated reporter, so there was no way she'd blow this off.

"Oh my goodness. Please, come in." She unlatches the chain and opens her door.

I step inside and she shuts the door behind me. Nice place. Her apartment is laid out as a mirror image of mine. Framed Jamaican and Italian art—mostly vivid watercolors of the ocean, mountains, and forests—adorns her walls. She's got a flat-screen smart TV, IKEA coffee table, and light blue couch set up almost exactly like I've got my furniture situated.

She was watching something on YouTube when I interrupted her. The image is paused on an Asian woman with electric blue and pink hair who's wearing a black T-shirt that reads "Not That Kind of Doctor." A moment later, I recognize the channel: Dr.

Kaz Chats. A lot of the other students in my classes watch her videos, and I've caught a few when I've had time. Interesting stuff.

"I didn't really know who to talk to." I gently set my adventure bag down on the floor. "I'm scared the police won't believe me."

"You can talk to me." She locks the door and puts the chain back in place. "You want some coffee? My grand-auntie in Kingston just sent me a care package. The really good beans we Jamaicans keep for ourselves and don't export."

"That's so nice of you. Yes, I would love that."

She steps past me toward her kitchen and I smoothly draw the dagger and drive it deep into the side of her neck.

Nurse Tesfaye gives a startled, strangled gasp—she can't really scream, since I've just severed her trachea along with her carotid artery—stumbles, half-turns toward me, her eyes wide. Shocked. Accusing. *Hurt.*

The orgasm shuddering through me has me pretty distracted, but I shove her down to the floor, yank the knife out, and press my mouth down on her jetting artery. Drinking her lifeblood deeply.

At first, nothing happens. But then, memories creep in. Memories that aren't mine, and which *can't* be hers. I'm racing across the frozen wilderness of Germania in Arminius's company, screaming, my sword raised to slaughter the Roman soldiers scattering in fear before us. I'm on the deck of a clipper ship beneath the creaking sails, seasick and sunburned, elated at finally seeing green on the horizon but desperately missing the lass I left behind in Glasgow. I'm picking grapes on the hills outside Rome, gossiping with my sisters as we enjoy the cool breeze. I'm stepping off a Sicilian tramp steamer in Asseb with my carpetbag, surveying the bustling port before me, praying that this strange, hot country with its relentless sun can become my new home. I'm tending goats in the scrublands at the foot of the majestic Mabla Mountains, pausing to shake a pebble from my sandal. I'm holding my big brother's strong, calloused hand as we step off the boat in

Kingston. "This is our new home, *wenidi liji*," he tells me. "Auntie is waiting for us!"

Ancestral memories. *This* is what the Two Archivists are recording from those they harvest. Thousands of lives are an intoxicating, immersive whirl in my mind. But it's not what I need. Not what I came here for.

I force a finger down my throat and vomit her blood onto her nice clean carpet. The memories lose their hold on my consciousness, fade. I dig the tack out of my shoe, crawl to my adventure bag, and fumble out my new circular saw. Find an outlet to plug it in. I know I have to work quickly.

As I cut into her skull, tiny bits of blood, scalp, and bone fly everywhere. The air fills with the stink of scorched bone. Her short hair is getting caught in the blade and making things extra messy and awkward. I should have brought a clipper with me and shaved her head first. But it's too late to worry about that now. I'll remember to do it next time.

I get the top of her skull off and slice open her dura mater with my box cutter. It is, indeed, a tough mother. But I get it peeled off and expose her raw brain. About three pounds of wrinkled gray matter glistens before me. It has a faint raw meat smell to it when I get close. Mostly, the air stinks of her blood and my vomit now. The aroma of coffee is a faint reminder of a pleasant, civilized world I no longer operate in.

I don't know enough about neurological anatomy to know where the memories of medical procedures she's learned are likely to be stored. I know these will be mostly explicit memories . . . but maybe implicit memory is involved as well? That might involve neurological clusters all over her brain.

Shit. Three pounds of brain is a *lot*. Will I have to eat the whole damn thing to get what I'm looking for?

No way to know. I just have to do this. So I dig my fingers into her gooshy neocortex and shove the fatty, gelatinous flesh into my mouth. It's disgusting, like thick boogers, and my throat closes, refusing it, but I've committed to this, so I force it down. Focus on mechanically scooping and swallowing.

Her memories flood into me—and almost immediately I'm regretting this terrible, utterly damning life choice I've made.

I'm reliving her childhood memories of Jamaica, Miami, and Cleveland. The little boy stepping off the boat in her blood-memory must be Gianni Tesfaye, her papa. He loved her and his other children so, so much. A kind, gentle, strong man who protected his children as they grew into happy, assured adults.

And I'm on my hands and knees on the sticky bloodstained carpet, ugly-crying my black little heart out. Because I thought a childhood like hers, a father like hers, was just fairy tales. Men like him don't exist outside Disney movies. I was sure of it. But her memories of her sweet, attentive, patient papa show me that my cynical conviction was a lie. Good fathers *do* exist. For other children. Other women. Not me.

I wail my heartbreak and fury into the polyester fibers. My siblings and I were *cheated*. Utterly, horribly cheated. I want to curse the gods who let this happen, but the ancient entities who are my masters now had nothing to do with the affairs of mankind. They wait impassive in the darkness between the stars. Waiting for me to get my shit together and get on with it.

So I crawl back to her skull and keep eating her brain, like a rat gorging itself on poisoned bait.

I can vividly imagine her ghost standing beside me, watching me defile her corpse. So vividly, I wonder if it's real and not my imagination at all.

Her ghost furiously shakes her head. "What goddamned, dirty, low-down white bullshit is this? I was nothing but good to you, and this is how you do me?"

*I'm sorry*, I want to say. *This was a mistake.*

"You lie about being raped! You think you some kind of

feminist, and you *lie* about that! To *me*. Do you have any god-damned idea how harmful that is? People would hold you up as an example. 'Oh, *she* lies, so they *all* lie about that.' Damn you *forever*."

Now I'm reliving her horror at going to the warehouse where they found all the trafficked men, women, and children. Women she saw as abused, exploited innocents. Not women like me.

"Nobody else would have known," I tell her. "I just said that to you because it was easy."

"Easy, huh? Easy to get me distracted and sympathetic? To come to me crying your white woman tears?" She spits for emphasis. "Just so you can betray and murder the one Black friend you had in your entire life."

That hits a weak spot in my armor, and I don't have a comeback. "Yeah. Sorry."

"People are counting on me! And now I can't help anyone ever again. Not *ever*. Your . . . your moral relativism is disgusting. And so is your work."

"Seriously?" I rock back onto my heels to glare at her. "My working in a brothel is *not* the problem here. There's nothing wrong with having a lot of consensual sex. There's nothing wrong with being good at sex, or being paid for sex. There's nothing wrong with giving other people pleasure. Oldest profession in the world, babe. If you wanna hate the game, that's fine, but don't hate us players. We're human beings the same as nurses are. No better, no worse. You get just as many body fluids in your face in a day as I do."

"I wasn't referring to your sex work, but okay. What *do* you think the problem is, Savannah?"

"I think the problem is I'm selfish." I stare down at the red, open cavity of her skull. "I'm descended from a long, long line of selfish people. People who murdered and enslaved other human beings when they damn well knew better, but they constructed elaborate justifications for themselves. Codified those dishonest justifications into laws. And I was raised up in a world of their creation."

I pause, swallowing against a stray tatter of dura mater that seems to have gotten stuck in the back of my throat. "That's why I hunted you. That's why I killed a nice woman who befriended me against her better instincts, instead of going out and finding a stranger. That's why I killed a strong, accomplished Black woman who was pretty much the living embodiment of the American Dream instead of going in search of a scrub. You looked *consumable*. And maybe I was still pissed off that you called me 'sheltered' that day."

I take a deep breath. "You'd have died soon anyway. An Archivist would take you. Tear you open. It wouldn't worry about making your death quick."

"Is that *justification* actually supposed to make me feel better?" She puts her fists on her hips. "Is that *actually* supposed to absolve you of what you've done here?"

"No. I guess not."

"How is this any different than the murder that got you in trouble with your gods? How is this not another transgression?"

"Your death serves them. I needed an education to do what they want, and you've given me one."

She shakes her head. "What you call 'selfish'? I would call it predatory. I would call it evil. Just straight-up evil."

I shrug, feeling profoundly ashamed and numb at the same time. "You could call it that, yes."

"So your eyes are opened," she says. "You know better than to do what you're doing. Are you going to do the decent thing and stop?"

"I don't know," I reply. "It depends on what the gods will let me do."

"The gods." Looking disgusted, she pokes at my discarded dagger with the toe of her slipper-shod foot. "You have the means to stop anytime you want to."

I stare down at the knife.

"Oh. *That* kind of stopping myself." I pause. "As a mental health care nurse, aren't you supposed to, you know, *not* tell people to kill themselves? Isn't that just a little frowned upon in your profession?"

"You ended my career as a nurse about an hour ago. Since then, I have had no professional obligations with regard to medical ethics," she replies coldly. "So the question remains: What are you going to do?"

"I think I'm going to think about it." I look at her body, and a fresh wave of regret washes through me. "I think I'm going to cover you, and I'm going to clean up some. Maybe have a cup of that coffee you offered me."

She rolls her eyes and throws up her hands. "Fine. Eat my brain. Drink my coffee. By all means, make yourself at home. But don't expect me to stay here. I have better things to do with my afterlife than haunt the mind of a psycho killer who betrayed me on my day off."

The shade of Nurse Tesfaye, the ghost of the woman who tried to be my friend, turns away from me and fades from existence. I am alone with her corpse. The sudden silence makes me nervous.

My belly is distended, aching from all the brains I've shoved down my throat. Frankly, I'm feeling more than a little sick. Kind of very, very sick, actually. But her skull isn't empty. Did I get what I was looking for? Can I keep from vomiting until I'm sure?

I can't keep reliving her memories. They'll destroy me. They need to be at a distance, filtered.

So I imagine her memories as a box of index cards. It appears in my hands: pink plastic with a flip top, just like the box I had in high school. Almost completely filled with white, ruled four-by-six cards. I flip through. *Antibiotics. Wound irrigation. Emergency first aid. Tracheotomies. Suturing.* Yes. The things I most wanted in my head are here. Even better: Now I also know the boundaries of my medical ignorance. I know what I *don't* know. And on one card, I have the address of a handsome young ER doctor named Craig, if I want to fill in those gaps later.

Elated, I run to her bathroom to puke her brains up.

# CHAPTER 18

Once I'm sure I'm done purging, I pull the purple satin comforter off her bed and wrap her body in it. Just to give her some dignity in death. Just so if the maintenance guy finds her, he doesn't have nightmares forever. Not that it will be any nicer for the forensics detectives, or the cleanup crew. God. The poor cleanup crews. I never thought of them before.

Devouring Allegra Tesfaye's brain has altered me. Some of her memories are mixed in with mine now. It's hard to tell them all apart. I'm . . . I'm not sure I know myself anymore.

I'm covered in her blood and fluids. Everything I'm wearing is incriminating garbage now. I get out a big plastic trash bag, strip, and sack my clothes and shoes. Take a long hot shower in Allegra's bathroom. Use her expensive boutique soap and shampoo. Towel off, then raid her closet and drawers for a new outfit.

Her clothes fit me surprisingly well. Even her sneakers. The red blouse I've picked out is pretty tight across the bust, but that's probably a feature. Nobody ever really expects a serial killer with nice tits.

I step back into the living room and survey the disaster I've made. Christ. The spinning saw blade threw blood and brains on the walls, onto the ceiling. Bits of nurse are *everywhere*. I need a better tool for next time. Maybe a machete? My arm will get tired, but it's probably good cardio.

This is where I should get to work with wipes and bleach to get rid of the evidence . . . but I'm absolutely bone-tired now. And something in the back of my head tells me that the cops are about to be way too busy to work this case in a timely fashion. If ever.

I pour myself a mug of the fragrant coffee and top it up with coconut creamer from her fridge. Sit down on her very lightly blood-speckled, sky-colored couch and wake up her TV. Hit the Play button to watch *Dr. Kaz Chats* while I sip my coffee.

". . . so I definitely have big news to share with your viewers," says a nerdy woman in a black T-shirt. "Do you want the good news first, or the bad?"

Dr. Kaz smiles at her. "Which does it make the most sense to talk about first?"

"The good, for sure." She clears her throat. "So, you know how there's been a massive uptick in false negative test results the past month, even with PCR? We figured out why that's happening."

"Is there a problem with the new batches of tests?"

She shakes her head. "The tests seem to be fine. As far as we can see, they work exactly the way they're supposed to. That's the good news."

The YouTuber's smile has faded. "So if it's not the tests . . . ?"

Black Tee makes a rewinding motion with her hands. "Let me back things up a little for your viewers. PVG has been classed as a pandoravirus. And pandoraviruses, as a group, were only identified recently, in 2013. These viruses are huge, and have enormous genomes. They're so big that the first scientists who observed them in amoebas thought that they were parasitic bacteria. You can see them with a regular light microscope; that's how big they are."

Dr. Kaz nods. "They're shockingly large compared to most other viruses."

"PVG has over two million base pairs in its genome, and its genes don't resemble any known cell lineages. We don't know what most of them actually do," says Black Tee. "It's got double-stranded DNA and a viral envelope. It *looks* like a bacterial cell.

The only thing stopping it from being one is that it doesn't have any ribosomes to make its own proteins, so it doesn't have any enzymes to make its own energy, and it can't divide to replicate itself. So it has to hijack another cell to do all that. A lot of people consider pandoraviruses to be a 'missing link' between viruses and bacteria."

"This is really interesting stuff, but how does it connect to the false negative tests?"

Black Tee nods and holds up her hands in a *be patient* gesture. "So, another interesting thing about pandoraviruses in general and PVG in particular? They can shuffle around their surface antigens to reduce or even eliminate host immune reactions. They do this before they invade a cell, but they can also do it once they're inside. And in an increasing number of people, PVG is taking up residence in infected people's cells and pretending to be an organelle like a mitochondrion. And once they've turned themselves into pseudo-organelles, there aren't any viral antigens floating around in their body fluids, so even the PCR tests come back negative."

"Ohhh, that's tricky!"

Black Tee nods vigorously. "We think the CDC probably figured this out a while ago, but they've been sitting on the information."

Dr. Kaz looks profoundly taken aback. "That would be completely unethical. Why would they do that?"

"Because if the virus isn't showing up in blood, saliva, urine, et cetera . . . the only way to know if a person has PVG or not is to do a biopsy of the specific infected tissue. And for a lot of people, that would mean needing to get a spinal tap. Which is painful, and dangerous, and expensive, and . . . can you imagine how much the public would freak out over that? People threw massive tantrums over getting vaccinated, and that's *easy*."

"Damn." Dr. Kaz sighs. "Yeah, that's a political hot potato, for sure."

I turn off the TV. Black Tee's discovery certainly explains a few things about my own situation. But not everything.

The mysteries that confound scientists compel me, too. I only know what I've witnessed and what the gods have shown me. I don't know their grand plan. The misery and chaos are a means to an end, and the question of what that end will be burns hot in my mind. Curiosity itches in me like a yeast infection.

I stand, drain the mug, and set it down on the coffee table. A reckless disregard for leaving DNA evidence behind. But I'm doing it.

I fucked a few dozen law enforcement officers my first few months at the brothel. Mostly city police, a few county deputies. A sheriff. They just aren't complicated men. Not deep thinkers, as a group. A bit smarter than the gangsters who sometimes come in from up north, but often cut from the same coarse cloth. Of course, I also know I've experienced a selection bias: those who go into the profession because they actually do want to protect and serve probably see visiting a brothel as unseemly or distasteful.

Part of me is hoping a cop comes knocking on my door, because it might be fun to see if I can get myself out of that kind of predicament. After all, Dahmer did. Straight-up had the cops find his teen victim Konerak Sinthasomphone on a street corner. Naked, bleeding from his ass, and disoriented because Dahmer had drilled a fucking hole in his skull and injected hydrochloric acid, trying to make him into a kind of zombie. But Dahmer played it totally cool, and they handed the kid right back to him. I'm a lot fucking smarter than Dahmer. I'd never flunk out of school.

"I'm not going to stop myself," I tell Nurse Tesfaye's corpse. "I need to find out what happens next. I need that very, very much. I need to be alive when it happens and see it with my own two eyes."

She doesn't answer me, but I didn't expect her to.

# CHAPTER 19

Michael comes to me a week later in all his blazing, profane, dong-hanging glory to tell me in ecclesiastic proclamations what a very good bad girl I've been and how pleased the gods are with my progress. And then he gives me a cryptic little homework assignment related to the future-precious She.

So I'm up at the crack of dawn, dressing in a nice soft-butch outfit that isn't *too* sexy—I don't want to attract the wrong kind of attention—and reloading my adventure bag. I hit the nearby Target as soon as it opens, to get an inexpensive but nice-looking gold cross necklace, pull a few hundred dollars out from a nearby ATM. Then I'm on the road heading southwest.

The flyspeck town Michael showed me is forty miles past the state line and twenty miles off the interstate. On one side of the road is a truck stop, a log cabin roadhouse called the Patriot Tavern, and a run-down motel called Sweet Zee's Lodge that looks like it was once a Knights Inn. The tall aluminum pole in front of the tavern is flying an American flag, a "Blue Lives Matter" flag, and a bright yellow Gadsden flag. Across the street is a small cemetery, a dingy white clapboard Baptist church, and an abandoned Dairy Queen with boarded-up windows.

The pothole-pocked parking lot of the motel is practically empty. It strikes me as the kind of place that's happy to take cash instead of a credit card and doesn't scrutinize fake IDs too closely. Its looks are not deceiving. I even get the front desk attendant, Clyde—who's apparently the grandson of Zee herself—to give me a discount on one of their suites, after I toss my hair a little and offer to keep him company after his shift is over that evening. If he tries to take me up on that, I know I'll be getting all my money back.

• • •

It's just before 2 p.m. when I put on my shiny new cross, stroll out into the chilly October air, and head across the cracked parking lot to the tavern. There's a laminated sign posted on the front door that reads "MASKS FORBIDDEN! No unconstitutional face-diapers allowed in here! Stop buying the government's bullshit and breathe free like God intended!"

Well, when in Rome, right? I pull my mask off, tuck it in my pocket, and push inside. The air smells like spilled beer, old peanuts, and stale cigarettes. It's so odd being in a place where smoking is allowed that I feel like I've gone back in time. Despite the overcast of the day, it takes my eyes a moment to adjust to the dimness inside. The tavern's decor is a mix of neon beer signs, Second Amendment fan art, and Cracker Barrel wall kitsch.

A couple of old white men wearing ill-fitting black leather biker vests over grubby tees and saggy jeans are sitting at the bar laughing at something with the bartender, a skinny young guy in a black tank top who's missing the ring and pinky fingers of his burn-scarred right hand. More white scars splash up his arm and onto his face. Nurse Tesfaye's expertise tells me that this was more likely an accident making homemade napalm than it was a war injury. They're all scrubs, and not who I'm here for.

I scan the rest of the room. In the far corner, by one of the few windows, is a tired-looking, bespectacled woman in her late twenties or early thirties. She's wearing a tan cardigan over a long, demure, blue chambray dress, and her brown hair is up in a bun. Her small-town librarian vibe is reinforced by the Amish romance paperback she's engrossed in. A white ceramic mug and a coffee carafe sit on the right side of the table with creamers lined up like bowling pins. She, too, is a scrub . . . but I can see the bright-edged aura of the person she would have become if she'd been planted in a place where she could flower. And that unrealized woman is extraordinary, though I can't see well enough to know why.

There's a ring on her left hand. A classic radiant-cut diamond solitaire. I'm pretty sure the rock is real, and considering how expensive it is compared to the rest of her outfit, I suspect it was bait. I saw a lot of bait at the brothel. Men hiding their abusive, possessive sides would give the girls fancy gifts and expensive jewelry. Probably many of these guys really did see themselves as white knights trying to "rescue" a beautiful fallen woman. They'd promise adoration, financial stability, and marital bliss, but instead they'd serve the girls jealous rages, cold silences, and bruises. The unluckiest ones got a baby in the bargain, too, which meant they had to spend years longer trying to pull free of the domestic tar pit they'd fallen into. Or they'd live with the guilt of abandoning their toddler with a man they knew would destroy the kid in one way or another.

The woman in the corner absolutely stinks of existential tar. I can see the exhaustion and tension in her shoulders and in the premature frown lines between her eyes. She's clearly hiding in here to get what respite she can from whatever's waiting for her back home.

I get the vibe that she in no way believes in white knights—but part of her is hoping for one anyway.

So I cross the room to her and stop a respectful social distance away. "Hi, I'm sorry to bother you, but what do you think of that book you're reading? I keep seeing ads for it online, but I can't tell if it's my thing or not."

"Oh. Hi. Yes, the book is great. I'm enjoying it a lot." The woman blinks at me in confusion, then glances around the tavern as if to check to see if I'm with anyone. "Not to be rude, but did . . . did you get lost?"

I laugh lightly. "Not exactly. I was supposed to meet with a client down here this afternoon, but she called it off at the last minute. I just couldn't face the drive back—five hours, can you believe?—so I thought, What the heck, and got a room at the motel next door. Normally I wouldn't be traveling so far out, but my office has lost a lot of people."

"Client?" she asks. "Are you a lawyer?"

"Oh, no. I work for Midwestern Empowerment Advocacy." A real organization that I knew about courtesy of Nurse Tesfaye. Sadly, I never once heard of it working at the brothel. "We help women—sometimes men, too—with families get themselves and their kids out of abusive relationships. Not just violent ones. We help people leave emotionally and psychologically abusive partners, as well as other difficult situations."

I can see a spark of cautious interest building in her eyes.

"What kind of difficult situations?"

"Well, our motto is 'If you don't know how to leave, you need MEA.' Sometimes folks don't realize they're in an abusive relationship, but if their partners have economically entrapped them so that they can't leave? It's abusive."

Her eyes have fallen on my cross. Or my cleavage. Or maybe both. "That's . . . very interesting."

"Hey, do you mind if I sit down?" I rest my hand on the chair opposite hers. "I made a bad decision putting on these shoes this morning."

She pauses, looking conflicted. "I hate to ask this, but have you gotten your vax?"

"Oh, absolutely." Keeping my thumb over my name, I pull my card out of the flap of my purse to show her. "My boss had us get ours right away."

Her shoulders relax a little. "That's good. I've gotten mine, too. Sure, please sit down."

"Thank you. My name is Vanna, by the way." I pull the chair out and settle into it.

"Nice to meet you. I'm Lee."

I put my vax card away. "I'm a little surprised you've picked a spot that's so antimask."

Lee shrugs. "That part isn't great, but nobody who knows me would ever come to this kind of place. It's quiet, and the coffee is really good." She nods toward the skinny, scarred bartender. "There aren't that many other places still open around here, anyway. I used to sit and read at the Starbucks in Cloverton. Billy was a barista there. But he got laid off after his accident, and then they shut the store down when the pandemic started."

"That makes sense," I say.

She takes a sip from her mug. "My husband doesn't approve of drinking caffeine or reading fiction, so I tell him I am going to a friend's church to play bingo. She covers for me. I know it's not right to lie to him . . . but I really do need this time to myself."

"You have kids?"

Lee nods wearily.

"Well, that definitely calls for coffee." I pause and bite my lower lip as though I'm thinking something over. "Hey, I bet Billy would let you take your carafe with you if you asked."

I reach across the table to put my hand over hers. She inhales sharply when I touch her. Her pupils dilate, and a faint flush rises in her cheeks.

*Gotcha, babe.*

"You seem like you could use a friend," I say. "I'm a really good listener. Why don't you come over to my room and we can chat on the sofa, where it's more comfortable?"

"I . . . I shouldn't." Her flush deepens under my gaze. Through my fingers, I can feel her desire building. "I only have the babysitter until my husband gets home at six . . ."

"That's hours from now. He'll never know. I promise."

●　●　●

In my motel room, Lee and I share her coffee and chat about books, and then we split the bottle of nice chardonnay that I left chilling in the mini fridge. She's an absolute lightweight and starts getting tipsy after half a glass. And anxious; she's terrified of going home drunk. I allay her worries by telling her that she'll be fine in an hour or two.

When she's two glasses in, I rest my hand on her thigh. And I'm ridiculously pleased with myself when she leans over and starts kissing me. Her mouth is hungry, her breath sweet with wine and musky with pheromones. She's been starving for this for a long time. Maybe her whole life.

We make out for a while on the couch, and I tease that hunger into a moaning ravening of raw need. When she's had about all I think she can take, I stand her up and lead her toward the king-size bed.

She resists me, just a little.

I stop, my hand still on her wrist. "What's the matter?"

She looks scared. Embarrassed, more likely. "I'm not as pretty as you. I have scars."

I smile reassuringly. "Real people have scars. You're beautiful to me. You're a goddess, and I want to worship at your altar."

From the look on her face, I've just spoken heresy. But she's absolutely into it just the same.

I slowly strip us both down and kiss her head to toe. I whisper sweet nothings into all those parts of herself that she probably hates seeing in the mirror. And then, when I know that her pussy has opened like a flower and is spilling nectar down her thighs, I take her to bed.

The moment my lips touch her slick labia, she arches her back and cries out. Twists the sheets in her shuddering fists. Her sudden orgasm makes me pretty sure that no one has gone down on her before. Possibly nobody has ever gotten her off properly, ever. She might have six kids, but in some ways she's still practically a virgin. So I give her flesh a moment to recover, then start again, taking my time.

I want to make sure that this is the best afternoon she's ever had in her life.

⬥ ⬥ ⬥

I make her come and come again until she's a sweaty rag doll, her nerves ringing with exhaustion, her eyes unfocused and barely able to stay open.

"Shh, it's okay to go to sleep." I kiss her neck and pull the cool white sheet up to her shoulders. "I'll make sure you get home in time."

"I think I'm in love with you," Lee murmurs as she drifts away.

I've had a few clients declare their love to me in the past, but this time it sends a Cupid's arrow pang through my heart. Poor woman. She really does deserve better than she's gotten.

Ah, well. There's no helping it. Michael's instructions were clear.

I wait until I'm sure she's deeply asleep, then I slide off the bed and quietly unzip my adventure bag. I pull out the heavy two-foot machete I recently found online—it's basically a meat cleaver with roid rage.

I step to the edge of the bed and grip the weapon. Focus on steadying my hands. *Don't fuck this up, bitch.* The last thing I want to do is whiff my swing and have her wake up in screaming torment.

It's time. I take a deep breath, raise the three-pound length of razor-sharp steel, and bring it down on her neck as hard as I can. Hot blood jets across my face, the wall, and the ceiling. I come so hard I nearly pass out. Her body jerks . . . and I'm relieved to see that it's just a reflex. She's gone. I severed her artery and her spine. Her head's only barely attached to her body by a strip of meat and skin now. I don't think she had a chance to wake. Thank the gods.

I pull the tip of the machete free of the mattress springs, reposition her head, take aim with the spine of the blade, and wreck her teeth so the local coroner won't be able to identify the body as quickly. Her pearly whites make a satisfying crunch as they shatter wetly in her jaw.

A series of short swings is all it takes to hack off the top of her head so I can get to her brains. I've made quite an incredible mess on the bed, but the blade is quieter than a saw. Eating her cerebrum is a whole lot less fun than eating her pussy was . . . but it's a whole lot more enlightening.

Because when I'm done, I have Lee's memory of the afternoon. Untainted by her death. Whenever I want, I can see myself desired and adored through this virgin mother's eyes. I can relive what it's like to receive all the very best things that I know how to give. A series of perfect erotic moments I can lose myself in whenever I want. Sweeter than a thousand boxes of chocolate.

But far more important to the gods? I know exactly who the future-precious She is. I have her name, her number, and her address. Once I've done the rest of my homework, I'll know her better than she might know herself.

And I can't wait to get my hands on her.

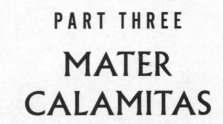

# PART THREE

# MATER CALAMITAS

Will matter then be destroyed or not?
The Savior said, All nature, all formations,
all creatures exist in and with one another,
and they will be resolved again
into their own roots. For the nature
of matter is resolved into the roots
of its own nature alone.

—The Gospel of Mary Magdalene

# CHAPTER 20

I first met Erin Holdaway a few months before the pandemic. We both had jobs at UCC but weren't coworkers, not at first. It was my second week in the network operations center, and the computer I'd been assigned to kept rebooting at random. Really, really annoying, especially when I was in the middle of administering another machine, so I called the company's tech support line. They sent Erin over to double-check my diagnosis and swap my computer out.

I had to work hard to stifle a gasp when she showed up at my workstation, because she could have been my sister Leila's identical twin. And part of my brain was *certain* she was Leila and was absolutely overwhelmed with joy. But the other part of my brain, the rational part, knew she couldn't possibly be Leila and was desperately trying to keep me from doing something socially unacceptable, like grabbing a complete stranger and hugging her.

*Don't be weird, Mar,* my rational brain lectured me. *You're always so weird.*

But I guess I must have beamed at her like she was Leila—half the time I have no idea what my face is doing—because she stopped, looked a little surprised in that *Have we met?* kind of way, smiled back at me, and then glanced down at her work tablet.

"Are you . . . Mareva Buduci?" she asked.

"Yes, that's me!" I tried to shift my expression to the normal kind of smile you'd give a coworker. Warm, but with professional distance. We're all one big happy family here at UCC—but if you lose your job, you're dead to everyone.

"I'm Erin from Desktop Support. So you're having a problem with your machine?" Her gaze shifted to my computer.

"Yes. I think it's overheating because of a bad fan."

"Well, let me check things out . . ."

I got up from my seat to let her work and tried not to stare at her. If I looked closely, I could see small features that weren't Leila's. She was a little paler and had a faint scattering of freckles across her nose and cheeks. Her hair was a lighter shade of brown, her eyebrows rounder. Her lips fuller.

But she had the same gorgeous cornflower blue eyes as my sister. And that, more than anything, made her resemblance astonishing. It made my heart ache around the Leila-shaped chasm inside me.

My rational brain tried to dismiss my feelings. It wasn't any surprise that I'd run into another woman who looked like Leila, was it? Not after the massive die-off that humanity suffered seventy thousand years ago. Our species had been reduced to just a few thousand individuals, and we hadn't recovered our diversity. There are only so many faces to go around these days.

•  •  •

I was my parents' surprise baby. They'd had Leila in January, and the doctor told my mother that she couldn't get pregnant while she was nursing. Well, the doctor was wrong. I was born a month early, in October, less than a year after Leila's arrival.

After we were both toddlers, a lot of people assumed she and I were fraternal twins. My body had grown quickly despite my prematurity, but my brain lagged hers by about a year. Sometimes more. She was so smart, and taught herself how to read when she was five. I didn't learn to read until first grade, despite Leila trying to help me, and even then I wasn't one of the first kids in my class to catch on. That was so frustrating, because I wanted to match Leila in every way I could.

I was Leila's adoring shadow from the time I could crawl, and

I was utterly heartbroken when she started kindergarten without me. Apparently I staged a hunger strike, but I don't remember that well. A week into my protest, my parents bargained with the school district to let me in early so my sister and I could be in the same class.

When we were little kids, we were as close as any two people have ever been. Before we learned to speak, we shared our own secret language. We ate together, laughed together, cried together. I think we shared our dreams.

But my fear, my sickness, drove us apart and disrupted that precious bond. I have spent most of my adult life regretting pushing her away.

What happened? I have a rare, previously undocumented genetic illness. I'm prone to growing chronic benign teratomas. "Benign" only in the sense that the cells that compose them aren't identifiably malignant. Not *cancer*. Not likely to kill me *directly*.

My first diagnosis came when I was just two years old. A lump in my upper belly, near my diaphragm, got bigger and bigger, and I started having trouble keeping food down. After the MRI showed a complicated mass, the pediatric surgeon operated on me and pulled out a baseball-size encysted tumor filled with distorted vertebrae, finger bones, teeth, and dark hair. The thing had been pressing on my gastroesophageal junction. He diagnosed me with fetus in fetu: a twin I'd absorbed in the womb had become a growing parasite inside my body.

Leila and I were much too young to understand what was happening, past the idea that I had gotten sick and had to go to the hospital. But our parents assured us that I'd get well again. She gave me her favorite teddy bear to take with me. The surgery was a success, and I healed up fine, and that seemed to be that. My parents were satisfied it was all over, and our family could go back to our normal lives.

But, like any kid, I was curious, and my curiosity about my surgical scars grew as I aged. My parents didn't like talking about it and answered my questions tersely or not at all. (Mom's typical response was "Oh, honey, don't think about such morbid things!") Finally, when I was eight or nine, my father pointed me to an article in a medical encyclopedia but didn't offer to discuss it with me afterward. Thanks to that text, I understood fetus in fetu just enough to get completely freaked out about what it all meant.

Around that same time, Leila and I were voraciously reading about carnivorous animals. She'd chosen wolves but I'd chosen sharks. And I'd learned about female sand tiger sharks, whose wombs routinely turned into Darwinian battles royale in which one unborn pup would mercilessly devour its fetal siblings.

Had I done that to my twin? Is that how I'd come to absorb it? Had I, as a fetus, been hatefully jealous of my mother's attention and just wanted there to be one of us? I pictured myself unhinging my jaw like a deep-sea creature and swallowing my twin whole as we floated in our amniotic sacs.

But I didn't remember hating my twin. Why would I hate it? After all, I loved Leila with all my heart. Didn't I?

I started to have nightmares about the vengeful ghost of the twin coming out of me at night and hurting Leila. Sometimes the ghost would smother her with a pillow, or push her down the narrow, dark basement stairs. Sometimes it would cut her up with knives from the kitchen.

My rational brain tried to push the dreams away, but it wasn't very strong back then. Science didn't have the same tight grip on my imagination that superstition did. I started to wonder: Would the act of loving Leila as much as I did make the ghost angry and envious? Was my adoration inadvertently endangering her?

So I decided to try to put some distance between us, for Leila's own good. Try to love her less. Try to do more things on my own. I could see the hurt and confusion in her eyes when I turned her down when she wanted to build Legos together or walk to the playground. She asked me why, but I couldn't bring myself to tell her the truth. What if voicing my fears made them become real, like saying "Bloody Mary" in front of a mirror?

She *knew* I was lying to her. And that made her pain so much more intense. I felt awful, but I figured if I had a choice between hurting her feelings or letting the ghost murder her, well. Eventually she'd get over feeling shunned.

Shortly thereafter, I got my second diagnosis: a tumor in the back of my upper left arm. I still remember seeing it on the MRI, curled up like a strange embryo. Crushing my radial nerve, so it had to come out.

The night before I went in for my surgery, I couldn't sleep and slipped downstairs to go sit on the porch. As I was sneaking through the living room, I overheard my parents talking in my father's study, and I stopped in the shadow of the entertainment center to eavesdrop.

"It's my fault," she said. "If I'd just double-checked the doctor's advice, we could have used protection. We could have had another baby after Leila was in preschool, like we planned."

"Honey, it's not your fault. I could have checked his advice, too. He should have checked himself!"

"Just a few months later, my body would've healed. It would've had the strength to make a normal baby."

My face burned with embarrassed horror when she said that. She sounded so bitter, so disappointed. Was I a burden? Did I not really deserve to be alive?

"It's not your fault," he repeated. "These things happen. Besides, she's not *that* bad off. She's a smart girl. Pretty, like you. As long as she doesn't get a tumor in her face, she'll be fine."

I wanted to throw up. I hurried back upstairs to hide under my sheets and quietly cry, my face to the wall.

Soon I heard the creak of Leila's mattress and the rustle of her slipping out from beneath her My Little Pony bedspread.

"What's wrong, Mar?" She put her hand on my shoulder.

How could I tell her the truth? I was too embarrassed.

"I'm scared about the surgery," I sobbed. It wasn't *exactly* a lie. I *was* afraid.

Leila climbed into bed behind me, the big spoon. She started to stroke my hair, like our mom did when we were sick, and quietly sang "You Are My Sunshine" to me.

And that made me cry even harder.

•  •  •

The surgery was a success. In eight weeks, the scar on my arm was nothing more than a thin pink line. I tried my best to forget what I'd overheard, as my body healed. But my parents' words stuck in my memory like a knife.

•  •  •

Years later, I'd want to punch my first pediatric oncologist for misdiagnosing my teratoma as fetus in fetu. I'd also want to kick my parents for never questioning what he told them. Never getting a second opinion even after I grew new tumors.

Because I never had a twin.

I hadn't absorbed anyone else.

I hadn't created a vengeful ghost anywhere except my imagination. All along, it was just my cells malfunctioning. I never needed to push my sister away. It wasn't for anyone's good, and it wounded us both. Forever. For *nothing*.

The damage was done. Leila withdrew from me in our teen years just the same as I had withdrawn from her. I knew she was lonely, because I could see that angry pain in her eyes. It mirrored what I felt in my own heart. But I was so embarrassed about my wild, childish ideas about a murder ghost, I didn't know how to explain it all to her. I didn't know how to fix things between us.

The worst part? Lonely seventeen-year-old girls are the perfect chum for a certain type of shark. One she had the misfortune to meet at my parents' church.

David was nearly a decade older than her. A young MD doing

his orthopedic surgery residency at a local hospital. She went absolutely crazy over him. He took her to nice places, brought her flowers, and made her feel like a princess.

Their age difference made me uneasy. What kind of fully grown, pushing-thirty man is interested in a teenager? *Love bombing* and *grooming* weren't terms I'd learn until I was in college, but I could see David use them on Leila. And I instinctively knew the situation wouldn't end well for her.

I tried to tell her that he was dangerous. But she got angry at me and accused me of being jealous. It drove us further apart.

My parents were in a much better position to get her away from David, but he was polite, intelligent, ambitious, and stood to make a very good salary later on. His father was the head of a local law firm. Aside from the sheer inappropriate creepiness of what he was doing, how could they object to her dating a doctor from a well-to-do family? That made him perfect husband material, right? He was camouflaging a huge red flag behind a bunch of fluttering gold-star pennants.

What none of us knew yet was that he absolutely believed that couples should only trust in God for their family planning. They eloped when Leila was eighteen, and she got pregnant on her wedding night. They didn't get much of a honeymoon because David couldn't take time away from his residency. She had her first baby at his hospital just a month shy of her nineteenth birthday.

Three months later, she was pregnant with twins. Just like our mother had gotten pregnant with me right after Leila. Jesus.

The twins ended up being a C-section, so all her kids after that were C-sections, too. David had an obstetrician friend of his handle all the deliveries. When she gave birth to her sixth child on her twenty-fourth birthday, that baby turned out to be her last, simply because David's buddy couldn't properly staple her uterus back together.

I almost never got to see my sister after she left with David.

He always had a plausible-sounding excuse to avoid our family gatherings. But during our rare, brief visits, I could see how perpetually exhausted Leila was. How motherhood was consuming her. I was profoundly angry with him for turning her into his personal incubator. Even if she claimed that her children were the shining lights of her life, she never got to go to college like she'd wanted to. She never got to become a veterinarian or a zookeeper, which she'd talked about so much when we were kids. Her life was cooking, cleaning, dirty diapers, and homeschooling. Because of *course* David felt that not even the private Christian academies in the city were good enough. Of *course*. Why would he pay his hard-earned money to put his children through school when he'd found a servant to handle all that?

What had happened to her seemed like a living nightmare from my perspective. Just absolutely one of the worst fates to befall a young woman with dreams and ambitions. And I felt so, so guilty. Mostly because I feared that by pushing her away, even though I'd done it with good intentions, I'd left her vulnerable to David.

But I also felt guilty because I was relieved that it hadn't happened to me. Even then, I knew I'd have fallen just as quickly if anyone had aimed a love bombing run at me when I was a teenager. It was pretty much dumb luck that no older man at church saw me as a target.

* * *

"Yep, you were right!" Erin announced.

"What?" I'd been lost in my grim memories.

"Your fan's dead," she said. "Gimme fifteen minutes and I'll be back here with a new machine for you."

She stood up and cheerfully hurried out, a woman on a mission.

*Gosh, she even walks like Leila*, I thought.

My superstitious mind chimed in: *This is a sign! You should follow her. Make friends! Maybe you can get back the kind of connection you had with your sister?*

But my rational brain was quick with a rebuttal: *Work friends almost never become real friends. You can't trust these relationships. Don't make things weird.*

*Are you sure?* I asked my rat brain.

*If it's meant to happen, it will happen,* replied my superstitious mind.

*Yes. Let things evolve naturally,* replied rat brain. *Don't be the office stalker, for Pete's sake.*

"Okay," I told myself. I sat down and waited for Erin's return.

# CHAPTER 21

Erin had to run to another call right after she set up my new computer. She and I didn't encounter each other again until the company's holiday party in December, just two months before the PVG pandemic started in the US. The event was at an enclosed pavilion at the zoo, which was all done up in poinsettias and strings of pretty lights for Christmas. I was in line for dessert when I overheard her talking.

"So did you hear about the megacephalopod they found in the North Pacific? The dodecapod?" she asked.

"No, uh-uh," the man she was talking to replied. Based on his designer shoes and clothes, I suspected he was an executive, but I didn't really know any of their faces. Judging by his puzzled expression, he had no idea what a cephalopod even was.

This was relevant to *my* interests, though. I veered out of line and stepped toward them. "Oh, yes, it's so amazing! I saw photos of it two days ago!"

"Isn't it?" she gushed at me. "Twelve arms! Four eyes! Bright red! Nine hundred pounds!"

Her C-suite acquaintance took my engagement as an opportunity to quietly step back and slip away.

"Just goes to show they have no idea what's down in those ocean trenches," I said.

"A shame it's so red, and so close to Christmas." She sipped her mulled cider. "I'm already seeing Photoshopped 'Santapod' memes online."

"Oh, yes. That 'You Better Watch Out' one? So funny!"

"It's funny, yeah, but . . . I dunno." Erin looked pensive. "I think a critter like that deserves some respect. It's majestic, and weird, and it kept itself hidden from us for so long . . . and now people are making fun of it."

"People often make fun of something they're trying to convince themselves they're not scared of. Humor's a coping mechanism."

"That tracks." She shrugged, then smiled at me. "Hey, have we met? You seem really familiar, but I don't think I know your name."

"Yes. You came by to get me a new computer about six months ago. My name's Mareva."

"Oh, right. Yours had a dead fan." She leaned in a little, looked around, and dropped her voice to a conspiratorial stage whisper. "I can't help but notice that not many people here are as enthusiastic about cephalopods as we are. So, do you have a background in science?"

"I do." I made myself smile. I hated telling this story, because it still felt like failure. "I moved to the city two years ago to start my Ph.D. in evolution, ecology, and organismal biology—"

Her eyes lit up. "Oh, wow, that's so cool!"

"But I got diagnosed with a tumor half a month after I got here, and I had to have surgery, *again*, and my recovery took longer than I expected. I just . . . couldn't catch up that term."

I sighed and rolled my neck, deciding I might as well give her the short version of the whole story, because why not?

"They told me that I could come back when I was ready," I said, "but I looked at my bank account and it told me I needed to get a jobby job right away. So I started hunting. I'd done mainframe work as part of my computational biology minor, so I got hired here at UCC. And so now I work with people who are mostly all well over fifty and who learned mainframes in the army. They never went to college at all and don't see much point to it unless it's business school. After all, *they* got jobs right out of high school, so why can't everybody else? As if, you know, shining yourself up to be the best possible cog in a corporation is the only reason to go to college. They're all about talking about their grandkids and football. And I just don't have a lot to contribute to those conversations."

Erin winced. "Yeah, that's the problem here. Way fewer geeks and nerds than you would expect at a computer company."

"I'm making two or three times what I'd be making as an adjunct or postdoc," I said. "It's hard to walk away from the paycheck and health insurance to go back to my Ph.D. Even if that's where my people are."

"I hear you." Erin nodded pensively. "I got my BS in environmental science at Northwestern. My mom died my junior year, and I got pretty depressed. Stopped showing up to class for a bit. Barely passed the term."

She shrugged sheepishly.

"I'm really sorry to hear about your mom," I said. "That's awful."

"Thank you." She gave me a quick, sad smile. "Upshot was, my grades weren't good enough for grad school funding. And I just couldn't find anything in my field. I'd hoped to work for a national park, or an environmental nonprofit, but no luck. I mean, there were a ton of unpaid internships out there that I could have landed in a heartbeat, but I needed money. So I looked at tech jobs, and landed here. I like the city and all . . . but it's not what I planned on."

"The city *is* nice," I said. "People on the coasts act like it's just cows and cornfields out this way, so I wasn't expecting much more than a big version of the town I grew up in. It's been a pleasant surprise."

"Hey." Erin bit her lip, looking as if she wasn't sure she should continue. "You said 'again' earlier, about the tumor. It wasn't your first one?"

I shook my head. "No. I'm prone to tumors. They're complicated, but they're not cancerous. I . . . had to have a hysterectomy because of one."

When I was twenty-one, my endometrium decided to go full teratoma and filled my entire uterus with hollow, bleeding orbs that the oncologist thought might be primitive eyeballs. What I thought was some bloating and a heavy period turned into a terrifying night of pain and hemorrhaging in the ER.

Afterward, my mother and father bore a palpable air of disappointment that never quite went away, no matter what else I managed to do with myself. Even though they would never, ever say so to my face, I knew that in failing to become a woman who could bear them grandchildren, I had failed in my most essential duty as a daughter. Especially compared to Leila and her bountiful brood.

Not on *purpose*, of course. I wasn't disobedient, or wicked. I was just *tragic*. Which was so much worse.

"Anyway," I said, "the kids-and-grandkids work conversations make me feel pretty left out."

"Ouch." She looked mortified. "Yeah. That really sucks. I'm so sorry."

I laughed bitterly. "Well, I'm kind of a buzzkill, aren't I?"

"Oh, not at all. I mean, I brought up the dead mom first, right?" She paused to take a sip of her cider. "So, uh, do you have any pets?"

"No. Not yet. My family got a couple of kittens when I was in high school: Droolius Caesar and Empurrer Clawdius—"

She burst out giggling. "Oh, wow, I love those names!"

"My parents still have them. They're the best boys. I miss them terribly. I'd like to get a kitten or two from one of the shelters, but I live by myself and I work a lot of overtime. And for all I know, I could get a new tumor tomorrow, and it could be bad . . . It doesn't seem fair to get pets when I'm not sure I could care for them properly."

"Yeah. That's how my boyfriend and I feel. I like cats, too, but Gregory's more a dog person. So we talk about getting dogs a lot, but the time hasn't seemed right." Erin paused briefly. Another nervous lip bite. "So, do you have a boyfriend? Girlfriend? Non-binary extra-friendly friend?"

I shook my head. "I tried dating a little in undergrad, but it just didn't feel right. I'm not really attracted to people like that. I mean, I like cuddling and going out, but fooling around . . . it's not really for me."

Her eyebrows rose in apparent curiosity. "Oh, you're an ace?"

I hedged. "Maybe? The hysterectomy definitely affected how I feel down there. Could be my hormones are off. I've been too busy to try to figure it all out. In some ways it seems like a blessing. I had friends in high school and college who got absolutely infatuated with someone who was just awful for them and derailed their whole lives . . ."

I trailed off, thinking of Leila.

"Yeah, the sexiest people do seem to be the hottest messes, don't they? I feel really lucky that I met Gregory. Things are nice. No drama. It's a good change from the people I dated before."

I smiled at her. "Maybe I'll meet someone like him someday. Who knows?"

"Hey." She glanced at the dessert tables. "Not to change the subject, but I saw you were in line, and it looks like the chocolate mousse is almost gone. It is *amazing*, and I'd hate for you to miss out."

"Okay," I laughed. "I love chocolate, so I definitely want to try it. It's been good talking to you."

"It's been great to get to know you better. Like, *authentically* get to know you." She raised her red plastic Solo cup. "Here's to good desserts, holiday pay, financial stability, and geeky new work friends."

My rat brain and superstitious mind victory danced with each other.

I smiled back at Erin and raised an imaginary glass. "Cheers."

• • •

I lost three coworkers right away in the pandemic: Sandy, Richard, and Joan. They'd shared the same shift for years and had a Thursday night poker game they all attended. Apparently, one of their friends got infected early and spread it to everyone there. Sandy and Richard had fatal hemorrhages in the ER, and Joan ended up having a stroke and had to go to a nursing home. It was really awful. PVG isn't kind to anyone, but it's particularly brutal for older folks.

The only upside, for the rest of us, was that they were all off on the days when they were asymptomatic and infectious. And that was absolutely blind luck. UCC hadn't implemented a mask mandate at our facility yet, but they certainly did after everyone learned we'd just lost all our senior mainframe computer operators and narrowly avoided a wipe of the whole shift.

So I was nervous and excited when I found out Erin would be joining us in network ops. Nervous because, obviously, I worried about catching PVG. Still, this was a prime opportunity for a real friendship to continue to evolve naturally, as my rat brain insisted it must.

But the Erin who came to work third shift? She was not the same woman I'd chatted with in December.

Her personality had radically shifted. She was withdrawn, seemed profoundly depressed—I mean, I would have been, too—and spoke so slowly I wondered if she'd had a stroke. But, surprisingly, her work was fine. I guess if you start out with a lot of brains, you can afford to lose a few before you end up unemployed, even at a place like UCC. Most everything we did was just a matter of following written procedures, and those were composed in simple, straightforward language, so that an average high school graduate could easily comprehend them in the middle of an emergency when everyone was yelling. Read the manual all day, every day. We weren't expected to be innovative, agile thinkers except on very rare occasions.

In later months, she got jumpy and seemed increasingly agitated. Paranoid. I sometimes heard her muttering about someone named Betty. I was curious about who that was. A little jealous, even. But at that point I was too afraid to get close enough to her to ask.

Erin's physical change was enormous, too. She'd lost twenty or thirty pounds—and those were not really pounds she had to lose. And she just kept losing weight. Within a couple of months, she looked like a starved refugee from a concentration camp. I didn't know if her hair fell out, because she kept her hoodie up all the time to shield her eyes from the overhead lights. Her scleras were mottled black and red from microhemorrhages, and she'd developed an awful gray pallor . . . She just didn't even look *alive* anymore, after a certain point.

And toward the end . . . her back. My goodness. I couldn't imagine what that growth might be, but it was enormous. It looked painful. She couldn't really sit in her chair, so I found her a stool from way in the back of the server room. I knew she had to see a doctor regularly, so I assumed that whatever was happening, her physician knew about it and it was under control. But it grew so fast, I knew it couldn't be good.

And it really, really wasn't.

# CHAPTER 22

I knew Erin was in a bad way the night before the incident. She'd come to work on time but it seemed like she could barely stand up. Barely speak. Quietly agitated—she didn't say anything but her knee was bouncing up and down in what looked like extreme anxiety. Way, way out of it. I wondered if I should message our supervisor and have him send her home. But I didn't, because I didn't want her to get into trouble. I've often wondered what would have happened if I'd followed my first instinct. Maybe nothing would have ultimately changed.

For most of the night, things went relatively well. We didn't have to work any difficult server alerts, didn't have to pull together as a team, so I don't know that anyone else was much aware that Erin was having some kind of crisis.

A little after 8 a.m., an hour before our shift ended, a new tech lead named Devin came in to ask Jorge about something. I didn't catch all of what they were chatting about. But Erin was staring at Devin, her eyes hollow. Her hands had gone slack on her keyboard. Nobody else noticed, I think.

"Sweet, it's a plan," Devin said to Jorge. "Well, I need to head upstairs for the Azure training class. Catch you later!"

And he got up and headed out, whistling a tune from a Pixar movie. Erin got up, grunting in pain, and strode after him. I was surprised she could move that quickly.

Something wasn't right. I *knew* it. I just didn't know what, or what to do about it. So I sat there for maybe a minute, but then I decided I should really go check on Erin. Maybe she just needed to go pee really badly, and her following Devin out was just a coincidence. But if not . . .

I didn't have a clear idea of what I planned to do, other than knock on the PVG-only restroom door and ask if she was okay. Which wasn't much. It probably wouldn't be anything helpful. But it felt wrong to just sit there stewing in my worries.

I set myself on Break, grabbed my purse, and went out to what had been the accessible restroom. Knocked. No answer. I tried the handle and opened the door. The green-tiled, claustrophobic little room was empty. The feeling that something was seriously wrong congealed to a hard lump in my chest. So I walked up and down the tall, glass-and-chrome atrium, casually poking my head into conference rooms and cubbies and behind potted sago palms to see if I could find her.

I was about fifteen feet away from the security guard's station with its banks of closed-circuit TV monitors when I heard him moan, "Oh my fucking God. Oh my *fucking God.*"

I heard him slap his panic button a moment before the emergency alarms went off.

He stood up, eyes wide, and hollered, "Everyone out to the parking lot! We have a situation! Everybody out, *now!*"

So we all herded out into the parking lot. Most of us didn't have our jackets with us, so we bounced on our toes and rubbed our arms to keep warm in the frosty fall morning air. The dew on the grass was still frozen.

A couple of minutes later, three police SUVs came tearing up and a whole squad of SWAT officers in black tactical armored hazmat gear and helmets with face shields swarmed into the building. Soon after, a red fire department ambulance rolled into the parking lot, lights on but no sirens. A pair of masked paramedics in white hazmat suits hurried into the building, pushing a wheeled stretcher with a gearbox on it.

"What the hell is *that?*" A woman was staring up into the clear blue sky, squinting in apparent disbelief.

I followed her gaze, and I saw something large and dark unsteadily flapping away. My first thought was that maybe it was a golden eagle or a turkey vulture. Those are big birds with six-foot-plus wingspans. Whatever this was, it was at least that big. But this creature, somehow, looked like it had long, thin arms. Birds don't have arms except in fun memes.

The other thing was that I had a hard time focusing on it. My brain registered it mostly as a dark shape and nothing else. Something about it was triggering a very old fear instinct in me; this creature was an actual monstrosity and did not belong in the world. *Do not look upon it, do not attract its attention by witnessing its existence. Avert your gaze, feeble monkey.*

So I looked at the other UCC workers crowded in the parking lot. Most of them were flinching and/or staring at the ground. It wasn't just me. That didn't make me feel a whole lot better, though.

And that's when the two paramedics, flanked by SWAT officers, wheeled out a corpse zipped up in a black vinyl body bag. Most stared grimly ahead of them, but a couple nervously scanned the now empty sky.

• • •

The police wouldn't let me or anyone else who'd been working with Erin that morning go home. They moved us into one of the conference rooms, closed the blinds, and told us that a trauma counselor would be on-site to talk to each of us individually. Why *we* needed a trauma counselor, and not the freaked-out security guard (who'd obviously seen something awful that we hadn't), wasn't clear. Or maybe he was off in another conference room and had a whole counselor to himself. The police officers didn't seem much inclined to answer many questions, and they discouraged us talking among ourselves. Not that any of us were in a chatty mood. The two stern officers watching us especially wouldn't answer any questions about Erin.

It wasn't that the thought of Erin being killed (or perhaps killing someone else) wasn't traumatic. The idea of it made me sad, and angry at the unknown physician who had clearly failed her. But all that didn't seem quite real. Not when I was sitting in that conference room, anyhow. I knew someone was dead, sure. But I didn't know if it was Erin. And if not her, I couldn't be absolutely sure it was Devin, either. For all I actually knew, they'd both run off into the woods and the body was someone else entirely.

And, honestly? I'd been mourning the loss of my could-have-been BFF, bit by bit, for months. It was obvious that she wasn't going to live much longer. I'd let go of the idea of her, or at least I thought I had.

•　•　•

About an hour into all that silent, uncomfortable awkwardness, an officer called my name and led me out to a different, much smaller conference room.

A short, redheaded woman sat in a chair at the table facing the door. She was wearing a black polo shirt and a black bullet-proof vest with a lot of tactical loops on it that read "Homeland Security" in white block lettering. Her mask matched her polo. She had wide shoulders and looked more physically capable of defending herself than some of the police I'd seen that day. I'd done a semester of judo in undergrad, and she would be deadly in that sport, because her center of gravity was so low.

"You're . . . you're a trauma counselor?" I asked her as the uniformed officer stepped out and shut the door behind me.

She nodded. "My name is Candy Kleypas, and I'm a licensed professional clinical counselor." Kleypas paused to look down at her tablet. "And you are Mareva Buduci?"

"Yes." I still wasn't wrapping my brain around all this. "You're with Homeland Security?"

"I am. Please, sit down." She gestured at the Aeron chair across the table from her. "Normally I work with PVG patients who are leaving care facilities," she said, "but they called me out today because they were shorthanded."

"What happened to Erin?" I blurted out as I sat.

"Well, that's why I'm here." She pushed her tablet to the side and looked at me very directly. "We're still trying to figure out why the incident today happened, and what we could do to prevent it in the future."

My pulse rose. "What was the incident?" I paused, thinking back. "Did . . . did Erin follow Devin into the elevator? Who was in the body bag?"

"Lord have mercy." She rolled her shoulders. "You seem like a smart gal. So you have to know that I cain't answer those questions. I ain't here to answer questions. You are here to answer them for *me*."

I flinched and nodded.

"So, you been working with Erin Holdaway since she got reassigned, correct?"

"Yes, ma'am."

"She been acting strange lately?"

"Strange compared to what?" I felt frustrated. "She wasn't the same person after she came back. Everything about her changed. And she just kept looking sicker and sicker, but she kept making it to work, mostly."

"But had she been worse *lately*?" Kleypas pressed.

"She got a little worse every day. Why aren't you asking her physician these questions?"

Kleypas closed her eyes, looking tired. "We would *love* to chat with Dr. Shapiro, but we cain't find her. Looks like she ain't been doing her job for a couple weeks now, maybe longer. So if you have any information on her whereabouts, that would be very helpful."

Homeland Security lost track of her *doctor*? And now they were checking with random coworkers to see if they knew anything?

Wow. I was getting the bad feeling that local authorities were completely losing control of the situation and things were about to get hairy.

"I don't," I said. "I didn't even know her name until now."

Kleypas reached into her pocket and pulled out a white business card. Pushed it across the table toward me. "Here's my contact information, just in case."

I reluctantly took the card and stuck it in the front flap of my purse.

She cleared her throat and launched into what sounded like a memorized spiel: "We know that this has been distressing. It's not uncommon to suffer trauma-related stress after an incident like this. You might feel nervous or anxious. Or have trouble sleeping, or have nightmares. Sometimes, people under a lot of stress see and hear strange things."

She paused, staring at me, studying my features. "Did you see anything unusual during or after the incident?"

I was afraid to lie. "I . . . saw something flying in the sky."

She didn't seem surprised. "What did you think it was?"

"An eagle or a vulture, maybe. But it didn't look right. I don't think it was really a bird."

Kleypas leaned forward, staring at me intensely. "See, this is exactly what I'm talking about. Stress makes your mind play tricks on you. Your brain knew something was wrong, so it was primed to take something just a little unusual and turn it into something unreal. Your mind couldn't figure out what was wrong, so it *made* something wrong. You understand?"

I nodded cautiously.

"And when your mind plays tricks on you like that, I personally think it's better to, you know, just try to set it aside. Tell yourself, 'That was just my imagination,' and move on."

"Okay." She would have had me mostly convinced, except for what she said next.

"Because the tough part happens if we hear that you've been

telling people you saw the Mothman or the Jersey Devil or whatever flying in broad daylight. Because then we gotta think, 'Hey,
this lady might have gotten infected with PVG.' And then we
have to take you in for a ten-day quarantine and observation, and
*that's* no damn fun. And you'd probably get stuck with the bill
for your stay. Could be thousands of dollars."

She leaned forward, eyebrows raised, speaking as if she was
letting me in on a secret. "And, to be honest? You might not have
a job anymore when you got out. I'm guessin' that after today,
your employer's gonna be pretty nervous about keeping anyone
they even *think* might be infected around. There would just be a
whole lot of consequences if you went around tellin' people you
saw something strange up there. And nobody wants that. You
feel me?"

My stomach churned. I loathed passive-aggressive, *I'm doing
this for your own good, see?* kinds of threats, but what could I do?
So I simply muttered, "Yes."

She nodded. "I'm glad we understand each other. You can go."

• • •

Thanks to my many biology classes, I do know what a bird looks
like. So after my "trauma counseling" with Kleypas, I was absolutely sure I'd seen something entirely non-avian that morning. Something real and strange and dangerous. Something that
Homeland Security didn't want anyone else to know about, since
it would probably cause a panic. Because it was something they
didn't know how to handle.

But I still had no idea what I'd seen.

# CHAPTER 23

I kept my mouth shut about what I'd seen in the sky, and so did everyone else I knew at UCC. We didn't even talk about it late at night in ops, when nobody else was around. Apparently the threat of losing a good job in the middle of a deadly pandemic was more than people could bear this time around.

At first, the PVG pandemic had been like the coronavirus years. Laid-off, healthy employees had plenty of options. But that had changed in the past couple of months. Many corporations had lost CEOs, owners, even entire C-suites, and private equity firms swooped in to loot the weakened businesses, deliberately crashing and burning them. The government saw it happening. But Congress deadlocked over trying to stop it, largely because a clique of senators were shareholders in those predatory firms. They were making too much money to willingly end it. The interconnected webs of ownership meant that big companies often took their smaller, seemingly independent subsidiaries down with them. So the pool of available jobs was shrinking even faster than the pool of uninfected job seekers.

But I was determined to figure out what I'd seen. So I did a ton of internet research at home, subscribed to a bunch of new YouTube channels. I'd been watching *Dr. Kaz Chats* since before the pandemic started. I'd actually met Alexandria Kasabian at a grad students' mixer the biology department hosted during the first week of my abandoned Ph.D. program. She seemed like a really cool lady. We'd exchanged emails, and although we never really corresponded much, she pinged me when she started her channel.

A week after Erin either died or disappeared, I got an alert that Dr. Kaz was doing a special livestream that evening, so I woke up a little early to watch it as I ate a microwaved box dinner.

"Hi, everyone! Welcome to my first livestream." She waved at the camera. "Today I'm talking with Gabriel Takahiro, a marine molecular geneticist at the University of Sydney who specializes in cephalopod genetics and evolution."

The image switched to a split-screen view of her on the right and a square-jawed Asian man with a mop of brown hair and a sunburned face. He was wearing a sky-blue T-shirt advertising a surfboard company. It was tight across his broad, muscular chest. When he pushed back his bangs, I saw a diving watch on his strong wrist.

I knew, objectively, that Dr. Takahiro was hot. And for the millionth time in my life, it bothered me just a little that I wasn't even slightly attracted to him on a physical level.

The biggest thing I noticed about him? He didn't look happy to be there. Dr. Takahiro had the same expression oncologists have every time they come into the room to tell me I have a new tumor that needs to come out.

"Hullo, everyone!" He had a thick Australian accent.

"So, Dr. Takahiro, you have some new information for us? Information you say is critical?"

"Right. I won't dance around this. I'm strongly advising all your viewers to avoid eating raw octopus. Right now. My lab, working in conjunction with virologists at my uni, has compelling evidence that raw octopus is how the PVG virus first spread to human populations, and it is still an important transmission vector."

I didn't generally eat octopus. Probably, if I'd thought about it more, I'd have decided it was unethical to eat such an intelligent creature. Erin probably never consumed octopus because of that. But honestly, I hadn't gotten past the part where eating octopus and calamari felt like chewing rubber bands most of the time.

"How do most people encounter raw octopus?" Dr. Kaz asked.

"There's takowasa and odorigui in Japan, sannakji in Korea. Outside those countries? Octopus sashimi, which you'll probably see listed as 'tako' on menus."

I think I tried a single piece of octopus sashimi in undergrad, when I'd gone out with friends to a Japanese restaurant to celebrate someone's birthday. It was just to be able to say I'd done it, and none had passed my lips since.

He continued: "The *one* thing that connected all the cities where the first cases were found—Tokyo, Hong Kong, London, Honolulu, Toronto, Los Angeles, Mexico City, and Seattle—is that they all got shipments of octopus from the same fishing grounds in northern Japanese waters. We've confirmed it. Outside Japan, the octopus went to high-end sushi restaurants that wanted authentic Japanese ingredients, all the way from the rice to the seaweed. My lab and the Branson virology lab are working on a formal joint press release, which we hope to send out tomorrow. But I felt that this information was too important to wait."

"Isn't most octopus exported for sushi frozen before it's served?"

"Right. For those of you in the US, your federal food code requires that seafood intended for raw consumption be frozen at negative twenty degrees Celsius for at least seven days. Or frozen to negative thirty-five degrees for at least fifteen hours. My colleagues in the Branson lab confirmed that those temperatures are *not* enough to destroy PVG viruses. In fact, samples survived immersion in liquid nitrogen."

Dr. Kaz looked concerned. "Cooking destroys it, though, right?"

He nodded. "Yup. A good solid boil at one hundred degrees will do the job. But a light sauté might not be enough if the inside doesn't get up to temperature."

"When did you find out about all this?"

"We've strongly suspected for a couple of weeks, but we didn't want to make an announcement until we were absolutely sure the connection was real. I got confirmation of the supply chain tracking today. The pieces fit. So I got in touch with you and a couple of other influencers right away to start spreading the word."

"A zoonotic infection spreading from octopuses to human beings . . . that's unusual."

"It's unprecedented, as far as I know. The closest thing I can think of is transmission of the anisakiasis nematode from squid to people who eat it raw. But that's a worm rather than a virus, and that disease is only rarely fatal."

"Aren't octopuses very different from human beings in terms of their immune systems?"

"Oh, absolutely. They lack the capability to develop acquired immunity, for one thing. So you can't give an octopus a vaccine—it just wouldn't do anything. There's a lot we don't know about how they protect themselves from diseases. They're just very, very different from us in every aspect of their biology, so this is a nasty surprise for everyone."

"You don't even study diseases, right?"

"Well, I do *now*. But not at all before this year."

"Then how did you and your lab mates make this discovery?"

"Right." Dr. Takahiro shifted in his seat. "Everyone buckle up, because this is quite a mad story. So, after the dodecapod was discovered near the Japan trench, I was quite keen to get my hands on a sample for genetic analysis so we could sort out which modern cephalopod species it's most related to. And from there, we could make some educated guesses about its evolutionary origins. But as you can imagine, the dodeck has been quite a popular beastie, so getting our hands on a sample took quite some time."

The geneticist swallowed anxiously. "So we sequenced its genetic structure, and it was just very unusual. Some gene sequences were a close match to *Enteroctopus dofleini*, the giant Pacific octopus. But others were sequences that we had *never* seen before, not even in distantly related mollusks. We just couldn't figure out what we were looking at. We all went out for beers one night and someone suggested cross-referencing the sequences against other genetics databases. It was a wild idea, but at that point, why not? So we ran it against pretty much everything we could get access to . . . and we got a match. From the fucking PVG virus."

Dr. Kaz blinked at him. "The dodecapod was infected?"

"No, you misunderstand me. The PVG viral genes were *incorporated into its genome*. It had hatched with those genes. Our best guess was that its mother or father—which we have to presume was a perfectly normal giant Pacific octopus—had been infected to such an extent that it spawned a radically altered offspring. A female of that species can lay 120,000 to 400,000 eggs in one go, so it's entirely possible that its brothers or sisters might have had different genetic alterations that were incompatible with life."

"But you couldn't know for sure."

"Right! So I pulled some strings and got myself and a couple of postdocs on board a fishing vessel that trolls the waters near the trench where the dodeck was caught. Hoping we'd find another. We didn't, not in the week we were able to stay at sea. But we caught a couple of common octopuses, members of *Octopus vulgaris*. We also found a longarm octopus, *Octopus minor*, that was a bit north of its expected range. We took the specimens back to our lab. Just to be thorough."

"And what did you find?"

"Ultimately, we found that all of our specimens were absolutely chockablock with PVG. Exactly the same as the first strain that popped up in the sashimi cities. It wasn't affecting them much. Asymptomatic carriers. The virus seemed strangely tuned to be a nonpathogenic rider on two species, but a genome-altering retrovirus in another."

"Do you think that this virus is naturally occurring?"

Dr. Takahiro shook his head. "I do not. I'm not a virologist, but based on what my colleagues in the Branson lab told me, there's a vanishingly small chance that this is not an engineered virus. And they don't think there's a single lab on earth that's capable of making something this complex and devious. Nobody who knows anything about octopuses would ever suspect that they could be carriers for a virus like this. *Nobody*. This is nothing short of diabolical."

"What are you saying?" Dr. Kaz's expression was a mix of disbelief, dismay, and amusement. "That this virus came from outer space or something?"

"Right. I know this sounds mad. But there's evidence. Giant Pacific octopuses typically live three to five years in the wild. The dodeck is a very big girl, but didn't appear to be elderly, so we'll assume that when she was captured she was plausibly four years old. And about four and a half years before she was caught, fishermen working near the Japan trench saw a meteorite streak through the sky and crash into the sea fifty nautical miles from where she was caught. It's well documented—sailors on four different vessels recorded video of it on their phones. But since the impact was in the open sea, well away from land, none of the news services paid much attention to it."

He paused. "Octopuses are extremely curious creatures. If there was a strange, shiny new rock in their hunting grounds—or possibly some kind of container that deployed after a protective rock exterior broke open on impact—they would defo take a look at it. Touch it. They would very easily be infected by a meteorite carrying a bioweapon."

Dr. Kaz stared speechless for a moment, then shook her head. "People will say that you're either crazy or you're deliberately starting a hoax as a publicity stunt. Or maybe to try to stop seafood companies from overfishing octopus populations? Either way, it'll be the end of your career, my friend."

Dr. Takahiro looked deeply unhappy. "While I would absolutely love to see fewer octopuses killed, I'm frankly a little offended you'd think I might lie about all this. I will email you whatever you want to see. I am *not* afraid of you or anyone else double-checking our work. Please do! We've meticulously documented every bit of this we can. But I'd actually love to be wrong about this, because the implications here are profoundly concerning on a global level. My continued career as a research scientist is the least of my worries right now."

He paused. "I owe a greater responsibility to let people know what I've discovered, in the hopes that they don't unknowingly endanger themselves. So, probable origins of the virus aside, don't eat raw octopus. It might kill you."

# CHAPTER 24

I spent my night at work sneaking peeks at social media and the PVG discussion boards to see what other people were saying. The life sciences community was exploding. A solid chunk of people were calling bullshit on Dr. Takahiro's claims, but he had plenty of supporters who pointed to his reputation and publications history. They said that a researcher of his stature would never knowingly lie about something like this. I still didn't quite know what to believe, but everything the marine geneticist had told Dr. Kaz had the ominous ring of uncomfortable truth to it.

The livestream was so interesting and disturbing that my worries over Erin and the thing in the sky had nearly left my mind by the time my shift was over. I barely noticed that we'd had our first snow of autumn overnight and the parking lot was a slick, gray mess. My thoughts were filled with the dodecapod, and images of strange cephalopod mutations living in the murk of the Japan trench.

So between my distracted imagination and my usual tiredness, I was not all that aware of my surroundings when I stopped at the Kroger near my apartment to pick up some milk, coffee, and baby carrots. I shuffled through the November slush, glad I'd worn relatively waterproof shoes and that my cotton mask was blunting the chill of the cold breeze.

But I woke up in a hurry when I heard several people toward the front of the store scream, followed by the sound of something large smashing through a front window, followed by even more screaming. Then the crash of shopping carts overturning, endcaps toppling, jars and cans shattering and clattering across the floor.

I was over in the produce section. A young couple close to the front stepped out to rubberneck, but the moment they saw whatever was going on, he swore in Spanish and she gasped, "¡Dios mío!," and they both came sprinting back down the aisle.

"What's going on?" I called to the woman as she charged past me.

"¡Sal de aquí! Vamos!" she hollered over her shoulder at me.

I didn't know much Spanish, but I knew *vamos*. So I dropped my basket and ran. People near the registers were still screaming. I chased after the couple, toward the back of the store, past the dairy fridges, through the swinging steel-clad doors into the fluorescent warehouse area. We dodged past stacked wooden pallets and towers of cardboard boxes and bundles of toilet paper. The air smelled like wet cardboard and old bananas. A bunch of other people had rushed in there, too, and grocery store employees yelled at us, confused and indignant.

We all spilled out onto the back dock and jumped or clambered off the concrete pier down to the pavement.

I took a few steps away from the others and paused, gasping for breath, scanning the strip of woods that ran beside and behind the grocery store parking lot. The not-quite-freezing air made my lungs ache. I knew there was a ravine in the longest section of woods, and my apartment complex was somewhere behind it. But where? What was the quickest way to get there? I knew the route in my car, and although it was certainly shorter on foot, I'd never tried it.

There came the rush of wings, and a nightmare landed right in front of me. Seven feet of dark, gnarled limbs and widespread, naked wings towering above me. The wings were batlike, certainly, but the rest . . . it wasn't really like any animal I'd seen. And I had a hard time looking at it. Focusing on it. There was something strange, something jittery and blurry about it that hurt my eyes. It was like trying to look into a strong light. Was it giving off some kind of invisible radiation? Or was it somehow out of phase with the physical world, and my pain a consequence of trying to force my mind to accept an utter impossibility?

The thing shrieked at me. Slimy, bloody drool sprayed out from its strange, elongated mouth. Off its weird, gnarled, swollen, sucking tongue covered with all those rasping sharky teeth. I froze like a bunny and covered my face with my hands. All I could think was *I'm about to die.*

But the thing didn't attack. It paused as I took shuddering, terrified breaths. It gazed down at me and shrieked again. It almost sounded like it was trying to say a word. *Ma. Re. Ra.*

Was . . . was it trying to say my name? I looked more closely into its awful face. There was a shadow of something human about its features, features I *did* recognize . . .

"Erin?" I breathed. "Erin. Is . . . is that you?"

The thing shrieked and bobbed its head. Barked something at me, a guttural noise.

"Back off, Archivist!" a woman shouted from a few yards away. "She's Chosen! Don't touch her!"

I turned. A tall blonde woman was striding toward us, expression fierce and determined. She wasn't wearing a mask. Her pretty face, designer denim jacket, and black pants were all spattered with gore. At first I thought she might be seriously injured, but then I saw she held a machete in her right hand. The broad blade dripped with blood and was caked with hair and bits of flesh. Somehow, she was even more disturbing than what Erin had become.

*Oh Jesus,* I thought. *Jesus, Jesus.*

Erin turned toward the woman and roared.

"She's *mine.*" The blonde pointed the bloody machete at her like a general with a saber. "I've been preparing for this all week. I don't care if you know her. This is *my* job. Don't push me, bitch."

Erin stepped back and furled her wings behind her, eyeing both of us.

*This is insane*, I thought. *I'm surrounded by insane people, and I'm insane now, too, and I'm gonna die in a Kroger parking lot.*

"So, hiii, my name's Savannah." The blood-soaked blonde stepped up beside me, smiling like an airline attendant. "I know all of this is probably a *lot*, but I want to assure you that you're perfectly safe with me. Perfectly safe."

She touched her bloody chest with her bloody left hand for emphasis and crossed her heart with her index finger. "I'm supposed to escort you to safety. Although you have been Chosen, some of the Archivists are . . . well, *overenthusiastic*. We wouldn't want you harvested by accident, would we?"

I could hear the capital *C* in *Chosen* because of her inflection.

"What . . . what the hell are you talking about?" I stammered. "Chosen *how*? Chosen why? What's happening?"

"Well, it's a little complicated, but the short version is: this is the first active phase of the harvesting and neutralization of the dominant technological species on this planet."

I blinked at her. "W-what?"

"The apocalypse, honey. Doomsday. The end of human civilization." She pointed her machete at people running terrified across the parking lot a few dozen yards away from us. Other creatures like Erin pursued them. "That lady's gonna get harvested soon, so's that guy, and one of us Slayers is just gonna put that sad loser over there out of everyone's misery. *She* gonna die, *he* gonna die, errybody gonna die. Maybe not today, maybe not tomorrow, but soon."

She turned back to me, beaming. "Except you. *You're* not gonna die. The gods have *plans* for you, sugar pie."

*God has a plan for us all.* My high school pastor's mellow voice echoed inside my head. *We shall all live immortal in His glory.*

Was this some weird, completely bonkers missionary encounter? Was this woman some kind of doomsday cultist? If so, what the hell was Erin in all this? A demon? A twisted angel?

"W-what plans?" I stammered.

"I'm not on a need-to-know on that. Yet. But it appears that you won the cosmic lottery, you lucky little bunny! You are useful to our eldritch lords and masters in mysterious ways that the rest of us are not."

Eldritch lords? Oh, no no no no . . . I had to be dreaming. Sick in the hospital with PVG, maybe. Hallucinating. People said they got all kinds of crazy dreams when they got infected.

"Can't . . . can't I just go back to my apartment?"

"Bad idea, I'm afraid," she singsonged. "It's Harvest season at all the apartment complexes around here. And it's only a matter of time before the government decides to send in the troops. Or panics entirely and decides to carpet-bomb cities with heavy Archivist activity. Wouldn't want you to end up as part of the collateral damage, either! So I really need to get you out of the city—"

Erin screamed something at her.

Savannah gave her an annoyed side glance. "No, I don't know *where* just yet—"

Erin barked out a torrent of harsh alien sounds that hurt my ears.

Savannah brightened, her eyebrows rising in surprise. "Oh, *really*? You did? Well, that's just fabulous."

The blonde turned back to me, grinning broadly. "It turns out, your former coworker here recently harvested the CEO of Mayne Sequence Solar. He has an off-grid mansion out in the hills. Isolated. Self-sustained, with its own power and water supply. It'll be *perfect*. You'll *love* it there."

I was very, very sure that whatever this madwoman had planned, I was *not* going to love it. So I bolted. Ducked past her arm and sprinted as fast as I could for the tree-lined ravine.

I made it about twenty paces before I felt the wind of Erin's wings. She landed in front of me, blocking any possible exit before she grabbed my flailing hands and held me fast in her gnarled talons.

"Gotta do this the hard way, I see," Savannah said behind me.

A moment later, she stabbed a hypodermic needle into my neck and I felt the cold burn of knockout chemicals jetting into my flesh.

I fell limp in Erin's grip, my eyelids fluttering, the world spinning.

"You'll learn that everything's going to be so much better if you just do as I say," Savannah told me as my consciousness faded. "You'll learn."

# CHAPTER 25

I wake up slowly, groggy, in a dark room. First: I'm aware of the sour-smelling paper mask clinging damply to my face. Second: This bed isn't mine. The sheets feel impossibly smooth and soft, and the mattress is plush, as if this is a high-end hotel room. But this doesn't smell like a hotel. My bladder aches, and that painful imperative forces me to throw off the covers and roll off the bed. My legs won't hold, and I fall to my knees.

"Here, let me help you," says a woman. The voice is familiar, but in my fuzzy-headed state, I can't place it. "I bet you need the toilet. It's this way."

I let the woman help me to my feet, take me by my elbow, and lead me through the maze of the dark room into an adjoining bathroom. The sudden light from the frosted glass windows hurts my eyes. Nothing is in focus. The bathroom seems huge. Beige marble tiles are hard but unexpectedly warm under my bare feet.

"In here." The woman ushers me through another door, into a toilet alcove.

I stagger in, fumble my jeans down, and do my business. Afterward, I just sit there for probably fifteen minutes, trying to clear my head and get my bearings. I gradually remember what happened just before I lost consciousness. All that seems . . . impossible. Surely it was a dream, a hallucination?

But I'm certain I am awake now. And I'm clearly not in my apartment. So where am I?

I check myself all over. These are my jeans and green knit cardigan set—I remember putting them on when I was getting ready for work. Nothing's askew, nothing makes me think I've been undressed aside from my shoes. No injuries aside from the swollen injection puncture, which aches like a hornet sting. My pounding headache isn't as bad as the pain in my neck. My mouth is sticky and dry, and my right side is sore, either because I've stayed in one position too long or because my liver is unhappy. Both are plausible.

But then something catches on my cuff as I pull my jeans up. A shiny stainless steel shackle is locked onto my left ankle over my sock. *That* definitely wasn't there before. I swing my left leg up onto my knee to take a closer look. The shackle isn't too tight; I can get two fingers under it. But of course there's no way to get it off over my foot. There's a shallow, round, recessed compartment inside the shackle, near the lock. Inside it, I can just barely feel the smooth outline of an Apple AirTag or something similar.

So it's a tracking bracelet. Wonderful. I look around the toilet alcove, trying to figure out what to do. Should I find a weapon? That's what the heroine would do in a thriller. It seems like a sensible step. But I've never had to physically defend myself before, and it doesn't look like there's anything in here that I could use as a knife or club. There isn't even a towel bar. Wait. The ceramic lid on the toilet tank . . . maybe I can swing it? I played softball when I was a kid. Could I pretend that my abductor's head is just a ball? A sudden grisly mental image of Savannah's smashed nose makes me feel sick to my stomach.

I swallow down my nausea and misgivings and carefully ease the lid off the commode. It's really heavy, but I think I can still swing it. I clutch it to my body with my left hand and slowly open the door with my right.

Savannah sits on the edge of a fancy Jacuzzi tub, sipping from a mug of coffee. She's showered, done her hair, and is wearing a clean blue dress and leather flats. Very professional, like she's just come from a downtown office.

But she's not wearing a mask, and I don't see one near her.

Another steaming mug of coffee sits on the edge of the Jacuzzi, about four feet away from her. A plastic and steel bath seat, the kind you buy for your invalid grandmother, sits near the coffee.

"You really gonna try to brain me with that thing?" She arches a perfectly shaped eyebrow. "You really think you can move faster than I can? In your condition?"

"I . . . um . . ." I can't think of what to say.

Savannah sighs and smiles. "Just put that silly thing down. Come over here, sit, and let's have a chat, alright? And have some coffee. It'll help you wake up. I promise it's not drugged or poisoned."

I lean the toilet lid against the doorframe but don't move out of the alcove. "You're not wearing a mask."

She shrugs. "That's true. I've already been infected, and I don't shed virus. So it's not a concern for me now."

"You could get infected again."

"I doubt that very much." She blows on her coffee and takes another sip.

"How do I know you're not shedding virus?"

She laughs and shakes her head. "Somehow I knew you'd ask that. Would a negative on a rapid antigen test be enough proof for you?"

"I suppose . . ."

I watch as she digs a plastic-wrapped box of rapid tests out of the under-sink cabinet, opens it, twirls the swab in her nose, and inserts it into the vial.

"See?" She shows me the single control bar on the readout. "Negative. So please come over here so we can chat more comfortably."

I shuffle over to the socially distanced bath seat. Pick up the coffee after I sit down. I take an experimental sip. It tastes like two lumps of sugar and a glug of cream. Not bad. No weird bitterness to make me think I'm being drugged again. It seems fine? Almost as important, I don't think I'm going to throw it up.

"So, I realize that yesterday morning was *not* the best way to establish trust and rapport," Savannah says. "We're off on the wrong foot. I hope we can fix that."

"Fix it? You stabbed me in the neck with a syringe." I glare at her. "Shot me up with God knows what."

"Because you ran from me! I had to get you out of there. More Archivists were coming."

"Of course I bolted. You were covered in *blood*. You'd obviously been murdering people. Did you really think I'd just . . . just say, 'Oh, okay, this seems fine' and come with you?"

"Clearly not." She shrugs and sips her coffee. "My plan A was entirely aspirational. My plan B went better than I expected. This is a *much* nicer safe house than an abandoned roadside motel in the sticks somewhere."

"I . . . I don't get why you've kidnapped me. My family doesn't have any money. *I* don't have any money."

"This isn't a kidnapping." She pauses, looking thoughtful. "Well, okay, yes, it is, but . . . I prefer to think of this as a rescue. If I hadn't intervened, an Archivist could have killed you."

"Erin wasn't going to kill me." I hope not, anyhow.

"No, she wasn't. Not then. But she'd have been compelled to harvest you, sooner or later, unless I intervened and changed her mission as I did. At best, you'd have made it to your apartment only to be dead by now."

"Where is she?"

"I sent her and another, named Betty, to go to your apartment and fetch your things. One load is in the living room. I'm afraid they may have ripped some of your clothes. Talons, you know."

She makes a raking motion in the air with her graceful hand.

"So why did you 'rescue' me?" I ask. "Why am I here?"

"I still don't know!" She shrugs cheerfully. "I just know that I'm supposed to keep you safe and healthy and cared for. I don't know for how long, but I suspect it might be quite a while. We just have to trust the gods' process!"

Her talk of the gods makes me nervous, but I don't know what to say about it.

So I point to the shackle on my ankle. "And I'm not allowed to go anywhere? I'm trapped here?"

"Well, trust is a two-way street. I can't do my job if I don't know where you are. If I'm sure, *absolutely* sure, that you'll return safely . . . then I'll remove the bracelet. But not before. And part of that calculation involves me feeling that the outside world is safe for you to explore."

My memory flashes on the chaos at the grocery store. How many people had been attacked? The seriousness and realness of the situation is sinking in. "My sister, Leila . . . my folks. I want to talk to them. I need to make sure they're okay."

"Sugar pie . . . I assure you, they're not okay. If they're okay right now? In a week, two weeks, they'll be gone. The sooner you're able to accept that, the better life will be for both of us."

"But I have to talk to them!" I'm starting to panic. Starting to cry.

"Then call them," she replies calmly. "The power's still on in most of the city, so we'll have cell service for at least another twenty-four hours. Your phone's in your purse, on the living room couch. Out that door, go down the stairs. Be careful you don't fall. Can't miss it."

●  ●  ●

When I get to the living room, I have to stand there staring in awe for a moment. Vaulted, skylit ceilings rise three stories high, hung with four squiggly, colorful Chihuly glass sculptures that probably cost $50,000 apiece. The Mayne family had already decorated for Christmas, and an LED-lit artificial balsam fir rises twenty feet tall in a juncture between the living room and a formal dining room. There's a wide stone fireplace hung with stockings and a huge flat-screen mounted above it. The sofa Savannah mentioned is a huge, blue, full grain leather sectional. Italian?

Probably Italian. The whole room cost more than I'd make in a decade at UCC. My rat brain admires everything I see, but my superstitious mind wants to set it on fire.

Meanwhile, some of my personal belongings sit in a sad-looking stack of awkwardly taped boxes that the monsters obviously found behind a grocery store. Stray talon marks gouge the sides. While the teetering cardboard pyramid would have filled my dining nook, it looks small, shabby, and lonely here. Just a plebian pile of Ph.D.-washout debris.

I retrieve my purse from the sectional and take it into the dining room so I can sit at the fancy, glossy, dark wood table that was probably hand-carved in Russia by vegan expatriate Coptic monks or someone. My phone still has a decent charge on it and is getting a reasonably strong signal. It doesn't look like Savannah tampered with my purse or took anything other than my apartment keys and the fob for my Prius.

Surprisingly, Candy Kleypas's card is still in the front pocket. Did Savannah overlook it? Or does she simply think Homeland Security is no threat? Does she believe the gods will protect her from Tasers, batons, or a barrage of federal bullets? That kind of faith worked out so well for people like David Koresh.

I tuck the card back in my purse and dial 911. And get a busy signal. Well, that's extremely not good. I dial and redial a few more times with no luck. A network problem? I hope it's a network problem.

I bring up my parents' number. Eight p.m. is a reasonable time to phone them—they usually don't go to bed before eleven. If this is my last chance to talk to them, I'll never forgive myself if I don't take it.

The call rings four times and goes to their voice mail. I briefly consider telling them that I've been kidnapped. But they're a half-day's drive away . . . what can they do if nobody can get through to the local police? Why worry them like that?

"Hey, this is Mareva. I'm worried about you two. Looks like

it's getting scary out there. I hope you're safe. I'm safe. Please call me if you get the chance to let me know you're okay? I love you both."

I'm supposed to be at work in a couple of hours, and obviously I'm not going to make it. So I call the ops number to let whoever's staffing the phones know that I won't be coming in and, hey, I've been kidnapped and could they maybe send the police to Mark Mayne's house? That, too, goes to voice mail.

This panics me even more than 911 being busy. The ops number should *never* go unanswered. Not unless there's an all-hands-on-deck emergency. Not unless the whole building's been evacuated.

Nausea's a heavy weight in the pit of my belly. *Please let this all be due to a phone system outage,* I think. I silently pray that my worst fears aren't coming true.

I haven't talked to Leila in an embarrassingly long time. It's just that our lives have become so different, it's hard to make conversation. What should I say to her now? Will it be horribly awkward if she's fine and nothing has happened in her sleepy little town? So it takes me a good minute before I work up the courage to dial her.

Three rings . . . and it connects. Yes!

But instead of Leila's voice, a young girl answers, quietly and tentatively: "Hello?"

I'm ashamed that I don't recognize the kid's voice, so I'm not sure which of my nieces she is. I know all their names start with *D*. Daniele? Denise? I am the worst aunt ever.

"Hi." I lower my voice to a whisper. "Is your mommy there?"

"She went out last week and didn't come back."

*Oh my Lord no.* "Is your daddy there?"

"He's in the yard. He won't move. A monster hurt him in his eye and he won't move."

"Is the monster still there?"

"I . . . I think it went away. But I'm scared."

"I know you are, baby." The awful reality of the situation hits me and I start to cry, even though I want to be a voice of calm for whichever little kid I'm talking to. My tears splash down on the fancy tabletop. "I'm so sorry about your mommy and daddy. I'm so, so sorry."

The child gasps, and my heart jumps.

"I . . . I think it's back." Her voice is tight with fear.

"Go hide! Go hide!" I whisper.

I hear something that might be the rush of wings but which might simply be connection static, or wind in the eaves.

Then the line is dead.

"So, how did your calls go?"

Savannah is standing by the Christmas tree. Arms crossed. Gazing at me dispassionately.

"I hate you," I sob. "I hope you die in flames." This is possibly the worst thing I've ever said out loud to another human being.

"Right." She looks down at her hands, inspects her flawless nails. "I'll just give you some time and space to process all this, then."

She crosses the room and disappears down the hallway.

I pull Candy Kleypas's card out of my purse. Open up Maps to figure out where I am, copy the unfamiliar address, and text the Homeland Security agent that I've been kidnapped by a woman named Savannah. I give her the address, and just in case she's too busy to bother with me, I tell her that Savannah has insider information about PVG patients going berserk. Really important information that Kleypas needs to hear.

For good measure, I straight-up lie and tell her that Savannah knows where Dr. Astrid Shapiro is hiding. I feel a little uncomfortable about doing that, but it's the only ace I have to play. I haven't forgotten how she tried to gaslight me. Covertly threatened me. Tried to silence me and anyone else who saw Erin in the sky. Kleypas will lie her butt off if those are her orders. So I only have so much good conscience to spend on her.

After I send the text, I try 911, with no better luck than before.

So I go to the couch, turn on the flat-screen above the fireplace, and watch the world thrash and burn on MSNBC and CNN as I weep for Leila, my parents, Erin, my coworkers, and everyone I've ever known.

# CHAPTER 26

About an hour later, Kleypas texts me back:

CK here. RU at Mayne residence?

   Yes, I type.

How do U still have your phone?
                S. didn't take it. Seems pretty cocky.
RU in immediate danger?
                No, but S. killed people at Kroger with a
                machete.
Accomplices?
                Maybe 2 others? Haven't seen. They might
                have killed Mark Mayne & his fam. Haven't
                seen them either
Are they human or flyers?

   Well, if she didn't believe the transformations were real before, she certainly knows now.
   Flyers, I text.

Other captives?

   Haven't seen, I reply.

OK. Stay put. Dont provoke her. Delete these
txts. When we get there, come out with yr

hands empty and up. Keep em high so you
dont get shot.

OK.

I delete the message thread as she asked and continue watching the news on TV. Most networks are playing and replaying
dramatic footage of a dozen Archivists descending on people leaving a horror movie premiere in Los Angeles. Most of the carnage
is blurred out. Director Eli Korman is gruesomely slaughtered,
along with a number of B-list celebrities. Talking heads debate
whether the footage is a deep fake or not. Someone on Fox News
scoffs that the whole thing is obviously an elaborate publicity
stunt. News anchors on other networks look unusually spooked.

My phone pings: I've just gotten an email that Dr. Kaz is
about to do a livestream. So I switch to YouTube.

Dr. Kaz appears, her anguished face lit blue by her phone in
the darkness. It looks like she might be hiding under a desk or in
the back of a closet.

"Hi, everyone. Thanks for joining me." She wipes away tears
with the back of her hand. "Welcome to my second livestream. I
hope it's not my last but . . ."

She trails off in nervous, sobbing laughter for a moment, but
gathers herself and continues: "So, I don't have a virology topic
tonight. My apartment building is under attack, and I can't get
through to nine one one, so. I mean. Things don't look so good
right now. If you've been watching the news and have been thinking, 'Oh, that stuff that people are saying about flying monsters
or vampires or whatever, that's all a crazy hoax' . . . I hate to be
the bearer of bad news, but it's real. It's happening. Please, get
someplace safe if you haven't already. Do not go walking outside.
These things are fast. If you're all 'photos or it didn't happen,' if
you stop to take a photo, you're probably going to die. So I have
no photos."

Dr. Kaz pauses to wipe her nose on her long-sleeved maroon

T-shirt. "I also . . . just wanted to give a shout-out to Dr. Gabriel Takahiro: I'm sorry I was so skeptical. I owe you an apology, my friend. And I just—"

There's a loud, crunching bang, like a door being knocked off its hinges. She jumps and the phone bobbles in her hands.

"Shit, shit, shit!" Her voice is a tight, terrified hiss.

The image swings wildly for a moment, and then the feed goes dark. The livestream ends.

I just sit there on the couch, staring numbly at my phone. Dr. Kaz isn't a friend, but I've seen her face practically every week, so my superstitious mind is certain that she's a buddy. And I've just come close to watching her get torn apart. She might be dead now. Dead like Leila, Leila's family, and my parents probably are.

Savannah's cheerful, casual voice echoes in my memory: *"She gonna die, he gonna die, errybody gonna die."*

But in this moment, I feel nothing. Inside me is a cold, blank absence. I can't bear to feel anything. Feeling would absolutely destroy what is left of my soul. Somewhere in the back of my mind, I'm aware that I've fully committed to the "denial" phase of grief. So be it.

●　●　●

Homeland Security pounds on the front door just after 10 p.m. I jump to my feet, expecting Savannah to come running into the living room, but she isn't there. I sprint into the foyer and pull the door open.

A cop in black armored hazmat gear kicks it the rest of the way open, painfully banging my hands and knees. He grabs me by the collar of my shirt before I can say anything. Jerks me outside into the glare of police floodlights. Hauls me down the broad stone steps and throws me face-first onto the freezing lawn. My front teeth cut a bloody groove on the inside of my lip. The cop jams his knees agonizingly into the backs of my thighs as he yanks my hands behind my back.

"Identify yourself!" another cop shouts down at me. My masked face is shoved down into the frosty blades of grass and I can't open my mouth to reply. I'm scared and furious. I'd tried to do what Kleypas told me to. I thought the police were supposed to make people safer, not make the situation ten times worse.

"Identify yourself! *Right now!*" I hear a pistol cocking.

I'm about to die. I'm sure of it. What a way to go.

"Whoa, whoa, Robocop, let her up," I hear Candy Kleypas say. "This is the woman who called me. You okay, Mareva?"

"Yes," I manage.

The two cops haul me to my feet. Blinking in the bright lights, I can barely see three black SUVs parked in the broad circular driveway in front of the mansion. Kleypas is a short, dark silhouette stepping toward me. Unlike the cops, she wears just a paper mask and a bulletproof vest for protection.

"Where's Savannah?" she asks me.

I shake my head. "I don't know. I thought she was in the house. Can you just . . . just get me out of here?"

"We need to find Savannah to determine what she knows about Dr. Shapiro," Kleypas says. "The doctor is considered a high-value target right now and we—"

The darkness around us comes alive. Monsters descend in a dizzying storm of wind and terrifying shrieks. Huge flapping wings obscure the lights as men and women scream and fire their weapons. The boom of shotguns, the explosive rattle of assault rifles, the firecracker bangs of pistols. My ears ring from the violent cacophony, and I can't think to do anything but drop to my knees and cover my head.

In seconds, the gunfire ends. The floodlights return, and I am bathed in their harsh whiteness again. All I can hear are muffled wails and the crack of bones. Slurping, wet crunching.

"Oh sweet Jesus," Kleypas groans just a few feet away from me.

I look up just in time to see Savannah's machete blade slam down on the crown of Kleypas's head, neatly shearing off the top of her skull.

Savannah, dressed now in a skirt and top made from black plastic trash bags, drops her machete. Moans and falls upon the twitching almost-corpse, shoving both hands into the counselor's open cranium. Digging out handfuls of pink-gray brains that steam in the cold air. Crams them into her mouth, swallowing them down.

Profoundly sickened, I turn away and vomit onto the frozen grass.

One of the Archivists snarls something. I can't see anything.

"You got a scrub?" Savannah replies around a mouthful of flesh. "Hold him. Don't kill him."

She rocks back on her heels and burps, staring down at Kleypas's emptied skull with glassy, excited eyes. Her face and arms are sheened with sweat. "Well, you've been the busiest little bee in the whole federal hive, haven't you?"

Savannah shakes bits of clinging offal from her gory hands. Picks up her machete. Stands and strides over somewhere behind the lights.

"No, no, don't," a man pleads.

Then the meaty *thunk* of a blade sinking into a body.

"Fuck yeah, that's *so* good," Savannah moans.

Oh my lord, she's literally getting off on this. What kind of a creature is she? Every time I'm certain the situation is as nasty as it can be, it manages to get worse.

My captor staggers back toward me, dragging the tip of her machete across the ground. Her face is flushed, her body trembling. Two gnarled, emaciated Archivists flap down to the empty paved driveway in front of the black SUVs and start spreading out a blue plastic sheet.

"Get the bodies and lay them out on the tarp," she calls to some Archivists I can't see. "And someone fetch my knife roll."

"What . . . what are you going to do?" My voice shakes, only partly from the cold.

"Well, there's a whole lot of nice fresh meat out here." Her tone is casual. "So I'm going to fill up the two empty chest freezers I found in the garage with some choice cuts. No sense letting all this go to waste."

It takes a moment for the full meaning of her words to sink in, because my mind flatly rejects what she tells me, at first.

"I'm not going to eat *people*!" I shriek at her.

"Well, you don't have to." She's the picture of calm. "But we're likely to be on this hill for quite some time, and we need to be prepared. I don't know what our hunting situation is going to be like, or if what we find to hunt will be edible. There's a big garden and greenhouse out back. So you can be a vegan come spring if you like, as long as it doesn't impact your health."

I slowly stand up, looking around at all the dead agents scattered across the driveway. I don't see any dead Archivists. Or even any who seem to be seriously injured. "You . . . you knew I would call Kleypas. You *planned* for this to happen."

"Of course I did, sugar pie. You seriously think I'd let you have your phone if I didn't? I wanted to know what the local authorities are planning. Thanks to sweet little Candy, now I do. I'll share that intel with the Archivists, and the Harvest will go *so* much more smoothly. There's a decent number of asymptomatic Type Zeros in local law enforcement, and the gods can turn them all to heroes. Like they did with me."

She kneels by one of the bodies on the tarp and starts to undress it. "And, as a bonus, it looks like we've got a nice little collection of firearms now. A couple of twelve-gauge Remington 870s, some AR-15s, a Heckler & Koch MP5, and of course some .357 SIGs and nine-millimeter Glocks. Early Christmas for us! Well, me, anyhow. It's going to be a few before I trust you with a gun."

"You're a monster," I say.

"I'm just doing my job. Doing our lords' work. Halle-fuckin'-lujah." She takes an olive drab canvas bundle from an Archivist and unrolls it. It's filled with a collection of hunting and kitchen knives. "While I'm more than happy to share with you what I've learned about butchery and meat cutting, I'm guessing you don't want to see what I'm about to do. So this is where you should go inside and watch some more TV."

I back toward the door. "I hate you."

"Oh, you'll learn to love me." She winks at me. "Now, don't go running off while I'm busy with this. It's cold out and I don't want you getting sick. And while you won't be able to see the Archivists in the woods, they'll be able to see and smell you just fine."

Savannah pulls out a knife with a sharp, hooked notch on its spine and starts humming "Santa Claus Is Coming to Town."

I stumble inside, shut the door, and go into the bathroom to lose what's left of my coffee.

# CHAPTER 27

The next morning, I hurt all over from being thrown on the ground. By midmorning I start to feel a bit feverish, just a little bit queasy. And that worries me. So I take one of the rapid antigen tests from the pack Savannah has in the bathroom.

It's positive.

I try very, very hard to keep myself together. After all, I don't feel very sick, and everyone says that the symptoms come on blindingly fast, if they come on at all. I don't tell Savannah, and by the time evening rolls around, my temperature is back to normal. I take another test, which returns a negative. So I figure all is well.

But when I take a bath that evening, I find a painful lump in my left breast. After a moment of heart-pounding panic, my rat brain tells me that this is just a bruise. A hematoma, from when the cop roughed me up. That's the simplest and most obvious explanation for it.

But over the next two weeks, the lump grows. Itches. Aches. It doesn't feel quite like the teratomas I've had before. My breast swells. And I am terrified.

My father's sister got inflammatory breast cancer when I was twelve. She and her doctor both thought it was mastitis at first. I remember her telling me that she was going to drink apple cider vinegar to treat it. But the vinegar didn't work, so the doctor prescribed her some antibiotics. And when those didn't work, he sent her for a mammogram and biopsy.

My aunt was dead within the year. It was not a good death. There aren't a whole lot of genuinely nice ways to die in this world, but if I had to choose between going out the way she did and being torn apart by Archivists? Archivists, definitely.

I don't want to tell Savannah about the lump. Because then she'll want to examine me. I don't want her touching me. Not anywhere, and especially not there.

Living with her is breathtakingly terrifying. She seems aware, occasionally, that she's become a complete maniac. If you crossed a savant with a perfect predator, gave that hybrid a cocaine high, and put it in the body of a model-poised, machete-swinging blonde . . . you'd have Savannah.

So no, I don't want to give her an excuse to put her hands on me.

Is there a physician left alive nearby, and could I get to him or her?

The tower-top bedroom that Savannah put me in has a set of white, curtained French doors that lead out onto an iron-railed stone balcony. It's empty right now, but it's probably big enough for a café table and a few tall chairs. A nice place for coffee and brunch in the spring. It's high enough to trigger my vertigo when I look over the railing, but tumbling over probably wouldn't kill a person. If you fell—or jumped—you'd hit the slope of the living room's slate roof, slide down, and if you couldn't grab onto the gutters, you'd most likely land in some bushy boxwood shrubs. This time of winter, it might be possible you'd get impaled on a branch, which seems like an unreliable, uncomfortable, slow way to die.

The balcony overlooks the city valley. Every morning I go out there with a pair of binoculars to watch smoke rise in the cold winter sky and listen for distant gunshots. In the first days of my captivity, I heard faint sirens from emergency vehicles; now those seem to be gone. The city looks more and more desolate. The only signs of life are Archivists circling downtown like huge vultures.

I am appalled at the scale of the death and destruction. But only on an intellectual level. It's just too big, too much to internalize emotionally. My mind just doesn't have the wherewithal to fret about more than my ongoing cancer scare. If I were a better, deeper person, I could probably do a better job at grieving for the world and the people in it. But I'm not that better person. I have to view the murder of the inhabitants of my own city more as a theoretical reality, the same as I'd looked at the famines in Africa or mass killings in South America or Asia that I only heard about on TV or Twitter. What's happened in my own city is huge and terrible and awful but I am apart from it. An observer. Emotionally detached, because my rat brain is sure that taking all this fully to heart will destroy me. My superstitious mind is buried in denial, pretending that my friends and family are still alive someplace, even though my rat brain knows that's unlikely.

Escape—assuming there's any place I could actually escape *to*—seems impossible because there are Archivists lurking nearby all the time. They don't like strong sunlight, but there are thick copses of arborvitae and other trees that give them good cover during the day. A few times I've strayed close to the boundary—a low, primitive wall they built by stacking whatever rocks, cinder blocks, and bricks they could find in a circle roughly half a kilometer from the mansion—and heard the vile coughing noise of one of them clearing its throat. Warning me.

The creatures continue to change. Over the past weeks they've sprouted dark plumage, long flight feathers on their wings, but shorter ones on their bodies, arms, and legs. Their faces mostly remain bare. Erin and a couple of the others still have a recognizable humanness in their faces and bodies, and they're starting to regrow the hair on their heads. Erin's is coming in thick and white. The rest, like Betty, are becoming more like beasts. It's easier and easier to tell them all apart. Betty's head reminds me of a lioness's: her nose is broad and her teeth are sharply feline. But there's an Archivist who looks like a bear to me, another a shark. A spider. A deep-sea angler. A bull. An eagle. A lion. A boar.

I've started to be able to understand what the Archivists say to me. Their language—if it's a language at all—hasn't changed. It's all shrieks and growls and snarls. But I know what they mean when they utter something. The beastly ones are hardest to understand; I don't get much more nuance than "Halt" or "Turn away" from them. But with Erin, and to a lesser extent the other humanlike Archivists, I understand a whole lot more.

I don't know how or why she and I are on the same wavelength, but obviously something in my brain has changed. So I suspect that my first PVG test wasn't a false positive. It's the most obvious thing. Maybe Erin infected me and those shared viral genes have rewired us both for mutual understanding, or the illusion of it. Or perhaps I was infected, directly or indirectly, by the person who exposed her to the virus.

Erin and Betty are my most frequent guards. They spend a lot of time wrapped around each other in the barn, growling and humming, licking each other's faces. But as distracted as they seem to be, my efforts to sneak past them have always failed.

But today, it's a bright, cold wintry day, and Erin and Betty are in the hayloft. At first they seemed to be canoodling as usual, but things have . . . escalated. The primal sounds and scattered meanings I overhear make my cheeks burn with embarrassment.

I've got a very warm coat on, and my good boots. I've packed some food, water, and a few other supplies in a sling pack . . . I don't think I'll get a better chance to escape than this.

So I take off at a sprint down the hillside. Jumping over fallen logs, ducking under branches. The impact of each step makes my breast ache sharply, but I can ignore the pain.

Soon I'm into the meadow, and I chance a glance behind me. Nobody is pursuing me. I can see the road, way down below, twisting like a blue racer snake. I just have to follow the highway east to get back to the city, and—

The sudden rush of wings, and a shadow envelops me.

Erin lifts me off my feet and flies to the shade of a stand of evergreen arborvitae.

"Thou cannot leave," she growls.

I struggle, but I can't break her grip. "Can't you just let me go? Pretend you didn't see me out here?"

She shakes her fearsome head. "I am commanded. Bound."

Up this close to her, I realize that the shorter feathers covering her arms and body aren't really feathers. Some look like thin, flat, distorted fingernails. Some are iridescent fish scales. I see toothy placoid, diamond ganoid, round cycloid, and fanlike ctenoid ones. And there are membranous, veined, vibrating insect wings mixed in, too.

It's amazing and horrifying in equal measure.

"I hate what they've done to you," I say. "I wanted us to be friends. When you came to my desk that first time? I wanted to follow you back to your office. Get to know you. But I was afraid of messing things up at work. So I didn't. But I wonder . . . if I had, maybe this wouldn't have happened to you?"

"I do not know," she replies. "But if this had not happened, I would be dead. I do not regret this. But . . . I do regret not knowing thine friendship. Perhaps in another world, another time, we shalt have the chance again."

"Savannah's supposed to protect me . . . which means that you also have to protect me, right?"

"Yes."

"I . . . I just want to get to a doctor. A real doctor."

"Art thou ill?"

"I found a lump in my breast. It could be cancer."

"Savannah will help thee."

"But what about Dr. Shapiro? You know her. You could . . . sniff her out, right? If she's still alive?"

Erin pauses. "I could find her, yes."

Hope soars in me. "You could fly me there. It wouldn't take long, would it?"

"I am bound. I cannot. Go back to the house."

"But—"

"*Go!*"

• • •

"Erin says you found a lump," Savannah says at dinner. "When were you going to tell me about it?"

I'm picking at my pulled pork. Savannah *says* it's pork; I'm hoping it's not Homeland Security. I've already eaten two potatoes and my peas, but I really want to eat the whole pile of meat, too. My hunger has gotten worse and worse ever since I found the lump growing. I don't know if it's from the stress of the situation or if it's a sure sign I have cancer.

Either way, I've been eating a lot more than usual, and haven't gained any weight.

"It's nothing," I say.

"Erin doesn't think it's nothing. She says your body odor has changed."

"Yes, well, I switched to a different kind of body wash, so that's probably—"

"Mareva." She gives me a hard look. "Please don't lie to me. I can't help you if you hide illnesses and injuries from me."

"The . . . uh, the lump's in my breast." I nervously eat a bite of meat. It certainly tastes like pork, but who can really tell what it is, under the sauce. "What are we going to do if it's another teratoma? What are we going to do if it's something worse?"

"I'll deal with it."

I set my fork down and stare at her. Does she seriously think I'd let her do surgery on me? Give me chemotherapy? Radiation? *Seriously?*

"How?" I ask. "You're not a doctor."

"I've eaten the brains of a nurse, a general practitioner, a gynecologist, an oncologist, and an ER trauma specialist." She counts those murders off like she's listing computer certifications. "And I've got a nice stack of medical texts. I think I can muddle my way through."

"I'd . . . be more comfortable with a traditionally trained physician."

"And I'd be shocked if any have escaped the Harvest. So you have me." She spears a baked potato from the serving tray and puts it on her plate. "I'll take a look at you after dinner."

"What about Dr. Shapiro?"

Savannah gives me a strange look. "I know of her, but haven't met her. She was instrumental in dozens of Archivists reaching their Becoming, simply because she watched their physical symptoms evolve rather than sending her patients to Greenlawn as she was supposed to. It could be that she was another kind of Type Five, but not a Slayer. Or maybe she was just burned out and morbidly curious. I don't know."

She pauses to chew her potato thoughtfully. "I guess it's possible she's still alive. Erin hasn't said."

"Could we go look for her, though? She's probably . . . more experienced?"

Savannah shakes her head. "She's not part of this. And until the Archivists and other Slayers are done mopping up the stragglers, it's too dangerous for me to take you anywhere. Most everyone who's survived until now is a well-armed scrub. It's, like, all neo-Nazi militias and drug gangs out there right now."

She makes a face and waves her hand dismissively. "I mean, they're fun to kill and all, but if you can't catch them alone, they're a real pain in the ass."

"But you could bring her here. How can you be sure she's . . . not part of this?"

"Michael would have showed her to me."

I sit back in the fancy dining room chair. "Michael? Who's Michael?"

"He's a monk I killed." She stares down at her half-eaten potato. "He comes to me in dreams. Shows me things the gods want me to see. I don't know why they're using him as their avatar of prophecy. Morgan Freeman would have been cooler. But it is what it is. The dreams are effective. They're how I knew to find you at the Kroger, for instance."

"But I—"

"Look, this isn't up for debate." She frowns at me. "Taking care of you is *my* job, not Shapiro's. And I'm going to do it if I have to get Erin and Betty to hold you down."

• • •

In the following days, which I mostly spend anxiously pacing the perimeter outside, Savannah turns the first-floor den—which has a wet bar—into something of a clinic. There's an exam table, surgical light, and an assortment of equipment, most still in boxes. Talon gouges told me Archivists carried everything in.

"Get up on the table, please," she says. "And take off your blouse."

I feel myself blush, but I do as she asks. My breast has gotten too painful for a bra.

"Oh, wow, yeah, something's not right." Savannah eyes my chest.

She touches my breast, presses her fingers in. A lance of pain shoots through me.

"Ow."

"Sorry. That's definitely a lump, for sure. I better do an ultrasound. Let me get the machine set up."

I sit there and play *Levelhead* on my phone while she pulls the ultrasound monitor out of the pantry and gets all the cords hooked up.

"Alright," she says. "Lie back and let me get this goop on you. It's gonna feel weird and cold."

She gels me up and presses the ultrasound wand into my flesh. It hurts, and I can't help but suck in my breath.

"This'll just be a minute." Savannah peers at the monitor, which I can't see.

The pressure of the wand hurts enough to make white spots bloom behind my eyelids, but it's more than just pain. There's a weird electricity in my flesh that makes me feel increasingly nauseated.

"I . . . I think I might throw up."

"Almost there."

Bile rises fast in my throat. "No, I—"

"Done." She pulls the wand away.

I take a couple of deep breaths to calm my stomach. "What . . . what do you think?"

"Not sure." She briskly wipes the wand off with a paper towel and hands me a damp washcloth.

"That's it? You're not sure?"

"I need to do some reading on teratomas. In the meantime, we should let it be and see what happens."

"Just . . . just see what happens?" Was she joking?

She gives me a look. "Did you *want* me to do surgery? Cut into your flesh?"

"N-no."

"I didn't think so. And right now, the only alternative to that is: we wait and see."

• • •

My breast keeps swelling. Hurting. Itching. The itching is the worst, because the moment I put any pressure on the area around the lump, blinding pain shoots through my chest and into my spine. I wake myself up at least three times a night by either touching my breast or accidentally pressing it when I roll onto my side.

And my fingernails are changing. Darkening. Thickening, but strangely. The layer of keratin closest to my nail bed seems extremely tough, but the layers above are brittle, prone to chipping away. The result is that my nails are getting very sharp and increasingly difficult to trim. The layered keratin reminds me of Damascus steel.

Savannah sees all this, and says we need to keep waiting.

— • • • —

It's two days before Christmas. Maddening itching wakes me in the darkest hours of the morning. I discover that my breast has swelled up even more, the skin shiny and tight as a balloon. The lump seems to be the size of an orange. Is this an infection? Or is it inflammatory cancer? Oh lord, is this cancer? Am I going to die in agony like my aunt died?

I have to calm down. But the itching is making that really difficult. Warm water often helps, so I decide the best thing would be to take a soak in the big fancy tub in the master bathroom.

I run the water, get undressed, and ease into the bath, up to my chin.

Suddenly there's a sharp cramp in my breast. No, not a cramp—it can't be a cramp. That part of my breast is just fat and glandular tissue. Unless the lump is a muscular teratoma?

Another cramp. A shuddering inside me. Twitching.

The teratoma is moving, shifting. Wriggling.

*Something is alive inside my breast,* digging deeper into my swollen flesh.

"Savannah!" I scream. "There's something in me! *Savannah!*"

In my terror, I grab my breast to try to stop whatever it is from burrowing into me farther. The agony brings vomit into my throat, but the pain is different now, somehow satisfying, triggering some kind of instinct in me to tear myself open.

Only able to breathe in heaving gasps, I dig my nails into the taut curve below my aureole. My skin ruptures beneath my nails as if I'd dug into a huge infected boil. Blood and yellow fluid cloud the water. My probing fingers encounter something like wriggling worms. I have to get the parasite out of there, so I grit my teeth and pull the hole open wider. The pain is awful, worse than anything I have endured before. Extreme. Transformative. I feel myself floating up, up into the sky, into the blackness of space, where ancient, inhuman gods in the dark spaces behold me . . . and find me adequate.

The sharp ripping sensation of the parasite squeezing itself free of my breast brings me back to the reality of the bathroom. It jets away from me in the warm water, a ragged-looking red thing that reminds me of a throbbing, disembodied heart trailing an improbable number of blood vessels behind it.

"*Savannah!*" I shriek, splashing up out of the bloodied water and lurching away from the tub. I stagger to the wall, blood and fluid pouring from my deflated breast, cascading pink and sticky down my body. It smells a little like menstrual blood. My heart strains in my chest and intense dizziness hits my skull like a hammer.

I realize I am losing consciousness, and I manage to grab the edge of the counter and mostly lower myself down to the marble floor before I pass out.

• • •

I awaken several hours later. I'm in bed under a sheet, still naked except for the bandages strapped tightly across my breast. The pain has subsided to a dull ache. My bedside lamp is dimmed, bathing the room in a gentle yellow glow that still hurts my eyes a bit. I blink against sticky crusts, trying to bring the world back into focus.

"Oh, look, Mommy's awake," Savannah says. "Say hi to Mommy!"

A cold dread washes over me. Grants me a shivering, unsteady wakefulness. I blink again, clearing the last bit of filmy mucus that has smudged my vision.

Savannah is sitting in a folding chair near the bed, smiling and petting something in a fluffy pink bath towel. Something red. Something that looks like a heart trailing blood vessels.

She lifts one of the vessels and waves it at me.

"Hi, Mommy!" she says in a high, Muppety voice.

"What. The . . ." I breathe.

Savannah gets up and brings the little bundle of squirm closer. What I'd thought was a heart is actually a round head with lidded eyes, and what I thought were vessels are curling cephalopod arms.

"Twelve little tentacles, one little beaky-weaky, a good set of lungs—*not* gills, thank goodness. He's already digging the Similac. I don't think he has your eyes, though."

As if on cue, the little teratomatic cephalopod squintingly peers out at me, and I catch a glimpse of sky-blue irises. My mother's eyes. My sister Leila's eyes.

"Oh my God," I whisper.

Savannah seems cheerfully oblivious to my profound, shuddering horror. "Isn't he *amazing*? I mean, who knows if he's really a he? Could be a she, or a they. Won't know until he learns words! *If* he learns words. I guess we'll find out, won't we? Yes, won't we, ooh!" she coos at it. "I think he looks like a Gregory, don't you?"

I open my mouth to say something, I'm not sure what, but I burst into wailing sobs instead.

"Oopsie, looks like Mommy's got a touch of the baby blues," she coos to the little creature. "But that's okay! We'll just let her get some sleep and you can hang out with Auntie Savannah!"

Savannah dances her charge out of the room, singing, "*Cancer Baby, dah de dah de dah da da da da da, de dah, Cancer Baby . . .*" as she disappears down the stairs.

I roll onto my good side, shivering, and don't go to sleep so much as faint.

— • • —

Itching in my thighs and belly wakes me at some ungodly hour. My scratching fingers find a total of five tiny new lumps in the flesh beneath my irritated skin. Not much bigger than uncooked barley grains, but I can definitely feel them. A pang of anxiety is quickly overwhelmed by muzzy exhaustion. I don't have anything left right now. I just need to sleep.

*But I'm just like Mom and Leila,* I think, as I drift off.

# CHAPTER 28

I dream of my mother. She and I are sitting in her favorite coffee shop, but instead of the usual downtown street view, the window overlooks the playground that Leila and I used to walk to when we were kids. The shop is empty except for us. I can't even see a barista. The playground equipment and the gentle hills of the park beyond are overgrown with vines of strange, beautiful crimson flowers. The blossoms resemble poppies, but I know that they don't belong here on Earth.

My mother sips her green tea latte. "My, what lovely flowers. Don't you think they're pretty, dear?"

"Yes, they're very nice."

I squint. Something's moving in the vines. Creatures. I give a start as I recognize Gregory, my red dodecapod teratoma infant. He's playing catch with a pink, naked spider creature, the pair chittering to each other as they toss a small skull back and forth. There are other weird, twisted hybrids out there, too: genetic remixes of cephalopods, arachnids, and crustaceans with human skin, human eyes, human hair. My skin. My and my sister's eyes. My hair.

The park expands and becomes an endless rolling field of crimson-flowered vines. There are dozens of the hybrids. Hundreds. Maybe thousands.

"I'm so proud of you, honey." Beaming, my mother reaches out and puts her hand over mine.

"Why?" I ask. "What did I do?"

"You're going to have so many babies. So *many*. You'll be the mother of multitudes. Your children will be legion. You will be fruitful and multiply and repopulate the world in the gods' images."

"What?" I look out at the hybrids playing in the endless field of flowers, and the truth of my role in this newly desolate world settles on me like heavy iron shackles.

"Oh my God. I'm a terraforming engine," I whisper.

"Well, that's a rather dry way of looking at things," my mother says disapprovingly. Her eyes are as black as outer space. "But if that's your path to understanding, so be it."

The innumerable hybrids stop playing, turn toward the coffee shop, and start chanting, "Mama, Mama, Mama, Mama . . ."

◆ ◆ ◆

I wake up screaming. Throw the covers off. Half-run, half-stagger out of my room, down the stairs, and into the kitchen.

I will not be an incubator for anyone, not even the gods. No. Absolutely not. I will *not* end up like Leila. This will stop today.

With shaking hands, I pull a sharp boning knife out of the maple block on the granite kitchen island and find the spot on my neck where my blood pulses. Ram the knife into it, severing my carotid and trachea. Blood pours down my windpipe, into my lungs. More spills down my naked body, staining the white bandages on my breast dark and gory.

I pull the knife free, drop it clattering on the tiles. Take three steps backward before my legs crumple under me and I collapse like a sack of wet sand. Drowning in my own blood. Suffocating.

I think I'll lose consciousness. Die. At any moment, I expect darkness to envelop my senses. But the relief of death never comes. I hang there in an agonizing liminal state, feeling the desperate pressure of suffocation, unable to move, unable to close my eyes.

"Shit! Shit, shit, shit."

Savannah has found me. I hear her footsteps pound across the floor. She kneels beside my body and presses her ear to my chest, listening for a heartbeat. There is none. My heart is trapped between beats, straining in the same uncanny liminality as the rest of my body.

"Jesus fucking Christ, Mareva." She shakes her head, gets up, and runs off.

An eternity seems to pass. An eternity of suffocating, drowning. Hanging suspended at the edge of death, spinning helpless above the abyss. My eyeballs start to dry out, and it is torture that I cannot blink.

Savannah returns with a surgical kit and a lot of gauze. She puts saline drops in my eyes. I'm grateful for this tiny bit of relief. Then she carefully cleans away the congealing blood with a handheld suction device that I never get a good look at. She opens up my neck with a scalpel so she can find the tissue layers I've severed. Sews them up again.

I feel every cut, every stitch. I cannot cry, cannot scream. Can only endure it in silence. Her surgery seems to take hours, and my nerves never grow dull. If birthing the dodecapod had been awful, this entirely eclipses it.

Finally, she finishes suturing me and ties off the thread. She wraps my neck in gauze and tapes it down. Then she opens my mouth and pours the contents of a small bottle inside, right into my clogged throat. It looks like honey but it tastes bitter, foul. The smell of it reminds me of the blood of Archivists.

My heart jerks to life in my chest. I gasp, and immediately begin to choke.

"Cough it up, cough it up."

Savannah helps me roll over onto my hands and knees, and I hack blood and mucus onto the expensive beige tiles.

"At least you didn't do this on the carpet," she says. "Christ, it's hard to get blood out of."

"Oh. Oh lord." I'm finally able to breathe again. My throat feels impossibly raw.

She sits me up.

"Mareva. I realize that all this has been a *lot*. I get that, okay? But you've been Chosen. You have a job to do, just like I do. And yours . . . well, I'm not gonna lie: it straight-up sucks. I'm as pro-choice as they come, but we're beyond that now. We don't get to just nope out. We have to do the work we've been selected to do."

"You . . . you can't possibly expect me to just breed . . . breed *monsters* . . ."

"Hey. Don't be a bigot. They're probably all going to be sentient on some level, and they'll be *yours*."

I just stare at her, sick and miserable.

"Look, you can't fight this," she says. "Did the Virgin Mary get a choice? Did Danaë? Did Leto? If they didn't, why do you think you get to be special? When the gods choose you, you're Chosen. *Forever.*"

I start to cry, from pain and frustration both. "I can't live like this."

"You can. And you *will*," says Savannah. "I am here to help you as much as I can, to try to make this as easy for you as I possibly can. But I have to say, this was a setback on the ol' trust front. I respect that you're almost certainly dealing with legitimate depression right now, and we can work on that. But if you try to kill yourself again? I will have to take serious measures. Measures you won't like one teeny-tiny little bit."

"What measures?" I ask.

"I can chop off your arms." She taps me on my elbow with her index finger. "I can give you a Dahmer-style lobotomy with acid. Or a more traditional one with an ice pick." She taps me on my forehead and I flinch. "Mind you, I don't want to do any of that, because if I disable you, or turn you into a shuffling zombie? Taking care of you becomes a whole lot more work. But you *know* I will. Don't force my hand, Mareva."

*Don't force my hand.* This was something my father used to say to me and Leila when he was angry with us but still trying to pretend he was being dispassionate and logical in his threats of punishment. Hearing that phrase come out of Savannah's mouth makes me feel squirmy and panicky. "Okay," I say, even though all this is very, very far from okay.

"And if I have to disable you? Your children—your sentient children who will build whatever passes for Earth's new civilization—will know *me* as their mother. I will teach them what I know about justice. I will teach them what I know about mercy. I will teach them what I know about love."

"You don't know anything about love, justice, or mercy," I reply.

"Exactly. *Exactly.* I *don't.*" She leans in very close to my face until we are practically eye to eye. "So it would be really great if you could summon up some maternal instinct and actually parent your squiddos, just in case there's a chance they don't have to be actual monsters."

She helps me up the stairs and puts me to bed. I roll onto my side, away from her. The silent treatment might be childish, but it's all I have the strength for.

"I want us to be friends, Mareva. We're all each other has now. And we could have a very nice life here together, if you'd just be open to it. Be willing to put the past behind you and embrace what you have now. I know you've been lonely, and so have I."

Savannah slides into the bed behind me and spoons me. I freeze up in her embrace as she starts to stroke my hair the way my mother used to.

"I've always wanted a friend like you," she whispers. "We could be best friends. We could be like sisters. Inseparable. Forever."

She starts to quietly sing "You Are My Sunshine."

And I know, deep in the pit of my churning stomach, that

she's the reason Leila disappeared days before the Archivists sent the world to hell. I know in my bones that Savannah murdered my sister and ate her brain.

I don't know what to do.

# CHAPTER 29

Something is wrong with Erin. There's some kind of new growth on her temple. It started a few days ago as a reddish lump that looked like the beginnings of a boil or cystic acne. But now it's a shiny, gray-headed protrusion about the size of a golf ball. A tumor? An infection? I can't really tell.

She pulls her coarse white hair down over it to try to hide it. I don't think Savannah has noticed it, or if she has, she hasn't remarked on it. It's possible that Betty spends too much time with her face buried between Erin's thighs to have noticed, either.

I'm worried about Erin. And I know I shouldn't be. She's a monster now. Obviously. She's one of my captors. But I can still see the old Erin in a look or a gesture sometimes. And that gives me a fragile bit of hope that maybe all is not lost here.

It's just past 10 p.m., and I've gone upstairs to get undressed and put on my pajamas. A rap at the French doors to the balcony startles me, and I hear Erin's low growl.

"I need to speak with thee," she says. "By the toolshed."

Then I hear the whoosh of her wings as she launches off the balcony and flies back down to the ground.

I pause. This seems pretty sketchy. She, like the other Archivists, is forbidden from hurting me, although they're allowed to use pain as a motivator to keep me from escaping.

And after all, would it actually be so bad if she did manage to kill me somehow? As long as it was reasonably quick?

So I put my shirt and shoes back on and creep downstairs. Savannah has fallen asleep on the couch with Gregory loosely wrapped around her neck and shoulders. He seems to be asleep, too. One of his scarlet arms is curled possessively around a plastic baby bottle.

Seeing them sleeping so cozily there makes me feel uneasy and guilty. And maybe a little envious. I haven't been able to pick up Gregory, and the idea of touching him makes me want to vomit. It horrifies me in ways I don't fully understand. Is he a sentient cancer? An alien child? Both? Neither? Was I an unwilling host, or an unwilling mother . . . and is there any difference between the two?

Nevertheless, he's a small, helpless thing, and I feel badly that he's at Savannah's mercy. But I don't know how to fix that right now. So I quietly get my coat and go outside to see what Erin wants.

She's pacing in a tight circle by the shed, her shaggy black wings dragging icy trails through the snow. Her face is shadowed under the glaring yellow security light. I can smell ichor and raw flesh, and I hear the tiny insect wings in her feathers buzzing like a fever.

"What's going on . . ." I start, but the words fail in my throat when Erin turns toward me and I can see that she's torn open the growth on her temple. There's nothing left but a ragged, cavernous gash. It's alarmingly deep. Looks like it goes straight into her brain cavity. Ichor and some other fluid, maybe pus, runs down the side of her face.

"I cannot ascend with these memories." She holds her taloned right hand out to me, and I see a jellylike blob of something in her palm. A thin, slimy, twisted gray cord still connects to it. The other end of the cord disappears inside the wound in her head. "Thou must take them. Thou must know me."

I stare at the blob . . . and my mind reels as it makes sense of what I'm seeing. It's a half-formed almond-size cerebrum floating in a transparent sac of yellowish fluid. The gray cord must connect to her pia mater. It's as if her brain got pregnant and Erin has just carved out the still-viable embryo with her claws.

"Thou must take them!" Erin growls. "I will be purged if these are recorded with my Harvest!"

"Take? How—"

As my lips are forming the *How,* Erin's left hand shoots forward and she clamps down on the hinge of my jaw with the sides of her thumb and forefinger, forcing my mouth open wider as if she's pilling a cat. In the next second, she pops the blob into my mouth and closes my jaw over it. My front teeth snap the rubbery cord, and a foul gel squirts up between my gums and lips. It burns just a little.

"Swallow!" she hisses, as I try to break free from her powerful grip. The effort makes the healing sutures in my neck and chest ache, and I'm worried about the stitches ripping.

"I shall not let thou spit them out!" she says. "They will not harm thee!"

The sac ruptures in my mouth, and bitter, sticky saltiness washes over my tongue. I'm desperate to spit everything out, but Erin starts stroking my throat, and the reflexive urge to swallow overcomes my nausea. The clammy cerebryo slides down my throat like a raw oyster. I hate oysters.

"Is it done?" she asks.

I nod as best I can.

"I shall release thee, but thou must not call for Savannah. Thou wilt not enjoy what she shalt do to remove mine memories from thee."

Two vivid images abruptly flash through my mind. The first is of an antique key down at the bottom of a Folgers can on a shelf in the basement. The second is of a hidden keyhole near a set of dusty shelves. I see myself putting the key in the lock, turning it, and watching the shelves swing out to reveal a secret room.

"What just happened?" I breathe when she lets me go.

"Explore not until the stars are right." Wincing, she carefully takes hold of the trailing, leaking cord and ties it off close to the wound in her skull. "Keep what thou seest to thyself."

"What . . . what have you done to me?"

"I hath given thee the ability to choose thine future." She severs the cord a few inches below the knot with the razor edge of her index finger talon and eats it, sucking it down like a noodle. "I shalt not pretend that thine choices are benign, but thou hast them now."

And with that, she turns and flies out into the darkness.

• • •

The next morning, after a night of fractured sleep and weird dreams, I awaken to the sound of Savannah stomping down the stairs, cursing. "God damn it, Michael! You could have told me about this weeks ago, but *no*, you have to spring this shit on me at the last minute. Not cool, Michael! Not cool!"

What on earth is going on now? I put on my robe and cautiously go downstairs. Savannah is having a full-on manic episode in the kitchen. She's yanking open silverware drawers and tossing all the sharp knives onto the kitchen island, all the while muttering and cursing to herself.

"Coulda gotten some scalpels," she fumes. "Coulda gotten sutures. But fine. Whatever! This is all fucking fine!"

She notices me standing there and shakes a knife at me. Her pupils are hugely dilated. I wonder if she's on drugs. "You know, it's a real goddamned pain in my ass that I ate those medical professionals, because every last one of them is backseat driving right now. Telling me what a goddamned shit show tonight is gonna be compared to how it should be if I just had time to gather real supplies. A God. Damned. Shit. Show!"

"What . . . what's going on?" I venture.

"The Cleaving," she seethes. "So special. So secret. So I wasn't on the need-to-know list until the actual day of. It isn't as if I have to make any preparations or anything! Oh, wait. I totally do! *Fuckers!* Goddamned ass rat fucking *fuckers*!"

Savannah finds a whetstone in the junk drawer and starts

aggressively sharpening the first boning knife she lays her hands on. This worries me on a profound level.

"What's the Cleaving?" I'm cringing before she even opens her mouth to answer.

"Well. The Cleaving is a very special time when . . ." She pauses, tapping the tip of the knife against the stone. Looking me up and down. Assessing me.

"On second thought," she says, "if I tell you, it *might* violate the rules about not letting any unnecessary harm come to you. So I think that, psychologically, ignorance is your friend and you should just spend the day chilling in your suite upstairs. Try out some of the spa shit Mrs. Mayne left behind. Catch up on your reading. Whatever. Just stay up there, stay out of my way, and don't go outside. Especially after sundown."

•  •  •

I know better than to cross Savannah when she's in this kind of mood. So I sit in the window seat in my room, watching her carry tarps, boxes of knives, and other supplies into the barn. And I fully intend to stay upstairs the rest of the day and into the night.

Except that I'm gradually snared in a partial memory of Erin's. It's not attached to any words or specific images. It's a blend of anticipation, fear, and desire that rises in me when I wonder what the Cleaving means. These emotions grow stronger, feel more and more like my own as the day marches on, and by dusk I'm caught in the grip of an intense urge to visit the barn.

This tension between my rat brain's insistence that it's most prudent to stay inside and my superstitious mind's conviction that this new instinct is absolutely something to obey—my nerves are wrecked. I can't read, can't even just sit still and go through mindfulness exercises on my phone.

So I go downstairs, purely intending to microwave some frozen mac and cheese in the hopes that comfort food might help.

Savannah's mania has passed and she's crashed, asleep on the couch with Gregory after another feeding. Apparently he's the physical embodiment of two doses of Xanax. Or maybe he's slowly draining her life energy. My skin still crawls at the thought of picking him up.

Then, I don't so much hear as *feel* Erin scream in passion and pain. It's like being punched in my spine.

The strange, alarming desire to find her, and Betty, is overwhelming.

So I get into my boots and my coat and go outside. Immediately, I hear more Archivists screaming. Gasping. Panting. Sobbing. Wailing. The cacophony is at once dreadful and thrilling. It sounds like the gods themselves are torturing them all to death. Anticipation and terror build with every step I take across the thawing mud and dead grass toward the huge red barn.

And I am not even remotely prepared for what I find.

The floor of the barn, including the stalls that haven't seen horses for fifty years, is entirely covered in a few inches of straw. Atop them is a patchwork of blue, green, red, and gray canvas and plastic tarpaulins. Archivists writhe upon the tarps in pairs, triads, and quads. The air is moist and rank with the stinks of carrion breath, ichor, sweat, urine, semen, and vaginal fluid.

They're rutting into each other . . . and slashing themselves open with knives, box cutters, and sometimes their talons. The scene before me is like something Hieronymus Bosch might have painted after he was kidnapped at church, drugged, and taken to an orgy in a slaughterhouse.

"All exist in and with one another!" Erin screams. I can't figure out where she is in this grisly congregation.

"Flesh to flesh, and blood to blood!" reply the others.

"The Mother of All beholds us!" cries Erin. "Let her see us rise from the forms of this world, and from the fetter of oblivion!"

"Flesh to flesh, and blood to blood!"

*There.* I see her. Erin is grinding against Betty's thigh on a red tarp near the middle of the barn. They've both cut themselves wide open from their clavicles to their pubic bones, their feathers matted with gore. Erin has carved open her left side, and Betty her right. I can see layers of seeping purple muscle. Shuddering pink viscera bulges through where they cut more deeply. Erin pulls Betty up for a wet, sticky, drooling kiss . . . and Betty lifts a big orange staple gun and begins to pinch their severed flesh together to join it with gleaming steel.

I look away . . . but it's happening everywhere. The trio to their left is stitching themselves together with huge leatherworking needles and dental floss. Another group is using awls and brass wire. They've cut the arms and legs off one Archivist to make him fit in their new flesh assembly. His severed limbs lie twitching on the floor, the taloned fingers and toes flexing, seeking purchase.

The Cleaving. I understand what this means now. I wish I didn't.

● ● ●

At first, my rat brain is convinced that the Archivists will certainly die after what they've done to themselves. I go out in the morning before Savannah awakens and peek into the barn to see how Erin's doing. Part of me doesn't want to know, but the rest of me is compelled. The stench inside is awful. And I can't see much but shaggy mounds of black feathers. But I can hear dozens of bodies shallowly breathing. They're still alive, or many of them are.

My rat brain tells me that this is an ideal time to run. Escape to the city and see if I can find Dr. Shapiro or Dr. Kaz. Thanks to Erin's memories, I think I might know where Dr. Shapiro is. I have an image of a street, and a doorway. It'll take awhile to find with no internet, but I think I could do it.

But my superstitious mind has latched on to a different set of memories, and it's convinced that I need to stay awhile longer.

I need to wait for . . . what? It's not clear. But the feeling that I shouldn't try to leave right now is very, very strong.

My indecision makes me feel ashamed. Am I giving my superstitious mind more faith than it deserves? Have I decided that staying is best because, deep down, I know that leaving here is a risk . . . and I'm fundamentally a coward?

The five teratomatic embryos are the size of chickpeas now. Gregory was the size of a big orange when he quickened and ruptured his cyst. For him, that took weeks. Will these grow faster? Slower? If I can actually escape Savannah, but can't find a doctor before I'm overcome . . . I shudder to think about it.

So I stay where I am and wait to see what happens.

• • •

On the fifth morning after the Cleaving, I hear a few of the Archivists moving through the straw, groaning. Coughing. But I can't see very much through the gap in the doors, and I can't bring myself to take a closer look.

That afternoon, I watch from the bedroom window seat as Savannah, wearing old, ragged gray sweats, hauls a hose out to the barn and disappears inside. Soon, rust-red water dotted with black feathers floods out under the sliding doors and soaks the dirt. I hear roars and screams, and I wonder if Savannah has done something to get herself attacked. Maybe killed? Can she die? If she's dead, what will the surviving Archivists do?

I watch, and wait. Just as I'm working up the nerve to go down and look in the barn, she emerges unharmed, wringing filthy water out of her sweatshirt.

• • •

On the sixth morning, just before sunrise, the bed starts to shake. At best half awake, I wonder if there's something strange going on with the HVAC system, or if the mattress has some weird built-in massage feature that somehow got tripped. But the shaking gets stronger and stronger. The headboard rattles against the wall, and one of the Maynes's framed watercolors bangs to the carpet.

A rhythmic low-frequency thrumming increases in volume along with the shaking, a nearly subsonic *voom voom voom* like the heartbeat of some unimaginably large creature. I can feel it in my bones, my skull, in my teeth.

Eerie purple and green lights like the aurora borealis undulate through the curtains over the French doors. We're too far south to see the northern lights like this. What could be happening outside? I get up, put on my robe, and start to open the rattling balcony doors. A blast of cold wind blows them open the moment I release the latch.

There's a gigantic hole in the sky above the city. It must be ten or twenty miles wide. The edges are ringed in dazzling purple and green plasma. Through the hole, I can see an enormous ringed planet silhouetted against a dim violet sun. I'm amazed, and terrified at the technology and power that creating this spectacular portal must have required.

And then I see the massive dark spaceship—or perhaps a space station—emerging through the rift between worlds. It's spherical, shaped like two wagon wheels interlocked with each other at ninety-degree angles. Round spokes from each ring join in a sphere in the middle of the structure. The miles-wide ship rotates like a small moon as it majestically lowers itself to hover high above the city. The outer surfaces of its huge rings are covered in glowing structures that look like amber eyes. They might be part of its propulsion system, or something else entirely.

Erin's scream cuts through the bass rumble: "We are released from this world! It is time to join our masters in the star shadows!"

I can't see the barn from this balcony, and I'm thinking about running downstairs to see what the Archivists are doing, when the four-winged creature that used to be white-haired Erin and lion-faced Betty flaps up from the yard and begins the flight toward the ship. Close behind, other Archivist fusions follow. I see creatures with four, six, and eight wings, and half as many heads. In the distance, I see the tiny dots of other Archivists from the city flying up to the ship.

Have they all truly left? I run downstairs and encounter Savannah in the foyer.

"You saw them ascend?" she asks.

I nod. "Are they all gone?"

"Ours are. It could be there are some leftovers in the city. Ones whose second transformations didn't take properly. But I don't know."

"Did you know this was going to happen?" I ask.

"It was the next obvious step after the Cleaving, but I didn't think it would happen so soon." She chews her lip uncertainly. "I thought we'd have their help a bit longer. We'll miss it. But I guess they've earned their trip to space, those lucky bunnies." Savannah sounds genuinely wistful. "Some day that bell will toll for me, and I'll get wings, too."

My stomach drops when I consider what the Ascension might mean with regard to Dr. Kaz and Dr. Shapiro. "Does . . . does this mean they killed all the survivors?"

She shrugs. "I don't know. There may still be some people out there, but there can't be very many. Either way, it's probably just you and me and Gregory now, sugar pie."

Then she winks. "At least until your next squiddo comes along."

# CHAPTER 30

With the Archivists gone, Erin's memory of the basement blossoms in my mind. I can't stop thinking about the key, and what might lie behind the hidden doorway in the secret room. But I manage to stay calm and keep my curiosity at bay until that night.

After I'm certain that Savannah is asleep, I head down to the basement. This part of the mansion wasn't renovated much at all, and the walls and floor are unpainted mortared limestone stained brown and black by mold and water. A derelict gravity furnace is down here, its metal arms spreading out to the rafters like an octopus. Savannah has been down here frequently and has wiped much of the dust off the old wooden shelves, possibly only incidentally, as she's pulled down boxes and crates to see what's inside.

But I spot the old, rusty red Folgers can down on a lower shelf, right where Erin's memory said it would be. I pick it up and sort through the debris of nuts, bolts, and old pennies until I find the green-patinaed antique brass key. I make my way farther back into the basement, where there are some warped board shelves stacked with obvious junk that Savannah hasn't paid much attention to. Things like old rusted watering cans, a coil of rotted red rubber hose, and parts of an old child's bicycle.

On a short section of wall near the shelves is a very old, extremely corroded push-button switch plate that clearly has been rendered obsolete by the newer overhead light fixture with an attached chain switch. The plate is missing its lower screw. I carefully pry the switch plate up a little with the key and push it to the left, revealing a keyhole that looks to be in much better condition.

I slot the key into the hole and twist. There's the click and whirr of some kind of mechanism behind the masonry, then a faint *clunk* and the shelves shift ever so slightly. I take hold of the nearest wooden shelf brace and pull, and the whole set of shelves swings wide to reveal a polished dark wood pocket door set into the stones.

As I slide the door open, a warm yellow light comes on in the room beyond. It's a large, wood-paneled study for some wealthy, educated gentleman of yesteryear, and my initial impression is that it's a perfect time capsule of the early 1920s. But as I step inside and start examining the furniture and fixtures, I realize that Mark Mayne definitely found this room and updated it. For one thing, the gilded gas lamps on the walls have been fitted with LEDs that mimic flickering flames. And the floor-to-ceiling bookshelves on either side of the mahogany desk have a few modern titles like *High Performance Habits* and *High Growth Handbook*, among leather-bound volumes from the nineteenth century and esoteric clothbound hardcovers from the early twentieth century.

Flanking a dark tufted leather love seat are a pair of Heathkit floor speakers. On top of the leftmost speaker is a Technics record player from the 1970s or 1980s. An album rests atop it. I feel a chill when I see the strange yellow symbol on the cover: Erin has a memory of seeing a sign like this in a courtyard at Greenlawn. I go to the album and inspect the cover more closely.

*Into the Hands of the Living God*
*An Etude in G Minor for Violin*
**Composed by Dunric Cage-Satin with Dr. Alexander Harroe**
**Performed by Caroline Cage-Satin**

I'm filled with a dreadful urge to listen to this strange album. My heart pounding, I slide it out of its paper sleeve, set it on the turntable, and set the needle on the vinyl.

There's an initial crackle from dust and faint scratches, and then I hear the melancholy strains of a solo violin. The music is atonal, unusual, and hearing it makes me strangely dizzy. I have to steady myself against the arm of the love seat. My vision starts to go dark at the edges.

Suddenly the room falls away and I find myself standing upon a high, barren cliff above a huge lake with driving waves. The air has an unhealthy odor to it, and in the sky there hangs a trio of strange, misshapen moons. Opposite the setting twin suns, three black stars rise, their bright coronas gleaming through the streaked clouds.

When the dark starlight touches my face, it's as if a supernova has gone off in my mind. I fall to my knees on the lichen-covered rocks, unable to even take a breath to scream as my mind burns with a transcendent darkness, hot as any stellar cataclysm.

I hear footsteps and the rustling of robes, and through my tears I see a regal iron boot beneath an ochre hem embroidered with the tiny white bones of birds and mice.

"At last, you've arrived," the stranger says, in a voice that makes me want to drive spikes into my brain. "The little mother. So much consequence in such an inconsequential form."

I look up at him. His face is blank, pale. It doesn't look like flesh at all.

"Why are you wearing a mask?" I ask, my mind still reeling.

"Mask? Why, I wear no mask." He sounds amused.

"Why am I here?" I stammer.

"I wish to give you a clearer glimpse of your future."

The stranger leans down and touches my forehead with a bone-thin finger.

Suddenly, I am hovering above the hilltop, a millennia in the future. The mansion, the barn, the solar panels are all gone. In their place is an enormous, shuddering amorphous mass of gray-white flesh. It has no legs, no arms, no eyes. Hundreds of mutated creatures—some look like spiders, others like millipedes, others like cephalopods, and every form in between—swarm over the bloated monstrosity, pulling squirming larvae from fleshy sacs that rupture like boils. The monstrosity moans, wracked by pain and pleasure in equal measure from this endless spawning process. Meanwhile, a steady train of other creatures brings food to the vast monster's hungry maw, a misshapen hole lined with rows of teeth that still look vaguely human . . .

"Oh my God," I gasp. I'm back at the stranger's feet, gripping lichen-covered rocks. "That's . . . that's what I become, isn't it? Oh God."

"It is," he replies evenly.

The fate I've just witnessed is unimaginably worse than death. "I . . . I can't . . . I won't . . ."

"But alas, you will. You will become the transformed Earth's new fertility deity. All-powerful yet helpless. Wise and yet mindless. Revered and yet an abomination. It's a terrible thing to become a living god."

"Please just kill me," I whisper.

"Oh, my adversaries have ensured that even I cannot." The stranger sounds amused again. "Your immortality is most irreversible."

"Jesus. Is there really nothing I can do?"

"There is one thing."

I look up at his uncanny face, afraid to hope. "What is it?"

"When you return to Earth, you will find a small gift from me. While you wear it, you shall not bear more offspring. You will have the power to escape and live out your immortality elsewhere."

"Why are you helping me?"

"I do not offer help. I offer a choice. The other gods offer you divinity and adoration. I offer a much more difficult, lonelier path."

"Why are you offering me this choice, then?"

"If you refuse the destiny for which you've been groomed, there will be no repopulation of this planet. The world will be silent but for the wind in the trees and the waves crashing upon the empty shores, just as I wish it to be. But the choice is yours."

• • •

I slowly regain consciousness in the study. The record has ended. I'm lying facedown on the wool Oriental carpet beside the love seat. It smells like dust and old mold.

A pale ring lies on the carpet, about a foot away from my face. I sit up and pick up the annulet. It's about three quarters of an inch in diameter, looks like it was carved from a cross section of bone—maybe a human radius—and has an inlay of the Yellow Sign. Putting it on is obviously a terrible idea. A terrible, awful, no-good idea. The only thing likely to be worse would be not putting it on.

"Here goes everything," I mutter.

And I slip the ring onto my right index finger. There's a bright flash of pain. Burning in my skin and a stabbing agony deep in the marrow of my finger bone. I try to pull the ring off, but that just makes it worse.

I stagger to my feet and go to one of the light sconces to see what the damage is. The ring has sprouted bony spikes through my skin and into my phalange. It's welded itself in place.

But on the plus side—and as far as I'm concerned, this is a *major* plus side—I can feel the ever-present itching around the five teratomatic encysted embryos subsiding. I touch one of the lumps and it feels softer. Like maybe it's dissolving.

"Hallelujah," I whisper.

• • •

"What the *shit* is that on your finger?" Savannah's eyes are wide, scared and furious.

I freeze, the platter of breakfast sausage in my hands. "It's a ring?"

"That's the fucking *Yellow Sign*. It does not belong on your goddamned hand. Take it off!"

"I . . . I can't?"

"The fuck you can't." Savannah gets up from her chair and storms around the dining room table. She grabs my hand and yanks on the ring. The pain makes me scream so loudly she almost lets me go.

"I told you I can't take it off!"

"Oh, I'll take it off, trust me." She grabs me by the wrist and drags me toward the kitchen.

"No! Stop!" I try to resist, but she's far too strong.

"I told you what would happen if you forced my hand." She pauses by the knife rack over the stove to grab a meat cleaver. "You've fucked around, and you're about to find out."

She's going to chop off my finger or my hand. No. I'll be maimed forever. I'll be one more step down the road to becoming that limbless breeding monstrosity.

The panic in me rises to a heat that pulses down my arm to the ring. Suddenly I've jerked my hand out of her grip, cocked it back, and slammed my fist into the side of her head. Savannah's knees buckle and she hits the floor like a sack of wet designer laundry. The meat cleaver clatters on the tiles and settles a few inches from my feet.

I've never hit anyone before in my entire life. When bullies messed with me at school, either Leila defended me or I just froze up, like I'm doing right now. I hit her really hard. It seems like my hand should hurt, but it doesn't. The ring still feels warm. I guess it redirected all the force of the blow into Savannah.

Have I killed her? I kneel and feel for a pulse in her neck. Her heart's still beating, strong and regular. I check under her eyelids. Her pupils both look the same. It seems that I only knocked her out.

But . . . should I kill her? She's definitely going to try to dismember me when she wakes up. Killing her would be the smart thing to do. I pick up the cleaver, put it to her throat . . . and I just can't do it. She's unconscious. It just feels like a lot, to jump directly from punching my first person to murdering my first person.

So, clearly, I need to get the heck out of here. I dig through her jeans pockets and find her keys so I can finally get the hateful shackle off my ankle. Then I drag her into the laundry room and wedge a chair under the doorknob. This won't hold her forever, but it should hold her long enough.

I run upstairs to start packing.

• • •

On my way out of the house with my stuffed-to-bursting external frame hiking backpack, I go into the nursery where Gregory lies sleeping on some folded towels, inside a large aquarium. I have only been in here once or twice, and I still haven't been able to get myself to pick him up.

"What am I going to do with you?" I mutter.

There are three obvious choices before me. First, I leave Gregory where he is and hope that Savannah takes care of him and doesn't turn him into a real monster. And that's supposing that I haven't put her in a coma. Because if I have, he'll slowly die of thirst in here.

Which leads to choice number 2: I kill him to preemptively put him out of his misery. But I don't actually know how to euthanize him quickly; I don't know how his anatomy works. Even if I did know what would constitute a fast, certain, killing blow, I'm not sure I have it in me. I could never sacrifice the rats in a biology lab. I don't even like killing hornets, and they're all absolutely vindictive jerks.

So, by default, that leaves choice number 3.

I take off my backpack, square my shoulders, and inhale

deeply. March forward to the aquarium and lift off the lid. I can do this. I can. I *will*.

I reach down, pick up Gregory, and lift him into my arms.

He's heavier than I expected, probably ten pounds or so. His red skin is covered in a short silver fuzz that feels like velvet. His arms and body are warm and firm, with just a touch of squishiness. He smells . . . a bit like sardines, if I'm being honest. Not exactly that good baby smell people always talked about. Probably some room for improvement there.

His blue eyes open sleepily, and he yawns at me, seemingly unconcerned that I'm holding him and Savannah is nowhere to be seen.

My rat brain is panicking right now. *You don't know anything about taking care of babies and this isn't even a baby oh Jesus what are you doing?*

Meanwhile, my superstitious mind says, *Have some faith. We can figure this out.*

I say to Gregory, "So, yeah. You wanna go look for Dr. Shapiro with me?"

He yawns again and smacks his tiny purple gums together. "Agafa."

"I will take that as a yes. Let's get your stuff together."

# ACKNOWLEDGMENTS

While writing is a solitary endeavor, it takes a whole lot of people to put a book into readers' hands. So I have a lot of people to thank! First, I'd like to thank my editor, Kelly Lonesome, and other Tor Nightfire staff: Jordan Hanley, Sarah Pannenberg, and Michael Dudding in marketing; Laura Etzkorn in publicity; Jessica Katz in production; and Lesley Worrell in art. I also owe deep thanks to my agent, Joanna Volpe, and her assistants, Abigail Donoghue and Jordan Hill, for representing my book. I'd also like to thank Jennifer Udden for getting the ball rolling at New Leaf Literary and Tor Nightfire.

I'd also like to thank my first readers and the subject matter experts I consulted as I was working on my manuscript: Alex Myers, Veronica Vega at Salt & Sage Books, Beverly Joseph Horsley, Elizabeth Lucas, Michael Lucas, Michelle R. Lane, Robert Pyatt, Scott Slemmons, and Tonia Ransom. And I must thank Julie Megchelsen and Mark Freeman for cheerfully accommodating my strange hours and generally feral state while I was under deadlines. Go Team Insomnia!

I'd also like to thank Slava Venske for the delightfully clacky Durgod Taurus mechanical keyboard that I composed most of this novel on.

I wouldn't have nearly as much time to write if it weren't for my Patreon, so I'd like to thank all my novel-level supporters: Alin Sari, Arasibo Campeche, Brit Marshalk, Donna Munro, Dora Knez, Eric Grizzle, Holly Zaldivar, Jim Leach, Joe and Gay Haldeman, Joel K., Kira Barnes, Linda Addison, Michael

Cieslak, Michelle Smith, Rebecca Allred, Roberta Slocumb, Sarah Hans, Scott A. Johnson, Shannon Eichorn, Stephanie Heminger, and Weston Kincade.

This book began its life as a couple of short stories that editors requested from me. I'd like to thank Doug Murano and Michael Bailey for soliciting "My Knowing Glance," which served as the seed of Savannah's story, for *Miscreations: Gods, Monstrosities & Other Horrors*. And I must thank Maurice Broaddus and Jerry Gordon for soliciting "Magdala Amygdala" for *Dark Faith: Invocations*. It was my first foray into this world, and Erin and Betty's story is vastly expanded in this novel.

I also have to thank Maurice for sending me my all-time favorite editorial acceptance for that piece:

"Lucy, what the fuck is wrong with you? Good grief that story was messed up. Thanks. I think."

# TUSCANY

*'Quaffing glass after glass of Chianti inspired
Elizabeth Barrett Browning to write her best poetry,
and there's no reason why the wines of Tuscany
shouldn't bring out the best in you as well.'*

Dana Facaros and Michael Pauls

# About the Guide

The **full-colour introduction** gives the authors' overview of the region, together with suggested **itineraries** and a regional **'where to go' map** and **feature** to help you plan your trip.

Illuminating and entertaining **cultural chapters** on local history, art, food, wine and everyday life give you a rich flavour of the region.

**Planning Your Trip** starts with the basics of when to go, getting there and getting around, coupled with other useful information, including a section for disabled travellers. The **Practical A–Z** deals with all the **essential information** and **contact details** that you may need while you are away.

The **regional chapters** are arranged in a loose touring order, with plenty of public transport and driving information. The authors' top **'Don't Miss'** 🟊 **sights** are highlighted at the start of each chapter.

A **language and pronunciation guide**, a **glossary** of cultural terms, ideas for **further reading** and a comprehensive **index** can be found at the end of the book.

Although everything listed in this guide is **personally recommended**, our authors inevitably have their own favourite places to eat and stay. Whenever you see this **Authors' Choice** ★ icon beside a listing, you will know that it is a little bit out of the ordinary.

## Restaurant Price Guide (*see also* p.73)

| | | |
|---|---|---|
| Very expensive | €€€€ | €60 + |
| Expensive | €€€ | €40–60 |
| Moderate | €€ | €25–40 |
| Inexpensive | € | under €25 |

## Hotel Price Guide (*see also* p.67)

| In Florence | | | Elsewhere in the Region | | |
|---|---|---|---|---|---|
| Luxury | €€€€€ | €250+ | Luxury | €€€€€ | €230+ |
| Very expensive | €€€ | €180–250 | Very expensive | €€€€ | €150–230 |
| Expensive | €€€ | €130–180 | Expensive | €€€ | €100–150 |
| Moderate | €€ | €75–130 | Moderate | €€ | €60–100 |
| Inexpensive | € | under €75 | Inexpensive | € | under €60 |

# About the Author

**Dana Facaros** and **Michael Pauls**, now based in southwest France, spent three years in a tiny Italian village, where they suffered massive overdoses of food, art and wine. They have written more than 40 guides for Cadogan.

5th Edition published 2010

A glass of wine before dinner on the garden terrace, the olives glinting in the last flash of the setting sun as the geometric vineyards lose their rigid order in the melting darkness, and only the black daggers of the cypresses stand out against the first stars of the evening – where could you be but Tuscany? It needs no introduction, this famous twilit land, where Titans of art five hundred years ago copied and then outdid nature, and where nature gets her gentle revenge by rivalling art.

Travellers have been coming to central Italy ever since the Middle Ages, to learn, to see and to understand. Most have come with their Baedekers or Ruskins or Berensons in hand, and even today it isn't easy to escape the weight of generations of worthy opinions or to avoid treading on those same old grapes of purple prose. After all, most of what we call Western civilization was either rediscovered or invented here, leaving behind works that have lost none of their power; at times it seems as if the artists of the early 1400s descended from outer space with their secret messages for the imagination. Anyway, to the mass of accumulated opinion we now add ours, for better or worse, but mostly in the hope of provoking some of your own.

But at the end of the day – or, as we are, at thee dawn of the 21st century, when times seem to be changing faster than we can or care to – the enduring charm of Tuscany is in that dreamy glass of wine, in those hills that look exactly as they did when Piero painted them, in the bartender who's a dead ringer for Lorenzo de' Medici, in those bewitching Etruscan smiles that seem to have been smiled only yesterday. Things have stayed the same way for

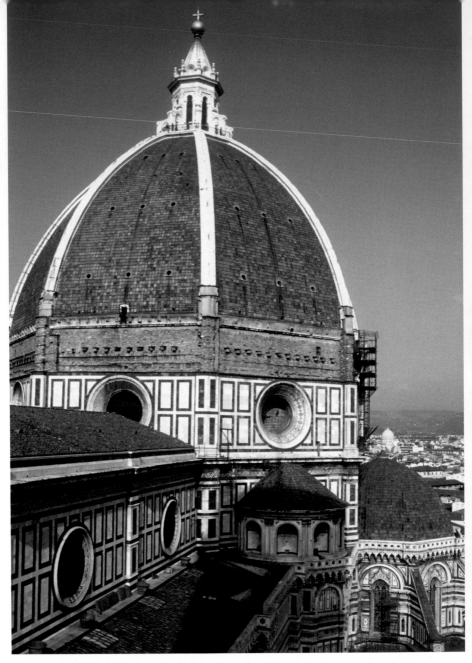

*The Duomo and campanile, Florence*

centuries not by any accident, or economic reason, or by divine decree of some Tuscan National Trust, but because that's the way people like them. People here make as few concessions to the new millennium as possible, and their Brigadoon may not be for everyone. They're not catching up with the world; the world's catching up with them.

# Top Ten Places to Visit

1 **Florence** il Magnifico, of course, p.79
2 The exquisite, medieval beauty of **Siena** – and the Palio if you can get a ticket, p.327
3 **Arezzo** and **Sansepolcro**, and their Piero della Francesca masterpieces, pp.414 and 421
4 Delightfully civilized **Lucca**, with its tree-lined walls and Puccini arias, p.257
5 **Pisa**'s Field of Miracles – much more than just a crooked tower, p.288
6 Unique hill towns – Etruscan **Volterra** and the many-towered **San Gimignano**, pp.362 and 368
7 **Monte Oliveto Maggiore** and Sodoma's frescoes, p.384
8 The handsome wine towns (and wines) of **Montalcino** and **Montepulciano**, pp.385 and 391
9 **Cortona** and its views over the Valdichiana, p.428
10 Nikki de Saint-Phalle's joyous **Tarot Garden**, p.326

*Below: The rooftops of Siena*

# Where to Go

Tuscany's extraordinary capital is the place to start. If you've already done **Florence** three or four times, you might have a good excuse to skip it: it's crowded, intense, and hard on the wallet. But with an outrageous portion of the Western world's most sublime art and architecture, it's also a big fat must.

Next up, just south of Florence, is fabled **Chianti**, where perfect Renaissance villas, villages and chapels dot rolling countryside, striped with the vines that produce the region's best known wine. North of Florence, the emerald green **Mugello**, the cradle of the Medici, is far more secretive.

*Above: Chianti landscape*
*Below: San Michele in Foro, Lucca*
*Bottom: Portoferraio, Elba*

In the busy **Valdarno**, west of Florence, **Empoli**, **Prato** and **Pistoia** have their share of great art and architecture; here too are the exquisite landscapes around **Vinci**, the relatively unspoiled Apennines to the north of Pistoia, and the atmospheric 19th-century spa, **Montecatini Terme**.

On to Puccini's birthplace, the urbane walled city of **Lucca**, before heading north into mountain micro-regions, dotted with sturdy hill towns: the beautifully rugged if relatively unvisited **Garfagnana** with the Grotto del Vento, Tuscany's best cave, and the even more remote **Lunigiana**, home to the intriguing prehistoric statue-*steles* in Pontrémoli.

From here we march down the **Tuscan coast**, north to south. After the marble mountains above **Carrara**, most of it is flat and dull, but ribboned with beaches and parasol pines. Here you'll find evergreen **Viareggio**, which also hosts Tuscany's biggest carnival, **Livorno**, famous for seafood, and **Pisa**, which needs no introduction. Here too are Tuscany's seven islands, from the big resort island of **Elba** to tiny **Montecristo**, plus the wetlands of the **Maremma**, home of Tuscany's cowboys, plus the swish resorts around Monte Argentario.

Next, **Siena**, Tuscany's most beautiful city, followed by the art-filled hill towns to the west: **San Gimignano**, **Volterra** and **Massa Marittima** with one of the best cathedrals in Italy. More stunning hill towns but far fewer tourists wait in **southern Tuscany**, with its lovely landscapes: highlights here include the planned Renaissance town of **Pienza**, Il Sodoma's frescoes at **Monte Oliveto Maggiore**, the wine towns of **Montalcino** and **Montepulciano**, and the Etruscan tombs around **Chiusi**.

Finally we head east to pretty **Arezzo**, famous for its frescoes by Piero della Francesca. There are more exquisite landscapes in the **Valtiberina** and **Valdichiana**, source of all the *bistecca alla fiorentina*, and last but not least, two splendid, arty hill towns, **Cortona** and **Sansepolcro**.

EMILIA-ROMAGNA

Pontremoli

10
LUCCA,
THE GARFAGNANA
& LUNIGIANA

Abetone

08
CHIANTI & THE
MUGELLO

Pistoia

Prato

11
THE
TUSCAN
COAST

Lucca

07
FLORENCE

09
THE
VALDARNO,
PRATO & PISTOIA

Florence

THE
MARCHES

Pisa

Livorno

Gorgona

Casciana Terme

08
CHIANTI & THE
MUGELLO

Sestino

15
AREZZO &
ITS PROVINCE

S. Gimignano

Castellina in Chianti

Volterra

TUSCANY

Arezzo

Siena

12
SIENA

13
HILL TOWNS
WEST OF SIENA

Montepulciano

Capraia

Massa
Marittima

UMBRIA

Piombino

14
SOUTHERN
TUSCANY

Elba

Pianosa

Orbetello

LAZIO

Montecristo

Giglio

N

Giannutri

20 km

10 miles

Tyrrhenian Sea

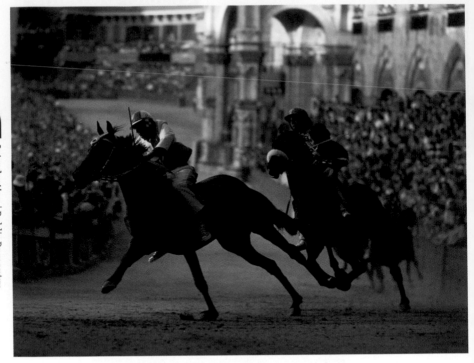

*The Palio, Siena*

# Public Pageantry

No one puts on a show like the Italians – this land of compulsive exhibitionists lays on spectacles to make your eyes pop, especially the Tuscans who like nothing better than swanning around in the gorgeous medieval and Renaissance costumes of their ancestors. For all the pageantry, the best thing about Tuscany's festivals is that they aren't put on for the benefit of the tourist industry: they are part of town life. The ten most lavish are:

- The **Palio**, the horse race around the Campo in Siena, in July and August, p.336
- *Calcio Storico* (historic football) in Piazza Santa Croce, Florence, in June, p.59
- **Joust of the Saracen**, Arezzo, in September, p.59
- **Giostra del Ponte**, traditional tug-of-war, Pisa, in June, p.59
- **Crossbow contest** in Sansepolcro, in September, p.59
- **Joust of the Bear**, Pistoia, in July, p.59
- **Palio dei Cerri**, Cerreto Guidi, in September, p.59
- **Crossbow tournament** in Massa Marittima, in May, p.59
- **Festa di San Ranieri**, a colourful historic regatta, Pisa, in June, p.59
- **Festa del Barbarossa**, commemorating the meeting of pope and emperor, San Quirico d'Orcia, in June, p.59

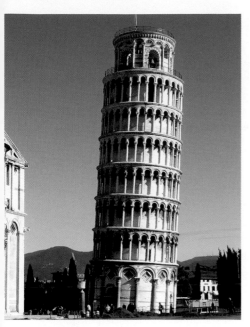

# Medieval Tuscany

Florence didn't invent the Renaissance out of thin air: wealthy through wool, banking and trade, the city and its medieval rivals Pisa, Siena, Pistoia, Prato, Lucca and Arezzo nurtured a pool of highly skilled and intelligent artists and architects who left masterpieces across the region. Not surprisingly, precocious Florence (p.79), with its baptistry, San Miniato, Orsanmichele, Bargello, Palazzo Vecchio and Duomo, has plenty to show. Outside Florence are:

- **Siena**, where the whole city is a medieval masterpiece, p.327
- **Pisa**, Field of Miracles, museums, and San Piero a Grado, p.287
- **Pistoia**, Sant'Andrea, the *centro storico*, San Giovanni Fuorocivitas, p.240
- **Massa Marittima**, the magnificent cathedral , p.377
- **San Gimignano**, Collegiata frescoes and medieval skyscrapers, p.362
- **Lucca**, cathedral and San Michele, p.257
- **Volterra**, civic buildings and art in the cathedral and San Francesco, p.368
- **Certaldo**, Boccaccio's well-preserved home town, p.228
- The bizarre **Pieve di Castelvecchio**, near Pescia, p.253
- **Empoli**, Collegiata and museum, p.223

*Above: Leaning Tower of Pisa*
*Below: San Gimignano*

*Above: Ruins in Fiesole*
*Below: Roman theatre, Volterra*

# Etruscans and Romans

Tuscany takes its name from the ancient Etruscans, and the mysterious ancestors of today's Tuscans left their mark across the region. Their stone effigies fill the museums, smiling mysteriously on the lids of the sarcophagi. What was the joke? After 2,500 years, we'll probably never know, but brushes with the Etruscans, after all, taught the Romans everything they knew. These are some of the best places to seek out the things they left behind:

- **Volterra** and its Etruscan arch, Roman theatre, and museum with the famous elongated Etruscan figure known as 'the Shadow', p.368
- **Chiusi** and the only painted Etruscan tombs in Tuscany, as well as a good museum, p.397
- **Florence**'s excellent but often overlooked Archaeological Museum, p.150
- **Fiesole**'s Etruscan walls, Roman walls, and museum, p.189
- The Etruscan gate, tombs and museum in **Cortona**, p.428
- **Arezzo**'s Roman amphitheatre and museum, p.414
- The Etruscan cities of the coast: **Populonia**, p.305, **Vetulonia**, p.319, **Roselle**, p.319, and **Ansedonia**, p.326
- Carved Etruscan rock tombs around **Pitigliano** and **Sovana**, p.403
- **Asciano**'s Museo Etrusco, p.383
- The 'Frontone' temple façade at **Orbetello**, p.321

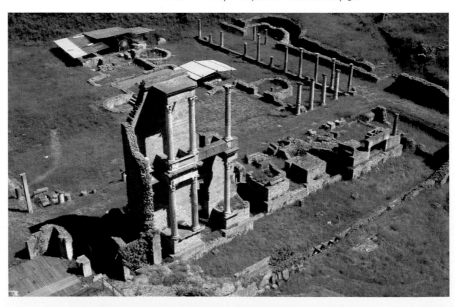

# Itinerary 1: Landscapes and Wines

Tuscany's artistry isn't confined to museums and churches; it also produces masterpieces in the bottle, many of which are unknown outside of Italy.

**Day 1** Start in Florence and head west to **Carmignano,** p.196, **Cerreto Guidi** and **Vinci**, p.226 (wines: Carmignano and Chianti)

**Day 2** 'The Valley of Mists': **Montecatini Alto**, p.251, **Collodi** (also famous as the hometown of Pinocchio, p.254) and **Montecarlo**, p.267 (wines: Bianco della Valdinievole and Montecarlo)

**Day 3** Head south of the Arno to the hill town of **San Minato**, p.227, and environs, and **Certaldo**, p.228 (wines: Bianco Pisano di S. Torpè and Chianti)

**Day 4 San Gimignano**, p.362, and **Colle di Val d'Elsa**, p.359 (wine: Vernaccia di San Gimignano and Chianti Colli Senesi)

**Days 5–6 Barberino Val d'Elsa**, p.208, and **San Casciano**, p.207, to the Chiantigiana (the Florence–Siena wine route) and **Greve in Chianti**, p.210 (wines: Chianti, Chianti Colli Fiorentini and Chianti Classico)

**Day 7 Panzano**, p.210, and **Radda in Chianti**, p.213 (wine: Chianti Classico)

**Day 8 Gaiole in Chianti**, p.214, **Castello di Brolio**, p.214, and on to **Siena** for a visit to the Enoteca Nazionale, p.353 (wines: Chianti Classico and Chianti Colli Senesi)

*Top to bottom: Oak barrels of Montepulciano; Montalcino vineyards; Vineyard in Orcia valley*

**Day 9 Montalcino**, p.385 (wine: Brunello)

**Day 10 Montepulciano**, p.391 (wine: Vino Nobile)

**Day 11 Cortona**, p.428 (wine: Bianco Vergine della Valdichiana)

**Day 12 Sovana**, **Pittigliano**, p.403, and **Saturnia**, p.404 (wines: Morellino di Scansano and Bianco di Pitigliano)

**Day 13** Check into the spa at Chianciano Terme, p.395, for liver repairs!

## The Tuscan Table

Just over the border in food-obsessed Emilia-Romagna, they tend
to sniff at the cooking in Tuscany. In fact, it has always come as
something of a surprise that Tuscany, for all its airs and graces in the
arts, doesn't really have a cuisine to match – other Italians call
Tuscans the 'bean-eaters'. And there's the lesson: even back in the
days of the Medici, the Tuscans took pride in their frugal peasant
roots. The ingredients are first-rate, the method of cooking simple
and the bottom line is that you'll eat here as well as anywhere on
the planet. Regional specialities to try (or avoid) include:

- *Ribollita*, a thick soup 'reboiled' from bread and cabbage, beans and
  other vegetables, p.51
- *Acqua cotta*, vegetable broth with mashed tomatoes poured on
  thick slices of country bread with a poached egg and grated
  cheese, p.51
- *Pappa al pomodoro*, fresh tomato soup with bread and
  olive oil, p.51
- *Cacciucco*, Livorno-style fish soup, p.51
- *Panzanella*, Tuscan gazpacho, p.51
- *Pici*, thick homemade spaghetti, p.51

- *Fagioli al fiasco*, beans cooked in an earthenware pot, p.51
- *Bistecca alla fiorentina*, a thick steak of Chiana beef, lightly grilled, p.51
- *Cibreo*, cockscombs with beans, chicken livers and egg yolks (don't worry, it's almost impossible to find these days), p.51
- *Panforte*, Siena's dense spicy cake of nuts and preserved fruits, p.52

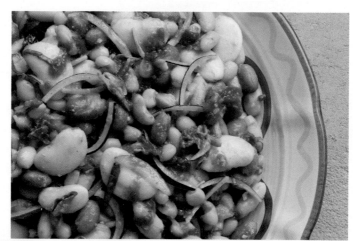

*Opposite: Pappa al pomodoro*

*Right: A typical Tuscan bean salad*

*Below: Panforte (left); Cacciucco (right)*

*Above: Villa Torrigiani*

# Villas and Gardens

Give the Medici credit for the lovely idea of escaping into the
Tuscan countryside into garden villas, for a total immersion into
Nature. But being the Medici they naturally brought along their
dear friend Art as well. The vast majority of the villas are centred
around Florence: come down from Fiesole and you'll be
surrounded by villas and gardens, or take a walk around Arcetri,
just outside the city walls of the Oltrarno.

- **Villa Careggi**, just outside Florence, the birthplace of humanism
  under Cosimo il Vecchio, p.193
- **Poggio a Caiano**, the first Renaissance villa and Lorenzo il
  Magnifico's favourite retreat , p.195
- **Villa Torrigiani** and the Baroque **Villa Mansi** near Lucca, splendid
  villa and gardens, p.266
- **Villa La Petraia** and **Villa di Castello**, two Medici villas just
  outside Florence, the latter famous for its gardens, p.194

- **Villa Stibbert**, for its gardens, and its eclectic art collection, p.160
- The 17th-century gardens at **Castello Garzoni**, near Collodi, p.254
- **Villa Medici** in Fiesole, built by Michelozzo, with lovely gardens, p.192
- **Villa Cafaggiolo**, the ancient Medici family seat in the Mugello, p.217
- **Villa Demidoff** at Pratolino, an ex-Medici spread up in the Mugello, with Giambologna's giant figure of *Appennino*, p.195
- **Castello di Brolio**, which has the added bonus of being one of Chianti's best known wineries, p.214

*Top, right: Villa Medicea, Poggio a Caiano; Above: Villa di Castello*

# Itinerary 2: Renaissance Loop Outside Florence

No place concentrates more superb Renaissance art per square foot than that great showcase Florence, but the rest of Tuscany is spectacular as well. This circular tour, beginning and ending in Florence, will take you through the best of it:

**Day 1 Impruneta** (Collegiata), p.206; Certosa del Galluzzo, p.197; Alberti's church in **Lastra a Signa**, p.223, and **Poggio a Caiano**, Lorenzo de' Medici's archetypal Renaissance villa, p.195

**Day 2 Prato** (Santa Maria delle Carceri, Filippo Lippi's fresco cycle in the cathedral, Donatello and Michelozzo's pulpit), p.230

**Day 3 Lucca**, for the sculpture of Matteo Civitali and Jacopo della Quercia, p.257

**Day 4 San Gimignano**, which has some of the best painting outside Florence, by Gozzoli, Ghirlandaio, Sodoma and more, p.362

**Day 5 Siena**, for the Sienese side of the Renaissance (most notably in the cathedral – the pavements, tombs, Piccolomini Library) and the Pinacoteca, p.327

**Days 6–7** The exquisite monastic complex and frescoes at **Monte Oliveto Maggiore**, p.384, on the way to Pius II's planned city of Pienza; nearby **Montepulciano** for Sangallo's church of San Biagio – the best of the classic Renaissance temples – as well as other churches and *palazzi*, p.391

**Day 8 Cortona** for its Renaissance temples and paintings by Signorelli and Beato Angelico, p.428, and **Monte San Savino**, p.425

**Day 9 Arezzo** (Piero della Francesca's fresco cycle and the church of Santa Maria delle Grazie), p.414

**Day 10** More Pieros in **Monterchi** and **Sansepolcro**, p.421

**Day 11** St Francis's **La Verna** (Andrea della Robbia), p.412, and over the Passo di Consuma back to Florence

*Top to bottom: Interior of Siena Cathedral; San Biagio in Montepulciano; Fresco by Piero della Francesca, Arezzo*

# CONTENTS

Contents

# History
# and Art

O2

# Historical Outline

At times, the history of Tuscany has been a small part of a bigger story – Rome's, or modern Italy's. However, the crucial eras of the Middle Ages and the Renaissance provided a tremendous chronicle of contending city-states, each with a complex history of its own. For that reason, we have included detailed histories of the most important towns – Florence, Siena and Pisa – and covered the rest to a lesser extent. Here is a brief historical outline for the region as a whole.

## The Etruscans

Neolithic cultures seem to have occupied this region of Italy since about 4500 BC without distinguishing themselves artistically or politically. The dawn of history in these parts comes with the arrival of the **Etruscans**, though where they came from and precisely when they arrived remains one of the major mysteries of early Mediterranean history. According to their traditions, the Etruscans migrated from western Anatolia, around 900 BC. Classical authors were divided on this point; some believed the migration theory, while others saw the Etruscans as the indigenous inhabitants of west-central Italy. Their language remains murky to modern scholars, but the discovery of Etruscan inscriptions on the Greek island of Lemnos, along with other clues, tends to support the Etruscan story.

Whatever it was, they were a talented people, and the great wealth they derived from intensive agriculture, manufacturing, and above all mining (Elba and the Metal Hills) allowed these talents to blossom into opulence by the 7th century BC. Though they gave their name to modern Tuscany, the real centre of Etruscan civilization lay to the south: roughly the coast from Orbetello to Cervéteri (Caere) in Lazio and around Lakes Bolsena and Trasimeno. Never a unified nation, the Etruscans preferred the general Mediterranean model of the independent city-state; the 12 greatest dominated central Italy in a federation called the **Dodecapolis**. Which cities were members is uncertain, but the 14 possible cities include *Veii, Cervéteri, Tarquinia* and *Vulci* (in Lazio), *Roselle, Vetulonia* and *Populonia* (on or near the Tuscan coast), *Volterra, Fiesole, Arezzo, Chiusi, Orvieto, Cortona* and *Perugia*.

The Etruscans always maintained extremely close trading and cultural ties with classical Greece. They sold Elban iron and bought Greek culture wholesale; the artistic thieving magpies of antiquity, they adapted every style of Greek art, from the Minoan-style frescoes at Tarquinia to the classical bronzes now in Florence's Archeology Museum, and created something of their very own. In expressive portrait sculpture, though, they surpassed even the Greeks.

A considerable mythology has grown up around the Etruscans. Some historians and poets celebrate them as a nation of free peoples, devoted to art, good food and easy living. A less sentimental view shows a slave society run for the benefit of a military, aristocratic élite. Whichever, the art they left behind gives them a place as the most enigmatic, vivid and fascinating people of early Italy. It isn't difficult to see echoes of their culture in everything that has happened in this part of Italy for the last 2,000 years.

## Romans

Etruscan kings once ruled in Rome, but, after the establishment of the Republic, this precocious city was to prove the end of the Etruscan world. All of southern Etruria was swallowed up by 358 BC, and internal divisions between the Etruscan cities allowed the Romans to push their conquest inevitably northwards. After the conquest of an Etruscan city, Roman policy was often diabolically clever: by establishing veterans' colonies in new towns nearby to draw off trade, Rome was able to ensure the withering of Etruscan culture and the slow extinction of many of Etruria's greatest cities.

Most of the Etruscan cities joined with neighbouring peoples, the Umbrii of Umbria and the Piceni of the Marches, in the Social Wars of 92–89 BC, the last doomed attempt of the Italians to fight free of Roman imperialism. Two distinct cultures occupied the northern fringes. The wandering **Celts**, who occupied all northern Italy, often made themselves at home in the Apennines and northern Etruria; their influence on the region's culture is slight. Finally there was the unnamed culture of the rugged **Lunigiana**, around Pontrémoli, a people who carried their Neolithic customs and religion (see the statue-*steles* in the Pontrémoli museum) well into the modern era.

Under the empire, Etruria was relatively quiet, though the region experienced a north–south economic split to mirror the bigger one beginning across Italy. Southern Etruria, the old Etruscan heartland, shrivelled and died under Roman misrule, never to recover. The north became more prosperous, and important new cities appeared: Lucca, Pisa, Florence and, to a lesser extent, Gubbio and Siena.

## The Dark Ages

Later Italians' willingness to create fanciful stories about the 'barbarian invasions' makes it hard to define what did happen in this troubled time. The first (5th-century) campaigns of the **Goths** in Italy did not seem to cause too much damage, but the curtain finally came down on Roman civilization with the Greek-Gothic wars of 536–563, when Eastern emperor Justinian and his generals Belisarius and Narsus attempted to recapture Italy for Byzantium. The chronicles of many cities record the devastation of the Gothic king, Totila (the sack of Florence), though the Imperial aggressors were undoubtedly just as bad. In any case, the damage to an already weakened society was fatal, and the wars opened the way for the conquest of much of Italy by the terrible **Lombards** (568), who established the Duchy of Spoleto, with loose control over much of central Italy. Lucca, the late Roman and Gothic capital of Etruria, alone managed to keep the Lombards out.

By this time, low-lying cities like Florence had practically disappeared, while the remnants of the other towns survived under the control of local barons, or occasionally under their bishops. Feudal warfare and marauding became endemic. In the 800s even a band of Arabs came looting and pillaging up the Valnerina, almost in the centre of the peninsula.

By the 10th century, things were looking up. Florence had re-established itself, and built its famous baptistry. The old counts of Lucca extended their power to become counts of Tuscany, under the Attoni family, lords of Canossa. As the leading power in the region, they made themselves a force in European affairs. In 1077, the great Countess Matilda, allied with the Pope, humbled Emperor Henry IV at Canossa – the famous 'penance in the snow' during the struggles over investiture. Perhaps most important of all was the growth of the maritime city of **Pisa**, which gave Tuscany a window on the world, building wealth through trade and inviting cultural influences from France, Byzantium and the Muslim world.

## Medieval Tuscany

By 1000, with the new millennium, all of northern Italy was poised to rebuild the civilization that had been lost centuries before. In Tuscany, as elsewhere, increasing trade had created a rebirth of towns, each doing its best to establish its independence from local nobles or bishops, and to increase its influence at the expense of its neighbours. Thus a thousand minor squabbles were played out against the background of the major issues of the day: first the conflict over investiture in the 11th century, evolving into the endless factional struggles of **Guelphs** and **Ghibellines** after 1215 (*see* pp.87–9). Throughout, the cities were forced to choose sides between the partisans of the popes and those of the emperors. The Ghibellines' brightest hours came with the reigns of strong Hohenstaufen emperors **Frederick I Barbarossa** (1152–90) and his grandson **Frederick II** (1212–46), both of whom spent much time in Tuscany. An early Guelph wave came with the papacy of **Innocent III** (1198–1216), most powerful of the medieval pontiffs, and the Guelphs would come back to dominate Tuscany after the invasion of Charles of Anjou in 1261. Florence, Arezzo and Lucca were the mainstays of the Guelphs, while Pisa, Pistoia and Siena usually supported the Ghibellines.

In truth, it was every city for itself. By 1200, most towns had become free *comuni*; their imposing public buildings can be seen in almost every corner of Tuscany. All the trouble they caused fighting each other (at first with citizen militias, later increasingly with the use of hired *condottieri*) never troubled the booming economy. Florence and Siena became bankers to all Europe; great building programmes went up, beginning with the Pisa cathedral complex in the 1100s, and the now tamed and urbanized nobles built fantastical skyscraper skylines of tower-fortresses in the towns. Above all, it was a great age for culture, the age of Dante (b. 1265) and Giotto (b. 1266). Another feature of the time was the 13th-century religious revival, dominated by the figure of St Francis of Assisi.

## Background of the Renaissance

Florence, biggest and richest of the Tuscan cities, increased its influence all through the 1300s, gaining Prato and Pistoia, and finally winning a seaport with the capture of declining Pisa in 1406. This set the stage for the relative political equilibrium of Tuscany during the early Renaissance, the height of the region's wealth and artistic achievement. The popes, newly established in Rome, sent Cardinal Albornoz across the territory in the 1360s with the aim of binding the region more closely to the Papal State; he built a score of fortresses across the neighbouring region of Umbria.

The **Wars of Italy**, beginning in 1494, put an end to Renaissance tranquillity. Florence was once more lost in its internal convolutions, twice expelling the **Medici**,

## Know Your Medici

The powerful Medici family started out, perhaps, as doctors or pharmacists (hence the name, which may derive from *medico*, denoting a medical trade), made it big as bankers, and ended up as grand dukes and even popes. From Giovanni de' Medici, the political boss who first took total control of a fractious urban republic, to the senile Gian Gastone, for more than 300 years the Medici *were* Florence. Along the way they patronized artists, from Donatello to Michelangelo, and did more than anyone else to finance the Renaissance.

Here's a little chart to help you to keep them all straight.

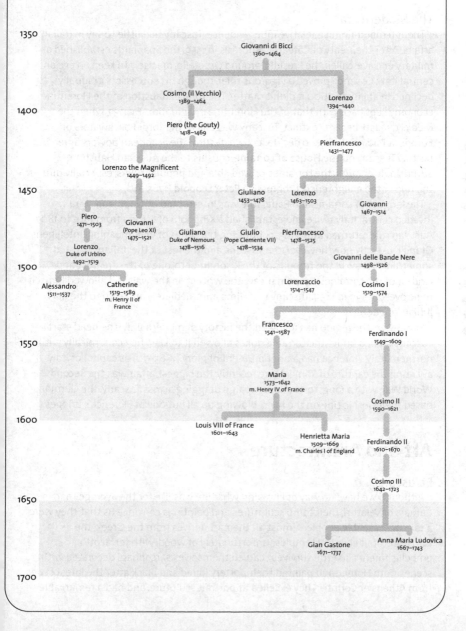

while French and Imperial armies marched over the two regions. When the dust had cleared, the last of the free cities (with the exception of Lucca) had been extinguished, and most of Tuscany came under the rule of the Grand Duke **Cosimo I** (1537–74), the Medici propped on a newly made throne by Emperor Charles V. Tuscany's economic and artistic decline was gentle until 1600. After that, it was precipitate; the old banking and textile businesses collapsed, and serious artistic production practically ceased.

### The Modern Era

Though maintaining a relative independence, Tuscany had little to say in Italian affairs. After the Treaty of Câteau-Cambrésis in 1559, the Spaniards established a military enclave, called the Presidio, around Orbetello, precisely to keep an eye on central Italy. Cosimo I proved a vigorous ruler, though his successors gradually declined in ability. By 1600 it didn't matter. The total exhaustion of the Florentine economy kept pace with that of the Florentine imagination. By 1737, when the Medici dynasty became extinct, Tuscany was one of the torpid backwaters of Europe. It had no chance to decide its own destiny; the European powers agreed to bestow Tuscany on the **House of Lorraine**, cousins to the Austrian Habsburgs. Surprisingly enough, the Lorraines proved able and popular rulers, especially during the rule of the enlightened, progressive **Peter Leopold** (1765–90).

The languor of Lorraine and Papal rule was interrupted by **Napoleon**, who invaded central Italy twice and established a Kingdom of Etruria from 1801 to 1807. Austrian rule returned after 1815, continuing the series of well-meaning, intelligent Grand Dukes. By now, however, the Tuscans and the rest of the Italians wanted something better. In the tumults of the Risorgimento, one of the greatest and kindest of the Lorraines, **Leopold II**, saw the writing on the wall and allowed himself to be overthrown in 1859. Tuscany was almost immediately annexed to the new Italian kingdom.

Since then, the region has followed the history of modern Italy. The head start Tuscany gained under the Lorraine dukes allowed it to keep up economically with northern Italy. Florence had a brief moment of glory (1865–70) as capital of Italy, awaiting the capture of Rome. More recently, the biggest affair was the **Second World War**, with a long, tortuous campaign dragging across Tuscany; the Germans based their Gothic Line on the Arno, blowing up all but one of Florence's bridges.

# Art and Architecture

### Etruscans

Although we have no way of knowing what life was like for the average man in Camars or Velathri, their tomb sculptures and paintings convince us that they were a talented, likeable people. Almost all their art derives from the Greek; the Etruscans built classical temples (unfortunately of wood, with terracotta embellishments, so little survives), carved themselves sarcophagi decorated with scenes from Homer, and painted their pottery in red and black after the latest styles from Athens or Corinth. They excelled at portrait sculpture, and had a remarkable gift for capturing personality, sometimes seriously, though never heroically, often with an entirely intentional humour, and with the serene smiles of people who truly enjoyed life.

Etruscan art in museums is often maddening; some of the works are among the finest productions of antiquity, while others – from the same time and city – are awkward and childish. Their talent for portraiture, among much else, was carried on by the Romans, and they bequeathed their love of fresco painting to the artists of the Middle Ages and Renaissance, who of course weren't even aware of the debt. After introducing yourself to the art of the Etruscans, it will be interesting to reconsider all that came later – in Tuscany, and indeed all Italy, you will find subtle reminders of this enigmatic people.

## Romans and Dark Ages

After destroying the Etruscan nation, the Romans also began the extinction of its artistic tradition; by the time of the Empire, there was almost nothing left that could be called distinctively Etruscan. Tuscany contributed little under the Empire. In the chaos that followed, there was little room for art. What painting survived followed styles current in Byzantium.

## The Middle Ages

In both architecture and sculpture, the first influence came from the north. Lombard masons filled Tuscany with simple Romanesque churches; the first (Spoleto, Bevagna, Grópina, Abbadia S. Salvatore and in the Garfagnana, to name a few) follow the northern style, although it wasn't long before two distinctive Tuscan forms emerged: the **Pisan style**, characterized by blind rows of colonnades, black and white zebra stripes and lozenge-shaped designs; and the '**Tuscan Romanesque**' that developed around Florence, notable for its use of dark and light marble patterns and simple geometric patterns, often with intricate mosaic floors to match (the Baptistry and San Miniato in Florence are the chief examples). In the cities in between – Lucca, Arezzo and Pistoia – there are interesting variations on the two different styles, often carrying an element like stripes or arcades to remarkable extremes. The only real example of French Gothic in Tuscany is San Galgano built by Cistercians in the 1200s, although the style never caught on here or anywhere else in Italy.

From the large pool of talent working on Pisa's great cathedral complex in the 13th century emerged Italy's first great sculptor, **Nicola Pisano**, whose Baptistry pulpit, with its realistic figures, derived from ancient reliefs. His even more remarkable son, **Giovanni Pisano**, prefigures Donatello in the expressiveness of his statues and the vigour of his pulpits; his façade of Siena cathedral, though altered, is a unique work of art. **Arnolfo di Cambio**, a student of Nicola Pisano, became chief sculptor-architect of Florence during its building boom in the 1290s, designing its cathedral and Palazzo Vecchio with a hitherto unheard-of scale and grandeur, before moving on to embellish Orvieto with statues and tombs. Orvieto, however, hired the more imaginative **Lorenzo Maitani** in the early 1300s to create a remarkable cathedral façade as individualistic as Siena's, a unique combination of reliefs and mosaics.

Painting at first lagged behind the new realism and more complex composition of sculpture. The first to depart from Byzantine stylization, at least according to the account in Vasari's *Lives of the Artists* (*see* **Topics**, p.39), was **Cimabue**, in the late 1200s, who forsook Greek forms for a more 'Latin' or 'natural' way of painting. Cimabue found his greatest pupil, **Giotto**, as a young shepherd, chalk-sketching sheep on a piece of slate. Brought to Florence, Giotto soon eclipsed his master's fame (artistic celebrity being a recent Florentine invention) and achieved the greatest advances on the road to the new painting with a plain, rather severe approach that shunned Gothic prettiness while exploring new ideas in composition and expressing psychological depth in his subjects. Even more importantly, Giotto through his intuitive grasp of perspective was able to go further than any previous artist in representing his subjects as actual figures in space. In a sense Giotto actually invented space; it was this, despite his often awkward and graceless draughtsmanship, that so astounded his contemporaries. His followers, **Taddeo and Agnolo Gaddi** (father and son), **Giovanni da Milano** and **Maso di Banco**, filled Florence's churches with their own interpretations of the master's style. In the latter half of the 1300s, however, there also appeared the key figure of **Andrea Orcagna**, the most important Florentine sculptor, painter and architect of his day. Inspired by the more elegant style of **Andrea Pisano**'s Baptistry doors, Orcagna broke away from the simple Giottesque forms for a more elaborate, detailed style in his sculpture, while the fragments of his frescoes that survive have a vivid dramatic power, which undoubtedly owes something to the time of the Black Death and social upheavals in which they were painted.

Siena never produced a Vasari to chronicle its accomplishments, though they were considerable; in the 13th and 14th centuries, Siena's Golden Age, the city's artists, like its soldiers, rivalled and often surpassed those of Florence. For whatever reason, it seemed purposely to seek inspiration in different directions from Florence: at first from central Italian styles around Spoleto, then, with prosperity and the advent of **Guido da Siena** in the early 1200s, from the more elegant line and colour of Byzantium. Guido's work paved the way for the pivotal figure of **Duccio di Buoninsegna**, the catalyst who founded the essentials of Sienese art by uniting the beauty of Byzantine line and colour with the sweet finesse of western Gothic art. With Duccio's great followers **Pietro and Ambrogio Lorenzetti** and **Simone Martini**, the Sienese produced an increasingly elegant and rarefied art, almost oriental in its refined stylization. They were less innovative than the Florentines, though they brought the 'International Gothic' style – flowery and ornate, with all the bright tones of May – to its highest form in Italy. Simone Martini introduced the Sienese manner to Florence in the early 1400s, where it influenced most notably the work of **Lorenzo Monaco**, **Masolino** and the young goldsmith and sculptor **Ghiberti**.

## The Renaissance

Under the assaults of historians and critics over the last two centuries, the term 'Renaissance' has become a vague and controversial word. Nevertheless, however you choose to interpret this rebirth of the arts, and whatever dates you assign to it, Florence inescapably takes the credit for it. This is no small claim. Combining art, science and humanist scholarship into a visual revolution that often seemed pure

# Masters and Students: the Progress of the Renaissance

The purpose of this chart is to show who learned from whom: an insight into some 300 years of artistic continuity.

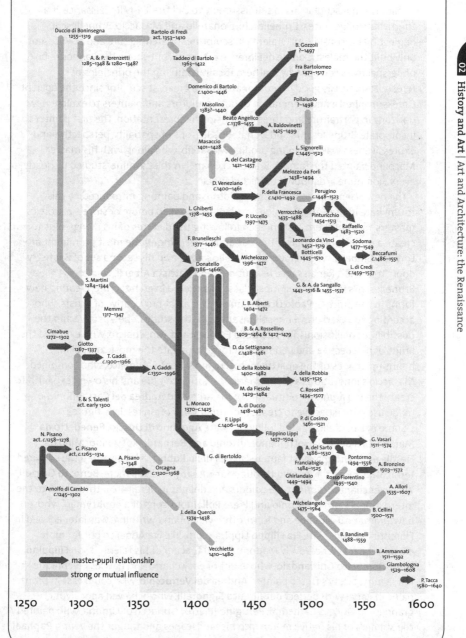

Duccio di Boninsegna
1255–1319

Bartolo di Fredi
act. 1353–1410

A. & P. lorenzetti
1285–1348 & 1280–1348?

Taddeo di Bartolo
1363–1422

Domenico di Bartolo
c.1400–1446

B. Gozzoli
?–1497

Fra Bartolomeo
1472–1517

Pollaiuolo
?–1498

Masolino
1383?–1440

Beato Angelico
c.1378–1455

A. Baldovinetti
1425–1499

Masaccio
1401–1428

L. Signorelli
c.1445–1523

A. del Castagno
1421–1457

Melozzo da Forlì
1438–1494

D. Veneziano
c.1400–1461

P. della Francesca
c.1410–1492

Perugino
c.1448–1523

L. Ghiberti
1378–1455

P. Uccello
1397–1475

Verrocchio
1435–1488

Pinturicchio
1454–1513

Raffaello
1483–1520

F. Brunelleschi
1377–1446

Leonardo da Vinci
1452–1519

Sodoma
1477–1549

Beccafumi
c.1486–1551

Michelozzo
1396–1472

Botticelli
1445–1510

L. di Credi
c.1459–1537

S. Martini
1284–1344

G. & A. da Sangallo
1443–1516 & 1455–1537

L. B. Alberti
1404–1472

Memmi
1317–1347

B. & A. Rossellino
1409–1464 & 1427–1479

Cimabue
1272–1302

Giotto
1267–1337

D. da Settignano
c.1428–1461

T. Gaddi
c.1300–1366

A. Gaddi
c.1350–1396

L. della Robbia
1400–1482

A. della Robbia
1435–1525

M. da Fiesole
1429–1484

C. Rosselli
1434–1507

F. & S. Talenti
act. early 1300

L. Monaco
1370–c.1425

A. di Duccio
1418–1481

F. Lippi
c.1406–1469

P. di Cosimo
1461–1521

N. Pisano
act. c.1258–1278

Filippino Lippi
1457–1504

G. Vasari
1511–1574

G. Pisano
act. c.1265–1314

A. Pisano
?–1348

Orcagna
c.1320–1368

G. di Bertoldo
?

A. del Sarto
1486–1530

Pontormo
1494–1556

A. Bronzino
1503–1572

Franciabigio
1484–1525

Ghirlandaio
1449–1494

Rosso Fiorentino
1495–1540

A. Allori
1535–1607

Arnolfo di Cambio
c.1245–1302

Michelangelo
1475–1564

B. Cellini
1500–1571

J. della Quercia
1374–1438

B. Bandinelli
1488–1559

B. Ammannati
1511–1592

Vecchietta
1410–1480

Giambologna
1529–1608

P. Tacca
1580–1640

master-pupil relationship

strong or mutual influence

1250   1300   1350   1400   1450   1500   1550   1600

sorcery to their contemporaries, a handful of Florentine geniuses taught the Western eye a new way of seeing. Perspective seems a simple enough trick to us now, but its discovery determined everything that followed, not only in art, but in science and philosophy as well.

Leading what scholars used self-assuredly to call the 'Early Renaissance' is a triumvirate of geniuses: Brunelleschi, Donatello and Masaccio. **Brunelleschi**, neglecting his considerable talents in sculpture for architecture and science, not only built the majestic dome of Florence cathedral, but threw the Pandora's box of perspective wide open by mathematically codifying the principles of foreshortening. His good friend **Donatello**, the greatest sculptor since the ancient Greeks, inspired a new generation of both sculptors and painters to explore new horizons in portraiture and three-dimensional representation. The first painter to incorporate Brunelleschi's and Donatello's lessons of spatiality, perspective and expressiveness was the young prodigy **Masaccio**, who along with his master Masolino painted the famous Brancacci Chapel in the Carmine, studied by nearly every Florentine artist down to Michelangelo.

The new science of architecture, sculpture and painting introduced by this triumvirate ignited an explosion of talent unequalled before or since – a score of masters, most of them Tuscan, each following the dictates of his own genius to create a remarkable range of themes and styles. Among the most prominent are: **Lorenzo Ghiberti**, who followed Donatello's advice on his second set of Baptistry doors to cause a Renaissance revolution; **Leon Battista Alberti**, who took Brunelleschi's ideas to their most classical extreme in architecture, creating new forms in the process; **Paolo Uccello**, one of the most provocative of artists, who according to Vasari drove himself insane with the study of perspective and the possibilities of illusionism; **Piero della Francesca** of Sansepolcro, who explored the limits of perspective and geometrical forms to create the most compelling, haunting images of the quattrocento; **Fra** (now **Beato**) **Angelico**, who combined Masaccio's innovations and International Gothic colours and his own deep faith to create the most purely spiritual art of his time; and **Andrea del Castagno**, who made use of perspective to create monumental, if often restless, figures.

Some of Donatello's gifted followers were **Agostino di Duccio**, **Benedetto da Maiano**, **Desiderio da Settignano**, **Antonio and Bernardo Rossellino**, **Mino da Fiesole** and, perhaps most famously, **Luca della Robbia**, who invented the coloured terracottas his family spread throughout Tuscany. And still more: **Benozzo Gozzoli**, whose enchanting springtime colours and delight in detail are a throwback to the International Gothic; **Antonio** and **Piero Pollaiuolo**, sons of a poultryman, whose new, dramatic use of line and form, often violent and writhing, was later echoed in Florentine Mannerism; **Fra Filippo Lippi**, a monk like Fra Angelico but far more earthly, the master of lovely Madonnas and teacher of his talented son **Filippino Lippi**; **Domenico Ghirlandaio**, whose gift of easy charm and flawless technique made him society's fresco painter; **Andrea del Verrocchio**, who could cast in bronze, paint, or carve with perfect detail; **Luca Signorelli**, who achieved apocalyptic grandeur in Orvieto Cathedral; **Perugino** (Pietro Vannucci) of Umbria, who painted the stillness of his native region into his landscapes and taught the young **Raphael** of Urbino; and finally **Sandro Botticelli**, whose intellectual but melancholy, mythological paintings are in a class of their own.

The 'Early Renaissance' came to a close near the end of the 1400s with the advent of **Leonardo da Vinci**, whose unique talent in painting, only one of his hundred interests, challenged the certainty of naturalism with a subtlety and chiaroscuro that approaches magic. One passion, however, obsessed the other great figure of the 'High Renaissance', **Michelangelo Buonarroti**: his consummate interest was the human body, at first graceful and serene as in most of his Florentine works, later contorted and anguished after he left for Rome.

## Mannerism

Michelangelo left in Florence the seeds for the bold, neurotic avant-garde art that has come to be known as Mannerism. The first conscious 'movement' in Western art can be seen as a last fling amidst the growing intellectual and spiritual exhaustion of 1530s Florence, conquered once and for all by the Medici. The Mannerists' calculated exoticism and exaggerated, tortured poses, together with the brooding self-absorption of Michelangelo, are a prelude to Florentine art's remarkably abrupt turn into decadence, and prophesy its final extinction.

Foremost among the Mannerist painters are two surpassingly strange characters, **Jacopo Pontormo** and **Rosso Fiorentino**, who were not in such great demand as the coldly classical **Andrea del Sarto** and **Bronzino**, consummate perfectionists of the brush, both much less intense and demanding. There were also charming reactionaries working at the time, especially **Il Sodoma** and **Pinturicchio**, both of whom left their best works in Siena. In sculpture **Giambologna** and to a lesser extent **Bartolomeo Ammannati** specialized in virtuoso *contrapposto* figures, each one more impossible than the last. With their contemporary, **Giorgio Vasari** (*see* p.89), Florentine art lost almost all imaginative and intellectual content, and became a virtuoso style of interior decoration perfectly adaptable to saccharine holy pictures, portraits of newly enthroned dukes, or absurd mythological fountains and ballroom ceilings. In the cinquecento, with plenty of money to spend and a long Medici tradition of patronage to uphold, this tendency soon got out of hand. Under the reign of Cosimo I, indefatigable collector of *pietra dura* tables, silver and gold gimcracks and exotic stuffed animals, Florence gave birth to the artistic phenomenon that modern critics call 'kitsch'.

## The Rest Compressed

In the long, dark night of later Tuscan art a few artists stand out – the often whimsical architect and engineer **Buontalenti**; **Pietro Tacca**, Giambologna's pupil with a taste for the grotesque; the charming Baroque fresco master **Pietro da Cortona**. Most of Tuscany, and particularly Florence, chose to sit out the Baroque – almost by choice, it seems – and we can race up to the 19th century for the often delightful 'Tuscan Impressionists' or Macchiaioli ('Splatterers'; the best collection is in the modern art section of the Pitti Palace); and, in the 20th century, **Modigliani** of the oval faces (from Livorno); the Futurist **Gino Severini** (from Cortona); and **Alberto Burri**, one of the first to use junk as a medium (from Città di Castello, where there's a museum). There is an exceptionally good collection of contemporary art, the

Centro per l'Arte Contemporanea Luigi Pecci, in Prato, with frequent exhibitions; others include a museum dedicated to sculptor **Marino Marini** in Florence, although newest and most entertaining of all is the late French artist **Niki de Saint-Phalle**'s Tarot Garden, south of Orbetello.

## Artists' Directory

This includes the principal architects, painters and sculptors of Tuscany and its nearby regions. The works listed are far from exhaustive, bound to exasperate partisans of some artists and do scant justice to the rest, but we have tried to include only the best and most representative works to be found locally.

**Agostino di Duccio** (Florentine, 1418–81). A precocious and talented sculptor, his best work is in the Malatesta Temple at **Rimini** – he was exiled from Florence after being accused of theft (**Florence**, Bargello; **Pontrémoli**, S. Francesco).

**Alberti, Leon Battista** (Florentine, b. Genoa, 1404–72). Architect, theorist and writer, also a sculptor and painter. His greatest contribution was recycling the classical orders and the principles of Vitruvius into Renaissance architecture; he was a consultant to the architecture-loving Duke of Urbino (**Florence**, Palazzo Rucellai, façade of S. Maria Novella, SS. Annunziata; **Lastra a Signa**, S. Martino).

**Allori, Alessandro** (1535–1607). Florentine Mannerist painter, prolific follower of Michelangelo and Bronzino (**Florence**, SS. Annunziata, S. Spirito, Spedale degli Innocenti).

**Ammannati, Bartolomeo** (1511–92). Florentine architect and sculptor. Restrained, elegant architect (**Florence**, S. Trínita bridge, courtyard of Pitti Palace); neurotic, twisted Mannerist sculptor (**Florence**, Fountain of Neptune, Villa di Castello).

**Andrea del Castagno** (c. 1423–57). Precise, dry Florentine painter, one of the first and greatest slaves of perspective. Died of the plague (**Florence**, Uffizi, S. Apollonia, SS. Annunziata).

**Angelico, Fra** (or **Beato**) (Giovanni da Fiesole, c. 1387–1455). Monk first and painter second, but still one of the great visionary artists of the Renaissance (**Florence**, S. Marco – spectacular *Annunciation* and many more; **Cortona**, cathedral museum; **Fiesole**, S. Domenico).

**Arnolfo di Cambio** (born in Colle di Val d'Elsa, c. 1245–1302). Architect and sculptor, pupil of Nicola Pisano and a key figure in his own right. Much of his best sculpture is in Rome, but he changed the face of Florence as main architect to the city's greatest building programme of the 1290s (**Florence**, cathedral and Palazzo Vecchio).

**Baldovinetti, Alesso** (Florentine, 1425–99). A delightful student of Fra Angelico who left few tracks; most famous for fresco work in **Florence** (SS. Annunziata, Uffizi, S. Niccolò sopr'Arno, S. Miniato).

**Bandinelli, Baccio** (1488–1559). Florence's comic relief of the late Renaissance; supremely serious, vain, and so awful it hurts – of course he was court sculptor to Cosimo I (**Florence**, Piazza della Signoria and SS. Annunziata).

**Barna da Siena** (active mid–late 1300s). One of the chief followers of Simone Martini, more dramatic and vigorous than the usual ethereal Sienese (**San Gimignano**, Collegiata).

**Bartolo di Fredi** (Sienese, active c. 1353–1410). Student of Ambrogio Lorenzetti, a genuine pre-Raphaelite soul, entirely at home in the Sienese trecento; employed colours never before seen on this planet (**Montepulciano**, Duomo; **San Gimignano**, Collegiata).

**Bartolommeo, Fra** (c. 1472–1517). Florentine painter, master of the High Renaissance style (**Florence**, San Marco, Pitti Palace).

**Beccafumi, Domenico** (c. 1486–1551). Sienese painter; odd mixture of Sienese conservatism and Florentine Mannerism (**Siena**, Pinacoteca, Palazzo Pubblico, cathedral pavement).

**Benedetto da Maiano** (Florentine, 1442–97). Sculptor, specialist in narrative reliefs (**Florence**, S. Croce, Strozzi Palace, Bargello; he also designed the loggia of S. Maria delle Grazie, **Arezzo**).

**Bigarelli, Guido** (13th century). Talented travelling sculptor from Como, who excelled in elaborate and sometimes bizarre pulpits (**Barga**; **Pistoia**, S. Bartolomeo, and **Pisa**, Baptistry).

**Bonfigli, Benedetto** (Perugia, *c.* 1420–96). Meticulous Umbrian painter, known for his painted banners in many **Perugia** churches; his best works, especially the Cappella dei Priori frescoes, are in that city's National Gallery.

**Botticelli, Sandro** (Florentine, 1445–1510). Though technically excellent in every respect, and a master of both line and colour, there is more to Botticelli than this. Above every other quattrocento artist, his works reveal the imaginative soul of the Florentine Renaissance, particularly the great series of mythological paintings (**Florence**, Uffizi). Later, a little deranged and under the spell of Savonarola, he reverted to intense though conventional religious paintings. He was almost forgotten in the philistine 1500s and not rediscovered until the 19th century, and thus many of his best works are probably lost (**Florence**, Accademia; **Montelupo**, S. Giovanni Evangelista).

**Bronzino, Agnolo** (1503–72). Virtuoso Florentine Mannerist with a cool, glossy, hyper-elegant style, at his best in portraiture; a close friend of Pontormo (**Florence**, Palazzo Vecchio, Uffizi, S. Lorenzo, SS. Annunziata).

**Brunelleschi, Filippo** (1377–1446). Florentine architect, credited in his own time with restoring the ancient Roman manner of building – but really deserves more credit for developing a brilliant new approach of his own (**Florence**, Duomo cupola, Spedale degli Innocenti, S. Spirito, S. Croce's Pazzi Chapel, S. Lorenzo). Also a sculptor (he lost the competition for the baptistry doors to Ghiberti), and one of the first theorists on perspective.

**Buontalenti, Bernardo** (1536–1608). Late Florentine Mannerist architect and planner of the new city of **Livorno**, better known for his Medici villas (**Artimino**; also the fascinating grotto in **Florence**'s Boboli Gardens, and Belvedere Fort, Uffizi Tribuna).

**Cellini, Benvenuto** (1500–71). Goldsmith and sculptor. Though a native of Florence, Cellini spent much of his time in Rome. In 1545 he came to work for Cosimo I and to torment Bandinelli (**Florence**, *Perseus*, Loggia dei Lanzi; also works in the Bargello). As famed for his catty *Autobiography* as for his sculpture.

**Cimabue** (*c.* 1240–1302). Florentine painter credited by Vasari with initiating the 'rebirth of the arts'; one of the first painters to depart from the stylization of the Byzantine style (**Florence**, mosaics in Baptistry, crucifix in Santa Croce; **Pisa**, cathedral mosaic).

**Civitali, Matteo** (Lucchese, *c.* 1435–1501). Sweet yet imaginative sculptor, apparently self-taught. He would be much better known if all of his works weren't in Lucca (**Lucca**, cathedral, Guinigi Museum).

**Coppo di Marcovaldo** (Florentine, active *c.* 1261–75). Another very early painter, as good as Cimabue if not as well known (**San Gimignano**; **Pistoia**, cathedral).

**Daddi, Bernardo** (active 1290–*c.* 1349). Florentine master of delicate altarpieces (**Florence**, Orsanmichele, S. Maria Novella's Spanish Chapel).

**Desiderio da Settignano** (Florentine, 1428/31–61). Sculptor, follower of Donatello (**Florence**, S. Croce, Bargello, S. Lorenzo).

**Dolci, Carlo** (Florentine, 1616–86). Unsurpassed Baroque master of the 'whites of their eyes' school of religious art (**Florence**, Palazzo Corsini; **Prato**, Museo del Duomo).

**Domenico di Bartolo** (Sienese, *c.* 1400–46). An interesting painter, well out of the Sienese mainstream; the unique naturalism of his art is a Florentine influence (**Siena**, Spedale di Santa Maria della Scala, Pinacoteca).

**Domenico Veneziano** (Florentine 1404–61). Painter, teacher of Piero della Francesca; master of perspective with few surviving works (**Florence**, Uffizi).

**Donatello** (Florentine, 1386–1466). The greatest Renaissance sculptor appeared as suddenly as a comet at the beginning of Florence's quattrocento. Never equalled in technical ability, expressiveness or imaginative content, his works influenced Renaissance painters as much as sculptors. A prolific worker, the favourite of Old Cosimo de' Medici, and a quiet fellow who lived with his mum, Donatello was the perfect model of the early Renaissance artist – passionate about art, self-effacing, and a little eccentric (**Florence**, Bargello – the greatest works including the original *St George* from Orsanmichele, *David* and *Cupid-Atys*, also the great pulpits, the masterpiece of his old age in San Lorenzo; other works in Palazzo Vecchio, and the cathedral museum; **Siena**, cathedral, baptistry).

**Duccio di Buoninsegna** (d. 1319). One of the first and greatest Sienese painters, Duccio was to Sienese art what Giotto was to Florence; he was ignored by Vasari, though his contributions to the new visual language of the Renaissance are comparable to Giotto's (**Siena**, parts of the great Maestà in the cathedral museum, also Pinacoteca; **Florence**, altarpiece in the Uffizi; **Massa Marittima**, cathedral; **Castelfiorentino**, Pinacoteca).

**Francesco di Giorgio Martini** (Sienese, 1439–1502). Architect – mostly of fortresses – sculptor and painter, his works are scattered all over Italy (**Siena**, cathedral, Pinacoteca; **Cortona**, S. Maria di Calcinaio).

**Franciabigio** (Florentine, 1482–1525). Most temperamental of Andrea del Sarto's pupils but only mildly Mannerist (**Florence**, Poggio a Caiano and SS. Annunziata).

**Gaddi, Taddeo** (c. 1300–c. 1366). Florentine; most important of the followers of Giotto. He and his son **Agnolo** (d. 1396) contributed some of the finest trecento fresco cycles (notably at S. Croce and S. Ambrogio, **Florence**).

**Gentile da Fabriano** (c. 1360–1427). Master *nonpareil* of the International Gothic style, from Fabriano in the Marches. Most of his work is lost (**Florence**, Uffizi).

**Ghiberti, Lorenzo** (1378–1455). Goldsmith and sculptor. The first artist to write an autobiography was naturally a Florentine. He would probably be better known had he not spent most of his career working on the doors for the Florence baptistry after winning the famous competition of 1401 (also **Florence**, statues at Orsanmichele; **Siena**, baptistry).

**Ghirlandaio, Domenico** (Florentine, c. 1448–94). The painter of the quattrocento establishment, master of colourful, lively fresco cycles (with the help of a big workshop) in which he painted all the Medici and Florence's banking élite. A great portraitist with a distinctive, dry, restrained style (**Florence**, Ognissanti, S. Maria Novella, S. Trínita, Spedale degli Innocenti; **San Gimignano**, Collegiata).

**Giambologna** (1529–1608). A Fleming, born Jean Boulogne; court sculptor to the Medici after 1567 and one of the masters of Mannerist virtuosity – also a man with a taste for the outlandish (**Florence**, Loggia dei Lanzi, Bargello, Villa della Petraia; **Pratolino**, the *Appennino*).

**Giotto** (c. 1266–1337). Shepherd boy of the Mugello, discovered by Cimabue, who became the first great Florentine painter – and recognized as such in his own time. Invented an essential and direct approach to portraying narrative fresco cycles, but is even more important for his revolutionary treatment of space and of the human figure (**Florence**, S. Croce, cathedral campanile, Horne Museum, S. Maria Novella).

**Giovanni da Milano** (14th century). An innovative Lombard inspired by Giotto (**Florence**, S. Croce; **Prato**, cathedral museum).

**Giovanni di Paolo** (d. 1483). One of the best of the quattrocento Sienese painters; like most of them, a colourful, often eccentric reactionary who continued the traditions of the Sienese trecento (**Siena**, Pinacoteca).

**Giovanni di San Giovanni** (1592–1633). One of Tuscany's more prolific, but likeable, Baroque fresco painters (**Florence**, Pitti Palace, Villa della Petraia).

**Gozzoli, Benozzo** (Florentine, d. 1497). Learned his trade from Fra Angelico, but few artists could have less in common. The most light-hearted and colourful of quattrocento artists, Gozzoli created enchanting frescoes (**Florence**, Medici chapel; **San Gimignano**, S. Agostino; **Pisa**, Camposanto).

**Guido da Siena** (13th century). One of the founders of Sienese painting, still heavily Byzantine in style; little is known about his life (**Siena**, Palazzo Pubblico, Pinacoteca; **Grosseto**, museum).

**Leonardo da Vinci** (1452–1519). We could grieve that Florence's 'universal genius' spent so much time on his scientific interests and building fortifications, and that his meagre artistic output was largely unfinished or lost. All that is left in Tuscany is the *Annunciation* (**Florence**, Uffizi) and also models of all his gadgets at his birthplace, **Vinci**. As the pinnacle of the Renaissance marriage of science and art, Leonardo requires endless volumes of interpretation. As for his personal life, Vasari records him buying up caged birds in the market-place just to set them free.

**Lippi, Filippino** (Florentine, 1457–1504). Son and artistic heir of Fra Filippo. Often seems a neurotic Gozzoli, or at least one of the most thoughtful and serious artists of the quattrocento (**Florence**, S. Maria Novella, S. Maria del Carmine, Badia, Uffizi).

**Lippi, Fra Filippo** (Florentine, 1406–69). Never should have been a monk in the first place. A painter of exquisite, ethereal Madonnas, with one of whom he ran off (the model, at least, a brown-eyed nun named Lucrezia). The Pope forgave them both. Lippi was a key figure in the increasingly complex, detailed painting of the middle 1400s (**Florence**, Uffizi; **Prato**, cathedral and Civic Museum).

**Lorenzetti, Ambrogio** (Sienese, d. 1348). He could crank out golden Madonnas as well as any Sienese painter, but was also a great innovator in subject matter and the treatment of landscapes. Created the first and greatest of secular frescoes, the *Allegories of Good and Bad Government* in **Siena**'s Palazzo Pubblico, while his last known work, the 1344 *Annunciation* in Siena's Pinacoteca, is one of the 14th century's most revolutionary treatments of perspective (also **Massa Marittima**, museum).

**Lorenzetti, Pietro** (Sienese, d. 1348). Ambrogio's big brother, and also an innovator, standing square between Duccio di Buoninsegna and Giotto; one of the precursors of the Renaissance's new treatment of space (**Siena**, S. Spirito; **Arezzo**, Pieve di S. Maria; **Cortona**, cathedral museum). Both Lorenzettis seem to have died in Siena during the Black Death.

**Lorenzo di Credi** (1439–1537). One of the most important followers of Leonardo da Vinci, always technically perfect if occasionally vacuous (**Florence**, Uffizi).

**Lorenzo Monaco** (b. Siena 1370–1425). A monk at S. Maria degli Angeli in Florence and a brilliant colourist, Lorenzo forms an uncommon connection between the Gothic style of Sienese painting and the new developments in early Renaissance Florence (**Florence**, Uffizi, S. Trinita).

**Manetti, Rutilio** (1571–1639). Quirky but somehow likeable Baroque painter, the last artist of any standing produced by Siena (**Massa Marittima**, cathedral).

**Margarito d'Arezzo** (Arezzo, 13th century). Also called Margaritone. A near-contemporary of Giotto who stuck firmly to his Byzantine guns (**Arezzo**, museum).

**Martini, Simone** (Sienese, d. 1344). Possibly a pupil of Giotto, Martini took the Sienese version of International Gothic to an almost metaphysical perfection, creating luminous, lyrical and exquisitely drawn altarpieces and frescoes perhaps unsurpassed in the trecento (**Siena**, Palazzo Pubblico; **Pisa**, Museo S. Matteo; **Florence**, Uffizi).

**Masaccio** (Florentine, 1401–c. 1428). Though he died young and left few works behind, this precocious 'shabby Tom' gets credit for inaugurating the Renaissance in painting by translating Donatello and Brunelleschi's perspective on to a flat surface. Also revolutionary in his use of light and shadow, and in expressing emotion in his subjects' faces (**Florence**, S. Maria del Carmine, S. Maria Novella; **Pisa**, Museo S. Matteo).

**Maso di Banco** (Florentine, active 1340s). One of the more colourful and original followers of Giotto (**Florence**, S. Croce).

**Masolino** (Florentine, d. 1447). Perhaps 'little Tom' also deserves much of the credit, along with Masaccio, for the new advances in art at the Carmine in **Florence**; art historians dispute endlessly how to attribute the frescoes. It's hard to tell, for this brilliant painter left little other work behind to prove his case (**Empoli**, civic museum; also attributed Tau chapel, **Pistoia**).

**Matteo di Giovanni** (Sienese, 1435–95). One Sienese quattrocento painter who could keep up with the Florentines; a contemporary described him as 'Simone Martini come to life again' (**Siena**, Pinacoteca, cathedral pavement, S. Agostino, S. Maria delle Neve; **Grosseto**, museum).

**Memmi, Lippo** (Sienese, 1317–47). Brother-in-law and assistant of Simone Martini (**Siena**, S. Spirito; **San Gimignano**, museum).

**Michelangelo Buonarroti** (Florentine, 1475–1564). Born in Caprese (now Caprese Michelangelo) into a Florentine family of the minor nobility come down in the world, Michelangelo's early years and artistic training are obscure; he was apprenticed to Ghirlandaio, but showing a preference for sculpture was sent to the court of Lorenzo de' Medici. Nicknamed *Il Divino* in his lifetime, he was a complex, difficult character, who seldom got along with mere mortals, popes or patrons. What he couldn't express by means of the male nude in paint or marble, he did in his beautiful but difficult sonnets. In many ways he was the first modern artist, unsurpassed in technique but also the first genius to go over the top (**Florence**, Medici tombs and library in San Lorenzo, three works in the Bargello, the *Pietà* in the Museo del Duomo, the *David* in the Accademia, Casa Buonarroti, and his only oil painting, in the Uffizi).

**Michelozzo di Bartolomeo** (Florentine, 1396–1472). Sculptor who worked with Donatello (**Prato**, pulpit of the Holy Girdle, and the tomb in **Florence**'s baptistry), he is better known as the classicizing architect favoured by the elder Cosimo de' Medici (**Florence**, Medici Palace, Chiostro of SS. Annunziata, library of San Marco; villas at **Trebbio** and **Cafaggiolo**; **Montepulciano**, S. Agostino; **Impruneta**, Tempietto).

**Mino da Fiesole** (Florentine, 1429–84). Sculptor of portrait busts and tombs; like the della Robbias a representative of the Florentine 'sweet style' (**Fiesole**, cathedral; **Empoli**, museum; **Volterra**, cathedral; **Florence**, Badia, Sant'Ambrogio; **Prato**, cathedral).

**Nanni di Banco** (Florentine, 1384–1421). Florentine sculptor at the dawn of the Renaissance (**Florence**, Orsanmichele, Porta della Mandorla).

**Orcagna, Andrea** (Florence, d. 1368). Sculptor, painter and architect who dominated the middle 1300s in Florence, though greatly disparaged by Vasari, who destroyed much of his work. Some believe he is the 'Master of the Triumph of Death' of Pisa's Camposanto (**Florence**, Orsanmichele, S. Croce, S. Maria Novella, *Crucifixion* in refectory of S. Spirito, also often given credit for the Loggia dei Lanzi).

**Perugino** (Pietro Vannucci, b. Perugia, *c.* 1450–1523). Perhaps the most distinctive of the Umbrian painters; created some works of genius, along with countless idyllic nativity scenes, each with its impeccably sweet Madonna and characteristic blue-green tinted background. Some of his later works are awful, although he may not always be responsible: in his cynical old age he let his workshop sign his name to anything (**Florence**, Uffizi, S. Maddalena dei Pazzi, Cenacolo di Foligno).

**Piero della Francesca** (c. 1415–1492). Painter, born at Sansepolcro, and one of the really unique quattrocento artists. Piero, a leading light in the famous court of Urbino, wrote two of the most important theoretical works on perspective, then illustrated them with a lifetime's work reducing painting to the bare essentials: geometry, light and colour. In his best work his reduction creates nothing dry or academic, but dreamlike, almost eerie scenes similar to those of Uccello. And, like Uccello or Botticelli, his subjects are often archetypes of immense psychological depth, not to be fully explained now or ever (**Arezzo**, S. Francesco and the cathedral; **Sansepolcro**, civic museum; **Monterchi**, cemetery church; **Florence**, Uffizi).

**Piero di Cosimo** (Florentine, 1462–1521). Painter better known for his personal eccentricities than his art, which in itself is pretty odd. Lived on hard-boiled eggs which he boiled along with his glue (**Florence**, Uffizi; **Fiesole**, S. Francesco).

**Pietro da Cortona** (Cortona, 1596–1699). The most charming of Tuscan Baroque painters; his best work is in Rome, but there are some florid ceilings in the Pitti Palace (**Florence**; also **Cortona**).

**Pinturicchio** (Perugia, 1454–1513). This painter got his name for his use of gold and rich colours. Never an innovator, but as an absolute virtuoso in colour, style and grace no one could beat him. Another establishment artist, especially favoured by the popes, and, like Perugino, he was slandered most vilely by Vasari (**Siena**, Piccolomini Library).

**Pisano, Andrea** (b. Pontedera, *c.* 1290–1348). Artistic heir of Giovanni and Nicola Pisano and teacher of Orcagna; probably a key figure in introducing new artistic ideas to **Florence** (baptistry, south doors). Not related to the other Pisani.

**Pisano, Nicola** (active *c.* 1258–78). The first great medieval Tuscan sculptor really came from down south in Apulia, which was then enjoying a flowering of classically orientated art under Emperor Frederick II. He created a little Renaissance all his own, when he adapted the figures and composition of ancient reliefs to make his wonderful pulpit reliefs in **Siena** and **Pisa**'s Baptistry. His son **Giovanni Pisano** (active *c.* 1265–1314) carried on the tradition, notably in the façade sculptures at **Siena** cathedral (also great relief pulpits in **Pisa** cathedral, Sant'Andrea, and **Pistoia**).

**Pollaiuolo, Antonio** (Florentine, d. 1498). A sculptor, painter and goldsmith whose fame rests on his brilliant, unmistakable line; he occasionally worked with his less gifted brother **Piero** (**Florence**, Uffizi and Bargello).

**Pontormo, Jacopo** (Florentine, b. Pontormo, 1494–1556). You haven't seen pink and orange until you've seen the work of this determined Mannerist eccentric. After the initial shock, though, you'll meet an artist of real genius, one whose use of the human body as sole means for communicating ideas is equal to Michelangelo's (**Florence**, S. Felicità – his *Deposition* – and Uffizi; **Carmignano**; **Poggio a Caiano**).

**Quercia, Jacopo della** (Sienese, 1374–1438). Sculptor who learned his style from Pisano's cathedral pulpit; one of the unsuccessful contestants for the Florence baptistry doors. Maybe Siena's greatest sculptor, though his most celebrated work, that city's Fonte Gaia, is now ruined (**Lucca**, cathedral *tomb of Ilaria del Carretto*; **San Gimignano**, Collegiata; **Siena**, baptistry; **Volterra**, cathedral).

**Raphael** (Raffaello Sanzio, 1483–1520). Born in Urbino, Raphael spent time in Città di Castello, Perugia and Florence before establishing himself in Rome. Only a few of the best works of this High Renaissance master remain in the region; those are in the Pitti Palace and Uffizi, **Florence**.

**Robbia, Luca della** (Florentine, 1400–82). Greatest of the famous family of sculptors; he invented the coloured glaze for terracottas that we associate with the della Robbias, but was also a first-rate relief sculptor (the *cantorie* in **Florence**'s cathedral museum; **Impruneta**, Collegiata). His nephew **Andrea della Robbia** (1435–1525; best works in convent of **La Verna** and the Tempietto at **Montevarchi**) and Andrea's son **Giovanni** (1469–1529; best work, **Pistoia**, Ospedale del Ceppo) carried on the blue and white terracotta 'sweet style' in innumerable buildings across Tuscany.

**Rosselli, Cosimo** (Florentine, 1434–1507). Competent middle-of-the-road Renaissance painter who occasionally excelled (**Florence**, S. Ambrogio).

**Rossellino, Bernardo** (1409–64). Florentine architect and sculptor best known as the planner and architect of the new town of **Pienza**. Also a sculptor (**Florence**, S. Croce, S. Miniato; **Empoli**, Pinacoteca). His brother **Antonio Rossellino** (1427–79) was also a talented sculptor (**Florence**, S. Croce).

**Rossi, Vicenzo de'** (1525–87). Florentine Mannerist sculptor of chunky male nudes (**Florence**, Palazzo Vecchio).

**Rosso Fiorentino** (Giovanni Battista di Jacopo, 1494–1540). Florentine Mannerist painter, he makes a fitting complement to Pontormo, both for his tortured soul and for the exaggerations of form and colour he used to create gripping, dramatic effects. Fled Italy after the Sack of Rome and worked for Francis I at Fontainebleau. (**Volterra**'s Pinacoteca has his masterpiece, the *Deposition*; **Florence**, Uffizi and S. Lorenzo; **Città di Castello**, Duomo).

**Salviati, Francesco** (Florentine, 1510–63). Friend of Vasari and a similar sort of painter – though much more talented. Odd perspectives and decoration, often bizarre imagery (**Florence**, Palazzo Vecchio and Uffizi).

**Sangallo, Antonio da** (brother of Giuliano, 1455–1537). Architect at his best in palaces and churches in the monumental style – notably at the great temple of S. Biagio, **Montepulciano**; the son, **Antonio da Sangallo the Younger**, also an architect, and the family's best, practised mainly in Rome.

**Sangallo, Giuliano da** (Florentine, 1443–1516). Architect of humble origins who became the favourite of Lorenzo de' Medici. Often tripped up by an obsession, inherited from Alberti, with making architecture conform to philosophical principles (**Poggio a Caiano**; **Florence**, S. Maddalena dei Pazzi; **Prato**, S. Maria delle Carceri).

**Il Sassetta** (Stefano di Giovanni; active *c.* 1390–1450). One of the great Sienese quattrocento painters, though still working in a style the Florentines would have found hopelessly reactionary; an artist who studied Masaccio but preferred the Gothic elegance of Masolino. His masterpiece, the Borgo Sansepolcro polyptych, is dispersed through half the museums of Europe.

**Signorelli, Luca** (b. Cortona, d. 1523). A rarefied Umbrian painter and an important influence on Michelangelo. Imaginative, forceful compositions, combining geometrical rigour with a touch of unreality, much like his master Piero della Francesca (**Cortona**, civic and cathedral museums; **Monte Oliveto Maggiore**; **Sansepolcro**, museum).

**Il Sodoma** (Giovanni Antonio Bazzi, 1477–1549). Born in Piedmont, but a Sienese by choice, he was probably not the libertine his nickname and Vasari's biography suggest. An endearing, serene artist, who usually eschewed Mannerist distortion, he got rich through his work, then blew it all feeding his exotic menagerie and died in the poorhouse (**Monte Oliveto Maggiore; Siena**, Pinacoteca and S. Domenico).

**Spinello Aretino** (b. Arezzo, late 14th century–1410). A link between Giotto and the International Gothic style; imaginative and colourful in his compositions (**Florence**, S. Miniato; **Siena**, Palazzo Pubblico; **Arezzo**, museum). His son **Parri di Spinello** did many fine works, all around Arezzo (**Arezzo**, S. Maria delle Grazie).

**Tacca, Pietro** (1580–1640). Born in Carrara, pupil of Giambologna and one of the best early Baroque sculptors (**Livorno**, *Quattro Mori*; **Florence**, Piazza SS. Annunziata fountains; **Prato**, Piazza del Comune).

**Taddeo di Bartolo** (Volterra, 1363–1422). The greatest Sienese painter of the late 1300s – also the least conventional; never a consummate stylist, he often shows a remarkable imagination in composition and the treatment of subject matter (**Siena**, Palazzo Pubblico, S. Spirito; **Colle di Val d'Elsa**, museum and Collegiata; **Volterra**, Pinacoteca; **San Gimignano**, Museo Civico).

**Talenti, Francesco** (early 14th century). Chief architect of **Florence** cathedral and campanile after Arnolfo di Cambio and Giotto; his son **Simone** made the beautiful windows in Orsanmichele (and perhaps the Loggia dei Lanzi) in **Florence**.

**Torrigiano, Pietro** (1472–1528). Florentine portrait sculptor, famous for his work in Westminster Abbey and for breaking Michelangelo's nose (**Siena**, cathedral).

**Uccello, Paolo** (Florentine, 1397–1475). No artist has ever been more obsessed with the possibilities of artificial perspective. Like Piero della Francesca, he used the new technique to create a magic world of his own; contemplation of it made him increasingly eccentric in his later years. Uccello's provocative, visionary subjects (**Florence**, *Noah* fresco in S. Maria Novella, and *Battle of San Romano* in the Uffizi, and cloister of San Miniato) put him up with Piero della Francesca and Botticelli as the most intellectually stimulating of quattrocento artists (also attributed frescoes, **Prato** cathedral).

**Vasari, Giorgio** (Arezzo, 1511–74). Florentine sycophant, writer and artist. Also a pretty good architect (**Florence**, Uffizi, Corridoio, and Fish Loggia, and the palace in **Città di Castello**).

**Il Vecchietta** (Lorenzo di Pietro, 1412–80). Sienese painter and sculptor, dry and linear, part Sienese Pollaiuolo and part Donatello. One wonders what he did to acquire his nickname, 'Little Old Woman' (**Siena**, Loggia della Mercanzia, baptistry).

**Verrocchio, Andrea del** (1435–88). Florentine sculptor who worked in bronze; spent his life trying to outdo Donatello. Also a painter, a mystic alchemist in his spare time, and interestingly enough the master of both Botticelli and Leonardo (**Florence**, Uffizi, S. Lorenzo, Orsanmichele, Palazzo Vecchio, and Bargello).

# Topics

03

# A Country Calendar

If there's a great sense of continuity in the land, it is the same with the rhythms of rural life in central Italy. Old traditions and seasonal changes are still of primary importance – Italians, for the most part, won't buy imported fruit or vegetables (although this is unfortunately changing); even in the cities it's difficult to find a decent tomato in January. Even chocolates disappear off the counter in July. Tuscany, like most of Italy, chooses to follow the calendar as a sort of sentimental journey through the rise and fall of the year.

The traditional Florentine New Year used to begin on Annunciation Day in March, the time when the countryside really did seem to awaken – until the Medici Grand Dukes finally aligned Tuscany to the papal calendar in the 1500s. **January** still hibernates; if the ground is soft farmers may put in peas and garlic; roast chestnuts, polenta, *bruschetta* and game dishes are the highlights of the table. **February** is the month of pruning and planting garden vegetables in frames. Sticky-sweet carnival pastries are unavoidable. In **March** new fruit trees are planted and the vines are pruned; potatoes, fennel, spinach, carrots, parsley and lettuce are planted directly in the garden. Blood oranges (from Sicily) and artichokes appear in the shops. The fruit trees burst into blossom, and continue through **April**, the time to plant sunflowers and corn, the other garden vegetables and most flowers. Lambs are slaughtered for Easter; young turkeys and pigs are purchased. The hunt for wild asparagus and salad greens is in full swing.

Strawberries and medlars are the fruits of **May**, central Italy's most glorious month, when the irises and roses bloom in profusion. *Fave* (broad beans) are the big treat, and in the mountains, in most years, you can finally stop lighting fires to stay warm in the evening. The first garlic, French beans and potatoes are harvested in **June**, which is also the time to plant cabbage and cauliflowers. Cherries, apricots, plums, the first watermelons and fresh tomatoes appear; everyone's eating melon and prosciutto *antipasti* and dishes with courgette flowers (*fiori di zucca*).

**July** brings an avalanche of *zucchini* and peaches. Country folk begin staying up past 10pm, and scorpions come into your house to cool off. In **August** chickens meet their maker, while the end of the month brings masses upon masses of tomatoes, which country families join together to conserve – a messy operation of steaming kettles and grinders that puts up a year's supply of tomato sauce. Apples, pears and fresh figs are harvested in **September**, a golden, placid month when the village stationery shops begin stocking the schoolbooks for the new year.

**October** is the *vendemmia*, or grape harvest, the highlight of the year for everyone outside the Umbrian Apennines; to make *vin santo* it's essential to pick out very mature bunches and hang them up to dry. The hunting season opens, and folks begin to poke around for wild mushrooms. **November** is a busy month, the time to hunt for truffles, harvest olives, pomegranates and chestnuts, and take care of wine business. In **December** the family pig is slaughtered for next year's *prosciutto* and sausages. Orange persimmons hang like ornaments on the trees and plague the table – no one likes them, but everyone has plenty to give away; if they are indeed the apples of the Hesperides, as some scholars suggest, the afterlife must be a major disappointment. Stick to the tiny tangerines from the south that flood the market. Christmas turkeys realize their time has come; and cakes are everywhere: dense confections of walnuts, raisins, chocolates and pepper (*panforte* of Siena) or tall, airy *panettone* sold in cylindrical boxes.

# The First Professional Philistine

Many who have seen Vasari's work in Florence will be wondering how such a mediocre painter should rate so much attention. Ingratiating companion of the rich and famous, workmanlike over-achiever and tireless self-promoter, Vasari was the perfect man for his time. Born in Arezzo, in 1511, a fortunate introduction to Cardinal Silvio Passerini gave him the chance of an education in Florence with the young Medici heirs Ippolito and Alessandro. In his early years, he became a fast and reliable frescoist gaining a reputation for customer satisfaction – a real innovation in an age when artists were increasingly becoming eccentric prima donnas. In the 1530s, after travelling around Italy on various commissions, he returned to Florence just when Cosimo I was beginning his plans to remake the city in the image of the Medici. It was a marriage made in heaven. Vasari became Cosimo's court painter and architect, with a limitless budget and a large group of assistants, the most prolific fresco machine ever seen in Italy – painting over countless good frescoes of the 1300s.

But more than for his paintings, Vasari lives on through his book, the *Lives of the Painters, Sculptors and Architects*, a series of exhaustive, gossipy biographies of artists. Beginning with Cimabue, Vasari traces the rise of art out of Byzantine and Gothic barbarism, through Giotto and his followers, towards an ever-improving naturalism, finally culminating in the great age of Leonardo, Raphael and the divine Michelangelo, who not only mastered nature but outdid her. Leon Battista Alberti gets the credit for drafting the first principles of artistic criticism, but it was Vasari who first applied such ideas on a grand scale. His book, being the first of its kind, and containing a mine of valuable information on dozens of Renaissance artists, naturally has had a tremendous influence on all subsequent criticism. Art critics have never really been able to break out of the Vasarian straitjacket.

Much of Vasari's world seems quaint to us now: the idea of the artist as a kind of knight of the brush, striving for Virtue and Glory, the slavish worship of anything that survived from ancient Rome, artistic 'progress' and the conviction that art's purpose was to imitate nature. But many of Vasari's opinions have had a long and mischievous career in the world of ideas. His blind disparagement of everything medieval – really the prejudice of his entire generation – lived on until the 1800s. His dismissal of Sienese, Umbrian and northern artists – of anyone who was not a Florentine – has not been entirely corrected even today. Vasari was the sort who founded academies, a cheerful conformist who believed in a nice, tidy art that went by the book. With his interior decorator's concept of Beauty, he created a style of criticism in which virtuosity, not imagination, became the standard by which art was to be judged; history offers few more instructive examples of the stamina and resilience of dubious ideas.

# Flora and Fauna

No one would come to this part of Italy expecting to find an unspoiled wilderness. Most of Tuscany, in particular, has been cultivated so long and so intensively that wildlife is completely pushed to the fringes. Nevertheless, there is a great variety of birds and beasts to complement the surprisingly wide range of landscapes. Cultivated Tuscany (*see* 'Landscapes', p.43) is another world, a land of vineyards and olive groves, cypresses, poplars and the occasional umbrella pine. The rest of the territory divides neatly into three parts: the coastal zone, with its beaches and wetlands, the central hills, and the mountains.

For nature-lovers, the **coast** will be by far the most interesting region; the malaria mosquito kept much of the southern Maremma undeveloped for centuries, leaving vast stretches of pine forest, along with cork oak and holm oak, a thriving wildlife (including, even, some wild horses) and marshlands that host a marvellous array of birds, from eagles to woodpeckers. Its protected nesting grounds (*see* the Monti dell'Uccellina, pp.319–20, Orbetello lagoons, p.322, and Lago di Burano, p.326) are Italy's greatest stopover for migrating waterfowl – herons, cormorants, storks, kingfishers, ospreys and the only flamingoes left on the mainland. Deforested land beyond the marshes is covered with the characteristic Mediterranean scrub, or *maquis* (*macchia*, in Italian): either *macchia alta* with shrub versions of pines (they harvest the pine nuts), oaks, beech, cypress and laurel; or the *macchia bassa* in drier regions, thick patches of broom, heather, lentisk and other fragrant plants.

As for the **animals**, there are pretty much the same characters throughout Tuscany starting with those two regional totems, the viper and the boar. The bad old viper, the only really unpleasant thing you may meet out in the woods and fields, proliferates especially where farmlands have been abandoned; he's brownish-grey, about a foot and half long (never more than a yard), and has a vaguely diamond-shaped head. Vipers are a nuisance only because there are so many of them, and because they object to being stepped on. If one bites you, you've got half an hour to find someone with the serum – or you can buy your own in any pharmacy and keep it in the fridge. The boar, a shy, well-mannered creature, flourishes everywhere despite the Italians' best efforts to turn him into salami or *prosciutto*. In summer, you may hear them nosing around the villages at night looking for water.

Beyond these, there are plenty of hares and rabbits, foxes and weasels, also polecats, badgers and porcupines in the wilder areas. Wolves, lynxes and deer were once common, and a few of each survive in the higher reaches of the Apennines; deer have been reintroduced in the Maremma coastal parks. There is a little isolated region in Tuscany, the Val di Farma north of Roccastrada, where you can find all of these, and even wildcats. The only mountain goats are found on the island of Montecristo.

Many writers on this part of Italy comment on the absence of **birdsong**. They're exaggerating. Italian hunters do shoot anything that flies, but there are still quite a few thrushes, starlings, wrens and such, along with the white doves that always make you think of Assisi and St Francis. Cuckoos unfailingly announce the spring, pheasants lie low during the hunting season, and an occasional owl can be heard in the country. Nightingales are rare, but there are supposed to be some around Lago di Massaccuccioli and the northern coasts – in the evening you're far more likely to see bats.

The **insect** world is well represented, and if you spend time in the country, you'll meet many of them: lovely butterflies and moths, and delicate white creatures with wings apparently made of feathers; rather forbidding black bullet bees, and wasps that resemble vintage fighter planes. Beetles especially reach disproportionate sizes – if you're lucky you may see a *diavolo*, a large black or red beetle with long, gracefully curving antlers that sings when you trap it; Leonardo drew one in his notebooks. There are enough mosquitoes, midges and little biting flies to be a nuisance in the summer, and, perhaps most alarming at first sight, the shiny black scorpion, who may crawl inside through the window or up drains (you may want to keep the plugs in) or come in with the wood if you have a fire. Once inside, they head for dark places like beds or shoes. One thwack with a shoe will do in even the largest scorpion (they're actually quite soft). If you happen to be stung, it may be painful but it's not deadly; the Italians recommend a trip to the doctor for treatment against an infection or allergic reaction. One of the most stunning insect spectacles is the fireflies in midsummer. In a cornfield it is a truly magical sight – and they are such dull little creatures in daylight.

As for the **forests**, oaks, chestnuts and beech predominate, along with tall, upright poplars ('Lombardy' type), pines, willows (not the weeping variety) and a few maples – with rounded leaves, not pointed as in northern Europe and America. Cypress trees are common. Incidentally the idea that there are erect, needle-like 'male' cypresses and blowsy 'female' ones is a misconception; the tidier ones have been planted, while shaggy cypresses are the wild variety. Parasol or umbrella pines (really the maritime pine), that most characteristic Italian tree, make a grand sight isolated on a hill crest, or in large groves along the Maremma coast. At higher altitudes, there are large beech forests, along with pines and firs – some beautiful groves of silver firs grow around Monte Amiata, while in the Casentino near Camaldoli is a vast stretch of old, protected beech and pine forest; another, primarily chestnut forest, is contained in the Garfagnana's Parco Naturale dell'Orecchiella.

Though at first the region's **wild flowers** may seem unfamiliar, many of the most common Italian wild flowers are close cousins to those seen in northern Europe and America. There are a million varieties of buttercup, usually tiny ones like the *ranuncolo* and *bottoncini d'oro*, and of bluebell, often called *campanella* or *campanellina*. Many of the common five-petalled pink blossoms in spring fields are really small wild geraniums (*geranio*), with pointed leaves like the anemone, and you'll see quite a few varieties of violets (*violette*) with round or spade-shaped leaves (a few species are yellow). A daisy, in Italian, is a *margherita*, and they come in all sizes. Tiniest of all are the wild pink and blue forget-me-nots (*non ti scordar di me*); you'll have to look closely to see them in overgrown fields. Large swatches of lavender are one of the charms of the hills of Chianti.

The real star of Italian fields is the poppy, bright red and thriving everywhere. Dandelions and wild mustard are also plentiful, along with white, umbrella-like bunches of florets called *tragosellino* or *podragraria*, similar to what Americans call

Queen Anne's Lace. More exotic flowers include wild orchids, some with small florets growing in spiky shoots, rhododendrons (in mountainous areas), five-petalled wild roses and water lilies in the coastal Maremma. The best wildflowers are found up in the Sibillini mountains; the Piano Grande blooming in early summer is an unforgettable sight.

There are other **plants** to look for; a dozen kinds of greens that go into somewhat bitter salads, anise, fennel, mint, rosemary and sage are common. The Italians beat the bushes with fervour every spring looking for wild asparagus and repeat the performance in autumn searching for truffles and *porcini* (boletus) mushrooms.

## A Florentine Puzzle

In a city as visually dry and restrained as Florence, every detail of decoration stands out. In the Middle Ages and Renaissance, Florentine builders combined their passion for geometry with their love of making a little go a long way; they evolved a habit of embellishing buildings with simple geometrical designs. Though nothing special in themselves – most are easily drawn with a compass and straight edge – in their context they stand out like mystic hieroglyphs, symbols upon which to meditate while contemplating old Florence's remarkable journey through the western mind.

The city is full of them, incorporated into façades, mosaics, windows and friezes. Here are eight of them, a little exercise for the eye while tramping the hard pavements of Florence. Your job is to find them. Some are really obvious, others obscure. For No.6 you should be able to find at least three examples (two across the street from each other) and if you're clever you'll find not only No.5, a rather late addition to the cityscape, but also the medieval work that inspired it. Don't worry too much about the last one. But if you're an art historian or a Florentinophile, it's only fair that you seek out this hard one too.

For the answers, *see* p.48.

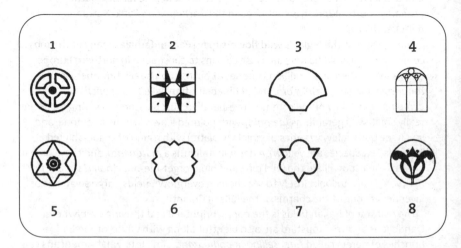

# Landscapes

Other regions in Italy are lusher, have taller mountains and more fertile valleys, support a far greater variety of flora and enjoy a more temperate climate. Yet, when all is said and done, the landscapes of Tuscany exert the most lasting charm. In the painting of the Renaissance, the background of rolling hills, cypresses, poplars and parasol pines, the vineyards and winding lanes are often more beautiful than the nominally religious subject in the foreground. Very early on, beginning with Giotto, artists took care to relate the figures in their composition to the architecture and the landscape around them, epitomized in the paintings of Leonardo da Vinci, where each tree and rock takes on an almost mystic significance.

Every Italian is born with an obsessive instinct to put in order, or '*sistemare*' things; with a history of wars, earthquakes, foreign rulers, and an age-old tendency to extremes of all descriptions, the race has had a bellyful of disorder and unpredictability. The tidy, ordered geometry and clipped hedges of an Italian garden are a perfect example of the urge to *sistemare* nature, and you'll find good examples of these in the Boboli Gardens and the Medici villas at Castello; the Tuscans, in the vanguard of Italy in so many ways, were the first to *sistemare* their entire territory. The vicious wars of the Middle Ages between cities and the Guelphs and Ghibellines devastated the countryside and much of the forests (as is visible in the harsh, barren brown and grey hills of trecento painting); the Black Death in the 1300s depopulated the cultivated areas, giving the Tuscans the unique opportunity to arrange things just so. Not entirely by coincidence, the late 14th century was the time when the élite, weary of the strife in the city, were discovering the joys of the country and building villas, playing the country squire and gentleman farmer whenever possible – already, in the *Decameron*, the nobles had estates in the environs of Florence. And they planted everything in its place according to elegance and discipline, each tree with its own purpose, a boundary marker, for shade, or to support a vine. Often cypresses and parasol pines stand strikingly along the crest of hills, not for aesthetics or as a study in perspective, but for a windbreak. Strongest of all is the feeling that nothing has changed for centuries, that in the quattrocento Gozzoli and Fra Angelico painted the same scene you see today. Few landscapes anywhere are more ancient, or civilized.

# Tuscany on Wheels

Tuscans have always loved a parade, and to the casual reader of Renaissance history it seems they're forever proceeding somewhere or another, even to their own detriment – during outbreaks of plague, holy companies would parade through an inflicted area, invoking divine mercy, while in effect aiding the spread of the pestilence. They also had a great weakness for allegorical parade floats. During the centuries of endless war each Tuscan city rolled out its war chariot or battle wagon, called the *carroccio*, invented by a Milanese bishop in the 11th century. A *carroccio*, drawn by six white oxen, was a kind of holy ship of state in a hay cart; a mast held up a crucifix while a battle standard flew from the yard-arm, there was an altar for priests to say mass during the battle and a large bell to send signals over the din to the armies. The worst possible outcome of a battle was to lose one's *carroccio* to the enemy, as Fiesole did to Florence. One is still in operation, in Siena, rumbling out twice a year for the Palio (*see* p.336).

Medieval clerical processions, by the time of Dante, became melded with the idea of the Roman 'triumph' (*trionfo*); in Purgatory, the poet finds Beatrice triumphing with a cast of characters from the Apocalypse. Savonarola wrote of a *Triumph of the Cross*; Petrarch and Boccaccio wrote allegorical triumphs of virtues, love and death. More interesting, however, are the secular Roman-style Triumphs that were staged by the Medici, especially at Carnival (the name of which, according to Burckhardt, comes from a cart, the pagan *carrus navalis*, the ship of Isis, launched every 5 March to symbolize the reopening of navigation). You can get a hint of their splendour from the frescoes at Poggio a Caiano; the best artists of the day would be commissioned to design the decorations – two particularly famous *trionfi* in Florence celebrated the election of the Medici pope Leo X. The last relics of these parades are the huge satirical carnival floats at Viareggio.

Two lovely memories of Florence's processions remain. One is Gozzoli's fairytale frescoes in the chapel of the Medici palace, of the annual procession staged by the Compagnia dei Magi, the most splendid and aristocratic of pageants (*see* p.144). The other comes from the Florentine Carnival, famous for its enormous floats, in which scenes from mythology were portrayed to songs and music. One year, for the masque of Bacchus and Ariadne, Lorenzo de' Medici composed the loveliest Italian poem to come out of the Renaissance, with the melancholy refrain:

> *Quanto è bella giovinezza,*      How fair is youth,
> *Che si fugge tuttavia!*      How fast it flies away!
> *Chi vuol esser lieto, sia:*      Let him who will, be merry:
> *Di doman non c'è certezza.*      Of tomorrow nothing is certain.

## Florentines 2, Giants 1

*Sono vulgari, quei Fiorentini...* You won't spend much time in Italy (or especially in Tuscany) before you hear someone commenting on the vulgarity of the Florentines. Such a remark may be occasioned by a lad standing next to an Alfa with Florence number plates, leaning on the horn and waking up the babies, or by a couple with sunglasses in a dark restaurant who manage to get in three cigarettes after each course. As everyone knows, Florentines are also the most arrogant and conceited people in the universe, surpassing even the Romans and Milanese.

After some initial dismay, you may find it refreshing to encounter a people with so many peculiar facets to their personality. We know about the Florentines of old, their fascination with mathematics and technology, and their matchless talent for art, and we know about the foppish prancing Florentine courtiers of the decadent 1600s. But more up-to-date models are not entirely without interest. Florentines are famous for their dry wit, and their penny-pinching economy, a talent for making a little go a long way. Their tenaciously conservative *dov'era com'era* mentality towards their museum city-home is extreme even by Italian standards. And a redeeming share of their old Renaissance craftsmanship remains, an attention to detail that makes them skilled seamstresses and the best art restorers in the world.

The refinement, as well as the arrogance and conceit, are one side of the coin; on the other we find a surprising streak of down-to-earth hillbilly cussedness. Florentines and the rest of the Tuscans are after all dismissed as *mangiafagioli*, 'bean-eaters', by other Italians. According to one perceptive observer, all the shortcomings of the Florentines are due to a diet of too much beans, tripe and cockscombs – the very mention of these conjures up the uneasy shade of the bloated, horrible Catherine de' Medici up in Paris, gorging herself on cockscombs and puking all over the Louvre.

For all these singular qualities, it is surprising that Florentines hardly ever make it into literature; it's hard to imagine a novel that could not be improved by giving a Florentine a small role. The only interesting one we have been able to find is the star of a fairy-tale heard in Pisa, one of those transcribed by Italo Calvino in his wonderful collection *Italian Folktales*. It seems there was this Florentine who had never in his entire life left Florence. Unable to talk knowledgeably about the comings and goings of the wide world, he felt at a loss in polite conversation, and finally he resolved to go out and do some travelling. He packed his bags and hit the road, in no particular direction, and along the way he met first a priest and then a farmer, both of whom felt the same way about their own lives and decided to join the Florentine as travelling companions. Eventually the three of them came to the house of a giant. The Florentine thought they should go and knock on the door, so that he could tell the folks back home about meeting a giant, and when they did they found the giant a rather courteous fellow who had need of a priest for his village church, and a farmer for his farm. He couldn't think of any particular use for a Florentine, but he took him in too.

Now, in fact this giant's courtesy was but a devious façade concealing a giant-size black-hearted stinker. He took the priest aside, supposedly to show him his duties, but once the door was closed he whacked off his head and kicked the corpse through a trap door. He did the same to the farmer – but the Florentine was watching through the keyhole this time, as Florentines will do, and, while he was pretty excited about the story he would have to entertain folks back home, it dawned on him that he would most certainly be next. At this point the storyteller, for lack of something better, gives the tale a turn straight from Homer (remember Odysseus and the Cyclops?). The giant had a squinty eye, and the Florentine had the presence of mind to tell him that he could cure it with a decoction made from a certain herb, which he had noticed growing in those parts. The giant was delighted to let him try, and the Florentine tied him to a marble table and poured the boiling mess into both his eyes. Now comes the chase scene, but the blinded giant couldn't very well catch a Florentine with a marble table tied to his back, and he tried to trick him by offering him his gold ring to finish the cure for his eyes. This was a magic ring, unfortunately, and when the poor guy put it on, his finger became as heavy as stone and weighed him to the ground. The Florentine couldn't get it off again (because it was a magic ring, remember), but he saved himself by chopping off the finger with a penknife. He made it home to Florence, finally, but he never bothered to tell anyone about his wonderful adventures, and whenever anyone asked him about the finger he said he'd had an accident while cutting the grass.

## The First Tuscans

Up in Rome's Capitoline Museum you can see the famous bronze statue of the she-wolf suckling Romulus and Remus, the symbol of Rome since ancient times. Not many people know that this was actually the work not of a Roman artist, but of an Etruscan. There are plenty of other things they never taught you in school about the Romans. Specifically, nearly every art or talent we usually give them credit for was bought or more likely stolen from somebody else. Roman painting, sculpture and architecture were seldom more than a grandiose pastiche of the Greek, and plenty of the other Roman trademarks – religion and superstition, gladiators, rectilinear surveying and town planning, portrait sculpture, sewers, togas and even concrete – were simply taken over whole from Rome's nearest neighbours and favourite victims, the Etruscans.

We often forget that, long before Brunelleschi and Donatello, Tuscany was home to another great civilization – Italy's first. But when Rome was still a collection of mud and timber huts among the miasmal swamps of the Tiber, the people of Etruria were collecting Greek urns, reclining on couches at their lavish banquets and dressing up for the races. Etruscan culture blossomed in the 8th century BC for the usual reasons – most importantly, a nice surplus of ready cash. Just as classical Athens's rise to prominence was financed by the silver mines at nearby Laurion, Etruria exploited the mineral wealth of the Colline Metallifere and Elba; there was plenty of iron, especially, for weapons and for exports. Cities grew opulent as trade boomed, and to protect their trade routes the cities developed powerful navys that dominated the Etruscan *mare nostrum*, the Tyrrhenian (so named because the Greeks called this people *Tyrrhenoi*; to the Romans they were *Tuscii* or *Etruscii*, while in their own language they are properly called the *Rasena*).

The overwhelming impression given by painting and sculpture is of a people who, whatever their flaws, were wonderfully alive. Etruscan art is full of expressive faces that either wear a smile, or are blissfully caught on the verge of breaking into one. Some of the jolly sculptures in the museums of Volterra and Rome must rank among the first conscious caricatures in art. Everything about this art paints a picture, true or not, of a people cheerfully devoted to the joys of this world. Indeed, their contemporaries dropped plenty of gossip about Etruscan hedonism and licentiousness (much of this comes from the devoutly male-chauvinist Greeks and Romans, shocked at a society where women seem to have enjoyed considerable rights and respect).

In any case, it would be difficult to find anyone in antiquity more fashion-conscious. Elaborately carved mirrors and make-up cases constitute a large part of the Etruscan collection in any museum, and the evidence from tomb frescoes suggests the ladies also liked to dye their hair blonde. The jewellery is remarkable – as good as anything between the Minoans and Fabergé. Some of it goes completely over the top, filigree work and granulation so ornate and flashy it could be worn in Las Vegas. Or whatever was the Etrurian equivalent thereof – after considering the Etruscans closely you'll begin to suspect they must have had one somewhere (perhaps Tuscany's thermal spas; the Etruscans, celebrated for their medical skills, were the first to develop these, and passed the habit down to the Romans). Coiffures and clothes could be equally elaborate; in art you will hardly ever find two Etruscan ladies with the same hairdo. Then, as now, Tuscan shoemakers were famous around the known world; the fashions of the 5th century, as shown in frescoes, featured pointed, curling toes.

Another of their talents was music; Etruscans are often pictured dancing or playing the trumpet, the lyre and, most commonly of all, a type of pan-pipes. According to a Hellenistic Greek account, they even used music in their hunting; pipers would play charmed melodies to draw the animals out of their lairs and towards the nets. Such a story is not surprising, considering another essential Etruscan trait, an attachment to magic and fortune-telling unsurpassed in the ancient world. Etruscan augurs, or *haruspices*, scrutinized the livers of sacrificed animals and scanned the skies for birds to foretell the future. Their skill was so great that *haruspices* were still employed around the Roman Empire in the 4th century AD, the last people on earth who understood the Etruscan language.

Nobody knows quite why, but after 500 BC everything started to fall apart for the Etruscans. Manufacture and art declined, slave revolts became common, and the archaeologists report that everything from tombs to pottery were being made less skilfully, more cheaply. The once-formidable Etruscan navy was getting regularly whipped by the Greeks, while the Celts destroyed the colonies in the north that had been built up with so much painstaking effort for so long. Most dire of all were the Romans. Rome's closest Etruscan neighbours, Fidenae and Veii, were captured and wiped out in 425 and 396. Veii suffered an epic siege of ten years, and, typically, during that time none of the other Etruscan cities did much to help. Chronic disunity among the members of the Dodecapolis allowed Rome to gobble up Etruria a bit at a time. The last important city, Volsinii, fell about 350, and from then on Etruria was nothing more than a Roman province – the first of many.

But the cultural heritage of these gifted people was too great to disappear completely. The Romans, as we have seen, swallowed Etruscan culture whole, and they passed quite a bit of it on to us. Hundreds of words in modern languages probably stem from the Etruscan, by way of Latin: *person*, for example, which originally meant an Etruscan theatre or ritual mask, or *temple* (this meant one of the 16 sections into which the Etruscan augurs divided the sky for divination by birdflight).

The Etruscan influence on the art of the Renaissance is a fascinating subject that has never been thoroughly explored. When medieval Tuscans revived the art of fresco painting, they probably had no idea they were simply following in the footsteps of their ancestors. Raymond Bloch, an authority on the Etruscans, noticed an eerily perfect resemblance between Donatello's famous *St George*, the very model of quattrocento *prontezza*, and an Etruscan head found long ago at Veii. In one of Michelangelo's sketchbooks we see an image of the Etruscan god Atia, undoubtedly copied from the frescoes in a tomb. And all those little faces we see staring out at us from Renaissance sculptural friezes, frescoes and book decorations are called 'grotesques', because Raphael found their originals in a painted 'grotto' in Rome. This was really a floor of buried rooms of Emperor Nero's palace, the famous Golden House, decorated in a style inherited from the Etruscans of old.

## Answers to 'A Florentine Puzzle' (p.42)

1 Façade of San Miniato
2 Baptistry, interior apse
3 Windows at rear of San Iacopo sopr'Arno, visible from Santa Trínita
4 Windows, Orsanmichele
5 Façade, Santa Croce (inspired by Orcagna's tabernacle in Orsanmichele)
6 Baptistry doors (Pisano's and Ghiberti's first set); portico of the Bigallo, interior apse, S. Croce
7 Loggia dei Lanzi
8 Rucellai Chapel, San Pancrazio

# Food and Drink

04

In Italy, the three Ms (the *Madonna*, *Mamma* and *Mangiare*) are still a force to be reckoned with, and, in a country where millions of otherwise sane people spend much of their waking hours worrying about their digestion, standards both at home and in the restaurants are understandably high. Everybody is a gourmet, or at least thinks he or she is, and food is not only something to eat but a subject approaching the heights of philosophy – two Umbrian businessmen once overheard on a train heatedly discussed mushrooms for over *four* hours. Although ready-made pasta, tinned minestrone and frozen pizza in the *supermercato* tempt the virtue of the Italian cook, few give in (although many a working mother wishes she could at times).

For the visitor this national culinary obsession comes as an extra bonus to the senses – along with Italy's remarkable sights, music and the warm sun on your back, you can enjoy some of the best tastes and smells the world can offer, prepared daily in Italy's kitchens and fermented in its countless wine cellars. Eating *all'italiana* is not only delicious and wholesome, but now undeniably trendy. Foreigners flock here to learn the secrets of Italian cuisine and the even more elusive secret of how the Italians can live surrounded by such a plethora of delights and still fit into their sleek Armani trousers.

# Regional Specialities

Regional traditions are strong in Italy, not only in dialect but in the kitchen. Tuscany is no exception and firmly maintains its distinctive cuisine.  Although Tuscany does not rank as one of  the great culinary regions of Italy, it offers good, honest, traditional dishes, often humble, rarely elaborate. The Medici may have put on some legendary feedbags, but the modern Tuscan is known by his fellow Italians as a *mangiafagioli*, or bean-eater. Some observers hold it as part of the austere Tuscan character, others as another sign of their famous alleged miserliness.

The truth is that, although beans and tripe often appear on the menu, most people when dining out want to try something different: from other regions,

## Restaurant Generalities

**Breakfast** (*colazione*) in Italy is no lingering affair, but an early morning wake-up shot to the brain: a *cappuccino*, a *caffè latte* or a *caffè lungo*, accompanied by a croissant (*cornetto*) or similar. This essential caffeine and sugar fuel can be consumed in any bar and repeated as often as necessary.

**Lunch** (*pranzo*), generally served around 1pm, is the most important meal of the day in rural areas, with a minimum of a first course (both or either *antipasti* or *primo piatto* – pasta dish, soup or risotto), a second (*secondo piatto* – meat or fish, plus a *contorno* or side dish), followed by fruit or dessert. In towns, however, where office workers (and tourists) don't want to spend a couple of hours at the table, bars serve simple first courses or *panini*.

**Dinner** (*cena*) is usually eaten around 8pm onwards, although many Italians wouldn't dream of showing up before 10pm.

The old hierarchy of **restaurants** – *ristorante*, *trattoria*, *osteria* and *vino e cucina*  – has been confused of late, though on the whole a *ristorante* is the most formal, a *vino e cucina* the most simple. Many offer a *menu turistico* – full, set meals of usually meagre inspiration for a reasonable price; others, with culinary ambitions, often offer a set-price *menu degustazione* – a 'tasting menu' of the chef's specialities.

## Siena's Salami

There are hundreds of different types of salami in Tuscany, each made to an age-old, much treasured recipe, and tasting far better than some of the ingredients might suggest. Siena has several of its own. *Buristo* is a cooked salami made from the blood and fatty leftovers of sausages and heavily spiced; *finocchiona* is peppered sausage meat seasoned with fennel seeds and stuffed into the sausage skin; *soppressata* is a boiled salami made from a mixture of rind and gristle; the alternative version, *soppressata in cuffia*, is made in the same way and then stuffed into a boned pig's head. The *salsiccioli secchi* are perhaps the most appetising salami of all, made from the leanest cuts of pork or wild boar, enhanced with garlic and black or red pepper.

perhaps, or the recent concoctions of Italian *nouvelle cuisine* or *cucina nuova*, or perhaps a recipe from the Middle Ages or the Renaissance. Some of the country's finest restaurants are in Tuscany; in practice, the diversity of dishes in the region, from traditional to bizarre, is almost endless.

# Food

Genuine Tuscan cooking is on the whole simple – calculated, as Tuscans will tell you, to bring out the glories of their wine. For *primo*, the Tuscan relies mostly on soups. Perhaps most traditional is *ribollita* ('reboiled'), made with chunks of yesterday's bread, beans, black cabbage and other vegetables. In summer look for *pappa al pomodoro*, another bread-based soup with tomatoes, basil and olive oil, and *panzanella*, a 'bread salad' of soaked stale bread, tomatoes, onions, basil, garlic and olive oil. Originally a one-course meal, *acqua cotta* is made by adding boiling water and tomatoes to sautéed vegetables, eggs and *pecorino* cheese; Livorno is famous for *cacciucco*, a heavenly fish soup. Other first courses include *pappardelle alla lepre* (wide egg noodles with a sauce of stewed hare) and *pici* (thick spaghetti), often served 'all'aglione' – with a garlic and tomato sauce. In Lucca look for *tortelli* – golden pasta parcels filled with spicy meat and topped with a rich *ragù*.

Tuscan bean classics include *fagioli al fiasco* (with oil and black pepper simmered in an earthenware pot), *fagioli all'uccelletto* (with garlic and tomatoes), and *zuppa di farro* (borlotti bean soup with spelt, a form of wheat going back to the Etruscans). Tuscany's tastiest cheese is ewe's milk *pecorino*; the best is from around Pienza, grated over pasta dishes when aged.

Grilled meats, salad and roast potatoes are typical *secondi*, reaching an epiphany in the *bistecca alla fiorentina*, a large, thick steak on the bone, cut from loin of beef and cooked over coals, served charred on the outside and pink inside, seasoned with salt and black pepper. Adventurous souls in Florence can try *cibreo* (cockscombs with chicken livers, beans and egg yolks). Tuscan tempura, *fritto misto*, can be divine: the classic version uses lamb chops, liver, sweetbreads, artichokes and courgettes. Other specialities are *arista di maiale* (pork loin with rosemary and garlic), *francesina* (meat, onion and tomato stewed in Vernaccia di San Gimignano), and *anatra* (duck).

It's fairly easy to find seafood as far inland as Florence – one traditional dish is *seppie in zimino*, or cuttlefish simmered with beets. Good Tuscan vegetable dishes are *piselli alla fiorentina*, peas cooked with olive oil, parsley and diced bacon; *tortino*

### Deluxe Virgins

Some day, on a trip to one of the fancier Italian food shops, you may pause near the section devoted to condiments and wonder at the beautiful display of bottles of unusually dark whiskies and wines, with corks and elegant labels – why, some is even DOC, though much is far more costly than the usual DOC vintages. A closer look reveals these precious bottles to be full of nothing but olive oil. Admittedly, *olio extra vergine di oliva* from Tuscany makes a fine salad dressing – according to those in the know, the oil of the Chianti brooks few rivals, Italian or otherwise. Its delicate, fruity fragrance derives from the excellent quality of the ripe olive and low acidity extracted from the fuit without any refinements. The finest, Extra Virgin, must have less than 1% acidity (the best has 0.5% acidity). Other designations are Soprafino Virgin, Fine Virgin, and Virgin (each may have up to 4% acidity) in descending order of quality.

As any Italian will tell you, it's good for you – and it had better be, because Tuscan chefs have put it in nearly every dish for centuries. The only difference is that it now comes in a fancy package at a fancy price, a victim of the Italian designer label syndrome and Tuscan preciosity. Not only does the oil have corks, but the trend in the early 1990s was for some of the smarter restaurants to offer an olive oil list similar to a wine list – one restaurant in Tuscany even had an oil *sommelier*. Many of these, perhaps fortunately, seem to have gone out of business.

*di carciofi*, a delicious omelette with fried artichokes; and *spinaci saltati* – fresh spinach sautéed with garlic and olive oil.

Typical sweets, to be washed down with a glass of *vin santo*, include Siena's *panforte* (a dense cake full of nuts and candied fruit), *castagnaccio* (chestnut cake, with pine nuts, raisins and rosemary), Florentine *zuccotto* (a cake of chocolate, nuts and candied fruits), *biscottini di Prato* (almond biscuits) or *crostate* (fruit tarts).

## Tuscan Wines

Quaffing glass after glass of Chianti inspired Elizabeth Barrett Browning to write her best poetry, and there's no reason why the wines of Tuscany shouldn't bring out the best in you as well. The first person to really celebrate Tuscan wines was a naturalist by the name of Francesco Redi in the 1600s, who, like many of us today, made a wine tour of the region, then composed a dithyrambic eulogy called 'Bacchus in Tuscany'. Modern Bacchuses in Tuscany will find quite a few treats, some of which are famous and some less so, along with plenty of cellars and *enoteche* (wine bars) where you can do your own survey – one particularly renowned place in Siena boasts a stock including every wine produced not only in Tuscany, but the rest of Italy as well.

Most Italian wines are named after the grape and the district they come from. If the label says DOC (*Denominazione di Origine Controllata*) it means that the wine comes from a specially defined area and was produced according to a certain traditional method; DOCG (the G stands for *Garantita*) means that a high quality is also guaranteed, and is a badge worn only by the noblest wines. *Classico* means that a wine comes from the oldest part of the zone of production; *Riserva*, or *Superiore*, means a wine has been aged longer.

Tuscany produces 19 DOC and DOCG wines, including some of Italy's noblest reds: the dry, ruby **Brunello di Montalcino** and the garnet **Vino Nobile di Montepulciano**, a lovely deep red with the fragrance of violets. The famous Chianti may be drunk either young or as a *Riserva*, especially the higher-octane **Chianti Classico**. There are seven other DOC Chianti wines (**Montalbano, Rufina, Colli Fiorentini, Colli Senesi, Colli Aretini, Colline Pisa** and simple **Chianti**). The chief grape in the Chianti region is sangiovese, shared by all the classified red wines of Tuscany.

Lesser known DOC reds include a dry, bright red named **Rosso delle Colline Lucchesi**, from the hills north of Lucca; the hearty **Pomino Rosso**, from a small area east of Rufina in the Mugello; **Carmignano**, a consistently fine ruby red that can take considerable ageing, produced just west of Florence; and **Morellino di Scansano**, from the hills south of Grosseto, a dry red to be drunk young or old. The three other DOC reds from the coast are **Parrina Rosso**, from Parrina near Orbetello, **Montescudaio Rosso**, and **Elba Rosso**, a happy island wine, little of which makes it to the mainland. All three have good white versions as well.

Of the Tuscan whites, the most notable is **Vernaccia di San Gimignano** (also a *Riserva*), dry and golden in colour, the perfect complement to seafood; delicious but more difficult to find are dry, straw-coloured **Montecarlo** from the hills east of Lucca and **Candia dei Colli Apuani**, a light wine from the mountains of marble near Carrara. From the coast comes **Bolgheri**, white or rosé, both fairly dry. Cortona and its valley produce **Bianco Vergine Valdichiana**, a fresh and lively wine; from the hills around Montecatini comes the golden, dry **Bianco della Valdinievole**. **Bianco di Pitigliano**, of a yellow straw colour, is a celebrated accompaniment to lobster.

Most Tuscan farmers also make a cask of *vin santo*, a dessert wine that can be sweet or almost dry, and which according to tradition is holy only because priests are so fond of it. It is made from semi-dried white grapes that are pressed in February and aged for a minimum of three years. Traditionally a wine made in small quantities in very old casks coated with generations of wild yeasts (the *madre*), it was the 'wine of hospitality' that a family would serve to guests.

# Italian Menu Vocabulary

## Antipasti

These before-meal treats can include almost anything; these are among the most common.

*antipasto misto* mixed antipasti
*bruschetta* garlic toast (sometimes with tomatoes)
*carciofi (sott'olio)* artichokes (in oil)
*frutti di mare* seafood
*funghi (trifolati)* mushrooms (with anchovies, garlic and lemon)
*gamberi ai fagioli* prawns (shrimps) with white beans
*mozzarella (in carrozza)* cow/buffalo cheese (fried with bread in batter)
*olive* olives
*prosciutto (con melone)* raw ham (with melon)
*salami* cured pork
*salsicce* sausages

## Minestre (Soups) and Pasta

*agnolotti* ravioli with meat

*cacciucco* spiced fish soup
*cannelloni* meat/cheese rolled in pasta tubes
*cappelletti* small ravioli, often in broth
*crespelle* crêpes
*fettuccine* long strips of pasta
*frittata* omelette
*gnocchi* potato dumplings
*lasagne* sheets of pasta baked with meat and cheese sauce
*minestra di verdura* thick vegetable soup
*minestrone* soup with meat, vegetables and pasta
*orecchiette* ear-shaped pasta, served with turnip greens
*panzerotti* ravioli with mozzarella, anchovies and egg
*pappardelle alla lepre* pasta with hare sauce
*pasta e fagioli* soup with beans, bacon, and tomatoes
*pastina in brodo* tiny pasta in broth
*penne all'arrabbiata* quill-shaped pasta with tomatoes and hot peppers
*polenta* cake or pudding of corn semolina

*risotto (alla milanese)* Italian rice (with stock, saffron and wine)
*spaghetti all'amatriciana* with spicy pork, tomato, onion and chilli sauce
*spaghetti alla bolognese* with ground meat, ham, mushrooms, etc.
*spaghetti alla carbonara* with bacon, eggs and black pepper
*spaghetti al pomodoro* with tomato sauce
*spaghetti al sugo/ragù* with meat sauce
*spaghetti alle vongole* with clam sauce
*stracciatella* broth with eggs and cheese
*tagliatelle* flat egg noodles
*tortellini* pasta caps filled with meat, cheese or vegetables
  *al pomodoro* with tomato sauce
  *con panna* with cream
  *in brodo* in broth
*vermicelli* very thin spaghetti

## Carne (Meat)

*abbacchio* milk-fed lamb
*agnello* lamb
*animelle* sweetbreads
*anatra* duck
*arista* pork loin
*arrosto misto* mixed roast meats
*bistecca alla fiorentina* Florentine beef steak
*bocconcini* veal mixed wih ham and cheese and fried
*bollito misto* stew of boiled meats
*braciola* chop
*brasato di manzo* braised beef with vegetables
*bresaola* dried raw meat
*capretto* kid
*capriolo* roe-buck
*carne di castrato/suino* mutton/pork
*carpaccio* thinly sliced raw beef
*cassueola* pork stew with cabbage
*cervello (al burro nero)* brains (in black butter sauce)
*cervo* venison
*cinghiale* boar
*coniglio* rabbit
*cotoletta* veal cutlet
  *alla milanese* fried in breadcrumbs
  *alla bolognese* with ham and cheese
*fagiano* pheasant
*faraona* guinea fowl
  *alla creta* in earthenware pot
*fegato alla veneziana* thinly sliced liver sautéed with chopped onion
*lepre (in salmì)* hare (marinated in wine)
*lombo di maiale* pork loin
*maiale (al latte)* pork (cooked in milk)
*manzo* beef
*osso buco* braised veal knuckle
*pancetta* rolled pork
*pernice* partridge

*petto di pollo* boned chicken breast
  *alla fiorentina* fried in butter
  *alla bolognese* with ham and cheese
  *alla sorpresa* stuffed and deep fried
*piccione* pigeon
*pizzaiola* beef steak in tomato and oregano
*pollo* chicken
  *alla cacciatora* with tomatoes and mushrooms, cooked in wine
  *alla diavola* grilled
  *alla Marengo* fried with tomatoes, garlic and wine
*polpette* meatballs
*quaglie* quails
*rane* frogs
*rognoni* kidneys
*saltimbocca* veal scallop with prosciutto and sage, cooked in wine and butter
*scaloppine* thin slices of veal sautéed in butter
*spezzatino* pieces of beef/veal, usually stewed
*spiedino* meat on a skewer/stick
*stufato* beef and vegetables braised in wine
*tacchino* turkey
*trippa* tripe
*uccelletti* small birds on a skewer
*vitello* veal

## Pesce (Fish)

*acciughe* or *alici* anchovies
*anguilla* eel
*aragosta* lobster
*aringa* herring
*baccalà* dried salt cod
*bonito* small tuna
*branzino* sea bass
*calamari* squid
*cappesante* scallops
*cefalo* grey mullet
*coda di rospo* angler fish
*cozze* mussels
*datteri di mare* razor (or date) mussels
*dentice* dentex (perch-like fish)
*dorato* gilt head
*fritto misto* mixed fried delicacies, mainly fish
*gamberetto* shrimp
*gamberi (di fiume)* prawns (crayfish)
*granchio* crab
*insalata di mare* seafood salad
*lampreda* lamprey
*merluzzo* cod
*nasello* hake
*orata* bream
*ostriche* oysters
*pesce spada* swordfish
*polipi/polpi* octopus
*pesce azzurro* various small fish
*pesce di San Pietro* John Dory
*rombo* turbot
*sarde* sardines

*seppie* cuttlefish
*sgombro* mackerel
*sogliola* sole
*squadro* monkfish
*stoccafisso* wind-dried cod
*tonno* tuna
*triglia* red mullet (*rouget*)
*trota* trout
*trota salmonata* salmon trout
*vongole* small clams
*zuppa di pesce* mixed fish in sauce or stew

## Contorni (Side Dishes, Vegetables)

*asparagi* asparagus
  *alla fiorentina* with fried eggs
*broccoli* broccoli
*carciofi (alla giudia)* (deep-fried) artichokes
*cardi* cardoons/thistles
*carote* carrots
*cavolfiore* cauliflower
*cavolo* cabbage
*ceci* chickpeas
*cetriolo* cucumber
*cipolla* onion
*fagioli* white beans
*fagiolini* French (green) beans
*fave* broad beans
*finocchio* fennel
*funghi (porcini)* (boletus) mushrooms
*insalata (mista/verde)* (mixed/green) salad
*lattuga* lettuce
*lenticchie* lentils
*melanzane* aubergine/eggplant
*patate (fritte)* (fried) potatoes
*peperoncini* hot chilli peppers
*peperoni* sweet peppers
*peperonata* stewed peppers, onions, etc.
  (similar to ratatouille)
*piselli (al prosciutto)* peas (with ham)
*pomodoro/i* tomato(es)
*porri* leeks
*radicchio* red chicory
*radice* radish
*rapa* turnip
*rucola* rocket
*sedano* celery
*spinaci* spinach
*verdure* greens
*zucca* pumpkin
*zucchini* courgettes

## Formaggio (Cheese)

*bel paese* soft white cow's cheese
*cacio/caciocavallo* pale yellow, sharp cheese
*caprino* goat's cheese
*fontina* rich cow's cheese
*groviera* mild cheese (Gruyère)
*gorgonzola* soft blue cheese
*parmigiano* Parmesan cheese

*pecorino* sharp sheep's cheese
*provolone* sharp, tangy; *dolce* is less strong
*stracchino* soft white cheese

## Frutta, Nocciole (Fruit, Nuts)

*albicocche* apricots
*ananas* pineapple
*arance* oranges
*banane* bananas
*cachi* persimmon
*ciliege* cherries
*cocomero* watermelon
*datteri* dates
*fichi* figs
*fragole (con panna)* strawberries (with cream)
*lamponi* raspberries
*limone* lemon
*macedonia di frutta* fruit salad
*mandarino* tangerine
*mandorle* almonds
*melagrana* pomegranate
*mele* apples
*mirtilli* bilberries
*more* blackberries
*nespola* medlar fruit
*nocciole* hazelnuts
*noci* walnuts
*pera* pear
*pesca* peach
*pesca noce* nectarine
*pinoli* pine nuts
*pompelmo* grapefruit
*prugna/susina* prune/plum
*uva* grapes

## Dolci (Desserts)

*amaretti* macaroons
*cannoli* crisp pastry tubes filled with ricotta,
  cream, chocolate or fruit
*coppa gelato* assorted ice cream
*crema caramella* crème caramel
*crostata* fruit flan
*gelato (produzione propria)* (home-made)
  ice cream
*granita* flavoured ice, often lemon or coffee
*monte bianco* chestnut pudding with cream
*panettone* sponge cake with candied fruit
  and raisins
*panforte* dense cake of chocolate, almonds and
  preserved fruit
*sant honoré* meringue cake
*semifreddo* refrigerated cake
*sorbetto* sorbet/sherbet
*spumone* a soft ice cream
*tiramisù* layers of sponge, mascarpone, coffee
  and chocolate
*torrone* nougat
*torta* cake, tart

*torta millefoglie*  layered pastry and custard cream
*zabaglione*  eggs and Marsala wine, served hot
*zuppa inglese*  trifle

## Bevande (Beverages)

*acqua minerale*  mineral water
  *con/senza gas*  with/without fizz
*aranciata*  orange soda
*birra (alla spina)*  (draught) beer
*caffè (freddo)*  (iced) coffee
*cioccolata*  chocolate
*gassosa*  lemon-flavoured soda
*latte (intero/scremato)*  (whole/skimmed) milk
*limonata*  lemon soda
*succo di frutta*  fruit juice
*tè*  tea
*vino*  wine
  *rosso*  red
  *bianco*  white
  *rosato*  rosé

## Cooking Terms (Miscellaneous)

*aceto (balsamico)*  (balsamic) vinegar
*affumicato*  smoked
*aglio*  garlic
*alla brace*  on embers
*bicchiere*  glass
*burro*  butter
*cacciagione*  game
*conto*  bill
*costoletta/cotoletta*  chop
*coltello*  knife
*cucchiaio*  spoon
*filetto*  fillet

*forchetta*  fork
*forno*  oven
*fritto*  fried
*ghiaccio*  ice
*griglia*  grill
*in bianco*  without tomato
*magro*  lean meat/pasta without meat
*marmellata*  jam
*menta*  mint
*miele*  honey
*mostarda*  candied mustard sauce
*olio*  oil
*pane*  bread
*pane tostato*  toasted bread
*panini*  sandwiches (in roll)
*panna*  cream
*pepe*  pepper
*piatto*  plate
*prezzemolo*  parsley
*ripieno*  stuffed
*rosmarino*  rosemary
*sale*  salt
*salmì*  wine marinade
*salsa*  sauce
*salvia*  sage
*senape*  mustard
*tartufi*  truffles
*tavola*  table
*tazza*  cup
*tovagliolo*  napkin
*tramezzini*  triangular sandwiches
*umido*  cooked in sauce
*uovo*  egg
*zucchero*  sugar

# Planning
# Your Trip

05

# When to Go

## Climate

The climate in Tuscany is temperate along the coasts and in the valleys, and cooler up in the mountains; the higher Apennines and Monte Amiata have enough snow for **skiing** until April.

**Summers** are hot and humid; in August Italians head for the sea or mountains. **Spring**, especially May, when it rains less, is pleasantly warm.

**Autumn**, too, is a classic time to visit; in October and November, before the rains, while the air is clear, the colours of the scenery are brilliant and rare. The hills of Tuscany are never less than beautiful but in October they're extraordinary – and it's the **truffle season**.

**Winter** can be agreeable for visiting indoor city attractions without the crowds, particularly in Florence, where it seldom snows but may rain for days at a time.

## Festivals

Some festivals in Tuscany are clearly meant to pull the tourists in, or are just an excuse to hang out under the stars, but this doesn't make them any less fun. The several

## Average Maximum Temperatures in °C/°F

|  | April | July | Oct |
|---|---|---|---|
| Florence | 13/55 | 25/77 | 16/60 |
| Livorno | 5/59 | 24/75 | 15/59 |
| Siena | 12/54 | 25/77 | 15/59 |

## Average Monthly Rainfall in Millimetres/Inches

|  | April | July | Oct |
|---|---|---|---|
| Florence | 74/3 | 23/1 | 96/4 |
| Livorno | 62/3 | 7/0.25 | 110/4 |
| Siena | 61/3 | 21/1 | 112/4 |

exceptions to this rule will generally add a note of pageantry or culture to your holiday. Some are great costume affairs, with roots dating back to the Middle Ages, and there are quite a few music festivals, antiques fairs, and most of all, festivals devoted to food and drink.

The box below has a calendar of the major events. There are countless others, especially in summer months; look out for banners and ask around when you arrive.

## National Holidays

See p.74.

## Calendar of Events

### January

**1st Sun of month** Feast of the Gift, the mayor's donation of gold, frankincense and myrrh, Castiglione di Garfagnana.

**24** Feast of San Feliciano, procession with a traditional fair, Foligno.

### February

**Carnival** is fêted in private parties nearly everywhere; Viareggio has a huge public one with floats, music and parades. In Bibbiena, the last day of Carnival is celebrated with a grand dance and massive bonfire.

### March

**18–19** Pancake festival, Montefioralle, near Greve- in-Chianti; San Giuseppe (with rice fritters) and *Torrita di Siena* (donkey race tournament), Siena.

### March or April

**Holy Week** Religious rites, torchlight processions and so forth.

**Good Friday** Way of the Cross procession, Grassina, near Florence.

**Easter** Easter morning, *Scoppio del Carro*, 11am explosion of the cart in Florence (see p.168); Mary's girdle displayed from Prato's pulpit.

**1st Sun after Easter** Kite Festival, San Miniato.

### April/May

**Ascension Day** Cricket Festival, with floats and crickets sold in little cages, Florence.

### May

**All month** Iris festivals, Florence, San Polo Robbiana (Chianti).

**1st Sun** Donkey *palio*, Querceta, near Lucca.

**1st–3rd wk** Sword derring-do and *palio*, Camerino (Macerata).

**4th Sun** Historical parade and crossbow tournament, Massa Marittima.

**Last Sun** Crossbow competition versus Sansepolcro; crossbow competition, wine festival and cart processions at Montespertoli.

**May and June** *Maggio Musicale Fiorentino* music festival, Florence.

## June

**2** *Festa della Repubblica.*

**Early June** Street parade on sawdust designs, Camaiore (Lucca).

**2nd Sun** *Bruschetta* festival, Montecatini Terme.

**Mid-June–Aug** *Estate Fiesolana* – music, films, ballet and theatre, Fiesole.

**16–17** *Festa di San Ranieri* – lights festival and historic regatta in Pisa.

**3rd Sun** *Festa del Barbarossa*, celebrating the meeting of the pope and emperor, with ballet, archery, snails, beans and *pici*, San Quirico d'Orcia.

**3rd Sun** *Palio di Rioni*, neighbourhood horserace, Castiglion Fiorentina.

**24** St John the Baptist's Day, with fireworks, Florence; *Calcio in Costume*, Renaissance football game, Florence (2 other games this month).

**Last Sun** *Gioco del Ponte*, a traditional tug-of-war on a bridge, with a cart in the middle, Pisa.

**Last Sun** *La Bruscellata*, a week of dancing and singing old love songs around a flowering tree, San Donato in Poggio (Florence province).

## July

**Every weekend** *Festa Medioevale*, Palazzuolo sul Senio.

**1** Versilian Historical Trophy, Querceta (Lucca).

**2** *Palio*, the famous horse race, Siena (also 16 Aug).

**2nd Sun** Archery contest, Fivizzano (Massa).

**3rd Sun** Feast of San Paolino, Lucca, a torch-light parade and crossbow contest.

**25** Joust of the Bear, Pistoia.

**Last week** Elban Wine Festival, Le Ghiaie.

**Late July** Medieval Festival, Monteriggione, near Siena.

**July–Aug** Concert and theatre festival, San Gimignano; opera, ballet and concerts at the Sferisterio, Macerata; Puccini Opera Festival, Torre del Lago.

## August

**1st weekend** Thanksgiving festival for San Sisto, Pisa.

**2nd Sun** Crossbow tournament, Massa Marittima.

**15** Beefsteak Festival, Cortona.

**16** *Palio*, dating from 1147, Siena.

**2nd Sun** *Palio Marinaro*, boat races, Livorno.

**15–30** International choir contest, Arezzo.

## September

**1st Sun** Saracen's Joust, Arezzo; *Palio dei Cerri* between neighbourhoods and Renaissance processions, Cerreto Guidi; lantern festival, Florence.

**2nd Sun** *Giostra della Quintana*, jousting, Foligno; crossbow contest with Gubbio, Sansepolcro.

**14** Holy Procession in honour of the Volto Santo by torchlight, Lucca.

**3rd Sun** Wine festival, Impruneta; donkey race, Carmignano.

## November

**22** Concerts in honour of Santa Cecilia, Siena.

## December

**8** Fair of the Immaculate Conception, Bagni di Lucca.

**24** Evergreen bonfire, Camporgiano (Lucca).

**25–26** St Stephen's feast and display of the holy girdle, Prato.

# Tourist Information

The city/provincial tourist offices (given in the area chapters) often have websites and usually provide lists of villas and farmhouses for rent, plus B&Bs and *agriturismi* (see p.67).

For information before you travel, contact the Italian National Tourist Office (*www.italiantourism.com*) in your own country.

## Italian Tourist Offices Abroad

**UK:** Italian State Tourist Board, 1 Princes St, London W1R 8AY, **t** (020) 7408 1254 *www.italiantouristboard.co.uk*; Italian Embassy, 14 Three King's Yard, Davies St, London W1K 4EH, **t** (020) 7312 2200, *www.amblondra.esteri.it*.

**USA:** 630 Fifth Ave, Suite 1565, New York, NY 10111, **t** (212) 245 5618; 12400 Wilshire Blvd, Suite 550, Los Angeles, CA 90025, **t** (310) 820

1898; 500 N. Michigan Ave, Suite 2240, Chicago 1 IL 60611, **t** (312) 644 0996.

**Australia**, Level 4, 46 Market St, Sydney, NSW 2000, **t** (02) 92 621666.

**Canada**: 175 Bloor St East, Suite 907, South Tower, Toronto, Ontario, M4W 3R8, **t** (416) 925 4882.

**New Zealand**: c/o Italian Embassy, 34 Grant Rd, Thorndon, Wellington, **t** (044) 947170.

For information on Italy and all the tourists boards in the world, visit *www.italiantourism.com*

Information may also be available from **Alitalia** (the national airline) or **CIT** (the state-run travel agency) offices in some countries.

## Embassies and Consulates

For a list of **Italian embassies abroad**, see *www.embassyworld.com*.

The UK and USA have consulates in Florence; the rest are all in Rome.

**UK**: Via XX Settembre 80a, Rome, **t** 06 4220 0001; Lungarno Corsini 2, Florence, **t** 055 284133.

**Ireland**: Piazza Campitelli 3, Rome, **t** 06 697 9121.

**USA**: Via Vittorio Veneto 119a, Rome, **t** 06 46741; Lungarno Amerigo Vespucci 38, Florence, **t** 055 2669 5232.

**Canada**: Via Zara 30, Rome, **t** 06 445981.

**Australia**: Via Alessandria 215, Rome, **t** 06 852721.

**New Zealand**: Via Zara 28, Rome, **t** 06 441 7171.

## Entry Formalities

### Passports and Visas

To get into Italy you need a valid passport. **EU citizens** do not need visas. Nationals from the **USA**, **Canada**, **Australia** and **New Zealand** do not need visas for stays of up to 90 days. For longer, you must get a *permesso di soggiorno*. For this you need to state your reason for staying and prove both a source of income and medical insurance.

The Italian law states you must register with the police within 8 days of arrival. If you check into a hotel this is done automatically; otherwise you should go to the local police station (in practice few people do this). If you need advice on the forms, call the Rome Police Office for visitors, **t** (06) 4686, ext. 2987.

## Customs

**EU nationals** over 17 can import and take out an unlimited quantity of goods for personal use. Arrivals from **non-EU countries** have to pass through Italian customs, which are usually benign, unless you're carrying more than 150 cigarettes or 75 cigars, 1 litre of hard liquor or 3 bottles of wine, a couple of cameras, one movie camera, 10 rolls of film for each, one tape-recorder, one radio, one record-player, one canoe less than 5.5m and one TV (though you'll have to pay for a licence for it), or sports equipment not for personal use. Pets must have a bilingual Certificate of Health from your vet. US citizens may return with $400 worth of merchandise – keep your receipts.

There are no limits to the amount of money you may bring into Italy, and no one is likely to check how much you leave with.

## Disabled Travellers

Access-for-all laws in Italy have improved the once-dire situation: the number of ramps and stairlifts has increased dramatically in the past decade, and nearly every hotel has one or two rooms with facilities for the disabled, though older ones may not have a lift, or not one large enough for a wheelchair.

Service stations on the *autostrade* have equipped restrooms, but you could get very stuck in the middle of a city – Florence, visited by zillions of tourists, lacks accessible loos. Local tourist offices (listed in the text) are helpful, and may even find someone to give you a hand, while the national tourist office (*see* p.59) can offer tips for difficult hilltowns.

Italian churches are a problem, with their long flights of steps in front.

## Insurance and EHIC Cards

National health services in the UK and Australia have **reciprocal healthcare agreements** with Italy (you need a European Health Insurance or **EHIC card**; see *www. dh.gov.uk/travellers* or pick up a form at a post office), but this only allows for state-

## Disability Organizations

### In Italy

**Centro Studi Consulenza Invalidi**, Via Gozzadini 7, 20148 Milan, **t** 02 4030 8339. Ask for the annual accommodation guide, *Vacanze per Disabili*.

**CO.IN (Consorzio Cooperative Integrate)**, Via Enrico Giglili 54a, 00169 Rome, **t** 800 271027, **t** 06 2326 7504, *www.coinsociale.it/turismoper tutti*. Its tourist information centre (Mon–Fri 9–5) offers advice and information on accessibility.

### In the UK and Ireland

**Tourism for All**, c/o Vitalise, Shap Road Industrial Estate, Shap Road, Kendal, Cumbria LA9 6NZ, **t** 0845 124 9971, *www.tourismforall.org.uk*. Information on accommodation, transport, equipment hire, services, tour operators and contacts.

**Irish Wheelchair Association**, Blackheath Drive, Clontarf, Dublin 3, **t** (01) 818 6400, *www.iwa.ie*. This publishes travel advice guides.

**RADAR**, 12 City Forum, 250 City Rd, London, EC1V 8AF, **t** (020) 7250 3222, *www.radar.org.uk*. Information and books.

**RNIB (Royal National Institute of the Blind)**, 105 Judd St, London WC1H 9NE, **t** 0303 123 9999, *www.rnib.org.uk*. The mobility unit has a 'Plane Easy' audio-tape with advice for visually impaired flyers, and also advises on finding accommodation abroad.

### In the USA and Canada

**American Foundation for the Blind**, 11 Penn Plaza, Suite 300, New York, NY 10001, **t** (212) 502 7600, *www.afb.org*. Info for visually impaired travellers.

**Federation for the Handicapped**, 211 West 14th St, New York, NY 10011, **t** (212) 747 4262. Organizes summer tours for members.

**SATH (Society for Accessible Travel and Hospitality)**, 347 5th Ave, Suite 610, New York, NY 10016, **t** (212) 447 7284, *www.sath.org*. Travel and access information. The website has good links and a list of online publications.

### Internet Sites

**Access-Able Travel Source**, *www.access-able.com*. Information for older and disabled travellers.

**Access Ability**, *www.access-ability.org/travel.html*. Information on travel agencies.

**Emerging Horizons**, *www.emerginghorizons.com*. An online newsletter for disabled travellers.

provided 'necessary' care, you should also take out your own **insurance** to cover the gap.

Those from elsewhere should check their current policies to see if they're covered abroad for mishaps such as cancelled flights and lost baggage, and under what circumstances, and judge whether they need an additional policy. Travel agencies sell policies, as well as insurance companies, but they are not cheap. First check whether your credit card company or bank account gives you some kind of cover. *See* also **Health and Emergencies**, p.73.

## Money

The **euro** is divided into 100 **cents**. There are banknotes in denominations of 5, 10, 20, 50, 100, 200 and 500, and coins in denominations of 1 and 2 euros, and 1, 2, 5, 10, 20 and 50 cents.

You can withdraw cash from most **ATMs/** cash dispensers with any of the common debit or credit cards; your bank may charge a small fee, but it won't work out any more expensive than normal commission rates. It's worth having a backup (e.g. traveller's cheques) in case your card is rejected; bring some euros for when you arrive, too..

**Credit and debit cards** are accepted by most hotels, resort-area restaurants, shops and car-hire firms, although some may take exception to American Express. Italians are wary of plastic, though, and you may be asked for some ID when paying by card.

**American Express**, Florence: Via Dante Alighieri 22R, off Piazza della Repubblica, **t** 055 50981.

For **banking hours**, *see* p.74.

## Getting There

### By Air from the UK and Ireland

At the time of writing there are a huge variety of flights from the UK and Ireland to Tuscany or cities handy for the region, many run by low-cost carriers.

From **London Heathrow**, Alitalia and British Airways (BA) fly to Milan Linate, Milan Malpensa and Rome (Fiumicino), BA also flies to Pisa, and Ethiopian Airlines to Rome (Fiumicino). From **London Gatwick** Meridiana

## Direct Flights from the UK and Ireland

**Aer Lingus**, Ireland t 0818 365 000; UK t 0871 718 5000, *www.aerlingus.com*.

**Alitalia**, t 08714 24 14 24, *www.alitalia.co.uk*.

**British Airways**, UK t 0844 493 0787; Ireland t 1890 626 747, *www.ba.com*.

**Ethiopian Airlines**, t (020) 8987 7000, *www.ethiopianairlines.com*.

### Low-cost Carriers

**easyJet**, t 0905 821 0905, *www.easyJet.com*.

**jet2.com**, t 0871 226 1 737, *www.jet2.com*.

**FlyGlobespan**, t 0871 271 9000, *www.flyglobespan.com*.

**Meridiana**, t 0871 222 9 319, *www.meridiana.it*.

**My Travel**, t 0871 895 0055, *www.mytravel.com*.

**Ryanair**, UK t 0871 246 0000, Ireland t 0818 30 30 30, *www.ryanair.com*.

**Thomsonfly**, t 0870 1900 737, *www.thomsonfly.com*.

## Direct Flights from the USA and Canada

**Alitalia**, US t 800 223 5730, *www.alitaliausa.com*.

**British Airways**, t 800 AIRWAYS, *www.ba.com*.

## Discounts and Youth Fares

### From the UK and Ireland

**Budget Travel**, 134 Lower Baggot St, Dublin 2, t (01) 631 1111, *www.budgettravel.ie*.

**Italflights**, 125 High Holborn, London WC1V 6QA, t (020) 7404 0470.

**Trailfinders**, 215 Kensington High St, London W8, t 0845 050 5945; 4–5 Dawson St, Dublin 2, t (01) 677 7888, *www.trailfinders.co.uk*; plus branches in other major UK cities.

**United Travel**, 2 Old Dublin Rd, Stillorgan, Co. Dublin, t (01) 219 0600, *www.unitedtravel.ie*.

Besides saving 25% on regular flights, under-26s can fly on on special discount charters. Contact:

**STA**, 6 Wright's Lane, London W8 6TA, t 0871 230 0040, *www.statravel.co.uk*. There are several other branches in London, and many in other major UK towns and cities.

**USIT Now**, 19–21 Aston Quay, Dublin 2, t (01) 602 1906 *www.usitnow.ie*. Ireland's no.1 specialist student travel agent, with other branches around the country.

### From the USA and Canada

It's also worth looking at the websites *www.xfares.com* (carry-on luggage only) and *www.smarterliving.com*.

**Airhitch**, 481 Eighth Ave, Suite 1771, New York, NY 10001-1820, t (212) 736 0505 or t 1 877 AIRHITCH.

**STA**, t 800 781 4040, *www.statravel.com*. There are branches at most universities and at 205 East 42nd St, New York, NY 10017, t (212) 822 2700, and ASUC Building, 1st Floor, University of California, Berkeley, CA 94720, t (510) 642 3000.

**TFI Tours**, 34 West 32nd St, New York, NY 10001, t (212) 736 1140 or t (800) 745 8000, *www.tfi-tours.com*.

**The Last Minute Club**, 1300 Don Mills Rd, Toronto, Ontario M3B 2W6, t (416) 449 5400, *www.lastminuteclub.com*.

**Travel Cuts**, 187 College St, Toronto, Ontario M5T 1P7, t (866) 246 9762, *www.travelcuts.com*. Canada's largest student agency, with branches in most provinces.

---

flies to Florence, BA and Thomsonfly to Pisa, and BA to Rome (Fiumicino), and easyJet to Rome (Ciampino), Milan Linate and Malpensa. From **London Stansted** Ryanair services Ancona, Bologna (Forlì), Genoa, Parma, Pescara, Pisa, Rome (Ciampino) and Milan (Bergamo).

From **Manchester** My Travel flies to Rimini, Alitalia and BA to Milan (Malpensa), Thomsonfly to Pisa, and jet2.com to Pisa and Rome (Fiumicino). From **Leeds/Bradford** jet2.com goes to Milan (Bergamo), Pisa and Rome (Fiumicino). From **Newcastle** jet2.com goes to Pisa, and easyJet to Rome (Ciampino).

From **Edinburgh** you can get to Pisa with Ryanair as well as jet2.com and Rome (Fiumicino) with FlyGlobespan; from **Aberdeen** you can get to Pisa with jet2.com and to Rome (Fiumicino) with British Airways and FlyGlobespan.

From **Dublin**, Aer Lingus flies to Bologna, Milan (Bergamo), Milan (Linate) and Rome (Fiumicino), Alitalia to Milan (Malpensa) and Rome (Fiumicino), Ryanair to Milan (Bergamo), Pisa and Rome (Ciampino). Aer Lingus also flies from **Cork** to Rome (Fiumicino).

When this guide went to press, Alitalia and BA return fares started at £80 one way if booked well ahead, and both airlines offered cheaper tickets on some flights for students and under-26s. Ryanair and easyJet can be much cheaper if booked well in advance on their websites or if you look out for special offers and sales which sometimes let you fly for free or a mere £5 (*see* listings opposite). It might also save you money to buy via UK **flight websites** such as *www.cheapflights.co.uk*, *www.ebookers.com*, *www.expedia.co.uk*, *www.flightline.co.uk*, *www.airflights.co.uk*, *www.flights4less.co.uk* and *www.flightsdirect.com*, and keep your eyes open for bargains and charters in the papers.

Alitalia often has **promotional perks** such as car hire or discounts on domestic flights, hotels or tours within Italy. BA does a fly-drive package to Pisa and Florence.

## By Air from the USA and Canada

From the **USA**, Alitalia flies to Rome or Milan from various destinations, and BA has a New York–London Gatwick–Pisa service. A travel agent may be able to find a much cheaper fare from your home airport to your Italian airport via London, Brussels, Paris, Frankfurt or Amsterdam. From **Canada**, only Alitalia flies direct to Italy (from Toronto/Montreal to Rome/Milan).

For **Apex fares**, you need fixed arrival and departure dates and to spend at least a week in Italy but no more than 90 days. Some Apex fares must be purchased at least 14 days (sometimes 21) in advance, and there are penalties if you change dates. At the time of writing, the lowest midweek Apex between New York and Rome in the off-season was around $800, rising to about $900 in summer; from Canada, low-season fares are about $1000–$1,250. Some carriers, including Alitalia, offer **promotions** that might include car hire or discounts on hotels, domestic flights or excursions; ask a travel agent for details. Under-2s usually travel free, and both BA and Alitalia offer cheaper tickets on some flights for students and under-26s.

It may be worth catching a cheap flight to London (New York–London fares are always competitive) then flying on using a British low-cost carriers such as easyJet and Ryanair (*see* box left). Prices are rather more from Canada, so it's best to fly from the USA.

For **discounted flights**, check the small ads in newspaper travel pages (e.g. *New York Times*, *Chicago Tribune*, *Toronto Globe & Mail*). Numerous travel clubs and agencies also specialize in discount fares but may require annual membership. You could also try some of the US **cheap flight websites** including: *www.priceline.com* (bid for tickets), *www.expedia.com*, *www.hotwire.com*, *www.bestfares.com*, *www.travelocity.com*, *www.cheaptrips.com*, *www.courier.org* (courier flights) and *www.ricksteves.com*. Other websites are listed in the box opposite.

## By Train

From London you can travel by Eurostar to France then take an onward train from there. The journey time to Florence is about 17hrs. Services run daily and return fares cost around £225. The journey involves changing trains and stations in Paris; sleepers or couchettes are available on the evening train from there.

Eurostar tickets, booking for onward journeys to destinations in Italy, and tickets and passes within Italy, can be bought via:

**Rail Europe, t** 08448 484064, *www.raileurope.co.uk* (in the States **t** 877 257 2887, in Canada **t** 800 361 RAIL, *www.raileurope.com*).

In an age of low-cost airlines, rail travel is not much of an economy unless you can take advantage of student, youth, family and young children or senior citizen discounts, although it is less environmentally harmful. **InterRail** (UK) or **Eurail** (USA/Canada) **passes** offer unlimited travel for all ages throughout Europe for a variety of timeframes. Various youth fares and inclusive rail passes are also available within Italy if you're planning on doing a lot of train travel solely in Italy; organize these before leaving home with:

**Rail Choice, t** 0870 165 7300, *www.railchoice.co.uk*.

The **Trenitalia Pass**, available to non-Italian residents, allows 1st- or 2nd-class travel on all Trenitalia trains for 4–10 days (consecutive or non-consecutive) within a 2-month period. It can be obtained at main Italian stations, or in travel agencies abroad. The versions are: Basic for over-26s, Youth for under-26s, and Saver for groups of 2–5. Prices for Basic 2nd-class tickets are £180 for 4 days, £290 for 10 days. You need to pay supplements if you take an Italian *Eurostar* (*see* p.64), or book a couchette or bed on an overnight train.

For more passes and discounts, contact **Rail Europe** or **Rail Choice** (for both, *see* above).

## By Coach

The coach is the last refuge of aerophobic bargain-hunters. The journey time from London to Florence is around 30hrs; the return full fare is around £115. There are discounts for students, senior citizens and children as well as off-peak travel.

**National Express/Eurolines, t** 08717 818 181, *www.nationalexpress.com/eurolines*.

## By Car

Driving to Italy from the UK is a lengthy and expensive proposition. No matter how you cross the Channel, it is a good two-day drive – about 1,600km from Calais to Rome. If you're only staying a short time, compare costs against Alitalia's or other airlines' **fly-drive schemes** (some airlines – *see* pp.61–3 – offer discounted car hire via their websites).

**Eurotunnel** trains shuttle cars and their passengers through the Channel Tunnel from Folkestone to Calais on a drive-on-drive-off system (journey time 35mins) 24hrs a day year-round (at least once an hour through the night). Standard return fares range from £124 to £398, but special offers can bring them as low as £98.

**Eurotunnel, t** 08705 353535, *www.eurotunnel.com*.

If you prefer to be above not below the sea, a good source of information on the many **ferry routes** is *www.ferrybooker.com*, which also offers discounts on bookings.

You can cut many of the costly **French motorway tolls** by going to Calais, driving to Basle, Switzerland, and from there through the Alps via the toll-free Gotthard Tunnel. In summer you can save the expensive tunnel tolls, and see some marvellous scenery, by taking one of the **mountain passes** instead.

Current motorway tunnel toll charges (one way) are:

**Fréjus Tunnel**, *www.tunneldufrejus.com*, Modane (France) to Bardonecchia. From €32.

**Gran San Bernardo**, *www.sitrasb.it*, Bourg St Pierre (Switzerland) to Aosta. From €25.

**Mont Blanc Tunnel**, *www.tunnelmb.com*. €32.

To **bring your car into Italy**, you need your registration document, a valid driving licence and valid insurance (a Green Card, obtained from your insurer, is not necessary unless you go through Switzerland, but is advisable). Make sure everything is in excellent working order; it's not uncommon to be stopped, checked and fined by the police, and **spare parts** for some non-Italian cars are hard to come by. For peace of mind, take out breakdown insurance from the well-reputed **Europ Assistance** (t 0844 338 5533, *www.europ-assistance.co.uk*).

## Getting Around

The republic has an excellent network of airports, railways, highways and byways, and you'll find getting around fairly easy – unless one union or another goes on strike (*sciopero*, pronounced SHO-PER-O). There's always a day or two's notice of one, and they usually last only 12 or 24 hrs, but this is long enough to throw a spanner in the works if you have to catch a plane, so keep your eyes and ears open for advance warnings. That said, they rarely happen in the main holiday season.

### By Train

**FS information from anywhere in Italy**: t 892021, *www.trenitalia.com*.

Italy's national railway, the FS (**Ferrovie dello Stato**), is well run and often a pleasure to ride. There are also several private rail lines around cities and in rural districts. We have tried to list them all in the 'Getting around' sections of the area chapters in this book. Some of these private companies don't accept InterRail or Eurail passes.

**Train fares** have increased greatly over the last five years or so, and only those without extra supplements can still be called cheap. Possible FS unpleasantnesses you may encounter, besides a strike, are delays and crowding, especially at weekends and in summer. **Reserve seats** in advance (*fare una prenotazione*); the fee is small and can save you hours of standing. For upper echelon trains (Italian *Eurostars* and some *Intercities*), reservations are mandatory. Check when you buy your ticket in advance that the date is correct; tickets are only valid the day they're purchased unless you specify otherwise.

**Tickets** are sold at stations and many travel agents (and some also online); it's wise to buy in advance as queues can be long. Make sure you ask which platform (*binario*) your train leaves from; the big permanent boards posted in the stations are not always correct.

Always **stamp your ticket** (*convalidare* or *obliterare*) in the not-very-obvious machine at the head of the platform before boarding – failure to do so may result in a fine. If you get on a train without a ticket you can buy one from the conductor, for an added 20%. You can also pay a conductor to move up to first class as long if places are available.

There is a strict **hierarchy of trains**. *Regionales* travel short-ish distances, and tend to stop at all stations. There are only a few *Espressi* left and they are in poor condition; most serve the long runs from the south of Italy. *Intercity* trains link Italian cities, with minimum stops. Some carry an obligatory seat reservation requirement (free); all require a supplement. The 'Kings of the Rails' are the swish, super-fast *Eurostars* (Florence–Rome 90mins). These make very few stops, offer 1st- and 2nd-class carriages, and carry a supplement that includes an obligatory seat reservation. For the **Trenitalia pass** for non-residents, *see* p.63.

**Refreshments** on routes of any great distance are provided by buffet cars or trolleys; you can usually get sandwiches and coffee from vendors along the tracks at intermediary stops. Station bars often have a good variety of takeaway travellers' fare. Bring a bottle of mineral water, as there's no drinking water on the trains.

Major stations have an *albergo diurno* ('day hotel', where you can shower, get a shave and haircut, etc.), information offices, currency exchanges open at weekends (not at the best rates), hotel reservation services, kiosks with foreign papers, restaurants, etc. You can also book a hire car to pick up at your destination, through Avis, Hertz or Maggiore (listed where relevant in the area chapters).

## By Coach and Bus

**Intercity coach travel** is often quicker than train travel and a bit more expensive. You will find regular coach links only where there's no train to offer competition. In many regions, buses are the only means of public transport and are well used, with frequent departures.

Coaches almost always depart from near the train station, and tickets usually need to be bought before boarding. Country bus lines are based in provincial capitals; we've done our best to explain the connections even for the most out-of-the-way routes, as well as listing coach companies in the relevant areas.

**City bus routes** are well labelled; all charge flat fees for rides within the city limits and immediate suburbs (around €1). Tickets must be purchased before you get on, either from a tobacconist's, a newspaper kiosk, many bars, or ticket machines near the main stops. Once you are on, you must '*obliterate*' (punch) your ticket in the machines at the front or back of the bus; controllers stage random checks, with fines for cheats about €40.

## By Car

The advantages of driving in Tuscany generally outweigh the disadvantages. Before you bring your own car or hire one, consider the kind of holiday you're planning. If it's a tour of major art cities, you're best off not driving: parking is impossible, traffic impossible, deciphering one-way streets, signals and signs impossible. In nearly every other case, a car gives you the freedom of making your way through Italy's delightful open countryside and stopping at smaller towns and villages.

Be prepared to encounter some of the highest **fuel costs** in Europe, to spend a very long time looking for a **parking place** in any town bigger than a peanut, and to face drivers who look at motoring as if it were a video game. No matter how fast you trip along on the *autostrade* (Italy's toll motorways, with an official speed limit 130km/80miles per hr), someone will pass you going twice as fast.

If you aren't intimidated, buy a good **road map** of Italy or a detailed one of the region you're travelling in (the Italian Touring Club produces excellent ones; see also p.74 for specialist travel bookshops selling maps). Most **petrol stations** close for lunch, and few stay open late at night, though you may find a 'self-service' one where machines accept nice, smooth banknotes. Autostrada **tolls** are high – www.autostrade.it helps calculate journey costs. Rest stops and petrol stations along motorways open 24hrs. Other roads are free.

Italians are good at signposting, and roads are almost all excellently maintained. Beware that you may be fined on the spot for speeding, a burnt-out headlamp, etc.; if you're especially unlucky you may be slapped with a super multa, or superfine, of €130–260 or more. You may even be fined for not having a portable **warning triangle** (these can be bought when you cross the Channel, at the border or from an ACI office). It is now law a) to keep **headlights on and dipped** on the autostrada and in rural areas at all times and b) to carry a bright **orange fluorescent jacket** in the car at all times and put it on if you break down.

The **Automobile Club of Italy** (ACI) (Via Marsala 8, Rome, t 064477, www.aci.it) is a good friend to the foreign motorist. Besides proffering useful info and tips, they can be reached from anywhere by calling t 116 – which is also the number to call if you have an accident or simply have to find the nearest service station. If you need **major repairs**, the ACI makes sure the prices charged are according to their guidelines.

### Car Hire

**Hiring a car** is fairly simple if not particularly cheap (an average of €85/day or €500/wk for a smallish car), although cheap deals can often be found online if you book well ahead. Italian car-hire firms are called autonoleggi. There are large international firms through which you can reserve a car in advance, and local agencies that often have lower prices; we've listed suggestions in the area chapters were relevant. Air or rail travellers should check out possible **discount packages**. Airlines (see pp.61–3) often offer deals through their websites; try www.easycar.com for the most competitive rates.

Most rental companies require a **deposit** amounting to the estimated cost of the hire, and there is 19% VAT added to the final cost. Rates become more advantageous if you take the car for a week with unlimited mileage. If you need a car for more than 3wks, **leasing** is a more economic alternative. The National Tourist Office (see p.59) has a list of firms in Italy that let **caravans** (trailers) and **campers**.

### By Taxi

Taxi tariffs from town to town start at €2.33; then add €0.78 per km (there is a minimum charge of €4.50). Each piece of baggage will cost you an extra €1.04, and there are surcharges for trips outside the city limits, between 10pm and 6am, and on Sundays and holidays.

### By Motorbike and Bicycle

The transport of choice for many Italians, motorbikes, mopeds and Vespas can be a delightful way to get between cities and see the countryside. You should only consider this, however, if you've ridden them before – Italy's hills and traffic make it no place to learn. Helmets are compulsory. A motorino (moped) costs from about €30/day to hire; scooters are somewhat more (from about €50).

Italians are keen cyclists, racing drivers up the steepest hills; if you're not training for the Tour de France, consider the hilliness of the region before planning a bicycling tour – especially in summer months. Bikes can be transported by train in Italy, either with you or within a couple of days; apply at the luggage office (ufficio bagagli). Hire prices range from about €10/day; to buy one, plan for upwards of €150, either in a bike shop or through local classified ads. If you bring your own bike, check with your airline first about their policies on transporting them.

## Where to Stay

### Hotels

Tuscany is well endowed with hotels (alberghi) of every description. These are rated by the government's tourism bureaucracy, on a 5-star scale. Ratings take into account such features as a restaurant on the premises, plumbing, air-con, etc., but not

## Hotel Price Ranges

Categories are based on a standard double room (en suite where available) in high season.

### In Florence

| luxury | €€€€€ | €250 + |
|---|---|---|
| very expensive | €€€€ | €180–250 |
| expensive | €€€ | €130–180 |
| moderate | €€ | €75–130 |
| inexpensive | € | – €75 |

### Elsewhere in the Region

| luxury | €€€€€ | €230 + |
|---|---|---|
| very expensive | €€€€ | €150–230 |
| expensive | €€€ | €100–150 |
| moderate | €€ | €60–100 |
| inexpensive | € | – €60 |

character, style or charm. And hotels may stay at a lower rating than they've earned, so a three-star could be as comfy as a four-star.

**Breakfast** is often included in the room rate. You might find that **half- or full-board** is obligatory, particularly in high season at hotels in seaside, lake or mountain resorts, spas or country villas.

## Prices

In general, the further south you go in Italy, the cheaper the rates. In **Florence**, prices are slightly higher (*see* box above). Prices are by law listed on the door of each room and printed in hotel lists available from local tourist offices. They may cost up to 50% less in the **low season**. In resorts, hotels may close down for several months of the year.

For a **single**, count on paying two-thirds of a double; to add an extra bed in a double adds 35% to the rate. Taxes and service charges are included in rates. **Non-en suite rooms** (i.e. sharing toilets and bathrooms in the hall) are about 20–30% cheaper.

A booking is valid once a **deposit** has been paid; different establishments have different policies about **cancellation charges** after a certain time. If you come in summer without reservations, call around for a place in the morning or put yourself at the mercy of one of the tourist office **hotel-finding services** (we've listed these in the area chapters).

The National Tourist Office (*see* p.59) has lists of and booking information for motels and 5- and 4-star hotels and chains. Besides classic hotels, there are an increasing number of alternatives, nearly always located in historic buildings.

## Inexpensive Accommodation

Bargains are few and far between in Italy. Most cheaper places are around railway stations. In small towns the tourist office may have a list of *affittacamere* (**rooms to rent**), which vary from basic accommodation in someone's house to more upmarket places.

Besides youth hostels (*see* below), there are **city-run hostels** with dorm-style rooms, open to all. In some cities **religious institutions** let extra rooms. Rural monasteries and convents sometimes take guests (bring a letter of introduction from your local priest or pastor).

## Youth and Student Hostels

You'll find hostels in Florence, Lucca, Tavarnelle Val di Pesa (Chianti), Abetone, Cortona, San Gimignano, Marina di Massa and Carrara. You can nearly always buy an **IYHF card** on the spot. There are no age limits, and senior citizens are often given added discounts. Accommodation – usually a bunk in a single-sex room, plus breakfast – costs around €10/day. Curfews are common, and you usually can't check in before 5 or 6pm. Avoid spring, when noisy school groups descend on hostels for field trips.

The **Centro Turistico Studentesco e Giovanile** (CTS; *www.cts.it*), with offices in most Italian cities (and one in London), can also book cheap accommodation for students.

## Self-catering Holidays: Villas, Farmhouses and Flats

Renting a villa, farmhouse, cottage or apartment has always been the choice way to visit Tuscany. The **Internet** has made finding a place easier than ever, with companies providing detailed listings and photos. Another place to look is the Sunday papers; or, if you're set on a particular area, contact its tourist office (or see its website) for a list of local rental agencies. These should provide photos; make sure all pertinent details are in your rental agreement to avoid misunderstandings later.

In general **minimum lets** are a week; rental **prices** (generally per week) usually include insurance, water and electricity, sometimes linen and maid service. Common problems are water shortages, insects (*see* p.41) and low kilowatts. Most companies offer **packages** with flights and car-hire. Book as far in advance as possible for summer.

## Rural Self-catering or Agriturismo

For a breath of rural seclusion, gregarious Italians head for **working farms**, offering accommodation (sometimes self-catering) that often approximates French *gîtes*. The real pull may be cooking by the hosts, using home-grown produce. In Tuscany hundreds of *agriturismo* farms offer rooms, varying enormously in standard and price, from quite modest to extremely upmarket. In general, prices, compared with overhyped 'Tuscan villas', are still reasonable.

This branch of the Italian tourist industry is run by **Agriturist** (*www.agriturist.it*), which has several offices in each region. Local tourist offices have information on such accommodation in their areas, or contact:

**Associazione Regionale Agriturist**, Via Degli Alfani 67, 50120 Florence, **t** 055 287838.

**Solemar**, Via G Modena 19, Florence, **t** 055 552131, *www.solemar.it*.

**Turismo Verde**, Via Jacopo Nardi 41, Florence, **t** 055 23389, *www.turismoverde.it*.

Alternatively, contact the individual provincial Agriturist offices (UPA) directly, as listed on the websites:

**Tuscany**: *www.agriturist.toscana.it*.

## Alpine Refuges

*Rifugi alpini* – mountain huts in the Apennines – vary from basic to grand; some are exclusively for hikers and climbers, others are reached by *funivie*, used by skiers in winter and holidaymakers in summer. Rates are about €10–28 a night, depending on whether you are a CAI member, but rise by 20% Dec–April. The club has a list of huts, dates available, and booking information.

**Club Alpino Italiano**: Via E Petrella 19, Milan, **t** 02 205 7231, *www.cai.it*.

## Camping

Most official campsites are near the sea, mountains or lakes; there is usually one within commuting distance of major tourist centres. Prices vary enormously. Details are published in the Italian Touring Club's *Campeggi e Villaggi Turistici*, sold in Italian bookshops (€20), or ask for a free abbreviated list from:

**Centro Internazionale Prenotazioni Federcampeggio**, Casella Postale 23, 50041, Calenzano (Florence), **t** 055 882391, *www.federcampeggio.it*.

You can camp outside an official site with the landowner's permission.

## Specialist Tour Operators

For **specialist courses for foreigners**, *see* p.76.

### In Italy

**Corymbus Viaggi**, Via Massetana Romana 56, 53100 Siena, **t** 0577 271654, *www.corymbus.it*. Etruscan tours, wine tours, art and cookery in Umbria and Tuscany, painting and stencil classes, and mountainbike tours of Chianti.

**Vitaly**, Piazza Massimo D'Azeglio 7, 50121 Florence, **t** 055 2001050, *www.vitaly.it*. Luxury tailor-made tours and holidays in Tuscany specializing in fulfilling unusual requests. Anything can be arranged: from wine, cooking or art tours, to private tours of the museums or a helicopter ride over vineyards, not to mention weddings.

### In the UK

**Abercrombie & Kent**, St George's House, Ambrose St, Cheltenham, Glos GL0 3LG, **t** 0845 070 0610, *www.abercrombiekent.co.uk*. City breaks in all major cities.

**Ace Study Tours**, Babraham, Cambridge CB2 4AP, **t** (01223) 835055, *www.study-tours.org*. Cultural tours through Tuscany and Umbria.

**Alternative Travel**, 69–71 Banbury Rd, Oxford OX2 6PE, **t** (01865) 315678, *www.atg-oxford.co.uk*. Walking, wildflower, garden and cycling tours – 'Piero della Francesca', 'The Palio in Siena' and 'Renaissance Tuscany' – plus truffle hunts and painting courses.

**Arblaster & Clarke Wine Tours**, Farnham Rd, West Liss, Petersfield, Hants GU33 6JQ, **t** (01730) 893344, *www.arblasterandclarke.com*. Tuscan wine tours, truffle hunts and cooking tours.

**Bellini Travel**, 7 Barb Mews, London W6 7PA, t (020) 7437 8918, www.bellinitravel.com. Tailor-made tours to Tuscany and other parts of Italy, including access to villas and gardens not usually open to the public.

**British Museum Traveller**, 38 Russell Square, London WC1B 3QQ, t 0800 085 0864, www.britishmuseumtraveller.co.uk. Occasional Tuscan art and architecture tours.

**Carrier Travel**, London Rd, Alderley Edge, Cheshire SK9 7JT, t (0161) 491 7650, www.carrier.co.uk. An award-winning holiday firm with lots of choice in the region.

**Citalia Holidays**, Atrium, London Rd, Crawley, West Sussex, RH10 9SR, t 0870 837 1371, www.citalia.co.uk. A wide range of escorted or independent holidays throughout Italy.

**Fine Art Travel**, 15 Savile Row, London W1X 1AE, t (020) 7437 8553, www.fineacttravel.co.uk. Cultural, art and historical tours.

**hush!**, No.1 Lakeside, Cheadle SK8 3GW, t (0161) 492 1392, www.hush-italy.com. 'Authentic' holidays in Tuscany and elsewhere.

**Inntravel**, near Castle Howard, York YO60 7JU, t (01653) 617945, www.inntravel.co.uk. Another award-winning firm particularly strong on walking holidays, including Tuscany.

**Inscape Fine Art Study Tours**, 1 Farley Lane, Stonesfield, Witney, Oxfordshire OX29 8HB, t (01993) 891726, www.inscapetours.co.uk. Escorted art 'study' tours with guest lecturers in Florence, Siena and southern Tuscany.

**Ilios Travel**, Bolney Place, Cowfold Road, Bolney, West Sussex RH17 5QT, t 0845 6752601, www.iliostravel.com. Specialists in beautiful villas and small boutique hotels in Tuscany with a wealth of local knowledge.

**JMB Travel Consultants**, 3 Powick Mills, Old Rd, Worcester, WR2 4BU, t (01905) 422282, www.jmb-travel.co.uk. Opera in Macerata and Pesaro.

**Italiatour**, 9 Whyteleafe Business Village, Whyteleafe, Surrey CR3 0AT, t (01883) 621900, www.italiatour.co.uk. Resort holidays, city breaks, self-catering accommodation, and watercolour and cookery courses.

**Kirker**, 4 Waterloo Court, 10 Theed St, London SE1 8ST, t 0870 112 3333. www.kirkerholidays.com. City breaks and tailor-made tours.

**Magnum**, 7 Westleigh Park, Blaby, Leicester, t (0116) 277 7123. Holidays in Florence especially suitable for elderly visitors.

**Martin Randall Travel**, Voysey House, Barley Mow Passage, Chiswick, London W4 4PH, t (020) 8742 3355, www.martinrandall.com. Imaginative cultural tours with expert guides – art, archaeology, history, architecture, music, and 'Medici Villas and Gardens'.

**Prospect Cultural**, 94–104 John Wilson Park, Whitstable, Kent, CT5 3QZ, t (01227) 773 545, www.prospecttours.com. Art tours in Florence, and specialist holidays devoted to local cultural figures such as Dante and Piero della Francesca.

**Ramblers**, Box 43, Welwyn Garden City, Hertfordshire AL8 7TR, t (01707) 331133, www.ramblersholidays.co.uk. Walking holidays.

**Real Holidays Ltd**, 66–68 Essex Rd, London N1 8LR, t (020) 7359 3938, www.realhols.co.uk. Quirky holidays.

**Sherpa Expeditions**, 131a Heston Rd, Hounslow, Middlesex, TW5 0RF, t (020) 8577 2717, www.sherpa-walking-holidays.co.uk. Walking and cycling holidays in Tuscany.

**Simply Tuscany & Umbria**, Kings Place, Wood Street, Kingston-upon-Thames, Surrey KT1 1SG, t (020) 8541 2222, www.simplytravel.com. Accommodation, from opulent villas with pools to country house hotels, plus cookery and painting courses.

**Tasting Places**, Unit 40, Buspace Studios, Conlan St, London W10 5AP, t (020) 8964 5333, www.tastingplaces.com. Cookery courses near Arezzo.

**Travelsphere**, Compass House, Rockingham Rd, Market Harborough, Leics LE16 7QD, t 0870 240 2428, www.travelsphere.co.uk. Coach tours of the Tuscan coast.

**Waymark**, 44 Windsor Rd, Slough, t 0870 950 9800, www.waymarkholidays.co.uk. Walking tours of San Gimignano and Tuscany.

### In the USA/Canada

**Abercrombie & Kent**, Suite 212, 1520 Kensington Rd, Oak Brook, IL 60523 2156, t 800 323 7308, www.abercrombiekent.com. City breaks and walking holidays.

**Archaeological Tours Inc.**, Suite 904, 271 Madison Ave, New York, NY 10016, t 1-800 554 7016, t (212) 986 3054, archtours@aol.com. Tours of Etruscan sites.

**Bike Riders' Tours**, PO Box 130254, Boston, MA 02113, t 800 473 7040, www.bikeriderstours.com. Cycling tours with stopovers at elegant hotels.

**CIT Tours**, 875 Third Ave, New York, NY 10022, t 1-800 CIT-TOUR, www.cittours.travel; 7007 Islington Ave, Suite 205, Woodbridge, Ontario L4L 4T5, t 800 387 0711. Customized tours.

**Europe Train**, 2485 Jennings Rd, Olin, NC 28660, www.etttours.com. Escorted tours by train and car.

**Italiatour**, 666 Fifth Ave, New York, NY 10103, t 800 845 3365 (US) and t 888 515 5245 (Canada), www.italiatourusa.com. Fly-drive holidays and sightseeing tours organized by flight operator Alitalia.

**Maupintour**, 2688 South Rainbow Bd, Las Vegas, NV 89146, *www.maupintour.com*. Escorted packages.

**Travel Concepts**, 307 Princeton, MA 01541, t (978) 464 0411. Gourmet wine and food holidays.

## Self-catering Operators

### In Italy

**The Best in Italy**, Via Ugo Foscolo 72, Florence, t 055 223064, *www.thebestinitaly.com*.

**Solo Affitti**, Via Scrivia 6, Grosseto, t 0564 416743, *www.soloaffitti.it*.

**Toscana Vacanze**, Piazza Silvio Pellico 1, 52047 Marciano della Chiana, t 0575 845348, *www.toscana-vacanza.com*.

**Toscanamare Villas**, Via W della Gheradesca 5, Castagneto Carducci (LI), t 0565 744012, *www.toscanamare.it*.

**Vela**, Via Colombo 16, Castiglione della Pescaia, t 0564 933495, *www.lavelaimmobiliare.it*.

### In the UK

**Accommodation Line**, 46 Maddox St, London W1R 9PB, t (020) 7499 4433, *www.accomline.com*.

**The Apartment Service**, 5–6 Francis Grove, London SW19 4DT, t (020) 8944 1444, *www.apartmentservice.com*.

**Citalia**, *see* p.68.

**CV Travel**, Thames Wharf Studios, Rainville Rd, London, W6 9HA, t (020) 7384 5897, *www.cvtravel.net*.

**The Individual Travellers**, Spring Mill, Earby, Barnoldswick, Lancs BB94 0AA, t 08700 780193.

**Inghams**, 10–18 Putney Hill, London SW15 6AX, t (020) 8780 4400/4433, *www.inghams.co.uk*.

**Interhome**, 383 Richmond Rd, Twickenham, Middx TW1 2EF, t (020) 8891 1294, *www.interhome.co.uk*.

**Simply Travel**, Wigmore Lane, Luton LU2 9TN, t 0870 166 4979, *www.simply-travel.co.uk*.

**Thomson Villas**, *www.thomson.co.uk* (check website to find your nearest branch)

**Topflight**, 3rd Floor, Jervis House, Jervis St, Dublin 2, t (01) 240 1700, *www.topflight.ie*.

**Travel à la Carte**, The White House, Drove Lane, Cold Ash, Thatcham, RG18 9NL, t (01635) 201250, *www.anotheritaly.co.uk*.

### In the USA

**At Home Abroad**, 405 East 56th St 6H, New York, NY 10022-2466, t (212) 421 9165, *www.athomeabroadinc.com*.

**CIT North America Ltd**, t (800) CIT-TOUR, 15 West 44th St, New York, NY 10173; in Canada, 7007 Islington Ave, Suite 205, Woodbridge, Ontario, L4L 4T5, t 905 264 0158; *www.cit-tours.com*.

**Hideaways International**, 767 Islington St, Portsmouth, NH 03801, t (603) 430 4433 or t 877 843 4433, *www.hideaways.com*.

**Homebase Abroad**, 29 Mary's Lane, Scituate, MA 02006, t (781) 545 5112, *www.homebase-abroad.com*.

**Italianvillas.com**, *www.italianvillas.com*.

**Rentals in Italy (and Elsewhere!)**, 700 E Main St, Ventura, CA 93001, t 1-800 726 6702, *www.rentvillas.com*.

# Practical A–Z

06

# Conversions:
# Imperial–Metric

## Length (multiply by)
Inches to centimetres: 2.54
Centimetres to inches: 0.39
Feet to metres: 0.3
Metres to feet: 3.28
Yards to metres: 0.91
Metres to yards: 1.09
Miles to kilometres: 1.61
Kilometres to miles: 0.62

## Area (multiply by)
Inches square to centimetres square: 6.45
Centimetres square to inches square: 0.15
Feet square to metres square: 0.09
Metres square to feet square: 10.76
Miles square to kilometres square: 2.59
Kilometres square to miles square: 0.39
Acres to hectares: 0.40
Hectares to acres: 2.47

## Weight (multiply by)
Ounces to grams: 28.35
Grammes to ounces: 0.035
Pounds to kilograms: 0.45
Kilograms to pounds: 2.2
Stones to kilograms: 6.35
Kilograms to stones: 0.16
Tons (UK) to kilograms: 1,016
Kilograms to tons (UK): 0.0009
1 UK ton (2,240lbs) = 1.12 US tonnes (2,000lbs)

## Volume (multiply by)
Pints (UK) to litres: 0.57
Litres to pints (UK): 1.76
Quarts (UK) to litres: 1.13
Litres to quarts (UK): 0.88
Gallons (UK) to litres: 4.55
Litres to gallons (UK): 0.22
1 UK pint/quart/gallon =
  1.2 US pints/quarts/
  gallons

## Temperature
Celsius to Fahrenheit:
multiply by 1.8 then
add 32

Fahrenheit to Celsius:
subtract 32 then multiply
by 0.55

# Italy Information

## Time Differences
Country: + 1hr GMT; + 6hrs EST
Daylight saving from last weekend in March
to end of October

## Dialling Codes
**Italy country code** 39

**To Italy from:** UK, Ireland, New Zealand 00 /
USA, Canada 011 / Australia 0011 then dial 39
and the full number including the initial zero

**From Italy to:** UK 00 44; Ireland 00 353; USA,
Canada 001; Australia 00 61; New Zealand 00
64 then the number without the initial zero

**Directory enquiries:** 12
**International directory enquiries:** 176

## Emergency Numbers
**Police:** 112/113
**Ambulance:** 118
**Fire:** 115
**Car breakdown:** 116

## Embassy Numbers in Italy
**UK:** (06) 422 0001; **Ireland** (06) 697 9121;
**USA:** (055) 2669 5232; **Canada** (06) 85 444 2911;
**Australia** (06) 852 721;
**New Zealand** (06) 853 7501

## Shoe Sizes

| Europe | UK | USA |
| --- | --- | --- |
| 35 | 2½ / 3 | 4 |
| 36 | 3 / 3½ | 4½ / 5 |
| 37 | 4 | 5½ / 6 |
| 38 | 5 | 6½ |
| 39 | 5½ / 6 | 7 / 7½ |
| 40 | 6 / 6½ | 8 / 8½ |
| 41 | 7 | 9 / 9½ |
| 42 | 8 | 9½ / 10 |
| 43 | 9 | 10½ |
| 44 | 9½ / 10 | 11 |
| 45 | 10½ | 12 |
| 46 | 11 | 12½ / 13 |

## Women's Clothing

| Europe | UK | USA |
| --- | --- | --- |
| 34 | 6 | 2 |
| 36 | 8 | 4 |
| 38 | 10 | 6 |
| 40 | 12 | 8 |
| 42 | 14 | 10 |
| 44 | 16 | 12 |

# Children

Children are the royalty of Italy: often spoiled, probably more fashionably dressed than you, and never allowed to get dirty. If you're bringing your own *bambini* to Italy, they'll be warmly received. Many **hotels** offer advantageous rates and have play areas, and most larger cities have permanent **Luna Parks** (funfairs). Other attractions young kids enjoy are the **Pinocchio Park** in Collodi, near Pisa, **Pistoia Zoo** and the **Nature Park** in Cavriglia in the Valdarno. If a **circus** visits town, you're in for a treat: it will either be a showcase of daredevil skill or a family-run modern version of Fellini's *La Strada*.

# Crime and the Police

**Police/Emergency, t** 113

Cities attract a fair amount of petty crime – pickpocketing, white-collar thievery (check your change) and car break-ins – but violent crime is rare. Stay on the inside of the pavement and hold on to your property; pickpockets most often strike in crowds; don't carry too much cash and don't keep what you have in one place; be extra careful in stations; don't leave valuables in hotel rooms; and park in garages, guarded car parks, or well-lit streets, with any temptations out of sight.

Purchasing small quantities of cannabis is legal, but 'small quantity' isn't defined and if the police dislike you already, it may be enough to get you into big trouble.

# Eating Out

When you leave a restaurant you will be given a receipt (*ricevuta fiscale*) that, according to Italian law, you must take with you out of the door and carry for at least 300m. If you aren't given one, the restaurant is probably fudging its taxes and thus offering you lower prices. There is a slim chance the tax police may have their eye on both you and the restaurant; if you don't have a receipt they could slap you with a heavy fine.

When you eat out, mentally add to the bill (*conto*) the bread and cover charge (*pane e coperto*, €1–3), and a 15% service charge. This is often included in the bill (*servizio compreso*); if not, it will say *servizio*

## Restaurant Price Categories

Categories are based on an average complete meal, Italian-style with house wine, for one.

| | | |
|---|---|---|
| *very expensive* | €€€€ | €60 + |
| *expensive* | €€€ | €40–60 |
| *moderate* | €€ | €25–40 |
| *inexpensive* | € | – €25 |

*non compreso*. Extra tipping is at your own discretion; *see* also p.77.

For further information about eating in Italy and a menu vocabulary, *see* pp.49–56.

# Electricity

For electric appliances you need a 220AC adaptor with two round prongs on the plug. American appliances need transformers too.

# Health and Emergencies

**Health emergencies, t** 118

Minor illnesses and problems that crop up in Italy will usually be handled free of charge in a public hospital **walk-in clinic** (*ambulatorio*). If you need minor aid, Italian **pharmacists** are highly trained and can probably diagnose your problem; look for a *farmacia* (all have a list in the window detailing which are open during the night and holidays). Extreme cases should head for the *Pronto Soccorso* (**A&E**) of the nearest hospital.

Italian doctors are not always great linguists; contact your embassy or consulate (*see* p.60) for an **English-speaking doctor**.

For **insurance and EHIC cards**, *see* p.60.

# Internet

Internet access has become much more widespread in Italy in recent years. Nearly all hotels and B&Bs now have their own website, which simplifies booking, and offer free Internet access (increasingly Wi-fi) for guests.

Most resorts and towns have at least one Internet point of some kind; ask for a list at the tourist office. Costs vary widely: in some cities there is free access for those under 26 or for students and there are an increasing number of cafés with free Wi-fi. Take a copy of your driving licence or passport otherwise they cannot let you log on.

## Maps and Publications

The maps throughout this guide are for orientation only; it is worth investing in a good, up-to-date regional map before you arrive in Italy, ideally from one of the following bookshops:

**Stanford's**, 12–14 Long Acre, London WC2 9LP, **t** (020) 7836 1321, *www.stanfords.co.uk*. There are also branches in Bristol and Manchester.

**The Travel Bookshop**, 13 Blenheim Crescent, London W11 2EE, **t** (020) 7229 5260.

**The Complete Traveller**, 199 Madison Ave, New York, NY 10016, **t** (212) 685 9007.

Excellent touring maps produced by Touring Club Italiano, Michelin and the Istituto Geografico de Agostini are available at major bookshops in Italy or sometimes on newsstands. Italian tourist offices can often supply good area maps and town plans.

Books are more expensive in Italy than the UK, but some excellent shops stock English-language books. A few useful ones are:

**Edison**, Piazza della Repubblica 27r, Florence, **t** 055 213110.

**Feltrinelli**, Via Cavour 12–20r, Florence, **t** 055 219524.

### National Holidays

Most museums, banks and shops are closed on the following national holidays:

**1 January** New Year's Day (*Capodanno*).

**6 January** Epiphany; better known to Italians as the day of *La Befana* – a kindly witch who brings *bambini* the toys that Santa Claus or *Babbo Natale* somehow forgot.

**Easter Monday**

**25 April** Liberation Day.

**1 May** Labour Day – lots of parades, speeches, picnics, music and drinking.

**2 June** *Festa della Repubblica*.

**15 August** Assumption (*Ferragosto*); the biggest holiday of all – woe to the innocent traveller on the road or train!

**1 November** All Saints (*Ognissanti*).

**8 December** Immaculate Conception of the Virgin Mary.

**25 December** Christmas Day.

**26 December** Santo Stefano.

**The Paperback Exchange**, Via delle Oche 4r, Florence, **t** 055 293460.

## Opening Hours

Don't be surprised if you find anywhere in Italy unexpectedly closed (or open for that matter), whatever its official stated hours.

Most of Italy closes down at 1pm until 3 or 4pm to eat and digest the main meal of the day. Afternoon hours are 4–7, or often 5–8 in summer. Bars are often the only places open early afternoon.

## Museums and Galleries

Most major museums open 9am–7pm; Sun afternoons and Mon they often close. Where possible we have given opening hours for individual museums; but note that they can change at short notice, particularly in summer.

With two works of art per inhabitant, Italy has a hard time financing the preservation of its national heritage; it's as well to enquire at the tourist office as to what is open and what is 'temporarily' closed before setting off on a wild-goose chase.

Entrance charges vary wildly; expect to pay €2–5 for museum entrance; expensive ones can be as high as €9.50 if there is a special exhibition. State museums and monuments are free to under-18s and over-60s (bring ID). One week a year – usually in late spring – all state museums are free of charge for the *Settimana dei Berri Culturali*.

For those staying in Florence for longer than a few days, it may be worthwhile to invest in an Amici Degli Uffizi card which, for €60 a year, will let you in free to all state-run museums and galleries, which in Florence includes practically everything. Best of all, with this card you can jump the queue.

**Amici degli Uffizi**, Via Lorenzo il Magnifico 1, **t** 055 4794422, *www.amicidegliuffizi.it*.

## Banks and Shops

**Banks** are open Mon–Fri 8.30–1/1.30 and 3–4 or 4–5 except on local and national holidays (*see* left). For **post offices**, *see* opposite.

**Shops** are generally open Mon–Sat 8–1 and 3.30–7.30. In bigger towns some supermarkets and department stores now open all day, but this varies from region to region. Food shops shut on Wed afternoons in winter, and Sat afternoons end June–beginning Sept; Sun opening is becoming more usual, particularly in the centre of town.

## Churches

Italy's churches have always been a prime target for art thieves and as a consequence are usually locked when there isn't a sacristan or caretaker. All churches, except the really important cathedrals and basilicas, close in the afternoon at the same hours as shops, and the little ones tend to stay closed.

Don't do your visiting during services, and don't come to see paintings and statues in churches the week preceding Easter – you will probably find them covered with mourning shrouds.

Always have a pocketful of coins for light machines in churches.

## Photography

Film and developing are very expensive in Italy, so a digital camera is handy.

You are not allowed to take pictures in most museums, or some of the churches.

## Post Offices

t 803160, *www.poste.it*.

City post offices usually open Mon–Sat 8.10–6; elsewhere it's Mon–Sat 8.10–1.25.

First-class mail, *posta prioritaria* (€0.60), is supposed to get to an address in Italy within 24hrs and to EU countries within 36. You can use registered delivery, *raccomandata*, for a €2.80 supplement. Stamps (*francobolli*) may also be purchased at tobacconists (*tabacchi*, identified by blue signs with a white T). Airmail letters to and from North America can quite often take up to 2 weeks.

Mail can be sent to you care of your hotel or addressed *Fermo Posta* (*poste restante*: general delivery) to the central post office where you are staying. When you go to pick up mail at the *Fermo Posta* window, take your passport as proof of ID. You will need to pay a nominal charge.

## Sports and Activities

Sports clubs are usually private and open only to members.

## Birdwatching

The islands, and coastal parks near the Argentario are great places to twitch; eco-friendly Giglio offers nature appreciation and classes for Italian speakers, based at the hotel Pardiui's Hermitage, t 0564 809034. The bird park at Lago Burano near Capalbio, t 0564 898829, is another good spot.

## Boats and Sailing

The sailing is beautiful among the coves of the Tuscan archipelago and around the Argentario; there's a good sailing school in Torre del Lago Puccini, t 0584 351211.

You can bring your boat by car to Italy for 6 months without paperwork; if you arrive by sea you must report to the authority of your first port to show passports and receive your *constituto*, which identifies you and allows you to purchase fuel tax-free. Boats with engines require a numberplate, and insurance if over 3 horsepower. To leave your boat in Italy for an extended period, you must have a Navigation Licence; after a year you have to start paying taxes on it. All yachts must pay a daily berthing fee in Italian ports.

The National Tourist office (*see* p.59) has a list of ports that charter yachts in Tuscan ports.

## Fishing

Fishing in the sea is possible from the shore or boats, or underwater (not with an aqualung) without a permit, though the Tyrrhennian sea has been so thoroughly fished commercially that the government declares 2- and 3-month moratoria on all fishing to give fish a break.

Artificial lakes and streams are well stocked, and, if you're more interested in the eating than in the sport, there are trout farms where you can almost pick the fish out of the water with your hands. To fish in fresh water you need a licence for foreigners (type D; about €40 for 3 months), available from the Federazione Italiana della Pesca Sportiva. Its offices in every province can inform you about local conditions and restrictions. Bait and equipment are readily available.

## Golf

There are courses in Florence, Montecatini Terme, Punta Ala, Tirrenia, Orbetello and Portoferraio on Elba.

## Horse-riding and Horse-racing

Horse-riding is popular; Agriturist (*see* p.68) offers villa and riding holidays in Tuscany.

There are race and trotting courses in Florence and Montecatini Terme.

## Hunting

The most controversial sport in Italy pits avid enthusiasts against a burgeoning number of environmentalists who oppose it. The Apennines are boar territory, and in the autumn months the woods are full of hunters. Pathetically tiny birds, as well as ducks and pigeons, are the other principal game for hunters.

## Medieval Sports

Some ancient sports such as the *palios* (two in Siena) are still popular, with rivalries between neighbourhoods and cities intense.

The Florentines play three games of Renaissance football (*calcio in costume*) a year; Sansepolcro stages an annual crossbow

## Specialist Courses for Foreigners

The **Italian Institute**, 39 Belgrave Square, London SW1X 8NX, **t** (020) 7235 1461, *www. icilondon.esteri.it*, or 686 Park Ave, New York, NY 10021, **t** (212) 879 4242, *www.iicnewyork.esteri.it*, is the main source of information on courses for foreigners in Italy, including Italian state scholarships and language courses for business students. Graduate students should also contact their nearest Italian consulate to find out about scholarships – many go unused each year because no one knows about them.

**Worldwide Classroom**, *www.worldwide.edu*, also has a database of educational organizations around the world.

### Language Courses

One obvious course to take in the linguistically pure land of Dante is Italian language and culture: there are summer classes at the Scuola Lingua e Cultura per Stranieri of the University of Siena, in Cortona, Viareggio (run by the University of Pisa) and, unsurprisingly, in Florence (sometimes there seem to be more US students than Florentines in the city).

The following offer courses year-round:

**British Institute**, Piazza Strozzi 2, Florence, **t** 055 267781, *www.britishinstitute.it*. Florentine art and history, Dante, opera and language.

**Centro Fiorenza**, Via di Santo Spirito 14, Florence, **t** 055 239 8274, *www.centrofiorenza.com*. History, literature and art at basic and advanced levels, plus cooking courses.

**Centro Linguistico Italiano Dante Alighieri**, Piazza Repubblica 5, Florence, **t** 055 211 211, *www.clida.it*. Language courses.

**Scuola Lorenzo de' Medici**, Via Alloro 14r, **t** 055 283142, *www.lorenzodemedici.it*. Classes in language and art.

**Scuola Macchiavelli**, Piazza Santo Spirito 4, Florence, **t** 055 239 6966, *www.centromachiavelli. it*. A small school run by a co-operative of teachers, with a personal approach. There are classes in Italian (including commercial Italian), art history, art and crafts, food and drink, and opera singing.

### Art Courses

There are courses on medieval art and the history of art, restoration and design at Florence's **Università Internazionale dell'Arte**, Villa Tornabuoni, Via Incontri 3, and workshops in art restoration at Florence's **Istituto per l'Arte e il Restauro**, Palazzo Spinelli, Borgo Santa Croce 10.

### Music Courses

Music courses complement the numerous music festivals: Certaldo's medieval music society, **Ars Nova**, sponsors a seminar in July. Siena's **Accademia Musicale Chigiana**, Via di Città, offers masterclasses for instrumentalists and conductors; and in July and August Barga holds an International Opera workshop.

### Cookery Courses

**Capezzana Wine and Culinary Centre**, Via Capezzana 100, 59011 Loc. Seano, Carmignano, 30km from Florence, **t** 055 870 6005, *www.capezzana.it*. A wine- and olive oil-producing estate running courses for food professionals, skilled cooks and all those involved with food and wine. Accommodation is available in a wing of the villa.

**A Taste of Florence**, Via Taddea 31, Florence, **t** 055 292578, *www.divinacucina.com*. Courses run by a long-time US expat from her home near the central market in Florence, starting with shopping sessions. Groups are limited to six, and day or week courses are offered.

match; while in Lucca archers compete from different city quarters.

Arezzo and Pistoia have annual jousts; in Pisa there's a medieval tug-of-war.

## Potholing

Spelunkers can find Tuscan caves to explore around Montecatini Alta, Monsummano and Sarteano.

## Rowing

When there's enough water, you can try your skills in the Arno (*see* p.171).

The annual rowing race between the four old maritime republics of Venice, Amalfi, Genoa and Pisa alternates between the cities.

## Skiing

Tuscany has major ski resorts at Abetone, north of Pistoia, and Monte Amiata.

## Swimming

The best (cleanest) swimming is on the islands, especially on beaches that look away from the mainland.

## Tennis

Each *comune* has at least one or two courts that you can hire by the hour, and many hotels have them too.

## Walking

Hiking and signed trails are best-developed in Tuscany; April–Oct is the best and safest time to go. There are several scenic routes through the mountains: one is the 4-day **High Trail of the Apuan Alps**, beginning from the Rifugio Carrara, above Carrara (for info call **t** 0585 841972, or the Italian Alpine Club/CAI, Via Giorgi, Carrara, **t** 0585 776782). A second trail, the **Grand Apennine Excursion** from Lake Scaffaiolo, goes along the mountain ridge that separates Tuscany from Emilia-Romagna, departing from Pracchia (info: **t** 0187 625154). There's a circular trail through the **Garfagnana**, from Castelnuovo di Garfagnana; contact the Comunità Montana Garfagnana, **t** 0583 644911. In southern Tuscany, trails cover **Monte Amiata** from Abbadia San Salvatore (Comunità Montana dell'Amiata, **t** 0564 969611).

Other fine day trails are in the **Casentino**, from Badia Prataglia or Stia, or in the nature parks of **Monti dell'Uccellina** from Alberese or the Maremma. Maremmagica (**t** 0564 20298) organizes trekking and walking tours with guides. For UK operators specializing in walks, *see* pp.68–9.

In Florence, you can get information from CAI, Via Mezzetta 2, **t** 055 612 0467.

# Telephones

Public phones for **international calls** may be found in the offices of Telecom Italia, Italy's telephone company. They are the only places where you can make **reverse-charge** (**collect**) calls (*a erre*), but be prepared for a wait, as they go through the operator in Rome. **Rates** for long-distance calls are among the highest in Europe (they're lowest after 11pm).

Direct international calls may be made by dialling the **international prefix** (for the UK 0044, Ireland 00353, USA and Canada 001, Australia 0061, New Zealand 0064) and then the full number without the initial zero.

Calls within Italy are cheapest after 10pm. Most phone booths now take only **phonecards** (*schede telefoniche*) available in €3, €5 and €10 denominations at tobacconists and newsstands – you will have to snap off the small perforated corner to use them. Avoid telephoning from hotels, which often adds 25% to the bill.

You now have to dial the full **town prefix**, including the zero, to call anywhere in Italy, even the town you are in. In this book we have given all phone numbers with the full town prefix. To **call Italy from abroad**, dial **t** 0039 followed by the area prefix, including the initial zero, e.g. 0039 06 for Rome.

Note that **mobile phone** numbers do NOT begin with an 'o'.

# Time

Italy is one hour ahead of UK time and six hours ahead of North American EST. Italian summer time runs from the last Sunday in March to the last Sunday in October; clocks change on those days.

## Tipping

If you're in a **bar**, leave the small change in the form of the copper-coloured coins if you are standing, and around 30-50 cents if you sat down. In **restaurants**, service is usually included (if not, leave 10%) but it's nice to reward good service with a few euros.

For **taxis**, 10% is the norm.

## Toilets

Don't get confused by Italian plurals: *signori* (gents), *signore* (ladies). There are very few holes in the ground left in Italy, but public loos only exist in places such as train and bus stations and bars; the latter are legally obliged to let you use their *bagno* without buying a drink. Stations, motorway stops and smarter cafés have toilet attendants who expect a small tip.

# Florence

*Unless you come with the right attitude, initially Florence can be disenchanting. It only blossoms if you apply your mind as well as your vision, if you go slowly and do not let the art bedazzle until your eyes glaze over in dizzy excess (a common complaint, known in medical circles as the Stendhal syndrome). You will come to realize that loving and hating Florence at the same time may be the only rational response. It is the capital of contradiction; you begin to like it because it goes out of its way to annoy.*

# 07

## Don't miss

⭐ **Italy's best picture gallery**
The Uffizi **p.120**

⭐ **The mystic egg that hatched the Renaissance**
The Baptistry **p.104**

⭐ **Florence's pride, and symbol**
Brunelleschi's dome **p.108**

⭐ **The greatest Renaissance sculpture**
The Bargello **p.130**

⭐ **The finest of frescoes**
Santa Maria Novella **p.137**

*See map overleaf*

07 Florence

250 metres
250 yards

N

Cenacolo di Sant'Apollonia

VIA SAN GALL

VIA GUELFA

Stazione di Santa Maria Novella

Lazzi Buses

VIA NAZIONALE

VIA PANICALE

PIAZZA DEL MERCATO CENTRALE

VIA TADDEA

VIA DE' GINORI

i

Sita Buses

PIAZZA DELLA STAZIONE

Cenacolo di Foligno

VIA SANT' ANTONINO

BORGO LANCO

VIA CAVOU

i Cappella degli Spagnuoli

VIA DELLA SCALA

VIA DELL' ARIENTO

VIA FAENZA

Medici Chapels

San Lorenzo

Palazzo Medici-Riccardi

VIA DE' MARTELLI

Santa Maria Novella

PIAZZA DELL'UNITÀ ITALIANA

VIA D. AVELLI

VIA DEL GIGLIO

PIAZZA MADONNA V.D.MELARANCIO

VIA DE' CONTI

Biblioteca Laurenziana

BORGO SAN LORENZO

PIAZZA SANTA MARIA NOVELLA

VIA DEI PANZANI

VIA DEI BANCHI

VIA DEI CERRETANI

Duomo

VIA MASO UNIGUERRA DELL'ALBERO

VIA DELLA PORCELLANA

VIA DEI FOSSI

Croce del Trebbio

Palazzo Antinori

VIA DE' RONDINELLI

PIAZZA DI SAN GIOVANNI

Baptistry

PIAZZA DEL DUOMO

BORGO OGNISSANTI

PALAZZUOLO

Ognissanti

VIA DEL MORO

VIA DELLE BELLE DONNE

San Gaetano

VIA DEGLI AGLI VIA DE'PECORI

ROMA

LUNGARNO AMERIGO VESPUCCI

PONTE AMERIGO VESPUCCI

VIA DEI FOSSI

San Pancrazio

VIA DELLA SPADA

Palazzo Rucellai

VIA D. CAMPIDOGLIO

VIA DELLE OCHE

VIA DELLO STUDIO

LUNGARNO

PIAZZA GOLDONI

Palazzo Corsini

VIA D. VIGNA NUOVA

PIAZZA STROZZI

VIA STROZZI

Palazzo Strozzi

PIAZZA DELLA REPUBBLICA

VIA DELLE

VIA DE' TORNABUONI

VIA SPEZIALI VIA DEL CORSO

Dante's House DANTE

VIA CALZAIUOLI

VIA DEL PARIONE

LUNGARNO CORSINI

Santa Trinita

Arte della Lana

Orsanmichele

VIA DEI CALIMALA

San Martino

San Fior

PIAZZA DI CESTELLO

P

LUNGARNO SODERINI

PONTE ALLA CARRAIA

Palazzo Davanzati

PORTA ROSSA

VIA

PIAZZA S. TRINITA

VIA DELLE TERME

Mercato Nuovo

VIA CONDOTTA

PIAZZA DELLA SIGNORIA

Palazzo Gondi

San Frediano in Cestello

BORGO SAN FREDIANO

Porta San Frediano 100m

LUNG. GUICCIARDINI

BORGO SS. APOSTOLI

Palazzo di Parte Guelfa

Loggia dei Lanzi

VIA POR S. MARIA

PONTE SANTA TRINITA

SS. Apostoli

LUNG. ACCIAIOLI

VIA LAMBERTESCA

PIAZZALE D. UFFIZI

Uffizi

VIA DE' CASTELLAN

PIAZZA DEL CARMINE

VIA DI S. SPIRITO

VIA S. MONACA

Santa Maria del Carmine

Santo Spirito

BORGO SAN JACOPO

PONTE VECCHIO

CORRIDOIO VASARIANO

Museum of the History of Science

Fiume

VIA DEL PRESTO DI S.MARTINO

PIAZZA SANTO SPIRITO

PIAZZA S. FELICITÀ

P

LUNGARNO TORRIGIAN

VIA DE' BARDI

VIA SANT' AGOSTINO

VIA DEI SERRAGLI

VIA MAGGIO

VIA DE' GUICCIARDINI

Santa Felicità

COSTA DI SAN GIORGIO

Casa Guidi

PIAZZA DEI PITTI

Grotta di Buontalenti

BORGO TEGOLAIO

VIA ROMANA

PIAZZA SAN FELICE

Pitti Palace

Kaffeehaus

La Specola Museum

Amphitheatre

Boboli

Belvedere Fort

Gardens

Porcelain Museum and Giardino del Cavaliere

Neptune Fountain

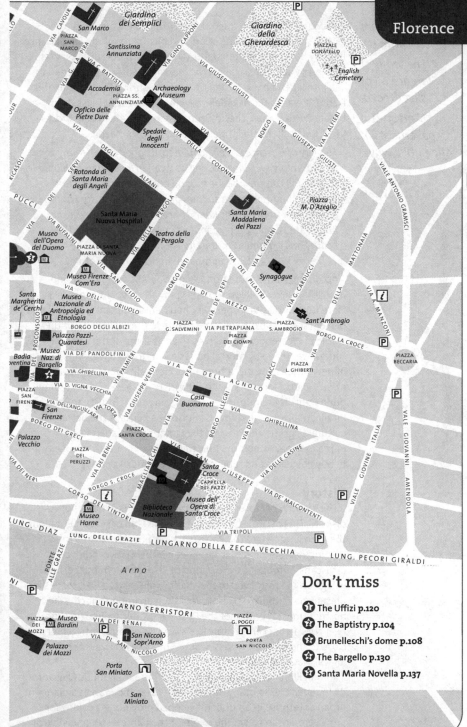

## Don't miss

⭐ The Uffizi **p.120**

⭐ The Baptistry **p.104**

⭐ Brunelleschi's dome **p.108**

⭐ The Bargello **p.130**

⭐ Santa Maria Novella **p.137**

*Fine balm let
Arno be;*

*The walls of
Florence all of
silver rear'd,*

*And crystal
pavements in
the public way...*

14th-century
madrigal by
Lapo Gianni

'*Magari!*' – 'If only!' – the modern Florentine would add to Gianni's vision, to this city of art and birthplace of the Renaissance, built by bankers and merchants whose sole preoccupation was making more florins. The precocious capital of Tuscany began to slip into legend back in the 14th century, during the lifetime of Dante; it was noted as *different* even before the Renaissance, before Boccaccio, Masaccio, Brunelleschi, Donatello, Leonardo da Vinci, Botticelli, Michelangelo, Machiavelli, the Medici...

*This city of Florence is well populated, its good air a healthy tonic; its citizens are well dressed, and its women lovely and fashionable, its buildings are very beautiful, and every sort of useful craft is carried on in them, more so than any other Italian city. For this many come from distant lands to see her, not out of necessity, but for the quality of its manufactures and arts, and for the beauty and ornament of the city.*

Dino Compagni in his *Chronicle* of 1312

According to the tourist office, in 2007, 885 years after Dino, more than seven million tourists spent at least one night in a Florentine hotel. Some, perhaps, had dental appointments. A large percentage of the others came to inhale the rarefied air of the cradle of Western civilization, to gaze at some of the loveliest things ever made by mortal hands and minds, to walk the streets of new Athens, the great humanist 'city built to the measure of man'. Calling Florence's visitors 'tourists', however, doesn't seem quite right; 'tourism' implies pleasure, a principle alien to this dour, intellectual, measured town. 'Pilgrims' is perhaps the better word, cultural pilgrims who throng the Uffizi, the Accademia, the Bargello to gaze upon the holy mysteries of our secular society, to buy postcards and replicas, the holy cards of our day.

## History

The identity of Florence's first inhabitants is a matter of dispute. There seems to have been some kind of settlement along the Arno long before the Roman era, perhaps as early as 1000 BC; the original founders may have been either native Italics or Etruscans. Throughout the period of Etruscan dominance, the village on the river lived in the shadow of Faesulae – Florence's present-day suburb of Fiesole was then an important city, the northernmost member of the Etruscan Dodecapolis. The Arno river cuts across central Italy like a wall. This narrow stretch of it, close to the mountain pass over to Emilia, was always the most logical place for a bridge.

Roman Florence can claim no less a figure than **Julius Caesar** for its founder. Like so many other Italian cities, it began as a planned urban enterprise in an underdeveloped province – a colony for army veterans in 59 BC. The origin of the name – so suggestive of

## Florentine Duality

Dante's *Vita Nuova*, the autobiography of his young soul, was only the beginning of Florentine analysis; Petrarch, the introspective 'first modern man', was a Florentine born in exile; Ghiberti was the first artist to write an autobiography; Cellini wrote one of the most readable; Alberti invented art criticism; Vasari invented art history; Michelangelo's personality, in his letters and sonnets, looms as large as his art. In many ways Florence broke away from the medieval idea of community and invented the modern concept of the individual, most famously expressed by Lorenzo de' Medici's friend, Pico della Mirandola, whose *Oration on the Dignity of Man* tells us what the God on the Sistine Chapel ceiling was saying when he created Adam: '...And I have created you neither celestial nor terrestrial, neither mortal nor immortal, so that, like a free and able sculptor and painter of yourself, you may mould yourself entirely in the form of your choice.'

To attempt to understand Florence, remember one historical constant: no matter what the issue, the city always takes both sides, vehemently and often violently, especially in the Punch and Judy days of Guelphs and Ghibellines. In the 1300s this was explained by the fact that the city was founded under the sign of Mars, the war god; but in medieval astronomy Mars is also connected with Aries, another Florentine symbol and the sign of the time of spring blossoms. (The Annunciation, at the beginning of spring, was Florence's most important festival.) One of the city's oldest symbols is the lily (or iris), flying on its oldest gonfalons. Perhaps even older is its *Marzocco*, originally an equestrian statue of Mars on the Ponte Vecchio, later replaced by Donatello's grim lion.

Whatever dispute rocked the streets, Great-Aunt Florence often expressed her schizophrenia in art – floral Florence versus stone Florence, epitomized by the irreconcilable differences between the two most famous works of art: Botticelli's graceful *Primavera* and Michelangelo's cold, perfect *David*. The 'city of flowers' seems a joke; it has nary a real flower, nor even a tree, in its stone streets; indeed, all effort has gone into keeping nature at bay, surpassing it with geometry and art. And yet the Florentines were perhaps the first since the Romans to discover the joys of the countryside. The rusticated stone palaces, like fortresses or prisons, hide charms as delightful as Gozzoli's frescoes in the Palazzo Medici-Riccordi. Luca della Robbia's dancing children and floral wreaths are contemporary with the naked, violent warriors of the Pollaiuolo brothers; the writhing, quarrelsome statuary in the Piazza della Signoria is sheltered by one of the most delicate *loggie* imaginable.

After 1500, all the good, bad and ugly symptoms of the Renaissance peaked in the mass fever of Mannerism. Then, drifting into a debilitating twilight, Florence gave birth to the artistic phenomenon known as kitsch – the Medici Princes' chapel is an early kitsch classic. Since then, worn out perhaps, or embarrassed, this city built by merchants has kept its own counsel, expressing its argumentative soul in overblown controversies about traffic, art restoration and the undesirability of fast-food counters and cheap *pensioni*. We who find her fascinating hope she some day comes to remember her proper role, bearing the torch of culture instead of merely collecting tickets for the culture torture.

springtime and flowers – is another mystery. First it was *Florentia*, then *Fiorenza* in the Middle Ages, and finally *Firenze*. One guess is that its foundation took place in April, when the Romans were celebrating the games of the Floralia.

The original street plan of Florentia can be seen today in the neat rectangle of blocks between Via Tornabuoni and Via del Proconsolo, between the Duomo and Piazza della Signoria. Its forum occupied roughly the site of the modern Piazza della Repubblica, and the outline of its amphitheatre can be traced in the oval of streets just west of Piazza Santa Croce. Roman Florentia never really imposed itself on the historian. One writer mentions it as a major town and river crossing along the Via Cassia, connected to Rome and the thriving new cities of northern Italy, such as Bononia and

# Getting to Florence

Florence is the central transport node for Tuscany, and harder to avoid than to reach.

## By Air

Florence's **Vespucci airport** was expanded in 1996, and now bustles with at least as much international traffic as Pisa. It is 4km out of the city centre at Peretola, *www.aeroporto.firenze.it*, flight information t 055 306 1300 (recorded message in Italian and English). There is a regular **bus** to Florence, terminating at Santa Maria Novella station (15mins). A **taxi** to the centre will cost €20–25.

**Alitalia:** reservations, t 06 2222, *www.alitalia.it*.
**British Airways:** t 199 712266, *www.ba.com*.
**Meridiana** (for London Gatwick): Peretola Airport 28r, t 892 928, *www.meridiana.it*.

## By Train

The central station is **Santa Maria Novella**; call t 892021 for information, *www.trenitalia.com*. Many long-distance trains arriving at night use **Campo di Marte** station, on bus routes 12 or 91 from the centre.

## By Bus

It's possible to reach nearly every city, town and village in Tuscany from Florence – once you know which of several bus companies to patronize. The tourist office has a complete list, but here are some of the most popular:

**SITA**, near station, Via S. Caterina da Siena 15, t 055 4782870, t 800 373760, *www.sitabus.it*: for towns in the Val d'Elsa, Chianti, Val di Pesa, Mugello and Casentino; Anghiari, Arezzo, Bibbiena, Castelfiorentino, Certaldo, Città di Castello, Consuma, Figline Valdarno, Firenzuola, Marina di Grosseto, Montevarchi, Poggibonsi (for San Gimignano and Volterra), Pontassieve, Poppi, Pratovecchio, Sansepolcro, Scarperia, Siena, Stia and Vallombrosa.

**LAZZI**, Piazza Stazione 47r, t 055 351061 Mon–Fri, *www.lazzi.it*: along the Arno to the coast, including Calenzano, Cerreto Guidi, Empoli, Forte dei Marmi, Livorno, Lucca, Marina di Carrara, Marina di Massa, Montecatini Terme, Montelupo, Montevarchi, Pescia, Pisa, Pistoia, Pontedera, Prato, Signa, Tirrenia, Torre del Lago and Viareggio.

**CAP**, Ligo Fili Alimani 9, t 055 214637, *www.capautolinee.it*: for Borgo S. Lorenzo, Impruneta, Pistoia, Prato.

**Blubus**, Ligo Fili Alimani 11, t 055 214637, *www.blubus.it*: for Abetone, Cerreto Guidi, Pistoia, Poggio a Caiano, and Vinci.

**GRIFORAMA**, Lazzi station, t 0564 475111, *www.griforama.it*: for Grosseto.

# Getting around Florence

Florence is a relatively easy city to get around, because nearly everything you'll want to see is within easy walking distance, and large areas in the centre are pedestrian zones. In addition, there are no hills to climb, and it's hard to lose your way for very long.

Just to make life complicated, however, Florence has two sets of **address numbers** on every street – red ones for business, blue or black for residences; your hotel could be either. However, there has been some improvement: every major piazza, landmark or monument now has a plaque offering relevant background information, and helpful maps have been posted in strategic positions throughout the city.

## By Bus

**City buses (ATAF;** *www.ataf.net*) can whizz or inch you across Florence, and are an excellent means of reaching sights on the periphery. Most useful lines begin at Santa Maria Novella station and pass by Piazza del Duomo or Piazza San Marco. ATAF supply a comprehensive booklet, including a clear map, with details of all bus routes, available at the information/ticket booth at the station, plus from tourist offices, some bars, and at ATAF's central office in Piazza della Stazione, t 800 424 500. **Ticket prices:** €1.20 for 70mins, €1.80 for 3hrs, €5 for 24hrs, €16 for a week, or €4 for 4 tickets valid for 70mins.

The most useful buses for visitors are:

**6** Via Rondinella–Piazza San Marco–Duomo–Stazione–Soffiano.

**7** Stazione –Duomo–San Domenico–Fiesole.

**10** Stazione –Duomo–San Marco–Ponte a Mensola–Settignano.
**11** Viale Calatafimi–San Marco–Piazza Indipendenza–Stazione–Porta Romana–Poggio Imperiale.
**11a** Viale Calatafimi–Duomo–Porta Romana–Poggio Imperiale.
**13** Stazione–Ponte Rosso–Parterre (car park)–Piazza Libertà–Viale Mazzini–Campo di Marte–
Piazzale Michelangelo–Porta Romana.
**14c** Rovezzano–Duomo–Stazione–Careggi (hospital).
**17** Cascine–Stazione–Duomo–Via Lamarmora–Salviatino (for the youth hostel).
**25** Stazione–San Marco–Piazza Libertà–Via Bolognese–Pratolino.
**28** Stazione–Via R. Giuliani–Castello–Sesto Fiorentino.
**37** Stazione–Ponte alla Carraia–Porta Romana–Certosa del Galluzzo.
**38** Porta Romana–Pian del Giullari (you need to book this one from the telephone near the bus stop at
Porta Romana, t 800 541200 toll free).

As part of the continuing campaign against city smog, a fleet of Lilliputian **electric buses**, routes A, B and D, have recently been introduced. These mainly serve the centre, often taking circuitous routes 'round the houses', and are a good way of seeing some of the sights if you've had enough walking. Details of routes can be found on the ATAF maps. A tram system is currently under construction.

## By Taxi

Taxis in Florence don't cruise; you'll find them in ranks at the station and in the major piazzas, or else ring for a **radio taxi**, t 055 4798 or 4242. Taxi meters start at €3.20 plus extras, €5.10 on Sundays and hols, adding c1 per km. There is a minimum charge of €5.

## By Car

Until the late 1980s, Florence had the most carcinogenic traffic problems in Italy. But in 1988, with great fanfares and accompanied by howls of protest, the city tried to do something about the cars that were choking it to death, by enlarging the limited access zone, the *zona di traffico limitato* (**ZTL**). Within the ZTL, only buses, taxis and cars belonging to residents are permitted; outside it, you are permitted to pay to park in one of the city's **car parks** (there's the underground car park at the station, or the cheaper, big park at the Parterre, near Piazza Libertà; see *www.firenzeparcheggi.it* for a full list) or take your chances on a side street or on metered parking areas as shown on the maps at the beginning of this chapter.

This new regulation was then followed by whole areas, especially around Piazza della Signoria and the Duomo, becoming totally traffic-free zones. The only danger is the odd ambulance or police car, the speeding mopeds (all of which you can easily hear), and the deadly silent bicycle.

### Bicycle, Scooter and Motorbike Hire

Hiring a **bike** can save you tramping time and angst but it's not risk-free. Watch out for cars and pedestrians.

You can hire bikes, mopeds and motorbikes at
**Alinari**, Via S. Zanobi 38r, t 055 280500, *www.alinarirental.com*.
**Florence by Bike**, Via S. Zanobi 120/122r, t 055 488992, *www.florencebybike.it*.

Between 8am and 7.30pm, visitors can now take advantage of one of the (almost) **free bicycles** supplied by the *comune* of Florence. The scheme is called Le Mille e Una Bici. There are various pick-up points around town, the most central being the Fortezza, the Parterre (for the car parks), Piazza Strozzi, Piazza Stazione, Piazza San Marco, the central market and Porta Romana. They cost about €1.50 for an hour, €8 for a day.

### Car Hire

When you can't take any more art, hire a car and escape into the ravishing countryside. Most rental firms are within easy walking distance of the station.
**Avis**, Borgo Ognissanti 128r, t 055 213629, *www.avis.it*.
**Europcar**, Borgo Ognissanti 53r, t 055 290438, *www.europcar.it*.
**Hertz**, Via M Finiguerra 33, t 199 112211, t 055 239 8205, *www.hertz.it*.
**Italy by Car**, Borgo Ognissanti 134r, t 055 287161, *www.italybycar.it*.
**Maggiore**, Via M. Finiguerra 31r, t 055 294578, *www.maggiore.it*.
**Targarent**, Borgo Ognissanti 133r, t 055 2654207.

Mediolanum (Bologna and Milan). At the height of the empire, the municipal boundaries had expanded out to Via de' Fossi, Via S. Egidio, and Via de' Benci. Nevertheless, Florentia did not play a significant role either in the Empire's heyday or in its decline.

After the fall of Rome, Florence weathered its troubles comparatively well. We hear of it withstanding sieges by the Goths around the year 400, when it was defended by the famous imperial general Stilicho, and again in 541, during the campaigns of Totila and Belisarius; all through the Greek-Gothic wars Florence seems to have taken the side of Constantinople. The Lombards arrived around 570; under their rule Florence was the seat of a duchy subject to the then Tuscan capital of Lucca. The next mention in the chronicles refers to Charlemagne spending Christmas with the Florentines in the year 786. Like the rest of Italy, Florence had undoubtedly declined; a new set of walls went up under Carolingian rule, about 800, enclosing an area that was scarcely larger than the original Roman settlement of 59 BC. Most likely throughout the Dark Ages the city was gradually increasing its relative importance and strength at the expense of its neighbours. The famous baptistry, which was erected some time between the 6th and 9th centuries, is the only important building from that troubled age in all Tuscany.

By the 1100s, Florence was the leading city of the County of Tuscany. **Countess Matilda**, ally of Pope Gregory VII against the emperors, oversaw the construction of a new set of walls in 1078, coinciding with the widest Roman-era boundaries. The city had recovered all the ground lost during the Dark Ages, and the momentum of growth did not abate. New walls again in the 1170s enclosed what was becoming one of the largest cities in Europe. In this period, Florence owed its growth and prosperity largely to the textile industry – weaving and 'finishing' cloth not only from Tuscany but wool shipped from as far afield as Spain and England. The capital gain from this trade, managed by the Calimala and the Arte della Lana, Florence's richest guilds, led naturally to an even more profitable business – banking and finance.

## The Florentine Republic Battles with the Barons

In 1125, Florence once and for all conquered its ancient rival Fiesole. Wealth and influence brought with them increasing political responsibilities; the city often found itself at war with its neighbours. Since Countess Matilda's death in 1115, Florence had become a self-governing *comune*, largely independent of the emperor and local barons. The new city republic's hardest problems, however, were closer to home. The nobles of the county, encouraged in their anachronistic feudal behaviour by representatives of the imperial government, proved irreconcilable enemies to the new merchant republic, and Florence spent most of the 12th century trying to keep them in line. Often the city actually declared war on a noble clan, as with the Alberti, or the counts of Guidi, and razed their castles whenever they captured one. To complicate the situation, nobles attracted by the stimulation of urban life – along with the opportunities for making money – often moved their families into Florence itself.

They brought their country habits with them: a boyish eagerness to brawl with their neighbours on the slightest pretext, and a complete disregard for the laws of the *comune*. Naturally, they couldn't feel secure without a little urban castle of their own, and before long Florence's skyline, like that of any prosperous Italian city of the Middle Ages, featured hundreds of tower-fortresses, built as much for status as for defence. Many were more than 60m in height. It wasn't uncommon for the honest citizen to come home from work hoping for a little peace and quiet, only to find siege engines in front of the house and a company of bowmen in the children's bedroom.

But just as Florence was able to break the power of the rural nobles, those in the town also eventually had to succumb. The last tower-fortresses were chopped down to size in the early 1300s. But even without the nobles raising all manner of hell, the Florentines managed to find brand new ways to keep the pot boiling. The rich merchants who dominated the government, familiarly known as the *popolari grossi*, resorted to every sort of murder and mayhem to beat down the demands of the lesser guilds, the *popolari minuti*, for a fair share of the wealth; the two only managed to settle their differences when confronted by murmurs of discontent from what was then one of Europe's largest urban proletariats. But even beyond simple class issues, the city born under the fiery sign of Mars always found a way to make trouble. Not only did Florentines pursue the Guelph-Ghibelline conflict with greater zest than almost any Tuscan city; according to chronicles, they started it. In 1215, men of the Amidei family murdered a prominent citizen named Buondelmonte dei Buondelmonti over a broken wedding engagement; this was the spark that ignited the factionalist struggles first in Florence, then quickly throughout Italy.

## Guelphs and Ghibellines

In the 13th century there was never a dull moment in Florence. Guelphs and Ghibellines, often more involved with some feud between powerful families than with real political issues, cast each other into exile and confiscated each other's property with every change of the wind. Religious strife occasionally pushed politics off the front page. In the 1240s, a curious foreshadowing of the Reformation saw Florence wrapped up in the **Patarene Heresy**.

This sect, closely related to the Albigensians of southern France, was as obsessed with the presence of Evil in the world as John Calvin – or as Florence's own future fire-and-brimstone preacher, Savonarola. Exploiting a streak of religious eccentricity that has always seemed present in the Florentine psyche, the Patarenes thrived in the city, even electing their own bishop. The established Church was up to the challenge; St Peter Martyr, a bloodthirsty Dominican, led his armies of axe-wielding monks to the assault in 1244, exterminating almost the entire Patarene community.

In 1248, with help from Emperor Frederick II, Florence's Ghibellines booted out the Guelphs – once and for all, they thought – but two years later the Guelphs were back, and it was the Ghibellines' turn to leave. The new Guelph regime, called the *primo popolo*, was for the first time completely in the control of the bankers and merchants. It passed the first measures to control the privileges of the turbulent, largely Ghibelline nobles, and forced them all to chop the tops off their tower-fortresses. The next decades witnessed a series of wars with the Ghibelline cities of Tuscany – Siena, Pisa and Pistoia, not just by coincidence Florence's habitual enemies. Usually the Florentines were the aggressors, and more often than not fortune favoured them. In 1260, however, the Sienese, reinforced by Ghibelline exiles from Florence and a few imperial cavalry, destroyed an invading Florentine army at the **battle of Montaperti**. Florence was at the Ghibellines' mercy. Only the refusal of Farinata degli Uberti, the leader of the exiles, to allow the city's destruction kept the Sienese from torching it – a famous episode recounted by Dante in the *Inferno*. (In a typical Florentine gesture of gratitude, Dante found a home for Uberti in one of the lower circles of hell.)

In Florence, a Ghibelline regime under Count Guido Novello made life rough for the wealthy Guelph bourgeoisie. As luck would have it, though, only a few years later the Guelphs were back in power, and Florence was winning on the battlefield again. The new Guelph government, the *secondo popolo*, earned a brief respite from factional strife. In 1289, Florence won a great victory over another old rival, Arezzo. This was the **battle of Campaldino**, where the Florentine citizen army included young Dante Alighieri. In 1282, and again in 1293, Florence tried to clean up an increasingly corrupt government with a series of reforms. The 1293 **Ordinamenti della Giustizia** once and for all excluded the nobles from the important political offices. By now, however, the real threat to the Guelph merchants' rule did not come so much from the nobility, which had been steadily falling behind in wealth and power for two centuries, but from the lesser guilds, which had been excluded from a share of the power, and also from the growing working class employed in the textile mills and the foundries.

Despite all the troubles, the city's wealth and population grew tremendously throughout the 1200s. Its trade contacts spread across Europe, and crowned heads from London to Constantinople found Florentine bankers ready to float them a loan. About 1235 Florence minted modern Europe's first gold coin, the florin, which soon became a standard currency across the continent. By 1300 Florence counted more than 100,000 souls, making it a little cramped, even inside the vast circuit of walls built by the *comune* in the 1280s. It was not only one of the largest cities in Europe but also one of the richest. Besides banking, the wool trade was also booming: by 1300 the wool guild, the Arte della Lana, had more than 200 large workshops in the city alone. Naturally, this opulence created new possibilities for culture and art. Florence's golden age began perhaps in the 1290s, when the *comune* started its tremendous programme of public buildings – including the Palazzo della Signoria and the cathedral; important religious structures, such as Santa Croce, were under way at the same time. Cimabue was the artist of the day; Giotto was just beginning, and his friend Dante was hard at work on the *Commedia*.

As in so many other Italian cities, Florence developed its republican institutions slowly and painfully. At the beginning of the *comune* in 1115, the leaders were a class called the *boni homines*, which was made up mostly of nobles. Only a few decades later, these were calling themselves *consules*, evoking a memory of the ancient Roman republic. When the Ghibellines took over, the leading official was a *podestà* appointed by the emperor. Later, under the Guelphs, the *podestà* and a new officer called the *capitano del popolo* were both elected by the citizens. With the reforms of the 1290s Florence's republican constitution was perfected – though it satisfied only a few citizens and guaranteed future trouble. Power was invested in the council of the richer guilds, the **Signoria**; the new Palazzo della Signoria was designed expressly as a symbol of their authority, replacing the old Bargello, which had been the seat of the *podestà*. The most novel feature of the government, designed to avoid the violent factionalism of the past, was the selection of officials by lot from among the guild members. In effect, politics was to be abolished.

## Business as Usual: Riot, War, Plagues and Revolution
Despite the reforms of the Ordinamenti, Florence found little peace in the new century. As if following some strange and immutable law of city-state behaviour, no sooner had the Guelphs established total control than they themselves split into new factions. The radically anti-imperial **Blacks** and the more conciliatory **Whites** fought each other through the early 1300s with the same fervour that both had once exercised against the

Ghibellines. The Whites, who included Dante among their partisans, came out losers when the Blacks conspired with the pope to bring Charles of Valois' French army into Florence; almost all the losing faction were forced into exile in 1302. Some of them must have sneaked back, for the chronicles of 1304 record the Blacks trying to burn them out of their houses with incendiary bombs, resulting in a fire that consumed a quarter of the city.

Beginning in 1313, Florence was involved in a constant series of inconclusive wars waged with Pisa, Lucca and Arezzo, among others. In 1325, the city was defeated and nearly destroyed by the great Lucchese general **Castruccio Castracani** (see p.260). Castruccio died of a common cold while the siege was already under way, in another instance of Florence's famous good luck, unfortunately one of the last. The factions may have been suppressed, but fate had found some more novel disasters for the city. One far-off monarch did more damage to Florence than its Italian enemies had ever managed – King Edward III of England, who in 1339 found it expedient to repudiate his foreign debts. Florence's two biggest banks, the Bardi and the Peruzzi, immediately went bust, and the city's standing as the centre of international finance was gravely damaged.

One constant throughout the history of the republic was the oppression of the poor. The ruling bankers and merchants exploited the labour of the masses and gave them only the bare minimum in return. In the 14th century, undernourishment, overcrowding and a large population of rats made Florence's poorer neighbourhoods a breeding ground for epidemics. Famine, plagues and riots became common in the 1340s, causing a severe political crisis. At one point, in 1342, the Florentines gave over their government to a foreign dictator, Walter de Brienne, the French-Greek 'Duke of Athens'. He lasted only for a year before a popular revolt ended the experiment. The **Black Death** of 1348, which provided the background for Boccaccio's *Decameron*, carried off perhaps one-half of the population. Coming on the heels of a serious depression, it was a blow from which Florence would never really manage to recover.

In the next two centuries, when the city was to stake its position as the great innovator in Western culture, it was already in relative decline, a politically decadent republic with a stagnant economy, barely holding its own among the changes in trade and diplomacy. For the time being, however, things didn't look too bad. Florence bought control of Prato, in 1350, and was successful in a defensive war against expansionist Milan in 1351. War was almost continuous for the last half of the century, constituting a strain on the exchequer but not usually a threat to the city's survival; this was the heyday of the mercenary companies, led by *condottieri* such as

**Sir John Hawkwood** (Giovanni Acuto), immortalized in Florence's cathedral. Before the Florentines made him a better offer, Hawkwood was often in the employ of their enemies.

Through the century, the Guelph party had steadily tightened its grip over the republic's affairs. Despite the selection of officials by lot, by the 1370s party organization bore an uncanny resemblance to some of the big-city political machines common not so long ago in America. The merchants and the bankers who ran the party used it to turn the Florentine republic into a profit-making business. With the increasingly limited opportunities for making money in trade and finance, the Guelph ruling class tried to make up the difference by soaking the poor. Wars and taxes stretched Florentine tolerance to breaking point, and finally, in 1378, came revolution. The **Ciompi Revolt** (*ciompi* were wage labourers in the textile industries) began in July, when a mob of workers seized the Bargello. Under the leadership of wool-carder Michele di Lando, they executed a few Guelph bosses and announced a new, reformed constitution. They were also foolish enough to believe the Guelph magnates when they promised to abide by the new arrangement if only the *ciompi* would go home. Before long di Lando was in exile and the ruling class firmly back in the seat of power, more than ever determined to eliminate the last vestiges of democracy from the republic.

## The Rise of the Medici

In 1393 Florentines celebrated the 100th anniversary of the great reform of the Ordinamenti, while watching their republic descend into oligarchy. In that year **Maso degli Albizzi** became *gonfaloniere* (the head of the Signoria) and served as virtual dictator for many years afterwards. The ruling class of merchants, more than a bit paranoid after the Ciompi Revolt, were relieved to see power concentrated in strong hands. In an atmosphere of repression and conspiracy, the Signoria's secret police hunted down malcontents while Florentine exiles plotted against the republic in foreign courts. Florence was almost constantly at war. In 1398 it defeated an attempt at conquest by Giangaleazzo Visconti of Milan. The imperialist policy of the Albizzi and their allies resulted in some important territorial gains, including the conquest of Pisa in 1406, and the purchase of Livorno from the Genoese in 1421, but unsuccessful wars against Lucca finally disenchanted the Florentines with Albizzi rule. An emergency *parlamento* (the infrequent popular assembly usually called when a coming change of rulers was obvious) in 1434 decreed the recall from exile of the head of the popular opposition, **Cosimo de' Medici**.

Perhaps it was something that could only have happened in Florence – the darling of the plebeians, the great hope for reform, was also the head of Florence's biggest bank. The Medici family had their roots in the Mugello region north of Florence. Their name seems to suggest that they once were pharmacists (later enemies would jibe at the balls on the family arms as 'the pills'). For two centuries they had been active in Florentine politics; many had acquired reputations as troublemakers; their names turned up often in the lists of exiles and records of lawsuits. None of the Medici had ever been particularly rich until **Giovanni di Bicci de' Medici** (1360–1429) parlayed his wife's dowry into the founding of a bank. Good fortune – and a temporary monopoly on the handling of the pope's finances – made the Medici Bank Florence's biggest.

Giovanni had been content to stay on the fringe of politics; his son, **Cosimo** (known in Florentine history as 'Il Vecchio', the 'old man'), took good care of the bank's affairs but aimed his sights much higher. His strategy was as old as Julius Caesar – the patrician reformer, cultivating the best men, winning the favour of the poor with largesse and gradually, carefully forming a party under a system specifically designed to prevent such things. In 1433 Rinaldo degli Albizzi had him exiled, but it was too late; continuing discontent forced his return only a year later, and for the next 35 years Cosimo would be the unchallenged ruler of Florence. Throughout this period, Cosimo occasionally held public office – this was done by lottery, with the electoral lists manipulated to ensure a majority of Medici supporters at all times. Nevertheless, he received ambassadors at the new family palace (built in 1444), entertained visiting popes and emperors, and made all the important decisions. A canny political godfather and usually a gentleman, Cosimo was also a useful patron to the great figures of the early Renaissance – including Donatello and Brunelleschi. His father had been one of the judges in the famous competition for the baptistry doors (*see* p.106), and Cosimo was a member of the commission that picked Brunelleschi to design the cathedral dome.

Under Cosimo's leadership Florence began Europe's first progressive income tax, and invented the concept of the national debt – endlessly rolling over bonds to keep the republic afloat and creditors happy. The poor, with fewer taxes to pay, were also happy, and the ruling classes were positively delighted; never in Florence's history had any government so successfully muted class conflict and the desire for a genuine democracy. Wars were few, and the internal friction negligible. Cosimo died in August 1464; his tomb in San Lorenzo bears the inscription *Pater patriae*, and no dissent was registered when his 40-year-old son **Piero** took up the boss's role.

## Lorenzo il Magnifico

Piero didn't quite have the touch of his masterful father, but he survived a stiff political crisis in 1466, when he outmanoeuvred a new faction led by wealthy banker Luca Pitti. In 1469 he succumbed to the Medici family disease, gout, and his 20-year-old son **Lorenzo** succeeded him in an equally smooth transition. He was to last for 23 years. As he was not necessarily more 'magnificent' than other contemporary princes, or other Medici, Lorenzo's honorific reveals something of the myth that was to grow up around him in later centuries. His long reign corresponded with the height of the Florentine Renaissance. It was a relatively peaceful time, and in the light of the disasters that were to follow, Florentines could not help looking back on it as a golden age.

As a ruler, Lorenzo showed many virtues. Still keeping up the pretence of being a private citizen, he lived relatively simply, always accessible to the concerns of his fellow citizens, who would often see him walking the city streets. In the field of foreign policy he was indispensable to Florence and indeed all Italy; he did more than anyone to keep the precarious peninsular balance of power from disintegrating. The most dramatic affair of his reign was the **Pazzi Conspiracy**, an attempt to assassinate Lorenzo plotted by Pope Sixtus IV and the wealthy Pazzi family, the pope's bankers and ancient rivals of the Medici. In 1478, two of the Pazzi attacked Lorenzo and his brother Giuliano during mass at the cathedral. Giuliano was killed but Lorenzo managed to escape into the sacristy. The botched murder aborted the planned revolt; the Florentines showed little interest in the Pazzis' call to arms, and before nightfall most of the conspirators were dangling from the cornice of the Palazzo Vecchio.

Apparently, Lorenzo had angered the pope by starting a syndicate to mine for alum in Volterra, threatening the papal monopoly. Since Sixtus failed to murder Lorenzo, he had to settle for excommunicating him, and declaring war in alliance with King Ferrante of Naples. The war went badly for Florence and, in the most memorable act of his career, Lorenzo walked into the lion's cage, travelling to negotiate with the terrible Neapolitan, who had already murdered more than one important guest. As it turned out, Ferrante was only too happy to dump his papal entanglements; Florence found itself at peace once more, and Lorenzo returned home to a hero's welcome.

In other affairs, both foreign and domestic, Lorenzo was more a lucky ruler than a skilled one. Florence's economy was entering a long, slow decline, but for the moment the banks and mills were churning out just enough profit to keep up the accustomed level of opulence. The Medici Bank was on the ropes. Partly because of Lorenzo's neglect, it came close to collapsing on several occasions – and it seems that Lorenzo blithely made up the losses with public funds. Culturally, he was fortunate to be the nabob of Florence at its most artistically creative period; later historians and Medici propagandists gave him a reputation as an art patron that is entirely undeserved. His own tastes tended towards bric-a-brac, jewellery, antique statues and vases; there is little evidence that he appreciated the extraordinary talents of the great artists around him. Perhaps because he was too nearsighted to see anything clearly, he did not commission a single important canvas or fresco in Florence (except for Luca Signorelli's mysterious *Pan*, which was lost in Berlin during the last war). His favourite architect was the hack Giuliano da Sangallo.

Lorenzo was brought up with some of the leading humanist scholars of Tuscany for tutors, and his real interests were literary. His well-formed lyrics and winsome pastorals have earned him a place among Italy's greatest 15th-century poets; they neatly reflect the private side of Lorenzo, the retiring, scholarly family man who enjoyed life better in one of the many rural Medici villas than in the busy city. In this he was perfectly in tune with his class and his age. Plenty of Florentine bankers were learning the joys of country life, reading Horace or Catullus in their geometrical gardens and pestering their tenant farmers with well-meant advice.

Back in town they had thick new walls of rusticated sandstone between them and the bustle of the streets. The late 15th century was the great age of palace-building in Florence. Following the example of Cosimo de' Medici, the bankers and merchants erected dozens of palaces (some of the best can be seen around Via Tornabuoni), each with blank walls and iron-barred windows to the street. Historians always note a turning inward, a 'privatization' of Florentine life in this period. In a city that had become a republic only in name, civic interest and public life ceased to matter so much. The rich began to assume the airs of an aristocracy, and did everything they could to distance themselves from their fellow citizens. Ironically, just at the time when Florence's artists were creating their greatest achievements, the republican ethos, the civic soul that had made Florence great, began to disintegrate.

## Savonarola

Lorenzo's death, in 1492, was followed by another apparently smooth transition of power to his son **Piero**. But after 58 years of Medicean quiet and stability the city was ready for a change. The opportunity came soon enough, when the timid and inept Piero allowed the invading king of France, **Charles VIII**, to occupy Pisa and the Tuscan coast. A spontaneous revolt chased Piero and the rest of the Medici into exile, while a mob sacked the family's palace. A new regime, under **Piero Capponi**, dealt sternly with the French and tried to pump new life into the dormant republican constitution.

The Florence that threw out the Medici was a city in the mood for some radical reform. Already, the dominating figure on the political stage was an intense Dominican friar from Ferrara named

**Girolamo Savonarola**. Perhaps unsurprisingly, this oversophisticated and overstimulated city was also in the mood to be told how wicked and decadent it was, and Savonarola was happy to oblige. A spellbinding revival preacher with a touch of erudition, Savonarola packed as many as 10,000 into the Duomo to hear his weekly sermons, which were laced with political sarcasm and social criticism. Though an insufferable prig, he was also a sincere democrat. There is a story that the dying Lorenzo called Savonarola to his bedside for the last rites, and that the friar refused him absolution unless he 'restored the liberty of the Florentines', a proposal that only made the dying despot sneer with contempt.

Savonarola also talked Charles VIII into leaving Florence in peace. Pisa, however, took advantage of the confusion to revolt, and the restored republic's attempts to recapture it were in vain. Things were going badly. Piero Capponi's death in 1496 left Florence without an able leader, and Savonarolan extremists became ever more influential. The French invasion and the incessant wars that followed cost the city dearly in trade, while the Medici, now in Rome, intrigued to destroy the republic. Worst of all, Savonarola's attacks on clerical corruption made him another bitter enemy in Rome – **Pope Alexander VI**, the most corrupt cleric ever – who scraped together a league of allies to make war on Florence in 1497.

This war proceeded without serious reverses for either side but Savonarola was able to exploit it brilliantly, convincing the Florentines that they were on a moral crusade against the hated and dissolute Borgias, Medici, French, Venetians and Milanese. The year 1497 was undoubtedly the high point of Savonarola's career. The good friar's spies – mostly children – kept a close eye on any Florentines who were suspected of enjoying themselves, and collected books, fancy clothes and works of art for the famous **Bonfire of Vanities**. It was a climactic moment in the history of Florence's delicate psyche. Somehow the spell had been broken; like the deranged old Michelangelo, taking a hammer to his own work, the Florentines gathered the objects that had once been their greatest pride and put them to the torch. The bonfire was held in the centre of the Piazza della Signoria; a visiting Venetian offered to buy the whole lot, but the Florentines had someone sketch his portrait and threw that on the flames, too.

One vanity the Florentines could not quite bring themselves to part with was their violent factionalism. On one side were the *Piagnoni* ('weepers') of Savonarola's party, on the other the party of the *Arrabbiati* ('the angry'), including the gangs of young delinquents who would demonstrate their opposition to piety and holiness by sneaking into the cathedral and filling Savonarola's pulpit with cow dung. A Medicean party was also gathering strength, a sort of fifth column sowing discontent within the city and undermining the war effort. Three times, unsuccessfully, the exiled Medici attempted to seize the city with bands of mercenaries. The Pisan revolt continued, and Pope Alexander had excommunicated Savonarola and was threatening to place all Florence under an interdict. In the long hangover after the Bonfire of Vanities, the Florentines were growing weary of their preacher. When the Arrabbiati won the elections of 1498, his doom was sealed. A kangaroo court found the new scapegoat guilty of heresy and treason. After some gratuitous torture and public mockery, the very spot where the Bonfire of Vanities had been held now witnessed a bonfire of Savonarola.

Pope Alexander still wasn't happy. He sent an army under his son, Cesare Borgia, to menace the city. Florence weathered this threat, and the relatively democratic 'Savonarolan' constitution of 1494 seemed to be working out well. Under a new and innovative idea, borrowed from Venice and designed to circumvent party strife, a public-spirited gentleman named **Piero Soderini** was elected *gonfaloniere* for life in 1502. With the help of his friend and adviser **Niccolò Machiavelli**, Soderini managed to keep the ship of state on an even keel. Pisa finally surrendered in 1509. Serious trouble returned in 1512, and once more the popes were behind it. As France's only ally in Italy, Florence ran foul of Julius II. Papal and Spanish armies invaded Florentine territory and, after their gruesome sack of Prato, designed specifically to overawe Florence, the frightened and politically apathetic city was ready to submit to the pope's conditions – the expulsion of Soderini, a change of alliance and the return of the Medici.

## The End of the Republic

At first, the understanding was that the Medici would live in Florence as private citizens. But **Giuliano de' Medici**, son of Lorenzo and current leader, soon united the upper classes for a rolling back of Savonarolan democracy. With hired soldiers to intimidate the populace, a rigged *parlamento* in September 1512 restored Medici control. The democratic Grand Council was abolished; its new meeting hall in the Palazzo Vecchio (where Leonardo and Michelangelo were to have their 'Battle of the Frescoes') became apartments for soldiers. Soldiers were everywhere, and the Medicean restoration took on the aspect of a police state. Hundreds of political prisoners were tortured in the Palazzo Vecchio's dungeons, among them Machiavelli.

Giuliano died in 1516, succeeded by his nephew **Lorenzo, Duke of Urbino**, a snotty young sport with a tyrant's bad manners. Nobody mourned much when syphilis carried him off in 1519, but the family paid Michelangelo to give both Lorenzo and Giuliano fancy tombs. Ever since Giuliano's death, however, the real Medici boss had been not Lorenzo, but his uncle Giovanni, who in that year became **Pope Leo X**. The Medici, original masters of nepotism, had been planning this for years. Back in the 1470s, Lorenzo il Magnifico had realized that the surest way of maintaining the family fortunes would be to get a Medici on the papal throne. He had little Giovanni ordained at the age of eight, purchased him a cardinal's hat at 13, and used bribery and diplomacy to help him accumulate dozens of benefices all over France and Italy. For his easy-going civility (as exemplified in his famous quote: 'God has given us the papacy so let us enjoy it'), and his patronage of scholars and artists, Leo became one of the best-remembered Renaissance popes. On the other side of the coin was his criminal mismanagement of the Church. Upper-class Florentines descended on Rome like a plague of locusts, occupying all the important sinecures and rapidly emptying the papal treasury. Their rapacity, plus the tremendous expenses involved in building the new St Peter's, caused Leo to step up the sale of indulgences all over Europe – disgusting reformers such as Luther and greatly hastening the onset of the Reformation.

Back in Florence, Lorenzo Duke of Urbino's successor Giulio, bastard son of Lorenzo il Magnifico's murdered brother Giuliano, was little more than a puppet; Leo found enough time between banquets to manage the city's affairs. Giulio himself became pope in 1523, as **Clement VII**, thanks to the newfound financial interdependence between Florence and Rome, and now the Medici presence in Florence was reduced to two more unattractive young bastards, Ippolito and Alessandro, under the guardianship of Cardinal Silvio Passerini. Clement attempted to run the city from Rome as Leo had done, but high taxes and the lack of a strong hand made the new Medici regime increasingly precarious; its end followed after the sack of Rome in 1527. With Clement a prisoner in the Vatican and unable to intervene, a delegation of Florentine notables informed Cardinal Passerini and the Medicis that it was time to go. For the third time in less than a century, Florence had succeeded in getting rid of the Medici.

The new republic, though initiated by the disillusioned wealthy classes, soon found radical Savonarolan democrats gaining the upper hand. The Grand Council met and extended the franchise to include most of the citizens. Vanities were cursed again, books were banned and carnival parades forbidden; the council officially pronounced Jesus Christ 'King of the Florentines', just as it had done in the heyday of the Savonarolan camp meetings. In an intense atmosphere of republican virtue and pious crusade, Florence rushed headlong into the apocalyptic climax of its history. This time it did not take the Medici long to recover. In order to get Florence back, the witless Clement became allied to his former enemy, **Emperor Charles V**, a sordid deal that would eventually betray all Italy to Spanish control. Imperial troops were to help subdue Florence, and Clement's illegitimate son Alessandro was to wed Charles' illegitimate daughter. Charles's troops put Florence under siege in December 1529. The city had few resources for the struggle, and no friends at all, but a heroic resistance kept the imperialists at bay all through the winter and spring. Citizens gave up their gold and silver to be minted into the republic's last coins. The councillors debated seizing little Catherine de' Medici, future queen of France but then a prisoner of the republic, and dangling her from the walls to give the enemy a good target. Few artists were left in Florence, but Michelangelo stayed to help with his city's fortifications (by night he was working on the Medici tombs in San Lorenzo; both sides gave him safe passage when he wanted to leave Florence).

In August of 1530, the Florentines' skilful commander, Francesco Ferruccio, was killed in a skirmish near Pistoia; at about the same time the republic realized that its mercenary captain within the walls, Malatesta Baglioni, had sold them out to the pope and emperor. When they tried to arrest him, Baglioni only laughed, and directed his men to turn their artillery on the city. The inevitable capitulation came on 12 August; after almost 400 years, the Florentine republic had breathed its last.

At first, this third Medici return appeared to be just another dreary round of history repeating itself. Again, a packed *parlamento* gutted the constitution and legitimized the Medici takeover. Again the family and its minions combed the city, taking back every penny's worth of property that had been confiscated from them. This time, however, was to be different. Florence had gone from being a large fish in a small Italian pond to being a minuscule but hindersome nuisance in the pan-European world of papal and imperial politics. Charles V didn't much like republics, or disorderly politicking, or indeed anyone who might conceivably say no to him. The orders came down from the emperor in Brussels: it was to be Medici for ever.

## Cosimo I: the Medici as Grand Dukes

At first little was changed; the shell of the republican constitution was maintained, but with the 20-year-old illegitimate **Alessandro** as 'Duke of the Florentine Republic'; the harsh reality was under construction above the city's west end – the Fortezza da Basso, with its Spanish garrison, demanded by Charles V as insurance that Florence would never again be able to assert its independence. If any further symbolism was necessary, Alessandro ordered the great bell to be removed from the tower of the Palazzo Vecchio – the bell that had always summoned the citizens to political assemblies and the mustering of the army. In 1537, Alessandro was treacherously murdered by his jealous cousin Lorenzaccio de' Medici. With no legitimate heirs in the direct line, Florence was in danger of falling under direct imperial rule, as had happened to Milan two years earlier, upon the extinction of the Sforza dukes. The assassination was kept secret while the Medici and the diplomats plotted for a solution. The only reasonable choice turned out to be 18-year-old **Cosimo de' Medici**, heir of the family's cadet branch. This son of a famous mercenary commander, Giovanni of the Black Bands, had grown up on a farm; both the elder statesmen of the family and the imperial representatives thought they would easily be able to manipulate him.

It soon became very clear that they had picked the wrong boy. Right from the start, young Cosimo had a surprisingly complete idea of the ways in which he meant to rule Florence, and also the will and strength of personality to see that his commands were carried out. No one ever admitted to liking him; his puritanical court dismayed even the old partisans of Savonarola, and Florentines enjoyed grumbling over his high taxes, going to support 'colonels, spies, Spaniards, and women to serve Madame' (his Spanish consort Eleanor of Toledo). More surprisingly, when bowing and scraping Italians were everywhere else losing their liberty, Cosimo held his own against both pope and Spaniard. To back up his growing independence, Cosimo put his domains on an almost permanent war footing. New fortresses were built, a big fleet was begun, and a paid standing army took the place of mercenaries and citizen levies. The skeleton of the old republic was revamped into a modern bureaucratic state.

Early in his reign Cosimo defeated the last-ditch effort of the republican exiles, unreconstructed oligarchs led by the banker Filippo Strozzi, at the **battle of Montemurlo**, the last threat ever to Medici rule. Cosimo's master stroke came in 1557, when with the help of an imperial army he took the entire Republic of Siena. Now the Medicis controlled roughly the boundaries of modern Tuscany; Cosimo was able to cap off his reign in 1569 by purchasing the title of Grand Duke of Tuscany.

## Knick-knacks and Tedium: the Later Medici

For all Cosimo's efforts, Florence was entering a very evident decline. Banking and trade did well throughout the late 16th century, which was a prosperous time for almost all of Italy, but there were few opportunities for growth. More than ever, wealth was going into land, palaces and government bonds; the tradition of mercantile venture was becoming a thing of the past. In terms of culture and art, Cosimo's reign turned out to be a disaster. It wasn't what he intended; indeed, the duke brought to the field his accustomed energy and compulsion to improve and organize.

07 **Florence** | History

Academies were founded, and research underwritten. Cosimo's emphasis on art as political propaganda helped change the Florentine artist from a guild artisan to a flouncing courtier, ready to roll over at his master's command. The city had as great an influence in its age of decay as in its age of greatness. The cute, well-educated Florentine pranced across Europe, praised as the paragon of culture and refinement, even in England – though that honest nation soon found him out:

*A little Apish hatte, couched fast to the Pate, like an Oyster,*
*French Camarick Ruffes, deepe with a witnesse,*
      *starched to the purpose,*
*Delicate in speach, queynte in arraye: conceited in all poyntes:*
*In Courtyly guyles, a passing singular odde man...*
                    *Mirror of Tuscanism*, Gabriel Harvey, 1580

Michelangelo, despite frequent entreaties, always refused to work for Cosimo. Most of the other talented Florentine artists eventually left for Rome or for places further afield, leaving lapdogs such as **Giorgio Vasari** to carry on the grand traditions of Florentine art. Vasari, with help from such artists as Ammannati and Bandinelli, transformed much of the city – especially the interiors of its churches and public buildings. Florence began to fill up with equestrian statues of the Medici, pageants and plaster triumphal arches displaying the triumphs of the Medici, sculptural allegories (including Cellini's *Perseus*) reminding us of the inevitability of the Medici and, best of all, portraits of semi-divine Medici floating in the clouds along with little Cupids and Virtues. It was all the same to Cosimo and his successors, whose personal tastes tended more to engraved jewels, exotic taxidermy and sculptures made of seashells. But it helped to hasten the extinction of Florentine culture.

Cosimo grew ill, abdicating most responsibility to his son **Francesco** from 1564 to his death 10 years later. Francesco, the genuine oddball among the Medici, was a moody, melancholic sort who cared little for government, preferring to lock himself up in the family palaces to pursue his passion for alchemy, as well as occasional researches into such subjects as perpetual motion and poisons – he received consignments of crates of scorpions every now and then. Despite his lack of interest, Francesco was a capable ruler, best known for his founding of Livorno.

Later Medici followed the general course established by other great families, such as the Habsburgs and Bourbons – each one was worse than the last. Francesco's death in 1587 gave the throne to his brother, **Ferdinando I**, founder of the Medici Chapels at San Lorenzo and another indefatigable collector of bric-a-brac. Next came **Cosimo II** (1609–21), a sickly nonentity who eventually succumbed to tuberculosis, and **Ferdinando II** (1621–70), whose long and uneventful reign oversaw the impoverishment of Florence and most of Tuscany. For this the Medici do not deserve much blame. A long string of bad harvests beginning in the 1590s, plagues that recurred with terrible frequency as late as the 1630s, and general trade patterns that redistributed wealth and power from the Mediterranean to northern Europe, all set the stage for the collapse of the Florentine economy. The fatal blow came in the 1630s, when the long-deteriorating wool trade collapsed with sudden finality. Banking was going too, a victim partly of the age's continuing inflation, partly of high taxes and lack of worthwhile investments. Florence, by the middle of the century, found itself with no prospects at all, a pensioner city drawing a barely respectable income from its glorious past.

With **Cosimo III** (1670–1723), the line of the Medici crossed over into the ridiculous. A religious crank and anti-Semite, this Cosimo temporarily wiped out free thought within the universities, allowed Tuscany to fill up with nuns and Jesuits, and decreed fantastical laws such as the one that forbade any man to enter a house in which an unmarried woman resided. In order to support his lavish court and pay the big tributes that were demanded by Spain and Austria (something earlier Medici would have scorned) Cosimo taxed what was left of the Florentine economy into an early grave. His heir, **Gian Gastone** (1723–37), was an obese drunkard, senile and slobbering at the age of 50. He had to be carried up and down stairs on the rare occasions that he got out of bed (mainly to disprove rumours that he was dead); on the one occasion he appeared in public, the chronicles report him vomiting out of the carriage window.

As a footnote on the Medici there is Gian Gastone's perfectly sensible sister, **Anna Maria Ludovica**. As the very last surviving Medici, it fell to her to dispose of the family's vast wealth and hoards of art. When she died, in 1743, her will revealed that the whole bundle was to become the property of the future rulers of Tuscany – whoever they should be – with the provision that not one bit of it should ever, ever be moved outside Florence. Without her, the great collections of the Uffizi and the Bargello might long ago have been packed away to Vienna or to Paris.

## Post-Medici Florence

When Gian Gastone died in 1737, Tuscany's fate had already been decided by the powers of Europe. The Grand Duchy would fall to **Francis Stephen**, Duke of Lorraine and husband-to-be of the Austrian empress Maria Theresa; his troops had been installed in the Fortezza da Basso a year before. For most of the next century, Florence slumbered under benign Austrian rule. Already the first

Grand Tourists were arriving on their way to Rome and Naples – sons of the Enlightenment such as Goethe, who didn't stop because 'nothing in Florence could interest him', or relics such as the Pretender Charles Edward Stuart, 'Bonnie Prince Charlie', who stayed two years. Napoleon's men occupied the city for most of two decades without making much impression.

After the Napoleonic Wars, the Habsburg restoration brought back the Lorraine dynasty. Between 1824 and 1859 Florence and Tuscany were ruled by **Leopold II**, that most likeable of all grand dukes. This was when Florence first became popular among the northern Europeans and was the time when the Brownings, Dostoevsky, Leigh Hunt and dozens of other artists and writers took up residence, rediscovering the glories of the city and of the early Renaissance. Grand Duke Leopold was decent enough to let himself be overthrown in 1859, during the tumults of the Risorgimento. In 1865, when only the Papal State remained to be incorporated into the Kingdom of Italy, Florence briefly became the new nation's capital. King **Vittorio Emanuele** installed himself in the Pitti Palace, and the Italian Parliament held meetings in the great hall of the Palazzo Vecchio.

It was not meant to last. When the Italian troops entered Rome in 1870, Florence's brief hour as a major capital came to an end, but it had given the staid old city a jolt towards the modern world. In an unusual flurry of exertion, Florence finally threw up a façade for its cathedral, and levelled the picturesque though squalid market area and Jewish ghetto in order to construct the dolorous Piazza della Repubblica. Fortunately, the city regained its senses before too much damage was done. Throughout the 20th century, Florence's role as a museum city was confirmed with each passing year. The **Second World War** allowed the city to resume briefly its ancient delight in black-and-white political epic. In 1944 and 1945 Florence offered some of the most outrageous spectacles of Fascist fanaticism, and also some of the most courageous stories of the Resistance – including that of the German consul Gerhard Wolf, who used his position to protect Florentines from the Nazi terror, often at great risk.

In August 1944, the Allied armies were poised to advance through northern Tuscany. For the Germans, the Arno made a convenient defensive line, a fact requiring that all the bridges of Florence be demolished. They all were, except for the Ponte Vecchio, which was saved in a last-minute deal, though the buildings on either side of it were destroyed in order to provide piles of rubble around the bridge approaches. After the war, all of them were repaired; the city had the Ponte della Trínita rebuilt stone by stone exactly as it was. No sooner was the war damage redeemed, however, than a greater disaster attacked Florence's heritage. The **flood of 1966**, when water reached a level of 6.5m, did more damage than Nazis or Napoleons; an international effort was raised to preserve and restore the city's art and monuments.

Since then the Arno has been deepened under the Ponte Vecchio and 5.5m earthen walls have been erected around Ponte Amerigo Vespucci; video screens and computers monitor every fluctuation in the water level. Should another flood occur, Florence will have plenty of time to protect itself. Far more insoluble a threat is terrorism, which touched the city in May 1993, when a bomb killed a family, destroyed the Gregoriophilus library opposite the Uffizi, and damaged the Vasari Corridor. Florence, which was shocked by this intrusion from the outside world into its holy of holies, repaired most of the damage in record time with funds that were raised by national subscription.

Careful planning has saved the best of Florence's immediate countryside from post-war suburbanization, but much of the other territory around the city has been coated by a suburban sprawl. Buildings on the marshland northwest of the city have been demolished, and a project for housing, shops, leisure facilities, and a new Fiat factory, have been built. The new university campus at Novoli boasts several new buildings, as architecturally uninteresting as the originals that they fail to blend in with, and the new law courts down the road have become Florence's one example of modern architecture (designed 30 years ago but only just erected).

Meanwhile Florence works hard to preserve what it already has. Although new measures to control the city's bugbear – the traffic problems of a city of 500,000 people that receives a staggering seven million visitors a year – have been enacted to protect the historic centre, pollution from nearby industry continues to eat away at monuments; Donatello's statue of St Mark at Orsanmichele, which was perfectly intact 50 years ago, is now a mutilated leper. Private companies, banks and even individuals finance 90 per cent of the art restoration that takes place in Florence, with techniques invented by the city's innovative Institute of Restoration. Increasingly, copies are made to replace original works. Naturally, half the city is for them, and the other half against. The proposed tram – for which you will see tracks being laid on the artery roads leading into town – has a controversial route planned, to take it right across the Piazza del Duomo. The idea is that by replacing the buses that rumble by, pollution will be greatly reduced and damage to historic buildings lessened, but Florentines do not really like the idea of their historic centre being dug up. In 2008 a referendum said a resounding 'no' to the route, but the politicians decided to go ahead with it anyway. In 2009, a young new mayor was elected who has promised to revitalize the city and look again at the tram routes. Only one thing

## Highlights of Florence

Florence's museums, palaces and churches contain more good art than perhaps any city in Europe, and to see it all without hardship to your eyes, feet and sensibilities would take at least three weeks. If you have only a few days to spend, the highlights will easily take up all of your time – the **cathedral** and **baptistry**, the paintings in the **Uffizi** (preferably not all in the same day) and the sculptures in the **Bargello**, which is more worthy of your brief time than the **Accademia**, where the rubbernecks pile in to see Michelangelo's *David*. Stop in for a look at the eccentric **Orsanmichele**, and see the Arno from the **Ponte Vecchio**, taking in some of the oldest streets in the city.

If your heart leans towards the graceful lyricism of the 1400s, don't miss the **cathedral museum** and the Fra Angelicos in **San Marco**; if the lush virtuosity of the 1500s is your cup of tea, visit the Pitti Palace's **Galleria Palatina**. Two churches on the edges of the centre, **Santa Maria Novella** and **Santa Croce**, are galleries in themselves; **Santa Maria del Carmine** has the restored frescoes of Masaccio. Devotees of the Michelangelo cult won't want to miss the Medici Chapels and library at **San Lorenzo**. Or head for the oasis of the **Boboli Gardens**. Finally, climb up to **San Miniato**, for the beautiful medieval church and enchanting view over the city.

Florence's 'secondary' sights are just as interesting. You could spend a day walking around old **Fiesole**, or 15 minutes looking at Gozzoli's charming fresco in the **Palazzo Medici-Riccardi**. The **Palazzo Vecchio** has more, but less charming, Medici frescoes. You can see how a wealthy medieval Tuscan merchant lived at the **Palazzo Davanzati**, while the **Museum of the History of Science** will tell you about the scientific side of the Florentine Renaissance; **Santa Trínita**, **Santo Spirito**, **Ognissanti** and the **Annunziata** all contain famous works from the Renaissance. **Casa Buonarroti** has some early sculptures of Michelangelo; the **Museo Archeologico** has even earlier ones by the Etruscans, Greeks and Egyptians; the Pitti Palace's **Museo degli Argenti** overflows with Medici jewellery and trinkets. Take a bus or car out to Lorenzo il Magnifico's villa at **Poggio a Caiano**, or to the other Medici garden villas: **La Petraia** and **Castello**, or **Villa Demidoff** at Pratolino.

There are two museums with 19th- and 20th-century collections to bring you back to the present: the recently expanded **Galleria d'Arte Moderna** in the Pitti Palace, and the **Collezione Alberto della Ragione**. There are two museums founded by Englishmen: the **Horne Museum**, with Renaissance art, and the eccentric **Stibbert Museum**, with everything but the kitchen sink. Strangest of all are the museums in **La Specola**, featuring stuffed animals and wax figures. Most of the important museums, excluding the Palazzo Vecchio, are run by the State and can be pre-booked; call **t** 055 294883.

is for sure: this is Florence, where modernity moves slowly and any decision reached will take many years to reach fruition.

# Piazza del Duomo

In the recently pedestrianized piazza, tour groups circle the three great spiritual monuments of medieval Florence like sharks around their prey. Postcard vendors prey on, and sax players play to, a human carnival from countless countries, who mill about the cathedral good-naturedly while ambulances of a medieval brotherhood dedicated to first aid stand at the ready in case anyone swoons from ecstasy or art-glut.

**㉔ Battistero di San Giovanni**
*open Mon–Wed and Sat 12–7, Thurs–Fri 12–11, Sun 8.30–2; bring small change for adm*

## The Baptistry

To begin to understand what magic made the Renaissance first bloom by the Arno, look here; this ancient, mysterious building is the egg from which Florence's golden age was hatched. By the quattrocento, Florentines firmly believed their baptistry was originally a Roman temple to Mars, a touchstone linking them to a legendary past. Scholarship sets its date of construction as between the 6th and 9th centuries, in the darkest Dark Ages, which makes it even more remarkable; it may as well have dropped from heaven. Its distinctive dark green and white marble facing, the tidily classical pattern of arches and rectangles that deceived Brunelleschi and Alberti, was probably added around the 11th century. The masters who built it remain unknown, but their strikingly original exercise in geometry provided the model for all Florence's great church façades. When it was new, there was nothing remotely like it in Europe; to visitors from outside the city it must have seemed almost miraculous.

Every 21 March, New Year's Day on the old Florentine calendar, all the children that had been born over the last 12 months would be brought here for a great communal baptism – a habit that helped make the baptistry not merely a religious monument but a civic symbol, in fact the oldest and fondest symbol of the republic. As such, the Florentines never tired of embellishing it. Under the octagonal cupola, the glittering 13th- and 14th-century gold-ground mosaics show a strong Byzantine influence, perhaps laid by mosaicists from Venice. The decoration is divided into concentric strips: over the apse, dominated by a 28ft (8.5m) figure of Christ, is a *Last Judgement*, while the other bands, from the inside out, portray the *Hierarchy of Heaven*, *Story of Genesis*, *Life of Joseph*, *Life of Christ* and *Life of St John the Baptist*, the last band believed to be the work of Cimabue. The equally beautiful mosaics over the altar and in the vault are the earliest, signed by a monk named Iacopo in the early 1200s. Lighting installed in recent years has vastly improved visitors' view of the ceiling.

To match the mosaics, there is an intricate tessellated marble floor, decorated with signs of the zodiac; the octagonal space in the centre was formerly occupied by the huge font. The green and white patterned walls of the interior are remarkable, combining influences from the ancient world and modern inspiration for something new, the perfect source that architects of the Middle Ages and Renaissance would strive to match. Much of the best design work is in the **galleries**, partially visible from the floor. The baptistry is hardly cluttered; besides a 13th-century Pisan-style baptismal font, only the **tomb of Anti-Pope John XXIII** by Donatello and Michelozzo stands out. This funerary monument, with marble draperies softening its classical lines, is one of the prototypes of the Early Renaissance. But how did Anti-Pope John, deposed by the Council of Constance in 1415, earn the privilege of a tomb here? Why, it was thanks to him that Giovanni di Bicci de' Medici made a fortune as head banker to the Curia.

## The Gates of Paradise

Historians used to pinpoint the beginning of the 'Renaissance' as the year 1401, when a merchants' guild, the Arte di Calimala, sponsored a competition for the baptistry's North Doors. The **South Doors** (the main entrance) had already been completed by Andrea Pisano in 1330 in the style of the day. Their 28 panels in quatrefoil frames – formal and elegant works in the best Gothic manner – depict scenes from the *Life of St John the Baptist* and the seven Cardinal and Theological Virtues. The celebrated competition of 1401 – perhaps the first ever held in the annals of art – pitted the seven greatest sculptors of the day against one another.

Judgement was based on trial panels of the *Sacrifice of Isaac*, and in a dead heat at the end of the day were the two by Brunelleschi and Lorenzo Ghiberti, now displayed in the Bargello. Ghiberti's more classical-style figures were eventually judged the better, and he devoted nearly the rest of his life to creating the most beautiful bronze doors in the world while Brunelleschi, disgusted by his defeat, went on to build the most perfect dome.

Ghiberti's first efforts, the **North Doors** (1403–24), are contained, like Pisano's, in 28 quatrefoil frames. In their scenes on the *Life of Christ*, the *Evangelists*, and the *Doctors of the Church*, you can trace Ghiberti's progress over the 20 years he worked in the increased depth of his compositions, not only visually but dramatically; classical backgrounds begin to fill the frames, ready to break out of their Gothic confines. Ghiberti also designed the floral frame of the doors; the three statues, of *John the Baptist*, the *Levite* and the *Pharisee*, by Francesco Rustici, were based on a design by Leonardo da Vinci and added in 1511.

Ghiberti's work pleased the Arte di Calimala, and they set him loose on another pair of portals, the **East Doors** (1425–52) – his masterpiece and one of the most awesome achievements of the age. Here Ghiberti (perhaps under the guidance of Donatello) dispensed with the small Gothic frames and instead cast 10 large panels that depict the Old Testament in Renaissance high gear, reinterpreting the forms of antiquity with a depth and drama that have never been surpassed. Michelangelo declared them 'worthy to be the Gates of Paradise'. The doors (they're actually copies – eight of the original panels, restored after flood damage, are on display in the Museo dell'Opera del Duomo, *see* pp.111–13) have been cleaned and stand in gleaming contrast to the others. In 1996, copies of Andrea Sansovino's marble statues of Christ and John the Baptist (1502) and an 18th-century angel were installed over the doors. The originals had begun to fall to bits in 1974; they too are now housed in the Museo dell'Opera.

Ghiberti wasn't exactly slow to toot his own horn; according to himself, he planned and designed the Renaissance on his own. His unabashedly conceited *Commentarii* was the first attempt at art history and autobiography by an artist, and was a work as revolutionary as his doors in its presentation of the creative God-like powers of the artist. In a typical exhibition of Florentine pride he also put busts of his friends among the prophets and sibyls that adorn the frames of the East Doors. Near the centre, the balding figure with arched eyebrows and a little smile is Ghiberti himself.

## The Duomo

**Duomo
(Cattedrale di Santa
Maria del Fiore)**
*www.duomofirenze.it
or www.operaduomo.
firenze.it; open Mon–
Wed and Fri 10–5, Thurs
10–3.30, Sat 10–4.45
(or 1st Sat of month
10–3.30), Sun 1.30–4.45*

For all its importance and prosperity, Florence was one of the last cities to plan a great cathedral. Work began in the 1290s, with the sculptor Arnolfo di Cambio in charge, and from the beginning the Florentines attempted to make up for their delay with sheer audacity. 'It will be so magnificent in size and beauty,' said a decree of 1296, 'as to surpass anything built by the Greeks and Romans.' In response, Arnolfo planned what in its day was the largest church in Catholicism; he confidently laid the foundations for an enormous octagonal crossing 146ft (44.5m) in diameter, then died before working out a way to cover it, leaving behind the job of designing the biggest dome in the world.

Beyond its presumptuous size, the cathedral of Santa Maria del Fiore shows little interest in contemporary innovations and styles; a visitor from France or England in the 1400s would certainly have found it somewhat drab and architecturally primitive. Visitors today often circle confusedly around its grimy, ponderous bulk. Instead of the striped bravura of Siena or the elegant colonnades of Pisa, they behold an astonishingly eccentric green, white and red pattern of marble rectangles and flowers – like Victorian wallpaper, or, as one critic expressed it, 'a cathedral wearing pyjamas'. In the sun, the cathedral under its sublime dome sports festively above the dullish dun and ochre sea of Florence; in dismal weather it sprawls morosely across its piazza like a beached whale tarted up with a lace doily front.

The fondly foolish **façade** cannot be blamed on Arnolfo. His original design, which was only one-quarter completed, was taken down in a late 16th-century Medici rebuilding programme that never got off the ground. The Duomo turned a blank face to the world until the present neo-Gothic extravaganza was added in 1888. Walk around to the north side to take a look at what many consider a more fitting door, the **Porta della Mandorla**, crowned with an *Assumption of the Virgin* in an almond-shaped frame (hence 'Mandorla'), made by Nanni di Banco in 1420.

**⭐ Cupola
Brunelleschi**
*open Mon–Fri 8.30–7,
Sat 8.30–5.40; adm*

## Brunelleschi's Dome

Brunelleschi's dome, more than any landmark, makes Florence Florence. Many have noted how the dome repeats the rhythm of the surrounding hills, echoing them with its height and beauty; from those city streets fortunate enough to have a clear view, it rises among the clouds with all the confident mastery, proportions and perfect form that characterize the highest aspirations of the Renaissance. But if it seems miraculous, it certainly isn't divine; unlike the dome of the Hagia Sophia, suspended from heaven by a golden chain, Florence's was made by man.

Losing the competition for the baptistry doors was a bitter disappointment to Filippo Brunelleschi. His reaction was a typically Florentine one: not content with being the second-best sculptor, he turned his talents to a field where he thought no one could beat him, launching himself into a study of architecture and engineering, visiting Rome and probably Ravenna to snatch secrets from the ancients. When proposals were solicited for the dome in 1418, he was ready with a brilliant *tour de force*. Not only would he build the biggest, most beautiful dome of the time, but he would do it without any expensive supports while work was in progress, making use of a cantilevered system of bricks that could support itself while it ascended.

Brunelleschi studied then surpassed the technique of the ancients. To the Florentines, who could have invented the slogan 'form follows function' for their own tastes in building, it must have come as a revelation: the most logical way of covering the space was a work of perfect beauty. Brunelleschi's dome put a crown on the achievements of Florence. After 500 years it is still the city's pride and symbol.

The best way to appreciate Brunelleschi's genius is by touring inside the two concentric shells of the dome (*see* p.110), but before entering note the eight marble ribs that define its octagonal shape; hidden inside are the three huge stone chains that bind them together. Work on the balcony around the base of the dome, designed by Giuliano da Sangallo, was halted in 1515 after Michelangelo commented that it resembled a cricket's cage. As for the lantern, the Florentines were famous for their fondness and admiration for Doubting Thomas, and here they showed why. Even though they marvelled at the dome, they still doubted that Brunelleschi could construct a proper lantern, and forced him to submit to yet another competition. He died before it was begun, and it was completed to his design by Michelozzo.

## The Interior

After the façade, the austerity of the Duomo interior is startling. There is plenty of room – contemporary writers mention 10,000 souls packed inside to hear Savonarola's sermons. But, the Duomo hardly seems a religious building – more a *Florentine* building, with simple arches and counterpoint of grey stone and white plaster, full of old familiar Florentine things. Near the entrance, on the right-hand side, are busts of Brunelleschi and Giotto. On the left wall, posed inconspicuously, are the two most conspicuous monuments to private individuals ever erected by the Florentine Republic. The one on the right, is to **Sir John Hawkwood**, the English *condottiere* whose name the Italians mangled to Giovanni Acuto, a commander who served Florence for many years and is perhaps best known to English speakers as the hero of *The White Company* by Sir Arthur Conan Doyle. Hawkwood made the Florentines promise to build him an equestrian statue after his death; it was a typical Florentine trick to pinch pennies and cheat a dead man, but they hired the greatest master of perspective, Paolo Uccello, to make a fresco that looked like a statue (1436). Twenty years later, they pulled the same trick again, commissioning Andrea del Castagno to paint the non-existent equestrian statue of another *condottiere*, Niccolò da Tolentino.

A little further down, Florence commemorates its own secular scripture with Michelino's well-known fresco of Dante, a vision of the poet and his *Paradiso* outside the walls of Florence. Two singular icons of Florence's fascination with science stand at opposite ends of the building: behind the west front, a bizarre clock painted by Uccello, and in the pavement of the left apse a gnomon fixed by the astronomer Toscanelli in 1475. A beam of sunlight strikes it every year at the summer solstice.

For building the great dome, Brunelleschi was accorded a special honour – he is one of the few Florentines to be buried in the cathedral. His **tomb** may be viewed in the **excavations of Santa Reparata** (the stairway descending on the right of the nave). Arnolfo di Cambio's cathedral was constructed on the ruins of the ancient church of Santa Reparata, which lay forgotten until 1965. Excavations have revealed not only the palaeo-Christian church and its several reconstructions, but also the remains of its Roman predecessor – a rather confusing muddle of walls that have been tidied up in an ambience that resembles an archaeological shopping centre. A coloured model helps explain what is what, and glass cases display items found in the dig, including the spurs of Giovanni de' Medici, who was buried here in 1351. In the ancient crypt of Santa Reparata are 13th-century tomb slabs, and in another section is a fine pre-Romanesque mosaic pavement.

There is surprisingly little religious art – the Florentines for reasons of their own have carted most of it off into the cathedral museum (*see* p.111). Under the dome are the entrances to the two sacristies, with terracotta lunettes over the doors by Luca

**Resti di Santa Reparata**
*open Sun–Wed and Fri 10–5, Thurs 10–3.30, Sat 10–4.45 (exc. 1st Sat of month 10–3.30); adm*

07
Florence | Piazza del Duomo

della Robbia; the scene of the Resurrection over the north sacristy is one of his earliest and best works. He also did the bronze doors beneath it, with tiny portraits on the handles of Lorenzo il Magnifico and his brother Giuliano de' Medici, targets of the Pazzi Conspiracy in 1478. In the middle apse is a beautiful bronze urn by Ghiberti containing relics of the Florentine saint Zenobius. The only conventional religious decorations are the frescoes some 60m up in the dome, mostly by Vasari. As you stand squinting at them, try not to think that the cupola weighs around 25,000 tons.

A door on the left-hand aisle near the Dante fresco leads up into the **dome** (*see* p.108). The complicated network of stairs and walks between the inner and outer domes (not too difficult, if claustrophobic and vertiginous) was designed by Brunelleschi, and offers an insight into how thoroughly the architect thought out the problems of the dome's construction, even inserting hooks to hold up scaffolding for future cleaning or repairs; Brunelleschi installed restaurants to save workers the trouble of descending for meals. There is also no better place to get an idea of the dome's scale; the walls of the inner dome are 13ft (4m) thick, and those of the outer dome 6ft (1.8m). These give the dome enough support to preclude the need for further buttressing.

From the gallery of the dome you can get a good look at the lovely **stained glass** by Uccello, Donatello, Ghiberti and Castagno, in the seven circular windows, or *occhi*, made during the construction of the dome, which are being restored one by one. Further up, the views through the small windows offer tantalizing hints of the breathtaking panorama from the marble lantern at the top. The bronze ball at the very top was added by Verrocchio, and can hold almost a dozen people when open.

## Giotto's Campanile

The dome steals the show, putting one of Italy's most beautiful belltowers in the shade both figuratively and literally. The dome's great size – 366ft to the bronze ball – makes the campanile look small, though 280ft is not exactly tiny. Giotto was made director of the cathedral works in 1334, and his basic design was completed after his death (1337) by Andrea Pisano and Francesco Talenti. It is difficult to say whether they were entirely faithful to the plan; Giotto was an artist, not an engineer. After he died, his successors realized the thing, then only 40ft high, was about to tumble over – a problem they overcame by doubling the thickness of the walls.

Besides its lovely form, the green, pink and white campanile's major fame rests with Pisano and Talenti's **sculptural reliefs** – a veritable encyclopaedia of the medieval world view with prophets, saints and sibyls, allegories of the planets, virtues and sacraments, the liberal arts and industries (the artist's craft is fittingly symbolized by a winged figure of Daedalus). All of these are copies of the originals now in the cathedral museum. If you can take another 400 steps or so, the **terrace** on top offers a slightly different view of Florence and of the cathedral itself.

**Campanile terrace**
*open daily*
*8.30–7.30; adm*

## Loggia del Bigallo

The most striking secular building on the Piazza del Duomo is the Loggia del Bigallo, south of the baptistry near the beginning of Via de' Calzaiuoli. This 14th-century porch was built for one of Florence's great charitable confraternities, the Misericordia, which still has its HQ across the street and operates the ambulances parked in front; during the 13th and 14th centuries members courageously nursed and buried victims of the plague. The Loggia itself originally served as a 'lost and found' office for children; if unclaimed after three days, they were sent to foster homes.

To the east of the Loggia del Bigallo is a stone bench labelled the 'Sasso di Dante' – **Dante's Stone** – where the poet would sit and take the air, observing his fellow citizens and watching the construction of the cathedral.

## Museo dell'Opera del Duomo

**Museo dell'Opera del Duomo**
*www.duomofirenze.it;*
*open Mon–Sat 9–7.30,*
*Sun 9–1.45; adm*

The cathedral museum (Piazza del Duomo 9, near the central apse) is one of Florence's finest museums, housing both relics from the construction of the cathedral and the masterpieces that once adorned it. The 2007 work completes a major restructuring to improve the layout and make it more visitor-friendly: there is now full disabled access, better information, a more logical layout, in a more or less chronological order, and greatly increased floor space. The courtyard has been covered by a glass roof and turned into an exhibition room; and there are long-term plans to incorporate a neighbouring 18th-century theatre into the museum, which has been closed for several centuries and was most recently used as a garage. When the restoration work is finished, the museum will have doubled in size.

The entrance leads into the ticket hall – which is pristine in marble and stone, the same materials that were used in the Duomo's construction – and past the bookshop. Just after the entrance are several fragments of Roman reliefs, then two anterooms containing restored statues or bits of statues that once adorned the façade of the Duomo.

The first hall is devoted to the cathedral's sculptor-architect Arnolfo di Cambio and contains the statues he made to adorn it: the unusual Madonna with the glass eyes, Florence's old patron saints Reparata and Zenobius, and nasty old Boniface VIII, who sits stiffly on his throne like an Egyptian god. There are the four Evangelists, including a *St John* by Donatello, and a small collection of ancient works – Roman sarcophagi and an Etruscan *cippus* carved with dancers. Note the 16th-century 'Libretto', a fold-out display case of saintly odds and ends. The Florentines were never enthusiastic about the worship of relics, and long ago they shipped San Girolamo's jawbone, John the Baptist's index finger and St Philip's arm across the street to this museum.

A nearby room contains a collection of altarpieces, triptychs and paintings of saints, including Giovanni del Biondo's *St Sebastian*. Also here are a series of marble relief panels by Baccio Bandinelli from the altarpiece of the cathedral. A small room next to this contains a section (several fragments pieced together) of the door known as the 'Porta della Mandorla' on the north side of the Duomo. This is an intricately carved marble relief, including a small figure of Hercules with his stick, significant in that it was the first representation of the adult male nude and a taste of things to come – more of a statue than a relief. Also in this room are two statues known as the *Profetini*, which once stood over the door and are attributed to the young Donatello.

On the landing of the stairs is the *Pietà* Michelangelo intended for his own tomb. The artist, increasingly cantankerous in old age, became exasperated with this complex work and took a hammer to Christ's arm, in the first known instance of an artist vandalizing his own work. His assistant repaired the damage and finished part of the figures of Christ and Mary Magdalene. According to Vasari, the hooded figure of Nicodemus is a self-portrait.

Upstairs, the first room is dominated by the two **Cantorie**, two marble choir balconies with exquisite bas-reliefs, made in the 1430s by Luca della Robbia and Donatello. Both rank among the Renaissance's greatest works. Della Robbia's delightful horde of children dancing, singing and playing instruments is a truly angelic choir, Apollonian in its calm and beauty. It is perhaps the most charming work ever to be inspired by the forms of antiquity. Donatello's *putti*, by contrast, dance, or rather race, through their quattrocento decorative motifs with fiendish Dionysian frenzy. Grey and weathered prophets by Donatello and others stand along the white walls. These originally adorned the façade of the campanile. According to Vasari, while carving the most famous of these, *Habbakuk* (better known as *lo Zuccone*, or 'baldy'), Donatello would mutter under his breath 'Speak, damn you. Speak!' The next room contains the original panels on the *Spiritual Progress of Man* from Giotto's campanile, made by Andrea Pisano.

The first thing you see as you enter the last room is Donatello's statue *Mary Magdalene*, surely one of the most jarring figures ever sculpted, ravaged by her own piety and penance, her sunken eyes fixed on a point beyond this vale of tears. This room is dedicated to works removed from the baptistry, especially the lavish silver altar

(14th–15th-century), made by Florentine goldsmiths, portraying scenes from the *Life of John the Baptist*. Antonio Pollaiuolo used the same subject to design the 27 needlework panels that once were part of the priest's vestments. There are two 12th-century Byzantine mosaic miniature masterpieces, and a *St Sebastian* triptych by Giovanni del Biondo that may well win the record for arrows; the poor saint looks like a hedgehog.

A ramp leads into the new part of the museum from the room containing the panels from the campanile. Cases on either side display the collection of pulleys and instruments that were used in the construction of the cathedral. At the bottom of the ramp on the left is Brunelleschi's death mask, facing a model of the lantern, which he was never to see. A window behind this model cleverly gives a close-up view of the cupola itself, which is topped by that self-same lantern.

A series of rooms off a long corridor contain bits and pieces brought out of storage, including the four carved façades, artists' models for the design of the cricket's-cage pattern round the base of the cupola. The corridor leads into a room with walls filled with drawings of the Duomo from the 1875 competition to design the façade. From here, a staircase leads down into the courtyard where eight of Ghiberti's panels from the *Gates of Paradise* are on display. The plan is to reconstruct the doors and their cornice once all the panels are restored. It is hoped that they will be ready to be placed in the new space next door to the museum by late 2010, but reconstructing the panels is proving notoriously difficult so the date is optimistic at best.

# Via de' Calzaiuoli and Piazza della Repubblica

Of all the streets that radiate from the Piazza del Duomo, it's the straight, pedestrian-only Via de' Calzaiuoli that most people almost intuitively turn down – the Roman street that became the main thoroughfare of medieval Florence, linking the city's religious centre with the Piazza della Signoria. The widening of this 'Street of the Shoemakers' in the 1840s has destroyed much of its medieval character, and the only shoe shops to be seen are designer-label. Its fate seems benign, though, compared with what happened to the Mercato Vecchio, in the fit of post-Risorgimento 'progress' that converted it into the **Piazza della Repubblica**, located a block to the right along Via Speziali.

On the map, it's easy to pick out the small rectangle of narrow, straight streets around Piazza della Repubblica; these remain unchanged from the little *castrum* of Roman days. At its centre, the old forum deteriorated through the Dark Ages into a shabby market square and the Jewish ghetto, a densely populated quarter known as the **Mercato Vecchio** – the epitome of the picturesque for 19th-century tourists but an eyesore for the movers and shakers of the new Italy, who tore it down. They erected a triumphal arch to themselves and proudly blazoned it with the inscription 'THE ANCIENT CITY CENTRE RESTORED TO NEW LIFE FROM THE SQUALOR OF CENTURIES'. The sad result, the Piazza della Repubblica, is one of the most ghastly squares in Italy, a brash intrusion of ponderous 19th-century buildings. Just the same, it is popular with locals and tourists alike, closed to traffic and full of outdoor cafés, something of an oasis among the narrow, stern streets of medieval Florence.

From Piazza della Repubblica the natural flow of street life will sweep you down to the **Mercato Nuovo**, the old strawmarket, bustling under a beautiful loggia built by Grand Duke Cosimo in the 1500s. Nowadays vendors hawk leather bags, purses, stationery, toys, clothes, umbrellas and knick-knacks. In medieval times this was the merchants' exchange, where any merchant who committed the crime of bankruptcy was publicly spanked before being carted off to prison; in times of peace it sheltered Florence's battle-stained *carroccio*. Florentines often call the market the '*Porcellino*' (piglet) after the large bronze boar erected in 1612. The current boar was put in place in 1999 – a copy of a copy of the ancient statue in the Uffizi. The drool spilling from the side of its mouth reminds us that Florence is no splashy city of springs and fountains. Rub the piglet's snout, and supposedly destiny will one day bring you back to Florence. The pungent aroma of the tripe sandwiches sold nearby may give you second thoughts.

## Orsanmichele

There is a wonderfully eccentric church on Via de' Calzaiuoli that looks like no other in the world: **Orsanmichele**, rising in a tall, neat three-storey rectangle. It was built on the site of ancient San Michele ad Hortum (popularly reduced to 'Orsan-michele'), a 9th-century church located near a vegetable garden, which the *comune* destroyed in 1240 to erect a grain market; after a fire in 1337 the current market building (by Francesco Talenti and others) was erected, with a loggia on the ground floor and emergency storehouses on top where grain was kept against a siege.

The original market had a pilaster with a painting of the Virgin that became increasingly celebrated for performing miracles. The area around the Virgin became known as the Oratory, and, when Talenti reconstructed the market, his intention was to combine both its secular and religious functions; each pilaster of the loggia was assigned to a guild to adorn with an image of its patron saint. In 1380, when the market was relocated, the entire ground floor

**Orsanmichele**
*in theory open Tues–Fri 10–5, Sat and Sun 10–6.30; closed 1st and last Mon of month; however, closed most of time due to lack of staff or redecoration (exc for summer concerts)*

was given over to the functions of the church, and Francesco Talenti's son Simone was given the task of closing in the arcades with lovely Gothic windows, later bricked in.

The church is most famous as a showcase of 15th-century Florentine sculpture, displaying the stylistic innovations through the decades. Each guild sought to outdo the others, commissioning the finest artists of the day to carve their patron saints and create elaborate niches to hold them. The first statue to the left of the door is one of the oldest: Ghiberti's bronze *St John the Baptist*, erected in 1416 for the Arte di Calimala, was the first life-sized Renaissance statue cast in bronze. Continue to the left on Via de' Lamberti to compare it with Donatello's *St Mark*, patron of linen dealers and used-cloth merchants. Finished in 1411, this is thought to be the first freestanding marble statue of the Renaissance.

The niches continue around Via dell'Arte della Lana, named after the Wool Merchants' Guild, the richest after that of the bankers. Their headquarters, the **Palazzo dell'Arte della Lana**, is linked by an overhead arch with Orsanmichele; built in 1308, it was restored in 1905 in a William Morris style of medieval picturesque. The first statue on this façade of Orsanmichele is *St Eligio*, patron of smiths, by Nanni di Banco (1415), with a niche embellished with the guild's emblem (black pincers) and a bas-relief below showing one of this rather obscure saint's miracles – apparently he shod a horse by cutting off its hoof, shoeing it, then sticking it back on the leg. The other two statues on this street are bronzes by Ghiberti, the Wool Guild's *St Stephen* (1426) and the Exchange Guild's *St Matthew* (1422), the latter an especially fine work.

On the Via Orsanmichele façade stands a copy of Donatello's famous *St George* (the original now in the Bargello) done in 1417 for the Armourers' Guild, with a dramatic predella of the saint slaying the dragon, also by Donatello, that is one of the first known works making use of perspective; next are the Stonecutters' and Carpenters' Guild's *Four Crowned Saints* (1415, by Nanni di Banco), inspired by Roman statues. Nanni also contributed the Shoemakers' *St Philip* (1415), while the next figure, *St Peter*, is commonly attributed to Donatello (1413). Around the corner back on Via de' Calzaiuoli stands the bronze *St Luke*, patron of the Judges and Notaries, by Giambologna, a work of 1602 in a 15th-century niche, and the *Doubting of St Thomas* by Andrea del Verrocchio (1484), made not for a guild but for the Tribunal of Merchandise, who like St Thomas wanted to be certain before making a judgement. In the rondels above some of the niches are terracottas of the guilds' symbols by Luca della Robbia.

Orsanmichele's dark **interior**, if you are lucky enough to find it open, is ornate and cosy, with more of the air of a guildhall than a church. It makes a picturebook medieval setting for one of the masterpieces of the trecento: Andrea Orcagna's beautiful Gothic **Tabernacle**, a large, exquisite work in marble, bronze and coloured glass framing a contemporary painting of the *Madonna* (either by Bernardo Daddi or Orcagna himself), replacing the miraculous one, lost in a fire. The Tabernacle was commissioned by survivors of the 1348 Black Death. On the walls and pilasters are faded 14th-century frescoes of saints, placed as if members of the congregation; if you look at the pilasters on the left as you enter and along the right wall, you can see the old chutes used to transfer grain.

## Piazza della Signoria

Now that this big medieval piazza is car-free, it serves as a great corral for tourists, endlessly snapping pictures of the Palazzo Vecchio or strutting in circles like pigeons. In the old days it would have been full of Florentines, as the stage-set for the tempestuous life of their republic. The public assemblies met here, and at times of danger the bells would ring and the piazza would fill with citizen militias, assembling under the banners of the quarters and guilds. Savonarola held his Bonfire of Vanities here, and only a few years later the disenchanted Florentines ignited their Bonfire of Savonarola on the same spot. (You can see a painting of the event at San Marco.) Today the piazza is still the city's favoured spot for hosting political rallies.

The three graceful arches of the **Loggia dei Lanzi**, next to the Palazzo Vecchio, were the reviewing stand for city officials during assemblies and celebrations. Florentines often call it the Loggia dell'Orcagna, after the architect who designed it in the 1370s. In its simple classicism the Loggia anticipates the architecture of Brunelleschi and all those who came after him. The city has made it an outdoor sculpture gallery, with some of the best-known works in Florence: Cellini's triumphant *Perseus*, radiant after recent restoration, and Giambologna's *Rape of the Sabines*, other works by Giambologna, and a chorus of Roman-era Vestal Virgins along the back wall. Cosimo himself stands imperiously at the centre of the piazza, a bronze equestrian statue also by Giambologna.

All the statues in the piazza are dear to the Florentines for one reason or another. Some are fine works of art; others have only historical associations. Michelangelo's *David*, a copy of which stands in front of the *palazzo* near the spot the artist intended for it, was meant as a symbol of republican virtue and Florentine excellence. At the opposite extreme, Florentines are taught almost from birth to ridicule the **Neptune fountain**, a pompous monstrosity with a giant marble figure of the god. Ammannati, the sculptor, thought he would upstage Michelangelo, though the result is derisively known as *Il Biancone* ('Big Whitey'). Bandinelli's statue of

*Hercules and Cacus* is almost as big and just as awful, according to Cellini looking like a 'sack of melons'.

## Palazzo Vecchio

**Palazzo Vecchio**
*open Mon–Wed and Fri–Sun 9–7, Thurs 9–2; adm, joint ticket available with Cappella Brancacci*

When Goethe made his blitz-tour of Florence, the **Palazzo Vecchio** (or Palazzo della Signoria) helped pull the wool over his eyes. 'Obviously,' thought the great poet, 'the people...enjoyed a lucky succession of good governments' – a remark which, as Mary McCarthy wrote, could make the angels in heaven weep. But none of Florence's chronic factionalism mars Arnolfo di Cambio's temple of civic aspirations, part council hall, part fortress. In many ways, the Palazzo Vecchio is the ideal of stone Florence: rugged and imposing, with a rusticated façade that inspired many of the city's private palaces, yet designed according to the proportions of the Golden Section of the ancient Greeks. Its dominant feature, the 308ft (94m) tower, is a typical piece of Florentine bravado.

The Palazzo Vecchio occupies the site of the old Roman theatre and the medieval Palazzo dei Priori. In the 13th century this earlier palace was flattened along with the Ghibelline quarter interred under the piazza, and in 1299 the now-ascendant Guelphs called upon Arnolfo di Cambio, master builder of the cathedral, to design the most impressive 'Palazzo del Popolo' (as the building was originally called) possible. The palace's unusual trapezoidal shape is often, but rather dubiously, explained as Guelph care not to have any of the building touch land once owned by Ghibellines. One doubts that even in the 13th century property realities allowed for such delicacy of sentiments; nor does the theory explain why the tower has swallowtail Ghibelline crenellations, as opposed to the square Guelph ones on the palace itself. Later additions to the rear of the palace have obscured its shape even more, although the façade is essentially as Arnolfo built it, except for the bet-hedging monogram over the door hailing Christ the King of Florence, put up in the nervous days of 1529, when the Imperial army of Charles V was on its way to destroy the last Florentine republic; the inscription replaces an earlier one left by Savonarola. The room at the top of the tower was used as a prison for famous people and dubbed the *alberghetto*; inmates in 'the little hotel' included Cosimo il Vecchio before his brief exile, and Savonarola, who spent his last months, between torture sessions, enjoying a superb view of the city before his execution in the piazza below.

### Inside the Palazzo Vecchio

Today the Palazzo Vecchio serves as Florence's city hall, but nearly all its historic rooms are open to the public. With few exceptions, the interior decorations date from the time of Cosimo I, when he moved his Grand Ducal self from the Medici Palace in 1540. To

**07 Florence | Piazza della Signoria**

politically 'correct' its acres of walls and ceilings in the shortest amount of time, he turned to his court artist Giorgio Vasari, who was famed more for the speed at which he could execute a commission than for its quality. On the ground floor of the *palazzo*, before you buy your ticket, you can take a look at some of Vasari's more elaborate handiwork in the **courtyard**, redone for the occasion of Francesco I's unhappy marriage to the plain and stupid Habsburg Joanna of Austria in 1565.

Vasari's suitably grand staircase takes you up to the vast **Salone dei Cinquecento**, which was added by Savonarola for meetings of the 500-strong Consiglio Maggiore, the reformed republic's democratic assembly. Leonardo da Vinci and Michelangelo were commissioned in 1503 to paint the two long walls of the *salone*, in a kind of Battle of the Brushes. Unfortunately, neither completed the project: Michelangelo only finished the cartoons of *The Battle of Cascina* before being summoned to Rome by Julius II, who required the sculptor of the *David* to pander to his own personal megalomania. Leonardo went back to Milan, but not before completing the central group of *The Battle of Angiari*, a seminal work in depicting motion and violence.

In 1563, Vasari was commissioned to fresco scenes of Cosimo's military triumphs over Pisa and Siena, with an apotheosis of the Grand Duke on the ceiling – busy scenes with all the substance of cooked pasta. But art detective Maurizio Seracini (the same who appears in *The Da Vinci Code*) is convinced that Vasari couldn't bear to destroy Leonardo's masterpiece, and hid it in a cavity behind the Medici fluff – one clue is the words Vasari himself wrote on his equestrian battle scene: '*Cerca Trova*' ('He who Seeks, Finds'). Currently a committee is studying how to reveal the work without ruining Vasari's frescoes.

The sculptural groups lining the walls of this large room (the Italian parliament sat here from 1865 to 1870 when Florence was the capital) are only slightly more stimulating; even Michelangelo's *Victory*, on the wall opposite the entrance, is more virtuosity than vision: a vacuous young idiot posing with one knee atop a defeated old man still half-submerged in stone, said to be a self-portrait of the sculptor. Its neighbour, a muscle-bound *Hercules and Diomedes* by Vicenzo de' Rossi, probably was inevitable in this city obsessed by the possibilities of the male nude.

Beyond the *salone*, behind a modern glass door, is a much more intriguing room the size of a closet. This is the **Studiolo of Francesco I**, designed by Vasari in 1572 for Cosimo's melancholic and reclusive son, where he would escape to brood over his real interests in natural curiosities and alchemy. The little study, windowless and more than a little claustrophobic, has been restored to its original appearance, lined with allegorical paintings by Vasari, Bronzino and Allori, and bronze statuettes by Giambologna and Ammannati, their refined, polished and erotic mythological subjects part of a carefully thought-out 16th-century programme on Man and Nature. The lower row of paintings conceals Francesco's secret cupboards where he kept his most precious belongings, his pearls and crystals and gold.

After the *salone* a certain fuzziness begins to set in. Cosimo I's propaganda machine, in league with Vasari's fresco factory, produced room after room of self-glorifying Medicean puffery. The first series of rooms, known as the **Quartiere di Leone X**, carry ancestor-worship to extremes, each chamber dedicated to a different Medici: in the first, Cosimo il Vecchio returns from exile amid tumultuous acclaim; in the second Lorenzo il Magnifico receives the ambassadors in the company of a dignified giraffe; the third and fourth are dedicated to the Medici popes, while the fifth, naturally, is for Cosimo I, who gets the most elaborate treatment.

Upstairs the next series of rooms, known as the **Quartiere degli Elementi**, contains more works of Vasari and his studio, depicting allegories of the elements. In a small room, the **Terrazzo di Giunone**, is the original of Verrocchio's boy with the dolphin, from the courtyard fountain. A balcony across the Salone dei Cinquecento leads to the **Quartiere di Eleonora di Toledo**, Mrs Cosimo I's private apartments. Her chapel is one of the masterpieces of Bronzino, who seemed to relish the opportunity to paint something else besides Medici portraits. The **Sala dell'Udienza**, found beyond the second chapel, has a magnificent quattrocento coffered ceiling by Benedetto and Giuliano da Maiano, and walls painted by Mannerist Francesco Salviati (1550–60).

The last room, the **Sala dei Gigli** ('of the lilies'), boasts another fine ceiling by the Da Maiano brothers; it also contains Donatello's restored bronze *Judith and Holofernes*, a late and rather gruesome work dating back to 1455; the warning to tyrants that is inscribed on its base was added when the statue was abducted from the Medici Palace and placed in the Piazza della Signoria.

Off the Sala dei Gigli are two small rooms of interest: the **Guardaroba**, or unique 'wardrobe', adorned with 57 maps painted by Fra Egnazio Danti in 1563, depicting all the world known at the time. The **Cancelleria** was Machiavelli's office from 1498 to 1512, when he served the republic as a secretary and diplomat. He is commemorated with a bust and a portrait. Poor Machiavelli would probably be amazed to learn that his very name had become synonymous with cunning, amoral intrigue. After losing his job upon the return of the Medici, and at one point being tortured and imprisoned on false suspicion of conspiracy, Machiavelli was forced to live in idleness in the country, where he wrote his political works and two fine plays, feverishly trying to return to favour. His concern throughout had been to advise realistically, without mincing words, the fractious and increasingly weak Italians on how to create a strong state. His evil reputation came from openly stating what rulers do, rather than what they would like other people to think they do.

The **Collezione Loeser**, a fine assortment of Renaissance art left to the city in 1928 by Charles Loeser, the Macy's department-store heir, is also housed in the Palazzo Vecchio, in the mezzanine before you exit the museum.

## Collezione Alberto della Ragione

**Collezione Alberto della Ragione**
*Piazza della Signoria 5; open by request; adm*

After the pomposity of the Palazzo Vecchio and a Campari cure at the Piazza della Signoria's Café Rivoire, you may be in the mood to reconsider the 20th and 21st centuries in Florence's only museum of modern art, the Collezione Alberto della Ragione.

There are typical still lifes by De Pisis, equally still landscapes by Carlo Carrà, mysterious baths by De Chirico, Tuscan landscapes by Mario Mafai, Antonio Donghi and Ottone Rosai, a speedy Futurist horse by Fortunato Depero and a window with doves by Gino Severini, a number of richly coloured canvases by Renato Guttuso, paintings after Tintoretto by Emilio Vedova, and many others.

# The Uffizi

**⭐ Uffizi**
*www.uffizi.com; open Tues 8.15am–9pm, Wed–Sun 8.15–6.50; adm exp; long queues very common in summer, so try to arrive early; you can pre-book by phone on t 055 294883, and pay at door when you pick up your ticket, or book ahead at Orsanmichele, Mon–Sat 10–5.30*

Florence has the most fabulous art museum in Italy, and as usual we have the Medici to thank for that; for the building that holds these treasures, however, credit has to go to Grand Duke Cosimo's much-maligned court painter. Poor Giorgio Vasari! His roosterish boastfulness and the conviction that his was the best of all possible artistic worlds, set next to his very modest talents, have made him a comic figure in most art criticism. On one of the rare occasions when he tried his hand as an architect, though, he gave Florence something to be proud of.

The Uffizi ('offices') were built as Cosimo's secretariat, incorporating the old mint (producer of the first gold florins in 1252), the archives and the large church of San Pier Scheraggio, with plenty of room for the bureaucrats who were needed to run Cosimo's efficient, modern state. The matched pair of arcaded buildings have coldly elegant façades that conceal Vasari's surprising innovation: iron reinforcements that make the enormous amount of window area possible and that keep the building stable on the soft, sandy ground. It was a trick that would be almost forgotten until the Crystal Palace and the first American skyscrapers. Almost from the start the Medici began to store some of their huge collection in parts of the building. There are galleries in the world with more works of art – the Uffizi counts some 1,800 – but the Uffizi overwhelms by the fact that everything in it is worth looking at.

The Uffizi has undergone major reorganization in the last few years. Some of this involved the restoration of remaining damage after the bomb of 1993 (all but a very few paintings are now back on display), but improvements have also been made on a practical level. Major restoration of the vaulted rooms on the ground floor has resulted in a vastly improved space; there are now three entrances (for individuals, for groups and for those with pre-paid tickets), bookshops, cloakrooms, video and computer facilities and information desks.

If you are particularly keen on seeing a certain painting, note that rooms may be temporarily closed when you visit; this often seems to depend on staff availability. There is a list of these closures at the ticket counters. Some works are still hung out of chronological order, and the rooms containing work by Caravaggio and Rubens are closed until further notice (although two of the Caravaggios are at present hung in Room 16).

From the ticket counter you can take the lift or sweeping grand staircase up to the second floor, where the Medici once had a huge theatre, now home to the **Cabinet of Drawings and Prints**. Although the bulk of this extensive and renowned collection is only open to scholars with special permission, a roomful of tempting samples gives a hint at what they have a chance to see.

Nowadays one thinks of the Uffizi as primarily a gallery of paintings, but when it first opened visitors came for the fine collection of Hellenistic and Roman marbles. Most of these were collected in Rome by Medici cardinals, and not a few were sources of Renaissance inspiration. The **Vestibule** at the top of the stairs contains some of the best, together with Flemish and Tuscan tapestries made for Cosimo I and his successors. **Room 1**, usually shut, contains excellent early Roman sculpture.

## Rooms 2–6: 13th and 14th Centuries

The Uffizi's paintings are arranged in chronological order, the better to educate its visitors on trends in Italian art. The roots of the Early Renaissance are most strikingly revealed in **Room 2**, dedicated to the three great **Maestà** altarpieces by the masters of the 13th century. All portray the same subject of the Madonna and Child enthroned with angels. The one on the right, by Cimabue, was painted around 1285 and represents a breaking away from the flat, stylized Byzantine tradition. To the left is the so-called *Rucellai Madonna*, painted around the same period by the Sienese Duccio di Buoninsegna for Santa Maria Novella. It resembles Cimabue's in many ways but has a more advanced technique for creating depth, and the bright colouring that characterizes the Sienese school. Giotto's altarpiece, painted some 25 years later, takes a great leap forward, not only in his use of perspective but in the arrangement of the angels, standing naturally, and in the portrayal of the Virgin, gently smiling, with real fingers and breasts.

To the left, **Room 3** contains representative Sienese works of the 14th century, with a beautiful Gothic *Annunciation* (1333) by Simone Martini and the brothers Pietro and Ambrogio Lorenzetti. **Room 4** is dedicated to 14th-century Florentines: Bernardo Daddi, Nardo di Cione, and the delicately coloured *San Remigio Pietà* by Giottino. **Rooms 5 and 6** portray Italian contributions to the International Gothic school, most dazzlingly Gentile da Fabriano's *Adoration of the Magi* (1423), two good works by Lorenzo Monaco, and the *Thebaid* of Gherardo Starnina, depicting the rather unusual activities of the 4th-century monks of St Pancratius of Thebes, in Egypt.

## Rooms 7–9: Early Renaissance

In the Uffizi, at least, it's but a few short steps from the superbly decorative International Gothic to the masters of the early Renaissance. **Room 7** contains minor works by Fra Angelico, Masaccio and Masolino, and three masterpieces. Domenico Veneziano's pastel *Madonna and Child with Saints* (1448) is one of the rare pictures by this Venetian master, who died a pauper in Florence. It is a new departure not only for its soft colours but for the subject matter, unifying the enthroned Virgin and saints in one panel, in what is known as a *Sacra Conversazione*. Piero della Francesca's famous *Double Portrait of the Duke Federigo da Montefeltro and his Duchess Battista Sforza of Urbino* (1465) depicts one of Italy's noblest Renaissance princes – and surely the one with the most distinctive nose. Piero's ability to create perfectly still, timeless worlds is even more evident in the allegorical 'Triumphs' of the duke and duchess painted on the backs of their portraits.

A similar stillness and fascination floats over into the surreal in Uccello's *Rout of San Romano* (1456), or at least the third of it still present (the other two panels are in the Louvre and London's National Gallery; all three once decorated the bedroom of Lorenzo il Magnifico in the Medici Palace). Both Piero and Uccello were deep students of perspective, but Uccello went half-crazy; the application of his principles to a violent battle scene has left us one of the most provocative works of all time – a vision of warfare in suspended animation, with pink, white and blue toy horses, robot-like knights, and rabbits bouncing in the background.

**Room 8** is devoted to the works of the rascally romantic Fra Filippo Lippi, whose ethereally lovely Madonnas were modelled after his brown-eyed nun. In his *Coronation of the Virgin* (1447) she kneels in the foreground with two children, while the artist, dressed in a brown habit, looks dreamily towards her; in his celebrated *Madonna and Child with Two Angels* (1445) she plays the lead before the kind of mysterious landscape Leonardo would later perfect. Lippi taught the art of enchanting Madonnas to his student Botticelli, who has some lovely works in this room and the next; Alesso Baldovinetti, a pupil of the far more holy Fra Angelico, painted the room's beautiful *Annunciation* (1447).

**Room 9** has two small scenes from the *Labours of Hercules* (1470) by Antonio Pollaiuolo, whose interest in anatomy, muscular expressiveness and violence presages a strain in Florentine art that culminated in the great Mannerists. He worked with his younger brother Piero on the refined *SS. Vincent, James and Eustace*, brought here from San Miniato. This room also contains the Uffizi's best-known forgery: *The Young Man in a Red Hat* or self-portrait of Filippino Lippi, believed to have been the work of an 18th-century English art dealer who palmed it off on the grand dukes.

## Rooms 10–14: Botticelli

To accommodate the bewitching art of 'Little Barrels' and his 20th-century admirers, the Uffizi converted four small rooms into one great Botticellian shrine. Although his masterpieces displayed here have become almost synonymous with the Florentine Renaissance at its most spring-like and charming, they were not publicly displayed until the beginning of the 19th century, nor given much consideration outside Florence until the early 20th century. Botticelli's best works date from his days as a darling of the Medici – family members crop up most noticeably in the *Adoration of the Magi* (1476), where you can pick out Cosimo il Vecchio, Lorenzo il Magnifico and Botticelli himself (in the right foreground, in a yellow robe, gazing at the spectator). His *Annunciation* is a graceful cosmic dance between the Virgin and the Angel Gabriel. In the *Tondo of the Virgin of the Pomegranate* the lovely melancholy goddess who was to become his Venus makes her first appearance.

Botticelli is best known for his sublime mythological allegories, nearly all painted for the Medici and inspired by the Neo-Platonic, humanistic and hermetic currents that pervaded the intelligentsia of the late 15th century. Perhaps no painting has been debated so fervently as *La Primavera* (1478). This hung for years in the Medici villa at Castello, and it is believed that the subject of the allegory of spring was suggested by Marsilio Ficino, one of the great natural magicians of the Renaissance, and that the figures represent the 'beneficial' planets able to dispel sadness. *Pallas and the Centaur* has been called another subtle allegory of Medici triumph – the rings of Athena's gown are supposedly a family symbol. Other interpretations see the taming of the sorrowful centaur as a melancholy comment on reason and civilization.

Botticelli's last great mythological painting, *The Birth of Venus*, was commissioned by Lorenzo di Pierfrancesco and inspired by a poem by Poliziano, Lorenzo il Magnifico's Latin and Greek scholar, who described how Zephyr and Chloris blew the newborn goddess to shore on a scallop shell, while Hora hastened to robe her – a scene Botticelli portrays once again with dance-like rhythm and delicacy of line. Yet the goddess of love floats towards the spectator with an expression of wistfulness – perhaps reflecting the artist's own feelings of regret. For artistically, the poetic, decorative style he perfected in this painting would be disdained and forgotten in his own lifetime. Spiritually, Botticelli also turned a corner after creating this haunting, uncanny beauty – his and Florence's farewell to a road not taken. Although Vasari's biography of Botticelli portrays a prankster rather than a sensitive soul, the painter absorbed more than any other artist the *fin-de-siècle* neuroticism that beset the city with the rise of Savonarola. So thoroughly did he reject his Neo-Platonism that he would only accept commissions of sacred subjects or supposedly edifying allegories such as his *Calumny*, a small but disturbing work, and a fitting introduction to the dark side of the quattrocento psyche.

This large room also contains works by Botticelli's contemporaries. There are two paintings of the *Adoration of the Magi*, one by Ghirlandaio and one by Filippino Lippi, that show the influence of Leonardo's unfinished but radical work in pyramidal composition (in the next room); Leonardo himself got the idea from the large *Portinari Altarpiece* (1471), at the end of the room, a work by Hugo Van der Goes that was brought back from Bruges by Medici agent Tommaso Portinari.

## Rooms 15–24: More Renaissance

**Room 15** is dedicated to the Florentine works of Leonardo da Vinci's early career. Here are works by his master Andrea Verrocchio, including the *Baptism of Christ*, in which Leonardo painted the angel on the left. Art critics believe the *Annunciation* (1475) is almost entirely by Leonardo – the soft faces, botanical details and misty, watery background would become his trademarks. Most influential was his unfinished *Adoration of the Magi* (1481), an unconventional composition that Leonardo abandoned when he left Florence for Milan. Although at first glance it's hard to make out much more than a mass of reddish chiaroscuro, the longer you stare, the better you'll see the serene Madonna and Child surrounded by anxious, troubled humanity, with an exotic background of ruins, trees and horsemen.

Other artists in Room 15 include Leonardo's peers: Lorenzo di Credi, whose religious works have eerie garden-like backgrounds, and the nutty Piero di Cosimo, whose dreamy *Perseus Liberating Andromeda* includes an endearing mongrel of a dragon that gives even the most reserved Japanese tourist fits of giggles. Tuscan maps adorn **Room 16**, as well as scenes by Hans Memling. Temporarily housed here, away from their normal home in Room 43, are Caravaggio's *Bacchus* and *The Head of Medusa*, believed to be self-portraits. In its day the fleshy, heavy-eyed *Bacchus*, half portrait and half still life, was considered highly iconoclastic.

The octagonal **Tribuna (Room 18)**, with its mother-of-pearl dome and *pietra dura* floor and table, was built by Buontalenti in 1584 for Francesco I and, like the Studiolo in the Palazzo Vecchio, was designed to hold Medici treasures. For centuries the best-known of these was the *Venus de' Medici*, a 2nd-century BC Greek sculpture, farcically claimed as a copy of Praxiteles' celebrated *Aphrodite of Cnidos*, the most erotic statue in antiquity. In the 18th century, amazingly, this rather ordinary girl was considered the greatest sculpture in Florence; today most visitors walk right by without a second glance. Other antique works include the *Wrestlers* and the *Knife Grinder*, both copies of Pergamese originals, the *Dancing Faun*, the *Young Apollo*, and the *Sleeping Hermaphrodite* in the adjacent room, which is usually curtained off.

The real stars of the Tribuna are the Medici court portraits, many of them by Bronzino, who was not only able to catch the likeness of Cosimo I, Eleanor of Toledo and their children, but could also aptly portray the spirit of the day – these are people who took themselves very seriously indeed. They have for company Vasari's posthumous portrait of *Lorenzo il Magnifico* and Pontormo's *Cosimo il Vecchio*, Andrea del Sarto's *Girl with a Book by Petrarch*, and Rosso Fiorentino's *Angel Musician*, an enchanting work entirely out of place in this stodgy temple.

Two followers of Piero della Francesca, Perugino and Luca Signorelli, hold pride of place in **Room 19**; Perugino's *Portrait of a Young Man* is believed to have been modelled on his pupil Raphael. Signorelli's *Tondo of the Holy Family* was to become the inspiration for Michelangelo's (*see* p.126). The room also contains Lorenzo di Credi's *Venus*, inspired by Botticelli.

The Germans appear in **Room 20**: Dürer's earliest known work, the *Portrait of his Father* (1490), done at age 19, and *The Adoration of the Magi* (1504). Also here are Lucas Cranach's Teutonic *Adam and Eve* and his *Portrait of Martin Luther* (1543), not someone you'd necessarily expect to see in Florence. **Room 21** is dedicated to the great Venetians, most famously Bellini and his uncanny *Sacred Allegory* (1490s), the meaning of which has never been satisfactorily explained. There are two minor works by the elusive Giorgione, and a typically weird *St Dominic* by Cosmè Tura.

Later Flemish and German artists appear in **Room 22**, works by Gerard David and proto-Romantic Albrecht Altdorfer, and a portrait attributed to Hans Holbein of *Sir Thomas More*. **Room 23** is dedicated to non-Tuscans Correggio of Parma and Mantegna of the Veneto, as well as Boltraffio's strange *Narcissus*.

## Rooms 25–27: Mannerism

The window-filled South Corridor, with its views over the city and its fine display of antique sculpture, marks only the halfway point in the Uffizi but nearly the end of Florence's contribution. In the first three rooms, however, local talent rallies to produce a brilliantly coloured twilight in Florentine Mannerism. By most accounts, Michelangelo's only completed oil painting, the *Tondo Doni* (1506), was the spark that ignited Mannerism's flaming orange and turquoise hues. Michelangelo was 30 when he painted this unconventional work, in a medium he disliked (sculpture and fresco being the only fit occupations for a man, he believed). It's a typical Michelangelo story that, when the purchaser complained the artist was asking too much for it, Michelangelo promptly doubled the price. As shocking as the colours are the spiralling poses of the Holy Family, sharply delineated against a background of five nude, slightly out-of-focus young men of uncertain purpose (are they pagans? angels? boyfriends? or just fillers?) – an ambiguity that was to become a hallmark of Mannerism; as the *Ignudi* they later appear on the Sistine Chapel ceiling. In itself, the *Tondo Doni* is more provocative than immediately appealing; the violent canvas in Room 27, Rosso Fiorentino's *Moses Defending the Children of Jethro*, was painted some 20 years later and at least in its intention to shock the viewer puts a cap on what Michelangelo began.

**Room 26** is dedicated mainly to Raphael, who was in and out of Florence from 1504 to 1508. Raphael was the sweetheart of the High Renaissance. His Madonnas, like *The Madonna of the Goldfinch*, have a tenderness that was soon to be overpopularized by others and turned into holy cards, a cloying sentimentality added over the centuries. It's easier, perhaps, to see Raphael's genius in non-sacred subjects, such as *Leo X with Two Cardinals*, a perceptive portrait study of the first Medici pope with his nephew Giulio de' Medici, later Clement VII. The same room contains Andrea del Sarto's most original work, the fluorescent *Madonna of the Harpies* (1517), named after the figures on the Virgin's pedestal. Of the works by Pontormo, the best is in **Room 27**, *Supper at Emmaus* (1525), a strange canvas with the Masonic symbol of the Eye of God hovering over Christ's head.

## Rooms 28–45

The Uffizi fairly bristles with masterpieces from other parts of Italy and from abroad. Titian's delicious nudes, especially the voluptuous *Venus of Urbino*, raise the temperature in **Room 28**; Parmigianino's hyper-elegant *Madonna with the Long Neck* (1536), displayed in **Room 29**, is a fascinating Mannerist evolutionary dead end. **Room 31** holds Paolo Veronese's *Holy Family with St Barbara*, bathed in a golden Venetian light, with a gorgeously opulent Barbara. Sebastiano del Piombo's *Death of Adonis*, in **Room 32**, is notable for its melancholy, autumn atmosphere, and for Venus's annoyed look. Tintoretto's shadowy *Leda* languidly pretends to restrain the lusty swan.

**Room 41** is a Flemish domain, with brand-name art by Rubens and Van Dyck; the former's *Baccanale* may be the most grotesque canvas in the whole of Florence. **Room 42**, the Sala della Niobe, was reopened in December 1998 after the bomb damage was repaired. A series of statues, *Niobe and her Sons* (18th-century copies of Hellenic works), are housed in the high, arched-ceilinged room, which is covered in pristine plaster and gold leaf. **Room 43** houses striking Caravaggios.

**Room 44** has three portraits by Rembrandt, including two self-portraits, and landscapes by Ruysdael. **Room 45**'s fine 18th-century works include portraits by Chardin, Goya and Longhi, and Venetian landscapes by Guardi and Canaletto. Even more welcome by this time is the **bar**, with a summer terrace.

**Contini Bonacossi Collection**
*visits by appointment, t 055 265 4321; Uffizi ticket is also valid for this*

The **Contini Bonacossi collection**, once housed in the Meridiana Pavilion at Palazzo Pitti, was moved to the Uffizi in 1999. There is a separate entrance in Via Lambertesca. This recent bequest includes works of Cimabue, Duccio and Giovanni Bellini, some sculpture and china, and also paintings by El Greco, Goya and Velázquez – the last represented by an exceptional work, *The Water Carrier of Seville*.

## Corridoio Vasariano

**Corridoio Vasariano**
*open for very limited periods of year, though now open to individual researchers not just groups; call t 055 265 4321 for information and bookings (obligatory); adm exp*

In 1565, when Francesco I married Joanna of Austria, the Medici commissioned Vasari to link their new digs in the Pitti Palace with the Uffizi and the Palazzo Vecchio in such a manner that the archdukes could make their rounds without rubbing elbows with their subjects. With a patina of 400 years, it seems that Florence wouldn't look quite right without this covered catwalk, leap-frogging on rounded arches from the back of the Uffizi, over the Ponte Vecchio, daintily skirting a medieval tower, and darting past the façade of Santa Felicità to the Pitti Palace.

The Corridoio not only offers interesting views of Florence: it has been hung with a celebrated collection of artists' self-portraits, beginning, reasonably, with Vasari himself before continuing in chronological order, past the Gaddis and Raphael to Rembrandt, Van Dyck, Velázquez, Hogarth, Reynolds, Delacroix and Corot.

## Museo di Storia della Scienza

**Museo di Storia della Scienza**
*open Mon and Wed–Fri 9.30–5, Tues and Sat 9.30–1; adm; partially closed for restoration at time of writing; only the ground floor is open*

For all that Florence and Tuscany contributed to the birth of science, it is only fitting to have the museum of the history of science in the centre of the city, behind the Uffizi in Piazza Giudici. Much of the first floor is devoted to instruments measuring time and distance: Arabian astrolabes and pocket sundials, Tuscan sundials in the shape of Platonic solids, enormous elaborate armillary spheres and a small reliquary holding the bone of Galileo's finger, erect, like a final gesture to the city that until 1737 denied him a Christian burial. Here, too, are two of his original telescopes and the lens with which he discovered the four moons of Jupiter. Other scientific instruments come from the Accademia del Cimento ('trial' or 'experiment'), which was founded in 1657 by Cardinal Leopoldo de' Medici, the world's first scientific organization, dedicated to Galileo's principle of enquiry and proof by experimentation. 'Try and try again' was its motto. Upstairs is a large room filled with machines used to demonstrate principles of physics, which the women who run the museum will operate if you ask. Two unusual ones are the 18th-century automatic writer and the instrument of perpetual motion. The rooms on medicine have a collection of 18th-century wax anatomical models, designed to teach budding obstetricians about unfortunate foetal positions, as well as a fine display of surgical instruments from the period.

# Ponte Vecchio and Ponte Santa Trínita

*Bent bridges seeming to strain like bows*

*And tremble with arrowy undertide...*

Elizabeth Barrett Browning, 'Casa Guidi Windows'

Often at sunset the Arno becomes a stream of molten gold – that is, during those months when it has a respectable flow of water. But even in the torrid days of August, when the Arno shrivels into muck and spittle, its two famous bridges retain their distinctive beauty. The most famous of these, the **Ponte Vecchio** or 'Old Bridge', crosses the Arno at its narrowest point; the present bridge, with its three stone arches, was built in 1345 to replace a wooden construction from the 970s, which in turn was the successor to a span that may well have dated back to the Romans. On this wooden bridge, at the foot of the *Marzocco*, or statue of Mars, Buondelmonte dei Buondelmonti was murdered in 1215, setting off the wars of the Guelphs and Ghibellines. The original *Marzocco* was washed away in a 14th-century flood, and Donatello's later version has been carted off to the Bargello.

Like old London Bridge, the Ponte Vecchio is covered with shops and houses. By the 1500s it had become the street of hog butchers, although, after Vasari built Cosimo's secret passage on top, the grand duke evicted the butchers and replaced them with goldsmiths. They have been there ever since, and shoppers from around the world descend on it each year to scrutinize the traditional Florentine talent for jewellery – not a few of the city's great artists began their careers as goldsmiths, beginning with Ghiberti and Donatello and ending with Cellini, whose bust adorns the middle of the bridge. In the 1966 flood the shops proved less resilient than the Ponte Vecchio itself, and a fortune of gold was washed down the Arno.

In the summer of 1944, the river briefly became a German defensive line during the slow painful retreat across Italy. Before leaving Florence, the Nazis blew up every one of the city's bridges, saving only, on Hitler's special orders, the Ponte Vecchio, though they blasted a large number of ancient buildings on each side of the span in order to create piles of rubble to block the approaches. Florence's most beautiful span, the **Ponte Santa Trínita**, was the most tragic victim. Immediately after the war the Florentines set about replacing the bridges exactly as they were: for Santa Trínita, old quarries had to be reopened to duplicate the stone, and old methods revived to cut it (modern power saws would have done it too cleanly). The graceful curve of the three arches was a problem: they could not be constructed geometrically, and considerable speculation went on over how the architect (Ammannati, in 1567) did it. Finally, recalling that Michelangelo had advised Ammannati on the project, someone noticed that the same form of arch could be seen on the decoration of the tombs in Michelangelo's Medici Chapel, constructed most likely by pure artistic imagination. Fortune lent a hand in the reconstruction; of the original statues of the 'Four Seasons', almost all the pieces were fished out of the Arno and rebuilt. Spring's head was eventually found by divers, completely by accident, in 1961.

## Dante's Florence

Dante would contemplate his Beatrice, the story goes, at Mass in the **Badia Fiorentina**, a Benedictine church on Via del Proconsolo across from the Bargello (entrance on Via Dante Alighieri), with a lovely Gothic spire to grace this corner of the Florentine skyline. The church has undergone many rebuildings since Willa, widow of a margrave of Tuscany, began it in around 990, but there is still a monument to Ugo, the 'Good Margrave' mentioned in Dante, and a painting of the Madonna appearing to St Bernard by Filippo Lippi.

Between the Badia and Via de' Calzaiuoli, a little corner of medieval Florence has survived the changes of centuries. In these quiet, narrow streets you can visit the **Casa di Dante**, which was actually built in 1911 over the ruins of an amputated towerhouse,

**Badia Fiorentina**
*cloister open Mon 3–6; church open Mon 3–6*

**Casa di Dante**
*t 055 219416; open daily 10–6; adm*

although scholars all agree that the Alighieri lived somewhere in the vicinity. Since 1960 this museum dedicated to Dante has made a game attempt to evoke Dante's life and times, in spite of neglect. Near the entrance is an edition of *The Divine Comedy*, all printed in tiny letters on a poster by a mad Milanese. Upstairs are copies of Botticelli's beautiful line illustrations for the *Commedia*.

Nearby, the stout medieval **Torre del Castagna** is all that remains of the original Palazzo del Popolo, residence of the *priori*, the governors of the city, before the construction of the Palazzo Vecchio. Dante himself was a *priore* once, and he would have spent his two-month term of office living here, as the law required.

After giving up on Beatrice, Dante married Gemma Donati, in **Santa Margherita** church on the same block. Another church nearby, **San Martino del Vescovo**, has a fine set of frescoes from the workshop of Ghirlandaio.

**San Martino del Vescovo**
*open Mon–Sat 10–12 and 3–5*

## Museo Nazionale del Bargello

**✪ Museo Nazionale del Bargello**
*www.polomuseale. firenze.it; open daily 8.15–1.50; closed 1st and 3rd Sun and 2nd and 4th Mon of month; adm*

Across from the Badia Fiorentina looms the Bargello, a battlemented urban fortress, well proportioned yet of forbidding grace; for centuries it served as Florence's prison. Today its only inmates are men of marble, gathered together to form Italy's finest collection of sculpture – a fitting complement to the paintings in the Uffizi. The Bargello is 'stone Florence' squared to the sixth degree, rugged and austere *pietra forte*, the model for the even grander Palazzo Vecchio. Even the treasures it houses are hard, definite, certain – and almost unremittingly masculine. The Bargello offers the best insight that is available into Florence's golden age, and it was a man's world indeed.

Completed in 1255, the Bargello was intended as Florence's Palazzo del Popolo, although by 1271 it served instead as the residence of the foreign *podestà*, or chief magistrate, who was installed by Guelph leader Charles of Anjou. The Medici made it the headquarters of the captain of police (the *Bargello*), the city jail and torture chamber, a function it served until 1859. In the Renaissance it was the peculiar custom to paint portraits of the condemned on the exterior walls of the fortress; Andrea del Castagno was so good at it that he was nicknamed Andrea of the Hanged Men. All of these ghoulish souvenirs have long since disappeared, as have the torture instruments – they were burned in 1786, when Grand Duke Peter Leopold abolished torture and the death sentence in Tuscany, only a few months after the Venetians led the way. Today the Gothic **courtyard**, the former site of the gallows and chopping block, is a delightful place, owing much to an imaginative restoration in the 1860s. The encrustation of centuries of *podestà* armorial devices and plaques in a wild vocabulary of symbols, the shadowy arcades and stately stairs combine to create one of Florence's most romantic corners.

The main **ground-floor gallery** is dedicated to Michelangelo and his century, although it must be said that the Michelangelo of the Bargello somewhat lacks the angst and ecstasy that one is accustomed to. The real star of the room is Benvenuto Cellini, who was, besides a good many other things, an exquisite craftsman and a daring innovator.

The stairway from the courtyard leads up to the shady **Loggia**, which has been converted into an aviary for Giambologna's charming bronze birds, created for the animal grotto at the Medici's Villa di Castello.

The **Salone del Consiglio Generale**, formerly the courtroom of the *podestà*, contains the greatest masterpieces of early Renaissance sculpture. When Michelangelo's maudlin self-absorption and the Mannerists' empty virtuosity begin to seem tiresome, a visit to this room will prove a welcome antidote. Donatello's originality and vision are strikingly modern – and mysterious. On the wall hang the two famous trial reliefs for the second set of baptistry doors (*see* p.106), by Ghiberti and Brunelleschi, both depicting the *Sacrifice of Isaac*. The remainder of the first floor houses fascinating collections of decorative arts that were donated to the Bargello.

Some of the most interesting items are in the next rooms, especially works in the **ivory collection** – Carolingian and Byzantine diptychs, an 8th-century whalebone coffer from Northumbria adorned with runes, medieval French miniatures chronicling *The Assault on the Castle of Love*, 11th-century chess pieces, and more.

A stairway from the ivory collection leads up to the **second floor**. It houses some of the finest enamelled terracottas of the Della Robbia family workshop, a room of portrait busts, works by Antonio Pollaiuolo and Verrocchio, including his *David* and lovely *Young Lady with a Nosegay*. There is also a collection of armour, and the most important collection of small Renaissance bronzes in Italy.

## Piazza San Firenze to the Duomo

The strangely shaped square that the Badia and the Bargello call home is named after the large church of **San Firenze**, now partially used as Florence's law courts. At the corner of the square and Via Gondi, the **Palazzo Gondi** is a fine Renaissance palace built for a merchant by Giuliano da Sangallo in 1489; it's not easy to pick out the discreet 19th-century additions. A block from the square on Via Ghibellina, the **Palazzo Borghese** (No.110) is one of the finest neoclassical buildings in the city, erected in 1822 for a party in honour of Habsburg grand duke Ferdinand III. The host was one of the wealthiest men of his day, the Roman prince Camillo Borghese, husband of Pauline Bonaparte and the man responsible for shipping many of Italy's art treasures off to the Louvre.

From Piazza San Firenze, Via del Proconsolo leads straight to the Piazza del Duomo, passing by way of the **Palazzo Pazzi-Quaratesi** (No.10), which was the 15th-century headquarters of the banking family that organized the conspiracy against Lorenzo and Giuliano de' Medici. No.12, the Palazzo Nonfinito – begun in 1593 but, as its name suggests, never completed – is now the home of the **Museo Nazionale di Antropologia ed Etnologia**, founded in 1869 and the first ethnological museum in Italy, with an interesting collection of Peruvian mummies, musical instruments collected by Galileo Chini (who decorated the Liberty-style extravaganzas at Viareggio), some lovely and unusual items of Japan's Ainu and Pakistan's Kafiri, and a large number of skulls from all over the world.

**Museo Nazionale di Antropologia ed Etnologia**
*open Mon, Tues, Thurs and Fri 9–1, Sat, Sun 9–5; adm*

## Florence As It Was

Borgo degli Albizi, the fine old street passing in front of the Palazzo Nonfinito, was in ancient times the Via Cassia, linking Rome with Bologna, and it deserves a leisurely stroll for its palaces (especially No.18, the cinquecento **Palazzo Valori**, nicknamed 'Funny Face Palace' for its surreal, semi-relief herm-busts of Florentine immortals on three floors of the façade). If Borgo degli Albizi, too, fails to answer to the Florence you've been seeking, take Via dell'Oriuolo (just to the left at Piazza G Salvemini) to reach the **Museum of Florence As It Was**, located at the big garden at No.24. The jewel of this museum is right out in front – the nearly room-sized *Pianta della Catena*, most beautiful of the early views of Florence. It is a copy; the original, made in 1490 by an unknown artist – that handsome fellow pictured in the lower right-hand corner – was lost during the last war in a Berlin museum. This fascinating painting captures Florence at the height of the Renaissance – a city of buildings in bright white, pink and tan; the great churches are without their façades, the Uffizi and Medici chapels have not yet appeared, and the Medici and Pitti palaces are without their later extensions.

**Museo di Firenze Com'Era**
*open Mon and Tues 9–2, Sat 9–7, plus Wed in winter 9–2; adm*

The museum is not large. At present it contains only a number of plans and maps, as well as a collection of amateurish watercolours of Florence's sights dating from the last century, and paintings of the city's surroundings by Ottone Rosai, a local favourite who died in 1957. Today's Florentines seem much less interested in the Renaissance than in the city of their grandparents. For further evidence of this, look around the corner of **Via Sant'Egidio**, where some recent remodelling has uncovered posters over the street from 1925, announcing plans for paying the war debt and a coming visit of the *Folies Bergère* – the Florentines have restored them and put them under glass.

From Via dell'Oriuolo, Via Folco Portinari takes you to Florence's main hospital, **Santa Maria Nuova**, which was founded in 1286 by the father of Dante's Beatrice, Folco Portinari. A tomb in the hospital's church, Sant'Egidio, is all that remains of the family. Readers of Iris Origo's *The Merchant of Prato* will recognize it as the workplace of the good notary, Ser Lapo Mazzei. The portico, by Buontalenti, was finished in 1612.

# Medieval Streets North of the Arno

Just to the west of Via Por S. Maria, the main street leading down to the Ponte Vecchio, you'll find some of the oldest and best-preserved lanes in all Florence. Near the **Mercato Nuovo** at the top of the street (*see* p.114) stands the **Palazzo di Parte Guelfa**, the 13th-century headquarters of the Guelph party, and often the real seat of power in the city, which was paid for by property confiscated from the Ghibellines; in the 15th century Brunelleschi added a hall on the top floor and an extension.

Next door is the guildhall of the silk-makers, the 14th-century **Palazzo dell'Arte della Seta**, still bearing its bas-relief emblem, or *stemma*, of a closed door, the age-old guild symbol. It's worth continuing around the Guelph Palace to Via Pellicceria to see the fine ensemble of medieval buildings on the tiny square near Via delle Terme, named after the old Roman baths.

## Palazzo Davanzati

**Palazzo Davanzati**
*t 055 238861; ground and first floor open, second floor by appt; open daily 8.15–1.50, closed 1st, 3rd and 5th Mon of the month, closed 2nd and 4th Sun of the month*

To get an idea of what life was like inside these sombre palaces some 600 years ago, stroll over to nearby Via Porta Rossa, site of the elegant **Palazzo Davanzati**, now the **Museo della Casa Fiorentina Antica**. One of the city's most delightful museums, it offers a chance to step back into domestic life of yore. Originally built in the mid-14th century for the Davizzi family, the house was purchased by merchant Bernardo Davanzati in 1578 and stayed in the family until the 1900s. Restored by an antique-collector in 1904, it is the best-preserved medieval-Renaissance house in Florence.

## Piazza Santa Trínita

Three old Roman roads – Via Porta Rossa, Via delle Terme and Borgo SS. Apostoli – lead into the irregularly shaped Piazza Santa Trínita. Borgo SS. Apostoli is named after one of Florence's oldest churches, Romanesque **Santi Apostoli** (11th century), in the sunken Piazzetta del Limbo, former cemetery of unbaptized babies.

Piazza Santa Trínita itself boasts an exceptionally fine architectural ensemble, grouped around the 'Column of Justice' from the Roman baths of Caracalla, which was given by Pius IV to Cosimo I, and later topped with a red statue of *Justice* by Francesco del Tadda.

Its pale granite is set off by the palaces of the piazza: the High Renaissance-Roman **Palazzo Bartolini-Salimbeni** by Baccio d'Agnolo (1520) on the corner of Via Porta Rossa, formerly the fashionable Hôtel du Nord where Herman Melville stayed; the medieval **Palazzo Buondelmonti**, with a 1530 façade by Baccio d'Agnolo, once home to the reading room and favourite haunt of such literati in the 19th century as Dumas, Browning, Manzoni and Stendhal; and the magnificent curving **Palazzo Spini-Ferroni**, the largest medieval palace in Florence, built in 1289 and retaining its original battlements. This is now home to the heirs of the Florentine designer Ferragamo and houses a retail outlet and a fascinating small **museum of Ferragamo's life and work**, including some of the most beautiful shoes in the world.

**Museo Salvatore Ferragamo**
*t 055 336 0456, www.salvatore ferragamo.it; open Wed–Mon 10–6*

## Santa Trínita

**Santa Trínita**
*open daily 7–12 and 4–7*

The church of **Santa Trínita** has stood here, in one form or another, since the 12th century; its unusual accent on the first syllable (from the Latin *trinitas*) is considered proof of its ancient foundation. Although the pedestrian façade that was added by Buontalenti in 1593 isn't especially welcoming, step into its shadowy 14th-century interior for several artistic treats, beginning with the **Bartolini-Salimbeni Chapel** (the fourth on the right), frescoed in 1422 by the Sienese Lorenzo Monaco; his *Marriage of the Virgin* takes place in a Tuscan fantasy backdrop of pink towers. He also painted the chapel's graceful, ethereally coloured altarpiece, the *Annunciation*.

In the choir, the **Sassetti Chapel** is one of the masterpieces of Domenico Ghirlandaio, completed in 1495 for wealthy merchant Francesco Sassetti and dedicated to the *Life of St Francis*, but also to the life of Francesco Sassetti, the city and his Medici circle: the scene above the altar, of Francis receiving the Rule of the Order, is transferred to the Piazza della Signoria, watched by Sassetti (to the right, with the fat purse) and Lorenzo il Magnifico; on the steps stands the great Latinist Poliziano with Lorenzo's three sons. The *Death of St Francis* pays homage to Giotto's similar composition in Santa Croce. The altarpiece, the *Adoration of the Shepherds* (1485), is one of Ghirlandaio's best-known works, often described as the archetypal Renaissance painting, with a contrived but charming classical treatment; the Magi arrive through a triumphal arch, a Roman sarcophagus is used as manger and a ruined temple functions as a stable – all matched by the sibyls on the vault; the sibyl on the outer arch is the one who supposedly announced the birth of Christ to Augustus.

Santa Trínita is a Vallombrosan church, and the first chapel to the right of the altar holds the Order's holy of holies, a painted crucifix formerly in San Miniato. The story goes that one Good Friday, a young noble named Giovanni Gualberto was on his way to Mass when he met the man who had recently murdered his brother. Rather than take his revenge, Gualberto pardoned the assassin in honour of the holy day. When he arrived at church to pray, this crucifix nodded in approval of his mercy. Giovanni was so impressed that he went on to found the Vallombrosan order in the Casentino. The **sanctuary** was frescoed by Alesso Baldovinetti, though only four Old Testament figures survive. In the second chapel to the left the marble **tomb of Bishop Benozzo Federighi** (1454) is by Luca della Robbia. In the fourth chapel, a detached fresco by Neri di Bicci portrays San Giovanni Gualberto and his fellow Vallombrosan saints.

# West of Piazza della Repubblica

The streets to the west of Piazza della Repubblica have always been the choicest district of Florence, and **Via de' Tornabuoni** has always been the smartest shopping street in the city. These days you won't find many innovations here, though: Milan's current status as the headquarters of Italy's fashion industry is a sore point with Florence.

In the bright and ambitious 1400s, however, when Florence was the centre of European high finance, Via de' Tornabuoni and its environs was the area the new merchant élite chose for their palaces. Today's bankers build great skyscrapers for the firm and settle for modest mansions for themselves; in Florence's heyday, things were reversed. Bankers and wool tycoons really owned their businesses. While their places of work were quite simple, their homes were imposing city palaces, all built in the same conservative style and competing with each other in size like some Millionaires' Row in 19th-century America.

The champion was the **Palazzo Strozzi**, a long block up Via de' Tornabuoni from Piazza Trínita. This rusticated stone cube of fearful dimensions squats in its piazza, radiating almost visible waves of megalomania. There are few architectural innovations in the Palazzo Strozzi, but here the typical Florentine palace is blown up to the level of the absurd: there are three storeys like other palaces, but each floor is as tall as three or four normal ones, and the rings to tie up horses could hold elephants. Like Michelangelo's *David*, Florence's other beautiful monster, it emits the unpleasant sensation of what Mary McCarthy called the 'giganticism of the human ego' – the will to surpass not only antiquity but nature herself. Nowadays, at least, the Strozzi Palace is moderately useful as a space for Florence's grandest temporary exhibitions.

## Palazzo Rucellai

There are two other exceptional palaces in the quarter. At the north end of Via de' Tornabuoni stands the beautiful golden **Palazzo Antinori** (1465, by an unknown architect), which has Florence's grandest Baroque façade, **San Gaetano** (1648, by Gherardo Silvani), as its equally golden companion, despite being decorated with statues that would look right at home in Rome but have the appearance of bad actors in Florence.

The second important palace, Florence's most celebrated example of domestic architecture, is the **Palazzo Rucellai**, in Via della Vigna Nuova. Its original owner, Giovanni Rucellai, was a quattrocento tycoon like Filippo Strozzi, but an intellectual too, whose *Zibaldone*, or 'commonplace book', is one of the best sources available on the life and tastes of the educated Renaissance merchant. In 1446 Rucellai chose Leon Battista Alberti to design his palace. Actually built by Bernardo Rossellino, it follows Alberti's precepts and theories in its use of the three classical orders; instead of the usual rusticated stone, the façade has a far more delicate decoration of incised irregular blocks and a frieze – elements influential in subsequent Italian architecture, though far more noticeably in Rome than Florence itself. Originally the palace was only five bays wide, and when another two bays were added later the edge was left ragged, unfinished – a nice touch, as if the builders could return at any moment and pick up where they left off. The frieze, like that on Santa Maria Novella, portrays the devices of the Medici and Rucellai families, whose alliance was fêted in the **Loggia dei Rucellai** across the street, also designed by Alberti.

## Piazza Goldoni and Ognissanti

Before taking leave of old Florence's west end, head back to the Arno and **Piazza Goldoni**, named after the great comic playwright from Venice. The bridge here, the Ponte alla Carraia, is new and nondescript, but its 1304 version played a leading role in that year's most memorable disaster: a company staging a water pageant of the *Inferno*, with monsters, devils and tortured souls, attracted such a large crowd that the bridge collapsed, and all were drowned.

The most important building on the piazza, the **Palazzo Ricasoli**, was built in the 15th century but bears the name of one of unified Italy's first prime ministers, Bettino 'Iron Baron' Ricasoli. Just to the east on Lungarno Corsini looms the enormous **Palazzo Corsini**, the city's most prominent piece of Roman Baroque extravagance, begun in 1650 and crowned with a bevy of statues. The Corsini, the most prominent family of 17th- and 18th-century Florence, were reputedly so wealthy that they could ride from Florence to Rome entirely on their own property. The **Galleria Corsini** (enter on Via del Parione) houses paintings by Giovanni Bellini, Signorelli, Filippino

**Galleria Corsini**
*t 955 218994;
currently closed for
restoration*

Lippi and Pontormo, and *Muses* from the ducal palace of Urbino, painted by Raphael's first master, Timoteo Viti. It also has the rarest of Florentine amenities: a garden, a 17th-century oasis of box hedges, Roman statues, lemon trees and tortoises. Further east on Lungarno Corsini stood the Libreria Orioli, which caused a scandal when it published the first edition of *Lady Chatterley's Lover* in 1927.

To the west of Piazza Goldoni lies the old neighbourhood of the only Florentine to have a continent named after him. Amerigo Vespucci (1451–1512) was a Medici agent in Seville, and made two voyages from there to America on the heels of Columbus. His

**Ognissanti**
*open 7.15–12.30 and 5–7.30*

parish church, **Ognissanti** (All Saints), is set back from the river behind a Baroque façade, on property donated in 1256 by the Umiliati, a religious order that specialized in wool-working. The Vespucci family tomb is below the second altar to the right, and Amerigo himself is said to be pictured next to the Madonna in the fresco of the *Madonna della Misericordia*. Also buried in Ognissanti was the Filipepi family, one of whom was Botticelli.

**Convent**
*open Sat, Mon and Tues 9–12 (you may have to ring the bell)*

The best art is to be found in the **convent**, just to the left of the church at No.42. Frescoed in the refectory is the great *Last Supper*, or *Cenacolo*, painted by Domenico Ghirlandaio in 1480. It's hard to think of a more serene and elegant *Last Supper*, akin to a garden party with its background of fruit trees and exotic birds; a peacock sits in the window, and cherries and peaches litter the lovely tablecloth. On either side of the fresco are two scholarly saints moved from the church itself; Ghirlandaio's *St Jerome* and, on the right, young Botticelli's *St Augustine*.

# Santa Maria Novella

**✪ Santa Maria Novella**
*open Mon–Thurs and Sat 9–5, Fri and Sun (exc. Aug) 1–5; adm*

As in so many other Italian cities, the two churches of the preaching orders – the Dominicans' Santa Maria Novella and the Franciscans' Santa Croce – became the largest and most prestigious in the city, where wealthy families vied to create the most beautiful chapels and tombs. In Florence, by some twitch of city planning, both of these sacred art galleries dominate broad, stale squares that do not invite you to linger; in the irregular **Piazza Santa Maria Novella** you may find yourself looking over your shoulder for the ghosts of the carriages that once raced madly around the two stout obelisks set on turtles, just as in a Roman circus, in the fashionable carriage races of the 1700s. The arcade on the south side, the **Loggia di San Paolo**, is much like Brunelleschi's Spedale degli Innocenti, although it suffers somewhat from its use as a busy bus shelter; the lunette over the door, by Andrea della Robbia, is the *Meeting of SS. Francis and Dominic*.

Santa Maria Novella redeems the anomie of its square with its stupendous black and white marble **façade**, the finest in Florence.

*(vertical margin text)* 07 Florence | Santa Maria Novella

The lower part, with its looping arcades, is Romanesque work in the typical Tuscan mode, finished before 1360. In 1456 Giovanni Rucellai commissioned Alberti to complete it – a remarkably fortunate choice. Alberti's half not only perfectly harmonizes with the original but perfects it with geometrical harmonies to create what appears to be a kind of Renaissance Sun temple. The original builders started it off by orientating the church to the south instead of west, so that at noon the sun streams through the 14th-century rose window. The only symbol Alberti put on the façade is a blazing sun; the unusual sundials, over the arches on the extreme right and left, were added by Cosimo I's court astronomer Egnazio Danti. The base of the façade is also the base of an equilateral triangle, with Alberti's sun at the apex. The beautiful frieze depicts the Rucellai emblem (a billowing sail), as on the Palazzo Rucellai. The wall of Gothic recesses to the right, enclosing the old cemetery, are *avelli*, or family tombs.

The **interior** is vast, lofty and more 'Gothic' in feel than any other church in Florence – no thanks to Vasari, who was set loose to remodel the church to 16th-century taste, painting over the original frescoes, removing the rood screen and Dominicans' choir from the nave and remodelling the altars; in the 1800s restorers did their best to de-Vasari Santa Maria with neo-Gothic details. Neither party, however, could touch two of the interior's most distinctive features – the striking stone vaulting of the nave and the perspective created by the columns marching down the aisles, each pair placed a little closer together as they approach the altar.

Over the portal at the entrance is a fresco lunette by Botticelli that has recently been restored. One of Santa Maria Novella's best-known pictures has also recently been restored and is at the second altar on the left: Masaccio's *Trinità*, painted around 1425, one of the revolutionary works of the Renaissance. Masaccio's use of architectural elements and perspective gives his composition both physical and intellectual depth. The flat wall becomes a deeply recessed Brunelleschian chapel, calm and classical, enclosed in a coffered barrel vault; at the foot of the fresco a bleak skeleton decays in its tomb, bearing a favourite Tuscan reminder: 'I was that which you are, you will be that which I am.'

Above this morbid suggestion of physical death kneel the two donors; within the celestially rational inner sanctum the Virgin and St John stand at the foot of the Cross, humanity's link with the mystery of the Trinity. In the nearby pulpit, designed by Brunelleschi, Galileo was first denounced by the Inquisition for presuming to believe that the Earth went around the Sun.

There is little else to detain you in the aisles, but the first chapel in the left transept, the raised **Cappella Strozzi**, is one of the most evocative corners of 14th-century Florence, frescoed entirely by

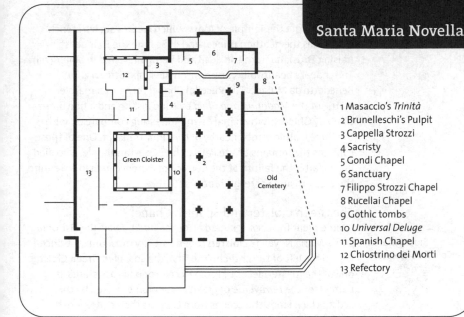

1 Masaccio's *Trinità*
2 Brunelleschi's Pulpit
3 Cappella Strozzi
4 Sacristy
5 Gondi Chapel
6 Sanctuary
7 Filippo Strozzi Chapel
8 Rucellai Chapel
9 Gothic tombs
10 *Universal Deluge*
11 Spanish Chapel
12 Chiostrino dei Morti
13 Refectory

Nardo di Cione and his brother, Andrea Orcagna; on the vault pictures of *St Thomas Aquinas* and the *Virtues* are echoed in Andrea's lovely altarpiece *The Redeemer Donating the Keys to St Peter and the Book of Wisdom to St Thomas Aquinas*; on the left wall is a crowded scene of *Paradise*, with the righteous lined up in a medieval school class photograph. On the right, Nardo painted a striking view of Dante's *Inferno*, with all of a Tuscan's special attention to precise map-like detail. Dramatically in the centre of the **nave** hangs Giotto's *Crucifix* (c.1300), one of the artist's first works. In the **Gondi Chapel** hangs another famous *Crucifix*, carved in wood by Brunelleschi, which, according to Vasari, so astonished his friend Donatello that he dropped the eggs he was carrying in his apron for their lunch when he first saw it.

The charming fresco cycle in the **sanctuary** (1485–90), painted by Domenico Ghirlandaio, is the *Lives of the Virgin, St John the Baptist and the Dominican Saints* portrayed in magnificent architectural settings; little Michelangelo was among the students who helped him complete it. Nearly all of the bystanders are portraits of Florentine quattrocento VIPs, including the artist himself (in the red hat, in the *Expulsion of St Joachim from the Temple*), but most prominent are the ladies and gentlemen of the Tornabuoni house. More excellent frescoes adorn the **Filippo Strozzi Chapel**, the finest work ever to come from the brush of Filippino Lippi, painted in 1502 near the end of his life; the exaggerated, dark and violent scenes portray the lives of St Philip (his crucifixion and his subduing of the dragon before the Temple of Mars, which creates such a stench that it kills the heathen prince) and of St John the Evangelist (raising Drusiana from the dead and being martyred in boiling oil). The chapel's beautifully carved tomb of Filippo Strozzi is by Benedetto da Maiano. The **Rucellai Chapel** contains a marble statue of the *Madonna and Child* by Nino Pisano and a fine bronze tomb by Ghiberti, which makes an interesting comparison with the three Gothic tombs nearby in the right transept. One of these contains the remains of the Patriarch of Constantinople, who died in here after the failure of the Council of Florence in 1439 to reunite the Western and Eastern Churches.

## The Green Cloister and Spanish Chapel

**Santa Maria Novella's cloisters**
*open Mon–Thurs and Sat 9–5, Fri and Sun 1–5; adm*

More great frescoes, restored after the flood, await the visitor in Santa Maria Novella's **cloisters**, open as a city museum (entrance just to the left of the church). The first, the so-called **Green Cloister**, one of the masterpieces of Paolo Uccello and his assistants, is named for the *terraverde* or green earth pigment used by the artist, which lends the scenes from Genesis their eerie, ghostly quality. Much damaged by time and neglect, they are nevertheless striking for their two Uccellian obsessions – perspective and animals. Best known, and in better condition than the others, is Uccello's surreal *Universal Deluge*, a composition framed by the steep walls of two arks, before and after views, which have the uncanny effect of making the scene appear to come racing out of its own vanishing point, a vanishing point touched by divine wrath in a searing bolt of lightning. In between the claustrophobic walls the flood rises, tossing up a desperate ensemble of humanity, waterlogged bodies, naked men bearing clubs, crowded in a jam of flotsam and jetsam in the dark waters. In the right foreground, amidst all the panic, stands a tall robed man, seemingly a visionary, perhaps even Noah himself, looking heavenward while a flood victim seizes him by the ankles.

The **Spanish Chapel** at the far end of the cloisters takes its name from the Spanish court followers of Eleonora di Toledo who worshipped here; the Inquisition had earlier made the chapel its headquarters in Florence. The chapel is, again, famous for its frescoes, the masterpiece of a little-known 14th-century artist named Andrea di Buonaiuto, whose subject was the Dominican cosmology, beautifully portrayed so that even the 'Hounds of the Lord' (a pun on the Order's name, the *Domini canes*) on the right wall seem more like pets than militant bloodhounds sniffing out unorthodox beliefs. The church behind the scene with the hounds is a fairy-pink confection of what Buonaiuto imagined the Duomo would look like when finished; it may well be Arnolfo di Cambio's original conception. Famous Florentines, including Giotto, Dante, Boccaccio and Petrarch, stand to the right of the dais supporting the pope, emperor and various sour-faced hierophants. Off to the right the artist has portrayed four urbane Vices with dancing girls, while the Dominicans lead stray sheep back to the fold. On the left wall, St Thomas Aquinas dominates the *Contemplative Life*, surrounded by Virtues and Doctors of the Church.

The oldest part of the monastery, the **Chiostrino dei Morti** (1270s), contains some 14th-century frescoes, while the **great cloister** beyond is now off limits, the property of the *Carabinieri*, the new men in black charged with keeping the Italians orthodox. Off the Green Cloister, the **refectory** is a striking hall with cross vaulting and frescoes by Alessandro Allori, now a museum.

### Around Santa Maria Novella

Opposite the basilica is one of Florence's newest museums, the **Museo Nazionale Alinari della Fotografia**, the national photography museum with permanent and temporary exhibitions, housed in a 15th-century building fronted by a lovely loggia.

**Museo Nazionale Alinari della Fotografia**
*Piazza Santa Maria Novella 14ar,* t 055 216310, www.mnaf.it; *closed at time of writing, call for opening hours*

Just behind, but a world apart, another large, amorphous square detracts from one of Italy's finest modern buildings – the **Stazione Centrale**, designed by Michelucci in 1935. Adorned by only a glass block canopy at the entrance (and an early model of that great Italian invention, the digital clock), the station is nevertheless remarkable for its clean lines and impeccable practicality.

Leading south from Piazza Santa Maria Novella, on Via della Scala is Florence's historic pharmacy, **Officina Profumo-Farmaceutica di Santa Maria Novella** – and one of the oldest in the world – where monks have been concocting remedies since 13th century. As well as goodies for sale, there is a museum and a bookshop **Via delle Belle Donne** was once known for its excellent brothels. Today it is worth a short stroll to see one of the very few crossroads in Italy that is marked by a cross, a Celtic custom that never really caught on here. According to legend, the **Croce del Trebbio** (from a corruption of '*trivium*') marks the spot where a massacre of Patarene heretics took place in the 1240s, after the masses had been excited by a sermon given by the fire-eating Inquisitor St Peter Martyr from the pulpit of Santa Maria Novella.

**Officina Profumo-Farmaceutica di Santa Maria Novella**
*Via della Scala 16,* t 055 216276, www.smnovella.it

# San Lorenzo and the Medici Chapels

**San Lorenzo**
*open Mon–Sat 10–5.30; Mar–Oct also Sun 1.30–5; adm*

The lively quarter just east of Santa Maria Novella has been associated with the Medici ever since Giovanni di Bicci de' Medici commissioned Brunelleschi to rebuild the ancient church of San Lorenzo in 1420; subsequent members of the dynasty lavished bushels of florins on its decoration and Medici pantheon, and on several projects commissioned from Michelangelo. The mixed result of all their efforts could be held up as an archetype of the Renaissance, described by Walter Pater as 'great rather by what it designed or aspired to do, than by what it actually achieved'. San Lorenzo's façade of corrugated brick was the most *non-finito* of all of Michelangelo's unfinished projects; commissioned by Medici Pope Leo X in 1516, the project never got further than a scale model, which may be seen in the Casa Buonarroti. To complete the church's dingy aspect, the piazza in front contains a universally detested 19th-century statue of Cosimo I's dashing father, Giovanni delle Bande Nere, who died at the age of 28 of wounds received fighting against Emperor Charles V.

The **interior**, completed after Brunelleschi's death to his design, is classically calm in good grey *pietra serena*. Of the artistic treasures it contains, most riveting are **Donatello's pulpits**, the sculptor's last works, completed by his pupils after his death in 1466. Cast in bronze, the pulpits were commissioned by Donatello's friend and patron Cosimo il Vecchio. Little in Donatello's previous work prepares the viewer for these scenes of Christ's Passion and Resurrection with their rough and impressionistic details, their unbalanced, emotional and overcrowded compositions, more reminiscent of Rodin than anything Florentine. Off the left transept, the **old sacristy** is a beautiful vaulted chamber with calmer sculptural decoration by Donatello. Just beyond the Bronzino a door leads into the 15th-century **cloister**, and from there a stair leads up to Michelangelo's **Biblioteca Laurenziana**.

**Biblioteca Laurenziana**
*open Sun–Fri 9.30–1.30*

## The Medici Chapels

San Lorenzo is most famous, however, for the Medici Chapels, which lie outside and behind the church. The entrance leads through the crypt, a dark and austere place where many of the Medici are actually buried.

**Capelle Medici**
*open Mon–Sun 8.15–4.50; closed 2nd and 4th Sun and 1st, 3rd and 5th Mon of month; adm*

Their main monument, the family obsession, located just up the steps, has long been known as the **Chapel of the Princes** – it's a stupefying, costly octagon of death that, as much as the grand dukes fussed over it, lends their memory an unpleasant aftertaste of bric-a-brac that grew and grew. Perhaps only a genuine Medici could love its trashy opulence; all Grand Duke Cosimo's descendants worked like beavers to finish it according to the plans left by Cosimo's illegitimate son, Giovanni de' Medici. Yet even today it is only partially completed, the *pietre dure* extending just part of the way up the walls. The 19th-century frescoes in the cupola are a poor substitute for the originally planned 'Apotheosis of the Medici' in lapis lazuli, and the two statues in gilded bronze in the niches over the sarcophagi are nothing like the intended figures to be carved in semi-precious stone. The most interesting feature is the inlaid *pietra dura* arms of Tuscan towns and the large Medici arms above, with their familiar six red boluses. (The balls probably derive from the family's origins as pharmacists or *medici*, and opponents called them 'the pills'. Medici supporters, however, made them their battle cry in street fights: 'Balls! Balls!')

A passageway leads to Michelangelo's **New Sacristy**, commissioned by Leo X to occupy an unfinished room originally built to balance Brunelleschi's Old Sacristy. Michelangelo's first idea was to turn it into a new version of his unfinished Pope Julius Tomb – an idea quickly quashed by his Medici patrons, who requested instead four wall tombs. Michelangelo only worked on two of the monuments but managed to finish the New Sacristy itself, creating a silent and gloomy mausoleum, closed in and grey, a chilly cocoon calculated to depress even the most chatty tour groups.

Nor are the famous tombs guaranteed to cheer. Both honour nonentities: *Night and Day* belongs to Lorenzo il Magnifico's son, the Duke of Nemours, and symbolizes the Active Life, while the *Dawn and Dusk* is of Giuliano's nephew, Lorenzo, Duke of Urbino (and dedicatee of *The Prince*), who symbolizes the Contemplative Life (true to life in one respect – Lorenzo was a disappointment to Machiavelli and everyone else, passively obeying the dictates of his uncle Pope Leo X). Idealized statues of the two men, in Roman patrician gear, represent these states of mind, while draped on their sarcophagi are Michelangelo's four allegorical figures of the *Times of Day*, so heavy with weariness and grief that they seem ready to slide off on to the floor. The most finished figure, *Night*, has always impressed the critics; she is almost a personification of despair, the mouthpiece of Michelangelo's most bitter verse:

*Sweet to me is sleep, and even more to be like stone*
*While wrong and shame endure;*
*Not to see, nor to feel, is my good fortune.*
*Therefore, do not wake me; speak softly here.*

Both statues of the dukes look towards the back wall, where a large double tomb for Lorenzo il Magnifico and his brother Giuliano was originally planned, to be decorated with river gods. The only part of this tomb ever completed is the statue of the *Madonna and Child* now in place, accompanied by the Medici patron saints, the doctors Cosmas and Damian.

In 1975, charcoal drawings were discovered on the walls of the little room off the altar – ask at the cash desk for a permit, as only 12 people can enter at once. They were attributed to Michelangelo, who may have hidden here in 1530, when the Medici had regained Florence and apparently would only forgive the artist for aiding the republican defence if he would finish their tombs.

07 **Florence** | San Lorenzo and the Medici Chapels

But Michelangelo had had enough of their ducal pretences and went off to Rome, never to return to Florence.

## Mercato Centrale and Perugino

What makes the neighbourhood around San Lorenzo so lively is its **street market**, which the Florentines run with an almost Neapolitan flamboyance. Stalls selling clothes and leather extend from the square up Via dell'Ariento (nicknamed 'Shanghai') towards the **Mercato Centrale**, Florence's main food market, a cast-iron and glass confection of the 1870s, brimful of fresh fruit and vegetables, leering boars' heads and mounds of tripe.

Beyond the market, at Via Faenza 42, is the entrance to Perugino's *Cenacolo di Foligno* fresco, housed in the **ex-convent of the Tertiary Franciscans of Foligno**. This 1490s Umbrian version of the *Last Supper* was discovered in the 1850s and has recently been restored.

## Palazzo Medici-Riccardi

A block from San Lorenzo and the Piazza del Duomo stands the palace that held Florence's unofficial court, where ambassadors would call, kings would lodge, and important decisions would be made. Built in 1444 by Michelozzo for Cosimo il Vecchio, it was the principal address of the Medici for 100 years, until Cosimo I abandoned it for larger quarters in the Palazzo Vecchio and the Pitti Palace. In 1659 the Riccardi purchased the palace, added to it and did everything to keep it glittering until Napoleon and his debts drove them to bankruptcy in 1809.

The palace is now used as the city's prefecture. In its day, though, it was the largest private address in the city, where the family lived with the likes of Donatello's *David* and *Judith and Holofernes*, Uccello's *Battle of San Romano* and other masterpieces now in the Uffizi and Bargello. Frescoes are much harder to move, however, and the Palazzo Medici is worth visiting to see the most charming one in Italy, Benozzo Gozzoli's 1459 *Procession of the Magi*, located in the **Cappella dei Magi** upstairs.

Painting in a delightful, decorative manner more reminiscent of International Gothic than the awakening Renaissance style of his contemporaries, Gozzoli took a religious subject and turned it into a merry, brilliantly coloured pageant of beautifully dressed kings, knights and pages, accompanied by greyhounds and a giraffe, who travel through a springtime landscape of jewel-like trees and castles. This is a largely secular painting, representing less the original Three Kings than the annual pageant of the Compagnia dei Magi, Florence's richest confraternity. The scene is wrapped around three walls of the small chapel – you feel as if you have walked straight into a glowing fairytale world. Most of the faces are those of the Medici and other local celebrities; Gozzoli certainly

**San Lorenzo street market**
*open Tues–Sat, plus Mon in summer*

**Mercato Centrale**
*open Mon–Fri 7–2; some stalls also open Sat pm*

**Convento delle Terziarie Francescane della Beata Angelina da Foligno**
*open Tues, Thurs and Sat 9–12; ring bell; donation requested*

**Cappella dei Magi**
*open Thurs–Tues 9–7; adm; only a few people allowed in at a time; in summer you can book, t 055 276 0340*

had no qualms about putting himself among the crowd of figures on the right wall, with his name written on his red cap. In the foreground, note the black man carrying a bow. Black people, as well as Turks, Circassians, Tartars and others, were common enough in Renaissance Florence, originally brought as slaves. By the 1400s, however, contemporary writers mention them as artisans, fencing masters, soldiers and one famous archery instructor, who may be the man pictured here. For an extraordinary contrast pop into the **gallery** (up the second set of stairs) with its 17th-century ceiling by Neapolitan Luca Giordano, showing the last, unspeakable Medici floating around in marshmallow clouds. In a small adjoining room is a lovely *Madonna and Child* by Filippo Lippi, placed here a couple of years ago after restoration.

## San Marco

**San Marco**
*convent open*
*Mon–Fri 8.15–1.50,*
*Sat and Sun 8.15–5;*
*closed 1st, 3rd and*
*5th Sun of month and*
*2nd and 4th Mon of*
*month; bring small*
*change for adm;*
***church** open daily*
*7–12 and 4–7*

Despite all the others who contributed to this Dominican monastery and church, it has always been best known for the work of its most famous resident. Fra Angelico lived here from 1436 until his death in 1455, spending the time turning Michelozzo's simple **cloister** into a complete exposition of his own deep faith, expressed in bright colours and angelic pastels. Fra Angelico painted the frescoes in the corners of the cloister, and on the first floor there is a small museum of his work, collected from Florentine churches, as well as several early-15th-century portraits by Fra Bartolommeo, capturing some of the most sincere spirituality of the age. The *Last Supper* in the refectory is by Ghirlandaio. Other works by Fra Angelico include the *Life of Christ* series, in which the Saved are well-dressed Italians holding hands. The Bad (mostly princes and prelates) are stripped to receive their interesting tortures.

Right at the top of the stairs to the monks' dormitory, your eyes meet the Angelic Friar's masterpiece, a miraculous *Annunciation* that offers an intriguing comparison with Leonardo's *Annunciation* in the Uffizi. The subject was a favourite with Florentine artists, not only because it was a severe artistic test – expressing a divine revelation with a composition of strict economy – but because the Annunciation, falling near the spring equinox, was New Year's Day for Florence until the Medici adopted the pope's calendar in the 17th century. In each of the monks' cells, Fra Angelico and students painted the *Crucifixion*, all the same but for some slight differences in pose; glancing in the cells down the corridor in turn gives the impression of a cartoon. One of the cells belonged to Savonarola, who was the prior here during his period of dominance in Florence; it has the simple furniture of the period and a portrait of Savonarola by Fra Bartolommeo. In a nearby corridor, you can see an anonymous painting of the monk and two of his followers being led to the stake on Piazza della Signoria. **Michelozzo's library**, located off the main corridor, is as light and airy as the cloisters below; in it is displayed a collection of choir books, one of which was illuminated by Fra Angelico.

Near San Marco, at Via G. La Pira 4, the University of Florence runs several small museums; nearly all the collections were begun by the indefatigable Medici. The **geology and palaeontology museum** has one of Italy's best collections of fossils, many of which were uncovered in Tuscany. The **mineralogy and lithology museum** houses a collection of strange and beautiful rocks, especially from Elba. The **botanical museum** is of less interest to the casual visitor, though it houses one of the most extensive herbariums in the world; most impressive here are the exquisite wax models of plants made in the early 1800s.

Also on Via La Pira is the entrance to the University's **Giardino dei Semplici**, the botanical garden created for Cosimo I, with medicinal herbs, Tuscan plants, flowers and tropical plants in its greenhouses.

## Sant'Apollonia and the Scalzo

*Cenacoli*, or frescoes of the Last Supper, became almost *de rigueur* in monastic refectories; in several of these the *Last Supper* is all that remains of a convent. Until 1860, the Renaissance **convent of Sant'Apollonia**, situated off Piazza San Marco at Via XXVII Aprile 1, was the abode of cloistered nuns, and the *cenacolo* within their refectory was a secret. When the convent was suppressed, and the painting discovered under the whitewash, the critics believed it to be the work of Paolo Uccello; it is only lately that is has been unanimously attributed to Andrea del Castagno, who painted it in from 1445 to 1450. The other walls have *sinopie* of the *Crucifixion*, *Entombment* and *Resurrection* by Castagno; in the vestibule are good works by Neri di Bicci and Paolo Schiavo.

Not far away you can enter a radically different artistic world in the **Chiostro dello Scalzo**, again off Piazza San Marco, at Via Cavour 69. Formerly part of the Confraternity of San Giovanni Battista, this cloister is all that has survived, frescoed (1514–24) with scenes of the life of St John the Baptist by Andrea del Sarto and his pupil Franciabigio. Del Sarto, Browning's 'perfect painter', painted these in monochrome *grisaille*, and while the *Baptism of Christ* is beautiful, some of the other panels are the most unintentionally funny things in Florence – the scene of Herod's banquet is reduced to a meagre breakfast where the king and queen look up indignantly at the man bringing in the platter of the Baptist's head as if he were a waiter who has made a mistake with their order.

**Museo di Geologia e Paleontologia**
*open Sun–Tues and Thurs–Fri 9–1, Sat 9–5; adm*

**Museo di Mineralogia e Litologia**
*open Sun–Tues and Thurs–Fri 9–1, Sat 9–5; adm*

**Museo di Botanica**
*open by request, t 055 275 7462*

**Giardino dei Semplici**
*open Thurs–Tues 10–7; adm*

**Sant'Apollonia**
*open daily 8.10–1.50; closed 2nd and 4th Mon and 1st, 3rd and 5th Sun of month*

**Chiostro dello Scalzo**
*open Mon, Thurs and Sat 8.15–1.50; ring bell*

# Galleria dell'Accademia

**Galleria dell'**
**Accademia**
*www.uffizi.com/*
*accademia-gallery-*
*florence; open*
*Tues–Sun 8.15–6.50,*
*Thurs late opening*
*8.15–9; Thurs nights*
*free 7pm–9pm; adm*

From Piazza San Marco, Via Ricasoli makes a beeline for the Duomo, but on most days the view is obstructed by the crowds milling around No.60; in the summer the queues are as long as those at the Uffizi, everyone anxious to get a look at *David*. Just over 100 years ago Florence decided to take this precocious symbol of republican liberty out of the rain and install it, with much pomp, in a specially built classical *exedra* in this gallery.

Michelangelo completed the *David* for the city in 1504, when he was 29, and it was the work that established the overwhelming reputation he had in his own time. The monstrous block of marble – 4.8m high but unusually shallow – had been quarried 40 years earlier by the cathedral works and spoiled by other hands. The block was offered around to several other artists, including Leonardo da Vinci, before young Michelangelo decided to take up the challenge of carving the largest statue since Roman times. And it is the dimensions of the *David* that remain the biggest surprise in these days of endless reproductions. Certainly as a political symbol of the Republic he is excessive – the irony of a David the size of a Goliath is disconcerting – but as a symbol of the artistic and intellectual aspirations of the Renaissance he is unsurpassed.

And it's hard to deny, after gazing at this enormous nude, that these same Renaissance aspirations by the 1500s began snuggling uncomfortably close to the frontiers of kitsch. Disproportionate size is one symptom; the calculated intention to excite a strong emotional response is another. In the *David*, virtuosity eclipses vision and commits the even deadlier kitsch sin of seeking the sterile empyrean of perfect beauty – most would argue that Michelangelo here achieves it, perhaps capturing his own feelings about the work in the *David*'s chillingly vain, self-satisfied expression. This is also one of the few statues to have actually injured someone: during a political disturbance in the Piazza della Signoria, its arm broke off and fell on a farmer's toe. In 1991 it was *David*'s toe that fell victim when a madman chopped it off. Since then, the rest of his anatomy has been shielded by glass.

In the Galleria next to the *David* you will find Michelangelo's famous *nonfiniti*, the four *Prisoners* or *Slaves*, which were worked on between 1519 and 1536, sculpted for Pope Julius' tomb and left in various stages of completion, although it is endlessly argued whether this is by design or through lack of time. Whatever the case, they illustrate Michelangelo's view of sculpture as a prisoner in stone just as the soul is a prisoner of the body. When he left them, the Medici snapped them up to decorate Buontalenti's Grotta fountain in the Boboli Gardens.

The Galleria was founded by Grand Duke Pietro Leopold in 1784 to provide Academy students with examples of art from every period. The big busy Mannerist paintings around the *David* are by Michelangelo's contemporaries, among them Pontormo's *Venus and Cupid*, with a Michelangelesque Venus among theatre masks. Other rooms contain a good selection of quattrocento painting, including the *Madonna del Mare* by Botticelli, a damaged Baldovinetti, the *Thebaid* by a follower of Uccello, and Perugino's *Deposition*. The painted frontal of the **Adimari chest** shows a delightful wedding scene of the 1450s with the baptistry in the background that has been reproduced in half the books that have ever been written about the Renaissance.

The hall off to the left of the *David* was formerly the women's ward of a hospital, depicted in a greenish painting by Pontormo. Now it is used as a gallery of plaster models by 19th-century members of the Accademia.

The excellent **collection of old musical instruments** once housed in the Palazzo Vecchio has moved to the Accademia. The collection of some 150 exhibits, including several violins and cellos by Cremona greats such as Stradivarius and Guarneri, is on display in a room on the ground floor, well organized and labelled.

## Piazza Santissima Annunziata

This lovely square, the only Renaissance attempt at a unified ensemble in Florence, is surrounded on three sides by arcades. In its centre, gazing down the splendid vista of Via dei Servi towards the Duomo, is the equestrian statue of Ferdinand I (1607) by Giambologna and his pupil, Pietro Tacca, made of bronze from Turkish cannons captured during the battle of Lepanto. More fascinating than Ferdinand are the pair of bizarre Baroque fountains, also by Tacca, that share the square. Though of a nominally marine theme, they resemble tureens of bouillabaisse any ogre would be proud to serve, topped by grinning winged monkeys.

**Spedale degli Innocenti**
*open Mon–Sat 8.30–7, Sun 8.30–2; adm*

In the 1420s Filippo Brunelleschi struck the first blow for classical calm in this piazza when he built the celebrated **Spedale degli Innocenti** and its famous portico – an architectural landmark, but also a monument to Renaissance Italy's long, hard and ultimately unsuccessful struggle towards some kind of social consciousness. Even in the best of times, Florence's poor were treated like dirt; if any enlightened soul had been so bold as to propose even a modern conservative 'trickle-down' theory to the Medici and the banking élite, their first thought would have been how to stop the leaks. Babies, at least, were treated a little better – the Spedale degli Innocenti was the first hospital for foundlings not only in Italy but in the world. At the left end of the loggia you can still see the original window-wheel where babies were anonymously abandoned until 1875. Today it is a nursery school.

The Spedale was Brunelleschi's first completed work and demonstrates his use of geometrical proportions adapted to traditional Tuscan Romanesque architecture. His lovely portico is adorned with the famous blue and white *tondi* of infants in swaddling clothes by Andrea della Robbia, added as an appeal to charity in the 1480s after several children died of malnutrition. Brunelleschi also designed the two beautiful cloisters of the convent; the **Chiostro delle Donne**, which was reserved for the hospital's nurses (located up the ramp on the right at No.13), is especially fine. Upstairs, the **Museo dello Spedale** contains a number of detached frescoes from Ognissanti and other churches, among them an unusual series of red and orange prophets by Alessandro Allori; other works include a *Madonna and Saints* by Piero di Cosimo, a *Madonna and Child* by Luca della Robbia, and the brilliant *Adoration of the Magi* (1488) that was painted by Domenico Ghirlandaio for the hospital's church – a crowded, colourful composition featuring portraits of members of the Arte della Lana, who funded the Spedale.

## Santissima Annunziata

To complement Brunelleschi's arches, the old church of Santissima Annunziata was rebuilt and given a broad arcaded portico by Michelozzo facing the street. Behind the portico the architect added the **Chiostrino dei Voti**, a porch that was decorated with a collection of early-16th-century frescoes, including two by Andrea del Sarto. The best of these, faded as it is, is a finely detailed *Nativity* by Alessio Baldovinetti, one of the quattrocento's underappreciated masters. The church itself is the gaudiest in Florence; its freshly gilded elliptical dome, its unusual polygonal tribune around the sanctuary and megatons of *pietra dura* have helped it become the city's high-society parish, where even funerals are major social events.

The huge candlelit chapel in the rear is the **Tempietta**, which is also by Michelozzo, sheltering a miraculous painting of the *Annunciation*. The church's **cloister** was long used by the Institute of Miltary Geography, but in 2005 restorers made an extremely interesting discovery off a secret staircase: Leonardo's Florentine studio, decorated with frescoes of birds, in which he painted at least one version of the *Virgin and Child with St Anne,* and perhaps also the *Mona Lisa.*

## Museo Archeologico

**Museo Archeologico** www.firenzemusei.it/ archeologico; open Mon 2–7, Tues and Thurs 8.30–7, Wed and Fri–Sun 8.30–2; adm

From Piazza SS. Annunziata, Via della Colonna takes you to Florence's archaeology museum, which is housed in the 17th-century Palazzo della Crocetta, originally built for Grand Duchess Maria Maddalena of Austria. Like nearly every other museum in Florence, this impressive collection was begun by the Medici, beginning with Cosimo il Vecchio and accelerating with the insatiable Cosimo I and his heirs. The Medici were especially fond of Etruscan things, while the impressive Egyptian collection was begun by Leopold II during the 1830s.

The **Etruscan collection** on the first floor includes the famous bronze *Chimera*, a remarkable beast with the three heads of a lion, goat and snake. This 5th-century BC work, dug up near Arezzo in 1555 and immediately snatched by Cosimo I, had a great influence on Mannerist artists. There is no Mannerist fancy about its origins, though; like all such composite monsters, it is a religious icon, a calendar beast symbolizing the three seasons of the ancient Mediterranean agricultural year. In the same corridor stand the *Arringatore*, or Orator, a monumental bronze of the Hellenistic period, a civic-minded and civilized-looking gentleman, dedicated to Aulus Metellus, and the statue of *Minerva*. Also to be found in this section are some other Etruscan bronzes, large and small. The cases here are full of wonderful objects – anything from tiny animals to jewellery, carved mirrors and household objects such as plates and even a strainer. All these show just how skilled the Etruscans were in casting bronze.

The beautifully lit **Egyptian collection**, which is also located on the first floor, has been expanded and modernized. It includes some interesting small statuettes, mummies, Canopic vases, and a unique wood and bone chariot, nearly completely preserved, found in a 14th-century BC tomb in Thebes.

On the second floor there is plenty of Greek art; Etruscan noble families were wont to buy up all they could afford. The beautiful Hellenistic horse's head once adorned the Palazzo Medici-Riccardi. The *Idolino*, a bronze of a young athlete, is believed to be a Roman copy of a 5th-century BC Greek original. There is an excellent *Kouros*, a young man in the archaic style from 6th-century BC Sicily. An unusual, recent find, the silver *Baratti Amphora*, was made in the 4th century BC in Antioch and covered with scores of small medallions showing mythological figures. Scholars believe that the images and their arrangement may encode an entire system of belief, the secret teaching of one of the mystic-philosophical cults common in Hellenistic times, and they hope some day to decipher it. There's a vast collection of Greek pottery (including the massive François vase in Room 2), and large Greek, Roman and Renaissance bronzes, recently brought out of storage. There are also several fabulous Greek marble sculptures dating from c. 500 BC.

There is virtually nothing displayed on the ground floor now, although temporary exhibitions are held there. In the garden are several reconstructed **Etruscan tombs**. The fabulous collection of precious stones, coins and, most notably, cameos (amassed by the Medici) is now permanently on display in the corridor which runs between the museum and the church of Santissima Annunziata.

**Tombe Etrusche**
*open Sat 8.30–2*

# South of Piazza Santissima Annunziata

## Santa Maria Maddalena dei Pazzi and the Synagogue

To the east of the archaeological museum, Via della Colonna becomes one of Florence's typical straight, boring Renaissance streets. It's well worth taking a detour down Borgo Pinti, to No.58, to visit one of the city's least-known but most intriguing churches, **Santa Maria Maddalena dei Pazzi**, which provides a fine example of architectural syncretism. The church itself was founded in the 13th century and rebuilt in the classically Renaissance style by Giuliano da Sangallo, then given a full dose of Baroque when the church was rededicated to the Counter-Reformation saint of the Pazzi family. Inside it's all high theatre, with a gaudy *trompe-l'œil* ceiling, paintings by Luca Giordano, florid chapels, and a wild marble chancel. From the sacristy a door leads down into a crypt to the chapterhouse, which contains a frescoed *Crucifixion* (1496), one of Perugino's masterpieces. Despite the symmetry and quiet, contemplative grief of the five figures at the foot of the Cross and the stillness of the luminous Tuscan-Umbrian landscape, the fresco has a powerful impact, giving the viewer the uncanny sensation of being able to walk right into the scene. The fresco has never been restored; during the 1966 flood, the water came within four inches (11cm) of it, and then stopped.

**Santa Maria Maddalena dei Pazzi**
*open Mon–Sat 9.30–12 and 5–7, Sun 9.30–11 and 5–7*

Florence's Jewish community, although today a mere 1,200 strong, has long been one of the most important in Italy, invited to Florence by the republic in 1430 but repeatedly exiled and readmitted until Cosimo I founded Florence's **Ghetto** in 1551. When the Ghetto was opened up in 1848 and demolished soon after, a new **synagogue** (1874–82) was built in Via L. C. Farini: a tall, charming, Mozarabic Pre-Raphaelite hybrid inspired by the Hagia Sophia and the Transito Synagogue of Toledo. Although seriously damaged by the Nazis in August 1944, as well as by the Arno in 1966, it has since been lovingly restored. There's a small **Jewish museum** upstairs, with a documentary history of Florentine Jews.

**Sinagoga**
*open April–Sept and Oct Mon–Thurs 10–6 and Fri 10–2, Sun 10–6; Oct–Mar Mon–Thurs 10–3, Fri 10–2, Sun 10–3; adm*

**Museo Ebraico**
*same opening hours as for synagogue*

## Sant'Ambrogio and the Flea Market

The streets of Sant'Ambrogio are among the most dusty and piquant in the city centre, a neighbourhood where tourists seldom tread. Life revolves around the church in **Sant'Ambrogio** and its neighbouring food market made of cast iron in 1873; the church (rebuilt in the 13th century, with a 19th-century façade) is of interest for its works of art: the second chapel on the right has a lovely fresco of the *Madonna Enthroned with Saints* by Orcagna (or his school), and the **Cappella del Miracolo**, just left of the high altar, contains Mino da Fiesole's celebrated marble tabernacle (1481) and his own tomb. The chapel has a fresco of a procession by Cosimo Rosselli, especially interesting for its depiction of 15th-century celebrities, including Pico della Mirandola and Rosselli himself (in a black hat, in the group on the left). Andrea Verrocchio is buried in the fourth chapel on the left; on the wall by the second altar is a *Nativity* by Baldovinetti. The fresco of an atypical *St Sebastian* in the first chapel on the left is by Agnolo Gaddi.

From Sant'Ambrogio, take Via Pietrapiana to the bustling **Piazza dei Ciompi**, named after the wool-workers' revolt of 1378. In the morning, Florence's fleamarket or *mercatino* takes place here – it's the best place in town to buy that 1940s radio or outdated ballgown you've always wanted. One side of the square is graced with the **Loggia del Pesce**, which was built by Vasari in 1568 for the fishmongers of the Mercato Vecchio; when that was demolished, the loggia was salvaged and re-erected here.

## Casa Buonarroti

**Casa Buonarroti**
*t 055 241752, www.
casabuonarroti.it; open
Wed–Mon 9.30–4; adm*

Michelangelo never lived in this house at Via Ghibellina 70, although he purchased it in 1508. That wasn't the point, especially to an artist who had no thought for his own personal comfort, or anyone else's – he never washed and never took off his boots, even in bed. Real estate was an obsession of his, as he struggled to restore the status of the semi-noble but impoverished Buonarroti family. His nephew Leonardo inherited the house and several works of art in 1564; later he bought the two houses next door to create a memorial to his uncle, hiring artists to paint scenes from Michelangelo's life. In the mid-19th century, the house was opened to the public as a Michelangelo museum.

The ground floor is dedicated to mostly imaginary portraits of the artist, and works of art collected by his nephew's descendants, including an eclectic Etruscan and Roman collection. The main attractions, however, are upstairs, beginning with Michelangelo's earliest known work, the beautiful bas-relief *Madonna of the Steps* (1490–91), the precocious work of a 16-year-old influenced by Donatello and studying in the household of Lorenzo il Magnifico. The relief of a battle scene, inspired by classical models, dates from the same period. Small models and drawings of potential projects line the walls; there's the wooden model for the façade of San Lorenzo, with designs for some of the statuary Michelangelo intended to fill in its austere blank spaces – as was often the case, his ideas were far too grand for his patron's purse and patience.

The next four rooms were painted in the 17th century to illustrate Michelangelo's life, virtues and apotheosis, depicting a polite, deferential and pleasant Michelangelo hobnobbing with popes. Those who know the artist best from *The Agony and the Ecstasy* may think they painted the wrong man by mistake. One of the best sections is a frieze of famous Florentines in the library. Other exhibits include a painted wooden *Crucifix* discovered in Santo Spirito in 1963 and believed by most scholars to be a documented one by Michelangelo, long thought to be lost; the *contrapposto* position of the slender body, and the fact that only Michelangelo would carve a nude Christ, weigh in favour of the attribution.

## Santa Croce

**Santa Croce**
*open Mon–Sat 9.30–5, Sun 1–5; adm (includes museum)*

No place in Florence so feeds the urge to dispute as the church of Santa Croce, Tuscany's 'Westminster Abbey', the largest Franciscan basilica in Italy and a must-see for every tour group. It was here that Stendhal gushed, 'I had attained to that supreme degree of sensibility where the divine intimations of art merge with the impassioned sensuality of emotion. As I emerged from the port of Santa Croce, I was seized with a fierce palpitation of the heart; I walked in constant fear of falling to the ground.' But don't be put off; most people manage to emerge without tripping over.

The contradictions begin in the **Piazza Santa Croce**, which has its interesting points – the row of medieval houses with projecting upper storeys, supported by stone brackets; the faded bloom of dancing nymphs on the **Palazzo dell'Antella**; the curious 14th-century **Palazzo Serristori-Cocchi**, opposite the church; a grim 19th-century **statue of Dante** (if Dante really looked like that, it's no wonder Beatrice married someone else). Because this piazza is the lowest-lying in the city, it suffered the worst in the 1966 flood, when 20ft (6m) of oily water poured in; note the plaque marking the waterline on the corner of Via Verdi.

Dominant over all is Santa Croce's neo-Gothic façade, which was built in 1857–63 and financed by Sir Francis Sloane, whose Sloane Square in London has more admirers than this black and white design, derived from Orcagna's Tabernacle in Orsanmichele. Yet, of all the modern façades that were built on Italy's churches to atone for the chronic Renaissance inability to finish anything, this is one of the least offensive.

## The Interior

Santa Croce was founded by St Francis himself; during repairs after the flood, vestiges of a small, early-13th-century church were discovered under the present structure. It went by the board in Florence's colossal building programme of the 1290s. The great size of the new church speaks for the immense popularity of Franciscan preaching. Arnolfo di Cambio planned it, and it was largely completed by the 1450s but, as in Santa Maria Novella, Giorgio Vasari and the blinding forces of High Renaissance mediocrity were unleashed upon the interior. Vasari never had much use for the art of Andrea Orcagna – he not only left him out of his influential *Lives of the Artists* but in Santa Croce he destroyed Orcagna's great fresco cycle that once covered the nave, replacing it with uninspired side altars.

For centuries it was the custom to install monuments to illustrious men in Santa Croce and, as you enter, you can see them lining the long aisles. Like many Franciscan churches, Santa Croce's large size, its architectural austerity and open timber roof resemble a barn, but at the end there's a lovely polygonal sanctuary, which shimmers with light and colour streaming through 14th-century stained glass. The whole interior has been treated to an overhaul, completed in 2000, including restoration of the ceiling.

Perversely, the greater the person buried in Santa Croce, the uglier their memorial. A member of the Pazzi Conspiracy, Francesco Nori, is buried by the first pillar in the right aisle, and graced by one of the loveliest works of art, the *Madonna del Latte* (1478), a bas-relief by Antonio Rossellino, while the **tomb of Michelangelo** (1570, the first in the right aisle) by Vasari is one of the least attractive. Michelangelo died in Rome in 1564, refusing for 35 years to return to Florence while alive but agreeing to give the city his corpse. Dante has fared even worse, with an 1829 neoclassical monument that's as disappointing (to the Florentines, anyway) as the fact that Dante is buried in Ravenna, where he died in exile in 1321.

Facing the nave, Benedetto da Maiano's marble **pulpit** (1476) is one of the most beautiful the Renaissance ever produced. Behind it, the **Vittorio Alfieri Monument** (1809) was sculpted by neoclassical master Antonio Canova and paid for by his lover, the Countess of Albany. Next is the nondescript 18th-century **monument of Niccolò Machiavelli**, then Donatello's *Annunciation* (1430s), a tabernacle in gilded limestone, the angel wearing a remarkably sweet expression as he gently breaks the news to a grave, thoughtful Madonna. Bernardo Rossellino's **tomb of Leonardo Bruni** (1447), another masterpiece of the Renaissance, is perhaps the one monument that best fits the man it honours. Bruni was a Greek scholar, a humanist, and the author of the first major historical

1 *Madonna del Latte*
2 Tomb of Michaelangelo
3 Monument to Dante
4 Benedetto da Maiano's Pulpit
5 Vittorio Alfieri's Tomb
6 Tomb of Machiavelli
7 Donatello's *Annunciation*
8 Tomb of Leonardo Bruni
9 Tomb of Carlo Malaspini
10 Tomb of Rossini
11 Castellani Chapel
12 Baroncelli Chapel
13 Medici Chapel
14 Sacristy

15 Rinuccini Chapel
16 Peruzzi Chapel
17 Bardi Chapel
18 Sanctuary
19 Bardi di Libertà Chapel
20 Bardi di Vernio Chapel
21 Niccolini Chapel
22 Bardi Chapel
23 Salviati Chapel
24 Monument to Alberti
25 Tomb of Lorenzo Ghiberti
26 Galileo's Tomb
27 Museo dell'Opera di Santa Croce

work of the period, *The History of Florence*, a copy of which his effigy holds. The tomb, with its Brunelleschian setting, proved a great inspiration to other artists, most obviously Desiderio da Settignano and his equally beautiful **tomb of Carlo Marsuppini** (1453) directly across the nave, and the less inspired, more imitative **monument to Rossini** crowded in to the left. The last tomb in the aisle belongs to poet and patriot Ugo Foscolo.

Santa Croce is rich in trecento frescoes, providing a unique opportunity to compare the work of Giotto with his followers. The south transept's **Castellani Chapel** has some of the later, more decorative compositions by Agnolo Gaddi (*Scenes from the Lives of Saints*, 1380s). The beautiful **Baroncelli Chapel** was painted with scenes from the *Life of the Virgin* by Agnolo's father Taddeo, Giotto's assistant in the 1330s, and includes a bright, gilded altarpiece, the *Coronation of the Virgin* by Giotto and his workshop. *The Annunciation to the Shepherds* by Taddeo, left of the window, is thought to be the first nocturnal scene in the history of Western art.

**Medici Chapel**
*open for Mass at 6pm*

The next portal gives on to a corridor and the **Medici Chapel**, both designed by Michelozzo, containing one of Andrea della Robbia's finest altarpieces and a 19th-century fake Donatello, a relief of the *Madonna and Child* that fooled the experts for decades. From the corridor a door leads to the **sacristy**, its walls frescoed by Taddeo Gaddi (*The Crucifixion*), Spinello Aretino and Niccolò di Pietro Gerini. Behind the 14th-century grille, the **Rinuccini Chapel** was frescoed by one of Giotto's most talented followers, the Lombard Giovanni da Milano, in the 1360s.

## Giotto's Chapels

The frescoes in the two chapels right of the sanctuary, the **Peruzzi Chapel** and **Bardi Chapel**, were painted by the legendary Giotto in the 1330s, towards the end of his life when he returned from Padua and his work in the Arena chapel. The frescoes have not fared well during the subsequent 660 years. Firstly Giotto painted large parts of the walls *a secco* (on dry plaster) instead of *affresco* (on wet plaster), presenting the same kind of preservation problems that bedevil Leonardo's *Last Supper*; secondly, the 18th century thought so little of the frescoes that they were whitewashed over as eyesores. Rediscovered some 150 years later and finally restored in 1959, the frescoes now, even though fragmentary, may be seen more or less as Giotto painted them. The Peruzzi Chapel contains scenes from the *Lives of St John the Evangelist and the Baptist*. In the Bardi Chapel is the *Life of St Francis*, which makes an interesting comparison with the frescoes in Assisi. The contrast between Giotto's frescoes and the chapel's 13th-century altarpiece, also showing the *Life of St Francis*, is a fair yardstick for measuring the breadth of the Giottesque revolution. Agnolo Gaddi designed

## The Legend of the True Cross

This popular medieval story begins with Noah's son Seth, as an old man, asking for the essence of mercy. The Angel Gabriel replies by giving Seth a branch, saying that 5,000 years must pass before mankind may know true redemption. Seth plants the branch over Adam's grave on Mount Sinai, and it grows into a magnificent tree. King Solomon orders the tree cut, but, as it is too large to move, the trunk stays where it is and is used as the main beam of a bridge. The Queen of Sheba is about to cross the bridge when she has a vision that the saviour of the world will be suspended from its wood, and that his death will mark the end of the Kingdom of the Jews. She refuses to cross the bridge and writes of her dream to Solomon, who has the beam buried deep underground. Nevertheless, it is dug up and used to make the cross of Christ.

The cross next appears in the dream of Emperor Constantine before the battle of Milvan Bridge, when he hears a voice saying that under this sign he will conquer. When it proves true, he sends his mother Helen to find the cross in Jerusalem. There she meets Judas Cyriacus, a pious Jew who knows where Golgotha is but won't tell until Helen has him thrown in a well and nearly starved to death. When at last he agrees to dig, a sweet scent fills the air, and Judas Cyriacus is immediately converted. To discover which of the three crosses they find is Christ's, each is held over the coffin of a youth; the True Cross brings him back to life. After all this trouble in finding it, Helen leaves the cross in Jerusalem, where it is stolen by the Persians. Their King Chosroes thinks its power will bring him a great victory, but instead he loses the battle, and Persia, to Emperor Heraclius, who decides to return the holy relic to Jerusalem. But the gate is blocked by the Angel Gabriel, who reminds the proud Heraclius that Jesus entered the city humbly, on the back of an ass. And so, in a similar manner, the emperor returns the cross to Jerusalem.

the stained glass around the sanctuary, as well as the fascinating series of frescoes on the *Legend of the True Cross*.

Further left are two more chapels frescoed by followers of Giotto: the **Bardi di Libertà Chapel**, by Bernardo Daddi, and the **Bardi di Vernio Chapel**, by Maso di Banco, one of the most innovative and mysterious artists of the trecento. They illustrate the little-known *Life of St Sylvester* – his baptism of Emperor Constantine, the resurrection of the bull, the closing of the dragon's mouth and resurrection of two sorcerers; on the other wall of the chapel are a *Dream of Constantine* and *Vision of SS. Peter and Paul*. In the corner of the transept, the richly marbled **Niccolini Chapel** offers a Mannerist-Baroque change of pace, built by Antonio Dossi in 1584 and decorated with paintings by Allori. Next, the second **Bardi Chapel** houses the famous crucifix by Donatello that Brunelleschi disdainfully called 'a peasant on the Cross'. The last funeral monuments, near the door, are of Lorenzo Ghiberti and Galileo, the latter an 18th-century work. For running foul of the Inquisition, Galileo was not permitted a Christian burial until 1737.

## Pazzi Chapel

**Pazzi Chapel**
*open Mon–Sat
9.30–5, Sun 1–5;
entrance through
Santa Croce; adm*

The **Pazzi Chapel** is well worth a visit, especially now that restoration on the frescoed ceiling is complete. Brunelleschi, who could excel on the monumental scale of the cathedral dome, saved some of his best work for small places. To make sense of the Pazzi Chapel, you need to have some knowledge of the architect and the

austere religious tendencies of the Florentines; it is a Protestant reformation in architecture unlike anything that preceded it. The 'vocabulary' is essential Brunelleschi, the geometric forms emphasized by the simplicity of the decoration: *pietra serena* pilasters and rosettes
on white walls, arches, 12 terracotta *tondi* of the *Apostles* by Luca della Robbia, coloured rondels of the *Evangelists* in the pendentives by Donatello, and a small, stained-glass window by Baldovinetti. Even so, that is enough. The contemplative repetition of elements makes for an aesthetic that posed a direct challenge to the International Gothic of the time.

Leaving the Pazzi Chapel (make sure you check out Luca della Robbia's terracotta decorations on the portico), you'll see a doorway on the left of the cloister that leads to Brunelleschi's **Second Cloister**, designed with the same subtlety and forming one of the quietest spots in Florence.

**Museo dell'Opera di Santa Croce**
*open Mon–Sat 9.30–5, Sun 1–5; adm*

The old monastic buildings off the first cloister now house the **Museo dell'Opera di Santa Croce**, where you can see Cimabue's celebrated *Crucifix*, devastated by the flood and partly restored after one of Florence's perennial restoration controversies. The refectory wall has another fine fresco by Taddeo Gaddi, of the *Tree of the Cross* and the *Last Supper*; fragments of Orcagna's frescoes salvaged from Vasari's obliteration offer powerful, nightmarish vignettes of *The Triumph of Death* and *Hell*. Donatello's huge, gilded bronze statue *St Louis of Toulouse* (1423) – a flawed work representing a flawed character, according to Donatello – was made for the façade of Orsanmichele. The museum also contains works by Andrea della Robbia, and a painting of Mayor Bargellini with a melancholy Santa Croce submerged in the 1966 flood for a backdrop; under the colonnade is a statue of Florence Nightingale, born in and named after the city in 1820.

## Around Santa Croce: the Horne Museum

The east end of Florence, made up of a rambling district packed with artisans and small manufacturers, traditionally served as the artists' quarter in Renaissance times. It is still one of the livelier neighbourhoods, with a few lingering artists lodged in the upper storeys, hoping to breathe inspiration from the very stones where Michelangelo walked. It is a good place to observe the workaday Florence behind the glossy façade.

**Museo Horne**
*www.museohorne.it; open Mon–Sat 9–1; adm*

From Santa Croce, the pretty Borgo Santa Croce takes you towards the Arno and the delightful **Horne Museum**, which is housed in a Renaissance palace, at Via de' Benci 6. Herbert Percy Horne (1844–1916) was an English art historian, the biographer of Botticelli and a Florentinophile, who bequeathed his collection to the nation when he died.

# North Bank Peripheral Attractions

## The Cascine

The newer sections of the city are, by and large, irredeemably dull. Much of Florence's traffic problem is channelled through its ring of avenues, or *viali*, laid out in the 1860s by Giuseppe Poggi to replace the demolished walls. On and along them are scattered points of interest, including some of the old city gates; the distances involved and danger of carbon monoxide poisoning on the *viali* make the idea of walking insane.

Bus 17C from the station or Duomo will take you through the congestion to the **Cascine**, the long (3.5km), narrow public park lining this bank of the Arno, originally used as the Medici's dairy farm or *cascina*, and later as a grand ducal hunting park and theatre for public spectacles. A windy autumn day here in 1819 inspired Shelley to compose his 'Ode to the West Wind'. Three years later Shelley's drowned body was burnt on a pyre in Viareggio, by his friend Trelawny; curiously, a similar incineration took place in the Cascine in 1870 when the Maharajah of Kohlapur died in Florence. According to ritual his body had to be burned near the confluence of two rivers, in this case, the Arno and Mugnone at the far end of the park, on a spot now marked by the Maharajah's equestrian statue. Florentines come to the Cascine by day to play; it contains a riding school, race tracks, a small amusement park and zoo for children, tennis courts, and a pool. At night they come to ogle the transvestites strutting their stuff on the *viale*.

Beyond the train station, cars and buses hurtle around and around the **Fortezza da Basso**, an enormous bulk built by Antonio da Sangallo on orders from Alessandro de' Medici in 1534. It immediately became the most hated symbol of Medici tyranny. Ironically, the duke who built the Fortezza da Basso was one of very few to meet his end within its ramparts – stabbed by his relative and bosom companion 'Lorenzaccio' de' Medici. As a fortress, the place never saw any action as thrilling or vicious as the Pitti fashion shows that take place behind the walls in its 1978 aluminium exhibition hall.

Just east of the Fortezza, at the corner of Via Leone X and Viale Milton, there's an unexpected sight rising above the sleepy residential neighbourhood – the five graceful onion domes of the **Russian church**, made even more exotic by the palm tree tickling its side. In the 19th century Florence was a popular winter retreat for Russians who could afford it, among them Dostoevsky and Maxim Gorky. Completed by Russian architects in 1904, the church is a pretty jewel box of brick and majolica decoration, open on the third Sunday of the month, when the priest comes from Nice to hold a morning service in Russian.

### Stibbert Museum

From Piazza della Libertà, walk 1km north along dull Via Vittorio Emanuele to reach Via Stibbert and the **Stibbert Museum** (alternatively, take bus 31 or 32 from the station). Those who make the journey to see the lifetime's accumulations of Frederick Stibbert (1838–1906), who fought with Garibaldi and hobnobbed with Queen Victoria, can savour not only Florence's most bizarre museum but also one of the city's most pleasant small parks, which was laid out by Stibbert, with a mouldering Egyptian temple sinking in a pond; just try to obey the sign on the door: 'Comply with the Forbidden Admittances!'

Stibbert's Italian mother left him a 14th-century house, which he joined to another house to create a Victorian's sumptuous version of what a medieval Florentine house should have looked like – 64 rooms to contain a pack-rat's treasure hoard of all things brilliant and useless, from an attributed Botticelli to snuff boxes and what a local guide intriguingly describes as 'brass and silver basins, used daily by Stibbert'.

Stibbert's serious passion, however, was armour, and he amassed a magnificent collection from all times and places. The best pieces are not arranged in dusty cases, but with a touch of Hollywood, on grim knightly mannequins ranked ready for battle.

## The Oltrarno

Over the Ponte Vecchio, a different Florence reveals itself: greener, quieter, and less burdened with traffic. The Oltrarno is not a large district: a chain of hills squeezes it against the river, and their summits afford some of the best views over the city.

Across the Arno, the Medici's catwalk becomes part of the upper façade of **Santa Felicità**, one of Florence's most ancient churches, believed to have been founded by the Syrian Greek traders who introduced Christianity to the city and established the first Christian cemetery in the small square in front of the church.

Rebuilt in the 18th century, it has one compelling reason to enter – here, in the first chapel on the right, is the *ne plus ultra* of Mannerism: Pontormo's weirdly luminous *Deposition* (1528), painted in jarring pinks, oranges and blues that cut through the darkness of the little chapel. The composition itself is highly unconventional, with an effect that derives entirely from the use of figures in unusual, exaggerated poses; there is no sign of a cross, the only background is a single cloud. Sharing the chapel is Pontormo's *Annunciation* fresco, a less idiosyncratic work, as well as four *tondi* of the Evangelists in the cupola, partly the work of Pontormo's pupil and adopted son, Bronzino.

# Pitti Palace

**Palazzo Pitti**
t 055 2654321,
www.palazzopitti.it

As the Medici consolidated their power in Florence, they made a point of buying up the most important properties of their former rivals, especially their proud family palaces. The most spectacular example of this was Cosimo I's acquisition of the Pitti Palace, built in 1457 by a powerful banker named Luca Pitti who seems to have had vague ambitions of toppling the Medici and becoming the big boss himself. The palace, with its extensive grounds, now the Boboli Gardens, was much more pleasant than the medieval Palazzo Vecchio, and in the 1540s Cosimo I and his wife Eleanor of Toledo moved in for good.

The palace remained the residence of the Medici, and later the House of Lorraine, until 1868. The original building, said to have been designed by Brunelleschi, was only as wide as the seven central windows of the façade. Succeeding generations found it too small for their burgeoning hoards of bric-a-brac, and added several stages of symmetrical additions, resulting in a long, bulky profile, resembling a rusticated Stalinist ministry, but a landscaped one, ever since the 1996 European Summit.

There are eight separate **museums in the Pitti**; the ticket office for them all is in the far right corner of the forecourt. They are a tribute to Medici acquisitiveness in the centuries of decadence, from which, in the words of Mary McCarthy, 'flowed a torrent of bad taste that has not yet dried up... if there had been Toby jugs and Swiss weather clocks available, the Grand Dukes would certainly have collected them'. For the visitor who wants to see everything, the Pitti is pitiless; it is impossible to see all in one day.

## Galleria Palatina

**Galleria Palatina**
open Tues–Sun
8.15–6.50; adm,
combined ticket with
Galleria d'Arte Moderna

The Pitti museum most people visit is the **Galleria Palatina**, with the grand dukes' famous collection of 16th–18th-century paintings, stacked on the walls in huge gilt frames under the berserk opulence of frescoed ceilings celebrating planets, mythology and, of course, the ubiquitous Medici. The gallery is on the first floor of the right half of the palace; the ticket office is on the ground floor, off Ammannati's exaggerated rustic courtyard, a Mannerist masterpiece.

After the entrance to the Galleria is the neoclassical **Sala Castagnoli**, with the *Tavola delle Muse* in its centre, itself an excellent introduction to the Florentine 'decorative arts'; the table, a paragon of the intricate art of *pietra dura*, was made in the 1870s. The Galleria's best paintings are in the five former reception rooms off to the left, with colourful ceilings painted in the 1640s by Pietro da Cortona, one of the most interesting Italian Baroque artists.

However, the set route takes you through the other part of the palace beforehand, starting with the adjacent **Sala di Prometeo** and Filippo Lippi's lovely *Tondo of the Madonna and Child* and

Baldassare Peruzzi's unusual *Dance of Apollo*. Next door you can peek into the **Sala di Bagni**, the Empire bathroom of Elisa Baciocchi, Napoleon's sister, who ruled the *Département de l'Arno* between 1809 and 1814, and seemingly spent much of those years redecorating the Pitti. Caravaggio's *Sleeping Cupid* is a couple of rooms up, in the **Sala dell'Educazione di Giove**. The next room to this is the pretty **Sala della Stufa**, frescoed with the *Four Ages of the World* by Pietro da Cortona.

The first of the reception rooms, the **Sala dell'Iliade** (which was frescoed in the 19th century), has some fine portraits by the Medici court painter and Rubens' friend, Justus Sustermans. Two *Assumptions* by Andrea del Sarto, *Philip II* by Titian and a Velàzquez equestrian portrait of Philip IV share the room with one of the most unusual residents of the gallery, *Queen Elizabeth*, who seems uncomfortable in such company.

The **Sala di Giove**, which was used as the Medici throne room, contains one of Raphael's best-known portraits, the lovely and serene *Donna Velata* (1516). The small painting *The Three Ages of Man* is usually attributed to Giorgione. Salviati, Perugino, Fra Bartolommeo and Andrea del Sarto are also represented. The **Sala di Marte** has two works by Rubens, *The Four Philosophers* and *The Consequences of War*, as well as some excellent portraits by Tintoretto and Van Dyck (*Cardinal Bentivoglio*). The newly restored *Annunciation of San Godenzo*, by Andrea del Sarto, is now back in place after a long absence, and there is also Titian's rather dashing *Cardinal Ippolito de' Medici* in Hungarian costume. Ippolito, despite being destined for the Church, was one of the more high-spirited Medici.

In the **Sala di Apollo** there's more Titian – his *Portrait of a Grey-eyed Gentleman*, evoking the perfect 16th-century English gentleman, and his more sensuous than penitent *Mary Magdalene* – as well as works by Andrea del Sarto and Van Dyck. The last reception room is the **Sala di Venere**, with several works by Titian, including his early *Concert*, believed to have been partly painted by Giorgione and a powerful *Portrait of Pietro Aretino*, Titian's close and caustic friend, who complained to the artist that it was all too accurate and gave it to Cosimo I. There are two beautiful landscapes by Rubens, painted at the end of his life, and an uncanny self-portrait, *La Menzogna* ('The Falsehood') by Neapolitan Salvator Rosa. The centrepiece statue, the *Venus Italica*, was commissioned by Napoleon from neoclassical master Antonio Canova in 1812 to replace the *Venus de' Medici*, which he 'centralized' off to Paris – a rare case of the itchy-fingered Corsican trying to pay for something.

The **Sala di Saturno**, with its restored ceiling, has several paintings from Raphael's Florence days. These include the *Maddalena and Agnolo Doni* (1506) and the *Madonna 'del Granduca'*, influenced by the paintings of Leonardo. Some 10 years later, Raphael had found his own style, which is beautifully evident in his famous *Madonna della Seggiola* ('of the chair') – perhaps the most popular work that the artist ever painted, and one that is far more complex and subtle than it first appears. The rounded, intertwining figures of the Madonna and Child are seen as if through a slightly convex mirror, bulging out – this is one of the first examples of conscious illusionism in the Renaissance.

Some of the more interesting paintings to ferret out in the remainder of the gallery include Filippino Lippi's *Death of Lucrezia* and Raphael's *Madonna dell'Impannata*, both in the **Sala di Ulisse**.

The right half of the Pitti also contains the **state apartments** (included as part of the visit to the Galleria Palatina). These were last redone in the 19th century by the dukes of Lorraine, with touches by the kings of Savoy.

## Galleria d'Arte Moderna

**Galleria d'Arte Moderna**
*open Mon–Sat 8.30–6.50, Sun 8.30–1.50; closed 2nd and 4th Sun and 1st, 3rd and 5th Mon of month; adm exp, combined ticket with Galleria Palatina; tickets from main ticket office on ground floor*

The second floor above the Galleria Palatina is where you will find Florence's modern – read late-18th–20th-century – art museum. Though the monumental stair may leave you breathless (the Medici negotiated it with sedan chairs and strong-shouldered servants), consider a visit for some sunny painting of the Italy of your great-grandparents. The Galleria was reopened after a major reorganization in 1999 and now consists of more 30 rooms. The most recent paintings on display are those in the last rooms, which cover the years 1900–23. There are plans eventually to open 13 more rooms covering 1923–45.

The 'Splatterers' or *Macchiaioli* (Tuscan Impressionists) illuminate Room 16 and the rest of the museum, forming an excellent introduction to the works by Silvestro Lega, Giovanni Fattori, Nicolo Cannicci, Francesco Gioli, Federigo Zandomeneghi and Telemaco Signorini, with an interval of vast Risorgimento battle scenes. What comes as a shock, especially if you've been touring Florence for a while now, is that the marriage between painting and sculpture that characterizes most of Italian art history seems to have resulted in a nasty divorce in the late 1800s: while the canvases radiate light, statuary becomes disturbingly kitsch, obsessed with death and beauty.

## Museo degli Argenti

**Museo degli Argenti**
*open April, May, Sept and Oct daily 8.15–6.30; June–Aug daily 8.15–7.30; Nov–Feb daily 8.15–4.30; Mar daily 8.15–5.30; exc 1st and last Mon of month; adm (combined ticket with Boboli Gardens, porcelain museum and museum of costumes)*

The ground floor on the left side of the Pitti was used as the Medici summer apartments and now contains the family's remarkable collection of jewellery, vases, trinkets and pricey curiosities. The grand duke's guests would be received in four of the most delightfully frescoed rooms to be found anywhere in Florence, beginning with the **Sala di Giovanni di San Giovanni**, named after the artist who painted it in the 1630s. The theme is the usual Medicean self-glorification – but nowhere does such dubious material achieve such flamboyant treatment. Here the Muses, chased from Paradise, find refuge with Lorenzo il Magnifico; Lorenzo smiles as he studies a bust of Pan by Michelangelo. His real passion, a collection of antique vases carved of semi-precious stones or crystal, is displayed in a room off to the left; the vases were dispersed with the rise of Savonarola, but Lorenzo's nephew Cardinal Giulio had no trouble in locating them, as Lorenzo had his initials LAUR.MED. incised into each. The three **reception rooms** were painted in shadowy blue *trompe l'œil* by two masterful Bolognese illusionists, Agostino Michele and Angelo Colonna.

The grand dukes' treasure hoard is up on the mezzanine. These golden toys are only a fraction of what the Medici had accumulated; despite the terms of Anna Maria's will, leaving everything to Florence, the Lorraines sold off the most valuable pieces and jewels to finance Austria's wars. Among the leftovers here, however, is a veritable apoplexy of fantastical bric-a-brac.

## More Pitti Museums

**Galleria del Costume/Museo delle Porcellane/Giardino di Boboli**
*open April, May, Sept and Oct daily 8.15–6.30; June–Aug daily 8.15–7.30; Nov–Feb daily 8.15–4.30; Mar daily 8.15–5.30; exc 1st and last Mon of month; adm (combined ticket with Museo degli Argenti)*

The **museum of costumes** is housed on the second floor of the Palace, near to the Galleria d'Arte Moderna. The highlight, perhaps, is a reconstruction of the dress that Eleanor of Toledo was buried in – the same one that she wears in Bronzino's famous portrait. The **porcelain museum** is housed in the casino of Cosimo III, which is located out in the Giardino del Cavaliere in the Boboli Gardens (follow the signs). It contains 18th- and 19th-century examples of chinaware from Sèvres, Meissen and Vienna.

Stretching back invitingly from the Pitti, the shady green of the **Boboli Gardens**, which is Florence's largest (and only) central public garden, provides an irresistible oasis in the middle of a stone-hard city. Originally laid out by Buontalenti, the Boboli reigns as queen of all formal Tuscan gardens, the most elaborate and theatrical – a Mannerist-Baroque co-production of Nature and Artifice laid out over a steep hill, full of shady nooks and pretty walks, and beautifully kept. The park is populated by a platoon of statuary; many of them are Roman works, others are absurd Mannerist pieces. There are three entrances and exits to the gardens: through the main courtyard of the Pitti Palace, from Via Romana and in Porta Romana. The main route, from the Pitti Palace, starts at the **amphitheatre**, which ascends in regular tiers from the palace, and was designed like a small Roman circus to hold Medici court spectacles. It has a genuine obelisk, of Rameses II from Heliopolis, which was snatched by the ancient Romans and shipped here by the Medici branch in Rome. The granite basin, which is large enough to submerge an elephant, came from the Roman baths of Caracalla. Straight up the terrace is the **Neptune fountain**; a signposted path leads from there to the pretty **Kaffeehaus**, a boat-like pavilion with a prow and deck offering a fine view of Florence; you can enjoy drinks here in the summer months. From here the path continues up to the **Belvedere Fort** (*see* p.186). Other signs from the Neptune fountain point the way up to the secluded **Giardino del Cavaliere**, located on a bastion on Michelangelo's fortifications. Cosimo III built the **casino** here in order to escape the heat in the Pitti Palace; the view over the ancient villas, vineyards and olives is pure Tuscan enchantment. This is where the porcelain museum (*see* left) resides.

At the bottom right-hand corner of the garden you will find the remarkable **Grotta di Buontalenti**, one of the architect's most imaginative works, anticipating Gaudí with his dripping, stalactite-like stone, from which fantastic limestone animals struggle to emerge. Casts of Michelangelo's *nonfiniti Slaves* in the corners replace the originals put there by the Medici; back in the shadowy depths stands a luscious statue of Venus coming from her bath by Giambologna. The Grotta di Buontalenti has been restored, but the fountains are not working yet due to technical problems.

**Grotta di Buontalenti**
*open April, May, Sept and Oct daily 8.15–6.30; June–Aug daily 8.15–7.30; Nov–Feb daily 8.15–4.30; Mar daily 8.15–5.30; exc 1st and last Mon of month; adm (combined ticket with Galleria Palatina)*

## Casa Guidi

**Casa Guidi**
*open April–Nov Mon, Wed and Fri 3–6; donations expected*

In the old days the neighbourhood around the Pitti was a fashionable address, but in the 19th century rents for a furnished palace were incredibly low. Shortly after their secret marriage, the Brownings settled in one of these, the Casa Guidi at Piazza San Felice 8; during their 13 years here they wrote their most famous poetry. The house is now owned by the Browning Institute. Dostoevsky wrote *The Idiot* while living nearby, at Piazza Pitti 21.

## Stuffed Animals and Wax Cadavers

**Museo La Specola**
*open Tues–Sun 9.30–4.30; adm*

Past the Pitti, at Via Romana 17, is one of Florence's great oddball attractions, the **La Specola museum**. Its **zoological section** has a charmingly old-fashioned collection of nearly everything that walks, flies or swims, from the humble seaworm to the rare Madagascar aye-aye or the swordfish, with an accessory case of different blades. The real horror show stuff, however, is kept hidden away in the **museum of waxes**. Dotty, prudish old Cosimo III was a hypochondriac and morbidly obsessed with diseases, which his favourite artist, a Sicilian priest named Gaetano Zumbo, was able to portray with revolting realism. His macabre anatomical models were one of the main sights for Grand Tourists in the 1700s.

## Piazza Santo Spirito

Piazza Santo Spirito, the centre of the Oltrarno, is home to a small market under the plane trees on Monday to Saturday mornings, as well as a quiet café or two. In the evening it changes face and the bars fill with people, who meet and chat in the piazza and on the church steps until the early hours of the morning.

At the southern end, a plain 18th-century façade hides Brunelleschi's last and perhaps greatest church. He designed **Santo Spirito** in 1440 and lived to see only one column erected, but subsequent architects were faithful to his elegant plan for the interior. This is done in the architect's favourite pale grey and *pietra serena* articulation, a rhythmic forest of columns with semicircular chapels is gracefully recessed into the transepts and the three arms of the crossing. The effect is unfortunately spoiled by the ornate 17th-century *baldacchino*, which sits in this enchanted garden of architecture like a 19th-century bandstand.

The art in the chapels is meagre, as most of the good paintings were sold off over the years. The best include Filippino Lippi's beautiful, restored *Madonna and Saints* in the right transept and Verrocchio's jewel-like *St Monica and Nuns* in the opposite transept. To the left of the church, in the **refectory** of the vanished 14th-century convent, are the scanty remains of a *Last Supper* and a well-preserved, highly dramatic *Crucifixion* by Andrea Orcagna.

**Santo Spirito**
*open Mon–Tues and Thurs–Sat 9.30–12.30 and 4–5.30, Sun and hols 3–5.30*

**Refectory**
*open Tues–Sat 10–1.30, Sun and hols 10–12.30; adm*

## Santa Maria del Carmine and the Cappella Brancacci

There is little to say about the surroundings, the piazza-cum-car park, the rough stone façade, or the interior of the Oltrarno's other great church, **Santa Maria del Carmine**, which burned down in 1771 and was reconstructed shortly after. Miraculously, the **Cappella Brancacci**, a landmark in Florentine art, survived both the flames and attempts by the authorities to replace it with something more fashionable. Three artists worked on the Brancacci's frescoes: Masolino, who began them in 1425, and who designed the cycle; his pupil Masaccio, who worked on them alone for a year before following his master to Rome, where he died at the age of 27; and Filippino Lippi, who finished them 50 years later. Filippino took care to imitate Masaccio as closely as possible, and the frescoes have an appearance of stylistic unity. Between 1981 and 1988 they were subject to one of Italy's most publicized restorations, cleansed of 550 years of dirt and overpainting, enabling us to see what so thrilled the painters of the Renaissance.

**Cappella Brancacci**
*open Mon and Wed–Sat 10–5 (last adm 4.45), Sun and hols 1–5; closed Tues; adm, combined ticket available with Palazzo Vecchio; 30 people admitted at a time, for 15mins; booking required, t 055 276 8224*

Masaccio in his day was a revolution and a revelation in his solid, convincing naturalism; his figures stand in space, without any fussy ornamentation or Gothic grace, very much inspired by Donatello's sculptures. Masaccio conveyed emotion with broad, quick brushstrokes and with his use of light, most obvious in the *Expulsion of Adam and Eve*, one of the most memorable and harrowing images created in the Renaissance. In *The Tribute Money*, the young artist displays his mastery of artificial perspective and light effects. The three episodes in the fresco show an official demanding tribute from the city, St Peter fetching it on Christ's direction from the mouth of a fish, and, lastly, his handing over of the money to the official. Other works by 'Shabby Tom' include *St Peter Baptizing* on the upper register, and *St Peter Healing with his Shadow* and *St Peter Enthroned and Resurrecting the Son of the King of Antioch*, the right half of which was finished by Filippino Lippi. The elegant Masolino is responsible for the remainder, except for the lower register's *Release of St Peter from Prison*, *St Peter Crucified* and *St Paul Visiting St Peter in Prison*, all by Filippino Lippi, based on Masaccio's sketches.

Among the detached frescoes displayed in the cloister and refectory is a good one by Filippino's papa, Fra Filippo Lippi, who was born nearby in Via dell'Ardiglione.

## Bardini Museum

**Museo Bardini**
*Via dei Renai 37, t 055 2342427, www. comune.firenze.it; open Sat, Sun, Mon 11–5*

At the other end of the Oltrarno, one street south of the Ponte alle Grazie, the newly reopened **Bardini Museum** is a jewel of a collection renowned for its Renaissance architectural decorations as well as Renaissance art. The works belonged to Stefano Bardini (1836–1922), an art dealer whose love of blue painted walls is as well known as his collection – the blue was imitated in Paris's Jacquemart-Andrè museum and the Isabella Stewart in Boston.

## Tourist Information in Florence

**ⓘ Florence >**
*Piazza Beccaria, Via Manzoni 16, t 055 23320, www. firenzeturismo.it; closed afternoons and weekends*

*Via Camillo Cavour 1r, t 055 290832; closed Sun afternoon*

*Borgo Santa Croce 29r, t 055 234 0444; open June–Sept daily 9.30–7.30, 21 Mar–May 10–7, Oct–20 Mar 10.30–4.30*

*Piazza della Stazione, t 055 212245, www. comune.firenze.it; closed Sun afternoon*

*Airport, t 055 315874*

Florence becomes more tourist-friendly all the time, and there is now a genuine effort on the part of the city administration to provide helpful tourist information. The *comune* publishes a leaflet listing bars and cafés that 'offer their clients a welcoming reception, politeness and, should they need it, bathroom facilities...'; believe it or not, finding a loo you could use in a bar or café used to be difficult. In addition, there are two guides for the disabled, both available at the tourist office. The more comprehensive is in Italian, but it has a good map and covers access to sites and restaurants, etc.

The **main tourist office** is a bit out of the way, near Piazza Beccaria. There are other branches around town, and on the south side of the **station** in Piazza della Stazione. There is an office at the **airport**. In the summer, look out for the temporary mobile '**Tourist Help Points**'

run by the Vigili Urbani (the traffic police), in the centre of town.

## Florence Practical A–Z

**American Express**: Via Dante Alighieri 22r, just off Piazza della Repubblica, t 055 50981.

**Central post office**: Via Pellicceria, near Piazza della Repubblica, t 055 273 6481; call t 160 for info. *Closed Sun.*

**Internet**: You can send e-mails, use the Internet or fax from all over the city nowadays; one such service is **Internet Train**, Piazza Stazione 14/38, t 055 239 9720, *www.internettrain.it*, or Via Guelfa 54–6, t 055 212204 (opening hours differ from branch to branch); they are also agents for the Swiss Post International if you want to avoid the bureaucratic slowpokes in the Posta Italiana. In addition many cafés have free Wi-fi; look for the sign in the window, and remember to take a photocopy of your passport.

**Libraries**: British Institute Library, Lungarno Guicciardini 9, t 055 2677

8270, *www.britishinstitute.it*; *closed Sat and Sun*. **American Library**, Via S. Gallo 10; *closed afternoons and weekends*. There are so many other libraries in Florence that one, the **Biblioteca del Servizio Beni Librari**, Via G. Modena 13, t 055 438 2655, does nothing but dispense information on the others.

**Lost property**: in Italian is *Oggetti smarriti* or *Oggetti ritrovati*. The office is in Via Circondaria 17b, t 055 328 3942.

**Medical**: For an ambulance or first aid, **Misericordia**, Piazza del Duomo 20, t 055 212222. **Doctor's night service**, t 055 287788. For general medical emergencies call t 118. The general **Hospital Santa Maria Nuova**, in Piazza S. M. Nuova, t 055 27581, is the most convenient. **Tourist Medical Service** (24hrs a day) is staffed by English- and French-speaking physicians at Via Lorenzo il Magnifico 59; ring first on t 055 475411. If you find yourself hospitalized while in Florence, the **AVO** (Association of Hospital Volunteers) has volunteer interpreters, t 055 425 0126/t 055 234 4567.

**Pharmacies**: Open 24hrs every day in S. Maria Novella station, also **Molteni**, Via Calzaiuoli 7r and **Taverna**, Piazza S. Giovanni 20r, by the baptistry.

**Police**: emergency t 113. The Ufficio Stranieri, in the Questura, Via Zara 2, t 055 49771 (*closed afternoons and weekends*) handles most foreigners' problems. Go there for residents' permits, etc.

**Tourist aid police**: Via Pietrapiana 50, t 055 203911; *closed Sat afternoon and Sun*. Interpreters are available to help you report thefts or resolve other problems.

**Towed-away cars**: call t 055 4224142, with the car's registration number.

# Festivals and Events in Florence

Traditional festivals in Florence date back centuries.

*Scoppio del Carro* (Explosion of the Cart), Easter Sunday. A commemoration of Florentine participation in the First Crusade, which took place in 1096. The Florentines were led by Pazzino de' Pazzi, who was the first over the walls of Jerusalem and who, upon returning home, received the special custody of the flame of Holy Saturday, with which the Florentines traditionally relit their family hearths. To make the event more colourful, the Pazzi constructed a decorated wooden ox cart to carry the flame. They lost the job after the Pazzi conspiracy in 1478, and since then the city has taken over the responsibility. In the morning, a firework-filled wooden float is pulled by white oxen from Il Prato to the cathedral, where, at 11am, during the singing of the Gloria, it is ignited by an iron 'dove' that descends on a wire from the high altar.

*Maggio Musicale Fiorentino*, Teatro del Maggio Musicale Fiorentino, Corso Italia 12 (off Lungarno Vespucci), t 055 277 9350 from abroad, *www.maggio fiorentino.com* (ticket information), late April–early July. The city's big music festival, bringing in big-name concert and opera stars. Some performances may also be held at Teatro della Pergola, or other venues.

**Flower and Plant Show**, Giardino di Orticoltura, Via Vittorio Emanuele 4, late April. A huge show, a must for horticulture fans, centred around a 19th-century glasshouse.

**International Iris Festival**, Piazzale Michelangelo, 2wks in May.

*Festa del Grillo* (cricket festival), Cascine, Ascension Day, May/June. Michelangelo was thinking of this festival's little wooden cricket cages when he mocked Ammannati's gallery on the cathedral dome (*see* p.108).

*Calcio Storico in Costume*, Piazza Santa Croce, June. Four matches of historical football played in 16th-century costume by 27-man teams from Florence's four quarters, in memory of a defiant football match played there in 1530, during the siege by Charles V. It's great fun, with flag-throwing and a parade in historical costume as part of the pre-game ceremonies. The only fixed date is 24 June; dates for the other matches are pulled out of a hat on Easter Sunday.

*Festa di San Giovanni*, 24 June. The festival of Florence's patron saint, marked by a big firework display near Piazzale Michelangelo at 10pm.

*Estate Fiesolana*, late June–Sept. One of the annual cultural events generally adored by Florentines. The old Roman theatre is made the venue for concerts, dance, theatre and films, at reasonable prices.

**Summer concerts**, Piazza Signoria, summer months. The piazza occasionally plays host to concerts and other events during the summertime. Countless smaller-scale concerts are also given, often outdoors or in cloisters, churches and villas. Look out for posters or ask at the tourist office.

*Maggio Musicale* festival closing concert, late June–early July. A free-for-all heralding the end of the annual music festival.

*MaggioDanza* ballet company, late June–early July. An evening of dance, held annually, also a free-for-all.

**Florence Dance Festival**, t 055 289276, *www.florencedance.org*, July. An interesting combination of classical and contemporary dance performances, usually held in Fiesole's Roman Theatre.

*Festa della Rificolona*, 6–7 Sept. A children's festival: Florentine kids gather in the evening in Piazza SS. Annunziata and along the river armed with paper lanterns, and then, after dark, they parade singing around the streets.

# Shopping in Florence

## Fashion

Though central Florence sometimes seems like one solid boutique, the city is no longer the queen of Italian fashion – the long lack of a central airport, more than anything else, sent most of the big designers to Milan. Even so, the big fashion names of the 1960s and '70s, and the international chain stores, are well represented in smart **Via Tornabuoni**, **Via Calzaiuoli** and around the **Duomo**.

## Leather

**Via della Vigna Nuova**. Leather is something Florence is still known for, and you'll see plenty of it here. Also try **Piazza Santa Croce**, **San Lorenzo** and **Mercato Nuovo**.

**The Leather School**, entrance at Piazza Santa Croce 16 or Via S. Giuseppe 5r. An unusual institution, occupying part of Santa Croce's cloister. Less expensive.

## Jewellery

**Ponte Vecchio**. Florence is famous for jewellery. The shops on and around the bridge are forced, by the nature of their location, into wide-open competition. Good prices for Florentine brushed gold (although much of it is made in Arezzo these days) and antique jewellery are more common than you may think.

Elsewhere, there is another store worth seeking out.

**Il Gatto Bianco**, Borgo SS. Apostoli 12r. Modern designs crafted on the premises in silver, gold and a variety of other metals with pearls and precious stones.

## Marbled Paper

Florence is one of the few places in the world that makes marbled paper, an art brought from the Orient in the 12th century. Each sheet is hand-dipped to create a delicate, lightly coloured clouded design; no two sheets are alike. The following shops (and many others) also carry Florentine paper with its colourful Gothic patterns.

**Giulio Giannini e Figlio**, Piazza Pitti 36r. The oldest manufacturer.

**Il Papiro**, three shops at: Via Cavour 55r; Piazza del Duomo 24r; and Lung. Acciaiuoli 42r.

**La Bottega Artigiana del Libro**, Lungarno Corsini 40r.

**Il Torchio**, Via dei Bardi 17, t 055 234 2862. A shop with the workbench in the shop so you can see the artisans in action.

## Books

Bookworms fare much better in Florence than in most Italian cities, and prices of books in English seem to have come down in recent years, so there are a fair number of places in which to browse.

**The Paperback Exchange**, Via delle Oche 4r. A wide selection of books in English, including many volumes about Florence.

**Seeber**, Via Tornabuoni 70r. A good selection.

**Feltrinelli**, Via Cavour 12–20r. Books in English and an excellent range of art books.

**BM Bookshop**, Borgo Ognissanti 4r. A similar proposition to Feltrinelli.

**Franco Maria Ricci**, Via delle Belle Donne 41r. A fabulous collection of art books.

**Edison**, Piazza della Repubblica 27r. Florence's biggest bookshop, with plenty in English, travel guides and maps (also in English), Internet points, video services and a café.

**Libreria Café La Cité**, Borgo San Frediano 20r, **t** 055 210387. Bookshop, café and cultural centre which has free Wi-fi, regular author readings, creative writing classes and even tango lessons, all in a space with a very cool, laid-back vibe.

## Antiques and Art Galleries

**Borgo Ognissanti** and the various **Lungarni** are the places to look. Also check out **Piazza dei Ciompi**'s fleamarket and the monthly fleamarket (2nd Sun of month) that is held in **Piazza Santo Spirito**.
**P. Bazzanti e Figli**, Lungarno Corsini 44. The place to pick up an exact replica of the bronze boar in the Mercato Nuovo.
**Atelier Alice**, Via Faenza 72r. Italian carnival masks (easier to carry than bronze boars) and more. For those who are keen to learn more about the art of the mask, the shop runs five-lesson courses (ring Professor Dessi on **t** 055 215961 for details).
**Via Maggio**. A street full of upmarket antique shops.

Serious collectors may want to check Florence's busy auction houses:
**Casa d'Aste Pandolfini**, Borgo degli Albizi 26, **t** 055 234 0888.
**Casa d'Aste Pitti**, Via Maggio 15, **t** 055 239 6382.
**Sotheby's Italia**, Via G. Capponi 26, **t** 055 247 9021 (*call for appt*).

## Cloth

**Casa dei Tessuti**, Via de' Pecori 20–24r, **t** 055 215961. A place keeping Florence's ancient cloth trade alive with its lovely linens, silks and woollens. During the lunch break, you might catch a lecture on the history of Florence with special reference to the textile industry.

## Silver, Crystal and Porcelain

**A Poggi**, Via Calzaiuoli 105r and 116r. One of the city's widest selections.

## Children's Toys and Clothes

**Anichini**, Via di Parione 59r. The oldest kids' clothes shop in Florence, with exquisitely produced dresses (made in store), silk party dresses, romper suits, christening robes and playwear.
**Città del Sole**, Via Cimatori 21r. The best toyshop in Florence.
**Cirri**, Via Por S. Maria 38–40r. A fairytale selection of dresses.

## Wine and Food

**Gastronomia di G. Tassini**, Borgo SS. Apostoli 24. A good place for items such as truffle cream.
**La Bottega del Brunello**, Via Ricasoli 81r. A two-part establishment: one for display and one for tasting the wine and specialities on sale.
**Casa del Vino**, Via dell'Ariento 16r, **t** 055 215609. Wine tastings plus snacks in the San Lorenzo street market.
**Enoteca dei Giraldi**, Via Giraldi. Tuscan wines from lesser-known producers, with more than 140 labels (you can also eat here).
**Ino**, Via de Georgofili 3/7r, **t** 055 219208. Slick bar and deli with good meats, cheeses, oils, vinegar and wine.
**Marchesi de' Frescobaldi**, Via di S. Spirito 11. One of the largest wine suppliers in Italy; you can visit their ancient cellars.
**Mercato Centrale**. The central market, housing some speciality food shops.
**Millesimi**, Borgo Tegolaio 33r. One of the best wine shops in town. Tastings are available by appointment.
**Pitti Gola e Cantina**, Piazza Pitti 16. A good selection of wines, oils and vinegars, and cookery books.
**La Porta del Tartufo**, Borgo Ognissanti 133r. A place specializing almost exclusively in different types of truffles or 'truffled' foods, ranging from grappa to salmon paste.
**Il Procacci**, Via Tornabuoni 64r. A high-quality *alimentari* (food shop) selling regional specialities as well as foreign foods. It's most famous as the venue for a lunchtime Prosecco and *panino tartufato* – a glass of sparkling

white wine and a truffle-filled sandwich. It's also a bar.

**Le Volpi e L'Uva**, Piazza de' Rossi 1. Situated behind the Ponte Vecchio, stocking lesser-known labels.

## Markets

Florence's lively street markets offer good bargains, fake designer glad-rags and even some authentic labels.

**San Lorenzo**. The largest and most boisterous market, selling food (*Mon–Sat 7–2*) and clothes and party gifts (*Tues–Sun 9–7.30, daily in summer*).

**Sant'Ambrogio**. A bustling and colourful food and clothes market, as yet undiscovered by tourists.

**Mercato Nuovo** (Strawmarket). The most touristy market.

**Piazza Santo Spirito**. Different markets on different days: food, clothes and shoes (small) *Mon–Sat*; craft and bric-a-brac (big) *2nd Sun of month*.

**Cascine**, along the river, *Tues 7–2*. A weekly market where many Florentines come to buy their clothes. Here you may easily find some designer clothes off the back of a lorry, shoes and lots more.

**Mercato delle Pulci** (fleamarket), Piazza dei Ciompi, *Tues–Sun 9–7.30 (daily in summer)*. Perhaps the most fun market, offering desirable junk. On the *last Sunday of every month*, the streets around here fill up with a huge antiques and bric-a-brac market.

# Sports and Activities in Florence

## On the Water

The one activity most summertime visitors begin to crave after tramping through the sights is a dip in a pool.

**Piscina le Pavoniere**, Cascine, **t** 055 333979. The prettiest in Florence. *Open June–Sept daily 10–6.30.*

**Bellariva**, up the Arno at Lungarno Aldo Moro 6. Olympic-sized pool and a rooftop restaurant and café are on offer. *Open June–Sept daily 10–6, Tues and Thurs 8.30pm–11pm.*

**Costoli**, Via Paoli, near Campo di Marte, **t** 055 623 6027. *Open all year.*

**The Flog**, Via Mercati 24b, Poggetto, **t** 055 477978, *www.flog.it. Open late May–end Aug daily 10–6.*

If there's enough water in the Arno, you can try rowing:

**Società Canottieri Comunali**, Lungarno Ferrucci 2 **t** 055 681 2151, *www.canottierifirenze.it.*

There is a **beach on the Arno** on the Oltrarno side *open July–Sept*. Turn left after the Ponte alle Grazie. It has beach volleyball, free yoga classes on Mondays, and showers.

## Horseracing and -riding

**Ippodromo Il Visarno**, Cascine, **t** 055 360549, *www.ippodromifiorentini.it.* Florence's flat racecourse.

**Ippodromo della Mulina**, Cascine, **t** 055 422 6076.

**Maneggio Marinella**, Via di Macia 21, **t** 055 887 8066. The nearest place to go riding in the Tuscan hills.

**Centro Ippico la Baita**, Cascine Park, **t** 055 307305, *www.clubippicolabaita.it.*

## Golf

**Golf Club Ugolino**, on Chiantigiana, **t** 055 230 1009, *www.golfugolino.it.* The nearest 18-hole golf course to Florence, in Grassina, 7km southeast of the city. It's a lovely course.

## Squash and Tennis

**Centro Squash**, Via Empoli 16, **t** 055 732 3055.

**Circolo di Tennis**, Via Scandicci Alto, **t** 055 252696.

**ASSI**, Viale Micheangelo, **t** 055 687858. Six clay courts overlooking the city.

# Where to Stay in Florence

### Florence ✉ 50100

Florence has some lovely hotels, and not all of them at grand ducal prices, although base rates are the highest in Tuscany. As in any city, the higher cost of living means you won't find much inexpensive accommodation. Florence, Venice and Rome are the most expensive places to stay in Italy, and you should count on having to pay around 25% more for a room here than you would anywhere else.

Historic old palace-hotels are the rule rather than the exception; those listed below are some of the more atmospheric and charming, but to be honest, few are secrets, so reserve as far in advance as possible. Note that many hotels will try to lay down a heavy breakfast charge that is supposed to be optional.

There are almost 400 hotels in Florence, yet that's not enough for anyone who arrives in June and September without a booking (Easter is even busier). But don't despair: there are several hotel consortia that can help you find a room in nearly any price range for a small commission. If you're arriving by car or train, the most useful will be ITA.

**ITA**, Santa Maria Novella station, **t** 055 282893, *open daily 8.30–7*. Bookings can be made by phone and a booking fee of between €3 and €8 is charged, according to the category of hotel.

**Florence Promhotels**, Viale A. Volta 72, **t** 055 553941, toll free **t** 800 866022, *www.promhotels.it*. A free service.

For *agriturismo* or farmhouse accommodation in the surrounding countryside (self-catering or otherwise), contact: **Agriturist Toscana**, Via degli Alfani 67, **t** 055 287838, *www.agriturist.it*; or **Turismo Verde Toscana**, Via Jacopo Nardi 41, **t** 055 2338911, *www.turismoverde.it*.

Besides hotels, a number of institutions and private homes let **rooms** – there's a complete list in the back of the annual provincial hotel book. Many take women only, and fill up with students in the spring.

A cheaper option can be a **bed and breakfast** (*affittacamere*). Ask for a list at the tourist office.

⭐ **Four Seasons Florence >**

### Luxury (€€€€€)
*****Four Seasons Florence**, Borgo Pinti 99r, **t** 055 26261, *www.four seasons.com/florence*. Seven years of restoration have gone into bringing a Renaissance *palazzo* and neighbouring convent back to life. Set in a beautiful private park just minutes from the Duomo, there are frescoes, bas reliefs and modern comforts aplenty, as well as a good restuarant, **Il Palagio**, and fashionable bar. The spa uses products exclusively devised for the hotel by the Farmacia di Santa Maria Novella, and there is a pool. The grounds are exceptional as is the slick service. If you have the money, check into the rooms on the *piano nobile*, all

individual and very special – choose from 18th-century Chinese wallpaper or the Royal Suite, 200 sq m of original tiles and frescoes fit for a prince. Florence's top hotel.

*****Excelsior**, Piazza Ognissanti 3, **t** 055 27151, *www.westin.com/ excelsiorflorence*. The former Florentine address of Napoleon's sister, Caroline. With lots of marble, it's neoclassically plush, lush and green with plants and immaculately staffed, with decadently luxurious bedrooms, many with river views (for a price). The restaurant serves innovative Mediterranean cuisine.

*****Helvetia & Bristol**, Via dei Pescioni 2, **t** 055 26651, *www. royaldemeure.com*. Luxury on a smaller scale, opposite Palazzo Strozzi, with 52 exquisitely furnished bedrooms, each one different but all with rich fabrics adorning windows, walls and beds; Stravinsky, Bertrand Russell and Pirandello stayed here. Additional attractions are the restaurant and the winter garden.

*****Savoy**, Piazza della Repubblica 7, **t** 055 27351, *www.hotelsavoy.it*. A crumbling old place that reopened in spring 2000 under the Forte Group and now strikes a minimalist tone with decor in shades of cream, beige and grey. It has a bar and restaurant, **L'Incontro**, where you can sit out on the piazza in fine weather, plus a spa and fitness centre.

****Boscolo Astoria**, Via del Giglio 9, **t** 055 2398095, *www.boscolohotels. com*. A grand 16th-century *palazzo* near San Lorenzo market, where Milton wrote *Paradise Lost*. It boasts more character than many hotels that are located near the station. The public rooms are impressive, as are some of the bedrooms – avoid those on the lower floors by the street.

****Gallery Hotel Art**, Vicolo dell'Oro 5, **t** 055 27263, *www.lungarno hotels.com*. Florence's shrine to contemporary interior design, although by no means stark. Its position (a mere two minutes from the Ponte Vecchio) is superb. It has a comfortable library, a smart bar for smart drinks and a restaurant serving trendy fusion food.

****J.K. Place**, Piazza Santa Maria Novella 7, **t** 055 2645181, *www.jkplace. com*. A tall, elegant townhouse on smartened-up Piazza Santa Maria Novella, offering rooms that overlook Alberti's glorious church façade. The interior is luxuriously designer-chic (and attracts the fashion crowd), but manages to be warm and welcoming at the same time. Some of the bedrooms are on the small side, but they are equipped with every mod con; there is a wonderful rooftop terrace and bar. Breakfast is served at a large communal table in a glassed-in courtyard, and a selection of complimentary soft drinks and snacks is available to guests.

****Kraft**, Via Solferino 2, **t** 055 284273, *www.krafthotel.it*. A place frequently used by upmarket tour groups, handy in the opera season (it is 2mins' walk from the Teatro del Maggio Musicale Fiorentino) and with the added advantage of a small rooftop pool. Bedrooms are light and sunny, comfortably furnished with cheerful fabrics, and fitted with Wi-fi. The suites on the top floor have great views. There is a restaurant.

****Lungarno**, Borgo San Jacopo 14, **t** 055 27261, *www.lungarnohotels.com*. A discreet hotel enjoying a marvellous location on the river, only 2mins' walk from the Ponte Vecchio. The ground-floor sitting/breakfast room and bar, and the new restaurant, which specializes in fish, look out on to the water. The building is modern, but incorporates a medieval tower. The smallish bedrooms are decorated in smart blue and cream. The best have balconies with 'The View'; book ahead for these. There are also some self-catering apartments.

***Beacci Tornabuoni**, Via Tornabuoni 3, **t** 055 212645, *www.tornabuonihotels. com*. Another excellent small hotel that puts you in the centre of fashionable Florence, on the top three floors of an elegant Renaissance palace. The rooms are comfortable, air-conditioned and equipped with minibars, though it's more fun to sit over your drink or meal on the panoramic roof terrace.

***Calzaiuoli**, Via Calzaiuoli 6, **t** 055 212456, *www.calzaiuoli.it*. A comfy hotel a few steps from Piazza Signoria and on a traffic-free street, with modern, pleasantly decorated rooms, an American bar, parking, and wonderful views from the top floor.

*****Relais Santa Croce**, Via Ghibellina 87, **t** 055 234 2230, *www.relaisantacroce.com*. Sumptuous Florentine swish, in the exquisitely restored early-18th-century palace of a papal treasurer, with a grand salon and music room, and 24 plush rooms with all mod cons, plus two royal suites with butler service. It shares *piano nobile* lobbies with the fabled Enoteca Pinchiorri (*see* p.178).

### Very Expensive (€€€€)

*****Villa La Vedetta**, Viale Michelangiolo 78, **t** 055 681631, *www.villalavedettahotel.com*. A luxury hotel occupying an elegant villa in a superb position near Piazzale Michelangelo, with panoramic views over the city from its terraces and some of the rooms. Downstairs, cool grey and white marble prevails; the bedrooms are sumptuously – but not ostentatiously – done out in silks. The superb restaurant, **Onice**, which was awarded a Michelin star just one year after opening, serves creative gourmet fare; in summer you can eat on the terrace overlooking the city lights.

****Villa Belvedere**, Via Benedetto Castelli 3, **t** 055 222501, *www. villabelvederefirenze.it*. Not the most interesting building in this part of peripheral Florence (1km above Porta Romana), but a pleasant alternative to central accommodation, with a beautiful garden, tennis court, a decent little outdoor pool and good views. Rooms are modern and comfortable with lots of wood and plenty of space. For trips into town, you can leave your car and catch a nearby bus. Light meals are served in the restaurant. It's excellent value.

****Villa Carlotta**, Via Michele di Lando 3, **t** 055 233 6134, *www. hotelvillacarlotta.it*. A Tuscan-Edwardian building in a quiet residential district in the upper Oltrarno, close to the Porta Romana, with 32 sophisticated rooms that have been tastefully refurnished and have every mod con. There's a garden and glassed-in veranda, where the large breakfasts are served, a restaurant; and a private garage offering safe parking.

****Monna Lisa**, Borgo Pinti 27, t 055 247 9751, *www.monnalisa.it*. A Renaissance palace, now owned by the descendants of sculptor Giovanni Dupré, with a stern façade and, it is said, staff to match. However, it is also one of the loveliest small hotels in Florence – well preserved and filled with family heirlooms and works of art. Rooms vary wildly; try to reserve one that overlooks the garden. There's private parking.

****Aprile**, Via della Scala 6, t 055 216237, *www.hotelaprile.it*. An old Medici palace convenient for the station and recently given a facelift, with a bust of Cosimo I above the door. Vaulted ceilings and frescoes remain intact, and the bedrooms all have period furniture although some are on the gloomy side; there's a shady courtyard.

***Hermitage**,Vicolo Marzio 1, t 055 287216, *www.hermitagehotel.com*. A little hotel tucked away behind the Ponte Vecchio on the north side of the river, built upside-down – the lift takes you to the fifth floor with its ravishing roof garden, reception and elegant blue and yellow sitting room. The bedrooms below are on the small side but are charmingly furnished with antiques and tasteful fabrics. Some have river views.

***Loggiato dei Serviti**, Via dei Servi 49, t 055 289592, *www.loggiato deiservitihotel.it*. A delightful hotel on Florence's most beautiful square, the Santissima Annunziata,, with front rooms overlooking Brunelleschi's famous portico. The 16th-century building was originally a convent, and many of the architectural features remain. Rooms are furnished with antiques and tasteful fabrics; each different from the next.

***Morandi alla Crocetta**, Via Laura 50, t 055 234 4747, *www.hotelmorandi. it*. A small but popular choice, with 10 rooms in the university area northeast of Piazza San Marco. The building was a convent in the 16th century, and some of the comfortable and pleasant rooms still have the odd fresco. Two rooms have private terraces.

***Torre Guelfa**, Borgo SS. Apostoli 8, t 055 239 6338, *www.hoteltorreguelfa. com*. A hotel boasting the tallest privately owned tower in Florence, in the middle of the *centro storico*. There's a grand double salon, a sunny breakfast room, and stylish bedrooms in pastel shades with wrought-iron and hand-painted furniture. You can sip your *aperitivo* while contemplating the 360° view.

**Casa Howard**, Via della Scala 18, t 06 6992 4555 (reservations made through Rome), *www.casahoward. com*. An elegant guesthouse following in the footsteps of the two very popular Casa Howards in Rome, only a stone's throw from the train station. It offers 11 individually decorated rooms (there is one for kids, one with a library in it, and one for dogs) at remarkably reasonable prices in a home-from-home atmosphere. All rooms have tea- and coffee-making facilities and some have a private terrace. There's also a Turkish hammam.

***Davanzati**, Via Porta Rossa 5, t 055 286 666, *www.hoteldavanzati.it*. A gem of a hotel in a 15th-century *palazzo*, right next to the Palazzo Davanzati, with wonderful, comfy, bright and airy rooms, friendly staff-owners, and Wi-fi. Breakfast is included. Book early.

### Expensive (€€€)
***Classic Hotel**, Viale Machiavelli 25, t 055 229351, *www.classichotel.it*. A good alternative in a very pleasant location just above Porta Romana on the way to Piazzale Michelangelo, a five-minute walk to a bus stop for the centre. The pink-washed villa stands in a shady garden (a welcome respite from the heat of the city), and breakfast is served in the conservatory in summer. There's private parking.

***Arti & Hotel**, Via dei Servi 38/A, t 055 267 8553, *www.artiehotel.it*. A nine-bedroom hotel under the same ownership as the Loggiato dei Serviti (*see* left), with a simpler, more rustic look than its big sister up the road. The stylish bedrooms are decorated in restful shades of green and cream and have wooden floors; a couple have pine four-posters. The three corner rooms are particularly spacious and light, and there is a pretty breakfast room on the top floor, with a wraparound terrace.

**Residenza il Villino >>**

***Silla**, Via dei Renai 5, **t** 055 234 2888, *www.hotelsilla.it*. An old-fashioned *pensione* 10mins' walk east of the Ponte Vecchio on the south bank of the river, in a quiet, quite green neighbourhood. It's on the first floor of a 16th-century *palazzo*, and the spacious breakfast terrace has great views over the Arno and beyond. There's an American bar and Wi-fi access.

**\*\*Alessandra**, Borgo SS. Apostoli 17, **t** 055 283438, *www.hotelalessandra.com*. A modest hotel in a *palazzo* designed by Michelangelo's pupil, Baccio d'Agnolo, on a central but quiet back street, with 25 rooms of varying standards. Not all have private baths; the best have waxed parquet floors and antiques and overlook the Arno.

**\*\*Casci**, Via Cavour 13, **t** 055 211686, *www.hotelcasci.com*. A 15th-century *palazzo* (once home to Rossini) run in a relaxed and cheerful way. The reception area is full of helpful information, the breakfast room has a frescoed ceiling, and the rooms are bright and modern. The choice few look on to a garden at the back.

**Locanda degli Artisti >>**

**\*\*La Scaletta**, Via Guicciardini 13, **t** 055 283028, *www.lascaletta.com*. A friendly *pensione* between the Ponte Vecchio and the Pitti Palace, with a roof garden and great views into Boboli. The 12 bedrooms (not all with bathrooms; and some sleeping up to four) are decently furnished, the best with some antique pieces. Moderately priced dinners are available.

**Antica Dimora**, Via San Gallo 72n, **t** 055 462 7296, *www.anticadimorafirenze.it*. A delightful new guesthouse, situated 10mins' walk north of the Duomo, with six beautifully furnished rooms and the warm atmosphere of an elegant private apartment. The four-posters are hung with fine linens and silks, and all rooms have DVDs.

**\*\*\*Relais Uffizi**, Chiasso de' Baroncelli/Chiasso del Buco 16, **t** 055 267 6239, *www.relaisuffizi.it*. The only hotel that overlooks Piazza della Signoria, hidden down a series of narrow lanes. The 13 rooms of varying shapes and sizes are decorated and furnished with style, and the overall atmosphere is

informal. You can relax in the sitting room and watch the ever-changing *piazza* below.

**Residenza il Villino**, Via della Pergola, **t** 055 200 1116, *www.residenzail villino.com*. A handsome 19th-century Tuscan complex near the Duomo, built around a courtyard and renovated to preserve all its original features. It has lovely owners and serene, spacious rooms (rates include a buffet breakfast; the garage is extra). It's essential to book well in advance.

**Tourist House Ghiberti**, Via M. Buffani 1, **t** 055 284858, *www.touristhouse ghiberti.com*. Five arty B&B rooms near the Duomo, equipped with original paintings and mosaics, and all the mod cons of a five-star hotel, including a sauna and Jacuzzi.

Moderate (€€)

**\*\*Belletini**, Via de' Conti 7, **t** 055 213561, *www.hotelbelletini.com*. A friendly place near the Medici chapels, decorated in traditional Florentine style; a couple of rooms have stunning views of the nearby domes. There's a good, generous breakfast. An annexe around the corner houses an additional six stylishly furnished rooms, slightly more expensive. There's TV, air-con, cots, and nearby parking.

**\*\*Locanda degli Artisti**, Via Faenza 88r, **t** 055 213806, *www.hotelazzi.it*. A hotel a stone's throw from the San Lorenzo market and the train station, with pleasant rooms and an arty, alternative feel to it. On the ground floor, the bedrooms are a little more sophisticated (there are even a couple of suites); upstairs, the rooms are clean but quite spartan. There's a sauna, a sunny terrace and a breakfast room where dishes made from organic produce are served, plus a free Internet access point.

**\*\*Boboli**, Via Romana 63, **t** 055 229 8645, *www.hotelboboli.com*. A modest hotel located near the back entrance of the Boboli Gardens. The brightest rooms are right at the top of the four-storey building; there is a lift. If you want quiet (Via Romana is quite noisy), go for a room on the inner courtyard. Breakfast is served on a little terrace in summer.

**Residenza Johanna II**, Via Cinque Giornate 12, t 055 473377, *www. johanna.it*. A villa representing good value for money in a city where bargains are few and far between, located some way from the centre (near Fortezza da Basso). It stands in its own garden and offers six comfortable rooms, each equipped with a breakfast tray and kettle, as well as a sitting room with plenty of reading material. Facilities are of a three-star standard, and parking is available. The staff are discreet.

**\*Bavaria**, Borgo degli Albizi 26, t 055 234 0313, *www.hotelbavariafirenze.it*. A once-crummy hotel in a grand, 16th-century *palazzo* with a façade said to be frescoed by Vasari. While only a handful of rooms have private baths, the rooms are stylish, and some have splendid views of the city.

**\*Maxim**, Via del Calzainoli 11, t 055 217474, *www.hotelmaximfirenze. it*. A centrally located hotel, with a bright, elegant reception area, and the bedrooms (which sleep two or three) are well furnished and modern. All are ensuite and one even has a Jacuzzi. There's air-conditioning, parking nearby, and free Internet.

**\*Orchidea**, Borgo degli Albizi 11, t 055 248 0346, *www.hotelorchideaflorence. it*. A hotel in a 12th-century building where Dante's in-laws once lived, run by an Anglo-Italian family. One of the seven cheerful rooms has a private shower; the best of the rest look on to a garden at the back.

**\*Pensione Sorelle Bandini**, Piazza Santo Spirito 9, t 055 215308. A perenially popular choice despite its state of disrepair and relatively high prices, partly due to the romantic loggia along one side, the fact that it features in Zeffirelli's film *Tea with Mussolini* and to its location on Piazza S. Spirito. Expect uncomfortable beds, cavernous rooms, heavy Florentine furniture and a certain shabby charm.

**Dei Mori B&B**, Via Dante Alighieri 12, t 055 211 438, *www.bnb.it/deimori*. One of the friendliest and best-value B&Bs in Florence, with pretty rooms (up a fair amount of stairs), many overlooking the courtyard, in a great location between the Duomo and Piazza della Signoria.

**Residenza Johanna I**, Via Bonifacio Lupi 14, t 055 481896, *www.johanna.it*. A building identified only by a tiny brass plaque over the bell, just north of Piazza San Marco. There are no TVs or phones in the rooms, no doorman, and not all rooms have private baths, but the furnishings are comfortable, the bedrooms are prettily decorated and there's lots of reading material to hand. Breakfast is on a do-it-yourself tray in each room, and there are kettles out in the corridor.

**Residenza Johlea**, Via San Gallo 76, t 055 463 3292, *www.johanna.it*. Another small hotel a few doors from the Johanna (*see* above), with which it shares ownership. Situated 10mins' walk north of the central market, it has comfortable rooms furnished with taste and style, with excellent bathrooms. Breakfast is supplied on trays in the rooms. On the top floor you can enjoy use of a small sitting room and a roof terrace with 360° views of the city. Ask the receptionist about the sister *residenza* (the **Johlea Due**) a few doors down.

**\*\*Ungherese**, Via G.B. Amici 8, t 055 573 474, *www.hotelungherese.it*. A wonderfully hospitable little hotel with a lovely garden terrace for *alfresco* drinks or breakfast. It's located outside the ZTL in the San Gervaso quarter (10mins from the centre by frequent bus); you can park on the street for a small fee.

### Inexpensive (€)

**\*Dali**, Via dell'Oriuolo 17, t 055 234 0706, *www.hoteldali.com*. A little hotel a few minutes' walk from the Duomo, run by a genuinely friendly young couple who have decorated the rooms with care and attention to detail in spite of the low prices. Only three of the 10 rooms have ensuite bathrooms, but all are bright and homely and have a small fridge. There's free parking in the internal courtyard but no breakfasts.

**\*Scoti**, Via de' Tornabuoni 7, t 055 292128, *www.hotelscoti.com*. A simple and cheap *pensione* with an upmarket address – the ideal spot if you would rather splurge on the wonderful clothes in the surrounding shops. All the plain rooms are ensuite, and there are wonderful faded floor-to-ceiling frescoes in the sitting room. The owners are friendly and there is a restaurant and bar.

**Istituto Gould**, Via dei Serragli 49, **t** 055 212576, *www.istitutogould.it*. An excellent budget choice near Santo Spirito, run by the Valdese church. Rooms vary in size from singles (just a couple) to quads, and not all have their own bathrooms; you need to book early to secure singles or doubles. The best rooms have access to a terrace; the noisiest are on Via dei Serragli.

## Youth Hostels

**Archi Rossi**, Via Faenza 94r, **t** 055 290804, *www.hostelarchirossi.com*. The nearest hostel to the station, purpose-built, fully wheelchair-accessible and well equipped. You can book a place anytime after 6am and occupy your room from 2.30pm. Phone bookings are accepted and there is a 12.30am curfew. There's a restaurant, a bar and Internet access.

**Ostello Villa Camerata**, Viale A. Righi 2/4 (bus from station), **t** 055 601451, *www.ostellionline.org*. Five hundred beds for IYHF card-holders. Located in an old *palazzo* with gardens, it is popular, and you'd be wise to show up at 2pm to get a spot in the summer. The maximum stay is three days.

**Ostello Santa Monaca**, Via Santa Monaca 6, **t** 055 268338, *www. ostello.it*. Just over 100 beds near the Carmine church, in a 15th-century convent; sign up for a place in the morning. Credit cards are accepted.

## Camping

There are a few campsites within easy striking distance of Florence. *See* also the pne in Fiesole, p.198.

**Camping Internazionale**, Via S. Cristofano 2, **t** 055 237 4704, *www. florencecamping.com*. A choice south of the city in Bottai Tavarnuzze, near the A1 exit *autostrada* Firenze–Certosa.

**Camping Michelangelo**, Viale Michelangelo 80, **t** 055 681 1977, *www.ecvacanze.it*. Fine views over the city and free hot showers; arrive early to get a spot. On the other hand, there's no shade and the disco goes on until 1am. Bus 13 will get you here from the station.

# Eating Out in Florence

Like any sophisticated city with many visitors, Florence has plenty of fine restaurants; even in cheaper places, standards are high, and if you don't care for anything fancier, there will be lots of good red Chianti to wash down your meal. By popular demand, the city centre is full of *tavole calde*, pizzerias and snackbars where you can grab a sandwich or a salad instead of a full sit-down meal (one of the best pizza-by-the-slice places can be found just across from the Medici Chapels).

You are advised to call ahead and reserve, even a day or two in advance, for the best places, many of which close for all or part of August.

**Very Expensive (€€€€)**

**Alle Murate**, Via del Proconsolo 16r, **t** 055 240618. A 'creative traditional' restaurant close to the Bargello, elegant but relaxed, serving two set menus. Ask for the 'Creative Menu': the modern take on Tuscan cuisine will amaze you. Highlights are veal rolls stuffed with aubergine, and octopus with potato purée. Book ahead. *Closed Mon and lunch.*

**Angiolino**, Via Santo Spirito 36l, **t** 055 239 8976. A reliable place to eat good Tuscan food. The vegetable *antipasti* are especially good, and the simple *pollastrina sulla griglia* (grilled spring chicken) is succulent. *Closed Mon.*

**Antico Ristoro di Cambi**, Via Sant' Onofrio 1r, **t** 055 217134. A place in the Oltrarno, to the west of the centre, that's very popular with the Florentine intelligentsia. The food is genuinely Florentine, the classic soups – *ribollita* and *pappa al pomodoro* – are tasty and warming, as is the *penne* with pumpkin flowers. *Closed Sun.*

**Beccofino**, Piazza degli Scarlatti, **t** 055 290076, *www.beccofino.com*. A trendy restaurant on the river under the British Institute. Inside you could almost be in London or New York, but the food is decidedly Italian. Dishes are enhanced with creative touches and elegantly presented. Both fish and meat dishes are excellent; the menu changes on a monthly basis but you might enjoy scallops with bitter greens, risotto with pears and pecorino cheese or a fabulous *bistecca alla fiorentina*. You can also eat a light meal in the wine bar, where prices are considerably lower. *Closed Mon, and Tues–Sat lunch.*

**Buca Lapi**, Via del Trebbio 1r, **t** 055 213768, *www.bucalapi.com*. Florence's oldest restaurant, open since 1880 in the old wine cellar of the lovely Palazzo Antinori complete with frescoes, serving traditional favourites, from *polenta al cinghiale* (with boar) to a *bistecca alla fiorentina con fagioli* that is hard to beat, downed with a wide selection of Tuscan wines. *Closed Sun, Aug, and Mon–Sat lunch.*

**Cibreo**, Via de Verrocchio 8r, **t** 055 234 1100, *www.fabiopicchi.it*. Fabio Picchi's most Florentine of Florentine restaurants has now spawned an empire of sorts on a corner close to Sant' Ambrogio market. The decor is simple yet elegant, but food is the main concern, and all of it is market-fresh. You can go native and order cold tripe salad, cockscombs and kidneys or rosemary-flavoured grilled baby goat chops, or you can play it safe with *prosciutto* from the Casentino, a fragrant soup (no pasta here) of tomatoes, mussels and bell peppers, and polenta with Parmesan and fresh herbs, topped off with a delicious lemon *crostata*, cheesecake or a chocolate cake that will answer every chocaholic's dream. Advance reservations are essential. *Closed Sun, Mon, Aug and 1st wk Jan.*

**Don Chisciotte**, Via C. Ridolfi 4r, **t** 055 475430. A small place located between the Fortezza Basso and Piazza dell'Indipendenza, serving inventive Italian food with a particular emphasis on fish and vegetables. Let yourself be tempted by the likes of squid filled with ricotta and Sardinian cheese, or tagliatelle with prawns and asparagus. *Closed Aug.*

**Enoteca Pinchiorri**, Via Ghibellina 87, near Casa Buonarroti, **t** 055 242777, *www.enotecapinchiorri.com*. One of the finest gourmet restaurants in all Italy, boasting two Michelin stars. The owners inherited the wine shop that it occupies and converted it into this beautifully appointed restaurant, with meals served in a garden court in the summer months. The cellars contain some 80,000 bottles of the best wines that Italy and France have to offer. The cooking, a mixture of *nouvelle cuisine* and traditional Tuscan, wins prizes every year. Italians complain about the minute portions. A meal will set you back more than €200 excluding wine; the sky's the limit if you go for a more interesting bottle. *Closed Sun, Mon–Wed lunch, and Aug.*

**Fuor d'Aqua**, Via Pisana 37r, **t** 055 222 299, *www.fuordacqua.org*. Florence's finest fish restaurant is located just outside the city gates at San Frediano. The elegant interior of stripped brick walls provides the perfect backdrop for preening Florentines as they tuck into the fresh fish and seafood. Try the seafood sampler for two, choose cooked or raw and watch as plate after plate lands on the table. Bring an appetite. Book ahead. *Closed Sun.*

**Oliviero**, Via delle Terme 51r, **t** 055 212421. A place five minutes from the Piazza della Signoria, with somewhat passé decor and a slightly bizarre clientele but excellent food. You can try such seasonal curiosities such as *gnudi di fiori di zucchini e ricotta* (ravioli stripped of its pasta coating with ricotta cheese and courgette flowers) and boned pigeon stuffed with chestnuts. Try the soufflé. *Closed lunch and Sun.*

**Ristorante Ricchi**, Piazza S. Spirito 8r, **t** 055 280830. A small fish restaurant with tables on magical Piazza Santo Spirito. Inside, the decor is both contemporary and elegant, with tables lined up against the walls. The generous plate of *antipasti* is good; main courses include ravioli filled with *burrata* cheese, lasagne with yellow pumpkin or radish, or fillet of pink tuna with carrots. There are a few meat dishes too. *Closed Sun (exc. 2nd Sun of month, when arts and crafts market takes place), last 2wks Aug, and Feb.*

**Targa**, Lungarno C Colombo 7, **t** 055 677377, *www.targabistrot.net*. The space is great, a delightfully warm wood-and-glass room on the Arno, and the food provides a creative take on regional dishes. Try the *garmugia ai tre caci*, with vegetables and typical Luccese cheeses, or a mixture of artichokes and Chinese cabbage with mussels. Leave room for the sinful hot chocolate soufflé, and choose a wine from the formidable list, which includes labels from all of Italy and beyond. *Closed Sun and 1st 3wks Aug.*

### Expensive (€€€)

**Antico Fattore**, Via Lambertesca 1/3r, **t** 055 288975. A traditional Florentine trattoria that suffered serious damage in the 1993 Uffizi bombing, serving excellent and reasonably priced local dishes. Try *pappardelle* with wild boar or deer sauce, the tender *lombatina all'aceto balsamico* (veal chops cooked in balsamic vinegar) or grilled pigeon. Book ahead. *Closed Sun and 2wks Aug.*

**Baldovino**, Via Giuseppe 22r (Piazza S. Croce), **t** 055 241773. An excellent trattoria/pizzeria where you can eat anything from a big salad, filled *focaccia* or pizza (from a wood-burning oven), *ribollita* or *bistecca alla fiorentina* and delicious home-made cakes. Nearby, at 18r, the **Enoteca Baldovino** offers a great list of wines. *Closed Mon.*

**Buca dell'Orafo**, Volta dei Girolami 28r, **t** 055 213619. One of Florence's traditional 'cellar restaurants', accessed via steep stairs down a little alley between the Ponte Vecchio and the Uffizi. Crowded and noisy, the tables are almost communal, and, if you come later, the American tourists will have given way to lively Florentines who love the fresh ingredients and excellent traditional cooking. In late spring, try the *spaghettini con piselli* (peas) or anything with artichokes. Book ahead. *Closed Sun, Mon and 2wks Aug.*

**Cantinetta Antinori**, Piazza Antinori 3, **t** 055 292234. This wine bar was opened by the Antinori wine clan in their *palazzo* 30 years ago, and is still one of Florence's most fashionable places. Seasonal recipes are designed to complement the wine; in winter try roast chestnuts with rum syrup, in summer a refreshing *panzanella* hits the spot. *Closed Aug.*

**Cavolo Nero**, Via dell'Ardiglione 22r, **t** 055 294744, *www.cavolonero.it*. A little restaurant in a side street near Piazza del Carmine, with quite a following among Florentine trendies. The interior is white on yellow, and as many tables as possible are crowded into the attractive room, though there's a pretty rear garden. The food is mainly Mediterranean with a twist (think gnocchi with tomato and *burrata* cheese, or risotto with scallops and rocket pesto, or monkfish tail and shrimp in a curry sauce or fried lamb fillet with stewed cabbage), but there are also plenty of local standards. Book ahead. *Closed Sun and 2wks Aug.*

**Coco Lezzone**, Via del Parioncino 26r (off Lungarno Corsini), **t** 055 287178. A restaurant with a name that means, in old Florentine dialect, 'big, smelly cook', but don't be put off. The atmosphere is informal and the food is classic Tuscan, with dishes featuring the highest-quality fresh ingredients, particularly meat. *Closed Sun and Aug.*

**Il Latini**, Via dei Palchetti 6r (by Palazzo Rucellai), **t** 055 210916. A place that's something of an institution in Florence – crowded (prepare to queue; they don't accept bookings) and noisy but great fun. You eat huge portions of Florentine classics at long tables – try one of the hearty soups followed by the *bistecca*, or, for a change, the *gran pezzo* – a vast rib-roast of beef. The house wine is good; try a *riserva*. *Closed Mon and Aug.*

**Nove**, Lungarno Guicciardini, **t** 055 2302756. Florence's newest, and hippest, restaurant is the brainchild of the man behind the Fashion Cafés of the 1990s. Equally beautiful staff work here too in this stylish modern interior with its acres of wood, back-lit bar and artful lighting. The food is a delectable fusion of Tuscan and international flavours; the *bistecca* is divine. Book ahead. *Closed Aug.*

**Sostanza**, Via della Porcellana 25r, **t** 055 212691. One of the last authentic Florentine trattorias, just west of Santa Maria Novella, and known as Il Troia. It's a good place to eat *bistecca*, but one of its most famous dishes is the simple but delectable *petto di pollo al burro* – chicken breast sautéed in butter. No credit cards are taken, and booking is strongly advised. *Closed Sat, Sun and Aug.*

**Zibibbo**, Via di Terzollina 3r, **t** 055 433383. A wonderful restaurant serving traditional Tuscan fare but in a stylish,

⭐ **Trattoria Cibreo (Cibreino) >>**

⭐ **Il Canapone >**

⭐ **Antica Porta >>**

⭐ **La Casalinga >>**

un-Tuscan setting (pink-varnished floorboards, contemporary furniture). Plenty of choice between meat and fish dishes; worth the trip. *Closed Sun.*

**Moderate (€€)**

**Aquacotta**, Via dei Pilastri 51r, t 055 242907. A restaurant north of Piazza Sant'Ambrogio, named for the simple but delicious bread soup that is one of its specialities; you could follow that by deep-fried rabbit accompanied by crisply fried courgette flowers. It also serves *acquacotta* ('cooked water'), a Maremman vegetable soup with onions, tomatoes and mushrooms. *Closed Sun and Aug.*

**Il Canapone**, Via Mazzetta 5, t 055 2381729. Bohemian little supper club by Santo Spirito; you have to ring the bell to get in. The duo running this place are good fun and they cook up a storm, mixing unusual flavours with Tuscan ingredients. Try the warming *peposo* in winter (a slow-cooked stew in which the meat melts in your mouth) and leave room for the chocolate soufflé which is the best in town. On Sunday they serve a good-value American brunch. *Closed Aug.*

**Il Cammillo**, Borgo San Jacopo 57r, t 055 212427. An Oltrarno favourite, rub shoulders with Florentine aristocracy in this unreconstructed trattoria. The food is reliably good too with all the usual Tuscan dishes on offer; try *ceciata del maiale* (salt pork with chickpeas and spinach). *Closed Tues, Wed and 2wks Aug.*

**Finisterrae**, Via de' Pepi 5–7r, t 055 2638675. A great place to come if you are tired of *ribollita* and the typical trattoria look, offering food from a range of Mediterranean countries, from southern Italy and France to Greece, Turkey, Tunisia and Spain. The standard of the food is not always what it might be, but the atmosphere is wonderful – a series of rooms decorated in the style of the various countries concerned.

**La Vecchia Bettola**, Viale Ariosto 32–34r, t 055 224158. A noisy trattoria located to the west of the Carmine, with great food; the menu changes daily, but you will nearly always find their classic *tagliolini con funghi porcini* on offer. Try the *bistecca* too.

The ice cream comes from Vivoli. *Closed Sun and Mon.*

**Trattoria Cibreo (Cibreino)**, Via dei Macci 114, t 055 234 1100. A little annexe to smart Cibreo (*see* p.178), constituting one of the best deals in town; the food is the same (excluding the odd more extravagant dish) but it's served in a rusticated setting on cheaper porcelain – with the result that your bill will be a third that of those who are dining around the corner. No reservations are taken, so make sure to come early to get a table. *Closed Sun, Mon and Aug.*

There aren't many **vegetarian restaurants** as such in Florence, though non-meat eaters will find plenty of choice (pastas, risotto, etc.) to tempt them. Specifically vegetarian restaurants in this range include:

**Ruth's**,Via Farini 2/A, t 055 248 0888. A bright and modern kosher vegetarian restaurant next to the synagogue, serving fish and Middle Eastern dishes. Try a *brik*, a savoury pastry filled with fish, potatoes or cheese that tastes better than it sounds. *Closed Fri eve and Sat lunch.*

**Il Vegetariano**, Via delle Ruote 30r, t 055 47030. Self-service place west of San Marco; with excellent fresh food, including a wide choice of soups, salads and more substantial dishes. *Closed Sat lunch, Sun lunch, 3wks Aug.*

**Inexpensive (€)**

**Antica Porta**, Via Senese 23r, t 055 220527. You have to step just outside the Porta Romana for what may be the best pizzas in town. You may have to queue but the excellent thin-crust pizzas are worth the wait. *Closed Mon and lunches.*

**La Casalinga**, Via Michelozzi 9r, t 055 218624. A family-run trattoria near Piazza Santo Spirito, and always busy, which is not surprising given the quality of the simple home cooking (the name means 'the housewife') and the low prices. Try the ravioli in rabbit sauce, *bollito misto*, and Limoncello sorbet for dessert. *Closed Sun, 1wk Jan, 3wks Aug.*

**Da Mario**, Via della Rosina 2r, t 055 218550. Mario's trattoria, located at the back of the central market, is always buzzing, and there is usually a queue for the few rather cramped tables; don't expect to get a table to yourself. The food is pure Tuscan, excellent and cheap: *ribollita, tortelli* stuffed with potatoes, roasted rabbit and tripe. Note that only cash is accepted. *Closed eves, plus Sun, hols and first 3wks Aug.*

**Da Rocco**, Sant'Ambrogio market. A family-run trattoria in the middle of the covered market, always bustling and staffed by comical characters. The tables are ranged round the middle; you have to get in from a gate on the outside and be prepared to share. The food is basic but good and very cheap, Rocco himself plays up for the regulars, doling out Tuscan profanities and clucking at children. *Closed Sun, Aug.*

⭐ Cibreo Caffè »

**Da Ruggero**, Via Senese 89r, t 055 220542. A tiny, family-run trattoria a little way from the centre of town outside the Porta Romana; it's always full, so make sure to book ahead. The traditional food is home-cooked; try the excellent *pappardelle alla lepre* (with hare sauce) and good puddings. *Closed Tues, Wed, and 3wks July/Aug.*

⭐ Santa Lucia ›

**Santa Lucia**, Via Ponte alle Mosse 102r, t 055 353255. A genuine Neapolitan pizzeria north of the Cascine, noisy, steamy and unromantic. But it makes up for its lack of glamour by serving what is possibly the best pizza in Florence, topped with the sweetest tomatoes and the creamiest *mozza?rella di buffala*. Note that payment is by cash only. *Closed Wed and Aug.*

**Al Tranvai**, near Carmine in Piazza Torquato Tasso 14r, t 055 225197. A cheerful little place done out like the buses of old, the *tranvai*, serving Tuscan favourites. There are two rows of tables that are always full; you may not get much elbow room. The menu changes daily, but everything is very good; this is the place to try *cervella* (fried brains). The *crostini misti* are always on offer, and there are lots of offal dishes. *Closed lunch and Sun.*

⭐ Trattoria del Carmine ›

**Trattoria del Carmine**, Piazza del Carmine 18r, t 055 218601. A traditional, bustling trattoria situated within the San Frediano district, and often full. The long menu includes such staples as *ribollita, pasta e fagioli* and roast pork, but also features seasonal dishes such as risotto with asparagus or mushrooms, pasta with wild boar sauce, *osso buco* and fish dishes. *Closed Sun and 3wks Aug.*

## Cafés and *Gelaterie*

**Badiani**, Viale dei Mille 20r. Out of the centre, but Florentines flock to this *gelateria* for its unique Buontalenti flavour.

**Caffè Italiano**, Via Isola delle Stinche 11/13r. A popular lunchtime stop for locals, right in the centre of town. It's on two levels: downstairs there's standing at the bar, upstairs you can sit down. The atmosphere is old-fashioned, particularly in the tearoom upstairs.

**Caffè Ricchi**, Piazza Santo Spirito 8r–9r, t 055 215864. A local institution that continues to serve excellent light lunches and wonderful ice cream. The outside tables enjoy the benefit of one of the most beautiful piazzas in Florence, though this comes at a price.

**Cibreo Caffè**, Via del Verrocchio 5r, t 055 234 5853. Another outpost of the Cibreo empire, this is probably the loveliest café in town. Light meals come from the restaurant across the road but at a fraction of the price. *Closed Sun, Mon, 3wks Aug.*

**Dolci e Dolcezze**, Piazza Cesare Beccaria 8r, t 055 234 5458. East of Sant'Ambrogio market, with the most delicious cakes, pastries and jams in the city – the *crostate, torte* and *bavarese* are expensive but worth every euro. It now has another shop at Via del Corso 41r. *Closed Mon.*

**Dolcissima Pasticceria**, 61r Via Maggio, Oltrarno. A tiny place with a divine selection of freshly made cakes, pastries, chocolates and sweets laid out in glass cases like precious jewels.

**Festival del Gelato**, Via del Corso 75r. More than 100 variations of ice cream.

**Gelateria de' Ciompi**, Via dell'Agnolo 121r. A traditional Florentine ice-cream parlour tucked around the corner from Santa Croce, priding itself on its authentic home-made recipes, some of which are more than 50 years old.

**Gilli**, Piazza della Repubblica 36–39r, t 055 213896. One of of Florence's old grand cafés dating back further than most, to 1733, when the Mercato Vecchio still occupied this area; its two panelled back rooms are especially pleasant in winter and the pastries are delicate and delicious. *Closed Tues*.

**Giubbe Rosse**, Piazza della Repubblica 13–14r, **t** 055 212280. Famous as the rendezvous of Florence's literati at the turn of the 19th century, with a chandelier-lit interior that has changed little since.

**Cucciolo**, Via del Corso 25r, **t** 055 287727. *Pasticceria*/café famous for its *bombolone* (doughnuts filled with cream, chocolate or jam). Look out for the contraption that transports them from kitchen to bar, via a long runway and a dunk in sugar at the end.

**Hemingway**, Piazza Piattellina 9r, **t** 055 284781. A beautifully appointed bar done out in pale blues with rattan furniture. You can enjoy teas and coffees, as well as cocktails and inter?esting light meals. The owner is a choc??aholic, so the hand-made choco?lates and puddings are a dream. Try the *sette veli* chocolate cake. Reserva?tions recommended. *Closed lunch, Sun*.

**L'Oasi**, Via dell'Oriuolo 5r, near Duomo. Sophisticated ice-cream flavours, and a good choice of cakes.

**Perché No** ('Why Not'), Via Tavolini 19r. Arctic heaven near Via Calzaiuoli, with wonderful ice cream served in 1940s surroundings.

**Rivoire**, Piazza della Signoria 5r. Florence's most elegant watering hole, with a marble-detailed interior as lovely as the Piazza della Signoria itself, plus a terrace on the square.

**GROM**, Via del Campanile 2. Near the Duomo, this newcomer may be a chain but its *gelato* is excellent. The apricot flavour is unrivalled.

**La Via del' Tè**, Piazza Ghiberti 22r. A place looking on to the Sant' Ambrogio food market, offering a huge range of teas to choose from plus sweet and savoury snacks.

**Vivoli**, Via Isola delle Stinche 7r, between Bargello and S. Croce. A place serving decadent confections and rich *semifreddi* that are partially responsible for Florence's claim to be the ice-cream capital of the world. Its rice *gelato* is famous. *Closed Mon*.

## Wine Bars

**Cantinetta dei Verrazzano**, Via dei Tavolini 18–20r, **t** 055 268590.

Part bakery (selling delicious bread and cakes), part wine bar, central and belonging to the Verrazzano wine estate – it serves its own very good wine exclusively. You can sip it with a plate of mixed *crostini* at hand.

**Enoteca Baldovino**, Via San Giuseppe 18r, **t** 055 234 7220. A bright and cheerful wine bar located down the northern side of Santa Croce, offering a range of snacks and pasta dishes. There is a comprehensive wine list and plenty of wines by the glass. *Closed Mon in winter*.

**Enoteca dei Giraldi**, Via dei Giraldi 4r, **t** 055 216518. A place near the Bargello, hosting art exhibitions and running wine-tasting courses as well as supplying excellent food and drink.

**I Fratellini**, Via dei Cimatori 38r. A hole in the wall, one of the last of its kind in Florence, where you can join the locals standing on the street, glass and *crostino* in hand. *Closed Sun*.

**Frescobaldi Wine Bar**, Vicolo dei Gondi (off Via della Condotta), **t** 055 284724. A pleasant little wine bar from one of Tuscany's best-known wine-growing families, forming an annexe to a full-blown (and very elegant) restaurant. The wines on offer are, naturally, all Frescobaldis produced on their estates in Tuscany and the rest of Italy; some are the result of joint ventures in California and Chile. Delicious snacks, or you can pop next door for dinner. *Closed Sun, and Mon lunch*.

**Fuori Porta**, Via Monte alle Croci 10r, **t** 055 234 2483. Possibly Florence's most famous wine bar of all, where there are some 600 labels on the wine list plus dozens of whiskies and *grappas*. Among the snacks and hot dishes, make sure to try one of the *crostoni* – huge slabs of local bread topped with something delicious and heated under the grill. *Closed Sun*.

**Pitti Gola e Cantina**, Piazza Pitti 16, **t** 055 212704. A delightful little place situated bang opposite the Palazzo Pitti, with a good choice of wines from Tuscany and beyond, snacks and other more substantial dishes, as well as a few outside tables. *Closed Mon*.

**Le Volpi e l'Uva**, Piazza dei Rossi 1, **t** 055 239 8132, *www.levolpieluva.com*. A place frequented by artists and run by knowledgeable and helpful owners who specialize in relatively unknown labels. Snacks include a marvellous selection of French and Italian cheeses. *Closed Sun.*

## Aperitivo Bars

**Il Rifrullo**, Via S. Niccolò 55r, **t** 055 234 2621. An older bar; probably the most popular of all, and certainly one of the first to attract people to the Oltrarno.

**Zoe**, Via de Renai 13r, **t** 055 243111. The city's coolest bar attracting the sexiest crowd, the Zoe metamorphoses from neighbourhood café/restaurant by day to the place to see and be seen by night. The *aperitivo* spread is generous and imaginative and DJs spin tunes in the back room. *Closed 3wks Aug.*

**Negroni**, Via de Renai 17r, **t** 055 243647. Giving the Zoe a run for its money, the Negroni attracts a slightly older 30-something crowd but the posing is equally compulsive. The two bars have made this innocuous street in the Oltrarno Florence's hottest night-time destination. *Closed 3wks Aug.*

**Moyo**, Via de Benci 23r, **t** 055 247 9738. Under the same ownership as the Zoe, Moyo's slick wooden interior is enhanced by the overflowing variety of *aperitivi* on offer. The first in Florence to have free Wi-fi access, it's still popular with American students.

**Sky Lounge**, Bar Continentale, Vicolo dell'Oro 6r, **t** 055 27262. Hotel Continentale's swanky bar gives incredible views over the city and serves a discreet *aperitivo* of mini brioche and raw vegetables.

**Fusion Bar**, Gallery Hotel Art, Vicolo dell'Oro 5, **t** 055 27263. Chic, contemporary bar popular with Florence's most sophisticated show-offs. The beautifully presented *aperitivo* features sushi, tempura and other Asian nibbles, and it just keeps coming. Dress up and join in the ever-so-discreet posing.

**Dolce Vita**, Piazza del Carmine, **t** 055 284595. The place where fashionable young Florentines have historically strutted their latest togs – a favourite pastime since the 14th century. Live music accompanies *aperitivi* on Wednesday and Thursday evenings. *Closed Mon and 2wks Aug.*

**Capocaccia**, Lungarno Corsini 12r, **t** 055 2345458. A place popular as a night-spot as well as a daytime bar and café, enjoying a great location on the river beside the British Consulate. A great spot for an *aperitivo* or as an evening venue for music and drinks. *Closed Mon.*

**Excelsior Hotel**, Pza Ognissanti 3, **t** 055 27151. The bar here has reopened and offers such wonderful views over the river and Ponte Vecchio that even die-hard Florentines are bagging a place.

# Entertainment and Nightlife in Florence

Nightlife with Great-Aunt Florence is still awaiting its Renaissance; according to the Florentines she's conservative, somewhat deaf and retires early – 1am is late in this city. However, there are plenty of people who wish it weren't so, and slowly, slowly, Florence by night is beginning to mean more than the old *passeggiata* over the Ponte Vecchio and an ice cream, and perhaps a late trip up to Fiesole to contemplate the lights.

Look out for listings of concerts and events in Florence's daily paper *La Nazione*. The tourist office's free *Florence Today* contains bilingual monthly information and a calendar, as does a booklet called *Florence Concierge Information*, which is available in hotels and tourist offices.

The monthly *Firenze Spettacolo*, which is sold at newsstands, contains a brief section on events in English, but the comprehensive listings (including anything from ecology and trekking events, film societies, clubs, live music, opera and concerts) are easy to understand even in Italian. The annual *Guida locali di Firenze* also gives listings. For all current films that are being shown in Florence, look in the local paper.

**Box Office**, Via Alamanni 39, **t** 055 210804, *www.boxoffice.it*. A central ticket agency for all the major events in Tuscany and beyond, including classical, rock, jazz, etc.

## Performance Arts

Florence's opera and ballet season runs from September to Christmas, and there are concerts from January to April at the **Teatro del Maggio Musicale Fiorentino**, and in the

*Maggio Musicale* festival, which features all three, running from mid-April to the end of June. There is usually more opera in July.

## Classical Concerts

Concerts are held mainly in the following venues:

**Teatro del Maggio Musicale Fiorentino**, Corso Italia 16, t 055 2779350, *www.maggiofiorentino.com*. Florence's municipal opera house, hosting symphony concerts, recitals, opera and ballet.

**Teatro della Pergola**, Via della Pergola 12–32, t 055 226 4316, *www.amicimusica.fi.it*. A stunning 18th-century theatre hosting an excellent chamber-music series promoted by the Amici della Musica.

**Teatro Verdi**, Via Ghibellina 99, t 055 212320, *www.teatroverdifirenze. it*. A red and gold theatre that's home to Tuscany's regional orchestra, who perform here on a regular basis from late Nov to May.

Many smaller events take place year-round in churches, cloisters and villas, and there are plenty of outdoor concerts in the summer months. Look out for posters: such events are not always well publicized.

## Rock and Jazz Concert Venues

**Auditorium FLOG**, Via M Mercati 24b, t 055 487145, *www.flog.it*. One of the best places in Florence to hear live music year-round, often hosting ethnic music events. Look out for the *Musica dei Popoli* festival in October. *Closed July and Aug.*

**Palasport Mandela Forum**, Viale Paoli, t 055 678841, *www.mandelaforum.it*. A venue in Campo di Marte, seating 7,000 people. Big-name rock and jazz bands nearly always play here.

**Saschall**, Lungarno Aldo Moro 3, t 055 650 4112, *www.saschall.it*. A 3,000-seat venue risen from the ashes (not literally) of the old Teatro Tenda, hosting all kinds of music (including musicals).

**Teatro Verdi**, *see above*.

**Tenax**, Via Pratese 46, t 055 308160, *www.tenax.org*. A spacious venue on the outskirts of town, which is very popular and so usually gets crowded. It stages lots of live rock concerts, with

bands ranging from international names to local groups. DJs take over after the live music stops.

In the summer months lots of live music venues spring up all over the city, many of them free, for when the Florentines move outdoors in order to cool off. Look out for concerts in the Piazze Signoria, Santo Spirito and SS. Annunziata.

## Cinemas

Summer is a great time to catch the latest films. English-language films are shown throughout the summer three evenings a week at the **Odeon** in Piazza Strozzi, and **open-air screens** are erected in several venues within Florence, showing two different films in Italian each evening from mid-June until mid-Sept. Details appear in the local newspapers.

The following shows original-language (usually English) films:

**Odeon Cinehall**, Piazza Strozzi, t 055 214068, *www.cinehall.it*. The latest releases on Mon, Tues and Thurs. *Closed Aug.*

## Clubs

Many clubs have themed evenings; keep an eye out for posters or handouts or buy the listings magazine *Firenze Spettacolo*. Places are somewhat seasonal as well.

**Caffè Decò**, Piazza della Libertà 45–46r, t 055 571135. Elegant Art Deco surroundings, where Florence's swells put on the dog, often hosting live jazz. *Closed Mon.*

**Caffè La Torre**, Lungarno Cellini 65r, t 055 680643, *www.caffelatorre.it*. A small club that hosts regular jazz and Latin events.

**Central Park**, Via Fosso Macinante 2, Parco delle Cascine, t 055 353505. Possibly the trendiest place in Florence during the summer months, full to bursting point with serious clubbers strutting their stuff to live music on three dance floors. *Closed Sun and Mon.*

**Jackie O**, Via dell'Erta Canina 24, t 055 234 2442. An old favourite for the 30ish crowd, including a piano bar. *Closed Mon, Tues and Wed.*

**Lido**, Lungarno Pecori Giraldi 1, t 055 234 2726. A small place in a pretty setting on the Arno, playing a wide variety of music to a mixed crowd. *Closed Mon.*

**Mago Merlino**, Via dei Pilastri 31r, **t** 055 242970. A relaxed tearoom/bar with live music, theatre, shows and games.

**Rex Café**, Via Fiesolana 23r, **t** 055 248 0331, *www.rexcafe.it*. The number one winter hotspot until Universale opened its doors, featuring an unusual decor, tapas, music and dancing. *Closed June–Aug.*

**Rio Grande**, Viale degli Olmi 1, **t** 055 331371, *www.riogrande.it*. A huge and hugely popular venue with an outside dance floor in summer. The music is mostly Latin. *Closed Mon exc. winter.*

**Tenax**, Via Pratese 46, **t** 055 308160, *www.tenax.org*. An ultra-trendy spot with live music out near the airport. *Closed Sun–Wed and mid-May–Sept.*

**Universale**, Via Pisana 77r, *www. universalefirenze.it* A vast ex-cinema, with designer decor, a restaurant, several bars and a pizzeria, all accompanied by live music and a giant cinema screen. Chic, sleek surroundings for a chic, sleek crowd; this is fast becoming the hottest hangout in town. *Closed Mon–Wed.*

⭐ **Teatro del Sale >**

**Teatro del Sale**, Via de Macci 111r, **t** 055 2001492, *www.teatrodelsale.com*. Part of the Cibreo empire, this is Fabio Picchi's stab at democracy. A private members' club (membership is €5 for visitors) where the food (an abridged version of that served in Cibreo across the road) is served buffet-style and costs just €15 for lunch and €30 for dinner for all you can eat, including wine and coffee. The price of dinner includes a show; after eating, everyone helps transform the room into a theatre where anyone from a tango duo to a chambre orchestra might be performing. *Closed Sun, Mon, Aug.*

## Pubs

Irish pubs are big in Florence, and you will also find the odd English and Scottish version too.

**The Fiddler's Elbow**, Piazza Santa Maria Novella 7r, **t** 055 215056. One of the original pubs in Florence, with some live music and an expat atmosphere. It's a handy place to wait for a train and has a terrace on the piazza, but otherwise it's a bit grim.

**James Joyce**, Lungarno B. Cellini 1r, **t** 055 658 0856. An Irish pub with literary pretensions, the James Joyce enjoys a pleasant location with a big garden near the river. Books and magazines are on hand for browsing.

**JJ Cathedral Pub**, Piazza San Giovanni 44r, **t** 055 280260. A pub sitting in the shadow of the Duomo, with an almost authentic atmosphere. The single table on the tiny terrace overlooking the cathedral itself is much sought-after.

**High Bar**, Via dei Renai 27a, **t** 055 234 7082. This little bar on the Oltrarno is the friendliest in town, with a terrace in the front, a garden out back and free Wi-fi. *Closed Sun and Sat during day.*

## Gay Clubs

There are a few gay clubs in Florence, including:

**Crisco**, Via Sant'Egidio 43r, **t** 055 248 0580. *Closed Tues.*

**Il Piccolo Café**, Borgo Santa Croce 23, **t** 055 200 1057. A minuscule, friendly, arty bar.

**Silver Stud**, Via della Fornace 9, **t** 055 688466, *www.silverstud.it*. A new bar in the Oltrano. *Closed Sun.*

**Tabasco**, Piazza Santa Cecilia 3r, **t** 055 213000, *www.tabascogay.it*. Italy's first gay bar, going since the 1970s.

## Summer Venues

A torrid Florentine summer evening is no time to sit indoors (unless there's air-conditioning), and in summer, nightlife in Florence moves out of doors, with a series of venues opening up between late May and mid-Sept in some of the city's squares and open spaces. These venues usually offer food and drink and some kind of live entertainment. Admission is usually free.

**Le Murate**, Via dell'Agnolo, **t** 338 506 0253. A venue taking over the courtyard of a former prison, offering music and dancing, food, drink, film and live music.

**Piazza Santissima Annunziata**. Live music and dance, plus a bar and pizzeria, against the incomparable backdrop of Brunelleschi's loggia.

**Le Rime Rampanti**. A great spot overlooking the river above Piazza Poggi, with a bar, snacks and live music and dancing.

# A City with a View

Great-Aunt Florence, with her dour complexion and severe, lined face, never was much of a looker from street level, but she improves with a bit of distance – either mental or from one of her hilltop balconies: the Belvedere Fort, San Miniato, Piazzale Michelangelo, Bellosguardo, Fiesole or Settignano.

## Belvedere Fort and Arcetri

One of Florence's best and closest balconies is the newly restored **Belvedere Fort**, a graceful six-point star designed by Buontalenti and built in 1590–95, not so much for the sake of defence but to remind any remaining Florentine republicans who was boss. Since 1958 it has been used for special exhibitions, but you can usually enjoy unforgettable views of Florence and the surrounding countryside from its ramparts. Leading up to it is one of Florence's prettiest streets, **Costa San Giorgio**, which begins in Piazza Santa Felicità, just beyond the Ponte Vecchio.

In this part of Florence, the countryside, a rolling landscape of villas and gardens, olives and cypresses, begins right at the city wall. Via San Leonardo winds its way out towards **Arcetri**; a 10-minute walk will take you to the 11th-century **San Leonardo in Arcetri**. There is a wonderful 13th-century pulpit here, originally built for San Pier Scheraggio, and a small rose window, which was made according to legend from a wheel of Fiesole's *carroccio*, captured by Florence in 1125.

*San Leonardo in Arcetri*
*usually open Sun mornings*

Half a kilometre further, past the Viale Galileo crossroads, Via San Leonardo changes its name to Via Viviani, where it passes the **astrophysical observatory** and **Torre del Gallo**. Another 1km further on, Via Viviani reaches the settlement of **Pian de' Giullari**, where Galileo spent the last years of his life, in the 16th-century **Villa il Gioiello**, virtually under house arrest after his encounter with the Inquisition in 1631. Milton is believed to have visited him here.

## San Miniato

*San Miniato*
*open Mon–Sat 8–7,*
*Sun 8–12.30 and 2–7*

From Porta San Miniato you can walk up to San Miniato church on the stepped Via di San Salvatore al Monte, complete with the Stations of the Cross, or take the less pious bus 13 up the scenic Viale dei Colli from the station or Via de Benci, near Ponte alle Grazie. High on its monumental steps, San Miniato's beautiful, distinctive façade can be spotted from almost anywhere in the city, although relatively few visitors take the time to actually visit what is in fact one of the finest Romanesque churches in Italy.

San Miniato was built in 1015, over an earlier church that marked the spot where the head of St Minias, a 3rd-century Roman soldier, bounced when the Romans axed it off. Despite its distance from

**Florence Environs**

N

5 km

2·5 miles

R. Ombrone

A11

Prato

Poggio a Caiano

Carmignano

Campi Bisenzio

SS66

Villa d'Artimino

Montelupo Fiorentino

To Pisa

Lastra a Signa

SS67

Signa

Firenze Signa

Arno

Settimello

Prato Calenzano

A11

Firenze Nord

AUTOSTRADA FIRENZE-MARE

Peretola

Peretola Airport

Quinto

Sesto Fiorentino

Cercina

Caldine

R. Mugnone

Villa Demidoff

Pratolino

Villa di Castello

Villa la Petraia

Villa Careggi

Castello

VIA BOLOGNESE

Fiesole

S. Domenico

Maiano

Settignano

Ponte a Mensola

Rovezzano

ARNO

S. Donato in Gollina

A1

Bagno a Ripoli

Nevoli

Firenze Nova

Rifredi

Stibbert Museum

Florence

Fortezza da Basso

Stazione Centrale

Ippodromo S. Pallai

Le Cascine

L'Isolotto

Vittoria

Bellosguardo

Ponte a Greve

Soffiano

Scandicci

Greve

Greve

Boboli Gardens

San Leonardo in Arcetri

Pian de' Giullari

Poggio Imperiale

Certosa del Galluzzo

Firenze Certosa

Campo di Marte

Stadio Comunale

Belvedere Fort

San Miniato

Gavinana

Badia a Ripoli

Ponte a Ema

Erna

AUTOSTRADA DEL SOLE

Firenze Sud

Grassina

Tavarnuzze

To Siena

Chiesanuova

T U S C A N Y

the centre, San Miniato has always been one of the churches dearest to Florentines' hearts. The remarkable geometric pattern of green, black and white marble that adorns its façade was begun in 1090, though funds only permitted the embellishment of the lower, simpler half of the front; the upper half, full of curious astrological symbolism (someone has written a whole book about it), was added in the 12th century, paid for by the Arte di Calimala, the guild that made a fortune buying bolts of fine wool, dyeing them a deep red or scarlet that no one else in Europe could imitate, then selling them back for twice the price; their proud gold eagle stands at the top of the roof. The glittering mosaic of Christ, the Virgin and St Minias came slightly later.

The Calimala was also responsible for decorating the interior, an unusual design with a raised choir built over the crypt. As the Calimala became richer, so did the fittings; the delicate intarsia marble floor of animals and zodiac symbols dates from 1207. The lower walls were frescoed in the 14th and 15th centuries, including an enormous St Christopher. At the end of the nave stands Michelozzo's unique, free-standing **Cappella del Crocifisso**, built in 1448 to hold the crucifix that spoke to St John Gualberto (now in Santa Trínita; see p.135); it is magnificently carved and adorned with terracottas by Luca della Robbia. Off the left nave is one of Florence's Renaissance showcases, the **chapel of the Cardinal of Portugal** (1461–6). The 25-year-old cardinal, a member of the Portuguese royal family, died in Florence at an auspicious moment, when the Medici couldn't spend enough money on publicly prominent art, and when some of the greatest artists of the quattrocento were at the height of their careers. The chapel was designed by Manetti, Brunelleschi's pupil; the ceiling exquisitely decorated with enamelled terracotta and medallions by Luca della Robbia; the cardinal's tomb beautifully carved by Antonio Rossellino; the frescoed *Annunciation* charmingly painted by Alesso Baldovinetti; the altarpiece *Three Saints* is a copy of the original by Piero Pollaiuolo.

Up the steps of the choir more treasures await. The marble transenna and pulpit were carved in 1207, with art and a touch of medieval humour. Playful geometric patterns frame the mosaic in the apse, *Christ between the Virgin and St Minias*, made in 1297 by artists imported from Ravenna, and later restored by Baldovinetti. The colourful **sacristy** on the right was entirely frescoed by Spinello Aretino in 1387 but made rather flat by subsequent restoration. In the **crypt** an 11th-century altar holds the relics of St Minias; the columns are topped by ancient capitals. The **cloister** has frescoes of the Holy Fathers by Paolo Uccello, remarkable works in painstaking and fantastical perspective, rediscovered in 1925. The monks sing magical Gregorian chant every afternoon at about 4pm.

The panorama of Florence from San Miniato is lovely to behold, but such thoughts were hardly foremost in Michelangelo's mind during the Siege of Florence. The hill was vulnerable, and to defend it he hastily erected the fortress (now surrounding the cemetery left of the church), placed cannons in the unfinished 16th-century campanile (built to replace one that fell over), and shielded the tower from artillery with mattresses. He grew fond of the small church below San Miniato, **San Salvatore al Monte**, built by Cronaca in the late 1400s; he called it his 'pretty country lass'.

With these associations in mind, the city named the vast, square terrace car park below **Piazzale Michelangelo**; this is the most popular viewpoint only because it's the only one capable of accommodating an unlimited number of tour buses (though now there are restrictions on the time buses are allowed to stop, the situation has improved a bit). On Sunday afternoons, crowds of Florentines habitually make a stop here during their afternoon *passeggiata*. Besides another copy of the *David* and a fun, tacky carnival atmosphere rampant with souvenirs, balloons and ice cream, the Piazzale offers views that can reach as far as Pistoia.

## Bellosguardo

Many people would argue that the finest view over Florence is from Bellosguardo, located almost straight up from Porta Romana at the end of the Boboli Gardens or Piazza Torquato Tasso. Non-mountaineers may want to take a taxi; the famous viewpoint, from where you can see every church façade in the city, is just before Piazza Bellosguardo. The area is a peaceful little oasis of superb villas and houses gathered round a square – there are no shops, bars or indeed anything commercial.

# Fiesole

Florence liked to regard itself as the daughter of Rome, and in its fractious heyday explained its quarrelsome nature by the fact that its population from the beginning was of mixed race, of Romans and 'that ungrateful and malignant people who of old came down from Fiesole', according to Dante. First settled in the 2nd millennium BC, it became the most important Etruscan city in the region. Yet from the start Etruscan Faesulae's relationship with Rome was rocky, especially after sheltering Catiline and his conspirators in 65 BC. Its lofty position made Fiesole too difficult to capture, so the Romans built a camp below on the Arno to cut off its supplies. Eventually Fiesole was taken, and it dwindled as the camp below grew into the city of Florence – growth the Romans encouraged to spite the old Etruscans on their hill. This easily defended hill, however, ensured Fiesole's survival in the Dark Ages.

When times became safer, families moved back down to the Arno to rebuild Florence. They returned to smash up most of Fiesole after defeating it in 1125; since then the little town has remained aloof, letting Florence dominate and choke in its own juices far, far below.

But ever since the days of the *Decameron*, whose storytellers retreated to its garden villas to escape the plague, Fiesole has played the role of Florence's aristocratic suburb; its cool breezes, beautiful landscapes and belvedere views make it the perfect refuge from the torrid Florentine summers. There's no escaping the tourists, however; we foreigners have been tramping up and down Fiesole's hill since the days of Shelley. A day-trip has become an obligatory part of a stay in Florence, and although Fiesole has proudly retained its status as an independent *comune*, you can make the 20-minute trip up on Florence city bus 7 from the station or Piazza San Marco. If you have the time, walk up (or, perhaps better, down) the old lanes bordered with villas and gardens to absorb some of the world's most civilized scenery.

## Around Piazza Mino

The long, sloping stage of Piazza Mino is Fiesole's centre, with the bus stop, the local tourist office, the cafés and the **Palazzo Pretorio**, its loggia and façade emblazoned with coats of arms. The square is named after a favourite son, the quattrocento sculptor Mino da Fiesole, whom Ruskin preferred to all others. An example of his work may be seen in the **Duomo**, with its plain façade dominating the north side of the piazza. Built in 1028, it was the only building spared by the vindictive Florentines in 1125. It was subsequently enlarged and given a scouring 19th-century restoration, leaving the tall, crenellated campanile its sole distinguishing feature. Still, the interior has an austere charm, with a raised choir over the crypt similar to San Miniato. Up the steps to the right are two works by Mino da Fiesole: the tomb of Bishop Leonardo Salutati and an altar front. The main altarpiece in the choir, *Madonna and Saints*, is by Lorenzo di Bicci, from 1440. Note the two saints frescoed on the columns; it was a north Italian custom to paint holy people as if they were members of the congregation. The crypt, with the remains of Fiesole's patron, St Romulus, is supported by columns bearing doves, spirals and other early Christian symbols.

**Museo Bandini**
*t 055 59477, www.comune.fiesole.fi.it; open April–Sept Wed–Mon 10–7, closed Tues; Oct Wed–Mon 10–6, closed Tues; Nov–Feb Thurs–Mon 10–4, closed Tues and Wed; Mar Wed–Mon 10–6, closed Tues; adm*

Located on Via Dupré, the **Bandini Museum** contains sacred works, including della Robbia terracottas and trecento paintings by Lorenzo Monaco, Neri di Bicci and Taddeo Gaddi.

**Area Archeologica**
*t 055 59477, www.fiesolemusei.it; open Mar–Oct Wed–Mon 9.30–6; Nov–Feb Wed–Mon 9.30–5; closed Tues*

## Archaeological Zone

Behind the cathedral and museum is the entrance to what remains of Faesulae. Because Fiesole avoided trouble in the Dark Ages, its Roman monuments have survived in much better shape

**Teatro Romano**
*open summer*
*daily 9.30–7; winter*
*Wed–Mon 9.30–6; adm*

than those of Florence; although hardly spectacular, the ruins are charmingly set amid olive groves and cypresses. The small **Roman theatre** has survived well enough to host plays and concerts in the summer; Fiesole would like to remind you that in ancient times it had the theatre and plays while Florence had the amphitheatre and wild beast shows. Close by are the rather confusing remains of two superimposed temples, the baths and an impressive stretch of Etruscan walls (best seen from Via delle Mure Etrusche, below) that proved their worth against Hannibal's siege.

**Museo Archeologico**
*open summer*
*daily 9.30–7; winter*
*Wed–Mon 9.30–6*

The **archaeology museum**, in a small 20th-century Ionic temple, has early bronze figurines with flapper wing arms, Etruscan urns and stelae, including the 'stele Fiesolana' with a banquet scene.

## Walking around Fiesole

From Piazza Mino, Via S. Francesco ascends steeply (at first) to the hill that served as the Etruscan and Roman acropolis. Halfway up is a terrace with extraordinary views of Florence and the Arno sprawl, with a monument to the three *carabinieri* who gave themselves up to be shot by the Nazis in 1944 to prevent them from taking civilian reprisals. The church nearby, the **Basilica di Sant'Alessandro**, was constructed over an Etruscan/Roman temple in the 6th century, reusing its lovely *cipollino* (onion marble) columns and Ionic capitals, one still inscribed with an invocation to Venus.

At the top of the hill, square on the ancient acropolis, stands the monastery of **San Francesco**, its church containing a famous early cinquecento *Annunciation* by Raffaellino del Garbo and an *Immaculate Conception* by Piero di Cosimo. A grab-bag of odds and ends collected from the four corners of the world, especially Egypt and China, is displayed in the quaint **Franciscan missionary museum** in the cloister; it also has an Etruscan collection.

**Museo Etnologico Missionario**
*open Tues–Fri*
*10–12 and 3–5,*
*Sat and Sun 3–5;*
*closed Mon*

There are much longer walks to be had along the hill behind the Palazzo Pretorio. Panoramic Via Belvedere leads back to Via Adriano Mari, and in a couple of kilometres to the bucolic **Montececeri**, a wooded park where Leonardo da Vinci performed his flight experiments, and where Florentine architects once quarried their dark *pietra serena* from quarries now abandoned but open for exploration. In Borgunto, as this part of Fiesole is called, there are two 3rd-century BC **Etruscan tombs** on Via Bargellino; east of Borgunto, scenic Via Francesco Ferrucci and Via di Vincigliata pass by Fiesole's castles, the **Castel di Poggio**, site of summer concerts, and the **Castel di Vincigliata**, dating back to 1031. Further down is American critic Bernard Berenson's famous **Villa I Tatti**, which he left, along with a collection of Florentine art, to Harvard University as the Centre of Italian Renaissance Studies.

The road continues down towards **Ponte a Mensola** (6km from Fiesole) and Settignano (*see* p.192), with buses back to Florence.

### San Domenico di Fiesole

San Domenico is a pleasant walk from Fiesole towards Florence down Via Vecchia Fiesolana, a steep, narrow road that passes the privately owned **Villa Medici** (Via Beato Angelico 2), constructed by Michelozzo for Cosimo il Vecchio; Lorenzo and his friends of the Platonic Academy would come here to escape the world within its lovely gardens, and it was also the childhood home of Iris Origo.

*Villa Medici*
*open by appt,*
*t 055 59417*

San Domenico, at the bottom of the lane, is where Fra Angelico first entered his monkish world. The church of **San Domenico** (15th century) contains his *Madonna with Angels and Saints*, in a chapel on the left, and a photograph of his *Coronation of the Virgin*, which the French snapped up in 1809 and sent to the Louvre. Across the nave there's a *Crucifixion* by the school of Botticelli, an unusual composition of verticals highlighted by the cypresses in the background. In the chapterhouse of the monastery (ring the bell at No.4) Fra Angelico left a fine fresco *Crucifixion* and a *Madonna and Child*, which is shown with its sinopia, before moving down to Florence and San Marco.

*Badia Fiesolana*
*open Mon–Fri 9–5,*
*Sat 9–12*

The lane in front of San Domenico leads to the **Badia Fiesolana**, Fiesole's cathedral, which was constructed in the 9th century by Fiesole's bishop, an Irishman named Donatus, and offers a fine view over the rolling countryside and Florence beyond. Although it was later enlarged, it preserves its original elegant façade, providing a charming example of the geometric black and white marble inlay decoration that characterizes Tuscan Romanesque churches, while the interior is adorned with *pietra serena* in the style of Brunelleschi. The ex-convent next door now houses the European University Institute.

## Settignano

The least touristy hill above Florence is beneath the village of Settignano (bus 10 from the station or Piazza San Marco). The road passes **Ponte a Mensola**, Boccaccio's childhood home; it is believed he set scenes of the *Decameron* at the Villa Poggio Gherardo. A Scottish Benedictine named Andrew founded its church of **San Martino a Mensola** in the 9th century and was later canonized. The church was rebuilt in the 1400s, and has three trecento works: Taddeo Gaddi's *Triptych*, his son Agnolo's paintings on St Andrew's casket, and high altar triptych by the school of Orcagna. Quattrocento works include Neri di Bicci's *Madonna and Saints* and an *Annunciation* by a follower of Beato Angelico.

Settignano is one of Tuscany's great cradles of sculptors, having produced Desiderio da Settignano and Antonio and Bernardo Rossellino; Michelangelo too spent his childhood here, at the

**Villa Buonarroti**. The curious thing is that they left behind no work as a reminder; the good art in **Santa Maria** church is by Andrea della Robbia (an enamelled terracotta *Madonna and Child*) and Buontalenti (the pulpit). However, there are more splendid views to be had from **Piazza Desiderio**, and a couple of decent places to quaff a glass of Chianti.

## Medici Villas

Like their Bourbon cousins in France, the Medici dukes whiled their time away acquiring new palaces for themselves, less as self-exaltation than as property speculation; they always thought generations ahead. As a result the countryside around Florence is littered with Medici villas, most now privately owned, though some are at least partly open to the public.

### Villa Careggi

**Villa Careggi**
*Viale Pieraccini 17,*
*(bus 14C from station);*
*open by appt,*
**t** *055 794 94612*

Perhaps the best-known of the villas is **Villa Careggi** ①, originally a fortified farmhouse but enlarged for Cosimo il Vecchio by Michelozzo in 1434. In the 1460s this villa became synonymous with the birth of humanism. The greatest Latin and Greek scholars of the day, Ficino, Poliziano, Pico della Mirandola and Argyropoulos, would sometimes meet here with Lorenzo il Magnifico and hold philosophical discussions in imitation of a Platonic symposium, calling their informal society the Platonic Academy. It fizzled out when Lorenzo died. Cosimo il Vecchio and Piero had both died at Careggi and, when he felt the end was near, Lorenzo had himself carried out to the villa, with Poliziano and Pico della Mirandola as company. After Lorenzo died, the villa was burned down by Florentine republicans, though Cosimo I later had it rebuilt, and Francis Sloane had it restored.

## Villa la Petraia

Villa la Petraia
*t 055 452 691/5007
210; open April, May
and Sept daily
8.15–6.30; June–Aug
daily 8.15–7.30; Nov–Feb
daily 8.15–4.30; Mar
and Oct daily 8.15–
5.30; exc 2nd and 3rd
Mon of month. It's hard
to reach: if you don't
have a car, take a
taxi or, if you are
adventurous, bus 28
from the station,
and get off after the
wastelands, by Via
Reginaldo Giuliano*

Further west, amid the almost continuous conurbation of power lines and industrial landscapes that blight the Prato road, **Villa la Petraia** ② remained Arcadian on its steeply sloping hill. It was bought by Grand Duke Ferdinando I in 1557 and rebuilt by Buontalenti, keeping the tower of the original castle intact. Unfortunately Vittorio Emanuele II liked it as much as the Medici, and redesigned it to suit his relentlessly bad taste. Still, the interior is worthwhile for its ornate Baroque court, frescoed with a pastel history of the Medici by 17th-century masters Volterrano and Giovanni di San Giovanni; Vittorio Emanuele II added the glass roof to use the space as a ballroom.

Of the remainder, you're most likely to remember the Chinese painting of Canton and the games room, with billiard tables as large as football fields and perhaps the world's first pinball machine, made of wood. A small room contains a most endearing statue by Giambologna, *Venus Wringing Water from Her Hair*. The villa was most recently owned by Harold Acton who arranged the collection on display here. It is now owned by New York University and there is a full programme of cultural events in the house and grounds.

La Petraia's beautiful gardens and grounds, shaded by ancient cypresses, are open in the afternoon.

## Villa di Castello

Villa di Castello
*t 055 454791;
from La Petraia, turn
right at Via di Castello
and walk about 450m;
open (gardens only)
April, May and Sept
daily 8.15–6.30;
June–Aug daily 8.15–
7.30; Nov–Feb daily
8.15–4.30; Mar and Oct
daily 8.15– 5.30; exc 2nd
and 3rd Mon of month*

One of Tuscany's most famous gardens is down from La Petraia, at **Villa di Castello** ③, bought in 1477 by Lorenzo di Pierfrancesco and Giovanni de' Medici, cousins of Lorenzo il Magnifico and Botticelli's best patrons, who hung it with his great mythological paintings now in the Uffizi. The villa was sacked in the 1530 siege then restored by Cosimo I; today it is the HQ of the Accademia della Crusca, dedicated to the study of the Italian language. The garden was laid out for Cosimo I by Tribolo, who also designed the fountain in the centre, with a statue, *Hercules and Antenaeus*, by Ammannati. Behind it is an artificial cavern, the **Grotto degli Animali**, filled by Ammannati and Giambologna with marvellous statues of every known creature, and lined with mosaics of pebbles and shells. The terrace above offers the best view over the garden's geometric patterns; a large statue by Ammannati of January, or *Gennaio*, emerges shivering from a pool among the trees.

A 20-minute walk north from Villa di Castello to **Quinto** are two unusual 7th-century BC **Etruscan tombs**. Neither has any art, but the chambers under their 25ft artificial hills bear an odd relationship with ancient cultures elsewhere in the Med – domed *tholos* tombs as in Mycenaean Greece, corbelled passages like the *navetas* of Majorca, and entrances that look like the sacred wells of Sardinia.

## Sesto Fiorentino

Museo di Doccia
*Via Pratese 31
(signposted); open
Sept–July Wed–Sat
10–1 and 2–6; other
days by appt; adm*

Change gear again by heading out a little further in the sprawl to Sesto Fiorentino, a suburb that since 1954 has been home to the famous Richard-Ginori china and porcelain firm. Founded in Doccia in 1735, the firm offers a neat chronological exhibition of its production of Doccia ware, including many Medici commissions (a ceramic *Venus de' Medici*), fine painted porcelain, and some pretty Art Nouveau works, at the **Doccia Museum**.

## Villa Demidoff at Pratolino

Villa Demidoff
*t 055 409427;
bus 25 leaves about
every 20mins from
Florence station;
open April–Sept
Thurs–Sun 10–7.30;
Mar and Oct Sun 10–6;
adm April–Sept
Sat and Sun*

It was to the village of Pratolino 12km north of Florence along Via Bolognese that Duke Francesco I bought the **Villa Demidoff** ④ in 1568 as a gift to his mistress, the Venetian Bianca Cappello. He commissioned Buontalenti – artist, architect and hydraulics engineer – to design the vast gardens, making Pratolino the marvel of its day, full of water tricks, ingenious automata and a famous menagerie. Sadly, none of Buontalenti's delights have survived, but the largest ever example of this play between art and environment has – Giambologna's massive *Appennino*, a giant rising from stone, part stalactite, part fountain himself, conquering the dragon, said to be symbolic of the Medici's origins in the Mugello just north of here. The rest of the park, made into an English garden by the Lorena family and named for Prince Paolo Demidoff who bought it in 1872 and restored Francesco's servants' quarters as his villa, is an invitingly cool refuge from a Florentine summer afternoon.

## Poggio a Caiano

Poggio a Caiano
*t 055 877012
CAP buses go past
every 30mins, departing
from in front of
McDonald's on north
side of Florence station;
open April, May and
Sept daily 8.15–5.30;
June–Aug daily
8.15–6.30; Nov–Feb
daily 8.15–3.30; Mar and
Oct daily 8.15–4.30;
exc 2nd and 3rd Mon
of month; adm*

Of all the Medici villas, **Poggio a Caiano** is the most evocative of the country idylls so delightfully described in the verses of Lorenzo il Magnifico; this was not only his favourite retreat but is generally considered the very first Italian Renaissance villa. Lorenzo bought a farmhouse here in 1480, and commissioned Giuliano da Sangallo to rebuild it in a classical style. It was Lorenzo's sole architectural commission, and its classicism matched the mythological nature poems he composed here, most famously 'L'Ambra', inspired by the stream Ombrone that flows nearby.

Sangallo designed the villa according to Alberti's description of the perfect country house in a style that presages Palladio, and added a classical frieze on the façade, sculpted with the assistance of Andrea Sansovino (now replaced with a copy). Some of the other features – the clock, the curved stair and central loggia – were later additions. In the interior Sangallo designed an airy, two-storey *salone*, which the two Medici popes had frescoed by 16th-century masters Pontormo, Andrea del Sarto, Franciabigio and Allori. The subject, as usual, is Medici self-glorification, and the frescoes depict family members dressed as Romans in historical scenes that parallel events in their lives. In the right lunette, around a large circular window, Pontormo painted the lovely *Vertumnus and Pomona* (1521), a languid summer scene under a willow tree, beautifully coloured. In another room, Francesco I and Bianca Cappello, his wife, died in 1587, only 11 hours apart; Francesco was always messing with poisons but in fact a nasty virus was the probable killer. In the grounds are fine old trees and a 19th-century statue celebrating Lorenzo's 'L'Ambra'.

## Carmignano and Villa Artimino

**San Michele**
*open daily 7.30–5 (until 6 in summer)*

A local bus continues 5km southwest of Poggio a Caiano to the village of **Carmignano**, which has, in its church of **San Michele**, Pontormo's uncanny painting *The Visitation* (1530s), a masterpiece of Florentine Mannerism. There are no concessions to naturalism here – the four soulful, ethereal women, draped in Pontormo's customary startling colours, barely touch the ground, standing before a scene as substantial as a stage backdrop. The result is one of the most unforgettable images produced in the 16th century.

**Tomba di Montefortini**
*t 055 44845222; open summer Fri and Sat 9–6; winter Mon–Sat 8–2*

Also to the south, at **Comeana** (3km, signposted), is the well-preserved Etruscan **Tomba di Montefortini**, a 7th-century BC burial mound, 35ft (10.5m) high and 260ft (79m) in diameter, covering two chambers. A long hall leads to the vestibule and tomb chamber, both covered with false vaulting; the latter preserves a shelf most probably used for gifts for the afterlife. Nearby, the equally impressive **Tomba dei Boschetti** was seriously damaged over centuries by local farmers.

**Villa Artimino**
*villa open for guided tours Tues, t 055 871 8124; museum open Feb–Oct Mon, Tues and Thurs–Sat 9.30–12.30, Sun 10–12, Wed by appt; Nov–Jan Sun 10–12, plus Thurs–Sat by appt; adm*

The Etruscan city of **Artimino**, 4km to the west, was destroyed by the Romans and is now the site of a small town and another Medici property, the **Villa Artimino** ('La Ferdinanda'), built as hunting lodge for Ferdinando I by Buontalenti. Its semi-fortified air with buttresses was aimed to fit its sporting purpose, but the total effect is simple and charming, with the long roofline punctuated by innumerable chimneys and a graceful stair, added in the 19th century from a drawing by the architect in the Uffizi. There is an **Etruscan archaeological museum** in the basement, containing findings from the tombs; among them a unique censer with two basins and a boat, bronze vases, and a red figured krater painted with initiation scenes, found in a 3rd-century tomb.

Also in Artimino is an attractive Romanesque church, **San Leonardo**, built of stones salvaged from earlier buildings.

## Poggio Imperiale and the Certosa del Galluzzo

**Villa di Poggio Imperiale**
*open Sept–July Wed by request, t 055 220151*

One last villa open for visits, the **Villa di Poggio Imperiale** ⑤, lies south of Florence, at the summit of Viale del Poggio Imperiale, which leaves Porta Romana with a stately escort of cypress sentinels. Cosimo I grabbed this huge villa from the Salviati family in 1565, and it remained a ducal property until there were no longer any dukes to duke. Its neoclassical façade was added in 1808, and the audience chamber was decorated in the 17th century by the underrated Rutilio Manetti and others. Much of the villa is now used as a girls' school.

**Certosa del Galluzzo**
*open summer Tues–Sun 9–11 and 3–6; winter Tues–Sun 9–11 and 3–5*

The **Certosa del Galluzzo** (also known as the Certosa di Firenze) lies further south, scenically located on a hill off the Siena road (take bus 36 or 37 from the station). Founded as a Carthusian monastery by 14th-century tycoon Niccolò Acciaiuoli, it has been inhabited since 1958 by Cistercians; there are 12 now living there, one of whom takes visitors around. The Certosa has a fine 16th-century courtyard and an uninteresting church, though the crypt-chapel of the lay choir contains some impressive tombs. The **Chiostro Grande**, surrounded by the monks' cells, is decorated with 66 majolica *tondi* of prophets and saints by Giovanni della Robbia and assistants; one cell is opened for visits, and it seems almost cosy. The Gothic **Palazzo degli Studi**, intended by the founder as a school, contains five lunettes by Pontormo, painted while he and his pupil Bronzino hid out here from the plague in 1522.

## Where to Stay around Florence

(i) **Fiesole >**
*Via Portigiani 3, t 055 598720 or t 055 597 8373, www. comune.fiesole.fi.it*

(★) **Villa San Michele >**

### Fiesole ✉ 50014

Many frequent visitors to Florence wouldn't stay anywhere else: it's cooler and quieter here, and at night the city far below twinkles as if made of fairylights.

\*\*\*\*\***Villa San Michele**, Via Doccia 4, t 055 567 8200, *www.villasanmichele. orient-express.com* (€€€€€). A hotel built as a monastery in the 15th century, and an unbeatable choice if money happens to be no object, set in a breathtaking location just below Fiesole, with a façade and loggia reputedly designed by Michelangelo himself. After suffering bomb damage during the Second World War, it was carefully reconstructed to create one of the most beautiful hotels in Italy, set in a lovely Tuscan garden, complete with a pool. Each of its 46 rooms is richly and elegantly furnished and air-conditioned; the more plush suites have Jacuzzis. The food is delicious, and the reasons to go down to Florence begin to seem insignificant; a stay here is complete in itself. Paradise, however, comes at a price. *Closed 19 Nov–21 Mar.*

\*\*\*\***Villa Aurora**, Piazza Mino 39, t 055 59363, *www.villaaurora.net* (€€€€). An agreeable 19th-century villa right on Fiesole's famous piazza, from where the no.7 bus whisks you down to central Florence in 20mins. The 25 air-conditioned bedrooms have rustic antiques and splendid views over the city, but some of the bathrooms are poky. There is a restaurant – on a terrace overlooking Florence in the summer – and the bar next door (noisy at times) is under the same ownership. There's parking too.

\*\*\*\***Villa Fiesole**, Via Beato Angelico 35, t 055 597252, *www.villafiesole.it* (€€€€). Once part of the San Michele convent, this hotel shares part of its driveway with the hotel of the same name. The smart, neoclassical-style interiors are variations on a fresh blue and yellow colour scheme. Light meals are served in a sunny dining room or on the terrace, and there is a fabulous pool with views. The facilities (and prices) here are decidedly four-star.

\*\*\***Pensione Bencistà**, Via Benedetto di Maiano 4, t 055 59163, *www.*

bencista.com (€€€). Another former monastery with views from its flower-decked terrace that are every bit as good as those at Villa San Michele; the welcome is more friendly. The bedrooms, each different from the next, are all comfortably furnished with solid antiques. The three little sitting rooms are inviting in cooler weather when fires are lit. Half- and full-board is available for a reasonable price. Credit cards are not accepted.

**Le Cannelle**, Via Gramsci 52–6, **t** 055 597 8336, *www.lecannelle.com* (€€). A friendly B&B run by two sisters on the main street. Rooms are comfortably rustic and there is a pretty breakfast room.

*****Villa Baccano**, Via Bosconi 4, **t** 055 59341, *www.villabaccano.it* (€). A villa in the hills 2km out of the centre of Fiesole, in a lovely garden setting.

*****Villa Sorriso**, Via Gramsci 21, **t** 055 59027, *www.albergovillasorriso.com* (€). An unpretentious, comfortable hotel in the centre of Fiesole, with a terrace overlooking Florence.

**Camping Panoramico Fiesole**, Via Peramonda 1, **t** 055 599069, *www.florencecamping.com*. A beautifully situated campsite just above Fiesole on a hill with fabulous views over Florence, but packed and expensive in summer.

## Villas in the Florentine Hills

If you're driving, you may consider lodging outside the city, where parking is hassle-free and the summer heat is less intense.

### Luxury (€€€€€)
******Grand Hotel Villa Cora**, Viale Machiavelli 18–20, **t** 055 271840, *www.villacora.it*. An opulent 19th-century mansion set in a beautiful formal garden overlooking the Oltrarno, near Piazzale Michelangelo. Built by Baron Oppenheim, it later served as the residence of the wife of Napoleon III, Empress Eugénie. Its conversion to a hotel has dimmed little of its splendour; some of the bedrooms boast frescoed ceilings and lavish 19th-century furnishings, and all are air-conditioned and have *frigo-bars*, and there's a pretty swimming pool. In the summer, meals are served in the garden, and there's a fine view of Florence from the roof terrace. Wi-fi access is available.

******Villa La Massa**, Via della Massa 24, **t** 055 62611, *www.villalamassa.com*. A lovely choice, up the Arno some 6km from Florence at Candeli. This is the former 15th-century villa of Count Giraldi, and it retains the old dungeon (which now houses one of the two restaurants), the family chapel (now a bar), and other early Renaissance amenities, with modern features such as tennis courts, a swimming pool, a beauty salon and air-conditioning. The recently refurbished interiors are fit for a Renaissance princeling, and there's dining and dancing by the Arno in the summer, a shady garden, and a hotel bus to whizz you into the city. The food is excellent.

*****Torre di Bellosguardo**, Via Roti Michelozzi 2, **t** 055 229 8145, *www.torrebellosguardo.com*. A tower built at Bellosguardo in the 15th century, plus a villa added later, enjoying one of the most breathtaking views over the city. The tower was purchased by the Cavalcanti, friends of Dante, and the villa added below it; after that, Cosimo I confiscated it, the Michelozzi purchased it from the Medici, Elizabeth Barrett Browning wrote about it, and finally, in 1988, it opened its doors as a small hotel. There are frescoes by Baroque master Poccetti in the entrance hall, and fine antiques adorn the rooms, each of which is unique and fitted out with a modern bath. The large, beautiful terraced garden has a pool. For a splurge, reserve the two-level tower suite, with fabulous views in four directions. Superb formal gardens look down to the city below, and lunch is served around the pool. Food and wine courses are also organized.

### Very Expensive (€€€€)
*****Paggeria Medicea**, Viale Papa Giovanni XXIII, Artimino, near Carmignano, **t** 055 875141, *www.artimino.com*. The refurbished outbuildings of Grand Duke Ferdinando's villa, where you can play the Medici. It offers some unusual amenities – a hunting reserve and a

lake stocked with fish, and a farm producing oil and wine. There's also a pool and tennis court, and many of the pleasant modern rooms have balconies (all are air-conditioned). There are some apartments. A short walk across the gardens brings you to the restaurant **Biagio Pignatta**, which specializes in Medici dishes, in the former butcher's quarters.

****Villa Le Rondini**, Via Vecchia Bolognese 224, **t** 055 400081, *www. villalerondini.it*. Several buildings in a pleasant setting 7km north of Florence, surrounded by olive and cypress trees. The most interesting rooms are in the 16th-century villa. There is a very pleasant swimming pool. Full- and half-board are available; the restaurant specializes in central Italian recipes.

***Villa Villoresi**, Via Campi 2, Colonnata di Sesto Fiorentino, **t** 055 443212, *www.villavilloresi.it*. Contessa Cristina Villoresi's family home, forming a lovely oasis in the middle of one of Florence's more unlovely suburbs. It hasn't been too pristinely restored, retaining much of its slightly faded appeal as well as its frescoed ceilings, antiques and chandeliers. The villa boasts the longest loggia in Tuscany, to which five of the grandest bedrooms have direct access. Other rooms are a good deal plainer and somewhat cheaper. There is a pool and a restaurant serving Tuscan cuisine.

**Villa Poggio San Felice**, Via S. Matteo Arcetri 24, **t** 055 220016, *www. villapoggiosanfelice.com*. A delightful alternative to city hotels – a 15th-century villa on a hill just south of Porta Romana, near the observatory, offering bed and breakfast. It was once owned by a Swiss hotel magnate, whose descendants have restored the house and gardens (designed by Porcinaie) and opened them up to guests. There are five double bedrooms, all furnished with family antiques, and all with stunning views. There is also a small pool, and a bus service to and from Florence. *Closed Dec–Feb*.

### Expensive (€€€)

***Hermitage**, Via Gineparia 112, Bonistallo, **t** 055 877085, *www. hotel hermitageprato.it*. A fine, quiet, affordable choice for families, several miles from Florence, near Poggio a Caiano. There's a pool in the grounds and air-conditioned rooms.

# Eating Out around Florence

**Bibé**, Via delle Bagnese 1r, **t** 055 204 9085 (€€€€). An old farmhouse with a lovely garden a couple of kilometres south of Porta Romana. Try the *pappardelle* with rabbit sauce, *ribollita*, lasagne with artichokes and *caciocavallo* cheese; grilled guinea fowl; or grilled chicken. Desserts here are creative and divine. They also sell local products. *Closed Wed, Thurs lunch, 3wks Nov, 3wks Feb*.

**Biagio Pignatta**, Artimino, near Carmignano, **t** 055 875 1406 (€€€). A place near the Medici villa in Artimino, named after a celebrated Medici chef, serving Tuscan dishes with a Renaissance flavour, using products directly from the farm. The terrace overlooks vines and olives. Book ahead. *Closed Wed, and Thurs lunch in winter, plus 3wks Nov*.

**Centanni** Via Centanni 8, Bagno a Ripoli, **t** 055 630122 (€€€). A spot east of Florence, set in an olive grove, with a lovely terrace. Dishes are along traditional lines – home-made pasta with pigeon or wild boar sauce, *bistecca*, chicken or brains – and there is an excellent 400-strong wine list. *Closed Sat and Sun eve, and Mon*.

**Da Delfina**, Via della Chiesa, Artimino, near Carmignano, **t** 055 871 8074 (€€€). A place worth the drive out for its enchanting surroundings, lovely views, charming atmosphere and sublime Tuscan cooking, including home-made tagliatelle with a sauce made from greens, risotto with vegetables, and rabbit with olives and pine nuts. There's outdoor seating. Only cash is accepted, and booking is advisable. *Closed Mon, and 3wks Aug*.

**Omero**, Via Pian de' Giuliari 11r, t 055 220053 (€€€). A rustic restaurant a 10min taxi ride from the centre of town, the main attraction of which is the wonderful view from the picture windows, over hills dotted with elegant villas, olive groves and cypresses – make sure you get a table in the top room. The typically Tuscan food is reliable without being exceptional, and the atmosphere is old-fashioned. *Closed Tues*.

# Entertainment around Florence

**Scuola di Musica di Fiesole**, Villa la Torraccia, San Domenico, Fiesole, t 055 597851, *www. scuolamusica.fiesole.fi.it*. One of the best-known music schools in Italy, which promotes a series of chamber music concerts.

# Chianti and the Mugello

*Chianti to the south and the Mugello to the north of Florence, one world-famous region and one obscure, are delightfully rural and endowed with every Tuscan charm. No Brunelleschi could have designed the grand stone farmhouses that crown every hill, offering endless variations of arches, loggias and towers, amidst an equally endless variety of rolling hills, vineyards, olives and cypresses. Towns are few, monuments scattered and of minor interest, paintings and sculpture very rare. But you'll find few places more enchanting to explore – by car, by bicycle, by foot – in a day or a lifetime.*

# 08

## Don't miss

⭐ **Wine-tasting**
Around Greve in Chianti
**p.211**

⭐ **Quattrocento charms**
Castellina in Chianti
**p.211**

⭐ **The Iron Baron's castle**
Castello di Brolio **p.214**

⭐ **Breathtaking views**
Passo della Futa **p.217**

⭐ **A Florentine outpost in the Mugello**
Scarperia **p.218**

*See map overleaf*

# Chianti and the Mugello

N

10 km
5 miles

Montecarelli · Marradi

Dovadola · Predappio
Predappio Alta
Rocca San Casciano

Barberino di Mugello
Scarperia
S. Piero a Sieve
Borgo S. Lorenzo

Portico di Romagna

EMILIA-ROMAGNA

Vaiano

Santa Sofia

Prato

M. Senario

Pratolino
Sesto Fiorentino

Campi Bisenzio

Signa

Florence
Fiesole
Scandicci
Pontassieve

S. Godenzo

Alpe di San Benedetto
M. Falterona
Pso. d. Calla

Stia
Pratovecchio

Bagno di Romagna

Badia Prataglia

S. Donato in Collina

M. Secchieta
M. Penna

S. Polo in Chianti
Strada in Chianti
Incisa in Val d'A.

Poppi
Bibbiena

Cerbaia
S. Casciano in Val di Pesa
Mercatale in Val di Pesa

Castelfranco di Sopra

Caprese Michelangelo

TUSCANY

Greve in Chianti

Subbiano

Tavarnelle in Val di Pesa
Barberino Val d'Elsa

S. Donato in Poggio

S. Giovanni Valdarno

Castiglion Fibocchi

Pietrafitta
Radda in Chianti
Badia Coltibuono

Montevarchi

Poggibonsi

Castellina in Chianti

Arezzo

Colle di Val d'Elsa

Ambra

Civitella in Val Chiana

Foce di Scopetone

Monteriggioni

Cast. di Brolio

Siena

p.222
p.358
p.382
p.406

Prato Monti d. Calvana

R. Bisenzio
R. Mugnone
R. Sieve
R. Pesa
R. Greve
R. Elsa
R. Arbia

Casentino
Pratomagno
R. Arno
Monti del Chianti

# Don't miss

① Greve in Chianti p.211

② Castellina in Chianti p.211

③ Castello di Brolio p.214

④ Passo della Futa p.217

⑤ Scarperia p.218

SLOVENIA
CROATIA
BOSNIA-HERZ.

Corsica

ITALY

Sardinia

Sicily

# Chianti

08

*From good Chianti, an aged wine, majestic and imperious, that passes through my heart and chases away without trouble every worry and grief...*

Francesco Redi, *Bacchus in Tuscany*

In the 17th century, naturalist and poet Francesco Redi was the first to note the virtues of 'Florentine red' from Chianti; since then Italians have invested a lot of worry into defining what 'Chianti' means. The name apparently derives from an Etruscan family named Clanti; geographically it refers, roughly, to the hilly region between Florence and Siena, bordered by the Florence–Siena Superstrada del Palio and the A1 from Florence to Arezzo. The part within Siena province is known as *Chianti Storico* or *Chianti Geografico*, once the territories of the Lega del Chianti, a consortium of barons formed in 1385 to protect their interests (and their wine).

But Chianti is an oenological as well as a geographical name, and, as such, first became official in 1716, when Grand Duke Cosimo III defined which parts of Tuscany could call their vintage Chianti, in effect making wine history – it was the first time a wine had its production area delimited. The Lorraine grand dukes promoted advances in wine-making techniques and the export of Chianti.

Yet the Chianti as we know it had yet to be developed, and it was largely the creation of one man – the 'Iron Baron', Bettino Ricasoli, briefly the second PM of unified Italy. The baron was very wealthy but not handsome, and Luigi Barzini, in *The Italians*, recounts how jealous he became when his new bride was asked to dance at a ball. Without ado, he ordered her into their carriage and told the driver to take her to the ancient family seat at Brolio in the Monti del Chianti – an isolated castle the poor woman rarely left ever after.

To pass the time the baron began to experiment with different vines and processes, eventually hitting upon a pleasing mix of red sangiovese and canaiolo grapes, with a touch of white malvasia. Meanwhile, the famous dark green flask , the *strapeso*, was invented, with its straw covering woven by local women. The end product took the Paris Exhibition of 1878 by storm; imitators soon appeared and, in 1924, the boundaries of Chianti Storico were more than doubled to create Chianti Classico, drawn by local producers to protect the wine's name, adopting the now familiar black cockerel as its symbol. In 1967 Chianti Classico, with Tuscany's six other Chianti vinicultural zones, was given its *denominazione di origine* status. Production soared, but quality and sales declined. To improve it, the Chianti Classico Consortium was upscaled to a DOCG rating to guarantee that all wines bearing the black cockerel would be tested and approved by a panel of judges.

But it was tales of Elizabeth Barrett Browning quaffing Chianti and finding her inspiration in its ruby splendour, as well as the sunny rural elegance of the region, that attracted first the English and Dutch, then Swiss, Americans, French and Germans, especially in the 1960s and 1970s; they form one of Italy's densest foreign

Prato

M. Senario
Bivigliano
Dicomano

Pratolino

R. Magnone

Florence

R. Sieve
Rufina

Fiesole

Pontassieve

Signa

Pelago

Pso. d.
Consuma

Scandicci

Bagno a Ripoli

Saltino
Vallombrosa
M. Secchieta

S. Donato
in Collina

Grassina

Rignano sull' Arno

Chiesanuova
Tavarnuzze

R. Pesa
Cerbaia

Impruneta

S. Andrea in
Percussina

S. Polo in Chianti

S. Casciano in Val di Pesa

Strada
in Chianti
Incisa in Val d'A.

R. Greve

Mercatale in
Val di Pesa

Cintoia

Bargino

Vicchiomaggio

Figline Vald.

Montefiridolfi

Verrazzano

TUSCANY

Passignano

Greve in Chianti

Tavarnelle
in Val di Pesa

Vignamaggio

S. Giovanni
Valdarno
Conv. Montecarlo

Barberino
Val d'Elsa

Montagliari

Panzano

Terranuova
Bracciolini

Cavriglia

S. Donato
in Poggio

Montevarchi

Granaio

Pietrafitta

Badia
Coltibuono

Rendola

Poggibonsi

Radda in
Chianti

Gaiole in Chianti

Castellina
in Chianti

Meleto

Staggia

Ambra

Colle di
Val d'Elsa

Cast. di Brolio

Monteriggioni

Quercegrossa

Osservanza

Castelnuovo
Berardenga

Siena

Monteaperti

Montecchio

Pievina

N

10 km
5 miles

## Getting around Chianti

Getting around by **bus** is fairly easy in Chianti, though you may not always find connections between towns very convenient; from Florence, SITA buses (**t** 055 47821, *www.sitabus.it*) go to Greve (25km/45mins), Gaiole (55km/90mins), Castellina in Chianti (44km/1hr), Mercatale, S. Casciano in Val di Pesa (17km/25mins), Tavarnelle Val di Pesa (29km/40mins), Panzano, Strada, and Radda (42km/1hr); CAP buses run frequently from Florence to Impruneta (14km/20mins). From Siena TRA-IN buses (**t** 0577 204111, *www.trainspa.it*) go to Castellina (20km/25mins), Radda (30km/40mins), Tavarnelle (38km/50mins) and S. Casciano (49km/90mins), Tavarnuzze and Strada.

The two main north–south routes through Chianti, the old Roman Via Cassia (SS2) and the Chiantigiana (SS222), rival one another in beauty. An ideal **motoring wine tour** would take in the east–west SS429 between the Badia a Coltibuono and Castellina. The distances aren't very great, though the single-lane winding routes make for fairly leisurely travel.

colonies, wryly nicknamed 'Chianti-shire'. The newcomers brought more money than Chianti's mouldering barons and *contessas* had seen since the Renaissance; property prices shot to the moon.

But just when this enchanting region was getting ready to nod off, a small band of wine-makers, looking towards Bordeaux and thinking their wines could be just as good, started to break the DOCG rules. Planting cabernet sauvignon, cabernet franc and merlot in Chianti was heresy enough, but in the early 1970s two estates began selling with them as *vino da tavola* (although hardly at *vino da tavola* prices): Tenuta San Guido's Sassicaia (75% cabernet sauvignon, 25% cabernet franc) and Antinori's Tiganello (80% sangiovese and 20% cabernet sauvignon). The Super-Tuscan revolution was born, and Chianti, instead of retiring, has become one of the hottest wine regions in Europe.

Some 800 farms and estates (only a selection of the most historic are listed in this chapter) produce wine in the 70,000 hectares of the Chianti Classico zone, and one of the chief pleasures is trying as many labels as possible – with the different mixtures of grapes, different soils and bottling methods, each should be, or at least strives to be, individual. Nor do estates limit themselves to Chianti; many produce *vin santo*, a white called Bianca della Lega, and many reds, as well as Chianti's other speciality, a delicate olive oil. Before setting out to any of them, call to check hours.

# Western Chianti:
# Florence to Tavarnelle Val di Pesa

Chianti begins 10km to the south of Florence, but on the way there you may want to follow the sign west off the SS222 just past the *autostrada*, to get to **Ponte a Ema** and the prettily sited 14th-century chapel of the Alberti, **Santa Caterina dell'Antella**, with its contemporary frescoes on St Catherine's life, one of Spinello Aretino's greatest works.

**Santa Caterina dell'Antella**
*open Mon–Sat*

Further along, at Grassina, there's a turn-off to **Impruneta**, a large town on a plateau noted for its terracotta tiles (including those on Brunelleschi's dome) and pottery, which is very much on sale, especially during St Luke's horse and mule fair in October. The fair takes place in the main piazza, in the shadow of Impruneta's pride and joy, the **Collegiata**, built to house a miraculous icon of the *Madonna and Child* attributed to St Luke, dug up by a team of oxen in the 10th century. After the Collegiata was bombed in the last war, restorers brought it back to its Renaissance appearance to match its two beautiful chapels, both designed by Michelozzo and richly decorated with enamel terracottas by Luca della Robbia. One houses the icon and the other a piece of the True Cross. In an adjacent chapel is a marble relief, the *Finding of the Icon*, by the school of Donatello; the bronze crucifix in the nave is attributed to Giambologna. The campanile dates from the 13th century, and the fine portico from 1634. Among the many terracotta shops, **Artenova** has creative designs and a good selection of gifts.

**Artenova**
*Via della Fonte 76,*
*t 055 201 1060*

## Macchiavelli in Exile, and Artistic Links

From the SS222 south of Florence, a byroad leads west from Tavarnuzze (8km) to **Sant'Andrea in Percussina**, long the country fief of the Macchiavelli. Here Niccolò spent his tedious exile, which he described in a letter as whiling away the day in his tavern 'playing at *cricca* and tric-trac, and this gave rise to a thousand arguments and endless exchanges of insults, most of the time there is a fight over a penny... and so surrounded by these lice, I blow the cobwebs from my brain and relieve the unkindness of my fate'. In the evening he would retire to work on *The Prince*. You can still eat and drink in the tavern (*see* opposite) and there's a small museum devoted to his life.

Near Chiesanuova, to the north, the 16th-century **Palazzo al Bosco**, attributed by some to Michelangelo, is a villa built atop a 13th-century structure. The stately, theatrical 15th-century **Villa Tattoli** to the west (on the Chiesanuova–Cerbaia road) features two levels of arcades.

**Villa Talente**
*t 055 825 9484,*
*www.villatalente.it;*
*call for opening hrs*

Near Cerbaia, 5km from San Casciano, **Villa Talente** is the former property of the artists who built Orsanmichele in Florence; you can buy Chianti, white wine and olive oil there.

## Where to Stay and Eat in Western Chianti

For Villa la Massa in Candeli and Centanni in Bagno a Ripoli, *see* p.198 and p.199 respectively.

In this part of Chianti, hotels tend to be on the small side and annexed to restaurants.

It's worth knowing that many of the larger wine estates let a few guestrooms or apartments.

ⓘ **Impruneta >>**
*Piazza Buondelmonti*
*29, t 055 231 3729, www.*
*proimpruneta.rtd.it*

### Impruneta ✉ 50023
**B&B Benedetta Bianchi**, Via Paolieri 26, t 055 231 2558, *www.bed-breakfast-bianchi.it* (€€). A spacious B&B located just off the main piazza, offering

well-furnished rooms and mini-apartments, and boasting lovely views over the hills.

**I Falciani**, Via Cassia 245, t 055 237 3298 (€€). A rustic, casual place full of locals, serving tasty *crostini*, *ribollita*, a hunters' roast-meat platter in autumn, pizza and home-made pasta. Booking is advised.

### Località I Falciani ✉ 50029

**Il Ciliegiolo**, Via Chiantigiana 22, t 055 232 6327 (€€). Sturdy dishes such as *rognone al ginepro* (kidneys with juniper) and *tagliolini* with truffles. Booking is required. *Closed Mon*.

### Tavarnuzze ✉ 50029

***Villa Ambrosina**, Via Montebuoni, t 055 202 0491, www.lavallombrosina.it

(€€€). A comfortable option with panoramic views of the Florence hills. Breakfast is included in the rates.

****Gli Scopeti**, Via Cassia 193, t 055 202 2666 (€€). Decent accommodation for the budget-conscious.

### Sant'Andrea in Percussina ✉ 50029

**Albergaccio di Machiavelli**, t 055 828471 (€€). A restaurant in Machiavelli's own tavern (*see* opposite), literally the 'nasty little inn'. Now owned by the Conti Serristori Wine Company, it serves simple Tuscan meals – try the refreshing *panzanella* in summer – and fine wines from the estate. You can also buy bottles to take home. *Closed Mon and Tues*.

# Along the Via Cassia (SS2)

Up-to-date **San Casciano in Val di Pesa**, 17km south of Florence, is the largest and busiest town in Chianti. Long an outpost of Florence, it suffered numerous vicissitudes until its walls were begun by the ill-fated Duke of Athens in 1342. Within these, near the gateway, the church of **Santa Maria del Prato** (1335) has retained its trecento interior and trecento art: a fine pulpit by Giovanni Balducci da Pisa, a pupil of Andrea Pisano, a crucifix attributed to Simone Martini, a triptych by Ugolino di Neri, and framed paintings on the pilasters by Giotto's pupil, Taddeo Gaddi.

**Museo di Arte Sacra**
*open summer Sat 9–12 and 5–7, Sun 10–12.30 and 5–7.30; winter Sat 4–7, Sun 10–12.30 and 4–7*

The **Museum of Sacred Art** includes the *Madonna and Child* that is considered the first work of Ambrogio Lorenzetti.

Around San Casciano, Florentine merchants and noblemen dotted the countryside with villas, including the late Renaissance **Fattoria Le Corti**, 2km east on the Mercatale road, owned by the princely Corsini family for the past six centuries and selling its own Chianti; and the 17th-century **Poggio Torselli**, just off the SS2, approached through a long avenue of cypresses and surrounded by a lovely garden.

**Fattoria Le Corti**
*t 055 829 9301; call for opening hrs*

## Mercatale, Bargino and Barberino Val d'Elsa

**Mercatale**, 5km east of San Casciano, grew up around its *mercato* (market), protected in the old days by the castle of the Florentine bishops but now a ruin fit only to protect the odd lizard.

More muscular, just east on the road to Passo dei Pecorai, is the **Castello di Greve**, bound by four round towers. The Bardi put it up in the 11th century, before they moved to Florence and founded the greatest pre-Medici bank. It sells its Chianti, *vin santo* and olive oil.

**Castello di Greve**
*t 055 821 101; tastings and lunches by appt*

Other villas worth visiting near Mercatale are Villa Caserotta, once property of the Strozzi, and the fortified Villa Palagio, on the Mercatale–Campoli–Montefiridolfi road, adapted from a 14th-century castle. The Mercatale–Panzano road will bring you to **La Torre a Luciana**, an unspoiled medieval hamlet once belonging to the Pitti family.

**Castello di Bibbione**
*t 055 8 24 92 31, www. castellodibibbione.com*

The Via Cassia, between San Casciano and Bargino, passes the ancient **castle of Bibbione**, once residence of the Buondelmonte family, who owned much of this territory in the days when they were throwing fat on the Guelph and Ghibelline fires in Florence. It has some apartments to rent.

Near **Bargino**, in the same bellicose spirit, is the impressive fortified hamlet of **Montefiridolfi**, just east of the Via Cassia. This road, meanwhile, rolls south through lovely hills towards **Tavarnelle Val di Pesa**, of mostly 19th-century origin, and medieval **Barberino Val d'Elsa**, with some Etruscan finds in the town hall and a good 10th-century Romanesque church, the Pieve di Sant'Appiano.

From here the Via Cassia continues to **Poggibonsi** (*see* pp.361–2), with a possible detour to **La Paneretta**, a sturdy 15th-century fort amid olive groves, with Baroque frescoes inside.

## Where to Stay and Eat along the Via Cassia

Most of the area's accommodation is in this area, as are some of Chianti's best restaurants.

### Cerbaia ✉ 50026

**La Tenda Rossa**, Piazza del Monumento 9/14, **t** 055 826132 (€€€€). A family-run shrine to *haute cuisine*, offering four tasting menus and particularly good home-made pasta. Try the wonderful *cappelletti* soup with dried cod; lamb with lard and peas; and tuna with saffron and basil. The wine list has some superb bottles. Booking is strongly advised. *Closed Sun, Mon lunch and Aug.*

(i) **San Casciano in Val di Pesa >**
*Piazza della Repubblica, t 055 822 9558, www.comune.san-casciano-val-di-pesa.fi.it*

⭐ **Villa il Poggiale >**

⭐ **La Trattoria del Pesce >>**

### San Casciano ✉ 50026

***Villa il Poggiale**, Via Empolese 69, **t** 055 828311, *www.villailpoggiale.it* (€€€). A lovely Renaissance villa overlooking a cypress-bordered lawn, with elegant rooms, some with four-posters, and a good pool. Great value, it feels like a grand but unstuffy private country home. Breakfasts (included) are hearty. Half-board is available, or there are self-catering apartments.

***Antica Posta**, Piazza Zannoni 1/3, **t** 055 822313, *www.anticaposta-chianti.it* (€€). Simple but comfortable rooms and a restaurant (€€€€–€€€) offering inviting Tuscan flavours: try the home-made potato dumplings with tomato sauce; grilled *filet mignon* with balsamic vinegar sauce; and fresh cream pudding in a wild berry sauce. *Closed Tues.*

**Nello**, Via IV Novembre 66, **t** 055 820163 (€€). Its simple decor belies its fashionability – Florentines flock here for Tuscan staples such as *ribollita* pasta with *funghi porcini* and beef braised in Chianti Classico, and a good wine list. *Closed Wed eve and Thurs.*

### Bargino ✉ 50024

***Bargino**, Via Cassia 122, **t** 055 824 9055 (€). Seven rooms in a garden along the old Roman road, with an excellent fish restaurant, **La Trattoria del Pesce** (€€). Breakfast is included.

### Mercatale ✉ 50026

***Hotel Paradise**, Piazza V. Veneto 28, **t** 055 821327, *www.hotelparadise.it* (€€). Simple rooms with TVs and kettles.

**Il Salotto del Chianti**, Via Sonnino 92, **t** 055 821 4429 (€€). A well-established spot on the local culinary scene – the

**ⓘ Barberino Val d'Elsa >>**
*Via Cassia 31a,* **t** *055 807 5622, www. barberinovaldelsa.net; closed Nov–Mar*

*ravioli con formaggio, pappardelle alla lepre* and wild boar are extraordinary, and the courgette cake with flowers and ricotta are recommended. *Closed lunch and Wed.*

## Tavarnelle ✉ 50028

**Osteria di Passignano,** Loc. Badia a Passignano, **t** 055 807 1278 (€€€). The abbey-fief of the Antinori clan, who have been making wine for more than 600 years and produced the first Super-Tuscans (*see* p.205). Try them here; seasonal menus bring out the best in the wines. *Closed Sun.*

**La Gramola,** Via delle Fonti 1, **t** 055 8050321 (€€). A pleasantly rustic restaurant in the heart of the town, with a seasonally changing menu: try ravioli with pumpkin and local truffles, vegetable lasagne, and peppery *Impruneta* beef stew.

## Barberino Val d'Elsa ✉ 50021

**\*\*Primavera,** Via della Repubblica, **t** 055 805 9223, *www.primavera-hotel. it* (€€). A pleasant, simple hotel. Rooms have bath and TV, and there's parking.

**Il Paese dei Campanell,** Loc. Petrognano Semifont, **t** 055 807 5318 (€€€). Traditional Tuscan dishes given an imaginative twist in this well regarded restaurant. Stone walls and candles make the atmosphere and the genial hosts provide the warmth. There is also a cookery school. Book ahead. *Closed lunches and Mon.*

## San Donato in Poggio ✉ 50028

**Villa Francesca,** Strada Monestiero 12, **t** 055 807 2849 (€€). A good place to come for roasts, risotto with *porcini,* and *bistecca. Closed Mon–Wed, and Thurs and Fri lunch.*

# Central Chianti: Along the Chiantigiana (SS222)

From Florence the scenic Chiantigiana (SS222) passes the Ugolino golf course (*see* p.171) and offers its first tempting detour at Petigliolo: turn left after 4km for the ivy-covered **Santo Stefano a Tizzano,** a Romanesque church built by the Buondelmonti, not far from an 11th-century castle-villa, the **Castello di Tizzano,** where you can buy Riserva, *vin santo naturale* and prizewinning olive oil.

**Castello di Tizzano** *t 055 495380; call for opening hrs*

The same road continues for 2km to **San Polo in Chianti,** the centre of Tuscany's iris industry, celebrated in an iris festival in May. On a hill from San Polo you can see a lonely building once belonging to the Knights Templar; an equally ancient church, **San Miniato in Robbiana,** was reconsecrated in 1077 by the bishop of Fiesole, according to a still legible inscription. San Polo's **Antico Toscano** is a wine shop with offerings from all over the region.

**Strada,** 14km from Florence along the Chiantigiana, is thought to take its odd name from an old Roman road. In the Middle Ages, the road to the south, towards the Valdarno, was protected by the **Castello di Mugano,** one of the best-preserved in the region. The rolling countryside is the dominant feature until **Vicchiomaggio,** with its distinctive castle where Leonardo da Vinci once stayed. This is now the British-run **Fattoria Castello di Vicchiomaggio,** offering own-label Chianti, *vin santo,* olive oil and honey, and plush rooms.

**Fattoria Castello di Vicchiomaggio** *t 055 854079, www.vicchiomaggio.it*

New Yorkers will recognize the name of nearby **Verrazzano** at once, thanks to Giovanni da Verrazzano, a captain who, in the service of François I of France, discovered New York harbour and

**Castello di Verrazzano**
*t 055 854243,
www.verrazzano.com;
tastings with
a week's notice*

**Castello di Uzzano**
*t 055 854 4851,
www.agricolauzzano.
com; tastings with
24hrs' notice*

**Macelleria Falorni**
*Piazza Matteotti 69/71,
t 055 853029,
www.falorni.it*

**Museo del Vino**
*Piazza Tirinnanzi 10,
t 055 854 6275,
www.museovino.it;
ring for opening
hours*

Manhattan island in 1524. He disappeared on his second voyage to Brazil but surely smiles down on the bridge named in his honour. His birthplace, the **Castello di Verrazzano**, sells wines and olive oils.

East of the Chiantigiana, 1.5km north of Greve, is the 13th-century **Castello di Uzzano**, built by the bishop of Florence and gradually converted into one of Chianti's most impressive villa estates.

## Greve in Chianti and Around

The biggest **wine fair** in Chianti occurs in September in medieval **Greve** (population 10,800), seen as the region's capital. On the banks of the river, it is celebrated for its charming, arcaded, funnel-shaped **Piazza del Matteotti**, studded with a statue of Verrazzano, for its specialized wine shops (*see* opposite), and for the **Macelleria Falorni**, one of the region's most famous butchers, acclaimed for its cured hams and *finocchiona* salamis flavoured with fennel seeds. The Falorni family is behind the new **Museo del Vino** nearby. In the church of **Santa Croce** is a triptych by Lorenzo di Bicci and a painting by the 'Master of Greve'. In a nearby hamlet, **Cintoia**, the little church of **Santa Maria a Cintoia** has a beautiful 15th-century panel attributed to Francesco Granacci.

The ancient village and castle of **Montefioralle**, 1km west of Greve, is where the townspeople lived in the bad old days. Now restored, it is an interesting place to poke around, with its intact octagonal walls, old towerhouses and Romanesque churches: **Santo Stefano**, housing early Florentine paintings, and the porticoed **Pieve di San Cresci a Montefioralle**, just outside the walls.

A minor road west passes the ruined castle of **Montefili**, built in the 900s as the eastern outpost of one of Chianti's most powerful religious institutions, the **Badia a Passignano**, a fortified complex now partly occupied by a restaurant (*see* p.212). The old abbey church, **San Michele**, has paintings by Ghirlandaio, Alessandro Allori and Domenico Cresti (better known as Passignano) and a bust of San Giovanni Gualberto, founder of the Vallombrosan order, who arrived here in the mid 11th century. Most buildings date from the 14th century, with a few 17th- and 19th-century remodellings.

Just east of Greve, the beautiful **Vignamaggio** villa was built by the Gherardini family, whose most famous member, Lisa, was born here. She married Francesco del Giocondo before posing for the world's most famous portrait. Used as a location for Kenneth Branagh's film, *Much Ado About Nothing*, it's now a hotel (*see* p.212).

**Panzano**, an agricultural centre 6km south of Greve on the Chiantigiana, played an important role in the Florence-Siena squabbles but retains only part of its medieval castle. Its butcher, Dario Cecchini, is famous for protesting when 'beef on the bone' was banned in 2001. He holds court in his shop at Via XX Luglio 11, selling his own condiments to accompany the meat, and has recently started a string of eateries (*see* p.213). Panzano is best known for its embroidery, and for the **Pieve di San Leolino**, 1km south, with its pretty 16th-century portico on a 12th-century Romanesque structure; inside is a triptych by Mariotto di Nardo. Another Romanesque church south of Panzano, Sant' Eufrosino, just off the SS222, enjoys especially fine views.

**Fattoria Montagliari**
*t 0555 852014,*
*www.montagliari.it;*
*call for opening hours*

Near Panzano, the **Fattoria Montagliari** sells a wide variety of its own wines, grappa, olive oil, cheese, salami, honey and so on. **Pietrafitta**, 9km further south and 4km from Castellina, is a lovely hamlet hidden in the woods.

## Castellina in Chianti and Around

**❷ Castellina in Chianti**

One of Chianti's most charming hilltop villages, **Castellina** (population 2,700) was fortified by Florence as an outpost against Siena, and for centuries its fortunes depended on who was on top in their endless war. It was lost to a combined Sienese-Aragonese siege in 1478, though after the fall of Siena itself in 1555 both cities lost interest in Castellina. Today it looks much as it did in the quattrocento: the circuit of walls is almost intact, with houses built into and on top of them. The **Rocca**, or fortress, is in the centre, its mighty donjon now home to the mayor; the covered walkway, Via delle Volte, is part of the 15th-century defensive works. Less historic but worth visiting is the **Bottega del Vino Gallo Nero**, which sells wines and olive oils. Visitors can explore the **Ipogeo Etrusco di Montecalvario**, a restored 6th-century BC Etruscan tomb.

**Bottega del Vino Gallo Nero**
*Via della Rocca 13*

West of Castellina on the SS429, **Granaio** has one of Chianti's most renowned wineries, the **Melini wine house**, established in 1705. There are also splendid old farmhouses and villas around Castellina, nearly all formerly fortifications along Chianti's medieval Maginot line, such as the **Villa La Leccia** southwest of Castellina, and the **Castello di Campalli** near **Fonterutoli**, an ancient hamlet south on the Chiantigiana. In the 13th century Florence and Siena often met here to work out peace settlements; none lasted long. Since 1435 the **Fattoria di Fonterutoli** has produced wine in traditional oak casks, including Chianti and Bianco della Lega, as well as lavender products, honey and Tuscany's finest *extra-vergine*.

**Fattoria di Fonterutoli**
*t 0577 741 385,*
*www.fonterutoli.com;*
*call for opening hours*

**Fattoria della Aiola**
*t 0577 322615,*
*www.aiola.net;*
*call for opening hours*

Further south, **Quercegrossa**, 10km from Siena but now practically a suburb of it, was the birthplace of quattrocento sculptor Jacopo della Quercia. A road forks northeast for Vagliagli, site of the medieval **Fattoria della Aiola** selling wines, grappa, oil, honey and vinegar.

## Wine-tasting in and around Greve

**❶ Wine-tasting around Greve**

**Bottega del Chianti Classico**, Via Cesare Battisti 4, **t** 055 853631. Wine/oil sales.
**Castello di Querceto**, Via A. François 2, just outside Greve, **t** 055 85921. A wide variety of wines, including Sangiovese aged in *barriques*, and olive oil. Tastings require one week's notice.
**Enoteca del Chianti Classico**, Piazzetta S. Croce 8, **t** 055 853297.
**Fontodi**, Via S. Leolino, on Chiantigiana, near Sant'Eufrosino, **t** 055 852005. Wine

aged in *barriques*, Chianti, Bianco della Lega and oil. One week's notice.

## Where to Stay in and around Greve

(i) **Greve in Chianti >**
*Viale G. da Verrazzano 59, t 055 854 6287*

### Greve ✉ 50022

**Villa Vignamaggio**, Via Petriolo 5, 5mins' drive from Greve on Panzano road, **t** 055 854 4661, *www.vigna maggio.it* (€€€). A historic villa (*see* p.210) with tennis facilities and a pool. Some of the accommodation is in the grounds. There's a minimum 2-night stay.

**Fattoria di Rignana**, Via di Rignana 15, **t** 055 852065, *www.rignana.it* (€€€). Wine estate and *agriturismo* up the dirt track from the Cantinetta (*see* below), it offers atmospheric and well-restored rooms and apartments. Stunning grounds, an infinity pool with views over the valleys and a room frescoed from wall to ceiling.

**\*\*\*Giovanni da Verrazzano**, Piazza Matteotti 28, **t** 055 853189, *www. verrazzano.it* (€€€–€€). Elegant rooms overlooking the pretty main square, with breakfast included in the rates, plus a restaurant (*see* below).

**\*\*\*Albergo del Chianti**, Piazza Matteotti 86, **t** 055 853763, *www. albergodelchianti.it* (€€). Comfortable, stylish rooms with baths and all comforts, near the centre, with a pool and a lovely garden.

★ **Villa le Barone >**

### Panzano ✉ 50022

**\*\*Villa le Barone**, Via S. Leolino 19, **t** 055 852621, *www.villalebarone.it* (€€€€). The 16th-century villa of the Della Robbia family, who still own it, just south of Greve. It's a lovely, intimate hotel, whether you need a base for visiting the region or a place to lounge – there's a pretty garden, an outdoor pool and a tennis court. Kids are very welcome. There's a minimum 3-night stay, and rates include break-fast and dinner. *Closed Nov–Mar.*

★ **La Cantinetta di Rignana >>**

**Villa Rosa**, Via San Leolino 59, **t** 055 852577, *www.resortvillarosa.it* (€€€). A pleasant, relaxed place on the road between Panzano and Radda, with a shady terrace and a hillside pool with beautiful views. Two of the rooms have private terraces.

### Castellina ✉ 53011

**\*\*\*\*Tenuta di Ricavo**, 3km north of town, **t** 0577 740221, *www.ricavo.com* (€€€€€–€€€€). An entire medieval hamlet of stone houses, wonderfully isolated in the pines, with a large garden and a pool. It's ideal for families. Breakfast is included in the rates, and there's a restaurant offering Chianti specialities. *Open April–Oct.*

**\*\*\*\*Villa Casalecchi**, **t** 0577 740240, *www.villacasalecchi.com* (€€€€–€€€). A comfy if rather sombre old house among trees and vineyards, with some elegant rooms full of antiques and others not so elegant, plus 3 apartments. It also has a large pool, a traditional restaurant and enchanting views over the hills. *Closed Nov–Mar.*

**\*\*\*Salivolpi**, Via Fiorentina, just outside town, **t** 0577 740484, *www. hotelsalivolpi.com* (€€). A smart place combining an old-fashioned atmosphere with modern comforts, set in two old farmhouses, with a garden and pool. Breakfast is included.

## Eating Out in and around Greve

### Greve ✉ 50022

**Osteria di Passignano**, Via Passignano 33, Badia a Passignano, **t** 055 807 1278 (€€€€–€€€). One of the best country restaurants in the area, set in the old wine cellars of a monastery (*see* p.210) on the famous Antinori wine estates. The atmosphere is rustically elegant, the creative food rooted in Tuscan and Italian traditions. Try *pici* with pigeon, red wine and bay leaf; or herb-crusted veal cutlet with potatoes and pumpkin flowers. It's essential to book. Ask about cookery courses. *Closed Sun, Jan and 2wks Aug.*

**La Cantinetta di Rignana**, Via Rignana, Greve, **t** 055 852601 (€€€). A trattoria in idyllic countryside between Greve and Badia in Passignano (to the south), with a panoramic terrace and serving the freshest local ingredients. Try home-made pasta with walnut sauce, or stewed beef with peppers. Best to book. *Closed Tues.*

**Ristoro di Lamole**, Via di Lamole 6, **t** 055 854 7050 (€€). A few miles out of town, this restaurant/wine bar offers excellent food and wine and views that go all the way to San Gimignano. **Giovanni da Verrazzano**, Piazza Matteotti 28, **t** 055 853189 (€€). One of Greve's most charming restaurants, furnished with antiques, overlooking the piazza. The main meat dishes are especially good – try *nana in sugo* (duck in wine sauce), turkey with olives or the *pappardelle* with wild boar. *Closed Sun eve and Mon.*

(i) **Castellina in Chianti >>**
*Via Ferruccio 40,*
*t 057 774 1392*

### Località Lucolena ✉ 50020

**Borgo Antico**, Via Case Sparse 115, **t** 055 851024 (€€). A place worth visiting for its tomato or bean *bruschetta*; *pappardelle* with wild boar or duck; little salami with truffles and other excellent salami and hams; and renowned Florentine beefsteak. It also has some rooms to let. *Closed Tues.*

(★) **Antica Trattoria La Torre >>**

(★) **Officina della Bistecca/ Solociccia/ MacDario >**

### Panzano ✉ 50022

**Officina della Bistecca**, Via XX Luglio 11, **t** 055 852020 (€€€). Butcher Dario Cecchini's passion for meat is expressed in three different eateries. His temple to *bistecca* offers two sittings for a fixed menu (€50) of glorious steaks. Book ahead and come hungry. *Open Fri, Sat dinner, Sun lunch.*
**Solociccia**, Via XX Luglio 11, **t** 055 852020 (€€). Solociccia concentrates on all the meat that is not *bistecca*. There are two sittings a night for the 6-course fixed menu (€30). The food is

delicious, Dario a fun host, and communal tables make it more like a dinner party. Book ahead. *Open Thurs, Fri, Sat eve, and Sun lunch.*
**MacDario**, *Via XX Luglio 11*, **t** 055 852020 (€). Cecchini's fast-food joint proves that fast food can also be good food. Two set menues available at two long communal tables; in the summer they are outside on the terrace. A plate of massive beef burger and fat chips is €10. *Open Mon–Sat lunch.*

### Castellina ✉ 53011

**Albergaccio di Castellina**, Via Fiorentina 63, on road to San Donato, **t** 0577 741042 (€€€). Creative fare such as lamb with saffron, and mushroom and chestnut soup, plus grilled meat and fish dishes. Booking is essential. *Closed Wed and Thurs lunch, Sun, last 2wks Nov, 1st week Dec.*

**Antica Trattoria La Torre**, Piazza del Comune 1, **t** 0577 740236 (€€). A popular family-run place with a cosy atmosphere, serving tasty rice or *pici* with *porcini*, *ribollita*, cheeses, Tuscan hams and salami, and more. *Closed Fri.*
**Pietrafitta Ristorante in Chianti**, Loc. Pietrafitta 41, **t** 0577 741123 (€€). An American-owned place offering good regional and international dishes, including imaginative Italian-Med food. Try the *Fiorentina* steak, grilled lamb or gnocchi with sheeps'-cheese fondue. *Closed Thurs and Feb.*

# Monti del Chianti: Radda and Gaiole

East of Castellina lies the more rugged region of the Monti del Chianti. Here in the ancient capital of the Lega del Chianti, **Radda in Chianti** (population 1,650), the streets follow a medieval plan, radiating from the central piazza and its stately, heraldry-encrusted Palazzo Comunale, and a 15th-century fresco *Madonna, St Christopher and St John the Baptist* in the atrium. Just outside town is the Franciscan **Monastero**, a pretty 15th-century church.

Two medieval villages are to be found nearby: **Ama**, with its castle, 8km to the south, near the attractive Romanesque church of San Giusto; and **Volpaia**, 7km north, with another ancient castle and walls, and an unexpected 'Brunelleschian' church called **La Commenda**. Also near Radda is the **Fattoria Vigna Vecchia**, where you can stock up on Chianti, grappa, *vin santo* and olive oil, and enjoy tastings (with three days' notice).

**Fattoria Vigna Vecchia**
*t 0577 738090,*
*www.vignavecchia.com;*
*call for opening hours*

On the way to Gaiole, 10km east of Radda, is the ancient **Badia a Coltibuono**, one of Chianti's gems. Set among centuries-old trees and gardens, the abbey is believed to have been founded in 770, passing to the Vallombrosan order in the 12th century. The Romanesque church, San Lorenzo, dates from 1049. The monastery was turned into a splendid villa, owned in the 19th century by the Poniatowski, one of Poland's greatest noble families, and now occupied by a wine estate, **Fattoria Badia a Coltibuono**. You can visit the cellars and Italianate garden, and it has a restaurant (*see* opposite).

**Gaiole in Chianti** (population 4,780) is an ancient market town: the **Agricoltori Chianti Geografico**, which sells Chianti, Vernaccia di San Gimignano, *vin santo* and olive oil, is the headquarters of a local co-operative; and the **Enoteca Montagnani** specializes in Chianti Classico. Gaiole is also a good base for visiting the impressive castles between the Arno and Siena. Just to the west are the walls and imposing donjon of the well-preserved 13th-century **Castello di Vertine**, one of the most striking sights in Chianti.

East of Gaiole is the ancient fortified village of **Barbischio**, and 3km south on the SS408 is the impressive medieval **Castello di Meleto** with its sturdy cylindrical towers. From here the road continues 4.5km up to the mighty **Castello di Castagnoli**, guarding a fascinating little medieval town in a commanding position.

Most majestic of all is the Iron Baron's isolated **Castello di Brolio** some 10km south of Gaiole along the SS484, high on a hill with views for miles around. Donated to the monks of the Badia in Florence in 1009, by Matilda of Tuscany's father Bonifacio, it passed to the Ricasoli in 1167. In 1478 the castle was bombarded for weeks by the Aragonese and Sienese, who later demolished it so that 'the walls levelled with the earth'. Florence rebuilt it, and in the mid-19th century Baron Ricasoli converted it into a splendid fortified residence, while experimenting with the modern formula for Chianti. You can sample the famous wines and olive oil and visit the cellars 10km south at the **Cantine Barone Ricasoli**. The **Fattoria dei Pagliaresi** near Castelnuovo Berardenga, between S. Gusmè and Pianella, offers older wines as well as new, and olive oil.

To the south, **Castelnuovo Berardenga** is an agricultural centre with the remains of a 14th-century castle. From here it's 16km to **Monteaperti**, where Florence almost went down the tubes. To continue south, *see* 'Monte Oliveto Maggiore and Around', p.384.

**Fattoria Badia a Coltibuono**
*t 0577 74481,*
*www.coltibuono.com*

**Agricoltori Chianti Geografico**
*Via Mulinaccio 10,*
*t 0577 749489,*
*www.chianti geografico.it*

**Enoteca Montagnani**
*Via B. Bandinelli 9,*
*t 0577 749517*

**Castello di Brolio**
*t 0577 731919,*
*www.ricasoli.it;*
*open Mar–Nov 10–5.30,*
*Dec gardens Sat, Sun only 10–4; adm*

**Cantine Barone Ricasoli**
*t 0577 730220,*
*www.ricasoli.it;*
*call ahead*

**Fattoria dei Pagliaresi**
*t 0577 359070;*
*call for opening hours*

## Where to Stay and Eat in the Monti del Chianti

**Radda ✉ 53017**
★★★★**Relais Vignale**, Via Pianigiani 9,
*t 0577 738300, www.vignale.it*

(€€€€€–€€€€). Well-equipped rooms furnished with antiques in a charming old house with fine views and an outdoor pool for hotter days, plus an excellent restaurant 300m down the road. Buffet breakfasts are included in the rates. *Closed Jan–Mar.*

ⓘ **Radda >**
*Piazza Castello 1,*
*t 0577 738494*

La Locanda, Loc. Montanino, Volpaia, t 0577 738832, www.lalocanda.it (€€€€€–€€€€). A little hotel on a wooded hill, in restored stone farm buildings, with a pool and good food. Breakfast is included.

Podere Terreno, 5km north of Radda on road to Volpaia, t 0577 738312, www.podereterreno.it (€€€). A working wine farm and agriturismo, with simple rooms (breakfast inc.) and a relaxed atmosphere – meals (half-board is available) are served at a communal table in a cluttered living room.

*Il Girarrosto Simplici, Via Roma 41, t 0577 738010 (€). Double rooms, some with bath, and a restaurant (€€) offering local cuisine. Closed Wed.

Antica Trattoria Botteganova, Via Chiantigiana 29, t 0577 284230 (€€€). Fish and meat in interesting combinations. The tagliolini with lemon, paprika and little squid is recommended. Come at lunch to eat for half the price. Closed Sun.

Il Vignale, Via XX Settembre 23, t 0577 738094 (€€€). A spot popular with locals for its refined Tuscan cooking using organic produce. Closed Thurs.

Badia a Coltibuono, next to old abbey of same name between Radda and Gaiole, t 0577 749424 (€€€). A menu degustazione, or tempting à la carte dishes such as risotto whisked with salt cod, tomato and olive pesto sauce; and guinea fowl roasted with lard, chestnuts and sausage. Closed Mon.

Il Carlino d'Oro, Via Brolio, San Regolo, t 0577 747136 (€). A small, family-run trattoria in an idyllic setting. Make sure to book ahead at weekends. Try the excellent bean soup, pappardelle with hare sauce, and deep-fried chicken and rabbit, and outstanding home-produced wine. Closed winter exc. Sat and Sun lunch.

## Gaiole ✉ 53013

Castello di Tornano, Loc. Lecchi, t 0577 746067, www.castelloditornano.it (€€€€€). A fortified farmhouse and castle with a 1,000-year-old tower commanding views of steep wooded hills. The castle and tower house luxurious double rooms and suites with original antiques; outbuildings have been converted into rustically styled self-catering apartments for 2–4. There is a restaurant, pool and tennis court. Breakfast is included.

Relais Borgo San Felice, Castelnuovo Berardenga, Loc. Borgo San Felice, t 0577 3964, www.borgosanfelice.com (€€€€€). A lovely renovated hilltop hamlet with rooms dotted around various buildings, surrounded by the vines of the famous San Felice estate. There is an excellent restaurant, a gym, a pool and a tennis court. Breakfast is included, and half/full-board is available. Closed Nov–Mar.

****Castello di Spaltenna, t 0577 749483, www.spaltenna.it (€€€€). A fortified monastery just by Gaiole. The delightful rooms have all comforts plus stunning views over the valley or courtyard. There is also an indoor pool, a sauna, a gym, a tennis court, billiards and a beauty centre. The restaurant in the ancient refectory serves both traditional and creative Tuscan dishes. Closed mid-Jan–Mar.

## Brolio ✉ 53013

Castello di Brolio, t 0577 730220, www.ricasoli.it (€€€€€). A chic farmhouse to let at this famous site (see opposite).

Osteria del Castello, t 0577 747277 (€€€). A delightful restaurant with an Irish chef who has a creative take on Tuscan cuisine. Booking is strongly recommended. Closed Thurs.

# The Mugello

Over the years, as their ambitions became less discreet, the Medici concocted a pretty story of how they were descended from knights of Charlemagne. In truth they came down to Florence from the Mugello, the hilly region just to the north – as did Giotto and Fra Angelico. As far back as Boccaccio's time, the Mugello was considered the loveliest region of the Florentine contada, and its

# Getting to and around the Mugello

The Mugello lies east of the A1 and north of Pontassieve. It has two **exits off the A1**: at Barberino (28km from Florence) and Roncobilaccio (47km from Florence) near the Passo della Futa. The two main roads north from Florence, the **SS65** (Via Bolognese) to the Medici villas and Passo della Futa and the **SS302** to Borgo San Lorenzo (28km), are pretty drives. North of the river Sieve, mountain roads make for slow travelling – allow at least 2hrs to get from Florence to Firenzuola (51km), more to Marradi (64km).

You can also loop through the Mugello by **train** (t 892021, *www.trenitalia.com*) from Florence, passing through Pontassieve, Dicomano, Vicchio, Borgo San Lorenzo, San Piero a Sieve, and Vaglia.

SITA **buses** (t 055 47821, *www.sitabus.it*) are more scenic and just as infrequent; check times before setting out (most pass through the junction at San Piero). Better still, hire a car.

bluish-green hills are dotted with elegant weekend and summer retreats, rather smarter than the typical stone *fattorie* of the Chianti. The Florentines come here whenever they can, and, if you find yourself stewing with them in the traffic gridlocks approaching Piazza della Libertà, know that all you have to do is turn up the Via Bolognese or Via Faentina and in 10 minutes you'll be in a cool, enchanting world immersed in green.

North of Florence altitudes rise appreciably towards the central Apennine spine that divides Tuscany from Emilia-Romagna. Tucked in these hills lies the Mugello basin, a broad valley along the Sieve and its tributaries that, in the Miocene era, held a lake. Most of the towns of the Mugello are here, surrounded by a sea of vines; olive groves cover the slopes but soon give way to cool, deep forests of pines, chestnuts and oaks, dotted with small resorts. Like any

The Mugello

fashion-conscious Florentine, the Mugello changes colours with the seasons, though it's strikingly beautiful at any time of year.

## The Original Medici Villa

Following Via Bolognese (SS65) north, past the gardens of **Pratolino**, one of the last Medici villas (*see* p.195), it's a panoramic and winding 30km to two of the very first. On the way, a slight detour east (from Pratolino or Vaglia) ascends to **Monte Senario** (820m) where, in 1233, seven Florentine noblemen founded the mendicant Servite Order, living in grottoes and building simple cells in the woods. The Servites later built Santissima Annunziata in Florence. Rebuilt in the 16th century, the monastery here has amazing views over the Arno valley and Mugello.

North, towards San Piero a Sieve, is a turn-off west on an untarred road for the Medici **Castello di Trebbio**, a family estate remodelled in 1461 by Michelozzo into a fortified villa with a tower. It has a formal Italian garden you can look around.

A bit further up looms the even grander **Villa Cafaggiolo**, favoured by Cosimo il Vecchio and Lorenzo il Magnifico, who spent as much of the summer as possible in its cool halls. Cosimo had Michelozzo transform this ancient family seat into an imposing castellated villa, its entrance protected by a bulging tower with an incongruous clock. It has apartments for rent (*www.villacafaggiolo.it*).

East, a minor road leads up to the wooded **Bosco ai Frati**, with a simple porticoed church also by Michelozzo; inside is a fine crucifix by Donatello, and another attributed to Desiderio da Settignano.

Beyond Cafaggiolo, towards Barberino, is the huge artificial **Lago di Bilancino**. The lake, which is dammed (the dam controls the water of the Sieve river), occupies nearly 5 sq km, has a beach with loungers and parasols, and is good for sailing, windsurfing, fishing and canoeing. Bars, restaurants and other facilities are springing up.

## To the Passo della Futa

Just off the *autostrada*, the largest town on the west rim of the Mugello basin is **Barberino di Mugello**, spread under the **Castello dei Cattani**. Its 15th-century Palazzo Pretorio is emblazoned with coats of arms; the open Loggie Medicee is another work by Michelozzo. On the SS65, 5km away at Colle Barucci, is one of the Mugello's grandest estates, the **Villa delle Maschere** ('of the masks').

**Barberino Outlet Village**
t 055 842161,
http://.barberino.
mcarthurglen.it

⊕ **Passo della Futa**

Signs will lead you to another tourist favourite: the **Barberino Outlet Village**, full of discount designer shops. Built to resemble a Renaissance village, it is surprisingly pleasant for a shopping centre.

Continue 14km north to appreciate the breathtaking views from the **Passo della Futa** (903m), a pass on the principal Apennine watershed; below, the whole Mugello extends like a relief map. In 1944, the pass was the Germans' strong point on the Gothic Line.

Beyond the pass the road winds under the craggy **Sasso di Castro** (1,276m); at La Casetta turn off for Firenzuola (*see* below) or hotfoot it over the mountains for dinner in Bologna, culinary capital of Italy.

## Scarperia and Around

At the major crossroads of the SS503 north and the SS551 along the Sieve, **San Piero a Sieve** is a busy little town defended by a mighty Medici citadel, the **Fortezza di San Martino**, designed by Buontalenti in 1571. Its Romanesque parish church, with a façade from 1776, contains a remarkable octagonal baptismal font in polychrome terracotta, by Luca della Robbia.

⭐ **Scarperia**

From here it's 4km to **Scarperia**, the most charming town in the Mugello, perched high above the valley. Florence fortified it in 1306, and laid out its simple rectangular plan, with one long main street. The **Palazzo dei Vicari**, from 1306, is so heavily decorated with stone and ceramic coats of arms that it resembles a page from a postage stamp album. Its atrium and upper halls have 14th- and 15th-century frescoes, the earliest ones by the school of Giotto. The **oratory of the Madonna di Piazza** has an attractive Renaissance front and a cinquecento fresco of the *Madonna and Child*, attributed to Iacopo del Casentino; the church dedicated to Our Lady of the Earthquakes has a fresco that some attribute to Filippo Lippi.

**Palazzo dei Vicari**
*open 16 Sept–31 May Sat, Sun and hols 10–1 and 3–6.30; 1 June–15 Sept Wed, Thurs and Fri 3.30–7.30, Sat, Sun and hols 10–1 and 3.30–7.30*

The *palazzo* houses the **Museo dei Ferri Taglienti**, a small museum of knife-making and cutting tools. From the 16th century, Scarperia supplied the duchy of Tuscany with knives, forks and scissors, as well as daggers and swords. By 1900 there were 46 thriving firms, though machine-made competition has reduced this. Firms still making knives, and selling bone- or horn-handled cutlery (at high prices), include **Conaz** (Via Roma 8), **Saladini** (Via Solferino 15), **Berti** (Via Roma 37) and **Giglio** (Via delle Oche).

**Museo dei Ferri Taglienti**
*open same hours as Palazzo dei Vicari; adm*

Scarperia is now better known for the **Autodromo Internazionale del Mugello**, a 5km track built by Florence's Auto Club in 1976, fairly well hidden in the hills east of town.

**Autodromo Internazionale del Mugello**
*www.mugellocircuit.it*

The Mugello's most fascinating historical relic, 4km northwest of Scarperia, is the 11th-century parish church of **Sant'Agata**, restored after an earthquake in 1919, with an unusual apse and a pulpit from 1175, decorated with white and green marble intarsia designs and animals. The chapel to the right of the altar houses Bicci di Lorenzo's painting *The Mystical Marriage of St Catherine*.

**Sant'Agata**
*open daily 7.30–5*

**Firenzuola**, 22km north of Scarperia, is famous for its production of 'Pietra Serena', the pale grey stone seen in buildings all over Tuscany. A small holiday resort, cool even in August, it was devastated in the Second World War and rebuilt along the lines of the original street plan between the Porta di Bologna and Porta di Firenze. Four kilometres west, in **Cornacchiaia**, is a church believed to date back to Carolingian times.

## Borgo San Lorenzo and Vicchio

**Borgo San Lorenzo** (population 16,300) on the Sieve is the boom town of the Mugello, partly due to its fast-train link to Florence. The main sights are the Romanesque churches: **San Lorenzo**, with an unusual hexagonal campanile built in 1263; and, 3km north, the parish church of **San Giovanni Maggiore**, with a belltower square at the base but octagonal on top, and a lovely 12th-century pulpit in marble intarsia.

To the north the road divides into the SS477 to **Palazzuolo sul Senio** and the SS302 to **Marradi**, also small resorts; Palazzuolo has a small **ethnographic museum** in the 14th-century Palazzo dei Capitani, and hosts an annual festival in July (*see* p.59).

Sleepy little **Vicchio**, east of San Lorenzo, was the birthplace of the Blessed Fra Angelico (Giovanni da Fiesole, 1387–1455) and often home from home for Benvenuto Cellini. Its **Museo Comunale Beato Angelico** has detached frescoes, Etruscan finds from nearby Poggio alla Colla, and a 13th-century holy-water stoup.

The nearby hamlet of **Vespignano** was the birthplace of Giotto di Bondone (1267–1337). The simple stone cottage where the father of Renaissance painting is said to have been born has been well restored as the **Casa di Giotto**. According to tradition, Cimabue discovered Giotto near the old (now restored) bridge over the Enza, where the young shepherd was sketching his sheep on a stone.

## The Valdisieve

The lower Sieve valley is mostly industrial: **Dicomano** can boast an interesting fresco by the school of Piero della Francesca but little else besides a big Saturday morning market and the junction for the SS67, which climbs east into a pretty range of mountains, the **Alpi di San Benedetto**. **San Godenzo**, 10km up the SS67, is the largest village, site of an 11th-century Benedictine abbey; its plain church has a raised presbytery and a polyptych by the school of Giotto.

From San Godenzo a road continues up to the birthplace of Andrea del Castagno, now called **Il Castagno d'Andrea** ('Andrew's chestnut'; 1,022m), a small holiday village. Wind a further 18km up to **San Benedetto in Alpe**, with a 9th-century Benedictine abbey that sheltered Dante (*Inferno*, Canto XVI, 94–105). Here you can hire horses to visit the enchanting **Valle dell'Aquacheta** with its waterfall.

In the old town of **Portico di Romagna** 11km further north, the Portinari family, including the beautiful Beatrice, spent their summers – their house still stands in the main street. Deeper into Romagna lie fascinating medieval **Brisighella**, the ceramic city of **Faenza**, and **Ravenna**, filled with ravishing Byzantine mosaics from the time of Justinian and the site of Dante's real tomb.

**Rufina**, 10km south of Dicomano, is dominated by the 16th-century Villa Poggio Reale, producing Chianti Rufina and Pomino wines.

---

**Museo della Civiltà Contadina ed Artigiana**
*t 055 844 6114; open Mar–June and Sept–Dec Sun 3–6; July and Aug daily 4–7; but call ahead*

**Museo Comunale Beato Angelico**
*t 055 849 7082; open Sat and Sun 10–12 and 4–7, plus Thurs 10–12 in summer; adm (combined with Casa di Giotto)*

**Casa di Giotto**
*t 055 843 9224; open winter Sat and Sun 10–12 and 3–6; summer Tues by appt, Thurs, Sat and Sun 10–12 and 3.30–6.30; adm (also allows entry to Museo Comunale Beato Angelico)*

**Castello di
Nipozzano**
*t 055 27141; open Mon
2.30–6.30, Tues–Fri
10.30–1 and 2.30–6.30,
Sat 10.30–1*

**Museo della
Vite e del Vino**
*t 055 839 7932;
open mid-April–Oct
Wed–Sat 10–1 and 2–7;
mid-Mar–mid-April
Wed–Sat 9–1 and 2–6;
but call ahead; adm*

Continuing east along the SS70 beyond Pontassieve, turn left after a few km for **Castello di Nipozzano**, one of the great Frescobaldi wine estates, producing prize-winning oak-aged red wines. For white wines, climb into the hills to the north to **Castello di Pomino**, another Frescobaldi property. **Poggio Reale** has a small wine museum.

Pause in **Pontassieve** to sample the region's best ice cream. **Sottani Gelateria** (*località* San Francesco) has been making ice cream for over 40 years; the rice flavour is famous. From **Pontassieve** the scenic SS70 leads up to the dramatic **Passo della Consuma** (1,022m) then descends into the Casentino (*see p.420*).

## Where to Stay and Eat in the Mugello

Nearly all Mugello hotels are in the countryside, so you need a car.

### Bivigliano ✉ 50030
****Giotto Park Hotel**, Via Roma 69, t 055 406608, *www.villagiotto.it* (€€€). A small, restful, comfy villa, and a cheaper *dipendenza*, in a garden with a tennis court. *Closed Nov–Feb.*

### Borgo San Lorenzo ✉ 50032
***Locanda degli Artisti**, Piazza Romagnoli 2, t 055 845 5359, *www.locandartisti.it* (€€). A neat, central little guesthouse; breakfast is included. **Ristorante degli Artisti**, Piazza Romagnoli 1, t 055 845 7707 (€€). An elegant spot for Mugello cooking, with a pretty courtyard terrace. *Closed Wed.*

(i) **Borgo San Lorenzo >**
*Via P. Togliatti 45,
t 055 845271,
www.mugellotoscana.it*

### Marradi ✉ 50034
**Palazzo Torriani**, Via Fabroni 58, t 055 804 2363, *www.palazzotorriani.it* (€€€€). A beautiful 16th-century *palazzo* in the centre, with 3 very comfy self-catering flats, one of which can be rented as two separate bedrooms. Breakfast is included, meals are available on request, and there are cookery courses. *Closed Jan–mid-Mar.*

⭐ **Il Giorgione >>**

### Scarperia ✉ 50038
***Hotel Cantagallo**, Viale Kennedy 17, t 055 843 0442, *hotelcantagallo@libero.it* (€€€). A tidy, quiet little hotel overlooking a shady garden, with a pool. **Teatro dei Medici**, Loc. La Torre 14, t 055 845 9876 (€€). An old house that once belonged to the Medici; book ahead in summer for country *antipasti*, pasta dishes and wild game. *Closed Mon.*

⭐ **Casa del Prosciutto >>**

### Palazzuolo sul Senio ✉ 50035
***Locanda Senio**, Borgo dell'Ore 1, t 055 8046019, *www.locandasenio.it* (€€€). Ancient buildings furnished with antiques. The food is excellent (breakfast is included; the restaurant serves mushroom, truffle and wild boar), and there is a pool and small spa.

### Vicchio ✉ 50039
****Villa Campestri**, Via de Campestri 19, t 055 849 0107, *www.villacampestri.it* (€€€€). An elegant Tuscan villa in a 300-acre park on a hill, with a pool with a view, exquisite rooms, a good restaurant, and a riding school. **Antica Porta di Levante**, Piazza Vittorio Veneto 5, t 055 840050 (€€). Creative Tuscan cuisine, including *tagliolini* with Mugello black truffles. There's a vine-covered terrace and a few rooms to let. *Closed Mon, 2wks Jan and summer exc. Sat lunch* (enoteca *open all year*). **La Casa di Caccia**, Loc. Farneto, t 055 840 7629 (€€). An isolated old hunting lodge north of Vicchio, with stunning views. Try ravioli with *scamorza* cheese. Book at weekends. *Closed Tues.*

### Sagginale ✉ 50032
**Il Giorgione**, between Borgo San Lorenzo and Vicchio, t 055 849 0130 (€€). A family-run restaurant at the back of a shop. Excellent rustic food; try rolled, stuffed rabbit. The owner has a small *bottega. Closed Thurs.*

### Ponte a Vicchio ✉ 50039
**Casa del Prosciutto**, Via Ponte a Vicchio, t 055 844031 (€). A grocer-cum-trattoria specializing in ham and local dishes, including potato-stuffed *tortelli. Closed eves, Mon and Tue, and Jan and July.*

# The Valdarno, Prato and Pistoia

*Half the people in Tuscany inhabit this strip between Florence and the sea. It's the hard-working, prosaic part of the region, full of factories and garden nurseries that churn out truly impressive quantities of motor scooters, bricks, fruit trees, straw hats, wool scarves, rail cars, raincoats, rooftiles and rose bushes.*

*There are two ways across it, both pretty crowded. To the south lies the Arno valley, to the north the modern A1 superstrada, passing Prato and Pistoia, estimable art towns with proud histories.*

*Between the routes are some charming hills to explore, the Monte Pisano and Monte Albano, where the star attraction is Leonardo's hometown of Vinci.*

# 09

## Don't miss

⭐ **A museum of Leonardo's inventions**
Vinci **p.226**

⭐ **Tiger-striped medieval churches**
Pistoia **p.240**

⭐ **The grandest of Italy's Belle Epoque spas**
Montecatini Terme **p.250**

⭐ **Italy's flower capital**
Pescia **p.253**

⭐ **Baroque gardens and a labyrinth**
Castello Garzoni **p.254**

*See map overleaf*

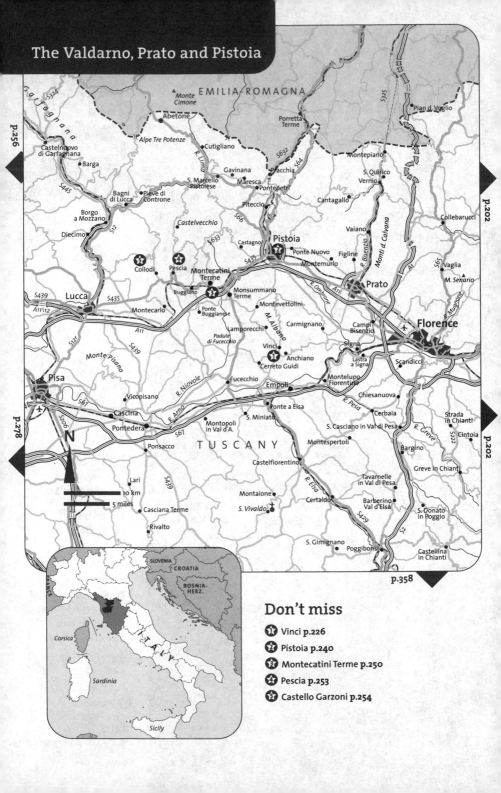

**Don't miss**

⭐ Vinci **p.226**

⭐ Pistoia **p.240**

⭐ Montecatini Terme **p.250**

⭐ Pescia **p.253**

⭐ Castello Garzoni **p.254**

# Down the Arno to Pisa

## Florence to Empoli

The old Florentine satellite town of **Scandicci** (6km west), once in the business of renting villas to foreigners like Dylan Thomas and D.H. Lawrence (who finished *Lady Chatterley's Lover* here), has since found more profit in industry. Most towns along the Arno specialize in certain products; in **Lastra a Signa** it's straw goods, sold in numerous village shops. Lastra retains its 14th-century walls and the **Loggia di Sant'Antonio**, all that survives of the hospital founded by Florence's Silk Guild in 1411; many believe Brunelleschi was the architect, and that the work was a prototype of Florence's Spedale degli Innocenti, funded by the same guild. Just outside Lastra, the church of **San Martino a Gangalandi** has a beautiful, semicircular apse with *pietra serena* articulation designed by Alberti. In **Signa**, the next village, the Romanesque **San Lorenzo** houses a remarkable 12th-century marble pulpit and trecento frescoes.

After Signa the road and river continue 12km through a gorge before **Montelupo Fiorentino**, celebrated since the Renaissance for its terracottas and delicately painted ceramics. The town hosts a ceramics fair at the end of June, which also features Renaissance music and costumes, demonstrations and exhibitions. The **Museo Archeologico e della Ceramica**, which has now been split into two museums, has examples from nearly every period, and a display on the lower Valdarno's prehistory, while Montelupo's shops sell more recent ceramic creations. The **Museo Contemporaneo** housed in the 16th-century Palazzo Pretorio includes modern ceramics alongside modern paintings and sculptures The old **castle** here was built in 1203 by the Florentines, during the wars against Pisa; the church of **San Giovanni Evangelista** contains a lovely *Madonna and Saints* by Botticelli and his assistants.

On the outskirts of Montelupo, you can see Buontalenti's **Villa Ambrogiana** (1587) from the outside, though you'll probably want to avoid being invited in – it's a mental hospital. From Montelupo a road leads southeast 20km to the town of San Casciano in Val di Pesa, in Chianti (*see* p.207).

### Empoli

The modern market town of Empoli, 32km from Florence, was witness to one of the turning points in Tuscan history: in 1260, the Ghibellines of Siena, fresh from their great victory over Florence at Monteaperti, held a parliament in Empoli to decide the fate of their arch enemy. Everyone was for razing Florence to the ground

**Museo Archeologico**
*Via Santa Lucia,*
*t 0571 541547; open*
*Tues–Sun 10–6; adm*

**Museo della Ceramica**
*Via Vittorio Veneto*
*8–10, t 0571 51352; open*
*Tues–Sun 10–6; adm*

**Museo Contemporaneo**
*Via Baccio Sinibaldi,*
*t 0571 51352; open*
*Thurs–Fri 10–1, Sat–Sun*
*10–6; adm; joint ticket*
*available for three*
*museums*

09

The Valdarno, Prato and Pistoia | Florence to Empoli

## Down the Arno to Pisa

once and for all, and waited for the approval of their leader, Farinata degli Uberti. The Uberti were Florentine gangster nobles famous for their hatred of their fellow citizens, and Farinata surprised all when he announced that, even if he had to stand alone, he would defend Florence for as long as he lived. The Sienese let their captain have his way, and lost their chance of ever becoming *numero uno* in Tuscany.

The prosperous new Empoli (pop. 45,000) produces green glass and raincoats. You'll find little to recall the days of Farinata, until you reach the piazza named after him; here is the palace where the parliament convened, across from the gem of a Romanesque church, the **Collegiata Sant'Andrea**, with its green and white marble geometric façade in the style of Florence's San Miniato. The lower portion dates from 1093; the upper had to wait until the 18th century, but it harmonizes extremely well.

**Museo della Collegiata**
*t 0571 76284;
open Tues–Sun 9–12
and 4–7; adm*

## Museo della Collegiata

Empoli has its share of 13th- and 14th-century Florentine art, much of it now in the small but choice **Museo della Collegiata** in the Collegiata's cloister. The most celebrated work is Masolino's *Pietà* fresco, with its poignant faces; upstairs there's an elegant relief of the *Madonna and Child* by Mino da Fiesole and his brother Antonio's painted tabernacle of St Sebastian. Lorenzo Monaco contributes a long-eyed *Madonna and Saints*; Lorenzo di Bicci's scene of San Nicola da Tolentino shielding Empoli from a rain of plague arrows is a quattrocento view of the city. There is a rare series of frescoes by Masolino's master, Starnina, as well as two saints by Pontormo, who was born nearby, and the fine *Tabernacle of the Holy Sacrament* by Francesco Botticini and his son Raffaello, with a good predella. The upper loggia has works by Andrea della Robbia, and the suspended wooden wings of the donkey that flies down on a wire from the church tower on *Corpus Domine* (though a papier-mâché donkey has of late replaced the original one).

**Santo Stefano**
*open Tues–Fri 9–12 by appt – enquire at the Museo della Collegiata*

Empoli's **Santo Stefano** church, restored after damage during the Second World War, has more beautiful frescoes by Masolino and a marble *Annunciation* by Bernardo Rossellini.

# Getting along the Arno between Florence and Pisa

If you're **driving**, persist: the Florentine sprawl finally gives way at Signa and after that the Arno road (S67) becomes even scenic in stretches. LAZZI **buses** take the main route to Pisa; SITA goes directly from Florence to Castelfiorentino or Certaldo; for Vinci, COPIT. **Trains** at least once an hour follow the Arno between Florence and Pisa, and at Empoli turn off for Castelfiorentino, Certaldo, Poggibonsi and Siena. Note that San Miniato and Fucecchio share a railway station; local buses commute from there to both centres.

## Around Empoli

Northwest of Empoli, in the Monte Albano, lies the old hill townlet of **Cerreto Guidi**, former property of the Counts of Guidi, taken over by Florence in 1237. It is known these days for its Chianti Putto, and for the **Villa Medicea**, rebuilt for Cosimo I by Buontalenti in 1564, relatively simple as Medici villas go, but approached by the 'Medici bridges', a grand double ramp of bricks. In 1576 Cosimo I's daughter Isabella was murdered here by her husband Paolo Orsini for her infidelities; look carefully and you will see the unhappy couple among the scores of Medici portraits in the villa. From the terrace there are fine views of the Monte Albano.

**Villa Medicea**
www.villamedicea.it;
open Tues–Sun
8.15–7; adm

From Cerreto it's 5km to **Vinci**, a tiny town most famous as the home of Leonardo, who was born in a humble house in Anchiano on 15 April 1452, the illegitimate son of the local notary and a peasant girl. In his honour, the town's landmark Conti Guidi Castle has been converted into the **Museo Leonardiano**, full of models of inventions he designed in his *Codex Atlanticus* notebooks, most of which this supreme 'Renaissance man' never had the time or attention span to build. There are descriptions in English for the 100 or so machines, including some inspired by those invented by Brunelleschi to build Florence's cathedral dome. This gentle fellow once said, 'I'll do anything for money' – one of the most startling quotes of the Renaissance. On the other hand, nothing could be more typical of the age than brilliance combined with immorality; while he often neglected his art, Leonardo was happy to help the bellicose princes who employed him with their military problems. Leonardo was baptized in **Santa Croce**, next to the museum.

**⭐ Museo Leonardiano**
www.museo
leonardiano.it, **t** 0571
933251; open Nov–Feb
daily 9.30–6; Mar–Oct
daily 9.30–7; adm

It's 3km southeast to **Anchiano** to see the simple stone house where Leonardo was born, the **Casa Natale di Leonardo**.

**Casa Natale di Leonardo**
open Nov–Feb daily
9.30–6; in summer
until 7; adm

## Where to Stay and Eat from Florence to Empoli

For Paggeria Medicea and Da Delfina in Artimino, *see* p.xxx and p.xxx.

**ⓘ Vinci >>**
Via delle Torri 11,
**t** 0571 568012,
www.terredel
rinascimento.it
(also serves Empoli)

### Santa Maria a Marciola
✉ 50018

**Fiore**, Via di Marciola 112, near Scandicci, **t** 055 768678 (€€). A good place to stop if it's time to eat just as you're leaving or approaching Florence, not only for its delicious crêpes and mixed meats on the grill, game, *bistecca*, etc., but for its lovely garden setting and pine-clad slopes. *Open for dinner daily and Sun and Sat lunch.*

### Vinci ✉ 50059

★★★**Alexandra**, Via dei Martiri 38, **t** 0571 56224, www.hotelalexandra

vinci.it (€€€). Vinci's one hotel; quiet and comfortable, with some apartments as well as rooms.

As for restaurants, there isn't much choice.

**Antica Cantina di Bacco**, Piazza Leonardo da Vinci 3, t 0571 568041 (€). A cosy wine bar with an attractive terrace, serving the usual *enoteca* fare; toasted *crostoni* with various toppings, a few pasta dishes, cheeses, desserts and, of course, wine. *Closed Mon.*

## Empoli ✉ 50053

Empoli isn't a posh town by any means, but it can be an agreeable place to stay over. It also has some good places to eat.

**\*\*\*Sole**, Piazza Don Minzoni, t 0571 73779 (€€). A good bargain, by the station, with baths in all rooms.

**Cucina Sant'Andrea**, Via Salvagnoli 43, t 0571 73657 (€€€). On the remains of the city walls, this *trattoria* run by a brother and sister serves creative versions of local dishes: pigeon terrine, courgette flan, risotto with artichokes, wild boar and game. *Closed Mon, 1 wk Dec/Jan, and Aug.*

**La Panzanella**, Via dei Cappucini 10, t 0571 922182 (€€). An old-fashioned trattoria, also by the station, which does an unusual artichoke soup and wonderful things with porcini mushrooms in season. Also a few fish dishes. *Closed Sat, Sun in summer and 2 wks Aug.*

# South of Empoli

## San Miniato

Just southwest of Empoli, the river Elsa flows into the Arno near San Miniato (pop. 23,000), a hill town that grew up at the crossroads of the Via Francigena (the main pilgrimage route from France to Rome) and the Florence–Pisa road. On a clear day the view reaches from Fiesole to the sea. Its strategic location made it the Tuscan residence of the emperors, from Otto IV to Frederick II; Matilda of Tuscany was born here in 1046, and in the 12th century it was an important imperial fortress, protecting the crossroads and levying tolls on travellers and merchandise.

Of the citadel, only two towers survive: the present campanile of the cathedral and the taller 'Torrione', in the shady Prato del Duomo that crowns San Miniato, with its peculiar chimney-like structures on top. It was from the top of this tower that Pier della Vigna, secretary and court poet to Frederick II's, falsely accused of treason, leapt to his death, to be discovered by Dante in the forest of suicides, as described in the *Inferno* XIII. Also in the Prato del

**San Martino Duomo**
*open summer Mon–Fri 9.30–5.45, Sat 9.30–6.45, Sun 9–9.50, 11.30–11.50 and 1–5; winter Mon–Sat 9.30–5*

Duomo stand the 12th-century **Palazzo dei Vicari dell'Imperatore** and the **Duomo** itself, with a Romanesque brick façade, incorporating pieces of sculpted marble and 13th-century majolica that catch the light as the sun sets. Most of the art in the interior is Baroque, except for a fine 13th-century holy water stoup; most of the earlier artworks from the region have been placed in the

**Museo Diocesano d'Arte Sacra**
*open Tues–Sun 10–12.30 and 3–6 (6.30 in summer); adm*

**Museo Diocesano d'Arte Sacra**, to the left of the cathedral. Among the prizes are the fresco of the *Maestà* by the 'Maestro degli Ordini' from Siena, a bust of Christ attributed to Verrocchio, Neri di Bicci's *Madonna con Bambino* and a *Crucifixion* by Filippo Lippi.

Since 1968, the Prato del Duomo has also been the site of the **National Kite Flying Contest** (*1st Sun after Easter*).

In the Piazza del Popolo's 14th-century church of **San Domenico** you can see minor works by Masolino, Pisanello and the della Robbias. Bernardo Rossellino carved the fine 15th-century tomb of Giovanni Chiellini, the Florentine founder of San Miniato's Hospital of Poor Pilgrim Priests. The tomb is modelled after Rossellino's famous tomb of Leonardo Bruni in Florence's Santa Croce. The beautiful church of **San Francesco** has fresco fragments by a follower of Masolino. Napoleon paid a visit in 1797, to see his relatives in the **Palazzo Bonaparte**. In the surrounding countryside are rich caches of white truffles, sought fervently in the autumn for the large market on the last Sunday in November; and many of what appear to be plain-looking Romanesque churches around San Miniato are actually tobacco-curing barns from the 1900s.

## Castelfiorentino and San Vivaldo

Some 12km south along the Valdelsa from San Miniato, **Castelfiorentino** (pop. 18,000) is another old hill town, though much rebuilt after damage in the Second World War. Its church of **Santa Verdiana** dates from the 18th century and houses the **Museo di Arte Sacra Santa Verdiana**, with some excellent trecento paintings, including a *Madonna* attributed to Duccio da Buoninsegna, another by Francesco Granacci, and a triptych by Taddeo Gaddi. In the **Biblioteca Comunale** are frescoes by Benozzo Gozzoli that were originally in the Tabernacle of the Madonna della Tosse, 'the coughing Madonna', in a nearby village, and also from the Cappella della Visitazione.

**Museo di Arte Sacra Santa Verdiana**
*open Sat 4–7, Sun and hols 10–12 and 4–7; guided tours by appt, call t 0571 64096; adm*

**Biblioteca Comunale**
*Via Tilli 41; open June–mid-Sept Mon, Tues and Thurs 3.30–8, Wed and Fri 9–1; rest of year Mon–Fri 2.30–7.30; adm*

One of the more unusual sights in Tuscany, the **Monastery of San Vivaldo**, lies to the southwest of Castelfiorentino, beyond the village of Montaione. Vivaldo, a hermit from San Gimignano, lived in a hollow chestnut tree where he was found dead in 1301, still in the attitude of prayer. A Franciscan community grew up in his footsteps, and in 1500, when the monastery was being rebuilt, one member, Fra Tommaso da Firenze, designed a 'New Jerusalem' in the monastery's wooded hills, with 34 **chapels** representing the sites of Christ's Passion. To render the symbolic journey more realistic for pilgrims, the 34 chapels combined polychrome terracottas by Giovanni della Robbia and other artists, set in frescoes – Pope Leo X immediately granted a fat indulgence to anyone who did the whole route. Today only 18 of the chapels survive .

**Capelle del Sacro Monte di San Vivaldo**
*www.sanvivaldo intoscana.com; open Nov–Mar daily 2–5; April–Oct Mon–Fri 3–7, Sat–Sun 10–7; to visit outside these hours, call t 0571 699252 for an appt*

## Certaldo

Certaldo (pop. 16,000), former seat of Florence's deputy, or Vicariate of the Valdelsa, is synonymous with Giovanni Boccaccio, who spent the last 13 years of his life in the old town, Castello Aldo,

## Where to Stay and Eat South of Empoli

### San Miniato ✉ 56027

****Miravalle**, Piazza Castello 3, t 0571 418075,*www.albergomiravalle. com* (€€€). Frederick II's 12th-century imperial palace, near the top of town.

**Il Canapone**, Piazza Bonaparte 5, t 0571 418121 (€€). A simple place where you can try the local truffles on spaghetti, in risotto, or with veal *scaloppine*; in the spring there's risotto with asparagus. *Closed Mon.*

### Certaldo ✉ 50052

****Il Castello**, Via della Rena 6, t 0571 668250, *www.albergoilcastello.it*

(€€€–€€). One of the more interesting of the three small hotels in town with a restaurant.

*****Osteria del Vicario**, Via Rivellino 3, t 0571 668228 (€€). A beautiful 12th-century ex-monastery with a garden, surrounded by a Romanesque courtyard. Rooms are simple, with terracotta floors, and the restaurant (€€€) serves creative fresh local fare. *Restaurant closed Wed.*

**Dolci Follie**, Piazza Boccaccio t 0571 668188 (€€–€). One place in Certaldo that can satisfy all your little vices at once. A fancy *pasticceria*, a wine bar and a fine little restaurant, where the cuisine (both fish and meat dishes) is more than a prelude to the exquisite desserts.

which could be a set for the *Decameron* itself (don't confuse it with the ugly sprawl of the new town, at the bottom of the hill).

Everything here is of good, honest brick, from the pavements to the *palazzi*, of which the most striking is the 14th-century castellated **Palazzo Pretorio**, studded with the arms of the former vicars. Inside it has a beautiful courtyard and museum containing Etruscan artefacts, frescoes and, in the annexed church and cloister, Gozzoli's *Tabernacle of the Punished*, not one of his more cheerful works. The walls of the old jail bear the forlorn graffiti of past prisoners.

The house traditionally associated with Certaldo's great author is the **Casa di Boccaccio**, which has been restored and is now the seat of the International Centre of Boccaccio Studies . Boccaccio died here in 1375 and lies buried in **Santi Michele ed Iacopo**, under an epitaph he penned himself; a 16th-century monument erected in his honour was destroyed by prudes in 1783. Boccaccio himself, in his later years, regretted the racy frivolity of his most famous book, wishing he had spent his time on serious Latin works – not a regret too many people have ever shared.

From Certaldo you can follow a pretty road to the south which leads to **San Gimignano** (*see* pp.362–8), about 13km away.

## Empoli to Pisa

There is no compelling reason to stop in the lower Valdarno unless you're low on petrol. If you're spending more time here, consider a visit to **Fucecchio** for its panoramic views, or better yet for the **Padule di Fucecchio**, claimed to be Italy's biggest inland swamp and certainly an excellent place for bird-watching.

## Where to Stay and Eat from Empoli to Pisa

### Fucecchio ✉ 50054

**Le Vedute**, Via Romana-Lucchese 121, t 0571 2977201 (€€€). A good inland seafood restaurant, pleasantly situated in the country. Serves good meats too. In summer you can linger on the veranda. *Closed Mon.*

**\*\*\*La Campagnola**, Viale Colombo 144, t 0571 260786 (€€). Twenty-five air-conditioned and plain, basic rooms.

### Montopoli in Val d'Arno ✉ 56020

**\*\*\*Quattro Gigli**, Piazza Michele da Montopoli 2, t 0571 466 878, *www. quattrogigli.it* (€€€). In this little place across the Arno, the old town hall has been converted into an inn with 28 rooms of varying quality. The restaurant (€€€) has a delightful terrace and an imaginative menu. Some of the dishes are based on centuries-old recipes, such as tripe with eggs and saffron. Others are more creative, such as fresh tuna soufflé with artichokes, *pici* with baby squid or duck with dried fruit. *Closed Mon, Sun eve in winter, 2wks Aug.*

Downriver lies industrial **Pontedera**, where the Piaggio Company produces most of Italy's motor scooters. Here you may detour south on the SS439 to Volterra (*see* p.368), by way of **Ponsacco** and the four-towered **Villa di Camugliano**, built by Alessandro and Cosimo I, an example of Medici real estate speculation. Between here and Volterra roll the Pisan Hills, some of the quietest, most rural countryside in Tuscany; the main attraction may be precisely its lack of art and history. Alternatively, from Ponsacco, you can head southwest to tiny **Lari**, with the remains of a Medici fortress, and for your rheumatism to **Casciana Terme**, famous for its cures in Roman times, and rebuilt by the Pisans in the 14th century.

**Vicopisano**, north of the Arno, defended the eastern frontier of Pisa from Lucca's ambitions, and its impressive *castello* was remodelled by Brunelleschi after the Florentine conquest of Pisa; vineyards now surround its walls and towers. Across the bridge, **Cascina** still has most of its medieval walls and Roman grid plan. It also has three churches that are worth a visit: **San Casciano**, an unusual 12th-century Romanesque church, with blind arches and some fine sculptural details; Romanesque **San Benedetto a Settimo**, adorned with a 14th-century alabaster altarpiece of Irish origin; and **San Giovanni Evangelista**, built by the Knights of St John, with trecento Sienese frescoes.

Further west lies the Certosa di Pisa (8km; *see* p.299) and Pisa itself (14km; *see* p.287).

# Prato

Prato is only 18km from Florence but it's a world away in atmosphere. This is a city that works for its living, where the population has doubled since the Second World War to 145,000,

## Getting to and around Prato

Prato is easily reached by **train** from Florence. It has two stations: the main Stazione Centrale, facing a pretty green square on the other bank of the river Bisenzio; and the Stazione Porta al Serraglio (not all trains stop), just north of the walls and closer to the centre, on the Florence–Pistoia line. This was one of Italy's first railways, built in 1848 for the Lorraine grand dukes by an Englishman, Ralph Bonfield, who so pleased the grand duke that he was made Count of St George of Prato. All Bonfields take note! The Prato tourist office is searching for his descendants, to claim the title and supply a likeness of Bonfield so they can erect a proper monument in his honour.

**Buses** from Prato depart from Piazza Ciardi or the Stazione Centrale; all pass through Piazza San Francesco (CAP or LAZZI buses, every half-hour to and from Florence with connections to the Mugello). LAZZI buses also serve Pistoia, Montecatini, Lucca, Pisa, Bologna and Viareggio.

Prato has two exits on the *autostrada* **A11** between Florence and Pisa (from Florence get on at Peretola). The centre is closed to traffic; Piazza Mercatale is a convenient place to **park**.

third largest in Tuscany after Florence and Livorno. And a vibrantly, joyously proletarian city it is, fond of Henry Moore, comic books, avant-garde theatre and heavy metal bars, full of people wanting you to sign petitions or buy encyclopaedias, all proud to live in 'the Manchester of Tuscany'. Living in Florence's shadow for the past thousand years has not dampened Prato's spirits; as in the days of the famous Francesco di Marco Datini, immortalized in Iris Origo's book *The Merchant of Prato*, this city still earns its keep from the manufacture of textiles, and especially the recycling of wool and rags. In the Renaissance, Prato made enough profit from these rags to hire the greatest artists of the day to embellish its churches and palaces.

## History

In the 9th century Prato was known as Borgo al Cornio. Outside the town was a meadow, or *prato*, the site of the market and fortifications, which gradually became so important that the whole town took the name.

It was first ruled by the Alberti, one of the region's more ambitious feudal families, who conquered lands all the way from the Maremma to the Mugello. In 1107 Countess Matilda personally led a combined Tuscan army against Prato in order to humble the Alberti; then, in 1140, the Pratesi rid their counts of most of their power and ran their city as a free *comune*. In 1193, at the height of the city's power, it even managed to snatch some of Florence's own *contado*. By this time the town of Prato had also become one of the most important manufacturers of woollen goods in Europe, and was so wealthy that the University of Paris created a special college for students from Pratesi.

Florence, however, could not countenance so near and so ambitious a rival, and in 1350, on charges of fomenting rebellion in the Valdelsa, Florence besieged Prato. An honourable peace was made; the next year Florence cemented its hold over its neighbour by purchasing it for the sum of 17,500 florins from its nominal overlord, the Angevin Queen of Naples.

Despite the ignominy of being bought, Prato functioned more as Florence's ally than its possession, retaining a certain amount of local autonomy. The late 14th century was the day of Francesco di Marco Datini, the Merchant of Prato, one of the richest men in Europe and history's first recorded workaholic businessman. However, although he built his palace in his home town of Prato, the big profits were to be had in Florence, and Datini spent most of his time there. Under the influence of Savonarola's preaching, Prato joined Florence in rebelling against Medici rule, but was soon to play the role of whipping boy, when the Spaniards, at the instigation of the Medici Pope Leo X, besieged and sacked the city with unheard-of brutality. Since that dark day, Prato's history has followed that of its imperious neighbour, until a few years ago, at least. You can't keep a good town down for ever, and Prato and its hinterlands have finally wriggled out from Florentine control and become a province in their own right – one of Italy's newest, and smallest.

## Castello dell'Imperatore

**Castello dell'Imperatore**
*t 0574 38207,*
*www.po-net.prato.it;*
*open Oct–Mar*
*Wed–Mon 9–1;*
*April–Sept Wed–Mon*
*9–1 and 4–7; adm*

Most people, whether arriving by car, bus, or at the Stazione Centrale, approach the walled core of Prato through the Piazza San Marco, embellished with a white puffy sculpture by Henry Moore from 1974. Viale Piave continues to the defiantly Ghibelline swallowtail crenellations of this castle. Built in 1237 by Frederick II, Holy Roman Emperor and heir to the Norman kingdom in southern Italy and Sicily, it marks a strange interlude in Prato's past. Frederick, unlike his grandfather Frederick Barbarossa, never spent much time in Tuscany, preferring his more civilized dominions in Apulia and Sicily, where he could discuss poetry, philosophy and falconry (in Arabic or Latin) with his court scholars. When he did come, it was in magnificent progress featuring dancing girls, elephants and the Muslim Imperial bodyguard. His Tuscan taxpayers were not impressed; nor did they much appreciate Frederick's tolerant, syncretistic approach to religion. The popes excommunicated him twice. He built this castle here because he had to, not so much to defend Prato, but to defend his Imperial *podestà* from the Pratesi, and perhaps impress the locals with its design – its clean lines must have seemed very sharp and modern in the 13th century.

Don't doubt for a minute that this castle is quite intentionally a work of art. The design, by a Sicilian named Riccardo da Lentini, is perfectly in tune with the south Italian works of the 'Hohenstaufen Renaissance' of Frederick's reign, a reminder of a rare age when artistically the south was keeping up with northern Italy, and often

N

250 metres
250 yards

Train Station

PIAZZA DELLA STAZIONE

Stadio Comunale

to Florence

VIA FIRENZE

VIA MACHIAVELLI

CORTELLI

VIA N. MACHIAVELLI

VIA P.

VIA G. MATTEOTTI

VIA TIZIANO

PIAZZA EUROPA

VIALE MONTE GRAPPA

VIA TACCA

VIA FRA BARTOLOMEO

VIALE VITTORIO VENETO

VIA F. FERRUCCI

VIA ABC MARTINI

Bisenzio

PIAZZA DEL MERCATALE

VIA G. MAZZINI

VIALE PIAVE

VIA S. CHIARA

VIA POMERIA

Museo dell'Opera del Duomo

Duomo

VIA DEI TINTORI

VIA G. GARIBALDI

VIA VERDI

VIA CAIROLI

Teatro Metastasio

Santa Maria delle Carceri

Castello dell'Imperatore

to Bologna   Stazione Porta al Serraglio

Sant' Agostino

PIAZZA S. AGOSTINO

VIA MAGNOLFI

VIA STUFA   VIA FILIPPINO

VIA DEL SERRAGLIO

CAP Bus Terminal

PIAZZA DEL DUOMO

VIA G. MAZZONI

Palazzo Comunale

PIAZZA DEL COMUNE

Palazzo Pretorio & Galleria Comunale

Palazzo Datini

VIA RICASOLI

PIAZZA S. MARIA DELLE CARCERI

San Francesco

PIAZZA S. FRANCESCO D'ASSISI

LAZZI Bus Terminal

VIA S. IACOPO

VIA FRASCATI

VIA CARBONAIA

VIA S. TRINITA

VIA ROMA

VIA S. FABIANO

PIAZZA LANDI

VIA C. GUASTI

VIA L. MUZZI

PIAZZA RINALDESCA

VIA BANCHELLI

VIA S. CATERINA

PIAZZA DEL COLLEGIO

VIA S. VINCENZO

VIA DEL SEMINARIO

San Domenico

CORSO SAVONAROLA

VIA DELLA MISERICORDIA

VIA CARRADORI

VIA DELL'ABBACO

to Pistoia

to Pistoia

VIA CAVOUR

VIA LUTI

VIA CURTATONE

Prato

a little in advance. There isn't much inside the castle now, though the city often uses the space for special exhibitions. Usually it is possible to walk up along its walls for a bird's-eye view of Prato.

## Santa Maria delle Carceri

Next to the castle stands the unfinished black and white marble façade of Santa Maria delle Carceri, begun in 1485 by Giuliano da Sangallo. Brunelleschian architecture was always a fragile blossom, as is clearly shown by the failure of this sole serious attempt to transplant it outside the walls of Florence, however Santa Maria always merits a mention in architectural histories. It was an audacious enterprise: Sangallo, a furiously diligent student of Vitruvius and Alberti, attempted to create a building based entirely on philosophical principles. Order, simplicity and correct proportion, as in Brunelleschi's churches, were to be manifest, with few frills allowed. Sangallo, the favourite of Lorenzo il Magnifico, unfortunately proved to be a better theorist than he was an architect. Santa Maria was a clumsy tombstone for the sort of theoretical architecture that was a fad in the 1400s, one more often expressed in paintings than actual buildings. The interior is better than the exterior, a plain Greek cross in the Brunelleschian manner with a decorative frieze and *tondi* of the four Evangelists by Andrea della Robbia. The church's name – *carceri* means prisons – refers to a local miracle, a speaking image of the Virgin painted on a nearby prison wall.

Behind the church is Prato's grand 1820's **Teatro Metastasio**, home to some of the most innovative theatre in Italy and also to frequent concerts.

## Piazza San Francesco and Datini

From Santa Maria delle Carceri you can see the apse of Prato's huge brick church of **San Francesco**, dating from the end of the 13th century, and embellished in front with white and green marble stripes. Inside, on the left wall is the Tomb of Gemignano Inghirami, one of Europe's crack lawyers of the quattrocento, the design attributed to Bernardo Rossellino (1460s); near the altar is the **tomb slab of Francesco di Marco Datini** (1330–1410) by Niccolò di Piero Lamberti. Off the elegant Renaissance cloister you'll find the entrance to the **Cappella Migliorati**, beautifully frescoed in 1395 by Niccolò di Pietro Gerini, one of the period's finest draughtsmen; here he depicts the *Lives of Sts Anthony Abbot and Matthew*.

**Palazzo Datini**
*Via Mazzei 33,*
*www.po-net.prato.it;*
*open Mon–Sat 9–12*
*and 4–6*

Niccolò also frescoed the nearby **Palazzo Datini**, the showplace palace built in the 1390s by the Merchant of Prato. If there were an Accountants' Hall of Fame, Francesco di Marco Datini would surely be in it; he helped invent that dismal science. The 150,000 documents, ledgers (all inscribed 'For God and Profit') and private letters stored in the archives in this palace formed the basis for Iris Origo's fascinating account of his life and times.

## Piazza del Comune and Around

Just north lies Prato's charming civic centre, the **Piazza del Comune**, decorated with a 19th-century **statue of Datini** with bronze reliefs of the merchant's life, and a pretty fountain by Tacca nicknamed 'Il Bacchino', or Little Bacchus (1659).

The city's **Palazzo Comunale**, behind the portico, retains only traces of its medieval heritage; drop in to see its **Sala di Consiglio** with its coffered ceiling, two quattrocento frescoes and portraits of the grand dukes.

The rugged **Palazzo Pretorio** is entirely medieval, a relic of the days when Prato governed itself without any help from the Medici; the stair on the façade leads up to the **Galleria Comunale 'Alberti'** with a good collection of mostly Florentine art. There's a tabernacle by Filippino Lippi, painted for his mother and later restored after damage in the war.

**Galleria Comunale 'Alberti'**
*open by appt, call t 057 4617359*

Up in the grand **Salone dell' Udienza** with the fine wood ceiling is Bernardo Daddi's *Story of the Holy Girdle*, a predella telling the tale of Prato's most famous relic, the Virgin Mary's belt. According to tradition she gave it to Doubting Thomas, from whom it was passed down until it became part of the dowry of a woman who married Michele, a knight from Prato during the First Crusade. Michele returned to Prato and hid the precious relic under his mattress; angels lifted him off, and the girdle was given into the care of the cathedral. In the same hall are fine 14th-century works by Giovanni di Milano, Michele di Firenze and Lorenzo Monaco, and a *tondo* attributed to Luca Signorelli. In an adjoining room is *Noli me tangere* by Battistello, a follower of Caravaggio; this curious work portrays Christ wearing a fedora at a rakish angle, doing a quick dance step to evade the Magdalene's touch.

**Museo del Tessuto**
*Via Santa Chiara 24, www.museodel tessuto.it; open Mon–Fri 10–6, Sat 10–2, Sun 4–7; for guided tours call t 0574 611503*

For a celebration of Prato's medieval and modern textile industry visit the **Museo del Tessuto**, which has a unique collection of fabrics and looms (some 6,000 pieces). It is housed in a stunning 19th-century textile mill.

**Duomo di Santo Stefano**
*www.diocesiprato.it; open July–Sept daily 7.30–12.30 and 4–7.30; rest of year Fri 7–12.30 and 3–6.30, Sun and hols 7–12.30 and 3–8; guided tours of chapel (inc. Lippi frescoes) Sat 10, 11, 4 and 5 and Sun 10 and 11, by appt with tourist office; adm*

## Cathedral of Santo Stefano

In the centre of Prato rises its cathedral, like a faded beauty who never recovered from the blow of a broken engagement. It was begun with great promise in the 13th century, and added to on and off for the next 200 years, with ever-dwindling passion and money. The best features are an exotic, almost Moorish campanile, a rather dirty Andrea della Robbia lunette of the *Madonna and St Stephen* over the door, a big clock on the half-striped façade that makes you smile when you notice it sitting where the rose window ought to be and, above all, the circular **Pulpit of the Sacred Girdle**, projecting from the corner of the façade. Perhaps no other church in Italy has such a perfectly felicitous ornament, something beautiful and special that the Pratesi look at every day as they walk through the piazza. Michelozzo designed it in 1428 and Donatello added the delightful reliefs of dancing children and *putti* along the lines of his *cantoria* in Florence's cathedral museum (the bas-reliefs are only casts, but you can see the originals in the Museo dell'Opera, *see* below). The Holy Girdle (*see* p.235) is publicly displayed here on Easter Day, 1 May, 15 August, 8 September and Christmas Day.

The Duomo's interior continues the motif of green and white stripes in its Romanesque arcades and ribs of the vaulting. The **Chapel of the Sacred Girdle**, just to the left as you enter, is protected by a screen, and the inside is covered with frescoes by Agnolo Gaddi on the legend of the girdle, and adorned with a beautiful marble statue, the *Madonna and Child*, by Giovanni Pisano.

In the left aisle there's a masterful **pulpit** carved by Mino da Fiesole and Antonio Rossellino, with harpies around the base. Filippo Lippi's celebrated frescoes on the *Lives of Saints John the Baptist and Stephen* (1452–66) are undergoing restoration and work is expected to continue for several years. While painting these frescoes, his first major work, Lippi is said to have fallen in love with a brown-eyed novice, Lucrezia Buti, who according to tradition posed for his magnificent *Herod's Banquet*, either as the melancholy Salome herself or as the figure in the long white dress, second from the right; Fra Filippo placed himself among the mourners for St Stephen, third from right, in a red hat. The less lyrical frescoes in the next chapel are by Uccello and Andrea di Giusto. There's a lovely, almost Art Nouveau candelabra on the high altar by Maso di Bartolomeo (1440s), closely related to his work in Pistoia cathedral.

**Museo dell'Opera del Duomo**
*t 0574 29339,*
*www.diocesiprato.it;*
*open Mon and*
*Wed–Sat 10–1 and*
*3–6.30, Sun 10–1; adm*

The **Museo dell'Opera del Duomo** is located next door in the cloister, one side of which retains its 12th-century geometric marble decorations and rambunctious capitals. The museum is currently undergoing long-term restoration work to enlarge it, and only two rooms are open. The most important works are now at the Museo di Pittura Murale (*see* below). The tragic star of the museum is the original pulpit of the Sacred Girdle, with Donatello's merry *putti* made into lepers by car exhaust. Lippi's *Death of San Girolamo* was painted to prove to the bishop that he was the man to fresco the cathedral choir. Other works include his son Filippino's *St Lucy*, blissfully ignoring the knife in her throat, and another full-length portrait, of *Fra Jacopone di Todi*, believed to be an early work by Uccello. More dancing *putti* adorn the *Reliquary of the Sacred*

*Girdle* (1446) by Maso di Bartolomeo, which was stolen but recovered at the Todi antique fair.

## Walking through Prato

Most of Prato's old streets are anonymous, self-effacing Tuscan. Sadly, some areas suffered bomb damage in the war, notably the great pear-shaped **Piazza del Mercatale** on the banks of the Bisenzio. This was long the working core of the city, surrounded entirely by porticoes and workshops; it was and is the site of Prato's big market and fairs. A few faded, peeling porticoed buildings remain, jostling for space with neon-lit themed restaurants, overlooking the river that has laundered the products of Prato's principal industry for eight centuries.

Sunday is a good day to visit the sturdy brick **San Domenico** on the west side of town, a large Gothic church begun in 1283 and completed by Giovanni Pisano, one side of it lined with arcades. There's not much to see inside, but the adjacent convent, the home of painter Fra Bartolommeo and Pratese address of Savonarola, holds the **Museo di Pittura Murale**, housing a collection of detached frescoes from surrounding churches, and currently holding some of the works of Prato's other museums while they undergo reorganization. There are charming quattrocento graffiti court scenes from the Palazzo Vaj, a sinopia from the cathedral attributed to Uccello, and Niccolò di Piero Gerini's *Tabernacle of the Ceppo*. Filippo Lippi painted the *Madonna del Ceppo* for the Ceppo offices in the Palazzo Datini; it portrays the tycoon himself, with four fellow donors, who contributed less and thus get portrayed as midgets.

**Museo di Pittura Murale**
*t 0574 44050; open Mon, Wed, Thurs 9–1; Fri–Sat 9–1 and 3–6; adm*

Just north of San Domenico, **San Fabiano**, at Via del Seminario 30, has an enchanting pre-Romanesque mosaic pavement, depicting mermaids, birds and dragons biting their own tails; north of San Fabiano, 15th-century **Sant'Agostino** contains Prato's most ridiculous painting, the *Madonna della Consolazione* (attributed, naturally, to Vasari), who does her consoling by distributing belts from heaven.

**Centro per l'Arte Contemporanea Luigi Pecci**
*Viale della Repubblica, t 0574 5317, www.centropecci.it; temporarily closed at time of writing; adm exp*

Despite all its artistic treasures, Prato doesn't sit on its Renaissance laurels. In the suburbs, the ambitious **Centro per l'Arte Contemporanea Luigi Pecci** has a collection of modern works from artists around the world, and holds temporary exhibitions by important artists, and concerts. Since the successful reception of Henry Moore's big lump by the train station in the 1970s, Prato has also accumulated outdoor abstract sculpture in a big way. Two that stand out, if only for their breathtaking pretentiousness, are Barbara Krueger's billboard *Untitled* (on Viale da Vinci), and Anne and Patrick Poirier's *Exegi Monumentum Aere Perennius*, in the grounds of the Centro Luigi Pecci.

## Shopping in Prato

Prato still makes its living from fine fabrics and clothing, and people from all over Tuscany come to visit the **factory outlets** where these are available at discount prices. Clothing designers from all over the world, including some of the biggest names, buy their fabric in Prato. One of the specialities is **cashmere**.

**Maglificio Denny**, Via Santa Gonda 3–7, t 0574 592350. Cashmere, wool and cotton knitwear.

**Anngorelle**, Via Vella, t 0574 467275. For cashmere and mohair.

**Tessiture Cecchi & Cecchi**, Via delle Calandre 53, t 0574 8878196. Does covers, scarves and such in cashmere, wool and silk.

There are also some good **clothing** outlets:

**M-Wear-Milior**, Via Pistoiese 755D, t 0574 818288. Women's clothes and accessories.

**Maglificio Pratesi**, Via Baccheretana 83, Seano, t 055 870 5467. Clothing for men, women and children.

## Where to Stay in Prato

### Prato ✉ 50047

Prato's hotels mostly cater for businessmen, but can be a good bet in the summer when Florence is packed to the gills.

**\*\*\*Flora**, Via Cairoli 31, near S. Maria dei Carceri, t 0574 33521, *www.prathotels.it* (€€€). Old-fashioned but decent modernized rooms. All rooms have a video machine and there is a small video library to borrow from.

**\*\*\*Villa Santa Cristina**, Via Poggio Secco 58, t 0574 595 951 (€€€). A relaxing spot with a garden, pool and most other comforts, over the river in the hills to the east of Prato. *Restaurant closed Sun.*

**\*\*\*Hotel Giardino**, Via Magnolfi 2, t 0574 26189, *www.giardinohotel.com* (€€€–€€). This smartly modernized and friendly hotel on Piazza del Duomo has a pleasant bar, a reading room and a private garage.

ⓘ **Prato** >
*Piazza Duomo 8,
t 0574 24112,
www.prato.turismo.it*

**\*\*\*San Marco**, Piazza San Marco 48, t 0574 21321, *www.hotelsanmarco prato.com* (€€). A pleasant place between the Stazione Centrale and the Castello, convenient if you arrive by train.

**Villa Rucellai**, Via di Canneto 16, 4km northeast of town, t 0574 460392, *www.villarucellai.it* (€€). A delightful, good value B&B in a Renaissance villa, with pool. Despite being surrounded by Prato's industrial sprawl, its formal gardens and the wonderful atmosphere of the house (filled with the family's books, pictures and furniture) is an oasis. The farm produces wine, oil, honey and jam.

**\*\*Toscana**, Piazza Ciardi 3, t 0574 28096, *www.hoteltoscana. prato.it* (€€). More economical, on a quiet square on the far side of the Stazione Porta al Serraglio, with recently renovated rooms.

## Eating Out in Prato

One reason for staying in Prato is the food, especially if you like fish.

**Osvaldo Baroncelli**, Via Fra Bartolomeo 13, t 0574 23810 (€€€€–€€€). A small establishment with an innovative chef and good value set menu. *A la carte* options include fricassée of salt cod, Tuscan bean and spelt soup with fish and frizzled leeks. The *sedano alla pratese* (celery with meat) is highly recommended, and there is a fabulous array of Italian and French cheeses. *Closed Sat lunch adn Sun.*

**Enoteca Barni**, Via Ferrucci 22, t 0574 607 845 (€€€). Has an excellent wine list; the food is good, with simpler, cheaper lunch menus and more interesting choices at night, in a more elegant setting – asparagus soufflé with foie gras sauce, red mullet with basil, black olives and tomato, bean and cabbage soup with lobster, lamb in a herb crust. *Closed Mon–Wed dinner, Sat–Sun lunch, Aug.*

**Il Pirana**, Via Valentini 110 (south of Viale Vittorio Veneto, between the central station and Piazza San Marco), t 0574 25746 (€€€). Maintains a justified reputation for some of the best seafood in inland Tuscany. An elegant place, hidden behind

⭐ La Vecchia
Cucina di
Soldano >>

reflecting glass windows. Try the *gran piatto* of raw marinated fish, *gnocchetti* with scampi and zucchini flowers, or fish ravioli in lobster sauce. *Closed Sat lunch and Sun and Aug.*

**Mattei**, Via Ricasoli 22 (€). The distinctive bright blue bags displayed in the window of this *biscotteria* and bar contain the best *biscotti (or cantucci) di Prato* around. Don't settle for anything less. *Closed Mon.*

**Osteria Cibbé**, Piazza Mercatale 49, t 0574 607509 (€). A small, family-run *osteria* with marble-topped tables set in a brick-vaulted room, serving delicious rustic dishes such as *pappa al pomodoro*, *garganelli* with aubergine and wild mushrooms, stock fish *in zimino* (spicy sauce with Swiss chard), and meatballs with ricotta cheese. Booking advisable. *Closed Sun.*

**La Vecchia Cucina di Soldano**, Via Pomeri 23, t 0574 34665 (€). A very gratifying trattoria for something less elaborate, with a traditional menu cooked and served on red-checked cloths by the Mattei family, that's full of *ribollita* and *pasta e fagioli*, stuffed celery and all the other old-fashioned soups and stews, including the house speciality, a hearty beef and onion stew known as *francesina*. Meat is the speciality, though, so try wild boar, roe deer, sheep or *sedano alla pratese* (see above). *Closed Sun.*

# North of Prato: the Val di Bisenzio

Prato's river begins some 40km up in the Apennines, and along its valley runs the SS325, a secondary highway towards Bologna. This valley was long the fiefdom of the Alberti counts, whose fortifications dot its sides. **Vaiano**, the first town on the main route, has a Romanesque abbey church and green-striped campanile as its landmark; just beyond are the ruins of the Alberti's **Rocca di Cerbaia** (12th century). The highway continues to **Vernio** and **San Quirico**, with another ruined Alberti castle up above.

From San Quirico's neighbour to the west, **Cantagallo** ('cock's crow'), a lovely walking path leads in just over an hour up to the **Piano della Rasa**, which is a panoramic valley with an **alpine refuge**.

**Refugio alpino**
*open April–Oct*

Further north on the SS325, at the small resort of **Montepiano**, the waters destined for the Tyrrhenian and Adriatic split and go their own ways. There is another ancient abbey here, the Vallombrosan **Badia di Santa Maria**, with good 13th- and 14th-century frescoes. From the abbey begins another fine walking path up to **Alpi di Cavarzano** (1,008m/3,306ft), and from there, it is another hour or so's walk up to the highest peak in the region, **Monte La Scoperta** (1,278m/4,192ft).

# Figline and Montemurlo

The old road between Prato and Pistoia passes near **Figline di Prato**, a medieval village well-known for its terracotta vases. Figline has a 14th-century parish church with contemporary mural paintings, including a 'primitive' *Last Supper* and also a *St Michael* with a finely detailed background; a small parish museum contains other 'primitives'.

**Montemurlo**, on its hill over the plain of Prato, is also medieval; in 1537 its castle, a stronghold of the Guidi counts, was the Alamo for the anti-Medici republican oligarchs of Florence, led by Filippo Strozzi, who were defeated here once and for all by the troops of Cosimo I. The old walled town is interesting, with an impressive and rather stylish **Rocca** for its crown, approached these days by a Mannerist ramp. The Romanesque church of 'Beheaded John' (**San Giovanni Decollato**) has a pretty campanile and some good art in its baroqued interior, including a miraculous Byzantine crucifix and a 16th-century painting by Giovanni da Prato illustrating its story.

# Pistoia

 **Pistoia**

You know Pistoia (pop. 94,000) is near when the road plunges into a Lilliputian forest of umbrella pines and cypresses, all in tidy rows. These are Italy's most extensive ornamental nurseries, a gentle craft that thrives in the rich soil at the foot of the Apennines. But Pistoia wasn't always content to cultivate its own garden peacefully; this is the place, after all, that gave us the word 'pistol' – which originally referred to the surgical knives made in the city, but later came to mean daggers, and finally guns.

Today it specializes in light rail trains (the Breda works built the cars for the Washington DC metro), mattresses, cymbals and baby trees. Although seldom sampled by the moveable feast of tourism, the historic centre of Pistoia is almost perfectly intact, and behind its medieval walls there is some fine art to be seen, part Pisan, part Florentine, reflecting its position between the two great rivals. On Wednesdays and Saturday a huge market takes over the city centre.

*...Proud you are, envious, enemies of heaven / Friends to your own harm and, to your own neighbour / The simplest charity you find a labour*

'Invective against the People of Pistoia', a sonnet by Michelangelo

## History

Pistoia's fellow Tuscans have looked askance at her ever since Roman times, when the city was called *Pistoria* and saw the death struggle of the Catiline Conspiracy, the famous attempted coup against the Roman Republic in 62 BC, which ended when the legions tracked down the escaped Catiline and his henchmen near Pistoia. Its position on the Via Cassia helped it prosper under the Lombards, who elevated it to a royal city. In 1158 Pistoia became a *comune*, and was seen as enough of a threat for Florence and Lucca to gang up against it twice. In the 13th century Pistoia's evil reputation gave it credit for having begun the bitter controversy between Black and White Guelphs that so obsessed Florence; Dante, himself a victim of that feud, made sure that in writing the *Divina Commedia* he never missed an opportunity to curse and condemn the fateful city. In 1306 Florence exacted revenge by

# Getting to and around Pistoia

There are frequent **trains** (*www.trenitalia.com*) along the main Florence–Lucca line from the station, just south of the city walls at the end of Via XX?Settembre.

Pistoia lies along the A11, and at the foot of two important routes north over the Appenines, the **SS64** towards Bologna and the **SS633** to Abetone.

COPIT **buses** (*www.copitspa.it*) for Vinci and Empoli (37km/2hrs – a beautiful, twisting road over the Monte Albano), Cutigliano (37km/1hr 45mins), Abetone (50km/2hrs 30mins), the zoo, Montecatini (16km/ 30mins), and other destinations in Pistoia's little province depart from Piazza San Francesco. LAZZI buses (*www.lazzi.it*) depart for Florence (35km/1hr), Prato, Lucca (43km/90mins), Montecatini, Viareggio and Pisa (65km/2hrs) from Viale Vittorio Veneto, near the train station.

**Cars** are banned from most of the centre (in theory), but there's plenty of parking around the Fortezza di Santa Barbara in the southeast corner of the walls.

capturing Pistoia, and as usual she adapted her politics to the nature of her conquest: Prato she made an ally, Pisa she held with fortresses, but Pistoia she controlled with factions. The only interlude came between 1315 and 1328, when Lucca's Castruccio Castracani held Pistoia as part of his empire; it was a short-lived respite, however: after his fall the Florentines soon returned. Pistoia, preoccupied with its own quarrels, carried on happily ever after, making a good living from its old speciality, ironworking. It proudly supplied the conspirators of Europe with fine daggers, and later, keeping up with technological advances, with pistols.

## Piazza del Duomo

Pistol-Pistoia no longer packs any heat, but it packs into the heart of its 16th-century diamond-shaped walls one of the finest squares in Italy, a lesson in the subtle medieval aesthetic of urban design, an art lost with the endless theorizing and compulsive regularity of the Renaissance. The arrangement of the buildings around the L-shaped Piazza del Duomo seems at first to be haphazard. The design is meant to be experienced from street level; if you try walking into the piazza from a few of its surrounding streets, you'll see how from each approach the monuments reveal themselves in a different order and pattern, like the shaking of a kaleidoscope; the windows of the Palazzo del Comune echo those on the Palazzo del Podestà, and the striped decoration of the baptistry is recalled in the campanile and Duomo. The piazza provides the perfect setting for Pistoia's great annual party in July, the colourful *Giostra dell'Orso* (Joust of the Bear, *see* 'Festivals', p.247).

The **Duomo**, dedicated to San Zeno, dates from the 12th century; the Pisan arcades and stripes of its façade, combined over the geometric patterns of the Florentine Romanesque and polychrome terracotta lunette by Andrea della Robbia, strike an uneasy balance between the two architectural traditions. The outsize **campanile**, originally a watchtower, tips the balance towards Pisa, with exotic, almost Moorish candy-striped arches at the top added in the 14th century when it was converted to church use – though you can still see the old Ghibelline crenellations on top. Inside the cathedral is a wealth of art – on the right a **font** with quaint medieval heads, redesigned by Benedetto da Maiano; the **tomb of Cino da Pistoia** (1337), a close friend of Dante, shown lecturing to a class of scholars; and a 13th-century painted crucifix by Coppo di Marcovaldo. The cathedral's most precious treasure is in the **chapel of St James**: a fabulous altar made of nearly a ton of silver, comprising 628 figures, begun in 1287 and added to over the next two centuries; among the Pisan, Sienese and Florentine artists who contributed to this shining *tour de force* was Brunelleschi, who added the two half-figures on the left before he decided to devote

**Cappella di San Jacopo**
*contact the sacristan to view; adm*

Pistoia

all his talents to architecture. Some of the oldest art, fine medieval reliefs of the *Last Supper* and *Gethsemane*, have been relegated to the dim and ancient crypt. By the altar there's a fine painting by Caravaggio's pupil, Mattia Preti, and Maso di Bartolomeo's bronze candelabra. On the left the **chapel of the Sacrament** contains a bust of a Medici archbishop attributed to Verrocchio, who also added the statues of Faith and Hope to the weeping angels on the **tomb of Cardinal Forteguerri**, just left of the main entrance.

Next to the Duomo stands the partly striped and partly brick **Palazzo dei Vescovi**, mangled by remodellings over the centuries. The tourist information office is here, and the restorations undertaken to install it uncovered some Etruscan *cippi* (gravestones), and the foundations of Pistoia's original cathedral. The Etruscan finds, along with relics of Roman Pistoia, have been arranged in an 'archaeological itinerary' in the Palazzo's basement,

**Museo San Zeno**
t 0573 369272; open
by appt Tues, Thurs and
Fri plus 2nd and 4th
Sun of month, 10–1
and 3–5; adm

and the old cathedral is now included in the **Museo San Zeno**, along with some interesting paintings and a fine reliquary by Lorenzo Ghiberti.

Across from the Duomo stands Pistoia's octagonal zebra of a baptistry, whose proper name is **San Giovanni in Corte**. Built over the site of a Lombard-era royal palace (the *corte*), it was finished in 1359, to a design by Andrea Pisano. It is one of the few outstanding

**San Giovanni in Corte**
open Tues–Sun 10–6

Gothic buildings in Tuscany, embellished with fine sculptural details on the outside. The interior has a remarkable conical ceiling of brick and a beautifully decorated font dating from 1226, designed by Lanfranco da Como. In Piazza della Sala, behind the baptistry, is a medieval well, topped by a Florentine *Marzocco*.

The Piazza del Duomo's other two palaces are civic in nature. The 14th-century **Palazzo Pretorio** on the west side has a decorated courtyard and an old stone bench where the judges once sat and where they often condemned malefactors to a unique punishment – they were ennobled. Not that Pistoia wanted to reward them; rather, to become noble meant losing one's rights as a republican citizen. The tower near here is known as the **tomb of Catiline**, who according to tradition was secretly buried here.

On the other side of the piazza stands the elegant **Palazzo Comunale**, begun in 1294, and prominently embellished with the usual Medici balls and the more unusual black marble head, believed to be that of a Moorish king captured by a captain from Pistoia on a freebooting expedition to Mallorca. Besides the town council and offices, the *palazzo* houses the **Museo Civico**, an excellent collection of great and odd paintings to suit even the most jaded of palates. Pistoiese patrons were uncommonly fond of the *Sacra Conversazione* – a group portrait of saints around the Madonna – and there are good ones by Mariotto de Nardo, Beccafumi, Lorenzo di Credi and Pistoia's own Gerino Gerini

**Museo Civico**
t 0573 371290,
www.comune.pistoia.
it/museocivico;
open winter Tues,
Thurs, Fri, Sat 10–5, Sun
11–5; summer Tues,
Thurs, Fri, Sat 10–6,
Sun 11–6; adm

(1480–1529), a follower of Raphael. From the 15th-century 'Maestro delle Madonne di Marmo' there's a sweetly smiling marble relief of the *Madonna and Child*; then two fancy *St Sebastians* with flowing curls, who precede the *Madonna della Pergola*, by local painter Bernardino di Antonio Detti (1498–1554), whose flaccid charwoman of a Madonna holds a child with a large housefly on his chubby arm before a crazy quilt of confusing iconography – children with dolls, the Judgement of Solomon, a child with a fruit-bowl, a floor littered with flowers, amulets, spoons and rags. On the mezzanine is the document centre of the great 20th-century Pistoiese architect Giovanni Michelucci; a comprehensive collection of models and drawings, as well as photos of his buildings and the media reaction to them. One example of his work is the large, angular Santa Maria Novella station in Florence, another is the restaurant in the Parco Collodi (*see* p.254).

Plod up another flight of stairs to see some screamingly lurid paintings from the 17th and 19th centuries, with enough historical canvases of murder and mayhem to suggest that the local taste for violence lingered on for some time, at least within the confines of art. There are two mythological paintings swathed in Caravaggiesque darkness by Cecco Bravo; a 17th-century *Young Woman with a Flower*, bathed in ghostly light; a sensuous, pouting *St Sebastian*, disdainfully plucking arrows from his chest; an absurd allegory of Medici rule in Pistoia, with *putti* scattering the family's lily symbol like flowers over the city; a Magdalene fondly patting a skull; as well as two rather nightmarish imaginary battle scenes by a 17th-century Neapolitan named Francesco Graziani.

Just off the Piazza del Duomo on Ripa del Sale, the 16th-century Palazzo Rospigliosi houses two small museums, the **Museo Rospigliosi**, with a collection of its original furniture and paintings *in situ*, the paintings mostly by a Pistoiese artist named Giacinto Gimignani, and the **Museo Diocesano**, displaying crosses and reliquaries from the early Middle Ages.

**Museo Rospigliosi / Museo Diocesano**
*t 0573 28740; both open Tues–Sat 10–1 and 3–6; joint adm*

## Ospedale del Ceppo and Sant'Andrea

In medieval Tuscany, it was customary to collect alms in a hollowed-out log (or *ceppo*) left in a public place, to be gathered and distributed to the poor at Christmas-time. *Ceppo* became synonymous with the word charity, as in Datini's famous foundation in Prato, and even earlier here in Pistoia, when the **Ospedale del Ceppo** was founded in the 13th century. Still functioning at the same address (walk down Via Filippo Pacini from the Palazzo Comunale), the building was given a fine arcaded porch in the 1500s, in the style of the famous Spedale degli Innocenti in Florence. And, as in Florence, the della Robbias were called upon to provide the decoration, in this case the usually insipid Giovanni, who with the help of his workshop and other artists created not only the typical della Robbian *tondi*, but a unique terracotta frieze that spans the entire loggia in resplendent Renaissance Technicolor, with scenes of the acts of mercy and theological virtues. Inside there's a small **Museo dei Ferri Chirurgici** dedicated to Pistoia's old iron industry, especially surgical knives. You can visit one of the city's wrought-iron 'laboratories', **Bartoletti** at Via Sestini 110.

**Bartoletti**
*t 0573 452784; open Mon–Sat , call for times*

**Sant'Andrea**
*open daily 8–12.30 and 3.30–6*

A short walk west of the hospital on Via Sant'Andrea is the 12th-century church of **Sant'Andrea** , with a Pisan façade and over the door, a charming bas-relief of the *Journey of the Magi*, dated 1166, and a pair of ghastly, leering lions. The real jewel is inside: Giovanni Pisano's hexagonal **pulpit** (1297), exquisitely carved in stirring high relief with scenes of the *Nativity*, *Massacre of the Innocents*, *Adoration of the Magi*, *Crucifixion* and *Last Judgement*, with sibyls in the corners and pedestals in the forms of the four Evangelists – one of the masterpieces of Italian Gothic. Sant'Andrea contains three other crucifixions: Giovanni Pisano's wooden crucifix in the right aisle; a medieval version over the main altar, portraying Christ crowned and dressed in a kingly robe; and, in the right nave, a large, rather mysterious painting of the saint crucified on a tree.

## San Francesco and the Madonna dell'Umiltà

Pretty striped churches circle the centre of Pistoia like zebras on a merry-go-round. The two plain ponies in the lot lie to the west. The large **San Francesco al Prato** in Piazza San Francesco d'Assisi, plain and Gothic like most Franciscan churches, has some notable 14th-century frescoes, especially in the chapel to the left of the altar, with Sienese scenes portraying the *Triumph of St Augustine*. On the side of the church there's an ancient olive tree and a memorial to assassinated prime minister Aldo Moro, a stark contrast with the heroic Fascist-era war monument in the piazza itself. South along Corso Gramsci is Pistoia's main theatre, the 1694 **Teatro Manzoni**; further south, on Via della Madonna, towers Pistoia's great experiment in High Renaissance geometry, the octagonal, unstriped **Basilica della Madonna dell'Umiltà** begun in 1518 by local architect and pupil of Bramante, Ventura Vitoni, who graced it with an imposing barrel-vaulted vestibule. In the 1560s Giorgio Vasari was called upon to crown Vitoni's fine start; not content to limit his mischief to Florence, he added a dome so heavy that the basilica has been threatening to collapse ever since. More work to shore it up is currently under way.

## San Giovanni Fuorcivitas and San Domenico

To the south of the Piazza del Duomo (Via Roma to Via Cavour) lies the tiny **Piazza San Leone**, the ancient Lombard centre of

Pistoia; its stubby tower once belonged to the nastiest Pistoian of them all, a 13th-century noble thug and church robber named Vanni Fucci whom Dante found in one of the lower circles of Hell, entwined in a serpent, cursing and making obscene gestures up at God. Around the corner of Via Cavour, the 12th-century **San Giovanni Fuorcivitas** claims the honour of being the most striped church in all Christendom, its green and white flank an abstract pattern of lozenges and blind arches that out-Pisas anything in Pisa. The gloomy interior holds a dramatic pulpit (1270) by Fra Guglielmo da Pisa, a pupil of Nicola Pisano, a holy water stoup supported by caryatids by Giovanni Pisano and a white, glazed terracotta group of the *Visitation* by Luca or Andrea della Robbia.

Piazza Garibaldi, also to the south, is adorned with a good equestrian statue of Garibaldi, some florid street lamps, and **San Domenico**, begun in the late 13th century. In its spacious, airy interior there's a splendid Baroque organ from 1617 and two Renaissance tombs: that of Filippo Lazzari, by the Rossellino brothers, portraying the deceased lecturing to his pupils (one of whom can't help yawning), and the other of Lorenzo da Ripafratta, with a fine effigy. In 1497, Benozzo Gozzoli died of the plague in Pistoia and is buried somewhere in the cloister of San Domenico; you can see a fresco he began of the *Journey of the Magi* nearby. Although the monastery is still in use, you can ring to see the frescoes in the chapter house, among them good Sienese works and a *Crucifixion* with its sinopia, dating back to the mid-13th century.

Even more interesting are the frescoes across the street in the little **Cappella del Tau**, so named after the blue 'T' its priests wore on their vestments. The vividly coloured scenes of Adam and Eve and assorted saints are attributed in part to Masolino. The convent of the chapel has become the **Fondazione Marino Marini**. The collection traces the career of this Pistoiese artist, who died in 1980, in both paint and sculpture; it includes the bronze *Young Girl* which recalls the antique tradition not only in her facial features but also her truncated arms. Next to it, at No.72, note the coat of arms over the pretty window of two dancing bears, recalling the Giostra dell'Orso. There's another good Gothic façade on **San Paolo**, a block to the east, with broader stripes and a statue of St James on the very top, attributed to Orcagna.

There are more old churches in central Pistoia, but only one other worth going out of your way to visit: **San Bartolomeo in Pantano** (St Bart in the Bog), on the east side of town, built on marshy land in the 8th century and sinking gently into the ground ever since. It has an attractive, partially completed façade, and contains a carved marble lectern of 1250 by Guido da Como.

**Cappella del Tau**
*open Mon–Sat
8.15–1.30*

**Fondazione
Marino Marini**
*t 0573 30285;
open Mon–Sat 10–5;
adm; joint ticket with
other museums
available*

## The Zoo and the Medici

**Giardino Zoologico
di Pistoia**
*Via Pieve a Celle,*
*t 0573 911219; open*
*Mon–Fri 9–6.30, Sat, Sun*
*and hols 9–7; adm exp*

**La Magia in
Quarrata**
*t 0573 7710;*
*open by appt*

The newest stripes in Pistoia may well be on the zebras in the **Pistoia Zoo**, 4km northwest of the city. Though the Medici always kept big menageries, modern Italians don't usually care for zoos.

Thirteen kilometres to the southeast, off the SS66, is yet another Medici villa, **La Magia in Quarrata**, begun in 1318. Its grand hall has 18th-century frescoes, and in 1536 Charles V and Alessandro de' Medici met here.

## Festivals in Pistoia

*Giostra dell'Orso* (Joust of the Bear), 25 July. The culmination of a month of concerts, fairs and exhibits. The Joust began in the 14th century, pitting 12 knights against a bear dressed in a checked cloak. The bear has been replaced by two wooden dummies, but the pageantry remains the same.

## Where to Stay in Pistoia

**① Pistoia ›**
*Piazza del Duomo, in*
*the bishop's palace,*
*t 0573 374541,*
*www.turismo.pistoia.it*

### Pistoia ✉ 51110

Pistoia gives the impression that it is more accustomed to lodging and feeding business travellers than pleasure-seekers. On balance, it might be better to make this city a day trip, or stay in nearby Montecatini Terme instead.

There are a couple of options if you travel a few kilometres outside town. **\*\*\*Il Convento**, Via S. Quirico 33, 5km east at Pontenuovo, **t** 0573 452651, *www.ilconventohotel.com* (€€€). A former convent, preserving its exterior if not all of its interior. The setting is quiet, with views over Pistoia; there's a pool and one of the city's better restaurants.

**⭐ Villa Vannini ›**

**⭐ La BotteGaia ››**

**Villa Vannini**, about 6km north of town, **t** 0573 42031 (€€€). Even more rural is this delightful, if slightly fading villa among the fir trees, where you can relax with wonderful hill walks on the doorstep; there are elegant, comfortable, good-value rooms, and a fantastic restaurant.

There are a few reasonable options if you need somewhere in Pistoia itself. **Tenuta di Pieve a Celle**, Via Pieve a Celle, **t** 0573 913087, *www.tenuta*

*dipieveacelle.it* (€€€). A stylish *agriturismo* right next to the zoo, this farmhouse has been converted into five guest rooms with great taste and style. The setting is lovely (the only sound that might disturb the peace is the odd animal roar) and there is a fine pool. Guests can order dinner.

**\*\*\*Hotel Patria**, Via Crispi 8, **t** 0573 25187, *www.patriahotel.com* (€€). Situated near San Domenico, this hotel has recently been revamped so is a bit more cheerful than the other hotels in town. You can even have bacon and eggs for breakfast.

**\*\*\*Leon Bianco**, Via Panciatichi 2, **t** 0573 26675, *www.hotelleonbianco.it* (€€). A bit dated, but reasonably comfortable, with views over the campanile and with free Wi-fi access.

**\*\*\*Piccolo Ritz**, Via Vannucci 67, **t** 0573 26775 (€€). A modern place near the station – nice, but somewhat noisy. The cheaper rooms share facilities.

**\*\*Firenze**, Via Curtatone e Montanara 42, **t** 0573 23141, *www.hotelfirenze.it* (€€). The closest thing to inexpensive accommodation, near Piazza del Duomo, but it's a bit woebegone.

## Eating Out in Pistoia

Pistoia has many simple trattorias and pizzerias, and also several places offering delicious local cuisine.

**La BotteGaia**, Via del Lastrone 17, **t** 0573 365602 (€€). Tucked away behind the baptistry, occupying a beautifully appointed vaulted room and a lovely terrace, this wine bar/restaurant serves snacks (selections of cheeses and meat, *bruschette* and salads) and full meals from a short, but ever-changing menu. The *menu degustazione* is excellent value and features such dishes as celery soup with pecorino cheese, leek flan, pesto lasagne, and duck breast with wild fennel. There are some 600 wines to choose from too. *Closed Sun lunch, Mon and 2wks Aug.*

**Trattoria dell'Abbondanza**, Via dell'Abbondanza 10, t 0573 368037 (€€). There is an abundance of tempting dishes at this cheerful trattoria near the Duomo. The food is rustic and delicious: porcini soup, *gnocchi all'Abbondanza* (with tomatoes, pesto and pecorino cheese), octopus and potato stew, and roast pork spiked with rosemary and garlic. *Closed Thurs lunch, Wed, 2wks in Oct.*

**San Jacopo**, Via Crispi 15, t 0573 27786 (€). A pleasant trattoria, serving top-

quality traditional food (both fish and meat dishes) on crisp white cloths; Tuscan soups, spaghetti with clams, tripe, *baccalà*, rabbit with olives and, in season, porcini mushrooms. *Closed Tues lunch, Mon.*

And outside the town itself:

**Rafanelli**, Via Sant'Agostino 47, Sant'Agostino, t 0573 532046 (€€). Local dishes, including *maccheroni* with duck, game dishes and lamb, served in a pretty country villa setting, also does a great *bistecca*, grilled over a wood fire. *Closed Sun eve, Mon and Aug.*

**Bar Pari**, Via C.E. Montenara 15 (€). A bar with a simple rear dining room serving up vast portions of tasty fare such as ravioli in walnut sauce, at the lowest prices in town.

# The Mountains of Pistoia

North of Pistoia rises a fairly unspoiled stretch of the central Apennines, luxuriantly forested and endowed with some lovely mountain escape routes, deep green in the summer and ski-white in the winter. Main routes include the beautiful Bologna road (SS64) known as the 'Porrettana', which follows the Bologna–Pistoia railway through the sparsely settled mountains, and the equally beautiful, parallel SS632, less encumbered with traffic. The main mountain resorts up to Abetone are along the SS66 and SS12, as easily reached from Lucca as from Pistoia.

Due north of Pistoia, 10km along a byroad towards Piteccio, is the ancient hamlet of **Castagno**, now converted into a unique open-air art gallery. Its lanes are embellished with 20th-century frescoes on the 12 months; modern statues pose in the nooks and crannies; and Castagno's ancient church and oratory dedicated to St Francis, both with interesting frescoes, have recently been restored.

A 4km backtrack takes you to the main SS66; at Pontepetri (20km) the SS632 veers north to the formerly popular little mountain resort of **Pracchia**.

Most visitors continue along the SS66 for the newer summer-to-winter resorts by way of the lovely state forest of Teso, at the fine old villages of **Maresca** and **Gavinana**. The latter is notorious in Florentine history for the defeat of its army by the imperial forces of Charles V, a battle that cost the lives of both commanders. The Florentine leader, Francesco Ferrucci, was knifed in the back; he has his own little museum in the main piazza.

The SS66 continues to **San Marcello Pistoiese**, 29km from Pistoia, the 'capital' of the mountains, in a lovely setting, where since 1854 the inhabitants have launched a hot-air balloon each year on 8 September as a farewell to summer. You can walk over the 720ft (220m) **suspension bridge of Mammiano** all year round, however. **Cutigliano**, a growing winter resort 7km north, has 27km of ski trails and a cable car up to its highest peak, Doganaccia (3,854ft/ 1,175m). In the village itself, the **Palazzo Pretorio** fairly bristles with the coats of arms of its former governors.

Near the northern border of Tuscany, through a lush and ancient forest, lies **Abetone** (4,592ft/1,400m), one of the most famous resorts in the central Apennines. Named after a huge fir tree, it grew up in the late 18th century, when Grand Duke Pietro Leopoldo built the road to the Duchy of Modena, designing it to not pass through the detested Papal States (the modern province of Bologna). Two milestones at Abetone mark the old boundary. The closest ski resort to Florence, it is highly developed, with 35km of trails, a new cable car and 23 chairlifts; in summer its cool climate, pools and other facilities make it popular, especially at weekends. In other seasons, rain is not exactly unknown.

## Where to Stay and Eat in the Mountains of Pistoia

There's nothing posh about this pretty but neglected corner of Tuscany – nearly all hotels are good bargains. In the mountains, many open only during the ski season and in July and Aug. There are some economical holiday villas near the towns and alpine refuges in the mountains nearby; the tourist office has a list.

ⓘ **Abetone >>**
*Piazza Piramidi,*
*t 0573 60231,*
*www.abetone.com*

ⓘ **San Marcello Pistoiese >**
*Via Marconi 70,*
*t 0573 630145,*
*www.comunesan marcello.it*

 **La Vecchia Cantina >**

ⓘ **Cutigliano >**
*Via Brennero 42/a,*
*t 0573 68029,*
*www.comune. cutigliano.pt.it*

### San Marcello Pistoiese ✉ 50128

**\*\*\*Il Cacciatore**, Via Marconi 87, t 0573 630533, *www.albergoilcacciatore.it* (€€). Pleasant, green, quiet. *Open all year.*

**La Vecchia Cantina**, Via Risorgimento 4, t 0573 64158 (€€). Menus are seasonal and dishes are rooted in local traditions: ravioli with goat's cheese, home-made pasta with courgette flowers and prosciutto, mushrooms or artichokes, boar stewed with wine and chestnuts and pork fillet with apple sauce. Good cheese and wine too. *Closed Tues in winter and 3wks Jan.*

### Cutigliano ✉ 50124

**\*\*\*Hotel Miramonte**, Piazza Catilina 12, t 0573 68012, *www.hotel miramonte.it* (€€). Quiet, with a nice garden and restaurant.

**L'Osteria**, Via Roma 6, t 0573 68272 (€). Top-class mountain food in the centre of town. Hearty soups, local lamb and pecorino cheeses. *Closed Tues lunch, Mon.*

### Abetone ✉ 51021

This ski resort is somewhat fancier.

**\*\*\*Regina**, Via Uccelleria 5, t 0573 60007, (€€€). On a quiet street. *Closed May, July and mid-Sept–Nov.*

**\*\*\*Il Granduca**, Via Brennero 289, t 0573 60067, *www.hotelgranduca.info* (€€). More elegant than most. *Closed May, June and Sept–Nov.*

**Ostello Renzo Bizzarri**, Via Brennero at Cosuma, t 0573 60117 (€). The youth hostel, with room for 92. *Closed April–June and Sept–Nov exc. by request.*

**Da Pierone**, Via Brennero 556, t 0573 60068 (€€). Rustic family-run restaurant serving local dishes, veal escalope with truffles, excellent choice of wine. *Closed Thurs, 2wks June and 2wks Oct.*

**La Capannina**, Via Brennero 520, t 0573 60562 (€€). Good choice: rustic décor, local dishes and a wide selection of wines. There are rooms too if you want to stay. *Closed Mon and Tues outside high season, 2wks June and 2wks Oct.*

# The Valdinievole

## Montecatini Terme

🕦 **Montecatini Terme**

West of Pistoia lies the Valdinievole, the 'Valley of Mists', a land obsessed with water, though mostly of the subterranean, curative variety, available in Montecatini (pop. 21,500), Italy's most glamorous thermal spa. Leonardo da Vinci's first known drawing was of a view towards Montecatini from Lamporecchio, near his home town of Vinci (*see* p.226), and it is believed that his lifetime fascination with canals, locks, currents and dams and the misty, watery backgrounds of his most famous paintings come from a childhood spent in the Valdinievole. He even designed a fountain for the baths of Montecatini in one of his notebooks, which after 380 years is now being built of Carrara marble as his monument.

Even in these days of holistic medicine, preventative medicine, herbal cures and pharmaceutical paranoia, the Montecatini tourist board despairs that Anglo-Saxons from both sides of the Atlantic refuse to believe that soaking in or drinking mere water can do anything as beneficial for them as imbibing a pitcher of Chianti. Unlike so many continental enthusiasts, we defy the wisdom of the ancients – especially the Romans, who spent the plunder accumulated from conquering the world on ever more fabulous baths. But taking the waters, no matter how hot, radioactive or chock-full of minerals, is only half the cure; the other is simply relaxation: the chance to stroll in gardens, listen to music, linger in a café, to indulge in a bit of the old *dolce far niente*. In Montecatini you can do just that without touching a blessed, unfermented drop, surrounded by Belle Epoque nostalgia from the days when the spa seethed with dukes, politicians, literati and actresses.

### Parco delle Terme

**Parco delle Terme**
*baths open May–Oct, exc. the Excelsior, which stays open all year; tickets for a day or subscriptions are available from the central office in Viale Verdi 41, t 0572 778428, www.termemonte catini.it*

A short stroll from the station, past Montecatini's trendy boutiques, cafés, cinemas and some of its 200 hotels, up to Viale Verdi, will take you to the town's mineral water Elysium, the immaculately groomed Parco delle Terme, where the high temples of the cult dot the shaded lawn. The Lorraine grand dukes, spa-soaks like their Habsburg cousins, were behind the initial development of Montecatini's springs, and many of the baths, or *terme*, are neoclassical pavilions – monumental, classical and floral architecture that lent itself nicely to the later Liberty-style embellishments of the 1920s.

You can take in some of these Art Nouveau fancies in Montecatini's Municipio, on Viale Verdi opposite the park, or in the most sumptuous and ancient of its nine major bathing establishments, **Tettuccio**. In the 1370s a group of Florentines attempted to extract mineral salts from the spring and built a little roof (*tettuccio*) over

# Getting to Montecatini Terme

Montecatini is easily reached by **train** from Florence (51km/1½hrs), Pistoia (16km/25mins) and Lucca (27km/45mins). The station, **t** 0572 78551, is on Via Toti, as is the LAZZI **bus** terminal, **t** 0572 911781, with hourly connections (at least until evening) to Florence, Lucca, Pisa, Viareggio and Montecatini Alto; also to Collodi via Pescia (6 daily).

it; and although they failed it was soon discovered that the water had a good effect on rotten livers – one of the first to come here was Francesco Datini, the Merchant of Prato, in 1401. By the 18th century, Tettuccio was in a state of ruin, and Grand Duke Leopold I had it splendidly rebuilt. His façade remains, while the interior was redone by Montecatini's greatest architect, Ugo Giovanozzi, in the 1920s, and embellished with paintings by Italy's Art Nouveau master, Galileo Chini, and ceramic pictures by Cascella in the drinking gallery; there's an elegant café, fountains, a reflecting pool and rotunda, a writing hall, music rooms – a little city within a city, all adorned with scenes from an aquatic Golden Age of languid nymphs – surely the perfect place to sip your morning glass of liver-flushing water.

Other establishments are nearby – the Palladian-style arcade of the **Regina** spring; the **Terme Leopoldine**, another grand ducal establishment, with mud baths housed in a temple-like building; the half-neo-Renaissance, half-modern **New Excelsior baths**; the pretty Tuscan rustic **Tamerici**, in its lush garden; the **Torretta**, with its phony medieval tower and afternoon concerts in the loggia.

## During Digestion

While the water works its way through your system, you can work your way through Montecatini's diversions. Just behind the Parco delle Terme is **Le Panteraie**, a wooded park with a swimming pool, where deer roam freely. You can play a round at the **Montecatini Golf Course**, among olive groves and cypresses, or have a game of tennis at the centrally situated courts of **La Torretta**. Alternatively you can try to win back your hotel bill at the trotting races at the **Ippodromo**. The **Kursaal**, with cinema, nightclub and games, is a popular meeting place. One of the prettiest excursions is to take the funicular up to **Montecatini Alto**, the original old hill town, with breathtaking views over the Valley of Mists and a charming little piazza with a small theatre; nearby you can visit the stalactites in the **Grotta Maona**.

**Montecatini Golf and Country Club**
*t 0572 62218, www.montecatinigolf.com*

**La Torretta**
*t 0572 78161*

**Grotta Maona**
*open April–Oct; call tourist office for details*

**(i) Montecatini ›**
*Viale G. Verdi 66, t 0572 772244, www.montecatiniturismo.it; open daily July–Dec 9–1 and 3–7*

## Where to Stay in Montecatini Terme

**Montecatini Terme** ✉ **51016**

Even if you don't care to take the waters, you'll have no difficulty finding a room. Italy's choicest spa has no fewer than six hotels that claim the title of 'Grand' and a half-dozen others that only decline to for discretion's sake. **Full board**, not counting breakfast, is the rule in most places; outside high season they might not require it, but ring ahead to make sure. The **APIA hotel association** on Via delle Saline 88, t 0572 72603, helps with bookings.

**\*\*\*\*\*Grand Hotel Bellavista**, Viale Fedeli 2, t 0572 78122, *www.pancioli hotels.it* (€€€€). Among the grandest, offering golf, tennis, an indoor pool, luxurious rooms, sauna, health club, and an infinite number of chances for self-indulgence. *Open Mar–Nov.*

**\*\*\*\*\*Grand Hotel & La Pace**, Corso Roma 12, t 0572 75801, *www.grand hotellapace.it* (€€€€). Renowned throughout the rest of Europe for its genuine Belle Epoque charm, this hotel has similarly impressive luxuries to the Bellavista; and the restaurant is unquestionably elegant, if expensive. *Open April–Oct.*

★ Enoteca da Giovanni >>

**\*\*\*Belvedere**, Viale Fedeli 10, t 0572 70251 (€€€). One of the more charming choices, featuring an indoor pool, tennis courts and friendly service, next to the Parco delle Terme.

**Villa Pasquini**, Via Vacchereccia 56 Massa e Cozile, 8km from Monte-catini, t 0572 72205, *www.villapasquini. it* (€€€). Charming, friendly and old-fashioned, set in lush gardens with rooms verging on the grand (some have frescoes), and a good restaurant.

**\*\*\*\*Grand Hotel Plaza e Locanda Maggiore**, Piazza del Popolo 7, t 0572 75831, *www.hotelplaza.it* (€€). This was apparently Verdi's favourite; it has a pool and air-conditioned rooms. *Open all year.*

**\*\*\*Corallo**, Viale Cavallotti 116, t 0572 78288, *www.golfhotelcorallo.it* (€€). Small but refined, with a pool and garden, on a quiet side street near the park. The restaurant serves Tuscan and Mediterranean specialities. *Open all year.*

★ Il Salotto di Gea >

Il Salotto di Gea, Via Talenti 2, t 0572 904318, *salottodigea@inwind.it* (€€). A small hotel (only 8 rooms) in the heart of the old town, a delightful and

good-value alternative to some of the rather overblown hotels in Monte-catini. Rooms are decorated with unfussy good taste. The restaurant offers tempting fish and meat dishes: warm octopus salad, aubergine ravioli with pesto, and fillet of beef with a Chianti sauce.

## Eating Out in Montecatini Terme

Most guests dine in their hotels, but there are some places that are well worth making the effort to leave the hotel for.

Enoteca da Giovanni, Via Garibaldi 25, t 0572 71695 (€€€€). Break loose at least once for the imaginative fare at this unique and much-honoured place, where game dishes – hare, venison, wild duck – and fish turn into impeccably *haute cuisine* in the hands of a master chef. *Closed Mon.*

**Ristorante il Cucco**, Via Salsero 3, t 0572 72765 (€€€€–€€€). Elaborate Tuscan cooking, both meat and sea-food, at more reasonable prices: try the spaghetti with fresh anchovies and breadcrumbs. *Closed Wed lunch, Tues.*

**Cucina da Giovanni**, Via Garibaldi (€€€). Next door to the Enoteca da Giovanni (*see* above), offering simple fare at more modest prices (try the wonderful *antipasti* and fabulous *maccheroncini* with duck sauce).

**La Torre**, Piazza Giusti, t 0572 70650 (€€). A wine bar/restaurant, up in the old town. If you want a full meal (rather than a drink and a snack), there are soups, good pastas and simple meat dishes.

When you get tired of immersing yourself in the waters, why not dip into the vintages at a wine bar?

**Enoteca**, Via Forini 13.

**Antinori 'Degustazione Vini'**, Viale Verdi 35.

# Around Montecatini Terme

## Monsummano and Serravalle

Narrow lanes crisscross the Valdinievole landscape, offering a wealth of tempting excursions further afield. Approximately 5km east of Montecatini is its sister spa, **Monsummano Terme**, which as its speciality offers vapour baths in natural grottoes. The first of these was discovered by accident in 1849, when the Giusti family moved a boulder and found the entrance to a stalactite cave. The **Grotta Giusti**, which is 325ft (100m) deep, has three small lakes fed by hot springs. These caves, including the steamy **Grotta Parlanti**, are only open to visitors seeking serious thermal treatment.

**Grotta Parlanti**
*info* **t** *0572 953029;*
*open May–Oct*

Monsummano meanwhile hasn't rested on its vapours, but has transformed itself into one of Italy's biggest shoe-making towns; like Montecatini it has an old antecedent atop a hill, **Monsummano Alto**, today all but abandoned, but with a pretty Romanesque church, a romantically ruined castle and splendid views. Another panoramic view may be had from **Montevettolini**, 4km from Monsummano, site of a villa built by Ferdinando I in 1597.

Continuing east, the old fortress at **Serravalle Pistoiese** 'locks the valley' between the Apennines and Monte Albano. Its old Lombard tower and 14th-century additions saw considerable action in Tuscany's days of inter-urban hooliganism.

## Pescia and Around

To the west of Montecatini, there's another attractive old hill town, **Buggiano Castello**, and, for those who imagine that frescoes went out of fashion years ago, there's San Michele in nearby **Ponte Buggianese**, freshly frescoed in stark colours by Pietro Annigoni. The colours are even more dazzling in **Pescia** (pop. 20,000), Italy's capital of flowers, a title snatched from San Remo on the Riviera. Some three million cut flowers are sent off every summer's day from Pescia's giant market; besides the gladioli, it is celebrated by gourmets for its tender asparagus and *fagioli*.

 Pescia

Pescia has several interesting monuments, beginning with a 14th-century church of **San Francesco**, containing Bonaventura Berlinghieri's 1235 portrait of *St Francis* with scenes from his life, considered to be one of the most authentic likenesses of the saint; also take a look at the *Crucifixion* by Puccio Capanna in the sacristy. The **Duomo** was rebuilt in the 1600s, but has a fine Romanesque campanile sporting a little cupola, and a late terracotta triptych by Luca della Robbia. On the long, narrow Piazza Mazzini stands the imposing **Palazzo del Vicario**; in nearby **Sant'Antonio**, from the 1360s, look up the 'Ugly Saints', a 13th-century wooden *Deposition from the Cross*.

The green, hilly region of prosperous villages north of Pescia in the upper Valdinievole is known as 'Little Switzerland'. In its cheerful core, some 12km from Pescia, stands one of Italy's most bizarre churches, the 12th-century **Pieve di Castelvecchio**, decorated with grinning and grimacing stone masks.

## Collodi and Pinocchio

Just west of Pescia is Collodi. As a child, Florentine writer Carlo Lorenzo (1826–90) often visited his uncle who worked in the castle, and took the name Collodi as his own when he published his *Adventures of Pinocchio*. In his honour the town has built the **Parco di Pinocchio**, with a bronze statue of the character by Emilio Greco and a piazza of mosaics with scenes from the book by Venturino Venturi, as well as other figures, all very much in the angular style of the late 1950s and early '60s; there's a lawn maze, a museum dedicated to the book, a playground and other amusements for the kids. Adults, meanwhile, can try to work their way through a much older labyrinth in the magnificent, recently restored hillside gardens of the **Castello Garzoni**, designed in the 17th century by Ottaviano Diodati of Lucca and considered one of the finest late Italian gardens, ornate with a labyrinth, fountains and statuary. The castle 'of a hundred windows' has a few grand rooms, and the kitchen where young Carlo sat and dreamed up Pinocchio.

**Parco di Pinocchio**
*t 0572 429342,
www.pinocchio.it;
open 8.30–sunset;
adm*

 **Castello Garzoni**
*t 0572 427314,
www.pinocchio.it;
gardens open Mar–
Oct 8.30–sunset; adm*

## Where to Stay and Eat around Montecatini Terme

### Monsummano Terme ✉ 51015

****Grotta Giusti**, Via Grotta Giusti 1411, **t** 0572 90771, *www.grottagiusti spa.com* (€€€€€–€€€€). Near the vaporous grottoes, the villa of the family of the poet Giuseppe Giusti. Recently upgraded and now a very comfortable hotel full of antiques, rich fabrics, etc. Half- or full-board obligatory in high season (Aug and Sept, Christmas, Easter). *Open Mar–Nov.*

### Montevettolini ✉ 51015

**Villa Lucia**, Via dei Bronzoli 144, **t** 0572 617790, *www.villaluciaoftuscany.com* (€€€€). An English-style B&B (the *padrona* is American/Italian), in a delightful setting on a hillside, with garden and pool.

**San Michele**, Piazza Bargellini 80, Montevettolini, **t** 0572 617 547 (€). A café-bar-restaurant with a tempting array of *antipasti* (smoked salmon, caviar, *carpaccio* with truffles), followed by spaghetti with lobster, perhaps, and prawns. *Closed Mon.*

### Pescia ✉ 51017

****Villa delle Rose**, Via del Castellare 21, **t** 0572 4670, *www.rphotels.com*

(€€€). Just outside Pescia, with a pleasant garden and pool and comfortable, modern rooms.

**Cecco**, Via Forti 96/98, **t** 0572 477955 (€€). Fine dining on seasonal dishes starring Pescia's famous asparagus, or wild mushrooms, truffles or zucchini flowers; for dessert, there's *torta di Cecco*, prepared according to an ancient recipe. *Closed Mon.*

**Monte a Pescia**, Via del Monte Ovest 1, Monte a Pescia, **t** 0572 476887 (€€). A rustic restaurant in a tiny, hilltop hamlet just outside Pescia, with a terrace overlooking the Valdinievole. Home-made pasta is served with asparagus, porcini or game sauce and meat is grilled over an open fire.

### Collodi ✉ 51014

**All'Osteria del Gambero Rosso**, Parco Collodi, **t** 0572 429 364 (€€€). Set in the grand Parco Collodi, this restaurant has made a name for its food as much as for its attractive surroundings. The building was designed by Giovanni Michelucci, arguably one of Italy's greatest 20th-century architects. Tuck into cannelloni, *tagliolini* with porcini mushrooms and prosciutto, and excellent crêpes stuffed with seafood or spinach. *Closed Mon eve and Tues plus Nov.*

# Lucca, the Garfagnana and Lunigiana

*Tuscany's northernmost corner is full of treats, starting with utterly urbane Lucca, birthplace of Puccini and home to an unusual set of medieval churches, a Roman amphitheatre turned into a piazza and a unique elevated promenade on top of the city walls.*

*Yet a hop and skip north, the mountainous micro-regions of the Garfagnana and Lunigiana are among Tuscany's best-kept secrets; here you can relax in the sleepy spa of Bagni di Lucca where romantic poets once lazed, explore the Cave of the Wind, or scratch your head over the statue-steles of Pontremoli.*

# 10

## Don't miss

⭐ **A luminescent and tender tomb**
Lucca cathedral p.262

⭐ **A church splendid as a cathedral**
San Michele in Foro, Lucca p.263

⭐ **The spa where roulette was born**
Bagni di Lucca p.269

⭐ **Rugged scenery and stout castles**
The Lunigiana p.273

⭐ **Mysterious statue-menhirs**
Pontremoli p.275

*See map overleaf*

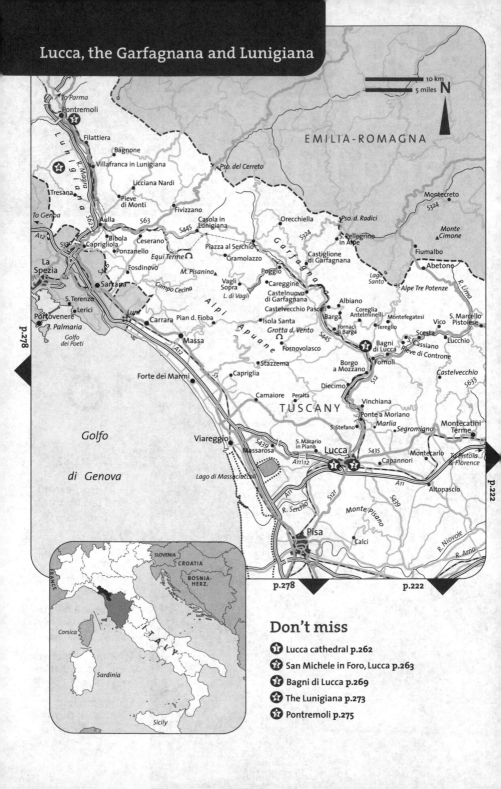

10 km
5 miles

**N**

*To Parma*

Pontremoli ✪

Filattiera

Bagnone

Villafranca in Lunigiana

Licciana Nardi

Tresana

*To Genoa*

Pieve di Monti

Fivizzano

Aulla

S63

Casola in Lunigiana

EMILIA-ROMAGNA

Montecreto

S324

Monte Cimone ▲

*Psp. del Cerreto*

Orecchiella

*Pso. d. Radici*

S. Pellegrino in Alpe

Fiumalbo

Abetone

R. Lima

La Spezia

S330

Bibola

Caprigliola

Ceserano

Ponzanello

Fosdinovo

Sarzana

Luni

Equi Terme ♫

S445

Piazza al Serchio

Gramolazzo

*M. Pisanino*

*Campo Cecina*

Vagli Sopra

*L. di Vagli*

Poggio

Castelnuovo di Garfagnana

Castelvecchio Pascoli

Isola Santa

Grotta d. Vento ♫

Fornovolasco

Castiglione di Garfagnana

*Lago Santo*

Alpe Tre Potenze

S. Marcello Pistoiese

Vico

Lucchio

Scesta

S. Cassiano

Pieve di Controne

*Castelvecchio*

S633

S. Terenzo

Lerici

Portovenere

*I. Palmaria*

*Golfo dei Poeti*

Carrara

Pian d. Fioba

Massa

*Alpi Apuane*

Careggine

Albiano

Coreglia Antelminelli

Barga

Fornaci di Barga

Tereglio

Montefegatesi

Borgo a Mozzano

Bagni di Lucca ✪

Fornoli

*Golfo*

*di Genova*

Forte dei Marmi

Capriglia

Stazzema

Peralta

Camaiore

Diecimo

**TUSCANY**

Vinchiana

Ponte a Moriano

*Marlia*

Segromigno

Montecatini Terme

Viareggio

Massarosa

*Lago di Massaciuccoli*

S439

S. Macario in Piano

S. Stefano

Lucca ✪ ✪

Capannori

Montecarlo

*To Pistoia & Florence*

A11

Altopascio

S439

A11 12

S435

*R. Sercho*

S121

*Monte Pisano*

*R. Niovole*

Pisa

Calci

*R. Arno*

p.278 ▼        p.222 ▼

*To Parma*
*To Genoa*

FRANCE
Corsica
ITALY
Sardinia
Sicily

SLOVENIA
CROATIA
BOSNIA-HERZ.

## Don't miss

✪ **Lucca cathedral p.262**

✪ **San Michele in Foro, Lucca p.263**

✪ **Bagni di Lucca p.269**

✪ **The Lunigiana p.273**

✪ **Pontremoli p.275**

# Lucca

Of all Tuscany's great cities, Lucca (pop. 92,500) is the most cosy, sane and domestic, a tidy gem of a town encased within its famous walls. Yet even these hardly seem formidable, more like garden walls than something that would keep the Florentines at bay. The old ramparts and surrounding areas, once the outworks of the fortifications, are now full of lawns and trees; on the walls, where the city's soldiers once patrolled, citizens ride their bicycles, walk their dogs, and stop to admire the view.

Like paradise, Lucca is entered by way of St Peter's Gate. Once inside you'll find tidy, well-preserved Romanesque churches and medieval towers that destroyed Ruskin's romantic notion that a medieval building had to be half-ruined to be beautiful, a revelation that initiated his study of architecture. Nor do Lucca's numerous Liberty-style shop signs show any sign of rust; even the mandatory peeling ochre paint and green shutters of the houses seem part of some great municipal housekeeping plan. Bicycles have largely replaced cars within the walls. At first glance it seems too bijou, but after its long and brave history it has earned the right to a little quiet. The hordes of tourists leave Lucca alone for the most part, though a small number of discreet visitors, many of them German and Swedish, come back every year. They don't spread the word, apparently trying to keep one of Italy's most beautiful cities to themselves.

## History

Lucca's rigid grid of streets betrays its Roman origins. It was founded as a colony in 180 BC as *Luca*, and it was here in 56 BC that Caesar, Pompey and Crassus met to form the ill-fated First Triumvirate. It was converted to Christianity early on by St Peter's disciple Paulinus, who became first bishop of Lucca. The city did especially well in the Dark Ages; in late Roman times it was the administrative capital of Tuscany, and under the Goths managed to repulse the murderous Lombards; its extensive archives were begun in the 8th century, and many of its churches were founded shortly after. By the 11th and 12th centuries Lucca emerged as one of the leading trading towns of Tuscany, specializing in the production of silk, sold by colonies of merchants in the East and West, who earned enough to make sizeable loans to Mediterranean potentates. A Lucchese school of painting developed, and beautiful Romanesque churches were erected, influenced by nearby Pisa. Ghibellines and Guelphs, and then Black and White Guelphs, made nuisances of themselves as they did everywhere else, and Lucca often found itself pressed to maintain its independence from Pisa and Florence.

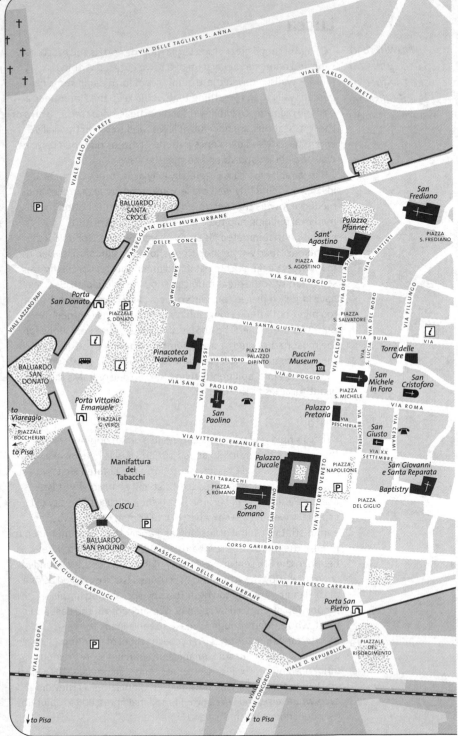

VIA DELLE TAGLIATE S. ANNA

VIALE CARLO DEL PRETE

VIALE CARLO DEL PRETE

P

BALUARDO
SANTA
CROCE

PASSEGGIATA DELLE MURA URBANE

San
Frediano

PIAZZA
S. FREDIANO

Palazzo
Pfanner

Sant'
Agostino

PIAZZA
S. AGOSTINO

VIA DELLE CONCE

VIA SAN GIORGIO

VIA DEGLI ASILI

VIA C. BATTISTI

VIA S. LUCIA

VIA FILLUNGO

VIA SAN TOMMASO

Porta
San Donato

P

PIAZZALE
S. DONATO

i

VIA SANTA GIUSTINA

PIAZZA
S. SALVATORE

VIA
BUIA

i

VIA LAZZARO PAPI

BALUARDO
SAN
DONATO

i

Pinacoteca
Nazionale

VIA DEL TORO

PIAZZA DI
PALAZZO
DIPINTO

Puccini
Museum

M

VIA DI POGGIO

VIA CALDERIA

VIA S. LUCIA

VIA DEL MORO

Torre delle
Ore

San
Michele
In Foro

San
Cristoforo

VIA ROMA

to
Viareggio

PIAZZALE
BOCCHERINI

to Pisa

Porta Vittorio
Emanuele

PIAZZALE
G. VERDI

VIA SAN GALLI TASSI

VIA SAN PAOLINO

San
Paolino

PIAZZA
S. MICHELE

Palazzo
Pretoria

VIA
PESCHERIA

VIA BECCHERIA

San
Giusto

VIA CENAMI

VIA VITTORIO EMANUELE

Manifattura
dei
Tabacchi

VIA XX
SETTEMBRE

San Giovanni
e Santa Reparata

Palazzo
Ducale

PIAZZA
NAPOLEONE

Baptistry

CISCU

P

BALUARDO
SAN PAOLINO

VIA DEI TABACCHI

PIAZZA
S. ROMANO

San
Romano

VICOLO SAN MARINO

i

VIA VITTORIO VENETO

P

PIAZZA
DEL GIGLIO

CORSO GARIBALDI

PASSEGGIATA DELLE MURA URBANE

VIA FRANCESCO CARRARA

VIALE GIOSUÈ CARDUCCI

Porta San
Pietro

VIALE EUROPA

P

VIALE D. REPUBBLICA

PIAZZALE
DEL
RISORGIMENTO

VIA DI
SAN CONCORDIO

to Pisa

to Pisa

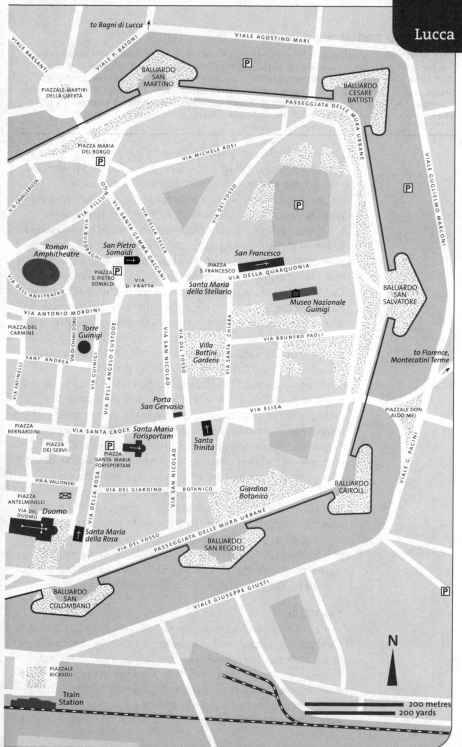

to Bagni di Lucca ↑

VIALE AGOSTINO MARI

VIALE BARSANTI

VIALE P. BATONI

PIAZZALE MARTIRI
DELLA LIBERTÀ

BALUARDO
SAN
MARTINO

BALUARDO
CESARE
BATTISTI

PASSEGGIATA DELLE MURA URBANE

PIAZZA MARIA
DEL BORGO

VIA MICHELE ROSI

V.D. CAVALLERIZZA

VIA FILLUNGO

VIA SANTA GEMMA GALGANI

VIA DELLA ZECCA

VIA DEL FOSSO

VIALE GUGLIELMO MARCONI

VIA BUSDRAGHI

Roman
Amphitheatre

San Pietro
Somaldi

San Francesco

PIAZZA
S. FRANCESCO

VIA DELLA QUARQUONIA

BALUARDO
SAN
SALVATORE

VIA DELL'ANFITEATRO

PIAZZA
S. PIETRO
SOMALDI

VIA
D. FRATTA

Santa Maria
dello Stellario

Museo Nazionale
Guinigi

to Florence,
Montecatini Terme
↗

VIA ANTONIO MORDINI

VIA DI CHIAVI D'ORO

Torre
Guinigi

VIA SANTA CHIARA

VIA BRUNERO PAOLI

PIAZZA DEL
CARMINE

VIA GUINIGI

VIA DELL'ANGELO CUSTODE

VIA SAN NICOLAO

VIA DEL FOSSO

Villa
Bottini
Gardens

PIAZZALE DON
ALDO MEI

SANT' ANDREA

VIA FATINELLI

Porta
San Gervasio

VIA ELISA

VIA G. PACINI

PIAZZA
BERNARDINI

VIA SANTA CROCE

Santa Maria
Forisportam

Santa
Trinità

PIAZZA
DEI SERVI

PIAZZA
SANTA MARIA
FORISPORTAM

VIA SAN NICOLAO

BALUARDO
CAIROLI

VIA A. VALLISNERI

VIA DELLA ROSA

VIA DEL GIARDINO

BOTANICO

Giardino
Botanico

PIAZZA
ANTELMINELLI

Duomo

VIA DEL
DUOMO

Santa Maria
della Rosa

VIA DEL FOSSO

PASSEGGIATA DELLE MURA URBANE

BALUARDO
SAN REGOLO

BALUARDO
SAN
COLOMBANO

VIALE GIUSEPPE GIUSTI

N

PIAZZALE
RICASOLI

Train
Station

200 metres
200 yards

## Getting to and around Lucca

The **railway** station is just south of the walls on Piazza Ricasoli, with lots of trains on the Viareggio–Pisa–Florence line, **t** 0583 892021. **Buses** leave from Piazzale Verdi, just inside the walls on the western end: LAZZI buses to Florence, Pistoia, Pisa, Prato, Bagni di Lucca, Abetone, Montecatini and Viareggio (**t** 0583 584876); and CLAP (that's right, CLAP) buses to towns within Lucca province, including Collodi, Marlia and Segromigno, as well as the Serchio valley (**t** 0583 587897). Get around Lucca itself like a Lucchese by hiring a **bicycle** from Poli (**t** 0583 493787) or Bizzarri (**t** 0583 496031), both in the Piazza Santa Maria.

In 1314, at the height of the city's wealth and power, the Pisans and Ghibellines finally managed to seize it. But Lucca had a trump card: a remarkable adventurer named Castruccio Castracani, an ambitious noble who lived for years in exile – part of it in England. When he heard the bad news he at once set forth to rescue his home town. Within a year he had chased the Pisans out and seized power for himself, leading Lucca into its most heroic age, capturing most of western Tuscany to form a Luccan empire, subjugating even Pisa and Pistoia. After routing the Florentines at Altopascio in 1325, Castracani was planning to snatch Florence too, but died of malaria just before the siege was to begin. Bickering between the powerful local families soon put an end to Lucca's glory days, though in 1369 the city managed to convince Emperor Charles IV to grant it independence as a republic, albeit a republic ruled by oligarchs like Paolo Guinigi, the sole big boss between 1400 and 1430.

But Lucca continued to escape being gobbled up by its voracious neighbours, surviving even after the arrival of the Spaniards – perhaps due not so much to its great walls as to its relative insignificance. Amazingly enough, after the Treaty of Câteau-Cambrésis, Lucca stood together with Venice as the only truly independent states in Italy. And, like Venice, the city was an island of relative tolerance and enlightenment during the Counter-Reformation, its walls proving stout enough to deflect the Inquisition. In 1805 Lucca's independence ended when Napoleon gave the republic to his sister Elisa Baciocchi, who ruled as its princess; it was given later to Marie-Louise, Napoleon's widow, who governed well enough to become Lucca's favourite ruler and earn a statue in the main Piazza Napoleone. Her son sold it to Leopold II of Tuscany in 1847, just in time for it to join the Kingdom of Italy.

### The Walls

Lucca's lovely bastions evoke the walled rose gardens of chivalric romance, enclosing a smaller, more perfect cosmos. They owe their charm to Renaissance advances in military technology. Prompted by the beginning of the Wars of Italy, Lucca began to construct the walls in 1500. The councillors wanted up-to-date fortifications to counter new advances in artillery, and their (unknown) architects gave them state-of-the-art examples, a model for the new style of fortification soon to transform the cities of Europe. Being Renaissance Tuscans, the architects also gave them a little more elegance than was strictly necessary. The walls were never severely tested. Today, with the outer ravelins, fosses and salients cleared away (such earthworks usually took up as much space as the city itself), Lucca's walls are just for decoration; under the peace-loving Duchess Marie-Louise they were planted with a double row of plane trees to create a 4km elevated garden boulevard, offering a continuous bird's-eye view over Lucca. They are among the best preserved in Italy. Of the gates, the most elaborate is the 16th-century **St Peter's Gate**, near the station, its portcullis still intact, with Lucca's motto of independence, LIBERTAS, inscribed over the entrance. One of the best ways to explore the walls is by bicycle; hire one (*see* p.left) and do a circular tour.

## Duomo

**Duomo**
*t 0583 957068;
open Sun–Fri
9.30–5.45, Sat
9.30–6.45; adm to
sacristy, joint adm
available with Museo
della Cattedrale and
San Giovanni e Santa
Reparata, see p.262
for both*

Through St Peter's Gate (Porta San Pietro), and then to the right, Corso Garibaldi leads to Lucca's cathedral, perhaps the most outstanding work of the Pisan style outside Pisa, begun in the 11th century and completed only in the 15th. Above the singular porch, with three different-sized arches, are three levels of colonnades, with pillars arranged like candy sticks, while behind and on the arches are exquisite 12th- and 13th-century reliefs and sculpture – the best work Lucca has to offer. Look out especially for the *Adoration of the Magi* by Nicola Pisano, for the column carved with the Tree of Life, with Adam and Eve crouched at the bottom and Christ on top, and a host of fantastical animals and hunting scenes, the months and their occupations, mermaids and dragons (*see* Pienza, p.390), and a man embracing a bear, even *Roland at Roncesvalles*, all by unknown masters. There is also a medieval maze on the right side of the portico, which you can trace with your finger. Walk round the back, where the splendidly ornate apse and transepts are set off by the green lawn. The crenellated **campanile** dates from 1060 and 1261.

The dark interior offers an excellent introduction to the works of Lucca's one and only great artist, **Matteo Civitali** (1435–1501), a barber until his mid-30s, when he decided he'd much rather be a sculptor. He deserves to be better known – but may never be, since everything he made is still in Lucca. His most famous work is the octagonal **Tempietto** (1484), a marble tabernacle in the middle of the left aisle, containing Lucca's most precious holy relic, the world-weary *Volto Santo* (Holy Image), a cedar-wood crucifix said to be a true portrait of Jesus, sculpted by Nicodemus, an eye-witness to the crucifixion. Saved from the iconoclasts, it was set adrift in an empty boat and floated to Luni, where the bishop was instructed by an angel to place it in a cart drawn by two white oxen, and where the oxen should halt, there should the image remain. They lumbered to Lucca, where the *Volto Santo* has remained. Its likeness appeared on the republic's coins, and there was a devoted cult of the image in medieval England; Lucca's merchant colony in London cared for a replica in old St Thomas's, and according to William of Malmesbury King William Rufus always swore by it, '*per sanctum vultum de Lucca*'. Long an object of pilgrimage, the image goes out for a night on the town in a candlelight procession each 13 September.

Further up the left aisle a chapel contains Fra Bartolommeo's *Virgin and Child Enthroned*. Here, too, is an altarpiece by Giambologna, *Christ with SS. Peter and Paul*. Civitali carved the cathedral's high altar, and also two tombs in the south transept. A door from the right aisle leads to the **sacristy**, where you can see Lucca's real icon, the remarkable **Tomb of Ilaria del Carretto** (1408), perhaps Jacopo della Quercia's most beautiful work, a tender effigy of the young bride of boss Paolo Guinigi, with a dog at her feet, waiting for his mistress to awaken. The city has always had a strange love-hate relationship with this lovely statue. Right after her husband was overthrown they hustled her out of the cathedral, and she didn't come back for centuries. Near the statue is a *Madonna Enthroned with Saints* by Domenico Ghirlandaio.

**⭐ Tomba di Ilaria del Carretto**

A side altar near the sacristy has a typically strange composition from the Venetian Tintoretto, a *Last Supper* with a nursing mother in the foreground and cherubs floating around Christ. In the centre, unfortunately often covered up, is a particularly fine section of the inlaid marble floor; on the entrance wall, a 13th-century sculpture of St Martin has been brought in from the façade.

## Around the Cathedral

An **antiques market** takes place in and around the cathedral's Piazza San Martino the third Saturday and Sunday of each month. Next to the cathedral is the **Museo della Cattedrale**. Its treasures, include the crown and garments of the *Volto Santo*, some good 13th-century reliquaries and pyxes, tapestries and paintings from Lucca's ancient cathedral, San Giovanni, and della Quercia's *St John the Evangelist*. The museum's upstairs windows afford a close-up view of some of the wonderful sculpture on the cathedral.

**Museo della Cattedrale**
*t 0583 4905330; open 10 Mar–2 Nov daily 10–6; 3 Nov–9 Mar Mon–Fri 10–2, Sat and Sun 10–5; 26 Dec–6 Jan 10–5; adm*

Across Piazza San Martino from the cathedral, **San Giovanni e Santa Reparata** was Lucca's original cathedral. The exterior has only parts of an 1187 portal to show for its old distinction, but inside there are some surprises. Excavations during the 1970s uncovered a series of buildings: the site of a 5th-century basilica, adjacent to it a huge, square **baptistry** from the 1300s, and under this the original Roman font – a walk-in model for total immersion baptisms – with bits of its mosaics, as well as later Romanesque pavements and a bishop's chair. San Giovanni also has a superb

**San Giovanni e Santa Reparata**
*open 15 Mar–2 Nov Mon–Fri 9.30–5.45, Sat 9.30–6.45, Sun 9.30–10.45 and 12–6; 3 Nov–14 Mar Mon–Fri 9.30–4.45, Sat 9.30–6.45, Sun 9.30–10.45 and 12–5; adm*

painted coffered ceiling and, above the main door, an attractive organ case, though the pipes have been removed. Lucca was once a city of organ-builders, and many of the churches have beautifully crafted instruments with elaborate cases.

## Piazza Napoleone and Piazza San Michele

San Giovanni lies on the Via del Duomo between Piazza San Martino and Lucca's shady twin squares, **Piazza del Giglio** and **Piazza Napoleone**, the focus of the Lucchesi evening *passeggiata*. The architectural hotchpotch of a palace on Piazza Napoleone, formerly seat of the republican council, has been called the **Palazzo Ducale** ever since it was used by Lucca's queen for a day, Elisa Bonaparte Baciocchi. In the 16th century, Ammannati had a go at it, and the courtyard, at least, still preserves signs of his Mannerist handiwork. One of Matteo Civitali's most beautiful works, the tomb of San Romano, is in the rarely opened church of **San Romano**, behind the Palazzo.

Via Vittorio Veneto leads from Piazza Napoleone into Piazza San Michele, with a church many people mistake for Lucca's cathedral. Built about the same time, and with a similar Pisan façade, it is almost as impressive. The full name, **San Michele in Foro**, stems from its location on what was Roman Lucca's forum. The ambitious façade rises high above the level of the roof, to make the building look even grander. Every column in the Pisan arcading is different; some doubled, some twisted like corkscrews, inlaid with mosaic Cosmati work, or carved with fanciful figures and beasts, exquisite work similar to the cathedral's, and recently completely restored. The whole is crowned by a giant statue of the Archangel – note the bracelet on his arm, set with real jewels. On the corner of the façade is a *Madonna* by Civitali; the graceful, rectangular campanile is Lucca's tallest and loveliest.

Inside, there's a glazed terracotta *Madonna and Child* attributed to Luca della Robbia, a striking 13th-century *Crucifixion* over the high altar and a painting of plague saints by Filippino Lippi. Giacomo Puccini began his musical career as a choirboy in San Michele (his father and grandfather had been organists in the cathedral) – he didn't have far to go, as he was born in Via di Poggio 30, just across the street. The house is now a little **Puccini museum**, with manuscripts, letters, mementos, the overcoat and odds and ends of the great composer, as well as the piano he used to compose *Turandot*.

## West of San Michele

Now that the state tobacco factory has been moved out of town, the quarter west of San Michele no longer smells of Toscanelli cigars; what will become of the factory is still undecided. Via San

*(Sidebar)*

**🕑 San Michele in Foro**
*open daily summer 9–12 and 3–6; winter 9–12 and 3–5*

**Casa Natale e Museo di Giacomo Puccini**
*t 0583 5840287; entrance in Corte San Lorenzo 9; open May–June and Sept daily 10–1 and 3–6; July–Aug 10–1 and 3–7; 16 Nov–31 Dec 10–1*

Paolino (the Roman *decumanus major*) leads to the **church of San Paolino** where little Puccini played the organ to earn some pin-money. It contains two beautiful works: a 13th-century French *Madonna and Child* brought back by Lucchese merchants from Paris, and an anonymous quattrocento Florentine *Coronation of the Virgin*, with Mary hovering over a city of pink towers; unusually she is crowned by God the Father instead of Christ.

**Pinacoteca Nazionale**
*Via Galli Tassi, t 0583 55570; open Tues–Sat 9–7, Sun 9–2; adm*

The **Pinacoteca Nazionale** is housed in the 17th-century Palazzo Mansi, in Via Galli Tassi. Most of the art, as well as the rich furnishings, dates from the 17th century. Portraits by Pontormo and Bronzino hang in the Prima Sala after the large hall: the Salone has a dark, damaged Veronese, and a follower of Tintoretto's *Miracle of St Mark Freeing the Slave*, showing the saint dive-bombing from heaven to save the day. There is also a set of neoclassical reliefs from the Palazzo Ducale of the *Triumphs of Duchess Maria Luisa*. The 1600s frescoes are more fun than the paintings, especially the *Judgement of Paris*, which Venus wins by showing a little leg. And one can't help but wonder what rococo dreams tickled the fancy of the occupants of the amazing bedroom.

## East of San Michele

East of San Michele, medieval **Via Fillungo** and its surrounding lanes make up the busy shopping district, a tidy grid of straight and narrow alleys where Lucca's contented cheerfulness seems somehow magnified. Along Via Fillungo you can trace the old loggias of 14th-century palaces, now bricked in, and the ancient **Torre delle Ore** (tower of hours), which since 1471 has striven to keep the Lucchesi on time, and perhaps now suggests that it's time for a coffee in Lucca's historic **Caffè di Simo** at Via Fillungo 58.

**Torre delle Ore**
*open spring 9.30–6.30; summer 9.30–7.30; winter 9.30–4.30; adm (joint adm available with Torre Guinigi, see opposite)*

At Via Fillungo's northern end stands the tall church and taller campanile of **San Frediano**, built in the early 1100s, and shimmering with the colours of the large mosaic on its upper façade, showing Christ and the Apostles in elegant flowing style. The 11th-century bronze Arabian falcon at the top is a copy – the original is kept in a safe. The palatial interior houses Tuscany's most remarkable baptismal font, the 12th-century *fontana lustrale* carved with reliefs, and behind it, a lunette of the *Annunciation* by Andrea della Robbia. On the left are several chapels, one with frescoes by Aspertini. The last chapel on the left has an altarpiece and two tomb slabs by Jacopo della Quercia and his assistants. The bedecked mummy is St Zita, patroness of maids and ladies-in-waiting; even in England maids belonged to the Guild of St Zita. The Lucchesi are very fond of her, and on 26 April they bring her body out to caress.

**Palazzo Pfanner**
*Via degli Asili, t (mobile) 340 923 3085; open Mar–Oct daily 10–6; Nov–Feb by appt only; adm*

Next to San Frediano, the **Palazzo Pfanner** has an 18th-century garden, a fine staircase, a collection of silks made in Lucca, and

17th- to 19th-century costumes. In the other direction, skirting Via Fillungo, narrow arches lead into something most visitors miss: the **Roman amphitheatre**. Only outlines of its arches are still traceable in the outer walls, while within the inner ring only the form remains – the marble was probably carted off to build San Michele and the cathedral – but the outline has been perfectly preserved. The foundations of the grandstands now support a perfect ellipse of medieval houses. Duchess Marie-Louise cleared out the old buildings in the former arena, and now, where gladiators once slugged it out, boys play football and the less active while away the time in cafés and shops around the piazza.

The streets in this quarter have scarcely changed in the past 500 years. Along Via Sant'Andrea and narrow Via Guinigi, you'll pass a number of resolutely medieval palaces, including that of the Guinigi family. Their lofty stronghold, the **Torre Guinigi**, stands next to their palace and is one of Lucca's landmarks, with a tree sprouting out of its top – the best example of that quaint Italian fancy. The tower has been restored, and it's worth the stiff climb up for the view over the city and the Apuan Alps.

**Torre Guinigi**
*open summer daily 9.30–7.30; winter daily 9.30–4.30; autumn daily 9.30–5.30; adm (joint adm available with Torre Ore, see* opposite*)*

## The East Side

Roman Lucca ended near the Guinigi palace, and when a new church was built in the early 12th century it was outside the gate, hence the name of **Santa Maria Forisportam** in Via Santa Croce, a pretty church in the Pisan style with blind arcades. Inside, it not only looks but smells terribly old, and contains two paintings by the often esoteric Guercino. Beyond the church is the best-preserved gate of 1260, the **Porta San Gervasio** giving on to the former moat, now a picturesque little canal running along Via del Fosso. Just across the canal from the gate is **Santa Trinità**, home of Civitali's *Madonna della Tosse* (Our Lady of the Cough), a bit too syrupy sweet, but perhaps that helped the cure. Nearby on Via Elisa is the entrance to the **Villa Bottini gardens**, one of the few green oases inside the city walls.

**Santa Trinità**
*if closed, ask for key in convent next door*

**Villa Bottini gardens**
*open Sun–Fri 9–7*

At the northern end of Via del Fosso stands a 17th-century column dedicated to another Madonna, and to the east, the church of **San Francesco**, a typical 13th-century Franciscan preaching church with the tombs of Castracani and Lucchese composer Luigi Boccherini (d. 1805) – he of the famous *minuet* – and some detached frescoes of the Florentine school. Beyond San Francesco stands the palatial brick Villa Guinigi, built in 1418 by the big boss Paolo Guinigi in his glory days. Now the **Museo Nazionale Guinigi**, its ground floor houses a collection of Romanesque reliefs, capitals and transennas, some of which are charmingly primitive – St Michael slaying the dragon, Samson killing the lion, a 9th-century transenna with birds and beasts, spirals and daggers.

**Museo Nazionale Guinigi**
*Via della Quarquonia 4, t 0583 496033; open Tues–Sat 8.30–7, Sun 8.30–1; adm*

Upstairs, room XI has a lovely *Annunciation* by Civitali. The painting gallery contains intarsia panels from the cathedral, each with scenes of Lucca as seen from town windows, some trecento works by the Lucca school and a charming quattrocento *Madonna and Child* by the 'Maestro della Vita di Maria'. Other rooms contain oversized 16th-century canvases, some by Vasari.

## Villas around Lucca

In 16th-century Lucca, as elsewhere in Italy, trade began to flounder, and merchants turned to the joys of property, where they could decline genteelly in a little country palace and garden. For the Lucchesi, the preferred site for such pleasure domes was in the soft, rolling country to the north and northeast of the city. Three of these villas or their grounds are open for visits. In **Segromigno**, 10km from Lucca towards Pescia, there's the charming, mid-16th-century but often modified **Villa Mansi**, embellished with a half-Italian (geometric) and half-English (not geometric) garden by the Sicilian architect Juvarra.

Nearby in **Camigliano**, the even more elaborate **Villa Torrigiani**, also begun in the 16th century , was celebrated for its fabulous parties and entertainments. Set in a lush park of pools and trees, it has 16th–18th-century furnishings. Elisa Bonaparte Baciocchi combined a villa and a summer palace to make her country retreat, now called the **Villa Pecci-Blunt ex-Villa Reale** in Marlia. Only the park and the Giardino Orsetti are open, but they are worth the trip .

## The Lucchese Plain

East and west of Lucca, what was swampland in the Middle Ages has been reclaimed to form a rich agricultural plain. One of its features are its 'courts' – farm hamlets not constructed around a central piazza, but with houses in neat rows. At one time there were 1,100 such courts on the plain. Among the highlights of the area is curious **Castello di Nozzano** just to the west, built by Matilda of Tuscany on a hill, its pretty tower now incongruously topped by a large clock. To the east, one of the first villages, **Capannori**, is the head town of several courts and has a couple of interesting Romanesque churches, especially the 13th-century **Pieve San Paolo**, around which a small village incorporated itself, using the campanile for defence. The most imposing monument nearby is the 19th-century **Acquedotto del Nottolini**, which is also visible from the *autostrada*. Just south is the pretty hilltop village of **Castelvecchio**, its tall houses forming an effective circular wall. **Altopascio**, on the Lucca–Empoli road, was built around an 11th-

**Villa Mansi**
*www.villelucchesi.net,*
*t 0583 920234;*
*open summer daily*
*10–1 and 3–6; winter*
*Mon–Sat 10–1 and 3–5;*
*adm exp*

**Villa Torrigiani**
*t (mobile) 330 644211;*
*villa and park open*
*Mar–Nov Wed–Mon*
*10–1 and 3–6; in winter*
*call ahead; closed Jan*
*and Feb; adm exp*

**Villa Pecci-Blunt**
**ex-Villa Reale**
*tours by appt, t 0583*
*30108; open Mar–Nov*
*Tues–Sun at 10, 11, 12, 3,*
*4, 5 and 6; Dec–Feb call*
*ahead; adm exp*

century hospice run by an obscure chivalric order called the Hospitaller Knights of the Order of Altopascio, who originally occupied themselves with rescuing travellers from the swamps. Only the campanile of their church remains in the village today. **Montecarlo** gives its name to a very good dry white wine produced in the immediate area.

## Shopping in Lucca

There is a big **antiques market** on the third weekend of each month in and around the Piazza San Martino, and a **crafts fair** on the last Sunday of each month in the Piazza San Giusto.

## Where to Stay in Lucca

### Lucca and Around ✉ 55100

Lucca can be less than charm city if you arrive without booking ahead; there simply aren't enough rooms (especially inexpensive ones) to meet demand.

**\*\*\*\*\*Locanda l'Elisa**, Via Nova per Pisa, Massa Pisana, t 0583 379 737, *www.locandalelisa.it* (€€€€€). Part of the Relais et Châteaux group, this bright blue, French-style 18th-century villa is set in a glorious mature garden. Public rooms and bedrooms are luxuriously appointed and furnished with antiques and elegant fabrics, with canopies over the beds. There is a conservatory restaurant (€€€) mixing tradition with modern trends and a pool. *Closed Jan.*

**\*\*\*\*Ilaria**, Via del Fosso 20, t 0583 47615, *www.hotelilaria.com* (€€€€€–€€€€). An elegant choice with smart comfortable rooms and a car park.

**\*\*\*\*Alla Corte degli Angeli**, Via degli Angeli 23, t 0583 469204, *www.alla cortedegliangeli.com* (€€€€). An upmarket, modern B&B with attractive, comfortable rooms; the bathrooms have Jacuzzis.

**\*\*\*La Luna**, Corte Compagni 12, t 0583 493634, *www.hotellaluna.com* (€€€). A cosy place in a quiet part of the centre, with a private garage and free Internet point.

**\*\*\*Universo**, Piazza del Giglio, t 0583 493678, *www.hoteluniversolucca.com* (€€€€). Within the walls, a slightly frayed, green-shuttered and delightful hotel, in the centre. Ruskin slept here, paving the way for nearly everyone else who followed him to Lucca. Some rooms are better than others. The restaurant serves fine food.

**\*\*\*Piccolo Hotel Puccini**, Via di Poggio 9, t 0583 55421, *www.hotelpuccini.com* (€€). A central, small, comfortable hotel with 14 rooms, but no air-con.

**\*\*Diana** Via del Molinetto 11, t 0583 492202 (€€). Friendly and well run, with some of the nicest inexpensive rooms in Tuscany, some with bath. Those in the more up-market annexe nearby are better.

**\*\*Villa Casanova**, Via Casanova, just outside the city at Balbano, t 0583 548429, *www.villacasanova.net* (€€). This has simple rooms but a pleasant garden, as well as a restaurant, tennis and a swimming pool to lounge by.

**Affittacamere S. Frediano**, Via degli Angeli 19, t 0583 469630, *www.san frediano.com* (€€). Six spotless, nicely furnished rooms (not all with private bath) near the Anfiteatro, with breakfast included. A nearby car park has special rates for guests.

**Da Elisa alle Sette Arti**, Via Elisa 25, t 0583 494539, *www.daelisa.com* (€). This good-value guest house offers 9 pretty and airy rooms in the centre of town with use of kitchen. Breakfast is taken at a neighbouring bar.

**Locanda Buatino**, Borgo Giannotti 508, t 0583 343207, *www.locanda-buatino.com* (€). Just outside the city walls to the north, with five simple but welcoming rooms above a restaurant of the same name (*see below*).

## Eating Out in Lucca

Within the walls:

**Giglio**, Hotel Universo, Piazza del Giglio, t 0583 494058 (€€€). Lucca's best seafood place, in Hotel Universo – river trout is a speciality or try spaghetti with crab pulp. *Closed Tues eve and Wed.*

### Sidebar

ⓘ **Lucca >**
*Palazzo Ducale, Cortile Carrara,* t 0583 919941
*Piazza S. Maria,* t 0583 919931, *www.luccaturismo.it (closed Sun)*

★ **Locanda l'Elisa >**

★ **Giglio >>**

**La Buca di Sant'Antonio**, Via della Cervia 3, t 0583 55881 (€€€). An inn dating back to 1782, offering old recipes like smoked herring and kid on a spit, plus some newer dishes like ravioli with ricotta and sage. *Closed Sun eve, Mon.*

**Da Giulio in Pelleria** Via Conce, t 0583 55948 (€€€). Less expensive, surprisingly sophisticated twists on 'peasant' fare including *farinata*, a spelt and bean soup. Booking advised. *Closed Sun and Mon.*

**Vineria I Santi**, Via dell'Anfiteatro 29a, t 0583 496124 (€€). Tucked behind Piazza dell'Anfiteatro, this restaurant/wine bar has a pretty terrace. Snack on a selection of cheeses, salamis and hams with your wine, or go for something more substantial such as honey-glazed turkey breast or baby squid (*moscardini*) soup. *Closed Wed.*

**Buatino**, Via Borgo Giannotti 508, t 0583 343207 (€€). Here you can enjoy good-value, excellent meals in lively surroundings: there's *zuppa di farro*, delicious roast pork, salt cod with leeks, and more. *Closed Sun.*

**Da Leo**, Via Tegrini 1, t 0583 492236 (€€). Pretty chaotic, full of both locals and tourists. Good *panzanella* (refreshing cold bread salad with tomato and basil). *Closed Sun.*

**Gli Orti di Via Elisa**, Via Elisa 17, t 0583 491241 (€). This cheerful *trattoria* is great for an inexpensive meal. Pizzas, salads, plus good pastas, etc. *Closed Thurs lunch, Wed.*

**Caffè di Simo**, Via Fillungo 58. Come here for a drop of java in a classic turn-of-the-century *gran caffè*.

Lucca's table service is particularly memorable if you have the horsepower to get out to some of the surrounding villages:

**La Mora**, Via Sesto di Moriano 104, Ponte a Moriano, t 0583 406402 (€€€). North of Lucca, in an old posthouse with four cosy rooms inside and dining outside under a pergola in the summer. According to the season, choose delicious ravioli flavoured with marjoram, roast lamb, pigeon or local freshwater fish. *Closed Wed.*

**Vipore**, in nearby Pieve Santo Stefano, t 0583 394065 (€€€). Located in a 200-year-old farmhouse, with views over the fertile plain of Lucca, serving up meals made of top-quality prime ingredients. *Closed Mon and Tues lunch.*

**Mecenate**, Via della Chiesa, Gattaiola, 4km from Lucca (follow signs frm *autostrada* exit), t 0583 512167 (€€). A little Slow Food place (with slow service) in an old hayloft. Try the delicious *tortelli* filled with meat and cinnamon. *Closed Mon.*

 **La Mora >>**

# The Garfagnana and Lunigiana

**Parco Regionale delle Alpi Apuane**
*The visitors' centre is at Piazza delle Erbe 1, Castelnuovo di Garfagnana,* t 0583 644242, www. parcapuane.toscana.it

The rugged northern finger of Tuscany encompasses the region's 'Alps', the tall and jagged **Alpi Apuane**, which like the real Alps wear brilliant white crowns, though not made of snow – that's marble up there, the 'tears of the stars', the purest and whitest in Italy. Historically the land is divided into two mini-regions: along the bank of the Serchio river, between the Apuan Alps and the Apennines, is the **Garfagnana**; while the region north of the village of Piazza al Serchio is the **Lunigiana**, former hinterland of the ancient Roman port of Luni.

The Garfagnana and Lunigiana are relatively undiscovered, and threaten to dispel many people's typical image of Tuscany: the mountains are too high, the valleys are too narrow, and you're more likely to find yourself amidst pine forests than vineyards and olive groves. However, a spell in this striking mountain scenery can be just what you need when the thought of cathedrals or art galleries begins to pall.

## Getting to and around the Garfagnana

CLAP **buses** from Lucca connect the city to Bagni di Lucca (27km/40mins), Barga (37km/1hr), and Castelnuovo di Garfagnana (50km/1½hrs).

The **railway station** is just south of the walls on Piazza Ricasoli. **Trains** on the scenic Lucca–Aulla line go up the Serchio valley, though beware that the stations for Bagni di Lucca and Barga are quite a distance from their centres and don't always have buses that connect; better to take the bus to begin with.

If you're **driving** from the south, the most convenient way into these mountains begins at Lucca; both the SS12 and SS445 routes follow the river Serchio.

# The Garfagnana

For many years the chief export of the Garfagnana has been Italians; the green hills and mountains, the narrow valley of the Serchio, between the Apennines and the Apuan Alps, the stone villages perched on slopes that look so picturesque on postcards, were simply never generous enough to provide a sufficient livelihood for their inhabitants. The chief staple of the district until recently was flour made from chestnuts, and chestnut groves still cover much of the region.

## Lucca to Bagni di Lucca

North of Lucca, the first tempting detour off the SS12 is to one of the many Romanesque churches in the region, **San Giorgio di Brancoli**, near Vinchiana, as notable for its lovely setting as for its 12th-century pulpit. **Diécimo**, across the river, has a name that survives from Roman times – it lies 10 Roman miles (18km) from Lucca. The town's main landmark is the mighty Romanesque campanile of the 13th-century church of **Santa Maria**, standing out starkly against the surrounding hills.

**Borgo a Mozzano**, 4km further upstream, is famous for its beautiful little hump-back bridge, with arches in five different shapes and sizes, which is dedicated to the Magdalene, or to the Devil. According to legend, he built it one dark and stormy night in exchange for the first soul to cross – the clever villagers outwitted him by sending a dog over in the morning. The real builder in this case was the slighty less lethal 11th-century Countess Matilda who, besides the bridge, endowed the villages around Borgo with a number of solid Romanesque parish churches. Inside Borgo's church you can see a wooden *San Bernardino* by Civitali.

To the north, just above the confluence of the Serchio river and the Torrente Lima, lie the long and narrow riverside hamlets that make up **Bagni di Lucca**, Lucca's once-grand old spa, first mentioned in the days of Countess Matilda. In the early 1800s, under the patronage of Elisa Bonaparte Baciocchi, it enjoyed a moment in high society's favour – long enough to build one of Europe's first official gambling casinos (1837; roulette was invented

🟦 **Bagni di Lucca**

here), an Anglican church in an exotic Gothic Alhambra style, and an unusual 1840 suspension bridge (the **Ponte alle Catene**) – before sinking into obscurity. In Bagni's heyday, though, Byron, Browning, Shelley and Heine came to take the sulphur and saline waters, and perspire in a natural vapour bath. Heine was particularly enthusiastic: 'A true and proper sylvan paradise. I have never found a valley more enchanting,' he wrote; even the mountains are 'nobly formed' and not 'bizarre and Gothic like those in Germany'. Little has changed, and these days Bagni di Lucca is a sleepy but charming little place, with some pretty villas, elegant thermal establishments that spring into action every summer, a miniature pantheon, and a fancy Circolo dei Forestieri, or foreigners' club (now a restaurant), on the river-front.

## Up the Lima Valley

From Bagni di Lucca, the SS12 leads towards San Marcello Pistoiese and the ski resort of Abetone (*see* p.249), following the lovely valley of the Lima. A byroad beginning at Bagni leads to picturesque, rugged stone hamlets like **Pieve di Controne** and **Montefegatesi** that only appear on the most detailed maps; from Montefegatesi, an unsealed road continues to the dramatic gorge of **Orrido di Botri** at the foot of the Alpe Tre Potenze (6,363ft/ 1,939m). As the byroad winds back towards the SS12 at Scesta, it passes **San Cassiano**, site of a fine 13th-century Pisan-style church with a delicately carved façade, in an isolated setting. Other byroads from the SS12 lead to tiny hamlets like **Vico Pancellorum** to the north and **Lucchio** to the south.

## To Barga and the Cave of the Wind

The Garfagnana proper begins where the Lima flows into the river Serchio at Fornoli. In the 14th century this area was ruled by the kinsmen of Castruccio Castracani; one of their prettiest mountain hamlets is **Tereglio**, along the scenic northeast road to the **Alpe Tre Potenze**, before it meanders on to Abetone. The Castracani had their base at **Coreglia Antelminelli**, high above the Serchio and the main SS445 (turn off at Piano di Coreglia). Coreglia's church contains a magnificent 15th-century processional cross, and there's a **Museo della Figurina di Gesso e dell'Emigrazione** devoted to the Garfagnana's traditional manufacture of plaster figures.

**Museo della Figurina di Gesso e dell'Emigrazione**
*t 0583 78082; open summer Mon–Sat 8–1, Sun 10–1 and 4–7; winter Mon–Sat 9–1; adm*

To the north, the hill town of **Barga** (pop. 11,000) stands above its modern offspring, Fornaci di Barga on the main SS445. Barga was astute enough to maintain its independence until 1341, when it decided to link its fortunes with Florence. At the very top of town stands Barga's chief monument, its **cathedral**, begun in the year 1000 on a terrace, with a panoramic view over the rooftops and of surrounding hills apparently clad in green velvet, and bare mountains scoured with white marble. Built of a blonde stone called *alberese di Barga*, its square façade is discreetly decorated with a shallow pattern, charming reliefs and two leering lions; on the side the campanile is incorporated into the church; over the portal, there's a relief of a feast scene with a king and dwarfs. There's yet another dwarf inside, supporting one of the red marble pillars of the **pulpit** by the idiosyncratic 13th-century Como sculptor, Guido Bigarelli. The other pillars required a pair of lions, one grinning over a conquered dragon, one being both stroked and stabbed by a man. Less mysterious are the naive reliefs around the pulpit itself, startlingly sophisticated versions of familiar scriptural scenes. In the choir note the venerable polychrome wood statue of St Christopher (early 1100s) and a choir screen with strange medieval carvings, including a mystic mermaid (*see* p.390). Around the back, the cathedral's garden has a magnificent Lebanon cedar.

Next to the cathedral stands the **Palazzo Pretorio**, with a small

**Museo Civico**

*open June–Sept daily 10–12.30 and 2.30–5; adm*

**Museo Civico,** and 14th-century **Loggetta del Podestà**; if you go down the stairs towards the dungeon you can see Barga's old corn measures – a medieval Trading Standards Office. The rest of Barga is a photogenic ensemble of archways and little *palazzi* piled on top of each other, with walls, gates and a ravine planted with kitchen gardens. Things get lively in July and August with the classes and performances of **Opera Barga** in the old Dei Differenti Theatre, founded in 1600. Between Barga and Fornaci di Barga, you can measure the showy success of the city's emigrants who returned to build modern palaces in the suburb of **Giardino**.

From Barga you can take a 17km potholing detour to

**Grotto del Vento**

*t 0583 722024, www.grottadel vento.com; open daily all year; guided 1hr tours at 10, 11, 12, 2, 3, 4, 5 and 6, 2hr tours for real cave fiends daily April–Oct; winter Sun and hols only at 11, 3, 4 and 5; sometimes only part of the cave is visited; less crowded in the mornings; adm exp*

**Fornovalasco** in the Apuan Alps to see Tuscany's best cave, the **Grotto del Vento**, a long cavern of fat stalactites, bottomless pits and abysses, and subterranean lakes and streams, set in a barren, eerie landscape.

## Castelnuovo di Garfagnana

Hanging over the Serchio, 11km north of Barga, is **Castelnuovo di Garfagnana**, the region's lively 'capital', guarded by its **Rocca**. Its most famous commander was Ludovico Ariosto, author of the epic poem of chivalry and fantasy, *Orlando Furioso*. Ariosto was employed by the Este Dukes of Ferrara to chase bandits and collect tolls here in the 1520s, but didn't take to it. 'I'm not a man to govern other men,' he wrote. 'I have too much pity, and can't deny the things they require me to deny.'

Castelnuovo makes a handy base for excursions into its often wild surroundings. Northeast, past the small resort of **Castiglione di Garfagnana**, a tortuous mountain road continues through 16km of magnificent scenery to the **Foce delle Radici** (the pass into Emilia-

**Museo Etnografico Campagna**
*t 0583 649072; open April–May Tues–Sun 9–12 and 2–5; June–Sept Tues–Sun 9.30–1 and 2.30–7 (daily July and Aug); Oct–Mar Mon–Sat 9–12 and 2–5; adm*

Romagna) and **San Pellegrino in Alpe**, with magnificent views, an ancient monastery and a good little museum, the **Museo Etnografico Campagna**. West of Castelnuovo a scenic road leads over the Apuan Alps to Carrara and the coast, through the desolate Turrite Secca, its sombre features relieved by the romantic oasis of **Isola Santa** (13km) – a tiny, slate-roofed village amid trees on a lake, once a hideout for medieval renegades; now it is abandoned, save for a few old folks and the sheep who lives behind the altar of the church.

North of Castelnuovo the road enters Garfagnana Alta, one of the least-known corners of Tuscany. Just north of town lies the **Parco Naturale dell'Orecchiella**, with eagles, mouflons, deer and a botanical garden, its mountains crisscrossed by paths; pick up a map at the visitor centre in Orecchiella. At Poggio, back on the Serchio, there's a turn-off for **Careggine**, a lofty old hamlet with commanding views, and the artificial **Lago di Vagli**. Creating this lake submerged the village of Fabbriche; the campanile may still be seen sticking stubbornly out of the water. There are more stunning views from **Vagli Sopra**, village of old marble quarries and an 18th-century road, deteriorated into a footpath, which leads into the Valle di Arnetola. Towering over all is **Monte Pisanino** (6,380ft/1,945m), the tallest of the Apuan Alps; the road up to the summit and the alpine refuge of Donegani, passing the lakelet of Gramolazzo, begins at **Piazza al Serchio**, leaving the Serchio and the Garfagnana behind.

## Where to Stay and Eat in the Garfagnana

There's nothing exceptional in Garfagnana, but the Italians firmly believe the further north in Tuscany you go, the better the cooking, graced by the kindly influences of Liguria and Emilia-Romagna; the pasta dishes in the region are especially good. Specialities include *torte di erbe* (vegetable pies), chestnut puddings and *pattona* (chestnut biscuits).

**ⓘ Bagni di Lucca >**
*Piazza Adolfo Betti, t 0583 805813, www.prolocobagnidilucca.it; open Sat am only*

### Bagni di Lucca ✉ 55022

Bagni di Lucca is wonderfully genteel, with a score of quiet, modest Victorian hotels.

**\*\*\*Regina Park Hotel**, Viale Umberto I 157, t 0583 805151, www.coronaregina.it (€€€€). A smart hotel with all mod cons housed in a Renaissance *palazzo* in the centre of Bagni. A lovely loggia overlooks the ample grounds, which back onto the river Lima. *Closed mid-Oct–Easter.*

**\*\*\*Corona**, Via Serraglia 78, t 0583 805151, www.coronaregina.it (€€€). Under the same ownership as the Regina, this is cheaper, but still very comfortable. The restaurant serves imaginative dishes such as *zucchini*, *taleggio* and truffle *timbale*, gnocchi with baby squid and chickpeas, and duck breast cooked with blackcurrants.

**\*Roma**, Via Umberto I 110, t 0583 87278, www.hotelromabagnidilucca.it (€). Toscanini, Puccini and Caruso all stayed here, a small, old-fashioned place with a shady garden at the back, also in Villa di Bagni. Most rooms have a bathroom.

**Circolo dei Forestieri**, Loc. Ville, t 0583 86032 (€€). Slightly smarter, where you can eat *filetto al pepe verde* and *crêpes ai funghi. Closed Mon.*

**Da Vinicio**, Via del Casino 8–10, t 0583 87250 (€). A chaotic and popular pizzeria a block west of Bagni's bridge, also serving good roast pigeon and seafood.

ⓘ **Barga** >
*Via di Mezzo,*
*t 800 028497,*
*www.comune.*
*barga.lu.it*

## Barga ✉ 55051

****Il Ciocco in Castelvecchio**, Pascoli, 6km north at Pascoli, t 0583 7191, *www.ciocco.it* (€€€). A huge resort hotel with some 260 rooms plus self-catering chalets, heliport, restaurant, bars, tennis court – in short, the works. Full-board available.

***Villa Libano**, Via del Sasso 6, t 0583 723059 (€). A lovely place in a courtyard, set next to Barga's city park; there's a restaurant with tables out in the garden.

**Terrazza**, Piazza San Michele, 5km north at Albiano, t 0583 766155 (€). Specialities of the region, plus some rooms. *Closed Wed.*

ⓘ **Castelnuovo di Garfagnana** >
*Via Cavalieri di Vittorio Veneto,*
*t 0583 641007,*
*www.castelnuovo garfagnana.org*

*The Visitors' Centre for the Parco Regionale delle Alpi Apuane is in Castelnuovo at Piazza delle Erbe 1, t 0583 644242, www. parcapuane.toscana.it*

## Castelnuovo di Garfagnana ✉ 55032

***Da Carlino**, Via Garibaldi 15, t 0583 644270 *www.dacarlino.it* (€€). A rustic old place with an alpine feel to it and comfy rooms. Excellent restaurant serves home-made organic produce, plus pizzas baked in a wood oven.

**La Ceragetta**, Via Ceragetta 5, t 0583 667065 (€). For a rustic feast with a majestic backdrop, seek out this alpine chalet-style restaurant just above Isola Santa. Your digestion will be challenged by a vast range of *antipasti*, home-made pastas, game and roast meats, mushrooms in season, good solid desserts and unlimited wine. *Closed Mon.*

**Osteria Vecchio Mulino**, Via Vittorio Emanuele 12, t 0583 62192 (€). This atmospheric wine bar, just outside the city walls, is a great place for a snack accompanied by some wonderful wines. Cold meats and superb cheeses are displayed on wooden boards at long tables, and there are excellent flans and marinated vegetables. *Closed Mon.*

## Camaiore ✉ 55041

**Peralta**, Via Pieve 321, t 0584 951 230, *www.peraltatuscany.com* (€€). A medieval village that was lovingly restored by sculptor Fiore de Henriquez over 30 years, this is a cross between holiday houses and an artists' retreat. Henriquez's sculptures dot the village and there are houses and apartments for rent, as well as courses on offer. The views are stunning, there is a nice swimming pool and the staff are lovely.

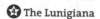 **The Lunigiana**

# The Lunigiana

Even less populous and less visited than the Garfagnana, the Lunigiana, separating Liguria and Emilia-Romagna from the rest of Tuscany, has traditionally been a tough nut for its would-be governors to crack. The Romans of Luni (founded in 180 BC to contain the fearsome Ligurians) found it a wild place; even in the 7th century, missionaries were still bashing revered ancient idols. This rugged territory of chestnut forests is crowded with the castles of would-be rulers and other toll-collecting gangsters. In the early 1900s the Lunigiana was a stronghold of rural anarchism, and in 1944 its partisans made it one of the bigger free zones in the north. Since then life has been fairly tranquil; rocky, forested landscapes, ruined castles (many bombed in the last war) and simple Romanesque churches form the main attractions.

## Piazza al Serchio to Aulla

Beyond **Piazza al Serchio**, the first town of consequence along the SS445 is fortified **Casola in Lunigiana** (20km); just beyond, a road veers south for the spa of **Equi Terme,** a tiny place where the medieval town is spectacularly perched on a rock above the new

# Getting to and around the Lunigiana

If you're approaching from the north, **trains** and *autostrade* from Genoa (A12) and Parma (A15) merge near Aulla. From here there are frequent trains to Massa-Carrara, Viareggio and Pisa, Pontremoli or Lucca. From Lucca, trains to Aulla take over 2hrs (85km) and to Pontremoli 2½hrs (108km).

**CAT buses** serve the Lunigiana, with Aulla as the main depot; there are services to Massa and Carrara, and to Bagnone, Filattiera, Fivizzano, Fosdinovo, Licciana Nardi, Pontremoli and Villafranca.

**Parco delle Grotte**
*t 0187 422598; open July–mid Sept 10.30–7; mid–Sept–Dec by appt; adm*

town. Equi is less known these days for its waters than for its splendidly sited **Parco delle Grotte**, where you can visit natural caves such as **La Buca** (The Pit), a caves museum and an archeopark, with reconstructed Palaeolithic and Neolithic settings. Our ancestors also apparently socialized with bears (or ate them), judging by the bones that have been found here. **Fivizzano** to the north (on the SS63 or by road from Casola) belonged to the Malaspina of Massa until the Medici snatched it and fortified it as a grand ducal outpost. The main square, Piazza Medicea, has a grand fountain paid for by Cosimo III, a few Florentine-style palaces, and the 13th-century parish church with the inevitable Medici balls on the front.

There are two interesting Romanesque chapels in the vicinity, **Santa Maria Assunta**, 3km towards Pognana, in a lovely isolated setting, and 12th-century **San Paolo a Vendaso** with carved capitals inside, on the SS63 towards the Passo di Cerreto.

From Ceserano, just south of the SS445, the SS446 heads southwest over the mountains to Sarzana, passing **Fosdinovo**, where the Malaspina **castle** that hosted Dante in 1306 is one of the most beautiful and majestic in the Lunigiana. Inside is a collection of arms and ornaments found in local tombs.

**Castello di Fosdinovo**
*t 0187 68891; guided tours winter Wed–Mon 10–11 and 4–5; summer Wed–Mon 10–11 and 4–6; adm*

## Aulla

**Aulla** grew up at the Lunigiana's hotly contested crossroads, guarding access into the Magra valley. The powerful 16th-century **Fortezza della Brunella** was built by the Genoese, who bought Aulla in 1543; Napoleon gave it to his sister Elisa in Lucca; it now contains a **natural history museum**. Nearby are the citadels of two other rivals for the town – the Bishop of Luni's **Caprigliola**, a fortified village still inaccessible to cars (6km southwest on the SS62), and the Malaspinas' fortified hamlet of **Bibola** and their romantically ruined **Ponzanello**, both due south of Aulla. The Malaspina also fortified the strategic road to the pass, to the northeast at **Licciana Nardi** (surrounded by immensely thick 11th-century walls with only narrow passageways giving access to its centre), and especially at **Bastia**, 4km further on.

**Museo di Storia Naturale**
*t 01867 409077; open Oct–Mar Tues–Sun 9–12 and 3–6; April–Sept Tues–Sun 9–12 and 3–7; adm*

From Aulla you can tack down into Liguria and the **Italian Riviera** to visit the 'Gulf of the Poets' (or, more prosaically, the Gulf of La Spezia), named after Byron, who swam across it, and Shelley, who last lived in San Terenzo near the Pisan town of **Lerici**. On the gulf's western shore (in Liguria) lies enchanting old **Portovenere**, named after the goddess of love herself. Near Carrara are the excavations of ancient Luni (*see* p.281).

North of Aulla is **Villafranca in Lunigiana**, along the Via Francigena, the pilgrimage route from France; here you can visit the 16th-century **church of San Francesco** and an **Ethnographic Museum** devoted to rural life in the Lunigiana, especially the chestnut industry. Yet another mighty castle beckons further up at **Bagnone**, 5km to the east.

**Museo Etnografico**
*t 0187 493417;*
*open Oct–May daily*
*4–7; June–Sept 9–12*
*and 4–7; adm*

## Pontremoli

Long and low-key, stretched lazily along the river Magra and the Torrente Verdi, is **Pontremoli** (pop. 11,000), chief town of the Lunigiana and the northernmost in Tuscany. The Via Francigena passes through the middle. Pontremoli is full of wonderful Belle Epoque details – lamp-posts, shop fronts and interiors, even the marble street names. The historical Liberty-style **Caffè Fratelli Aichta** in Piazza della Repubblica, with its old carved wood cabinets and counters, is well worth a visit. The town wasn't always so peaceful: in 1322 Guelph and Ghibelline quarrels led Castruccio Castracani to build a fortress, called *Cacciaguerra* ('drive-away war'), in the town centre to keep the two parties apart until they made peace. Of this noble effort only the **Torre del Campanone** and what is now the campanile of the **Duomo** survive. The Duomo itself has a fine, ballroom interior hung with dozens of glittering chandeliers, unusual for Tuscany. Over the Torrente Verdi, the church of **San Francesco** contains a lovely polychrome relief of the *Madonna and Child* attributed to Agostino di Duccio. Between the centre and the station, the oval 18th-century church of **Nostra Donna** is a rare example of Tuscan rococo.

**Museo delle Statue-stele della Lunigiana**
*t 0187 831439;*
*open Oct–April*
*Tues–Sun 9–12 and 2–5;*
*May–Sept 9.30–12.30*
*and 2.30–5.30*

The gloomy 14th-century **Castello del Piagnaro** is home to a small museum of statue-*steles*, large and carved, by an unknown culture that flourished in the Lunigiana between the 3rd millennium BC and 2nd century BC. The *steles*, rather like menhirs with personality, include stylized warriors with daggers or axes, and women with little knobbly breasts. They are displayed in semi-darkness, adding to their mystery. The oldest (3000–2000 BC) have a U for a face and a head hardly distinguishable from the trunk; the middle period (20th–8th century BC) sport anvil heads and eyes; the last group (7th–2nd century BC) are mostly warriors, with a weapon in each hand, just as Virgil described the Gauls who invaded Lazio. They were often found near sources of water, and some scholars think they may have symbolized the heavens (the head), the earth (the arms and weapons) and the underworld (the lower third, buried in the ground). Some had their heads knocked off – a sure sign that the pope's missionaries in the 8th century were doing their job. Curiously, in the nearby hamlet of **Vignola**, a folk memory survives of the destruction of idols; during the patron saint's festival they make little wooden idols strangely similar to Pontremoli's statue-*steles* and burn them to celebrate the triumph over the pagans.

In 1471 the Virgin made an appearance a mile south of Pontremoli, and to honour the spot the church of **Santissima Annunziata** was built with a lovely marble Tempietto by Jacopo Sansovino, a quattrocento fresco of the *Annunciation* by Luca Cambiaso, an elegant triptych of uncertain hand or date, and some fun *trompe l'œil* frescoes by a Baroque painter from Cremona named Natali.

## Where to Stay and Eat in the Lunigiana

⭐ Da Bussé >>

### Equi Terme ✉ 54022

\*La Posta in Via Provinciale, t 0585 97937 (€€). Friendly little place with a bright restaurant and attractive rooms. Eat ravioli stuffed with ricotta and nettles or the house special, 'La Spagnola' (a kind of cheesy strudel). *Closed Jan, Feb and Tues in winter.*

### Bagnone ✉ 54021

I Fondi, Via della Repubblica 26, t 0187 429086 (€€). Up in fortified Bagnone, you can fortify yourself with good, solid country cooking – lasagne with pesto or mushrooms, ravioli filled with gorgonzola and *radicchi, testeroli in pesto*. In summer you can eat overlooking the river. Booking advisable

⭐ Osteria Caveau del Teatro >>

### Fivizzano ✉ 54013

\*\*Il Giardinetto, Via Roma 151, t 0585 92060 (€). A delightful, old-fashioned place overlooking Piazza Medicea. Rooms are comfortable, and there's a little garden. The restaurant (€€) was established in 1882, the *antipasti* are especially tempting. Booking required. *Closed Mon.*

ⓘ Fivizzano >
*Via Roma, t 0585 92625, www.tdl.it*

### Pontremoli ✉ 54027

Pontremoli is rich in good restaurants, and has several hotel options.

\*\*\*Golf Hotel, Via Pineta, t 0187 831573 (€€). Modern and out of town in a

ⓘ Pontremoli >
*Piazza della Repubblica, t 0187 833701, www.tdl.it*

pine wood, offering a restaurant and 80 very comfortable rooms, suites and apartments all with bath and TV.

Da Bussé, Piazza del Duomo 31, t 0187 831371 (€€). An age-old restaurant featuring Pontremoli's special *pasta testaroli* with pesto, *involtini* (little meat parcels) in tomato sauce, stuffed pigs' trotters, and a delicious Swiss chard and ricotta pie. A sign on the door announces that they don't cook mushrooms. Finish with *spongata*, a local chocolate tart. *Open lunch only Mon–Thurs, lunch and dinner Sat, Sun; closed Fri.*

Osteria Caveau del Teatro, Piazza Santa Cristina, t 0187 833328 (€€). Elegant yet cosy cellar restaurant offering a change from rustic fare. The menu features such dishes as pâté of foie gras with port, potato *tortelli* with a Parmesan cream, roast pork with orange, and chocolate mousse with apricot *coulis*. The adjoining 17th-century tower houses seven delightful bedrooms, which are beautifully furnished with antiques and named after musicians.

La Manganella, Via Garibaldi 20, t 0187 830653 (€€). If you want mushrooms, here they do them every way under the sun: grilled, raw in salad, *trifolati* (sautéed), with pasta... *Closed Mon.*

Trattoria del Giardino da Bacciottini, Via Ricci Armani 13, t 0187 830120 (€€–€). In the old town, you'll find *fritelle* of salt cod, marinated herrings and excellent *testaroli* with pesto and lamb. *Closed Sun eve and Mon.*

# North of Livorno: The Coast and Inland

## Riviera della Versilia: Carrara to Viareggio

### Carrara

In the centre of dynamic, up-to-date Carrara (population 69,000) is a garden square, Piazza Gramsci, with an unusual fountain: a large, snow-white sphere of marble that revolves hypnotically, glistening with water, as the Apuan Alps tower in the background, streaked with the white quarries from which the sphere was 'liberated'. Carrara actually means marble; its name is believed to come from 'kar', the Indo-European for stone. The Romans were the first to extract it 2,000 years ago; they drove wooden wedges soaked in water into natural cracks in the stone; when the wedges swelled the marble broke off and was rolled away on iron balls and sent to Rome to become Trajan's column or Apollo Belvedere.

The same techniques were being used when Carrara began its revival in 1502, when Pope Julius II sent Michelangelo to find marble for his tomb. These mountains are haunted by the memory of the 'divine' sculptor, in his old clothes and smelly goatskin boots, going to the most inaccessible corners to discover new veins of perfect white stone. Michelangelo thought quarrying just as serious an art as sculpture; he loved to spend time here with his rock, and he claimed with his usual modesty to have 'introduced the art of quarrying' to Carrara. Marble has also made the Carraresi traditionally a breed apart – although their official past is dominated by the rule of godfatherish noble clans such as the Malaspina and Cybo-Malaspina, the undercurrents were always fiercely independent, leaning strongly towards anarchism.

Some of Carrara's marble went into its one outstanding monument, the **cathedral**, a distinctive Romanesque church begun in the 11th century with marble stripes and an arch of marble animals, and later embellished with an exquisite 14th-century rose window of marble lace, and marble art and statues inside, including a huge bowl in the baptistry. In the little piazza is a bulky sculpture by Florentine hack Bandinelli, generally known as

### Beach Life, Tuscan-style

The sea along the Tuscan coast isn't as clean as it might be, and the closer you get to the mouth of the Arno and Livorno, the less savoury it becomes. For a spell on the beach, you may find Tuscany's archipelago of seven islands more congenial – the sea is cleaner and the coast and beaches prettier. Unless you go to the smallest islands, Italian beach culture is hard to escape here. Much of the shore is privately owned and you have to pay to access a veritable wall of deckchairs and beach umbrellas, as densely as possible; behind this there's inevitably a busy road, where the traffic is mainly with loudspeakers and motorcycles; behind the busy road is another wall of hotels, and perhaps a woods. As always, you'll find it more pleasant and less frenzied outside July and August.

# Getting around North of Livorno

Transport is very easy along the coast, especially by **bus**. CAT (**t** 800 570530, *www.catspa.it*) links the Marinas of the coast with Massa and Carrara, and with the towns of the Lunigiana; CLAP (**t** 800 602525, *www.clapspa.it*) links Forte dei Marmi and Viareggio with Lucca; LAZZI (**t** 055 351061, *www.lazzi.it*) connects the coast with Lucca, Montecatini, Pistoia and Florence.

There are regular **trains** along the coastal line, which hugs the shore except at the mouth of the Arno and the Maremma. Trains to Massa or Carrara leave you between the beach and the centre, but CAT bus links to both are frequent. The stations at Pietrasanta and Camaiore are inland, not at the Marinas.

By **car** you can whip through the dull stretches on the A12, or follow the Via Aurelia (SS1), the main Roman route, though both keep their distance from the sea.

the Giant, though it is supposed to be *Andrea Doria in the Guise of Neptune*. Next to Piazza Gramsci, on Via Roma 1, is the **Accademia delle Belle Arti**, in a medieval castle converted into a palace in the 16th century by Alberico Cybo-Malaspina, Marchese di Massa, whose descendants ruled Massa and Carrara until they died out in 1829, when the state joined the duchy of Modena until unification. The courtyard has sculptures from Luni and the *Edicola dei Fantescritti*, a Roman tabernacle from the Fantescritti quarry, with bas-reliefs of Jove, Hercules and Bacchus, arm-in-arm like old chums, surrounded by graffiti by Giambologna and other sculptors who visited the quarries.

## Marble Quarries and Roman Ruins

Carrara exports half a million tonnes of different marbles a year, but there is little danger of it running out soon (though locals will gravely tell you there are only a few cubic kilometres of good stone left). The **quarries** surrounding Carrara are an unforgettable sight; usually they extend straight up to the sky, forming a blinding white scar down the mountain, with a narrow access road zigzagging perpendicularly to the top. Signs from the centre of Carrara direct you to the quarries, or **Cave di Marmo – Colonnata** (8km, founded as a colony of Roman slaves and famous for *lardo di Colonnata*, a fat bacon salted in marble vats), **Fantiscritti** (a Roman quarry still in use) and **Ravaccione** (with fine mountain views). The **Museo Civico del Marmo** has photos of the marble-workers of a century ago and of the surreal world of the quarries; halls of polished slabs introduce the amazing variety of marbles and travertines from the area, and the rest of the world; and there's marble art and a room of modern marble to prove it's not limited to churches.

**Museo Civico del Marmo**
*Viale XX Settembre (main road between Carrara and train station)*, **t** 0585 845746; open May, June and Sept Mon–Sat 10–6; July and Aug Mon–Sat 10–8; Oct–April Mon–Sat 9–5; adm

The Apuan Alps, only a few kilometres from the sea, give this coast a certain majesty. The beach at **Marina di Carrara** is divided in two by the marble port, which sends the big blocks all over the world; in July and August the port-resort puts on a large show of marble arts and crafts.

Just north, on the border of Liguria near Marinella, is the site of Roman **Luni**, built as a bulwark against the fierce Ligurians. The city survived until the Middle Ages; the power-hungry bishopric of Luni survived until 1929, when it was combined with that of La Spezia. You can see a large amphitheatre, forum, houses, temples and so on; the **Museo Nazionale di Luni** has marble statuary, coins, jewellery, portraits and more, as well as a display of modern techniques used in the excavation of the site, which can be toured with a guide.

East off the SS446, 20km into the mountains, **Campo Cecina** has an extraordinary panoramic view over the marble quarries. The city of Carrara has an alpine refuge here; it's a good base for exploring the trails across the Apuan Alps (the tourist office has maps).

**Museo Nazionale di Luni**
t 0187 66811,
www.archeoge.liguria.
beniculturali.it; open
Tues–Sun 8.30–7.30
(amphitheatre
Tues–Sun
10.30–3.30); adm

## Massa

Massa (population 66,200), nearly the same size as Carrara and co-capital of the province, was the principal seat of the Cybo-Malaspina dukes. They were never great builders or patrons, except when it came to their own digs – the polychrome 17th-century **Palazzo Cybo-Malaspina** on central Piazza degli Aranci, with its orange trees and obelisk, and, up the hill, the **Castello Malaspina**, an 11th-century castle with Renaissance additions, including a beautiful, ornate courtyard, loggias and frescoed rooms.

From Massa there are other marble quarries to visit, near **Pasquilio** 11km east, a balcony with views over the gulf of La Spezia; in the same area, the **Pian della Fioba**'s botanical garden features the flora of the Apuan mountains, more stunning views, and another alpine refuge open all year.

**Marina di Massa**, which is situated on a drained marsh, is a lively proletarian resort with lots of pine trees. Its neighbour, **Cinquale**, the 'Marina' of the old hilltown of Montignoso, is smaller and prettier; between it and Forte dei Marmi you'll find a long stretch of free beach. Near **Montignoso** stand the picturesque ruins of the **castle of Aghinolfi**, a Lombard outpost that was constructed in AD 600 by King Agilufo.

**Castello Malaspina**
*Via della Rocca,*
*t 0585 44774; open*
*Tues–Sun 9.30–12.30*
*and 4–8; adm*

**Castello Aghinolfi**
*t 0585 8271204; open*
*summer Tues–Sun 4–7;*
*winter Sun 3–5.30; adm*

## Around Forte dei Marmi

**Forte dei Marmi**, one of the larger, smarter resorts, full of chic shops, bars and restaurants, is a playground for the rich and famous. Founded in 1788, when Grand Duke Leopoldo constructed the fortress and seaport in order to serve the marble quarried from Seravezza, it has an old loading pier that is now a promenade. In the 1860s the first holiday villas were built along the white sandy beach. Piazza Marconi holds an excellent market on Wednesdays.

**Marina di Pietrasanta** to the south isn't quite so upmarket, but in its **Parco della Versiliana** you will find the last section of the coastal forest, lush with parasol pines, holm oaks and myrtles. This was a favourite haunt of Gabriele D'Annunzio; in summer the La Versiliana Arts Festival includes concerts, plays and ballets, put on in its small outdoor theatre. **Lido di Camaiore**, the last resort before Viareggio, caters mainly for families, and has an elevated garden terrace along the beachfront.

Inland from Forte dei Marmi is the marble town of **Seravezza**, where Michelangelo lived in 1517 during his marble pilgrimage to Monte Altissimo; it's rich in statue stone known as *statuario*. Not long after, Duke Cosimo I commissioned Ammannati to build the **Villa Medicea** with its Mannerist courtyard. The **cathedral** contains works by Florentine goldsmiths, including a crucifix attributed to one of the Pollaiuolo brothers; 5km away, the **Pieve alla Cappella** has a fine rose window, the 'Eye of Michelangelo'.

Pretty **Stazzema** has a Romanesque church and stunning views. Quarries nearby produce the blue and white streaked 'flowered' marble used in the Medici's Princes' Chapel. Among the mountains is the curious **Monte Forata** (1,212m), with a hole near its summit.

## Pietrasanta

Pietrasanta is a mellow old town rich in marbly traditions, patronized by well-heeled Italian holidaymakers and home to a sub-culture of foreign artists attracted by its proximity to one of the world's greatest sources of marble and by the facilities around it, from marble studios to bronze foundries. Henry Moore, Fernando Botero and Igor Mitoraj, among others, have been residents.

The town's walls date from 1255, though its regular street plan suggests a Roman origin. Life centres around Piazza del Duomo with its Florentine *Marzocco* on a pillar (1514) and the **Duomo di San Martino**, begun in 1256, with a rose window carved from a single block of marble. There's more marble inside, plus a bronze crucifix by Tacca and a 13th-century fresco by the school of Giotto. It shares the piazza with the **Palazzo Pretorio** and **Sant'Agostino** (14th century) with an attractive minimalist Pisan façade. From here a road leads up to the citadel, or **Rocca Arrighina**, built in the 1300s by Castruccio Castracani and lit up at night, which often hosted emperors on their way to Rome. Or turn right from the main gate for the central market building, its parking area adorned with an erotic statue of a woman *en déshabille* pulling a young bull after her. There is often a sculpture exhibition in the pretty piazza or cloisters of Sant'Agostino. **Cosmave** can give information about the work of local artists.

**Cosmave**
*t 0584 283128,*
*www.cosmave.it*

## The Mountains Beyond Pietrasanta

From Pietrasanta a road heads inland to **Valdicastello Carducci** (birthplace of poet Giosuè Carducci) passing the 9th-century **Pieve di Santi Giovanni e Felicità**, the oldest church in the Versilia, with 14th-century frescoes. The road winds up into the mountains, giving lovely views, particularly at **Capezzano** and **Capriglia**.

**Camaiore** (from the Roman *Campus Major*; population 31,000) is an industrial town on the road to Lucca, with two Romanesque churches – the **Collegiata**, **Santi Giovanni e Stefano** (with a stately belltower and Roman sarcophagus for a font), and **Badia dei Santi Benedettini**, 8th-century with 11th-century additions. In Via IV Novembre, the **Museo d'Arte Sacra** has good Flemish tapestries.

**Museo d'Arte Sacra**
*open summer*
*Tues, Thurs and Sat*
*4–7.30, Sun 9–12;*
*winter Thurs and Sat*
*3.30–6, Sun 10–12*

A road from Camaiore leads up to **Monteggiori**, with more fine views. Other destinations include **Pieve a Elici**, near Massarosa, with a fine Romanesque church, 12th-century **San Pantaleone**. From here a minor road continues up through chestnut groves to **Montigiano**, one of the best balconies in the Apuans.

# Where to Stay and Eat on the Riviera della Versilia

At many hotels in coastal resorts, half-board is obligatory in high season (mid-July–mid-Aug). There are lots of camp-sites along the public beach between Massa and Carrara Marinas.

(i) **Carrara >**
*Viale XX Settembre,
t 0585 844136, www.
aptmassacarrara.it*

(i) **Pietrasanta >>**
*Piazza Statuto,
t 0584 283284 or
t 0584 284877*

(i) **Marina di Pietrasanta**
*Via Donizetti 14,
t 0584 20331*

(★) **Enoteca Marcucci >>**
(i) **Marina di Massa >**
*Viale Vespucci 24,
t 0585 240063*

(i) **Forte dei Marmi >**
*Via Franceschi 8b,
t 0584 80091*

## Carrara ✉ 54033

Look out for Candia, the white wine eked from Carrara's mountain terraces, and for local speciality *lardo* – pork-fat lard preserved in salt and rosemary in marble vats.

***Michelangelo**, Corso F Rosselli 3, t 0585 777161, *hm.carrara@tin.it* (€€). Modern rooms, most with baths, a restaurant and parking facilities.

**Da Venanzio**, Piazza Palestro 3, Colonnata, t 0585 758062 (€€€). A place among the quarries, serving a wonderful risotto with mushrooms. *Closed Thurs, and Sun eve.*

**Locanda Apuane**, Colonnata, t 0585 768017 (€€). Delicious *antipasti*, *tordelli* (meat, spinach and ricotta-filled ravioli), potato cake and local *panizza*. *Closed Mon, Sun eve, Jan.*

**Roma**, Piazza Battisti, t 0585 70632 (€€). A favourite for simple Tuscan cooking in the town centre, including *osso buco* with peas, and *scaloppine* with mushrooms. *Closed Sat lunch.*

## Marina di Massa ✉ 54037

**Ostello Apuano**, Viale delle Pinete 237, t 0585 780034, *ostelloapuano@hotmail. com* (€). A youth hostel. Rates include breakfast. *Closed Oct–mid-Mar.*

## Forte dei Marmi ✉ 55042

Forte is expensive, but many places offer big reductions in June and Sept.

*****Augustus**, Viale A Morin 169, t 0584 787200, *www.augustus-hotel.it* (€€€€€). A lovely villa in large grounds, with elegant rooms (breakfast is included). Facilities include a pool, private beach and two restaurants, one on the lido. *Closed mid-Oct–April.*

***Hotel Franceschi**, Via XX Settembre 19, t 0584 787114, *www.hotelfranceschi.it* (€€€€€). A lovely villa in a shady garden. Many of the bedrooms have balconies; breakfast included. The restaurant (€€€) is excellent; try the speciality,

*pesce in pane* (whole fish baked in a bread crust). Prices almost halve out of season. Balloon trips over town.

***Hotel Mignon**, Via G Carducci 58, t 0584 787495, *www.hotelmignon.it* (€€€). Bright and airy rooms (breakfast included), a garden, a pool, saunas, a solarium and a fitness centre a couple of blocks from the sea. The restaurant serves local and international cuisine.

**Da Lorenzo**, Via Carducci 61, t 0584 874030 (€€€€). Beautifully and imaginatively prepared seafood such as steamed octopus. Reserve. *Closed Mon exc. July and Aug, mid-Dec–Jan, and lunch July and Aug.*

## Pietrasanta ✉ 55045

This is one of the best places to stay in the area, and full of great eateries.

****Albergo Pietrasanta**, Via Garibaldi 35, t 0584 793726, *www.albergopietra santa.com* (€€€€€). An upmarket hotel in a 17th-century *palazzo*, with contemporary Italian art in public rooms and bedrooms. Rooms and suites have original frescoes too, and breakfast is taken in a conservatory or in the pretty courtyard garden.

****Palazzo Guiscardo**, Via Provinciale 16, t 0584 735298, *www.palazzo guiscardo.it* (€€€€). Nine plush rooms in a Liberty-style *palazzo*, the main feature being the bathrooms, each a different sort of local marble.

**Enoteca Marcucci**, Via Garibaldi 40, t 0584 791962 (€€€). More a restaurant with a fabulous wine list than a wine bar. Very popular among the rich and famous (book ahead) and justifiably so, the food is fantastic. Highlights include anchovies with lemon. *Closed lunch, Nov and Mon in winter.*

**Da Sci**, Vicolo Porta a Lucca 3, t 0584 790983 (€€). A simple trattoria serving vegetable flans, *pappa al pomodoro* and more. Booking advisable. *Closed Sun.*

## Camaiore ✉ 55043

**Locanda delle Monache**, Piazza XXIX Maggio 36, t 0584 984282, *www. lemonache.com* (€€). An excellent hotel and restaurant in a former convent.

**Emilio e Bona**, Loc. Candalla, Via Lombrici 22, just outside town, t 0584 989289 (€€). Excellent dishes, many featuring meat, mushrooms and truffles. *Closed Mon, and Tues lunch.*

# Viareggio to the Parco Naturale Migliarino San Rossore e Massaciuccoli

## Viareggio

**⓫ Viareggio**

Up until the 1820s **Viareggio** (population 59,000), Tuscany's biggest seaside resort, was little more than a fishing village, named after the medieval royal road, the 'Via Regia' between Migliarino and Pietrasanta. After the 14th-century battles with Pisa, Genoa and Florence, this village was the republic of Lucca's only port. Fortifications were built – Forte del Motrone (lost in 1441), the **Torre del Mare**, and **Torre Matilde** near the canal. Lucca's beloved duchess Maria Louisa drained the swamps, developed the shipyards and fishing and resort industries, and laid out the neat grid of streets; by the 1860s the first *cabanas* and beach umbrellas had arrived, and by 1900 Viareggio was booming. Playful, intricate wooden Art Nouveau buildings lined its promenade, the Passeggiata Viale Regina Margherita.

**Torre del Mare/
Torre Matilde**
*open by request;
ask at tourist office
(see p.286)*

A massive fire in 1917 led to major rebuilding in the 1920s; the most important buildings were designed by Galileo Chini and the eclectic Alfredo Belluomini. Chini (1873–1956), one of the founders of Italian Art Nouveau, or the Liberty Style, was especially known for florid ceramics. He also designed stage sets for the New York Metropolitan Opera's premieres of his friend Puccini's operas: *Turandot*, *Manon Lescaut* and *Gianni Schicchi*, as well as the throne room of the King of Siam (1911–14). With Belluomini he produced what has become the symbol of Viareggio, the colourful **Gran Caffè Margherita**, in a kind of Liberty-Mannerism, as well as the **Bagna Balena** and what is now the **Supercinema**, all located on the Passeggiata. You can compare their work with the 1900 **Negozio Martini**, the only wooden building to survive the 1917 fire. Chini and Belluomini also designed a number of hotels (*see* p.286), as well as Puccini's villa on Piazza Puccini and the buildings at Piazza d'Azeglio 15 and Viale Manin 20.

Viareggio's famous **Carnival**, which began in the 1890s, has grown to rival the much older ones of Rome and Venice, and in pure frivolity it surpasses them all. At the centre of the action are large papier-mâché floats, often lampooning public figures and politicians. If you can't make the huge parade that takes place on *Martedì Grasso* (Shrove Tuesday, and also on the four previous Sundays), you can see the floats all year round at the **Cittadella del Carnivale** near the Aurelia in the northwest of the town. This vast modern workshop and performance space is also the setting for concerts (mostly jazz and rock) in summer. Viareggio also has an open-air **fleamarket** around Piazza Manzoni on the fourth Saturday and Sunday of each month.

**Cittadella
del Carnivale**
*Via Maria Goretti;
visits by appt on t 0584
51176; closed for much
of winter while
floats being made*

**11**

**The Tuscan Coast | Viareggio**

**Museo Pucciniano**
*t 0584 341445; buses
from Piazza d'Azeglio;
open Mar and April
Tues–Sun 10–12.30 and
3.30–5.30; May–Oct
Tues–Sun 10–12.30 and
3–6.30; Dec–Feb 10–12.30
and 2.30–5; adm*

**Festival Pucciniano**
*Piazzale Belvedere
Puccini, Torre del Lago,
t 0584 350567, www.
puccinifestival.it; adm*

**Parco Naturale
Migliarino**
*www.parks.it; open
summer Tues, Thurs, Sat
and Sun 9.30–11.30 and
3.30–5.30; winter Tues,
Thurs, Sat and Sun
9.30–11.30 and 2–4; for
guided tours call
t 050 989084*

ⓘ **Viareggio >**
*Viale Carducci 10,
and at station in high
season, t 0584 962233,
www.aptversilia.it*

★ **Plaza e de
Russie >**

# Torre del Lago and Puccini

Puccini spent most of his later years in his villa at **Torre del Lago** 6km south of Viareggio. Now the **Museo Pucciniano**, it is on the banks of Lake Massaciuccoli, where he could practise his 'second favourite instrument, [his] rifle' on passing coots. The villa has its original furnishings, old photos, the piano on which Puccini composed many operas, his rifles and other mementos. The maestro, along with his wife and son, is buried in the adjacent chapel. In July and August the **Torre del Lago Opera Festival** presents famous and more obscure works by the composer. The stage is built out on the lake and spectators sit on the lakeside – beware the mosquitoes.

Most of Lake Massaciuccoli and the *macchia* (marshlands) and beaches to the south are part of the **Parco Naturale Migliarino San Rossore Massaciuccoli** (reached by boat from Torre del Lago, or drive to tiny Massaciuccoli). The wild beaches from Viareggio and Torre del Lago, with low dunes and pine forest, are free and undeveloped.

# Where to Stay and Eat in Viareggio

## Viareggio ✉ 55049

There are lots of hotels along the beach, especially inexpensive ones.

★★★★**Plaza e de Russie**, Piazza d'Azeglio 1, t 0584 44449, www.plazaederussie.com (€€€€). An elegant option with marble and Murano glass in the public rooms and a lovely rooftop breakfast room and restaurant where you can enjoy Mediterranean cuisine. Half- and full-board are available.

★★★★**Grand Hotel Excelsior**, Viale Carducci 88, t 0584 50726, www.excelsiorviareggio.it (€€€). One of the most extravagant Chini-Belluomini ventures, built in 1923. The public rooms preserve their original decor. Breakfast is included, and there's a restaurant and a babysitting service. *Closed Nov–Mar.*

★★**Apollo**, Viale Carducci 76, t 0584 407 383, www.hotelapolloviareggio.it (€€). A Liberty villa by the seafront, with original Belle Epoque features. Bedrooms are spartan but have baths and sea views, and there's a garden and a restaurant.

★★**Al Piccolo Hotel**, Via Duilio 16, t 0584 51014, alpiccolohotel@cheapnet.it (€€). An old villa a few blocks from the sea, now a modest hotel offering half- and full-board. *Closed winter.*

**Da Romano**, Via G. Mazzini 122, t 0584 31382 (€€€€). An elegant restaurant with an interior garden, offering creative cooking and delicious seafood such as squid stuffed with vegetables and shellfish. Book ahead. *Closed Mon, Tues lunch in July and Aug, 1wk in Jan, and 1wk in July.*

**L'Imbuto**, Via Fratti 308, t 0584 48906 (€€€). A lively, informal place for innovative fish dishes such as anchovies with fried green tomatoes. Booking is advisable. *Closed Mon.*

**L'Oca Bianca**, Via M. Coppino 409, t 0584 388477 (€€€). A restaurant overlooking the yacht harbour, and a cheaper adjoining *taverna*. Try the squid in basil sauce. *Closed lunch Mon–Sat, Tues in winter.*

**Piccolo Tito**, Lungomolo del Greco, t 0584 962016 (€€€). A lively, popular restaurant overlooking the canal. No-nonsense fish dishes include Catalan lobster. There are pizzas too.

**Al Porto**, Via M. Coppino 118, t 0584 383878 (€€€). A stunning restaurant overlooking the port, with wonderful home-made tagliatelle in San Pietro sauce, sea bass cooked in salt, and more. *Closed Sun eve and Mon in winter; Sun and Mon lunch in summer.*

**La Darsena**, Via Virgilio 150, t 0584 392785 (€€). A hugely popular place for *bavette* (pasta) with anchovies, fried squid and more. *Closed Sun.*

# Pisa

Pisa (population 104,000) is at once the best-known and most mysterious Tuscan city. Its most celebrated attraction has become a symbol for all Italy; even the least informed recognize the 'Leaning Tower of Pizza'. Tour buses disgorge thousands of people into the Field of Miracles every day, to spend a couple of hours 'doing' the sights before heading back to Florence, Elba or Rome. At night even the Pisani make a mass exodus into the suburbs, as if they sense that the city is too big for them – not physically, but in terms of unfulfilled ambitions, of past greatness nipped in the bud.

In 1100, Pisa was 'the city of marvels', the 'city of 10,000 towers' – or so it seemed to the awed writers of that century, who, at least outside Venice, had never seen such an enormous, cosmopolitan city in Christian Europe since the fall of Rome. Its population stood at 300,000. Pisan merchants travelled all over the Med, bringing back new ideas and styles in art, as well as riches. Pisa contributed much to the rebirth of Western culture: Pisan Romanesque, with its stripes and blind arcades, which had such a wide influence in Tuscany, was inspired by the Moorish architecture of Andalucía; Nicola Pisano, first of a long line of great sculptors, is as important to the renaissance of sculpture as Giotto is to painting.

Pisa has put all its efforts into one fabulous spiritual monument, while the rest of the city wears an undemonstrative, almost anonymous face. It is a subtle place, a little sad and run-down perhaps, but strangely seductive if you give it a chance. After all, one can't create a Field of Miracles in a void.

## History

Pisa used to like to claim that it began as a Greek city, founded by colonists from Elis. Most historians won't accept anything earlier than around 100 BC, when a Roman veterans' colony was settled here. Records of what followed are scarce, but Pisa, like Amalfi and Venice, must have had an early start in building a navy and establishing trade connections. By the 11th century, the effort had blossomed into opulence; it had acquired a small empire, including Corsica, Sardinia and, for a while, the Balearics. Around 1060, work began on the great cathedral complex and many other buildings, inaugurating the Pisan Romanesque.

In 1135 Pisa captured and sacked Amalfi, its greatest rival. The First Crusade, when Pisa's archbishop led the entire fleet in support of the Christian knights, was an economic windfall for the city. And when the Pisans weren't fighting the Muslims of Spain and Africa, they were learning from them: much medieval Arab science, philosophy and architecture came into Europe through Pisa. Pisa's architecture, the highest development of the Romanesque in Italy,

## Getting to and around Pisa

Pisa's **international airport**, Galileo Galilei (**t** 050 849300, *www.pisa-airport.com*) 3km to the south, is 10mins from Piazza Stazione (in front of the main station south of the Arno) by bus no.5. It also has a station with regular daily trains to the centre and a special train service to Florence (1½hrs, every 1–2hrs daily), as well as the Terravision bus which goes regularly to Florence (1½hrs, two an hour). **Car hire** companies at the airport include Hertz, **t** 050 43220, *www.hertz.it*, Maggiore, **t** 050 42574, *www.maggiore.it*, easyCar, **t** 091 6751711, *www.easycaritalia.it*, and Auto Europa, **t** 050 506883, *www.autoeuropa.it*.

Pisa has three **train stations** (**t** 892021, *www.trenitalia.com*): some coastal trains stop at San Rossore, near Campo dei Miracoli, and some trains from Florence stop at Pisa Aeroporto (*see* above), but it's best to plan trips through the Stazione Centrale south of the Arno, where all trains call.

**Intercity buses** depart from near Piazza Vittorio Emanuele II, the big roundabout just north of the central station: CPT buses (*www.cpt.pisa.it*) for Volterra, Livorno and the coastal resorts (to the west on Via Nino Bixio, **t** 800 012773) and LAZZI buses (*www.lazzi.it*) to Florence, Lucca, La Spezia (on Via d'Azeglio, **t** 050 46288). Many of these buses also stop at Piazza D. Manin, just outside the walls at the cathedral.

The **Parco Naturale Migliarino San Rossore Massaciuccoli** can be reached by city bus no.11 from Piazza Vittorio Emanuele. For taxis, call **t** 050 555330, or **t** 050 541600.

Pisa lends itself well to **bikes**; you can hire one at A Ruota Libera, Via Galli Tassi 6, near the Leaning Tower.

---

saw its influence spread from Sardinia to Puglia in southern Italy; when Gothic arrived in Italy, Pisa was one of the few cities to take it seriously, and the city's accomplishments in that style rank with Siena's. In science, Pisa contributed a great if shadowy figure, the mathematician Leonardo Fibonacci, who either rediscovered the principle of the Golden Section or learned it from the Arabs, and also introduced Arabic numerals to Europe. Pisa's scholarly tradition was crowned in the 1600s by its most famous son, Galileo Galilei.

Pisa was always a Ghibelline city, the greatest ally of the emperors in Tuscany if only for expediency's sake. But the real threat eventually came from the rising mercantile port of Genoa. After years of constant warfare, the Genoese devastated the Pisan navy at the battle of Meloria (an islet off Livorno) in 1284. All chance of recovery was quashed by an even more implacable enemy: the Arno. Pisa's port was gradually silting up, and, when the cost of dredging became greater than the traffic could bear, the city's fate was sealed. The Visconti of Milan seized the economically enfeebled city in 1396, and nine years later Florence snatched it from them.

Except in 1494–1505, when the city rebelled and kept the Florentines out despite an almost constant siege, Pisa's history as a key locale ended. The Medici dukes did the city one big favour, in supporting the university and even removing Florence's university to Pisa. In the last 500 years of Pisa's pleasant twilight, this institution has helped the city stay alive and vital, and in touch with the modern world; one of its students was nuclear physicist Enrico Fermi.

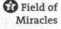 **Field of Miracles**

*for info on the Campo and all its attractions, www.opapisa.it, t 050 3872211*

## Field of Miracles (Campo dei Miracoli)

Almost from its conception, the **Field of Miracles** was the nickname given to medieval Italy's most ambitious building programme. Too many changes were made over two centuries to tell exactly what the original intentions were, but of all the unique things about the complex, the location is most striking. Whether their reasons had to do with aesthetics or land values, Pisans built their cathedral on a broad expanse of green lawn at the northern edge of town, just inside the walls. The cathedral was begun in 1063, the famous Leaning Tower and the baptistry in the middle 1100s, at the height of Pisa's fortunes, and the Campo Santo in 1278.

The Leaning Tower is not the only strange thing in the Field of Miracles. The more time you spend here, the more you notice: little monster-griffins, dragons and such, peeking out of every corner of the oldest sculptural work, or the big bronze griffin on a column atop the cathedral apse (a copy) and a rhino by the door, Muslim arabesques in the Campo Santo, perfectly classical Corinthian capitals in the cathedral nave and pagan images on the pulpit. The elliptical cathedral dome, in its time the only one in Europe, shows that the Pisans had not only audacity but the mathematical skills to back it up. You may notice that the baptistry too is leaning – about 1.5m in the opposite direction to the tower. And the cathedral façade leans outwards about 30cm; it's hard to notice, but disconcerting if you see it from the right angle. This could hardly be accidental. So much in the Field of Miracles gives evidence of a very sophisticated, strangely modern taste for the outlandish. Perhaps the medieval master masons in charge here simply thought that plain perpendicular buildings were becoming just a little trite.

## Baptistry

**Battistero**
*open daily Mar–Sept
8–7.30; Oct 9–7;
Nov–Feb 10–4.30; adm;
joint adm available
with cathedral, Campo
Santo, Museo delle
Sinopie and/or
Museo del Duomo*

This is the biggest of its kind in Italy. Its original architect, Master Diotisalvi ('God save you'), saw the lower half done in the Pisan-style stripes-and-arcades. A second colonnade was intended, but, as the Genoese gradually muscled Pisa out of trade routes, funds ran short. In the 1260s, Nicola and Giovanni Pisano redesigned and completed the upper half in a harmonious Gothic crown of gables and pinnacles. They also added the dome over Diotisalvi's original prismatic dome, still visible from inside. Both domes were among the largest attempted in the Middle Ages.

Inside, the austerity of the simple, striped walls and heavy columns of grey Elban granite is broken by two superb works of art. The great **baptismal font** is by Guido Bigarelli, the 13th-century Como sculptor who made the crazy **pulpit** in Barga (*see* p.271). Its 16 exquisite marble panels are finely carved in floral and geometric patterns of inlaid stones, an almost monochrome variant on the Cosmati work of medieval Rome and Campania. Nicola Pisano's pulpit (1260) was one of that family's first, and established the form for their later pulpits, the columns resting on fierce lions, the relief panels crowded with intricately carved figures in New

11

The Tuscan Coast | Pisa

to Genoa

LARGO COCCO GRIFFI

VIA CONTESSA MATILDE

VIALE DELLE CASCINE

VIA CAMMEO

Stazione San Rossore

Camposanto

Baptistry

Duomo

Leaning Tower

VIA PIETRO MAFFI

PIAZZA ARCIVESCOVADO

Museo del Duomo

VIA ANDREA PISANO

PIAZZA MANIN

PIAZZA DUOMO

PIAZZA DUOMO

Museo delle Sinopie

VIA DELLA FAGGIOLA

DON BOSCHI

VIA ANDREA PISANO

VIA BONANNO PISANO

Botanical Gardens

VIA MILLE

VIA PAOLO SAVI

VIA ROMA

VIA SANTA MARIA

VIA PAOLI

VIA GABBA

VIA DERNA

VIA VOLTA

VIA ARANCIO

PIAZZA DANTE

VIA RISORGIMENTO

San Nicola

PIAZZA CARRARA

VIA NICOLA PISANO

VIA E FERMI

Museo Nazionale di Palazzo Reale

LUNGARNO PACINOTTI

VIA VOLTURNO

PIAZZA SOLFERINO

PONTE SOLFERINO

Santa Maria della Spina

VIA BONANNO PISANO

Arsenal

LUNGARNO SIMONELLI

PIAZZA A. SAFFI

VIA SANT' ANTONIO

VIA FRANCESCO CRISPI

Citadel

LUNGARNO SONNINO

Sant'Agata

San Paolo a Ripa d'Arno

PONTE DELLA CITTADELLA

PIAZZA SAN PAOLO A RIPA D'ARNO

VIA F NIOSI

PONTE FERROVIA

Arno

LUNGARNO COSIMO

VIA NINO BIXIO

APT Buses

VIA S GIOVANNI AL GATANO

VIA CONTE FAZIO

VIA CESARE BATTISTI

VIA ALDO MORO

VIA LIVORNESE

to Livorno

to Lucca, Florence

VIA LUIGI BIANCHI

VIA DEL BRENNERO

Porta
Lucca

San Zeno

VIA SAN ZENO

VIA FILIPPO BUONARROTI

VIA VITTORIO VENETO

VIA ANGELO BATTELLI

Roman Baths

PIAZZA
S. CATERINA

Santa
Caterina

VIA SAN GIOVANNI BOSCO

VIA MARTIRI

S. APOLLONIA

PIAZZA
MARTIRI
DELLA
LIBERTA

VIA SAN LORENZO

San
Francesco

VIA SAN FRANCESCO

VIA MARIO CANAVARI

Palazzo
dell'Orologio

Palazzo della
Carovana

PIAZZA
DEI
CAVALIERI

Santo
Stefano

VIA DINI

VIA S. CECILIA

VICOLO TINTI

VIA R. FUCINI

VIA S. ANDREA BERLINGHIERI

PIAZZA
D'ANCONA

VIA DE AMICIS

VIA CASTELLETTO

VIALE TAVOLERIA

VIA SAN FRANCESCO

PIAZZA
PAOLO
ALL'ORTO

VIA SAN FREDIANO

VIA CAVALCA

VIA CAVOUR BATICHIODI

VIA BORGO STRETTO

San Michele
in Borgo

Universita
degli Studi

PIAZZA
VETTOVAGLIE

VIA SANTA MARTA

VIA PALESTRO

PIAZZA
REPUBBLICA

VIA GIUSEPPE GARIBALDI

VIA DELLE BELLE TORRI

PONTE DI
MEZZO

LUNGARNO MEDICEO

Palazzo
Toscanelli

PIAZZA
MAZZINI

Palazzo dei Medici
(Prefettura)

LUNGARNO GAMBACORTI

Logge di
Banchi

LUNGARNO GALILEI

Museo di
San Matteo

VIA GIUSEPPE MAZZINI

VIA SAN MARTINO

San
Sepolcro

PONTE DELLA
FORTEZZA

VIA S BERNARDO

VIA DEL BORGHETTO

CORSO ITALIA

VIA DEL CARMINE

FILIPPO TURATI

VIA GIORDANO BRUNO

VIA G BOVIO

Giardino
Scotto

VIA D'AZEGLIO

LAZZI
Buses

PIAZZA
VITTORIO
EMANUELE II

VIA BENEDETTO CROCE

Bastione del
Sangallo

PONTE DELLA
VITTORIA

VIA G. MATTEOTTI

VIALE BONAINI

PIAZZA
GUERRAZZI

Arno

N

VIA COLOMBO

VIA A. FRATTI

VIA CARLO CATTANEO

PIAZZA DELLA
STAZIONE

Stazione Centrale

VIA AMERIGO VESPUCCI

VIA FILIPPO CORRIDONI

400 metres

400 yards

Testament episodes – a style that seems to owe much to the reliefs on Roman triumphal arches and columns. The baptistry is famous for its uncanny acoustics; if you have it to yourself, sing a few notes from as near the centre as guards will allow you to go. If there's a crowd the latter will be waiting for someone to bribe them to do it.

## Duomo

**Duomo**
*t 050 3872211,
www.opapisa.it; open
April–Sept Mon–Fri
10–7.45, Sat–Sun 1–7.45;
Mar and Oct Mon–Fri
10–5.30, Sat–Sun 1–5.45;
Nov–Feb Mon–Fri
10–12.30, 3–4.30,
Sat–Sun 3–4.30; adm;
joint adm available
with baptistry, Campo
Santo, Museo delle
Sinopie and/or
Museo del Duomo*

One of the first and finest works of the Pisan Romanesque, the cathedral façade, with four levels of colonnades, is a little more ornate than Buscheto, the architect, planned in 1063. These columns, with similar colonnades around the apse and the Gothic frills later added around the unique elliptical dome, are the only showy features on the calm, restrained exterior. On the south transept, the late 12th-century **Porte San Ranieri** has fine bronze doors by Bonanno, one of the architects of the Leaning Tower. The biblical scenes are enacted among real palms and acacia trees; the well-travelled Pisans would have known what they looked like.

On the inside, little of the original art survived a fire in 1595, and a coffered Baroque ceiling and some poor painting were added during the reconstruction. Some fine works remain: a few patches of the Cosmati pavement; the great mosaic of *Christ Pantocrator* in the apse by Cimabue; and some portraits of the saints by Andrea del Sarto in the choir and his *Madonna della Grazia* in the right nave.

The **pulpit** (*c.* 1300), by Giovanni Pisano, is his family's acknowledged masterpiece, and one of the key works of Pisan sculpture. After the 1595 fire it was left unassembled in crates until the 20th century. It shows a startling mix of classical and Christian elements. St Michael, as a telamon, supports the pulpit with Hercules and the Fates, as prophets, saints and sibyls look on. The relief panels, full of expressive faces, are equal to the best work of the Renaissance.

## The Leaning Tower

**La Torre**
*www.opapisa.it,
t 050 3872211; open
April–Sept daily 8–8;
Nov–Feb daily 9–5; Mar
and Oct daily 9–6; max.
30 people at a time,
with guide;
book well in advance;
300 steps to top; no
under-8s, 8–12 year-olds
must be hand-held by
adult, 12–18 year-olds
must be accompanied
by adult; adm exp*

The architects who measured this campanile's stones concluded that its lean was intentional when it was begun in 1173, but say this to a Pisan and they will be mortally offended. Whatever, it is a unique and beautiful building – and a very expensive bit of whimsy, with some 190 marble and granite columns. It has also been expensive to local and national governments, who have had to shore it up – $80 million since 1990, when rescue operations began. Most dramatically, in 1995, while workers were freezing the ground to mute vibrations, the tower suddenly groaned and tipped another few millimetres; to prevent similar scares it was given a girdle of steel braces, attached by a pair of 72ft (22m) steel cables to a counterweight system hidden among buildings on the north end of the Campo. This, combined with other moves, seems to have worked; the tower is not only stable but has righted itself about 16 inches (40.5cm) (to a lean of about 15ft or 4.5m).

## Campo Santo

**Campo Santo**
*open April–Sept daily
8–8; Oct daily 9–7;
Nov–Feb daily 10–5;
Mar daily 9–6; adm;
joint adm available
with baptistry,
cathedral, Museo
delle Sinopie and/or
Museo del Duomo*

This remarkable cloister is as unique in its way as the Leaning Tower. Basically, the cemetery is a rectangle of gleaming white marble, unadorned save for the blind arcading around the façade and the beautiful Gothic tabernacle of the enthroned Virgin Mary over the entrance. With its uncluttered, simple lines, the Campo Santo seems more like a work of our own times than of the 1300s.

The cemetery began, according to legend, when the battling archbishop Lanfranchi, who led the Pisan fleet into the Crusades, came back with boatloads of soil from the Holy Land for extra-blessed burials. Over the centuries an exceptional hoard of frescoes and sculpture accumulated here. Much went up in flames in July 1944, when an Allied incendiary bomb set the roof on fire. Many priceless works of art were destroyed and others, including most of the frescoes, were damaged beyond hope of being perfectly restored. The biggest loss, perhaps, was the set of frescoes by Benozzo Gozzoli – including the *Tower of Babylon*, *Solomon and Sheba*, the *Life of Moses* and the *Grape Harvest*; in their original state they must have been as fresh and colourful as his famous frescoes in Florence's Medici Palace.

Even better known, and better preserved, are two 14th-century frescoes by an unknown artist (perhaps Buffalmacco, described by Boccaccio in the *Decameron*): the *Triumph of Death*, a memento of the century of plagues and trouble in which Death (in Italian, feminine: *La Morte*) swoops down on frolicking nobles; and the *Last Judgement*, with the damned variously cooked, wrapped in snakes, poked, disembowelled, banged up and chewed on. These are some of the best paintings of the trecento.

Another curiosity is the *Theological Cosmography* of Piero di Puccio, a vertiginous diagram of 22 spheres of the planets and stars, angels, archangels, thrones and dominations, cherubim and seraphim, and so on; in the centre, the small circle trisected by a T-shape was a common medieval map pattern for the known earth. The three sides represent Asia, Europe and Africa, and the three lines the Mediterranean, the Black Sea and the Nile.

## Other Museums

**Museo delle
Sinopie**
*open April–Sept daily
8–7.30; Mar and Oct
daily 9–5.30; Nov–Feb
daily 9–4.30; adm; joint
adm available with
baptistry, cathedral,
Campo Santo and/or
Museo del Duomo*

**Museo del Duomo**
*Piazza Arcivescovado;
open April–Sept daily
8–7.20; Mar and Oct
daily 9–5.20; Nov–Feb
daily 9–4.20; joint adm
available with baptistry,
cathedral, Campo Santo
and/or Museo delle
Sinopie*

Opposite the cathedral, the **Museo delle Sinopie** contains the pre-painting sketches on plaster of the frescoes lost in the Campo Santo fire. Many are works of art in their own right, and, though faint, give an idea of how the frescoes once looked.

Near the Leaning Tower, the **Museo del Duomo** in the old chapterhouse boasts descriptions in English in each room. The first rooms contain the oldest works – beautiful fragments from the cathedral façade and altar, plus two Islamic works, the strange, original bronze **griffin** from the top of the cathedral, believed to have come from Egypt in the 11th century, and a 12th-century bronze basin with an intricate decoration. Statues from the baptistry by the Pisanos were brought in from the elements too late; worn and bleached, they resemble a convention of mummies. The sculptures in the next room survived better: Giovanni Pisano's grotesque faces, his gaunt but noble *St John the Baptist* and the lovely *Madonna del Colloquio*, so named because she speaks to her child with her eyes.

In the next room are fine works by Tino di Camaino, including the tomb of San Ranieri and his sculptures from the tomb of Emperor Henry VII, sitting among his court like some exotic oriental potentate. In Room 9 you'll find works by Nino Pisano, and, in Rooms 11–12, the cathedral treasure. Giovanni Pisano's lovely ivory *Madonna and Child* steals the show, curving to the shape of the elephant's tusk; there's an ivory coffer and the cross that led the Pisans on the First Crusade.

Upstairs are some extremely large angels used as candlesticks, intarsia and two rare illuminated 12th- and 13th-century scrolls ('exultet rolls'), perhaps the original visual aids – the deacon would unroll them from the pulpit as he read so the congregation could follow the story with the pictures. Remaining rooms have Etruscan and Roman odds and ends (including a good bust of Caesar) and prints and engravings of the original Campo Santo frescoes made in the 19th century. The courtyard has a unique view of the Leaning Tower, which seems to be bending over to spy inside.

## North Pisa

With the cathedral on the edge of town, Pisa has no real centre, but Pisans are very conscious of the division made by the Arno; every June neighbourhoods on either side of it fight it out on the Ponte di Mezzo in the *Gioco del Ponte*, in a medieval tug-of-war where opponents try to push a big decorated cart over each other.

From the Field of Miracles, Via Cardinale Pietro Maffi leads eastwards to ruined **Roman baths** near the Lucca Gate. Also in the neighbourhood are **San Zeno**, in a corner of the walls, with some parts as old as the 5th century, and **Santa Caterina**, a Dominican church with a beautiful, typically Pisan façade, and, inside, an *Annunciation* and a sculpted Saltarelli tomb by Nino Pisano, and a large 1340s painting of the *Apotheosis of St Thomas Aquinas*, with Plato and Aristotle in attendance and defeated infidel philosopher Averroës below, attributed to Francesco Traini.

One long street near the Campo dei Miracoli begins as Via della Faggiola, leading into the **Piazza dei Cavalieri**. Duke Cosimo I started what was probably the last crusading order of knights, the Cavalieri di Santo Stefano, in 1562. The crusading urge ended long before, but the duke found the knights a useful tool for placating the anachronistic fantasies of the Tuscan nobility – most of them newly titled bankers – and for licensing out freebooting expeditions against the Turks. Cosimo had Vasari build the **Palazzo della Carovana** for the order, demolishing the old Palazzo del Popolo, symbol of Pisa's lost independence. Vasari gave the palace an outlandishly ornate *graffito* façade; it now holds the Scuola Normale Superiore, founded by Napoleon in 1810.

Next door, **Santo Stefano**, the order's church, is also by Vasari, though the façade was by a young Medici dilettante; inside are some war pennants the order's pirates captured from the Muslims in North Africa. Also on the piazza, the **Palazzo dell'Orologio** was built around the 'Hunger Tower' (right of the big clock), famous from Dante's story in the *Inferno* of Ugolino della Gherardesca, the Pisan commander walled in here with his sons and grandsons after his fickle city began to suspect him of intrigues with the Genoese. The **university**, founded by his family in 1330 and still one of Italy's most important, is just south of here, while Via dei Mille leads west to the **botanical gardens**, created under Cosimo I in 1544, for the university; the institute, in the grounds, has an extraordinary façade covered with shells and mother-of-pearl.

**Orto Botanico di Pisa**
*open Mon–Fri 8.30–5.30, Sat 8.30–1, museum open by appt; call t 050 221 1316*

From Piazza dei Cavalieri, Via Dini takes you south into the twisting alleys of the lively market area, around **Piazza Vettovaglie** ('victuals square') where every morning except Sunday the city's ancient mercantile traditions are renewed. Tucked in the main street, old arcaded **Borgo Stretto**, is one of the most gorgeous façades in the city, belonging to **San Michele in Borgo**, a 10th-century church redone in the 14th century, with three tiers of arcades. Much of the interior collapsed during the bombing raids of 1944.

Off to the east, Via San Francesco leads to the church of **San Francesco** – Gothic, with a plain marble façade but some good paintings – a polyptych over the altar by Tommaso Pisano, frescoes by Taddeo Gaddi, Niccolò di Pietro Gerini (in the chapterhouse) and, in the sacristy, *Stories of the Virgin* by Taddeo di Bartolo (1397). The unfortunate Count Ugo and sons are buried in a chapel near the altar.

## Museo Nazionale di San Matteo

**Museo Nazionale di San Matteo**
*Lungarno Mediceo, t 050 9711395; open Tues–Sat 9–7, Sun 9–2; adm; joint adm available with Museo Nazionale di Palazzo Reale (see p.296)*

An old convent that also served as a prison now holds much of the best Pisan art from the Middle Ages and Renaissance: works by Giunta Pisano, believed to be the first artist ever to sign his work (early 1200s); excellent 1300s paintings by Pisans and other schools from the city's churches; a polyptych by Simone Martini; paintings by Francesco Traini, Taddeo di Bartolo, Agnolo Gaddi, Antonio Veneziano and Turino Vanni; sculptures by the Pisanos; and medieval ceramics brought from the Middle East by Pisan sea-dogs.

In Room 7, after all the trecento works, the Early Renaissance comes as a startling revelation, as it must have been for the people of the 15th century: here is Neri di Bicci's wonderfully festive *Coronation of St Catherine* bright with ribbons, a *Madonna* from the decorative Gentile da Fabriano, a sorrowful *St Paul* by Masaccio, with softly moulded features and draperies, an anonymous *Madonna with Angel Musicians*, and a beautifully coloured *Crucifixion* by Gozzoli, which looks more like a party than an execution. The last great work is Donatello's gilded bronze reliquary bust of *San Lussorio*, who could pass for Don Quixote.

## Along the Lungarno

Pisa's **Prefettura** is housed in the lovely 13th-century stone, brick and marble Palazzo Medici, once a favoured residence of the magnificent Lorenzo. Nearby is the beautiful 16th-century **Palazzo Toscanelli** (once attributed to Michelangelo), where Byron lived in 1821–2 and wrote six cantos of *Don Giovanni*. Behind it, picturesque **Via delle Belle Torri** has 12th- and 13th-century houses interspersed with modern constructions that fill in the gaps left by bombs.

Further down the Lungarno, the former Palazzo Reale, begun in 1559 by Cosimo I, has a new life as the **Museo Nazionale di Palazzo Reale**, an annexe to the Museo di San Matteo, housing old armour that gets dusted off every June for the *Gioco del Ponte*, and some 900 other pieces from the 15th–17th centuries. There are plans for a section with paintings, sculptures and collectables (mostly 15th–18th-century) from the Medici and Lorraine archducal hoards.

Just behind the Palazzo Reale is Pisa's other famous belltower, belonging to 12th-century **San Nicola**, designed by Nicolò Pisano. Cylindrical at the bottom, octagonal in the middle and hexagonal on top, it has exactly the same kind of tilt as the Leaning Tower – it was built to lean forward before curving back towards the perpendicular. Ask the sacristan to show you the famous spiral stair inside, claimed by Vasari to have inspired Bramante's Belvedere stair in the Vatican. The church contains a fine *Madonna* by Traini, a wooden sculpture, also of the Madonna, by Nino Pisano, and a painting from the quattrocento of St Nicholas of Tolentino shielding Pisa from the plague (fourth chapel on the right).

**Museo Nazionale di Palazzo Reale**

*entrance at Lungarno Pacinotti 46, t 050 926511, www.libero logico.com/sbaaaspi; open Mon–Fri 9–2.30, Sat 9–1.30; adm; joint adm available with Museo Nazionale di San Matteo (see p.295)*

# Pisa South of the Arno

After the Campo dei Miracoli, what most impresses Pisa's visitors is its languidly curving stretch of the Arno – an exercise in Tuscan gravity, with the river lined with mirror-image lines of blank-faced yellow and tan buildings, all the same height, with no remarkable bridges or any of the picturesque quality of Florence. Its uncanny monotony is broken by only one landmark, but it is something special: **Santa Maria della Spina**, sitting on the bank opposite the Palazzo Reale like a precious Gothic jewel box. Although its placement on the Lungarno Gambacorti is perfect, it was built at the mouth of the Arno, where it suffered so many floods that it was on the point of vanishing in 1871, when it was dismantled and rebuilt by the city on this new site. Although it's an outstanding achievement of Italian Gothic, it wasn't originally Gothic at all. Partially rebuilt in 1323, it was turned by its new architect – perhaps one of the Pisanos – into an extravaganza of pointed gables and blooming pinnacles. All of the sculptural work is first-class, especially the figures of Christ and the Apostles in the 13 niches facing the streets. The chapel takes its name from a thorn of Christ's crown of thorns, a relic brought back from the Crusades. Inside the luminous zebra interior, the statues of the Madonna and Child, St Peter and St John are by Andrea and Nino Pisano.

Just down from Santa Maria della Spina, the church of **San Paolo a Ripa del Arno** has a beautiful 12th-century façade similar to that of the cathedral. It stands in a small park, and is believed to have been built over the site of Pisa's original cathedral; perhaps building cathedrals in open fields was an old custom. Behind it, the unusual and very small 12th-century chapel of **Sant'Agata** has eight sides and an eight-sided prismatic roof like an Ottoman tomb.

Down the Arno, the monotony is briefly broken again by the arches of the 17th-century **Logge di Banchi**, the old silk and wool market, at the Ponte di Mezzo and at the head of Pisa's main shopping street, the Corso Italia. A bit further down is another octagonal church, **San Sepolcro**, built for the Knights Templar by Diotisalvi.

Behind it, picturesque **Via San Martino** was Pisa's old casbah, the main street of the Chinizica, the medieval quarter of Arab and Turkish merchants. At No.19 a Roman relief was incorporated into the building, known since the Middle Ages as Kinzica, after a maiden who saved Pisa when the Saracens sailed up to the famous Golden Gate, medieval Pisa's door to the sea.

At the east end of the Lungarno is a shady park, **Giardino Scotto**, in the former Bastion Sangallo. Shelley lived nearby, in the Palazzo Scotto (1820–22), where he wrote *Adonais* and *Epipsychidion*.

## Festivals in Pisa

***Gioco del Ponte***, Ponte di Mezzo, last Sun in June. A 13th-century tug-of-war held on the bridge, with costumes, processions and music (*see* p.294).

**Regatta and lights festival of San Ranieri**, 16–17 June. An event when the banks of the Arno glimmer with tens of thousands of candles.

**San Sisto**, 6 Aug. Folklore displays.

**Old Maritime Republics boat race**. A contest between old sea rivals Pisa, Venice, Genoa and Amalfi, hosted by Pisa every four years (next one 2010).

## Shopping and other Activities in Pisa

Pisa abounds in tacky souvenirs, especially around the Campo dei Miracoli, including light-up Leaning

Towers in all sizes. For boutiques, head down Via Oberdan and Corso Italia.

You can **horse-ride** at the Cooperativa Agrituristica in Via Tre Colli in Calci, and **swim** in the pool in Via Andrea Pisano.

## Where to Stay in Pisa

**ⓘ Pisa >**
*Piazza dei Miracoli,*
*t 050 560464*

*Piazza Vittorio*
*Emanuele II 16,*
*t 050 42291*

*airport, t 050 503700,*
*www.pisaturismo.it*

**★ Ristoro dei Vecchi Macelli >>**

**★ Royal Victoria >**

**Pisa ✉ 56100**

Many of the moderate hotels are around the central train station. Inexpensive hotels, spread throughout town, are often full of students, particularly around the start of the university term, so book ahead.

**★★★★★Relais dell'Orologio**, Via della Fagiola 12–14, **t** 050 830361, *www.hotelrelaisorologio.com* (€€€€€). An elegant option in the 13th-century home of the owner's ancestors. The bedrooms are rather small but the swish public rooms make up for it.

**★★★★Grand Hotel Duomo**, Via S. Maria 94, **t** 050 561894, *www.grandhotelduomo.it* (€€€€). An unexciting choice near the Campo dei Miracoli, with a restaurant serving national and international cuisine. Breakfast is included in the rates.

**★★★Hotel di Stefano**, Via Sant'Apollonia 35, **t** 050 553559, *www.hoteldistefano.it* (€€€). A good central choice; rates, which are much lower for rooms without baths, include breakfast.

**★★★Il Giardino**, Piazza Manin, **t** 050 562101, *www.hotelilgiardino.pisa.it* (€€€). A smart little hotel just outside the walls off Piazza dei Miracoli. Rooms are modern and quite stylish (breakfast is included), and there is a pleasant terrace.

**★★★Royal Victoria**, Lungarno Pacinotti 12, **t** 050 940111, *www.royalvictoria.it* (€€€). An atmospheric 1839 hotel overlooking the Arno; guests have included Dickens and Ruskin. Rooms (still in 1930s style) have antiques. Breakfast is included, and the rooms minus baths are nearly half the price.

**★★★Verdi**, Piazza Repubblica 5, **t** 050 598947, *www.verdihotel.it* (€€€). A good choice in a well-restored palace in the centre. Breakfast is included.

**Villa Kinzica**, Piazza Arcivescovado 2, **t** 050 560419, *www.hotelvillakinzica.it*

(€€€). Fairly basic and rather worn bedrooms, from which you can practically touch the Leaning Tower. Breakfast is included; staff are friendly.

**★Helvetia**, Via Don G. Boschi 31, **t** 050 553084 (€€). A clean budget option, with some ensuite rooms.

**Youth hostel**, Via Pietrasantina 15, **t** 050 890622. A hostel 1km from the Campo dei Miracoli (no.3 bus), with cooking facilities.

## Eating Out in Pisa

Pisa is a good place for walks on the wild side of the Tuscan kitchen – eels, *baccalà*, tripe, wild mushrooms, 'twice-boiled soup' and dishes waiters can't satisfactorily explain. There are also a good many unpretentious trattorias, many near the university.

**Ristoro dei Vecchi Macelli**, Via Volturno 49, **t** 050 20424 (€€). A gourmet stronghold on the north bank of the Arno, near Ponte Solferino, with especially good fish. Booking is a must. *Closed Wed and 2wks in Aug.*

**Cagliostro**, Via del Castelletto 26–30, **t** 050 575413 (€€). An extraordinary restaurant/*caffè*/*enoteca*/art gallery/ nightclub and general trendy hang-out, known for its good cheeses. *Closed Tues.*

**Osteria dei Cavalieri**, Via San Frediano 16, **t** 050 580858 (€€). Several fixed-price menus featuring seafood, meat and veggie dishes, and good game. The spaghetti with octopus and clams is recommended. Book for Saturday evenings. *Closed Sat lunch and Sun.*

**Il Nuraghe**, Via Mazzini 58, **t** 050 44368 (€€). A trattoria offering Tuscan and Sardinian specialities, including octopus, and ravioli with ricotta cheese. *Closed Mon.*

**Osteria I Santi**, Via Santa Maria 71/73, **t** 050 28081 (€€). Come here for *baccalà* or excellent *zuppa Toscana*, or just for the lively atmosphere and the kitsch decor. The tables are long and the service is friendly.

**Osteria La Grotta**, Via San Francesco 103, **t** 050 578105 (€€). A cosy place situated in an impressive old wine cellar, with a regularly changing menu of comforting, very traditional dishes. Try *spaghettone dell'Osteria.* *Closed Sun.*

**Re di Puglia**, Via Aurelia Sud 7, Loc. Mortellini, **t** 050 960157 (€€). A converted farmhouse 1km from the Pisa Sud *autostrada* exit, famous for its home-produced organic meat and vegetables, much of which is cooked over an open grill. *Closed Mon and Tues, and lunch Wed–Sat.*

**Pasticceria Federico Salza**, Borgo Stretto 46, **t** 050 580144 (€). Pisa's most elegant bar/*pasticceria*, with tables under Borgo Stretto's portico – great for watching the world go by. Come for morning coffee, a light lunch, a delicious afternoon pastry or an evening aperitif. *Closed Mon.*

**Trattoria S. Omobono**, Piazza S. Omobono 6, **t** 050 540847 (€). A rustic trattoria in a square just off the main market place. Good risotto with porcini, *spaghetti alla marinara*, *stoccafisso* (stockfish) with potatoes, and fish *fritto misto*. It's always crowded, so come early. *Closed Sun.*

**Vineria di Piazza**, Piazza delle Vettovaglie 13, **t** 050 3820433 (€). Tables right in the market, where you can enjoy simple but very tasty food such as bean soup with *pioppini* mushrooms, and risotto with radicchio and gorgonzola. *Closed lunch, Sun and 2wks in Aug.*

## Around Pisa

A couple of kilometres upriver to the east is 'Pisa's second leaning tower', the campanile of the Romanesque **San Michele degli Scalzi**, built between 1152 and 1171. Under the slopes of Monte Pisano, **Calci** has a good 11th-century church and an eroded giant of a campanile.

**Certosa di Pisa**
*open Tues–Sat 9–6.30, Sun 9–12; natural history collections Tues–Sat 9–9, Sun and hols 10am–7; adm*

In a prominent site overlooking the Arno, the ornate **Certosa di Pisa** was founded in 1366 but completely Baroqued in the 18th century, in a kind of 1920s Spanish-California exhibition style with three fine cloisters. There are some lavish pastel frescoes by Florentine Baroque artist Bernardo Poccetti and his school, plus a giraffe skeleton, stuffed penguins, Tuscan minerals and even wax intestines – all part of the university's **natural history collections**, founded originally by the Medici.

Towards the coast, 6km from Pisa, is the beautifully isolated **basilica of San Piero a Grado**. According to tradition it was founded in the first century by St Peter himself, and in the Middle Ages it was a popular pilgrimage destination. It was first documented in the 8th century but the current buildings are 11th-century, embellished with blind arcades and ceramic *tondi*. Like many early churches and basilicas, it has an apse on either end, though of different sizes; the columns were brought in from various ancient buildings. The altar stone, believed to have been set there by St Peter, was found in excavations that uncovered the remains of several previous churches. Frescoes in the nave by a 14th-century Lucchese, Deodato Orlandi, tell the story of *St Peter* with effigies of the popes up to the turn of the first millennium AD (John XVIII). The retreating German army blew up the campanile.

In 1822, a strange ceremony took place on the wide, sandy beach of **Gombo**, near the mouth of the Arno, described in morbid detail by Edward Trelawny: 'the brains literally seethed, bubbled, and boiled as in a cauldron, for a very long time. Byron could not face this scene, he withdrew to the beach and swam off to the *Bolivar*.' Such was Shelley's fiery end, after he drowned sailing from Livorno. Gombo, and Pisa's other beaches, the **Marina di Pisa** and **Tirrenia**, are often plagued by pollution, although Marina di Pisa makes a pretty place to stroll, with its Liberty-style homes and pine forests.

# The Livorno Coast and Tuscan Islands

## Livorno

*...There is plenty of space; it is a fully registered cemetery with an attendant keeper. So, if any of you have the intention of retiring to this very interesting part of Tuscany you will be well taken care of!*

Horace A. Hayward on the British cemetery in Livorno

From its founding in 1577, the English spent so much time in this city, and grew so fond of it, they renamed it. It's time the bizarre anglicization, Leghorn, be put to sleep; the city that Duke Cosimo founded to replace Pisa's silted-up harbour is named Livorno. It hasn't much in common with other Tuscan cities: instead of frescoes, it has perhaps the best seafood on the Tyrrhenian coast; instead of rusticated *palazzi* and marble temples, it has canals, docks and a very lively citizenry famous for free-thinking and tolerance; and instead of winding country lanes, there are big white ferries to carry you off to the Tuscan Islands, Corsica or Sardinia.

### History

The site had always been a safe harbour, and in the Middle Ages there was a small fortress here. The Pisani briefly considered making a port here in the 1300s, when it was becoming clear that Pisa's own port would fill up with the sands of the Arno. Eventually the fortress fell into the grasp of the Genoese, who sold it to Florence in 1421. Cosimo I, in his attempts to build Tuscany into a modern state, first saw the advantage of having a good port to avoid trading at the mercy of the Spaniards and Genoese. Cosimo expanded the fortress, but it was not until the reign of his successors, Francesco and Ferdinando, that Livorno really got off the ground. The first stone was laid on 28 March 1577, and a regular gridiron city soon appeared, designed by Buontalenti, and surrounded by fortresses and canals.

Almost from the start there was an English connection. Sir Robert Dudley, Queen Elizabeth's favourite, son of the Earl of Leicester, left England in 1605 after failing to prove his legitimacy in the Star Chamber court. Dudley built warships for the grand dukes, fortified the port of Livorno and drained the coastal swamps, making the region healthy and habitable. In 1618, Livorno was declared a free port – free not only for trade but for the practice of any faith and for men of any nationality. It was a brilliant stroke, designed to fill out the population of this very rough and dangerous new town, and it is, to the credit of the Medici dukes, an act of tolerance

# Getting to and around Livorno and its Coast

Livorno's **train station** is on the edge of the city, with plenty of services to Pisa and Florence and along the Tyrrhenian coast. Some trains to Pisa go on to Lucca–Pistoia–Florence. There are some connections to Volterra, with a change down the coast at Cecina. The station is about 2km from the city centre; take bus no.1 (most other city buses also pass through the centre, but routes are circuitous).

**Buses** for all villages in Livorno province (the strip of coast down as far as Follonica) leave from Piazza Grande. LAZZI buses (**t** 055 363041, *www.lazzi.it*) for Florence depart from Scali A. Saffi, on the Fosse Reale, just off Piazza Cavour.

Livorno is the main port for **ferries** to Corsica and Sardinia, with Corsica Ferries (**t** 0586 881380, *www. corsicaferries.com*) and Moby Lines (**t** 0586 899950, *www.mobylines.it*). Some ferries call at Elba, *see* p.307.

---

almost unthinkable in the Catholic Mediterranean of the 1600s. Before long, Livorno was full of persecuted Jews, Greeks, English Catholics, Spanish Muslims and loose ends from around Europe. The only safe trading port in a sea full of Spaniards acquired thriving communities of English and Dutch merchants. In the 1700s progressive, tolerant Livorno was a substantial city, a breath of fresh air in the decadent Mediterranean and a home from home for British travellers. Shelley wrote *The Cenci* here, as well as 'To a Skylark'; he bought his fatal sailing boat in Livorno's port.

Livorno declined a little once the same low tariffs and trading advantages became available in other Mediterranean ports. The Austrian dukes, especially Leopold II, helped keep it ahead of its rivals; still, true to its traditions, the city contributed greatly to the mid-century revolutionary movements and the wars of the Risorgimento. After unification it was still a lively place, full of many nationalities; it also began to make cultural contributions to the new Italy – the operatic composer Mascagni, the painter Modigliani, and several other artists of the Macchiaioli school. The Second World War hit Livorno harder than anywhere in Tuscany, but the city rebuilt itself quickly. Long before other ports, Livorno realized the importance of container shipping. As the Mediterranean's first big container port, Livorno today has become the second city of Tuscany, and Italy's second-largest port after Genoa.

## Four Moors, Inigo Jones and the American Market

Though the streets are usually brimming, a combination of north Tuscan austerity and an excess of dreary architecture make Livorno a disconcertingly anonymous city. The **port**, however, is a busy, fascinating jumble of boats, cranes, docks and canals. Close to the port entrance, the **Fortezza Vecchia** conceals the original Pisan fortress and an 11th-century tower built by Countess Matilda. Piazza Micheli, Livorno's front door to the sea, is decorated with its only great work of art, the **Quattro Mori** by Carraran sculptor Pietro Tacca (1623). The monument's original design became somewhat mangled, and Tacca's brilliant figures now sit in chains under a silly earlier statue of Duke Ferdinando I. The four Moors are a symbol of

*Gulf*

*of Genoa*

*Isola di Gorgona*

Tirrenia

To Pisa

Ponsacco

Lari

Montaione

Livorno

Casciana Terme

Ardenza

Antignano   Montenero

Golfo Aranci/ Olbia/
Portoferraio/ Capraia/
Bastia/ Porto Torres/
Palermo

Castiglioncello

Rosignano Solvay

Rosignano
Marittimo

Montecatini
Val di Cecina

Volterra

Vada

Cecina

R. Cecina

Pomarance

Marina di Cecina

Guardistallo

*Isola di Capraia*

Capraia

Sto. Stefano

Bolgheri

Colline

Metallifere

Donoratico

Castelnuovo
di Val di Cecina

Castagneto
Carducci

Lago
Boracifero

Monterotondo
Marittimo

S. Vincenzo

Campiglia
Marittima

Suvereto

Massa Marittima

*Golfo di
Baratti*

Populonia

To
Grosseto

*Portoferraio*

Piombino

Follonica

*Isola d'Elba*

Rio Marina

*Punta Ala*

Porto Azzurro

*Isola Pianosa*

N

10 km

5 miles

*I. di Montecristo*

*Isola del Giglio*

Sardinia, but the statue's intent was to commemorate the successes of the great Tuscan pirates, the Order of Santo Stefano, against North African shipping.

From here, the arcaded **Via Grande** leads into the centre; every original building on this street was destroyed in the bombings of 1944. **Piazza Grande** has the **cathedral**, designed on a bad day by Inigo Jones in 1605; the present building is a post-war reconstruction. Jones took a little bit of Livorno home with him: his plan for Covent Garden (originally arcaded all round, without the market) is a copy of this piazza, with St Paul's church in place of the cathedral.

Via Grande continues to ghastly **Piazza della Repubblica**, a treeless, paved-over section of the **Fosso Reale**, the curving canal that surrounded the original city. Just north, the sprawling, brick **Fortezza Nuova** is on an island in the canal, landscaped as a park and a popular resort for the Livornese on Sundays. Nearby, on Via della Madonna, three adjacent churches, Greek Orthodox, Catholic and Armenian (all recycled for other uses) make a fitting memorial of Livorno's career as a truly free city. On the other side of Piazza della Repubblica, Piazza XX Settembre is the site of the Saturday **American market**, so called for the vast stores of GI surplus sold here after the war, and still a street market for clothes and odd items.

## Little Venice and the Museo Civico

Just off Piazza della Repubblica is a neighbourhood unlike any outside Venice; in fact, it's known as 'Nuova Venezia', or 'Piccola Venezia', and for picturesque tranquillity it may even outdo its famous precursor. On a few blocks square, **Little Venice** is laced with quiet canals that flow between the Fortezza Nuova and the port, lined with sun-bleached tenements hung with laundry. The pseudo-Baroque **Santa Caterina** church is typical of the ungainly, functional buildings of early Livorno. In late July or August restaurants stay open late for the *Effetto Venezia*, a 10-day festival with evening shows and concerts and *cacciucco* (*see* p.304) stalls.

Leading east towards the train station from Piazza della Repubblica, **Viale Carducci** is Livorno's *grand boulevard*. It passes the **Cisternone**, a neoclassical palace built to house the waterworks Leopold II had constructed in the 1830s.

Along the coast south of the centre, Viale Italia leads past the **Terrazza Mascagni**, a grandiose overlook on the sea. A few streets inland, in a park called the Villa Mimbelli, the **Museo Civico Giovanni Fattori** has a good collection of works by the Macchiaioli, Italy's late 19th-century Impressionists, and one work by Modigliani plus a wealth of paintings that lead up to his art. Other painters represented include Ulivi Liegi, Mario Puccini, that rare blossom Lodovico Tommasi and Livorno's own Giovanni Fattori, one of the leading figures of the Macchiaioli. Together, they make a natural

**Museo Civico Giovanni Fattori**
*3rd floor of city library; open Tues–Sun 10–1 and 4–7; adm*

11 The Tuscan Coast | Livorno

progression from the Biedermeier art of the 1860s – including stirring scenes of Italian volunteers leaving for the front – to the sweet haziness of the Belle Epoque 1890s.

South of Terrazza Mascagni, Viale Italia continues past the **Italian naval academy** (you may glimpse one of the exquisite old sailing ships the navy uses for training), then through neighbourhoods full of surprisingly blatant neo-Gothic and Art Nouveau villas from the 1890s, on the way to **Ardenza**, with its seafront park and marina.

### The English Cemeteries and Montenero

For a sentimental journey into Livorno's cosmopolitan past, visit the **English cemeteries**. Crotchety old Tobias Smollett, who never stopped crabbing about Italy and never quite got around to leaving it, is interred here, along with numerous members of the British trading community and quite a few Americans. Many of the tombs (dating back to 1670) are truly monumental, some with inscriptions from scripture or Shakespeare; some are charmingly original.

Many members of the British community, including Byron and Shelley, passed their time up on the suburban hill of **Montenero** to the south. Byron and Shelley spent six weeks in 1822 at **Villa delle Rose**, a fascinating romantic ruin. There is a charming, old-fashioned funicular railway to the top, where there's been a sanctuary and pilgrimage site since an apparition of the Virgin Mary in the 1300s. The present church, full of *ex votos*, is the work of 18th-century architect Giovanni del Fantasia; there is also a small museum, an ancient pharmacy and some caves, the **Grotte del Montenero**.

**Cimiteri Inglesi**
*Via Pisa and Via Adua, next to Anglican church; to visit, ask at Archiconfraternità della Misericordia on Via Adua*

**Villa delle Rose**
*open by request of owner Signor di Valentina at No.57*

ⓘ **Livorno >**
*Piazza Cavour 6 (2nd floor), t 0586 204611; there are also 2 summer (June–Sept) booths at port, on Porto Mediceo, t 0586 895320, www. costadeglietruschi.it*

## Where to Stay in Livorno

**Livorno ✉ 57100**

As this is a port, there's an abundance of inexpensive hotels, many across the piazza from the train station or around the port and Via Grande. Some are dives; Corso Mazzini, a few blocks south of the Fosso Reale, has some good ones.

***La Vedetta di Montenero**, Via della Leccetta 5, in the suburb of Montenero, t 0586 579957, *www. hotellavedetta.it* (€€€€). A modern hotel overlooking the sea, with comfortable rooms and a restaurant (half-board and full-board available). *Restaurant closed May–Sept.*

***Gran Duca**, Piazza Micheli 16, t 0586 891024, *www.granduca.it* (€€€). Livorno's most interesting hotel, built into a section of the walls right on the piazza near the harbour. Inside it's

modern; some rooms overlook the Quattro Mori and the port. Breakfast is included in the rates, and you can stay half- or full-board: the restaurant specializes in fresh fish.

****Giardino**, Piazza Mazzini 85, t 0586 806330, *www.parkingiardinohotel.it* (€€). Ensuite rooms near the port.

## Eating Out in Livorno

**Livorno ✉ 57100**

The main reason for coming to Livorno is to eat seafood. Livornese ways of preparing it, especially *cacciucco*, the famous fish stew, are now much copied throughout Tuscany, but restaurants here are generally better value. After a rich meal, try a *bomba livornese*, with equal quantities of coffee and rum.

**Ciglieri**, Via Ravizza Giuseppe 43, Ardenza, t 0586 508194 (€€€€). An elegant, intimate, highly regarded restaurant serving high-quality fish dishes such as spaghetti with clams, dried tomatoes and basil, and stuffed sea bass with mushrooms. For dessert, don't miss the chocolate ravioli filled with *gianduja. Closed Wed.*

**La Barcarola** >

**La Barcarola**, Viale Carducci 39, t 0586 402367 (€€€€–€€€). A big, noisy place near the train station, set up in 1935 and serving up the likes of gnocchi with prawns, smoked salmon ravioli, squid *au gratin*, and shellfish soup. *Closed Sun and Aug.*

**Da Oscar**, Via Franchini 78, Ardenza. t 0586 501258 (€€€). A longstanding favourite in a seaside suburb, serving good grilled fish in a garden in summer. Booking is advisable. *Closed Mon and 3wks in Jan.*

**La Chiave**, Scali delle Cantine 52, t 0586 829865 (€€). A restaurant renowned for its seafood: spaghetti with clams, smoked mullet roe and courgettes, oysters, caviar, and risotto with crustacea flavoured with gin. It's small, so book ahead. *Closed Wed, lunch, and mid-Aug–mid-Sept.*

**Da Motorino**, Via Oberdan 30, t 0586 896485 (€€). A spartan trattoria with a brusque owner, one of the best places to eat *cacciucco* in town. Booking essential. *Closed Mon.*

**Vecchia Livorno**, Via Scali delle Cantine 34, t 0586 884048 (€€). A lively trattoria in the *centro storico*, serving interesting variations on traditional dishes. The baked sea bream, squid rings and fish *fritto misto* are good; note that you have to book the *cacciucco* in advance. Reservations are highly advisable. *Closed Tues.*

**Trattoria da Galileo**, Via della Campana 20, t 0586 889009 (€€). A friendly trattoria that has been serving up *cacciucco* since 1959, seemingly mainly to Italian celebs – the walls are lined by signed pictures. The huge serving of fried fish and seafood is also good. *Closed Wed.*

## Livorno's Coast

Livorno's canny tourist office calls this shore the 'Etruscan Riviera', conjuring up the irresistible idea of Etruscans lounging in beach chairs the way they do on funerary urns. Beyond Antignano, the shoreline becomes jagged and twisting, dotted with beaches that are usually more than well exploited, including **Castiglioncello**, a pretty corner with narrow beaches packed with Italians all summer. **San Vincenzo** is an awful, booming resort, but it does have kilometres of good beaches on either side – perhaps your best chance on this strip of coast for a little seaside peace and quiet.

Next is the half-moon **Golfo di Baratti**, with tranquil beaches and some Etruscan tombs from the once-mighty town of **Populonia**. Modern Populonia has an impressive medieval castle and a small

**Museo Archeologico del Territorio di Populonia**
*t 0565 226445; call for opening hours*

**archaeological museum**; ask there about visiting the ruins of the Etruscan city and tombs, which include a so-called 'arsenal' where the Etruscans turned Elban iron into armaments. **Piombino**, at the tip of this stubby peninsula, mercilessly flattened during the war, and mercilessly rebuilt, is the major port for Elba.

Towns of interest up in the hills include **Bolgheri**, centre of a DOC wine area (Bolgheri is a little-known dry white wine); **Castagneto Carducci**, a pretty strawberry-growing town; and **Suvereto**, a seldom-visited medieval village with an arcaded Palazzo Comunale and the 12th-century Pisan church of San Giusto.

## Where to Stay and Eat on Livorno's Coast

**San Vincenzo >**
*Via Aliata 1,*
*t 0565 707111*

**La Pineta >>**

### San Vincenzo ✉ 57027

**Gambero Rosso**, Piazza della Vittoria 72, **t** 0565 701021 (€€€€). One of Italy's top restaurants, renowned not only for its fish but also for its delicate crustacea, pasta, pheasant and pigeon with foie gras. Try the *zuppa di ceci* with shellfish, the fish ravioli, the sea bream with artichokes, or the squab casserole, or order the *menu degustazione*. It's a wonderful place to eat and watch the sun set over the sea. *Closed Mon, Tues, Nov and Dec.*

### Bibbona ✉ 57020

**Podere Le Mezzelune**, Loc. Mezzelune 126, **t** 0586 670266, *www.lemezzelune. it* (€€€€). A little 19th-century house situated near Cecina, with charming owners, antique furnishings, an open fire for cold days and a shady terrace for hot ones.

**La Pineta**, Via dei Cavalleggeri Nord 27, Marina di Bibbona, **t** 0565 600016 (€€€). No more than a shack on the beach, but serving reputedly the best seafood in Tuscany with the best view. Order the catch of the day or a perfect *spaghetti alla vongole*. There are only 15 tables so book ahead. *Closed Mon.*

# The Tuscan Islands

The Tuscan archipelago is a broad arch stretching from Livorno to Monte Argentario; Elba is its only large and heavily populated member. Fate has not been kind to these islands as a whole: with deforestation, Saracen and Turkish pirates, and finally the Italian government, not much is left. Two islands are still prison camps; another is a nature reserve where no one can stay overnight.

# Capraia

Capraia, 65km from Livorno, measuring about 10 x 5km and home to about 400 people, is the third largest of the Tuscan islands. Like Elba, it is mountainous, but it has fewer trees; most of the island is covered with scrubby *macchia*. In Roman times Capraia seems to have been a private estate, and the ruins of an extensive villa can be seen. In the days of the Empire, the island was occupied by Christian monks. The setting was perfect for withdrawal and contemplation but it also prevented Church authorities from keeping a close watch on the colony, and the monks slipped into unorthodoxy and loose behaviour; an armed mission from Pope Gregory the Great forced them back in line in the late 6th century.

When Saracen pirates began to infest the Tyrrhenian Sea, Capraia, like most of the group, became deserted. The Pisans thought it important enough to repopulate and fortify in the 11th century. Genoa eventually gained control, as she did in Corsica only 32km away. This proximity gave Capraia its one big moment in history; in 1767 the revolutionary forces of Corsican nationalist leader Pasquale Paoli, and the weakness of the Genoese, resulted in, of all things, an independent Capraia, which learned to support itself by piracy. French occupation put an end to that four years later.

## Getting to and around the Tuscan Islands

There's a daily trip from **Livorno** to Capraia, plus a daily (16 June–30 Sept) afternoon run to Portoferraio, Rio Marina and Porto Azzurro on Elba, run by TOREMAR (Via Calafati 6, Livorno, **t** 0586 896113, *www.toremar.it*).

Gritty **Piombino** is the main point of departure for ferries to **Elba**. Any train down the Tyrrhenian coast will take you as far as Campiglia Marittima station; from there the FS operates a regular shuttle train to Piombino (don't get off at the central station; the train continues to the port). TOREMAR (**t** 0586 896113; on Elba at Calata Italia 23, Portoferraio, **t** 0565 960131; in Piombino at Piazzale Premuda, **t** 0565 31100) runs services on this route too, as do Moby Lines (Piazzale Premuda, Piombino, **t** 0565 9361, *www.mobylines.it*). The most frequent passage is the 1hr Piombino–Cavo–Portoferraio trip; there are also TOREMAR **hydrofoils** that go from Piombino to Rio Marina (45mins) and on to Porto Azzurro (1hr 20mins) or Portferraio (1hr). Services to Elba can be as frequent as every half-hour in July, down to two or three a day in winter. Moby Lines connects Piombino to Portoferraio and Livorno to Bastia and Olbia.

Elba has just room enough for an **airport** (**t** 0565 976011, *www.elbaisland-airport.it*), and there are plenty of flights in summer – mainly to Germany, Switzerland and Austria. There's also an infrequent service to Pisa, Florence and Milan.

An efficient **bus** service goes to every corner of Elba frequently. Portoferraio is the hub of the system, with buses leaving and returning to the terminal by the Grattacielo, facing the harbour.

There are plenty of **car hire** agencies in Elba's main towns. You can hire **scooters and bikes** everywhere too, and the tourist office (*see* p.314) has itineraries for bike/mountainbike trips around the island.

---

The main draw is Capraia's natural setting, deep-sea diving and marine grottoes. The northern quarter has long been an agricultural penal colony, and the civilian population is almost entirely concentrated in the port and only town, **Capraia Isola**, where the Baroque church and convent of **Sant'Antonio**, used as a barracks in the last century, is crumbling and abandoned. On the outskirts are the ruins of the **Roman villa**, apocryphally the abode of Augustus' profligate daughter Julia, and an 11th-century Pisan chapel dedicated to the **Vergine Assunta**. Overlooking it all is the impressive fortress of **San Giorgio**, begun by the Pisans and completed by the Genoese. The well-preserved **watchtower** at the port was built by the Genoese Bank of St George. On the eastern side of town, the beach under the cliffs has an interesting tower built by the Pisans, connected to the cliff by a natural bridge.

From Capraia Isola a road leads southwest across the island, passing another Pisan church, **Santo Stefano**, built on the ruins of a 5th-century church used by the early monks and destroyed by the Saracen pirates. Near Monte Pontica is a sacred cave, the **Grotta di Parino**, used as a place of meditation by the monks. The road ends at a lighthouse on the west coast. Just south is a sea-cave, the **Grotta della Foca**, where Mediterranean seals are reported still to live. At the southern tip of the island is another Genoese watchtower, the **Torre dello Zenobito**.

Capraia can be reached by a daily boat from Livorno, of which it is administratively part. The same goes of nearby **Gorgona**, where the boat stops to drop off new prisoners and supplies on the way to Capraia; you, however, can't alight there (there's nothing to see anyway, except maquis and a handful of olive trees).

# Elba

When the government closed the steel mills on Elba after the war, local authorities sought to make up lost income by promoting tourism. They have been singularly successful: it is one of Europe's most popular holiday playgrounds, with nearly two million visitors a year, making its 30,000 inhabitants prosperous once more.

It's a comfortable, unglamorous place attracting families, especially Germans, who have bought up most of the southern coast. There is no single big, crowded tourist ghetto but plenty of quiet, small resorts around the coast. In an unspectacular way, however, Elba is beautiful. Pink and green predominate – pink for the granite outcrops and houses, green for the heavy forests. Like its neighbour Corsica, it is a chain of mountains rising out of the sea, the tallest to the west, grouped around Monte Capanne (3,546ft/1,080m). For a mineralogist, it's a dream – besides iron ore, dozens of common and rare minerals are found here, from andalusite to zircon. For most people, however, Elba's big draw is beaches and mild climate – it hardly ever rains. The coastline, all bays and peninsulas, is more than 150km long, and there are beaches everywhere, large and small, sand or pebbles. Even in August, there's plenty of Elba-room.

## History

Elba is close enough to the Italian mainland to have been inhabited from the earliest times. When Neanderthals were tramping through the neighbourhood about 50,000 years ago, Elba may still have been linked to the peninsula. Later peoples, a seemingly unending parade, colonized the island after 3000 BC,

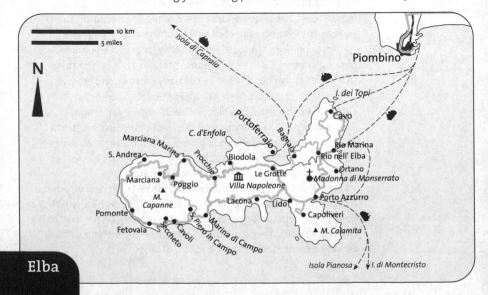

Elba

drawn by the treasure hoard of metals. In the Copper Age they mined its copper; in the Bronze Age they alloyed the copper into bronze. The copper gave out just in time for the Iron Age – and Elba had vast deposits of this as well. Competition was fierce: the Etruscans and Greeks fought over the island and established colonies of miners to extract the iron, but archaeologists have been unable to find evidence of permanent settlements.

For Rome, expanding across the Italian peninsula in the 4th century BC, Elba was an important prize. After conquering the island at the end of the century, the Romans founded towns to consolidate their hold. From then on, whenever Roman legions ran their swords through Teutons, Persians, Gauls, Carthaginians or each other, they were usually made from Elban iron. The mines and forges, then as now, were concentrated on the eastern third of the island, while the beautiful beaches everywhere else became a holiday spot for wealthy Romans, as demonstrated by the archaeological remains of large villas discovered near Portoferraio.

The fall of Rome brought invasions, disorder, depopulation and pirates; the Lombards in the 6th century, under the murderous Gummarith, subjugated the island with their usual bloodshed; Saracens and adventurous barons from Italy fought for the scraps. By the 11th century Pisa had complete control, as the island lay across its most important trade route. It held Elba for almost 500 years, constructing fortresses at Luceri and Volterraio and exploiting the mineral resources. At the time the capital was called *Ferraia*, of which the modern capital of Portoferraio was only the port. Nowadays not a trace remains of the medieval city; archaeologists are still trying to locate its site.

From the 13th century, Genoa contested Pisa's possession. In the 16th century, Duke Cosimo I saw his opportunity and seized it for Florence. He built Portoferraio and the walls around it but soon had to contend with the growing power of Spain in the western Med, and after inconclusive skirmishes Elba was partitioned between Tuscany and Spain. Spain built the town and fortress of Porto Azzurro as a counter to Portoferraio, an arrangement that lasted through the 18th century, despite French efforts to grab the island.

## Portoferraio

Portoferraio (population 11,000) is the capital, and indeed the only city of Elba. The massive walls built by Cosimo remain, though Portoferraio has spilled west along the bay. Here the ferries dock at the Calata Italia, where the visitor's introduction to Elba is the hideous **Grattacielo** (skyscraper), a 10-storey pile of peeling paint built in the 1950s, which contains a tourist office, most of the ferry offices, and the bus terminal. Follow Calata Italia and its various pseudonyms beneath the walls, next to the old U-shaped harbour.

On the far side rises the **Torre del Martello**, from which in the old days a chain was stretched across the harbour in times of danger. The main gate of the city is the **Porta a Mare** at the base of the U, over which can be seen the inscription of Duke Cosimo reminding us, with the usual Medicean vanity, how he constructed the whole town 'from the foundations upwards'; the new town had originally been dubbed Cosmopolis.

Directly inside the Porta a Mare is **Piazza Cavour**. Portoferraio is a big natural amphitheatre; from the piazza the town slopes upwards in all directions towards the walls on the high cliffs. North of the piazza, Via Garibaldi leads up to the main attraction, Napoleon's house, the **Villa dei Mulini**, yellowing, unloved, unchanged since Napoleon had it built according to his simple tastes; inside are furnishings, books and other paraphernalia, including the flag with three golden bees that he bestowed on the Elbans, and political cartoons mocking him. The gardens, equally uncared for, offer fine views over the walls. On either side, two Medici fortresses dominate the highest points in the city: **Forte Falcone** to the west, and **Forte Stella**.

On the way down Via Garibaldi are two parish churches: the **Holy Sacrament**, which has a copy of Napoleon's death mask, and the **Misericordia**, which on 5 May holds a procession to commemorate Napoleon's death, with a replica of his coffin. The **town hall**, which

**Villa dei Mulini**
*t 0565 915846; open daily 9–7; adm; joint adm available with Villa di San Martino (see opposite)*

**Forte Falcone**
*open summer Wed–Mon 10–1 and 3.30–7.40; rest of year Wed–Mon 10–1; adm*

**Forte Stella**
*open summer daily 10–6; adm*

## Napoleon on Elba

During the Napoleonic wars, Elba was occupied for a time by the English, and Portoferraio was unsuccessfully besieged for more than a year by Napoleon's troops in 1799. Napoleon finally annexed it in 1802, with no premonitions that the 1814 Treaty of Fontainebleau would put a temporary end to the First Empire and send him there.

Napoleon chose Elba, from the variety of small Mediterranean outposts offered him, for 'the gentleness of its climate and its inhabitants'. Also, perhaps because on clear days he could see his own island of Corsica. No one, however, seems to have consulted the Elbans themselves on the matter, and they can be excused for the cold indifference with which they received their new ruler, who arrived on 4 May 1814 with some 500 of his most loyal officers and soldiers and a British commissioner charged with keeping an eye on him. But he soon won the hearts of the Elbans, by being the best governor they had ever had. New systems of law and education were established, the last vestiges of feudalism were abolished, and what would today be called economic planning was begun; he reorganized the iron mines and started work on Elba's modern network of roads.

Not that Napoleon ever really took his stewardship seriously. Remaking nations and institutions was a reflex by then; he'd done it all across Europe for 20 years. It was the return to France that occupied his attention. The atmosphere was thick with intrigues and rumours, and secret communications flowed incessantly between Napoleon and his partisans on the continent. On 20 February 1815, just nine months after his arrival, the Elbans and the embarrassed British watchdog awoke to find the emperor missing. The 'Hundred Days' had begun. Later, after Waterloo, a smaller, gloomier and more distant island (St Helena) would be found to keep Napoleon out of trouble.

Elba was returned to Tuscany, and soon afterwards it joined the new Kingdom of Italy. It was hit hard by the Germans. In 1944, in one of the most disgraceful episodes of the war, Elba was 'liberated' by Free French and African troops, with more murder, pillage and rape than had been seen in the Med since the days of the pirates.

was originally a bakery for Cosimo's troops, was the boyhood home of Victor Hugo, whose father was the French military commander in Elba. There's a **Roman altar** in the courtyard.

Two blocks west, the tiny but surprisingly grand **Teatro dei Vigilanti** was rebuilt by Napoleon from an abandoned church. East of Via Garibaldi, **Piazza della Repubblica** is the throbbing heart of Portoferraio, with its crowded cafés, 18th-century **cathedral** (not a cathedral at all these days) and nearby market.

Outside the walls, on the eastern side of the port, a converted salt warehouse is now home to the **Museo Civico Archeologico**, which displays items from the Roman patrician villas, one of which was discovered here.

**Museo Civico Archeologico**
*t 0565 901215; open Fri–Wed 10–1 and 4–7.40 but afternoon hours may vary in winter; adm*

### Around Portoferraio

Most of Portoferraio's hotels and restaurants are in the modern extension outside the walls. There are pebble beaches on the north side (**Le Ghiaie**) and under the walls near Forte Falcone (**Le Viste**). One of the two roads from the capital leads along the northern coast to the small resorts of **Acquaviva** and **Viticcio**, and to **Capo d'Enfola**, a lovely headland rising sheer out of the sea, barely connected to the rest of the island. The second road runs south to the junction of **Bivio Boni**, where it branches east and west. Nearby is a thermal spa at **San Giovanni**, and the ruins of a Roman villa at **Le Grotte**, on the south shore of the gulf of Portoferraio, more interesting for its view than its scant remains. There are beaches here, at Ottone, Magazzini and **Bagnaia**, the latter the site of the simple, beautiful 12th-century church of **Santo Stefano**, the best Pisan monument in the archipelago.

At **Acquabona** you can shoot some bogeys at one of Elba's two golf courses (nine holes), or continue west from Bivio Boni to the resort at **Biodola Bay** and the **Villa Napoleone di San Martino**. The emperor soon tired of life in Portoferraio and built this as his country retreat. In later years the husband of his niece (daughter of Jérome) bought it and added a pretentious neoclassical façade with big Ns pasted everywhere; it's now another Napoleonic museum, with a little art gallery including a *Galatea* by Canova.

**Villa Napoleone di San Martino**
*open Tues–Sun 9–7; adm; joint adm available with Villa dei Mulini, see opposite*

### Eastern Elba

**Rio nell'Elba** is the old mining centre, although it's as pleasant and pastel as any other Elban town, set in the hills overlooking the eastern coast. Archaeological sites, the scanty remains of mines and Etruscan mining camps dot the surrounds. There are many undeveloped beaches on the western side of Rio's peninsula, including Nisporto and Nisportino. The road between Portoferraio and Rio passes the steep hill of **Volterraio**, and you can make the long climb to the 11th-century Pisan castle perched on the summit.

**11**

The Tuscan Coast | Elba

**Museo dei Minerali dell'Elba e dell' Arte Mineraria**
*Palazzo Comunale; open April–June, Sept and Oct Tues–Sun 9.30–12.30 and 3.30–6.30; July and Aug Tues–Sun 9.30–12.30, 4.30–7.30 and 9–11pm; adm*

**Parco Minerario**
*visits April–June, Sept and Oct daily at 10am; July and Aug daily at 6pm; for guided visits, call **t** 0565 962088*

**Rio Marina**, as its name implies, is the port for Rio nell'Elba. Here, the **mineralogical museum** has displays of the island's unusual rocks and minerals – few places on earth have such a variety. Devoted rock-hounds should continue to the **Parco Minerario**, located in an old mine. Rio Marina has a busy harbour, its many small fishing boats bobbing under the vigilant eye of an octagonal Pisan watchtower. The eastern side of this peninsula, like the western side, has fine beaches where you can sometimes escape the crowds – **Ortano**, **Porticciolo** and **Barbarossa** among others.

## Porto Azzurro and Capoliveri

South of Rio, the road passes through some difficult terrain towards **Porto Azzurro**, built by the Spaniards and now a large holiday town, with a beach. Until 1947 it was called Porto Longon. The fortress, built in 1603 to withstand the Austrians and French, was converted into a famous Italian calaboose that hosted many political prisoners and criminal celebrities.

Several other beaches nearby include a bizarre one at **Terrenere**, where a yellow-green sulphurous pond festers near the blue sea in a landscape of pebble beach and ancient mine debris. In season, day excursions run from Porto Azzurro to the island of Montecristo.

Just north of Porto Azzurro is the **sanctuary of Monserrato**, a famous shrine with a 'Black Madonna' icon. The Spanish governor built this here in 1606 because the mountain (Monte Castello) reminded him of the odd mountain of Montserrat near Barcelona. Similar Black Madonnas are revered from Portugal to Poland; over the centuries the oxidization of yellow paint has darkened them.

South of Porto Azzurro is another Spanish fortress at **Capo Focardo**, on a large oval-shaped peninsula consisting of Monte Calamita and the rough hill country around it. On this peninsula is **Capoliveri**, one of the oldest inhabited sites on the island. The town takes its name from the Roman *Caput Liberi*, which may refer either to the worship of Liber, an Italian equivalent of Dionysus (this has always been a wine-growing area) or to the free men (*liberi*) who lived here – in Roman times, Capoliveri was a refuge for any man who could escape to it. It has had a reputation for independence ever since, giving a bad time to the Pisans, the Spanish, and even Napoleon. Today it is peaceful, with fine views from its hilltop over the surrounding countryside and sea, though much of its scenic coast is privately owned.

South, near the coast, is the **sanctuary of the Madonna delle Grazie**, with a *Madonna and Child* by the school of Raphael, miraculously saved from a shipwreck. The coast west of Capoliveri is marked by two lovely broad gulfs, **Golfo Stella** and **Golfo di Lacona**, separated by a steep, narrow tongue of land. Both are developed resorts, with centres at Lacona and Lido Margidore.

## Western Elba

Beyond Biodola, the scenic corniche road west from Portoferraio passes through the resorts of **Procchio** and **Campo all'Aia**; the former is larger and one of the more expensive resorts on Elba. **Marciana Marina**, 7km west, is another popular resort, with a 15th-century Pisan watchtower, the **Torre Saracena**. This is the port for **Marciana**, the oldest continuously inhabited town on Elba. In the 14th and 15th centuries, when life near the coast wasn't safe, Marciana was the 'capital' of the feudal Appiani barons, the most powerful family on the island. Today, high in the forests on the slopes of Monte Capanne, it is surprisingly beautiful, with narrow streets, stone stairs, archways and belvederes. Sections of the old city wall and gate are still intact, and the old Pisan **fortress** hangs over the town.

**Fortezza di Marciana**
*t 0565 901215; open usually Easter–Oct mornings and 6pm–11pm; adm; joint adm available with archaeology museum*

The palace of the Appiani may be seen on a narrow *vicolo* in the oldest part of town. Marciana's **archaeology museum** has some prehistoric and Roman objects found in the area. In season, a **cable lift** climbs to the summit of Elba's highest peak, **Monte Capanne** (3,342ft/1,019m), with stupendous views over Corsica, the Tuscan archipelago and the mountains of Tuscany itself.

**Museo Civico Archeologico**
*t 0565 901215; open mid-June–mid-Sept daily 9.30–2.30 and 5–midnight, rest of the year Thurs 10.30–1.30 and 4–8, adm; joint adm available with Fortezza*

Three churches outside Marciana are of interest: the ruined Pisan **San Lorenzo**; the **sanctuary of San Cerbone**, who escaped here from the troublesome Lombards (later his body was buried in a rainstorm, so they wouldn't see); and the 11th-century **sanctuary of the Madonna del Monte**, one of the island's most important shrines, with a Madonna painted on a lump of granite. Pagan Elbans may have worshipped at this site as well, as did Napoleon for two weeks, after a fashion, with his Polish mistress, Maria Walewska.

**Impianto di Risalita (cable lift)**
*daily mid-April–Oct 10–12.15 and 2.30–4.45; €10 return*

Another mountain village is **Poggio**, just east, with a natural spring where Elbans bottle their *acqua minerale* – called Napoleone, of course. It's very good, but the Elbans keep it all to themselves.

On the rugged coast west and south of Marciana are more beaches and resorts: **Sant'Andrea**, **Patresi**, **Chiessi**, **Pomonte**, lovely **Fetovaia**, **Seccheto** and **Cavoli**. Seccheto has ancient granite quarries from which the stone was cut for the Pantheon in Rome.

Elba's pocket-sized plain, the **Campo nell'Elba**, stretches 7km east of Marciana, extending from Procchio to Marina di Campo and separating the western mountains from the central range. Elba's airport is here – it's the only place they could put it. Two old towns lie on the edge of the plain: **Sant'Ilario in Campo** and **San Piero in Campo**. San Piero's parish church of **San Niccolò** has interesting frescoes; it was built on the ruins of an ancient temple to Glaucus.

Halfway between the towns are the ruins of the Pisan church of **San Giovanni**, with a watchtower you can view from outside. On the coast is **Marina di Campo**, Elba's first resort, with the largest beach. The harbour watchtower was built by the Medici.

# Pianosa and Montecristo

Two other members of the Tuscan archipelago are included in Livorno province: one you won't want to visit, and the other you usually can't. **Pianosa** is the black sheep of the chain. Its name, taken from the Roman *Planasia*, explains why – it's as flat as a pool table. Like Gorgona, Pianosa's unhappy fate was to serve as a prison island. There are some substantial ruins of a Roman villa, from the days when Pianosa was the playground of Cornelius Agrippa, Emperor Augustus' great general, but to see them you need special permission from the prison authorities in Rome.

Tiny **Montecristo**, the tip of an ancient volcano 40km south of Elba, and the hunting preserve of King Vittorio Emanuele III, is now a nature reserve. Private boats and day-trips organized from Porto Azzurro on Elba may dock at Cala Maestra, but visitors must stay on the cove and its beach; the mountain, ruins of a medieval monastery and royal villa (now the custodian's house) are out of bounds. In Roman times this was an important religious site, *Mons Jovis*, with a famous temple of Jupiter; not a trace remains. The early Church wasted no time Christianizing the place, renaming it Montecristo. None of *The Count of Monte Cristo* is really set here; like the count himself, seeing the place on a map is probably as close to it as Alexandre Dumas ever got.

## Where to Stay on the Tuscan Islands

(i) Capraia >

*Via Assunzione,
Capraia Isola,*
t *0586 905138, www.
prolococapraiaisola.it*

### Capraia ✉ 57032

The tourist office in Capraia Isola will provide a list of accommodation – a decade or so ago, this consisted of one hotel and two tiny *pensioni*; today, by a miracle of 21st-century Eurotourism, these have all grown into 3- or 4-star hotels, and two more have sprouted to join them.

(i) Elba >

*Grattacielo building,
Calata Italia 43,
Portoferraio, across
from ferry dock,*
t *0565 914671,
www.aptelba.it*

### Elba ✉ 57037

There are more than 150 hotels on the island, especially mid-priced resorts for families, but this a big package-tour destination, so you must book ahead. Many hotels require half-board in high season (mid-June–mid-Sept). Lots stay open all year, offering substantial off-season discounts.

Prices tend to be slightly lower at Cavo, on the east coast, which has plenty of campsites and holiday apartments. The same is true of most beaches on the southeastern peninsula around Capoliveri. Among the resorts to the west, there are some smart places near Procchio, more modest hotels at Sant'Andrea and Pomonte, and a few that are blissfully out of the way.

For self-catering accommodation, see *www.tuscany-charming.it*.

****Villa Ottone**, at Ottone, t 0565 933042, *www.villaottone.com* (€€€€€). A 19th-century villa with its white-sand beach, with a shady garden and a tennis court. Full board is available.

****The Hermitage**, Loc. Biodola, Portoferraio, t 0565 9740 (€€€€). A sprawling resort hotel by a white-sand beach, with lots of facilities for families, including a tennis court. Rooms are quite luxurious, and all have a patio or balcony. Breakfast and dinner are included in the rates. *Closed mid-Oct–Easter.*

***Hotel Ilio**, Capo Sant'Andrea 24, t 0565 908018, *www.ilio.it* (€€€). A whitewashed modern villa and outbuildings, with pretty bedrooms with rattan furniture. Breakfasts (included) are huge, and evening meals excellent (half-board is obligatory April–mid-Oct).

**\*\*L'Ape Elbana**, Salità de' Medici 2, Portoferraio, t 0565 914245, *www.ape-elbana.it* (€€). The oldest hotel on the island, where Napoleon's guests were entertained. All rooms are ensuite, and half- and full-board are available.

**\*\*La Conchiglia**, Cavoli, t 0565 987010, *www.laconchigliacavoli.it* (€€). A small family-run hotel with air-conditioning. There's a good restaurant; in high season it's full-board only.

**\*\*La Voce del Mare**, Naregno beach, t 0565 968455, *www.hotelvocedelmare.it* (€€). One of many pleasant hotels on the beach, with its own private stretch of sand. Half-board is required, or you can opt for full-board. There are also apartments let by the week, and some rooms have kitchenettes.

## Eating Out on the Tuscan Islands

### Piombino (mainland)

**Ristorante Terrazza**, Piazza Premuda, t 0565 226135 (€€). Somewhere to wait for the ferry, above the bar in the port, with delicious *spaghetti alle vongole*.

### Elba ✉ 57037

Elba's DOC wines, Elba Rosso and Elba Bianco, complement any meal.

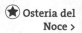 Osteria del Noce >

**Osteria del Noce**, Via della Madonna 27, Marciana Alta, near Poggio, t 0565 901284 (€€€). An *osteria* in a hilltop village, with fabulous views to the sea. You sit at tables carved from old wine barrels to eat dishes marrying the flavours of Elba, Liguria and Sardinia: anchovies marinated in lemon juice, mussel and bean soup and oven-baked fish of the day. Booking is essential. *Closed Oct–Mar*.

**Rendezvous**, Piazza della Vittoria, Marciana Marina, t 0565 99251 (€€€). Famous for serving its fresh fish perfectly grilled without drying it out. Always excellent. *Closed Wed*.

**La Lucciola**, Viale degli Eroi, Marina di Campo, t 0565 976395 (€€€). A few metres from the sea with a colonial decor, there is not only wonderfully imaginative Elban seafood on offer, but bags of atmosphere and fun.

**Capo Nord**, Località Fenicia 1, next to the old harbour, Marciana Marina, t 0565 996983 (€€€). Simple and chic, with beautiful views over the sea, this is the place for a romantic dinner. Try the pasta with swordfish or risotto with octopus. Booking advised.

**Stella Marina**, Via Vittorio Emanuele 2, Portoferraio, t 0565 915983 (€€€). Next to the ferry port. Of all the excellent dishes on offer at this family-run place, perhaps there is none more unusual and stunning than the seafood *carbonara*. Quite incredible.

**Il Chiasso**, Via Nazario Sauro 20, Capoliveri, t 0565 968709 (€€). This fun and lively place is where you should try stuffed fresh anchovy spaghetti with fish roe, *risotto al nero di seppia* (with cuttlefish in ink) and a fabulous octopus soup with onions and potatoes. *Closed Tues, and lunch mid-Oct–mid-Apr*.

**Osteria Libertaria**, Calata Matteotti 12, Portoferraio, t 0565 914978 (€€). A traditional *osteria* serving local seafood: try mussel and clam soup, or *cozze alla marinara* (mussels with lemon and oil). Come early for a seat in the garden or one of two tables on the pier, with great views. *Closed Mon*.

**Solemar**, Loc. Lacona, just outside Capoliveri, t 0565 964248 (€). A pleasant trattoria with the best pizzas on Elba. Booking is advisable. *Closed Mon in winter*.

# South of Piombino

# The Maremma

In a sense, this flat, lonely stretch of coast really belongs to Italy's south. History has been unkind to the Maremma, domain first of the Etruscans, later of the anopheles mosquito. Like many southern coastal regions, the Maremma was a prosperous agricultural region until Roman times. The Romans gave it its name: the 'maritime' zone (as in names such as Massa Marittima), gradually mangled into Maremma.

Historians sometimes give the Romans too much credit for capable governance; their grasping, bureaucratic state slowly corroded and eventually destroyed the Italian economy. Many centuries of Roman misgovernment – impossible taxes, cheap imported grain and especially, in this case, neglect of the Etruscans' system of drainage canals – doomed the Maremma to a slow death. When the canals failed, much of the land was abandoned and reverted to swamps, breeding the malarial mosquitoes that made the Maremma of the Middle Ages a place of suffering and death, inhabitable only by the *butteri*, tough Tuscan cowboys who tended the herds in the abandoned marshy pastures. A considerable body of folklore has grown up around the *butteri*; the Maremma's proudest moment came in the 19th century when some of them went to Rome and defeated Buffalo Bill and his travelling Wild West show in a test of cowboy know-how.

The first work of reclamation began with the Austrian grand dukes. The Italian Kingdom that followed forgot all about the Maremma, and it was not until after the Second World War that the task was completed. The Maremma today is back on its feet, a new region and a little rough around the edges but prosperous once more.

## Follonica and Punta Ala

After Piombino, the coast bends eastwards into a broad arc, the Golfo di Follonica. There are some wonderful beaches between Piombino and Follonica, notably **La Sterpaia**, which partly backs on to a nature reserve.

Since the Second World War, new resort towns have been popping up like toadstools all along the Tuscan coast. One of the biggest and least likeable is **Follonica**, 21km east of Piombino, partially redeemed by the long pine groves that follow its crowded beaches. Follonica has some other enchantments, notably the **Museum of Iron and Cast Iron**, in an 1830s foundry where Elban iron was once smelted. There is also **CARAPAX**, the European Centre for the Protection of Turtles and Tortoises, who study turtles, save endangered ones and reintroduce them into the wild. Visitors can look at the turtle clinic and nursery, and see exotic species. The centre is also working to reintroduce the stork to Italy, and has a colony of them in Italy's biggest aviary.

On the promontory that closes the gulf, 14km south, **Punta Ala** is a modern, entirely synthetic resort built in the suburban style of the Costa Smeralda. It's an attractive location, with a fine sandy beach and views around the gulf, and it attracts a well-heeled clientele with diversions rare in Tuscany, such as golf (at the Golf Hotel, Via del Gualdo) and polo (at the Polo Club).

**Castiglione della Pescaia**, attached to an attractive ancient fishing village to the south, is much less exclusive. The beach isn't great, but the town on its hill, with trees and ivy-covered walls, is one of the more pleasant detours on this coast. The Spanish left a 16th-century castle, and the church of San Giovanni has an tower that could pass for a minaret. From the harbour, Navimaremma offers summer island cruises; ask at the tourist office (*see* p.320).

## Grosseto

Under the prevailing prosperity, the natural Tuscan sense of order and propriety has slowly been asserting itself in this place that we described, in the original edition of this book, as 'a city of

**Museo del Ferro e della Ghisa**
*t 0566 59006; open summer Wed 8.30–1.30 and 5–8, Fri and Sat 8.30–1.30 and 5–11pm, Sun 5–11pm; winter Wed and Sun 4.30–7.30, Fri and Sat 9–12 and 4.30–7.30*

**CARAPAX**
*t 0566 902387, www.carapax.org; open April–20 June daily 9.30–6; 21 June–20 Sept daily 9–7; 21 Sept– 31 Oct daily 9–5; closed Nov–Mar (feeding time 9am)*

# Getting to and from Grosseto

Seven **trains** a day (t 892021, *www.trenitalia.com*) leave Grosseto for Siena, via Roccastrada and Buonconvento (some continue to Florence). There are also services along the coastal line for Livorno, or Orbetello and Rome.

GRIFORAMA (t 0564 25215, *www.griforama.it*) runs **buses** from Grosseto to Siena (7 a day) and every town in Grosseto province, including 2 a day to Massa Marittima (*see* Hilltowns West of Siena), and 5 daily to Arcidosso and Pitigliano (*see* Southern Tuscany). Buses leave from the train station.

Art Nouveau buildings and perverse teenagers, a city conducive to hallucinations, its streets alive with swirls of dust and flying plastic bags'. Instead of punk music, there are dance and chamber music concerts and scholarly conferences, and Italy's Most Improved Town, always a likeable place, grows steadily more normal, even pleasant – though you still can't buy a decent slice of pizza.

Via Carducci leads from the station towards the fearful hexagon of walls that enclose Grosseto, passing Mussolini's contribution to the city, the circular Piazza Fratelli Rosselli, or **La Vasca** (which can mean 'tub' or 'toilet bowl'). Here the starring role is played by an exuberant **Mussolini post office**, with heroic statuary in travertine. The main gate is only a block away. Cosimo's walls are perfectly preserved, done in tidy, reddish brick festooned with Medici balls.

Much of the old city looks very Spanish; the Art Nouveau pharmacies and shoe shops along the main street, Corso Carducci, contribute to the effect, as does the arcaded Piazza del Duomo, very like a Spanish *plaza mayor*. The **Duomo** (1190–1250) suffered grievously from overambitious restoration in the 1840s; the façade looks like a Hollywood prop. Inside is a genuinely lovely painting, Matteo di Giovanni's *Madonna delle Grazie* (1470). Around the side of the Duomo is an interesting sundial, and the piazza has an allegorical monument to the Maremma's benefactor, the Lorraine grand duke Leopold II; the woman he is raising up represents the suffering Maremma, and the snake he's crushing is Malaria.

**Museo Archeologico e d'Arte della Maremma**
*t 0564 488754, www.archeologia toscana.it; open May–Sept Tues–Sun 10–1 and 5–8; Oct and April Tues–Sun 9.30–1 and 4.30–7; Nov–Feb Tues–Fri 9–1, Sat and Sun 9.30–1 and 4.30–7*

Around the corner in Piazza Baccarini, two museums, collectively called the **Museo Archeologico e d'Arte della Maremma**, show you something of life in this region before there ever was a Grosseto. Thousands of years ago, Grosseto and most of its plain were underwater; by the time of the Etruscans, the sea had receded, leaving a large lake on the plain. Two wealthy Etruscan cities, Vetulonia and Roselle (*see* opposite), stood on the hills above the lake, and they contributed most of the items here: cinerary urns with scenes from Homer, architectural fragments and delicate terracottas, some with bits of their original paint. Up on the third floor, the **Pinacoteca** has some good Sienese art, including an amazing, very Byzantine *Last Judgement* by 13th-century artist Guido da Siena.

**Pinacoteca**
*open as Museo Archeologico, above*

Just north of the museum, San Francesco has an early work by Duccio di Buoninsegna, the crucifix above the high altar, and some good 13th-century frescoes. From here you can walk around the

Medicean walls. After Italian unification, the bastions were landscaped into beautiful semi-tropical gardens; some are still well kept, others have decayed into spooky jungles.

The liveliest parts of Grosseto are the shopping streets around **Piazza del Mercato**; nearby, just outside the walls, mornings see a large, almost picturesque street market.

## Roselle and Vetulonia

You actually learn more about these two Etruscan towns from the Grosseto museum (*see* opposite) than from seeing the ruins, but a visit can be fun. **Roselle**, 7km north of Grosseto, survived Roman rule better than many other Etruscan cities, but by the 5th century it was almost abandoned. The bishops of Roselle hung on until 1178, when the seat was transferred to Grosseto. Like many other Etruscan towns, Roselle is a high plateau and is surrounded by more than 3km of walls. A Roman road leads up to the complex, where there are still a few foundations, remains of the baths, the imperial forum and the outline of the amphitheatre, a medieval tower, and necropoli. North of the site are the ruins of a **Roman villa** with parts of its original mosaic floor paving. The last occupant operated a forge here to melt down bronze statues.

**Domus dei Mosaici**
*open daily 9–dusk*

**Vetulonia**, 17km from Grosseto, above the Via Aurelia west of Braccagni, lives on in its worthy successor, Massa Marittima (*see* pp.377–9). On the site itself, a miniature hilltown survives, in rugged but lovely countryside with occasional views over the Tyrrhenian and the islands. Like Roselle, it lasted until the Middle Ages, and was probably destroyed in a 14th-century revolt against its Pisan overlords. Bits of old Vetulonia can be seen in the **Aree Archeologiche** (signposted) and nearby **museum**. The scanty ruins are more Roman and medieval than Etruscan, but the periphery has some interesting tombs (also signposted): the massive **Tomba della Pietrera** and the unique **Il Diavolino** (7th century BC). Both have a long corridor under a tumulus, with an arched burial chamber in the centre; the Diavolino has a window to the sky.

**Aree Archeologiche and Museo Archeologico**
*t 0564 402403; open Nov–Feb 8.30–5.30 Mar–April and Sept–Oct 8.30–6.30; May–Aug 8.30–7; joint adm*

## Monti dell'Uccellina: The Maremma Nature Park

One effect of the Maremma's history of abandonment is a lovely, unspoiled coast. In the 1950s and 1960s developers followed the DDT where they could, but the government set aside a few of the best parts. The **Monti dell'Uccellina**, a ragged chain of hills south of Grosseto, largely covered with umbrella pines, is an important stop for migratory birds between Europe and Africa, hence the name.

For such a small area (roughly 5x15km), the park has a lot to see: nine old defence towers, dozens of caves and the ruins of an 11th-century monastery, **San Rabano**, that belonged to the Knights of Malta. It retains its campanile and some early medieval stone

**⊕ Monti dell'Uccellina**
*visitor centre: Alberese, west of coastal Via Aurelia/SS1 (regular shuttle service from car park), t 0564 407098, www.parks.it; open daily 8am–1hr before sunset; adm; guided tours in English in summer, or private guides available for about €12/hr; visitors limited to 500/day; call ahead at busiest times (Easter, 29 April–1 May, July and Aug); no cars or dogs; bring good shoes and some water*

carvings. Where the park meets the sea is a strip of fabulous beaches. Despite the park status, some people still make their living here, herding cattle, cutting cork oak and gathering pine nuts for Italy's pastry cooks. The landscape ranges from swamps to heather and scented *macchia* to pine groves, and the fauna includes wild horses, deer and boar, along with the *uccellini* themselves – herons, eagles and falcons, ospreys and kingfishers, every sort of duck, and that most overdressed of waterfowl, the *cavaliere d'Italia*. Some peripheral areas can be toured on horseback, and **Il Rialto** at Albarese can fix you up with a steed, plus bikes and canoes.

**Il Rialto**
*t 0564 407 1020*

Nine walks have been laid out in the park, lasting 2–6 hours, and visitors are expected to keep to them. One walk begins from a separate park entrance at Talamone, further south, and doesn't connect to the others. Note that in summer some areas can only be visited by guided tour.

## Talamone

The Sienese Republic never really had a port, gravely hampering foreign trade. Now and then it tried to make one out of Talamone, a fishing village at the tip of the Monti dell'Uccellina, but the little harbour couldn't be kept clear – a continuing embarrassment for the republic; even Dante dropped a jibe about foolishly 'hoping from Talamone'. Garibaldi had better luck: when in 1860 he and his 'Thousand' chose to stop here rather than Sardinia, they avoided the orders for their arrest sent by the treacherous Count Cavour; Garibaldi also found a cache of weapons in Orbetello, which came in handy during the conquest of Sicily.

The walled village on its rock has become a discreet, laidback resort with a small marina. Above, a 16th-century Spanish castle sits like an abstract modern sculpture, set to house a new museum devoted to nature in the Monti dell'Uccellina.

## Where to Stay and Eat in the Maremma

(i) **Castiglione della Pescaia >**
*Piazza Garibaldi, harbour, t 0564 933678, www.col-castiglionegr.it*

(★) **L'Andana >**

### Castiglione della Pescaia
✉ 58043

Castiglione lacks appealing beaches but has a good choice of inexpensive hotels. Most insist on half- or full-board in mid-July–mid-Sept.

**L'Andana**, Tenuta la Badiola, t 0564 944800, *www.andana.it* (€€€€€). Stunning Alain Ducasse property set in a wonderful park and fragrant gardens. Rooms range through all degrees of luxury and there are two swimming pools, one outdoor and one inside the world-class spa. The food is inspired and the trattoria in the old barn has been cited by Michelin. There are fine wines to try from the estate, and plans for a golf course. The sea is less than 10 minutes away.

**\*\*Rossella**, Via Fratelli Bandiera 18, t 0564 933832, *www.albergorosella.it* (€€€). Good rooms, most with a balcony, plus a solarium and a restaurant with a terrace, serving Tuscan specialities.

**Ristorante Miramare**, Via Vittorio Veneto 35, t 0564 933524 (€€€). An excellent seafood restaurant offering seasonal dishes such as prawns with beans, or pumpkin tart. There are also some comfy rooms and flats (€€).

(i) **Grosseto >**
*Viale Monterosa 206,*
*t 0564 462611,*
*www.lamaremma.info*

(★) **Castello di Vicarello >>**

**Grosseto** ✉ 58100

****Bastiani Grand Hotel**, Via Gioberti 64, t 0564 20047, *www.hotelbastiani. com* (€€€€). An elegant city-centre hotel in a gracious 1890s *palazzo*, with a restaurant. Breakfast is included.

**Buca di San Lorenzo**, Via Manetti 1, t 0564 25142 (€€€). A restaurant dug into the Medicean walls, serving local cuisine. *Closed Sun, Mon, 3wks in Jan and 2wks in July.*

**Da Remo**, Rispescia Stazione, a few km south of Grosseto, just off Aurelia, t 0564 405014 (€€€). Fish brought directly from the daily market: try the

spaghetti with prawns and lemon. *Closed Wed and mid-Oct–mid-Nov.*

**Poggi del Sasso** ✉ 58044

**Castello di Vicarello**, Poggi del Sasso, t 0564 990718, *www.vicarello.it* (€€€€€). 11th-century castle deep in the Maremma countryside with 7 beautifully restored suites and a country house party atmosphere courtesy of the delightful owners Carlo and Aurora. There is excellent food and wine from their own estates – cookery classes can be arranged. Two swimming pools, vast views and a lovely spa make this a very special place to stay.

# Monte Argentario

(✪) **Monte Argentario**

In the last decade or so, this curiosity of the Tuscan coast has grown popular. It has much going for it: attractive old towns, a genuine Mediterranean feeling and matching scenery. Long ago, **Monte Argentario** was an island, the closest of the Tuscan archipelago to the shore. No one can explain how it happened, but the Tyrrhenian currents gradually built up two symmetrical sandbars connecting the rugged, mountainous island to the mainland. In between, there was a peninsula with the Etruscan then Roman city of Orbetello; the Romans built a causeway on to Argentario that split the natural lagoon in half. It is said that sailors named the Argentario in classical times, noticing the bright flashes of silver from the olive trees that still cover its slopes.

Most books describe Porto Santo Stefano and Porto Ercole as 'exclusive'. The Argentario does attract its share of the high life, particularly the yachting crowd from Rome, and it's pricier than other resorts, but the peninsula has not become an overcrowded beach Babylon like Elba. The beaches are not special, and Tuscany's art and other attractions are far. On balance, though, the Argentario is a contender for the best place for a seaside holiday in the region.

## Orbetello

Go to the northern tip of the peninsula of Orbetello (population 13,500), near the causeway, and look over the water; below the modern breakwater are bits of ancient wall in huge irregular blocks – the sole remnants of Etruscan Orbetello, probably the biggest port on the Etruscan coast, and defensible enough to give the city a minor historical role over the centuries. The Byzantines held out longer here than anywhere else on this coast; the city then fell into the hands of the Three Fountains Abbey in Rome, who handed it to

# Getting around the Monte Argentario

**Orbetello** is the centre for public transport around the Argentario, with a bus station just off Piazza della Repubblica. There are regular **buses** for Porto Ercole, Porto S. Stefano, Grosseto for and the **train** station, about 2km east of town, on the Grosseto–Rome coastal line, plus daily buses to Capalbio and Pitigliano.

the pope – until 1980 the pope was also bishop of Orbetello. After the treaty of Cateau-Cambrésis in 1559, Orbetello became capital of a new province – the Spanish military Presidio, from which imperialist Spain could menace both Tuscany and the Pope, ruled by a viceroy directly responsible to the King. The Presidio lasted only until 1707 but had a strong impact on the area's buildings and its people.

Orbetello was briefly a resort but passed this role on to Porto Ercole and Porto Santo Stefano; its most recent flash of glory was in the 1930s, when Mussolini made it Italy's main seaplane base. Fascist hero Italo Balbo began his famous transatlantic flight from the lagoon in 1933, landing at the opening of the Chicago World's Fair.

Confined on its peninsula, with its palm trees and sun-bleached Spanish walls, this is a charming town, where buses barely squeeze through the main gate. Viale Italia, the main street, runs down the centre of the peninsula; just north on Piazza della Repubblica, is the **cathedral** with a sculpted portal and rose window from 1376.

**Laguna di Orbetello**

*visitor centre: coast road between Orbetello and Albinia, **t** 0564 820297; open for guided tours Oct–April (outside nesting period) Thurs, Sat and Sun 10 and 3; adm*

Orbetello's **lagoons**, on average about 90cm deep, are partly used for fish farms, but most of the north half has been declared a **WWF nature reserve**. Like the Monti dell'Uccellina, the area is a breeding ground for marine birds, and also storks and a species of eagle, not to mention the stilt plover, bee-eater and lesser hen harrier.

## Porto Ercole and Porto Santo Stefano

Over the causeway from Orbetello on to Monte Argentario, you can go north or south to begin the *gita panoramica*, the 24km road that circles the island (it offers some exceptional views, but it's not surfaced the whole way and you won't get round without a Jeep).

South, **Porto Ercole** wraps itself around a yacht-filled harbour, guarded by Spanish fortresses. Forte Stella and Forte San Filippo were probably the last word in 16th-century military architecture, with low, sloping walls and pointed bastions draped over the cliffs; today they are an ominous, surreal sight. San Filippo is the more interesting, though you can't visit – it's been converted to holiday apartments. Above the souvenir shops and seafood restaurants of the harbour is a fine old town, entered through a Gothic gate built by the Sienese. Piazza Santa Barbara has the dignified 17th-century **palace** of the Spanish governor, and a view over the harbour. Caravaggio was buried in the church of **Sant'Erasmo** in 1609 after dying of malaria in a tavern nearby, on his way back from Malta to Rome, where he'd hoped the pope would pardon him for a murder committed years before.

Beyond Porto Ercole, the coast road twists and turns under the slopes of **Il Telegrafo**, Argentario's highest peak (2,083ft/635m). One feature of the *gita panoramica* is the many defence towers, some built by the Sienese, others by the Spaniards.

On the northern side of the Argentario, **Porto Santo Stefano** makes a matching bookend for Porto Ercole. Larger than its sister town, this also began as a sleepy fishing village. Now the fishing boats are elbowed off to the side of the port by speedboats, shiny yachts and the Giglio ferries, and the old town is lost in the agglomeration of hotels and villas on the surrounding hills. However, it remains less exclusive than Porto Ercole and more of a real community than an exclusive yachting port. There are really two harbours: the first, larger one has the ferries and fish markets; the yachts – some real dreadnoughts – call at the western harbour.

The spits of land joining Argentario to the mainland are made up of two long beaches, the **Giannella** and the **Feniglia**. The latter is backed by a beautiful protected pine forest (a nature reserve) with a path along it. You can hire bikes and ride the 7km of its length, branching on to the beach at various points. The Giannella is backed by the main road but faces west, so you get lovely sunsets.

## Where to Stay and Eat in the Monte Argentario

ⓘ **Orbetello >**
*Piazza della Repubblica,*
*t 0564 860447*

★ **San Biagio Relais >**

★ **I Pescatori >**

### Orbetello ✉ 58035

***Hotel Relais Presidi**, Via Mura di Levante 34, **t** 0564 867601, *www.ipresidi.com* (€€€€). Lagoon views, a restaurant and a beautiful American bar. Most rooms have balconies.

***San Biagio Relais**, Via Dante 34, **t** 0564 860543, *www.sanbiagiorelais.com* (€€€€). A classy hotel in an elegant *palazzo* in the centre, with comfortable rooms and suites, a gym and fitness centre, and a restaurant. There's a minimum two-night stay in high season. Rates include breakfast.

***Piccolo Parigi**, Corso Italia 169, **t** 0564 867233 (€€). A delightful, very friendly spot with a Mediterranean feel. Breakfast is included.

**Osteria del Lupacante**, Corso Italia 103, **t** 0564 867618 (€€). Wonderful fresh seafood, including risotto with shrimps and pine nuts, and mussels with Marsala wine. *Closed Tues in winter, and 3wks Dec/Jan.*

**I Pescatori**, Via Leopardi 9, **t** 0564 860611 (€€). A simple restaurant run by the local fishermen's cooperative, serving only fish caught in the lagoon, on plastic plates from a self-service counter. Try *bottarga d'Orbetello* (tuna eggs), smoked eels, or grilled lake fish. *Closed lunch, Mon–Thurs eves in winter.*

### Porto Ercole ✉ 58018

****Il Pellicano**, Sbarcatello (cove near Porto Ercole), **t** 0564 858111, *www.pellicanohotel.com* (€€€€€). A Relais et Châteaux hotel popular with yachtsmen and Italian TV stars, with a beach, a pool, watersports, tennis and two fish restaurants, plus golf nearby. Half-board obligatory mid-June–Sept.

****Torre di Calapiccola**, **t** 0564 825111, *www.torredicalapiccola.com* (€€€€€). An apartment complex perched spectacularly above the sea, with a beach, a pool and lots of activities. *Closed late-Oct–Mar.*

***Don Pedro**, Via Panoramica, **t** 0564 833914, *www.hoteldonpedro.it* (€€€). An option above the town, some way from the nearest beach, with a fish restaurant. Breakfast is included and half board available. *Closed Nov–Mar.*

***La Conchiglia**, Via della Marina 22, **t** 0564 833134 (€€). One of the few moderate places on Argentario proper, comfortable, with breakfast included.

**★ Osteria
I Nobili Santi >**

**ⓘ Porto Santo
Stefano >**

*Piazzale S. Andrea,
t 0564 814208*

**Osteria I Nobili Santi**, Via dell'Ospizio 8, t 0564 833015 (€€€). Elegant fish dishes in an elegant setting; try the *maltagliati* with squid and tomatoes. Booking is advisable. *Closed Mon, and lunch Tues–Sat in summer.*

**Porto Santo Stefano** ✉ **58019**

**\*\*\*Filippo II**, Loc. Poggio Calvella, t 0564 811611, *www.filipposecondo.it* (€€€€€). Plush suites and apartments with a restaurant, close to beaches.

**\*\*\*La Caletta**, Via Civinini 10, t 0564 812939, *www.hotelcaletta.it* (€€€€). Pleasant rooms overlooking the sea; rates include breakfast. Half- and full-board are available.

**\*\*Alfiero**, Via Cuniberti 12, t 0564 814067 (€€). A simple hotel by the harbour. Rates include breakfast.

**Dal Greco**, Via del Molo 1, t 0564 814885 (€€€). An elegant place on the harbour, serving great spaghetti with lobster. *Closed Tues in winter.*

**I Due Pini**, Loc. La Soda, on coast road into Porto Santo Stefano, t 0564 814012 (€€€). A stunning beachside setting for some of the best seafood in the area, including *spaghetti al nero di seppia*. There's live music at night.

**Da Orlando**, Via Breschi 3, t 0564 812788 (€€). A relaxed, lively place facing the islands. Try sea bream, black sea bass or lake bass. *Closed Wed.*

# Giglio and Giannutri

## Giglio

Giglio is the largest Tuscan island after Elba (about 21km by 8km). It is also second in population, with about 1,600 souls, almost all in its little villages: Giglio Porto, Giglio Castello and Giglio Campese. Like many Italian islands, Giglio suffered from deforestation and abandonment of the land in the 18th and 19th centuries. Though much of it remains green and pretty, large expanses are now almost barren. In latter years, however, a switch in environmental consciousness has occurred – there's no camping, no noise, no riding over the wildflowers, and no collecting rocks.

*Giglio* means 'lily', and the lily is the island's symbol, though it has nothing to do with its name. The Romans called it *Aegilium* or *Gilium*. Under them, Giglio, like most Italian islands, was a resort for the very wealthy. Pisa, Aragon and various feudal families held it in the Middle Ages. Duke Cosimo seized it for Tuscany in the 16th century but did little to protect it against its great danger, pirates. But the Giglians had the holy right arm of San Mamiliano to protect them. This 6th-century Sicilian bishop, fleeing Arian heretics, became a hermit on Montecristo. When he died, a divine signal alerted fishermen from Elba, Giglio and even Genoa, who arrived and began to fight over the remains. In the true tradition of Christian brotherhood they struck a deal and cut Mamiliano in three. Giglio got the arm, which proved its worth by chasing away Turkish pirates in 1799. On other occasions it wasn't so helpful. The redoubtable pirate Barbarossa carried off most of the population in 1534, and his understudy Dragut came back for the rest in 1550.

**Giglio Porto**, the island's metropolis, has red and green lighthouses, and pink and beige houses straggling up the hills. There are two beaches south of the town, at **Cala delle Canelle** and **Cala delle**

# Getting around Giglio and Giannutri

Porto Santo Stefano is the port for **Giglio** (1hr); **ferries** are run by TOREMAR (**t** 0564 810803, *www.toremar.it*) and Maregiglio (**t** 0564 812920, *www.maregiglio.it*), both in Porto S. Stefano. Boats run at least twice daily (more in summer). The **train** station (**t** 892021, *www.trenitalia.com*) for Porto S.Stefano, along the main Livorno–Rome line, is Orbetello Scalo; buses meet the trains to carry passengers to the port. On Giglio, **buses** run fairly regularly from the ferry dock to Giglio Castello and Giglio Campese.

**Giannutri** can be reached regularly only in July and August, on a daily boat from Porto S. Stefano.

**Caldane**, and one to the north at **Punta Aranella**; all are more or less developed. In the town itself is the world's smallest beach, tucked behind the houses on the left side of the port.

From Giglio Porto a difficult mountain road leads up to **Giglio Castello**, the only secure refuge in pirate days, and until recently the only real town. The fortress itself was begun by the Pisans and completed under the grand dukes. The picturesque town inside, all medieval alleys and overhanging arches, has plenty of gulls and swallows, a few German tourists, and a small Baroque church with an odd tower and the famous arm of San Mamiliano.

From Giglio Castello, a road leads south past **Poggio della Pagana**, the island's highest peak (1,633ft/498m), to Punta del Capel Rosso, at the southern tip, then back along the coast to Giglio Porto. The main road from Giglio Castello continues on to **Giglio Campese**, a growing resort with an old watchtower and a large sandy beach.

## Giannutri

Giannutri, the southernmost of the Tuscan islands, is a rocky crescent about 5km long, with little water and no fertile ground, and little history to speak of. The ancient Greeks knew it as *Artemisia*, the Romans as *Dianium*; perhaps the associations with the moon goddess came from the crescent shape. In Roman times it was an estate of the noble Ahenobarbus family; there are the substantial ruins of a **Roman villa** (1st century AD) near Cala Maestra, a popular destination among day-trippers from Porto Santo Stefano in summer. Though Giannutri has no permanent population, there is a tourist village and some holiday cottages near the well-protected bay, **Cala Spalmatoio**, on the eastern coast.

## Where to Stay and Eat on Giglio

**Giglio** ✉ 58012

**\*\*\*Campese**, Via della Torre 18, Giglio Campese, **t** 0564 804003, *www.hotelcampese.com* (€€€€). A good, modern beach hotel (half/full-board).

**\*\*Pardini's Hermitage**, Cala degli Alberi, **t** 0564 809034, *www.hermit.it* (€€€€). A little hotel in a quiet cove,

reached by boat. There are sports and nature activities, or just lie back and enjoy the sea and mountains. It's full- or half-board only in summer. The farm produes oil, wine, milk and meat. *Closed mid-Oct–Mar.*

**\*\*\*Arenella**, Via Arenella 5, **t** 0564 809340, *www.hotelarenella.com* (€€€). An option near the beach, with a pretty garden, a sauna, Turkish bath and gym, and a good restaurant. Rates include breakfast.

***Demo's**, Via Thaon De Revel 31, t 0564 809235, *www.hoteldemos.com* (€€€). A hotel right in the port, in a 1960s Miami Beach style. Breakfast is included, and there's a restaurant serving fish and seasonal specialities.

****La Pergola**, Via Thaon De Revel 30, t 0564 809051 (€€). A cosy little option; breakfast is included.

**Da Maria**, Via Casamatta 12, Giglio Porto, t 0564 806062 (€€€). A family-run trattoria with excellent seafood. *Closed Wed in winter and 3wks Jan.*

**La Margherita**, Via Thaon De Revel 5, Giglio Porto, t 0564 809237 (€€). One of the most popular seafood restaurants around the harbour, with a terrace on the beach. Booking is recommended. *Closed Mon.*

**Da Santi**, Via Marconi 20, Giglio Porto, t 0564 806188 (€€). An old-fashioned restaurant in the old town, run by a former ship's cook. Try the octopus, and sample local white wine, rarely on sale. It's tiny, so book ahead. *Closed Mon outside high season, and Feb.*

# Capalbio and the Tarot Garden

Back on the coast south of Orbetello, almost nothing is left of **Ansedonia**, destroyed by the Sienese in 1330: there's a beach, a few hotels, and an unusual Etruscan attempt to stop Cosa's harbour silting up – deep channels hewn from solid rock. Climb up to **Cosa**, settled by Romans in the 3rd century BC to keep an eye on the restless Etruscan cities – and maybe accelerate their decline by draining off trade. Cosa was sacked by Visigoths in the 5th century, but the ruins and small museum give a fair idea of the Roman city,.

Before the Via Aurelia (SS1) passes into Lazio, it skirts another World Wide Fund for Nature project, a nature reserve at the **Lago di Burano**. Though small, the lagoon attracts the same birds as the Monti dell'Uccellina and Orbetello lagoons; including, in summer, perhaps the only cranes left on the Italian mainland.

**Capalbio**, 6km inland, is one of the loveliest villages in southern Tuscany – a circular hilltop enclave built around a castle. Head a few kilometres east for the unsignposted **Tarot Garden**, the project of French artist Niki de Saint-Phalle (who died in 2002), known for her works at the Pompidou Centre in Paris, and for her *nanas*, colossal, brilliant figures scattered over Europe. In this garden, created for meditation, monumental sculptures represent the 22 key arcana of the Tarot – mad, brilliant works harking back to Gaudí.

**Lago di Burano**
*tours Sept–April Sun at 10 and 2.30; summer by advance booking on t 0564 898829; adm*

🔆 **Tarot Garden**
*turn off SS1 to Capalbio then right just before 1st petrol station; www.nikidesaintphalle. com; open April–mid-Oct daily 2.30–7.30; adm exp (free to groups in winter)*

# Over the Border

There are a few attractions on the way to Rome. The wealthiest Etruscan cities were here, so the finest painted tombs are on the north Lazio coast at **Tarquinia** and **Cervetri**. Inland are the remains of Etruscan **Vulci**; the fortress of Castello dell'Abbadia holds an Etruscan museum, and an Etruscan bridge spans the gorge.

**Tuscania** has two unusual early medieval churches in the style of medieval southern Italy. Further inland is a chain of lakes, including tranquil **Lake Vico**, and the city of **Viterbo**, once home to the popes.

# Siena

*Draped on its three hills, Siena is the most beautiful city in Tuscany, a flamboyant medieval ensemble of palaces and towers cast in warm, brown, Siena-coloured brick. Its soaring skyline, dominated by the blazing black and white banner of a cathedral and the taut needle of the Torre di Mangia, is its pride, yet the Campo, the very centre, is only four streets away from olive groves and orchards. The contrast is part of the city's charm: dense brick urbanity, neighboured by a fine stretch of long Tuscan farmland that fills the valleys within the city's walls.*

*Here art went hand-in-hand with a fierce civic desire to make Siena a world of its own, and historians go so far as to speak of 'Sienese civilization' when summing up the achievements of this unique little city.*

# 12

## Don't miss

*See map overleaf*

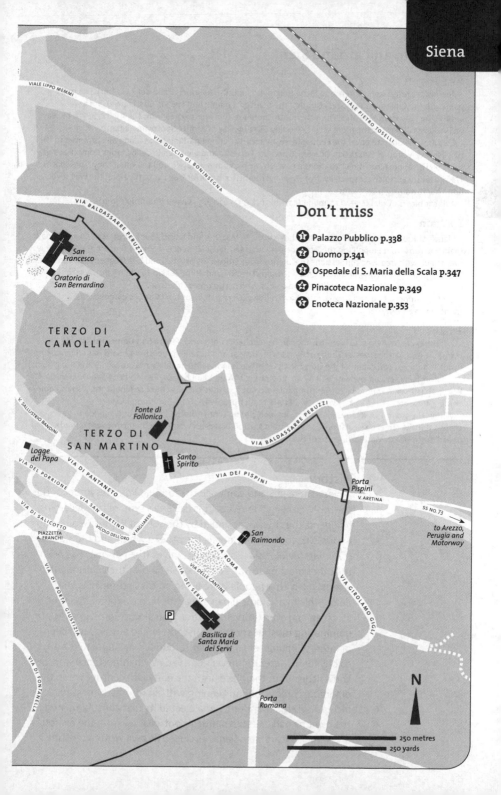

Siena

## Don't miss

1. Palazzo Pubblico p.338
2. Duomo p.341
3. Ospedale di S. Maria della Scala p.347
4. Pinacoteca Nazionale p.349
5. Enoteca Nazionale p.353

VIALE LIPPO MEMMI

VIALE PIETRO TOSELLI

VIA DUCCIO DI BONINSEGNA

VIA BALDASSARRE PERUZZI

San Francesco

Oratorio di San Bernardino

TERZO DI CAMOLLIA

V. SALLUSTRIO BANDINI

Fonte di Follonica

TERZO DI SAN MARTINO

VIA BALDASSARRE PERUZZI

Logge del Papa

VIA DI PANTANETO

Santo Spirito

VIA DEI PISPINI

Porta Pispini

V. ARETINA

VIA DEL PORRIONE

VIA DEL SALICOTTO

VIA SAN MARTINO

VICOLO DELL'ORO

V. PAGLIARESI

PIAZZETTA A. FRANCHI

San Raimondo

SS NO. 73

to Arezzo, Perugia and Motorway

VIA ROMA

VIA DELLE CANTINE

VIA DI PORTA GIUSTIZIA

VIA DEI SERVI

P

VIA GIROLAMO GIGLI

Basilica di Santa Maria dei Servi

VIA DI FONTANELLA

Porta Romana

N

250 metres
250 yards

# Getting to and around Siena

## By Car

The fastest route from Florence to Siena (68km) is the toll-free Superstrada del Palio (1hr). The most scenic are the Chiantigiana (SS222) through the heart of Chianti, and the Via Cassia (SS2); both weave amidst the hills. Both take 2hrs. From the south, there are two approaches from the A1: the SS326 by way of Sinalunga (50km) or the more scenic, winding SS73 by way of Monte Sansovino (44km).

Cars are forbidden to enter the centre; there are clearly defined **parking areas** along all entrances to the city, especially around Piazza San Domenico and the Fortezza and along Viale dello Stadio. Computerized signs on the approaches direct you to the city-run car parks and garages, and tell you if they have spaces. They're pretty expensive, especially if you stay overnight; look out for free car parks along the way if you don't mind walking a bit further.

Avis **car hire** is available at Via Simone Martini 36, **t** 0577 270305, *www.avisautonoleggio.it*.

## By Train

Siena's **station** is 1.5km from the centre down Viale G. Mazzini, and linked to it by frequent buses. Siena's main line runs from Empoli (on the Florence–Pisa line) to Chiusi (Florence–Rome). There are trains roughly every hour, with frequent connections to Florence from Empoli (97km/1hr), and less frequent ones to Pisa from Empoli (125km/2hrs), and from Chiusi towards Umbria and Rome (65km to Chiusi, 1hr). A secondary line runs towards Grosseto (70km/1hr) – 8 a day, of which 3 go on to Orbetello.

For train information and tickets, call **t** 892021 (*www.trenitalia.it*), or try Il Carroccio agency, Via Montanini 73, **t** 0577 226964.

## By Bus

Almost every town in southern Tuscany can be reached by bus from **Piazza San Domenico**, the big transport node on the western edge of Siena, with tourist and hotel info booths. A board has all departure times and the exact location of the stop; the ticket office is in the little building next to San Domenico church.

The company serving the whole of Siena province is TRA-IN, Viale F. Tozzi, just north of San Domenico, **t** 0577 204111, *www.trainspa.it*, Other companies depart for cities such as Florence (about 1hr; also to Rome, Perugia, Pisa, etc.; SITA, **t** 055 47821, *www.sitabus.it*). All buses leave from San Domenico.

Within the walls, TRA-IN runs a service using *pollicini* or 'Tom Thumbs': little buses designed to get around narrow streets. Regular buses to the train station and everywhere else in the modern suburbs depart from Piazza Matteotti, north of the Campo.

---

## History

Everywhere in Siena you'll see the familiar Roman symbol of the she-wolf suckling the twins. This is Siena's symbol too; according to legend, the city was founded by the sons of Remus, Senius and Ascius. One rode a black horse, the other a white, and the simple *comunal* shield of black and white halves (the *balzana*) has been the other most enduring symbol of Siena over the centuries. It is most likely that people were living on these three hills long before this mythological pair; excavations have found traces of Etruscan and even Celtic habitation. The almost impregnable site, dominating most of southern Tuscany, would always have been of interest. Roman-era *Sena Julia*, refounded by Augustus as a colony for his veterans, never achieved much importance, and we know little about the place until the early 12th century, when the emerging *comune* began keeping written records. In 1125, an increasingly independent Siena elected its first consuls. By 1169, the *comune* had wrested political control away from the bishop, and some 10 years later Siena developed its own written constitution.

The political development of the city is complex, with good reason. Twelfth-century Siena was a booming new city: having control over its rich countryside, supplying some of the best wool in Italy, helped start an important cloth industry, and a small silver mine, acquired from Volterra in the 1160s, provided seed capital for what became one of the leading banking towns of Europe. Like so many other Italian cities, Siena was able early on to force its troublesome rural nobles to live within its walls, where they built scores of tall defence towers, fought pitched battles in the streets and usually kept the city divided into armed camps; in the narrowest part of the city, the *comune* once had to lay out new streets parallel to Via Camollia because of one particularly boisterous nobleman whose palace most Sienese were afraid to pass. Yet Siena was never completely able to bring its titled hoodlums under control. The businessmen made the money, and gradually formed their city into a sophisticated self-governing republic, but the nobles held on to many of their privileges for centuries, giving an anachronistically feudal tinge to Siena's life and art.

Like its brawling neighbours, medieval Siena enjoyed looking for trouble; in the endless wars of the 13th century, they never had to look far. Originally a Guelph town, Siena changed sides early to avoid being in the same camp with arch-rival Florence. With Pisa, Siena carried the Ghibelline banner through the Tuscan wars with varying fortunes. Its finest hour came in 1260, when a Florentine herald arrived with the demand that Siena demolish its walls and deliver up its large population of Ghibelline exiles from Florence; if they didn't, the armies of Florence and the entire Guelph League – 40,000 men – were waiting outside to raze the city to the ground. The Sienese determined to resist. They threw the keys of the city on the altar of the as yet unfinished cathedral, dedicating Siena to the Virgin Mary (a custom they have repeated ever since when the city is endangered, most recently just before the battle for liberation in 1944). In the morning they marched out to the **battle of Monteaperti** and beat the Florentines so badly they captured their *carroccio*.

After the battle, Siena had Florence at her mercy and, naturally, was anxious to level the city and scatter the ground with salt. One of the famous episodes in the *Inferno* relates how the Florentine exiles, who made up a large part of the Sienese forces, refused to allow it. Unfortunately for Siena, within a few years Florence and the Tuscan Guelphs had the situation back under control and Siena never again came so close to dominating Tuscan affairs. Yet the city was a constant headache to Florence for the next three centuries.

When things were quiet at the front, the Sienese settled for bashing each other. The constant stream of anti-Siena propaganda in Dante isn't just Florentine bile; medieval Siena earned its reputation for violence and contentiousness. The impressive forms and rituals of the Sienese Republic were a façade concealing endless pointless struggles between the factions of the élite. Early on, Siena's merchants and nobles divided themselves into five *monti*, syndicates of self-interest that worked like political parties only without any pretence of principle. At one point, this Tuscan banana republic had 10 constitutions in 27 years, and more often than not its political affairs were settled in the streets. Before the Palio, Siena's favourite civic sport was the *Gioco del Pugno*, a 300-a-side fistfight in the Campo. Sometimes tempers flared and the boys would bring out the axes and crossbows.

## Siena's Golden Age

For all its troubles and bad intentions, Siena often ran city business disinterestedly and with intelligence. An intangible factor of civic pride always made the Sienese do the right thing when something important was at hand, such as battling the Florentines or selecting a new artist to work on the cathedral. The battle of Monteaperti was a disappointment territorially but inaugurated the most brilliant period of Sienese culture, and saw the transformation of the hilltop fortress town into today's beautiful city.

In 1287, under pressure from the Guelphs and their Angevin protectors, Siena actually allied itself with Florence and instituted a new form of government: the '**Council of the Nine**'. Excluding nobles from office, as Florence would do six years later, the Rule of the Nine lasted until 1355, and gave Siena a more stable regime than at any other period. Business was better than ever. The city's bankers came to rival Florence's, with offices in all the trading

## Ancient Rivals

Few rivalries have been more enduring than that between Florence and Siena. Long ago, while Florence was off at university busily studying her optics and geometry, Lady Siena spent her time dancing and dropping her scarf for knights at the tournament. Florence thought she had the last laugh in 1555, when Duke Cosimo and his black-hearted Spanish pals wiped out the Sienese Republic and put this proud maiden in chains. It's frustrating enough today, though, when Florence looks up in the hills and sees Siena, an unfaded beauty with a faraway smile, sitting in her tower like the Lady of Shalott.

For two towns built by bankers and wool tycoons, they could not have less in common. Siena may not possess an Uffizi or a David, but nor does it have to bear the marble antimacassars and general stuffiness of its sister on the Arno, nor her smog, traffic, tourist hordes and suburban squalor. Florence never goes over the top; Siena loves to, especially around the race of the Palio, the wildest party in Tuscany, a worthy successor to the fabulous masques and carnivals, bullfights and bloody free-for-alls of the Sienese Middle Ages. In fact, Florence has clicked its tongue at Siena since the time of Dante, who refers sarcastically in his *Inferno* to a famous club, the *Brigata*, made up of 12 noble Sienese youths who put up 250,000 florins for a year of nightly feasting; every night they had three sumptuously laid tables, one for eating, one for drinking and the third to throw out the window.

But there's more to Siena than that. This is a city with its own artistic tradition (*see* p.26); in the 1300s, Sienese painters gave lessons to the Florentines. Always more decorative, less intellectual than Florence, Siena fell behind in the quattrocento, but by then the greatest achievement of Sienese art was nearing completion – Siena herself.

centres and capitals of Europe. A sustained peace, and increasing cultural contacts with France and Naples, brought new ideas and influences into Siena's art and architecture, in time to embellish massive new building programmes such as the **cathedral** (begun in 1186 but not substantially completed until the 1380s) and **Palazzo Pubblico** (1295–1310). Beginning with Duccio di Buoninsegna (1260–1319), Sienese artists explored new concepts in painting and sculpture and, through the 1300s, contributed as much as or more than the Florentines in laying the foundations for the Renaissance. Contemporary records show an obsession on the part of bankers and merchants with decorating Siena and impressing outsiders.

At its height, in the early 14th century, Siena ruled most of southern Tuscany. The very pinnacle of civic pride and ambition came in 1339, with the fantastical plan to expand the still-unfinished cathedral into the largest in Christendom. The walls of that effort, a nave that would have been longer than St Peter's in Rome, stand as a monument to the event that snapped off Siena's career in full bloom. The **Black Death** of 1348 carried off a third of the population – a death toll perhaps no greater than in some other Italian cities, but it struck Siena at a moment when its economy was vulnerable, and started a decline that continued for centuries. Economic strife led to political instability, and in 1355 a revolt of the nobles, egged on by Emperor Charles IV, then in Tuscany, overthrew the Council of the Nine. In 1371, seven years before the Ciompi revolt in Florence, the wool workers staged a genuine revolution. Organized as a trade union of sorts, the **Compagnia del Bruco** seized the Palazzo Pubblico and instituted a government with greater popular representation.

The decades that followed saw Siena devote more and more of its diminishing resources to buying off the marauding mercenary companies that infested much of Italy. By 1399 the city was in such dire straits it surrendered independence to **Giangaleazzo Visconti**, tyrant of Milan, who was attempting to surround and conquer Florence. After his death, Siena reclaimed its freedom. Political confusion continued through the century, with only two periods of relative stability. One came with the pontificate (1458–63) of Pius II, the great Sienese scholar **Aeneas Silvius Piccolomini**, who exerted a dominating influence over his native city while he ruled at Rome. In 1487, a nobleman named **Pandolfo Petrucci** took over the government; as an honest broker, regulating the often murderous ambitions of the *monti*, he and his sons kept control until 1524.

## The Fall of the Republic

Florence, always waiting in the wings to swallow Siena, had its chance in the 1500s. The real villain of the piece, however, was not Florence but that most imperious emperor, **Charles V**. After the fall of the Petrucci, factional struggles resumed immediately, with frequent assassinations and riots, and constitutions changing with the spring fashions. Charles, who had bigger prey in his sights, cared little for the fate of the perverse little republic; he feared, though, that its disorders, religious tolerance and wretched finances were diseases that might spread. In 1530, he took advantage of riots in the city to install an imperial garrison. Yet even the emperor's representatives, usually Spaniards, could not keep Siena from sliding further into anarchy and bankruptcy several times, largely thanks to Charles's war taxes. Cultural life was stifled as the Spaniards introduced the Inquisition and the Index. Scholars and artists fled, while poverty and political disruptions meant that Siena's once-proud university ceased to function.

In 1550, Charles announced he was going to build a fortress within the city walls, for which the Sienese were going to pay. Realizing that the trifling liberty still left to them would soon be extinguished, the Sienese ruling class began intrigues with Charles's great enemy, France. A French army, led by a Piccolomini, arrived in July 1552. Inside the walls the people revolted and locked the Spanish garrison in its own new fortress. The empire was slow to react but inevitably, in late 1554, a huge force of imperial troops, along with those of Florence, entered Sienese territory. The **siege** was prosecuted with remarkable brutality by Charles's commander, the **Marquis of Marignano**, who laid waste much of the Sienese countryside, tortured prisoners and even hired agents to start fires inside the walls. After a brave resistance, led by a republican Florentine exile, **Piero Strozzi**, and assisted by France, Siena was starved into surrender in April 1555. Two years later, Charles's son Philip II sold Siena to Duke Cosimo of Florence and the republic was consumed by the new Grand Duchy of Tuscany.

If nothing else, Siena went out with a flourish. After its capture, some 2,000 republican bitter-enders escaped to make a last stand at Montalcino. Declaring 'Where the *Comune* is, there is the City', they established the world's first republican government-in-exile. With control over much of the old Sienese territory, the '**Republic of Siena at Montalcino**' held out against the Medici for four years.

With independence lost and a ruined economy, Siena withdrew. For centuries there was no recovery, little art or scholarship, and no movements towards reform. The aristocracy, decayed into a parasitic *rentier* class, made its peace with the Medici dukes early on; in return for their support, the Medici let them keep much of their power and privileges. The once-great capital of trade and finance shrank rapidly into an overbuilt farmers' market, its population dropping from a 14th-century high of 60–80,000 to around 15,000 by the 1700s. This explains largely why medieval and Renaissance Siena is so well preserved – nothing happened to change it.

By the Age of Enlightenment, with its disparaging of everything medieval, the Sienese seem to have forgotten their own history and art, so it is no surprise that the rest of Europe forgot them too. During the first years of the Grand Tour, no self-respecting northern European so much as considered visiting Siena. It was not until the 1830s that it was rediscovered, with the help of literati such as the Brownings, who spent several summers here, and later that truly Gothic American, Henry James. The Sienese were not far behind in rediscovering it themselves. The civic pride that had lain dormant for centuries yawned and stretched like Sleeping Beauty and went diligently back to work.

Before the 19th century was out, everything that could still be salvaged of the city's ancient glory was refurbished and restored. More than ever fascinated by its own image and eccentricities, and more than ever without any kind of economic base, Siena was ready for its present career as a cultural attraction, a tourist town.

## Orientation: *Terzi* and the *Contrade*

The centre of Siena (population 59,000), the site of the Palio and, importantly to the Sienese, the 'farthest point from the world outside', is the piazza called **Il Campo**. The city unfolds from it like a three-petalled flower along three ridges. It has been a natural division since medieval times, with the oldest quarter, the **Terzo di Città**, to the southwest; the **Terzo di San Martino**, to the southeast; and the **Terzo di Camollia**, to the north.

Siena is tiny, covering little more than 2.5 square kilometres. The density, and especially the hills, make it seem much bigger when you're walking. There are no short cuts across the valleys between the three *terzi*. There are few cars in the centre, but taxis and motorbikes will occasionally try to run you down.

### Contrade

The Sienese have taken the *contrade* – the 17 neighbourhoods into which Siena is divided – for granted for so long that their history is almost impossible to trace. Like the *rioni* of Rome, the *contrade* were the original wards of the ancient city – not merely geographical boundaries but self-governing entities; the ancients with their long racial memories often referred to them as the city's 'tribes'. In Siena, the *contrade* survived and prospered through classical times and the Middle Ages, maintaining the city's traditions and sense of identity through the dark years after 1552. Incredibly, they're still here now, unique in Italy and perhaps all Europe. Once Siena counted more than 60 *contrade*. Now there are 17, each with a sort of totem animal for its symbol, ranging from a snail to a dragon. Sienese and Italian law recognize these as legally chartered communities.

## The Palio

The thousands of tourists who come twice a year to see the Palio, Siena's famous horse race around the Campo, probably think the Sienese are doing it purely for their benefit. Yet, like the *contrade* that contest it, the Palio is an essential aspect of Sienese culture, as significant to the city today as it was centuries ago. Here are the plain facts on Italy's best-known annual festival.

The oldest recorded Palio was run in 1283, though no one knows how far the custom goes back. During the Middle Ages, besides the horse races there were violent street battles, bloody games of primeval rugby and even bullfights. (Bullfights were also common in Rome and there's an argument to be made that Italy is actually the place where the Spaniards got the idea, back in the 16th and 17th centuries when Spain's own medieval passion for such things was all but forgotten.) At present, the course comprises three laps around the periphery of the Campo, although in the past the race has been known to take in some of the city's main streets.

The *palio* (Latin *pallium*) is an embroidered banner offered as a prize to the winning *contrade*. Two races are held each year, on 2 July and 16 August, and the *palio* of each is decorated with an image of the Virgin Mary; after political violence, the city's greatest passion has always been Mariolatry. The course has room for only 10 horses per race, so some of the 17 *contrade* are chosen by lot each race so they all have a fair chance. The horses, too, are selected by lot, but the *contrade* select their own jockeys.

Though the race itself lasts only 90 seconds, an hour or two of pageantry precedes it; the famous flag-throwers or *alfieri* of each participating *contrada* put on dazzling shows, while the medieval *carroccio*, drawn by a yoke of white oxen, circles the Campo, bearing the prized *palio* itself.

The Palio is no joke; baskets of money ride on each race, not to mention the sacred honour of the district. To obtain divine favour, each *contrada* brings its horse into its chapel on race morning for a special blessing (and if a little horse manure drops during the ceremony, it's taken as a sign of good luck). The only rule stipulates that you can't seize the reins of an opponent. There are no rules against bribing opposing jockeys, making alliances with other *contrade* or ambushing jockeys before the race.

The course around the Campo has two right angles. Anything can happen; recent Palii have featured not only jockeys but *horses* flying through the air at the turns. The Sienese say no one has ever been killed at a Palio. There's no reason to believe them. They wouldn't believe it themselves, but it is an article of faith among the Sienese that fatalities are prevented by special intervention of the Virgin Mary. The post-Palio carousing, while not up to medieval standards, is still impressive; in the winning *contrada* the party might go on for days on end, while the losers shed bitter tears.

No event in Italy is as infectiously exhilarating as the Palio. There are two ways to see it, either from the centre of the Campo, packed tight and always very hot, or from an expensive (€130–260) seat in a viewing stand, but book well in advance if you want one of these. Several travel agencies offer special Palio tours (*see* pp.68–9); otherwise make sure you book by April.

Today a *contrada* functions as a combination of social-and-dining club, neighbourhood improvement association, religious confraternity and mutual assistance fund. Each *contrada* elects its own officials annually in May. Each has its own chapel, museum and fountain, its own flag and colours, and its own patron saint, who pulls all the strings he can in Heaven twice a year to help his beloved district win the Palio.

Sociologists, not only in Italy, are becoming ever-more intrigued by this ancient yet very useful system, with its built-in community solidarity and tacit social control. (Siena has almost no crime and no social problems, except a lack of jobs.) The *contrade* probably function much as they did in Roman or medieval times, but it's surprising just what up-to-date, progressive, adaptable institutions they can be, and they are still changing today. Anyone born in a *contrada* area, for example, is automatically a member; besides their baptism into the Church, they receive a sort of 'baptism' into the *contrada*, conducted in the pretty new fountains constructed all over Siena in recent years as centrepieces for the neighbourhoods.

The best place to learn more about the *contrade* is one of the 17 little *contrada* museums; the tourist office (see p.354) has a list of addresses (most ask visitors to contact them a week in advance), plus details of the annual *contrada* festivals and other shows and dinners they are wont to put on; visitors are always very welcome.

### Walking in Siena

If you keep your eyes open while walking the back streets of Siena, you'll see the city's entire history laid out for you in signs, symbols and scores of other clues. Little ceramic plaques with the *contrada* symbol appear on buildings and street corners, not to mention flags in the neighbourhood colours, bumper stickers on cars and fountains, each with a modern sculptural work, usually representing the *contrada*'s animal.

Look for the coats of arms of nobles above doorways; aristocratic, archaic Siena has more of these than almost any Italian city. In many cases, they are still the homes of the original families, and often the same device is on a dozen houses on one block, a reminder of how medieval Siena was largely divided into separate compounds, each under the protection (or intimidation) of a noble family. One common symbol is formed from the letters IHS in a radiant sun: Siena's famous 15th-century preacher, San Bernardino, was always pestering nobles to forget their contentiousness and vanity, and proposing that they replace their heraldic symbols with the monogram of Christ. The limited success his idealism met with can be read on the buildings of Siena today.

They don't take down old signs in Siena. One, dated 1641, informs prostitutes that the Most Serene Prince Matthias (the Florentine governor) forbids them to live on his street (Via di Salicotto). Another, a huge 19th-century marble plaque on the Banchi di Sotto, reminds passers-by that 'in this house, before modern restorations reclaimed it from squalidness, was born Giovanni Caselli, inventor of the pantograph'. A favourite, found on Via del Giglio, announces a stroke of the rope and a 16-lira fine for anyone throwing trash in the street, with proceeds to go to the accuser.

## The Campo

There is no lovelier square in Tuscany, and none more beloved by its city. The Forum of ancient *Sena Julia* was on this spot, and in the Middle Ages it evolved into its present fan shape. The Campo was paved with brick as early as 1340; the nine sections into which the fan is divided are in honour of the Council of the Nine (*see* p.332), rulers of the city at the time. Thousands crowd over the bricks every year to see the Palio run on the periphery.

For a worthy embellishment to their Campo, the Sienese commissioned for its curved north end the **Fonte Gaia** from Jacopo della Quercia, their greatest sculptor, who worked on it from 1408 to 1419, creating the broad rectangle of marble with reliefs of Adam and Eve and allegorical virtues. It was to be the opening salvo of Siena's Renaissance, an answer to the baptistry doors of Ghiberti in Florence (for which Della Quercia himself had been a contestant). What you see now is an uninspired copy from 1868; the badly eroded original is up on the loggia of the Palazzo Pubblico.

The republic always made sure each part of the city had access to good water; medieval Siena created the most elaborate engineering works since ancient Rome to bring the water in. Fonte Gaia, and others such as Fontebranda, are fed by underground aqueducts that stretch for miles across the Tuscan countryside. Charles V, when he visited the city, is reported to have said that Siena is 'even more marvellous underground than it is on the surface'.

The original Fonte Gaia was completed in the early 1300s; there's a story that, soon after, some Sienese citizens dug up a beautiful Greek statue of Venus signed by Praxiteles himself. The delighted Sienese carried it in procession through the city and installed it on top of their new fountain. With the devastation of the Black Death, however, the preachers were quick to blame God's wrath on the indecent pagan on the Fonte Gaia. Throughout history, the Sienese have been ready to be shocked by their own sins; in this case, with their neighbours dropping like flies around them, they proved only too eager to make poor Venus the scapegoat – they chopped her into little bits, and a party of Sienese disguised as peasants smuggled the pieces over the border and buried them in Florentine territory to pass the bad luck on to their enemies.

## Palazzo Pubblico

 **1** Palazzo Pubblico

If the Campo is like a Roman theatre, the main attraction on stage since 1310 has been the brick and stone **Palazzo Pubblico**, the enduring symbol of the Sienese Republic and still the town hall. Its façade is the face of Siena's history, with the she-wolf of Senius and Ascanius, Medici balls, the IHS of San Bernardino, and squared Guelph crenellations, all in the shadow of the **Torre di Mangia**, the graceful, needle-like tower Henry James called 'Siena's Declaration of Independence'. At 332ft (101m), the tower was the second-tallest raised in medieval Italy (behind the campanile in Cremona). At the time, the cathedral tower on its hill dominated Siena's skyline; the Council of the Nine wouldn't accept that the symbol of religious authority or any of the nobility's fortress-skyscrapers should be

**Torre di Mangia**
*t 0577 226230; open daily Mar–mid-Oct 10–7; mid-Oct–Feb 10–4; adm; joint adm available with Musei Comunali, see opposite*

taller than the symbol of the republic, so its Perugian architects, Muccio and Francesco di Rinaldo, made sure it would be hard to beat. There was a practical side to it, too. At the top hung the *comune*'s great bell, which had to be heard in every corner of the city tolling the hours and announcing the curfew, or calling citizens to assemble in case of war or emergency. One of the first bell-ringers gave the tower its name: fat, sleepy Mangiaguadagni ('eat the profits'), Mangia for short; there is a statue of him in one of the courtyards. Climb the tower's endless staircase for the definitive view of Siena – on the clearest days, you'll see about half of the medieval republic's territory. At the foot of the tower, the marble **Cappella della Piazza**, with its graceful rounded arches, stands out clearly from the Gothic earnestness of the rest of the building. It was begun in 1352, in thanks for deliverance from the Black Death, but not completed until the mid 15th century.

**Musei Comunali**
*t 0577 226230;
open 16 Mar–Oct
daily 10–7; 1 Nov–16 Nov
and 16 Feb–15 Mar
daily 10–6.30;
26 Nov–22 Dec and
7 Jan–15 Feb daily
10–5.30; 23 Dec–6 Jan
daily 10–6.30; adm;
joint 2-day adm
available with Palazzo
delle Papesse, see p.341,
and Ospedale di Santa
Maria della Scala,
see p.347*

Most of the Palazzo's ground floor is still city offices, but the upper floors house the city museum, the **Musei Comunali**. Here the main attraction is the state rooms done in frescoes, a sampling of the best of Sienese art throughout the centuries. First, though, come the historical frescoes in the **Sala del Risorgimento**, done by A.G. Cassioli in 1886: the meeting of Vittorio Emanuele II with Garibaldi, his coronation, portraits, epigrams of past patriots and an 'allegory of Italian Liberty', all in a colourful, photographically precise style. Next, on the same floor, the **Sala di Balia** has frescoes depicting the life of Alessandro VII, vigorous battle scenes by the Sienese Spinello Aretino (1300s) and the *Sixteen Virtues* by Martino di Bartolomeo. The adjoining **Anticamera del Concistoro** has a lovely *Madonna and Child* by Matteo di Giovanni. In the **Sala del Concistoro**, Gobelin tapestries adorn the walls, while the great Sienese Mannerist Beccafumi contributed a ceiling of frescoes in the 1530s celebrating the political virtues of antiquity; that theme is continued in the **vestibule to the chapel**, with portraits of ancient heroes from Cicero to Judas Maccabeus, all by Taddeo di Bartolo. These portrayals, plus more portraits of the classical gods and goddesses and an interesting view of ancient Rome, bear witness to a real fascination with antiquity even in the 1300s. Intruding among the classical crew is a king-sized St Christopher covering an entire wall; before setting out on a journey, it was good luck to catch a glimpse of this saint, and in Italy and Spain he is often extra large so you won't miss him. In a display case in the hall, some of the oldest treasures of the Sienese Republic are kept: the war helmet of the Captain of the People, and a delicate **golden rose**, a gift to the city from the Sienese Pope, Pius II.

The chapel (**Cappella del Consiglio**) is surrounded by a lovely wrought-iron grille by Jacopo della Quercia; when it is open, you can see more frescoes by Taddeo di Bartolo, an altarpiece by

Il Sodoma and exceptional carved wood seats by Domenico di Nicolò (*c.* 1415–28). In the adjacent chamber (**Sala del Mappamondo**), only the outline is left of Lorenzetti's cosmological fresco, a diagram of the universe including all the celestial and angelic spheres, much like the one in the Campo Santo at Pisa. Above it is a very famous fresco by Simone Martini (*c.* 1330), showing the redoubtable *condottiere* **Guidoriccio da Fogliano** on his way to attack the castle of Montemassi, during a revolt against Siena. Also by Martini is an enthroned Virgin or *Maestà*, believed to be his earliest work (1315).

## The Allegories of Good and Bad Government

When you enter the **Sala dei Nove** (or Sala della Pace), meeting room of the Council of the Nine, you understand at a glance why they ruled Siena so well. Whenever one of the councillors had the temptation to skim some cream off the top, or pass a fat contract over to his brother-in-law, or tighten the screws on the poor by raising the salt tax, he had only to look up at Ambrogio Lorenzetti's great frescoes to feel like a worm. There are two complementary sets, with scenes of Siena under good government and bad, and allegorical councils of virtues or vices for each. Enthroned Justice rules the good Siena, with such counsellors as Peace, Prudence and Magnanimity; bad Siena groans under the thumb of one nasty piece of work, sneering, fanged Tyranny and his cronies: Pride, Vainglory, Avarice and Wrath, among others. The good Siena is a happy place, with buildings in good repair, well-dressed folk dancing in the streets, and well-stocked shops. Bad Siena is almost a mirror image, except that the effects of the Tyrant's rule are plain to see: urban blight, crime in broad daylight, buildings crumbling, and business bad for everybody – a landscape that for many of us modern city-dwellers will seem all too familiar. Lorenzetti finished his work, probably the most ambitious secular painting attempted up to that time, around 1338. Fittingly, Good Government has survived more or less intact, while Bad Government has not aged so well and parts have been lost.

In the next room is Guido da Siena's large *Madonna and Child* (mid-1200s), the earliest masterpiece of the Sienese school. If you're not up to climbing the tower, take the long, unmarked stairway by the Sala del Risorgimento up to the **loggia**, with the second-best view over Siena and disassembled pieces of Della Quercia's reliefs from the Fonte Gaia, worn and damaged.

## Around the Campo

Part of the Campo's beauty lies in the element of surprise; one usually enters from narrow arcades between the medieval palaces that give no hint of what lies on the other side. Two of Siena's three main streets form a graceful curve around the back of the Campo;

where they meet the third, behind the Fonte Gaia, is the corner the Sienese call the **Croce del Travaglio** (a mysterious nickname: the 'Cross of Affliction'). Here, the three-arched **Loggia della Mercanzia**, in a sense Siena's Royal Exchange, was where the republic's merchants made their deals and settled their differences before the city's famed commercial tribunal. The Loggia marks the transition from Sienese-Gothic to early Renaissance style – begun in 1417, it was probably influenced by Florence's Loggia dei Lanzi. The five statues of saints on the columns are the work of Antonio Federighi and Vecchietta, the leading Sienese sculptors after Della Quercia.

The three streets that meet here lead directly into the three *terzi* of Siena. All three are among the city's most beautiful, in particular the gracefully curving **Banchi di Sotto**, main artery of the Terzo di San Martino. Just beyond the Campo, this street passes Siena's most imposing *palazzo privato*, the **Palazzo Piccolomini**, done in the Florentine style by Rossellino in the 1460s. This palace houses the old **Sienese state archive** – not a place you might consider visiting but for the presence of the famous *Tavolette della Biccherna* (the account books of the Biccherna or state treasury). From the 1200s, the republic commissioned the best local artists to decorate the covers of the *tavolette*, portraying such prosaic subjects as medieval citizens coming to pay their taxes, city employees counting their pay and earnest monks trying to make the figures square. Among other manuscripts and documents are Boccaccio's will.

**Palazzo Piccolomini**
*t 0577 247145; state archive open for visits at 9.30, 10.30 and 11.30; adm*

## Terzo di Città

Southwest from the Croce del Travaglio, Via di Città climbs up to the highest and oldest part of Siena, the natural fortress of the Terzo di Città. Among the palaces that it passes is the grandiose **Palazzo Chigi-Saracini**, home to internationally important music school, the Accademia Musicale Chigiana, and a large collection of Sienese and Florentine art .

**Palazzo Chigi-Saracini**
*open to public limited times of year; call t 0577 246928 for info*

Next door is yet another reminder of the Piccolomini, the **Palazzo delle Papesse**, now home to the **Centro Arte Contemporanea**, with permanent and changing exhibitions of modern works. The Piccolomini family, along with the Colonna of Rome and Correr of Venice, was one of the first to really exploit the fiscal possibilities of the papacy; Aeneas Silvius (Pius II) built this palace, also designed by Rossellino, for his sister, Caterina.

**Centro Arte Contemporanea**
*Via di Città 126, t 0577 224820; open Tues–Sun 11–7; adm; joint 2-day adm available with Musei Comunali, see p.339, and Santa Maria della Scala, see p.347*

### The Duomo

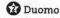 **Duomo**

All approaches from Via di Città to Siena's glorious cathedral, spilling over the highest point in the city, are oblique. Easiest, perhaps, is Via dei Pellegrini, which winds around the back, past the unusual crypt-baptistry tucked underneath (*see* p.347), up the steps

**Duomo**
*t 0577 283048,
www.operaduomo.
siena.it; open Mar–May
and Sept–Oct Mon– Sat
10.30–7.30 and Sun
1.30–5.30; June–Sept
Mon–Sat 10.30–8, Sun
1.30–6.30; Nov–Feb
Mon–Sat 10.30–6.30,
Sun 1.30–5.30; adm*

to the Piazza del Duomo, and through a portal in a huge, freestanding wall of striped marble arches, a memorial to that incredible ill-starred 1339 rebuilding plan confounded by the Plague. The cathedral the Sienese had to settle for may not be a transcendent expression of faith, and it may not be a landmark in architecture, but it is one of the most delightful, decorative ornaments in Christendom.

Begun around 1200, and one of the first Gothic cathedrals in central Italy, it started in the good medieval tradition as a communal effort, not really a project of the Church. There doesn't seem to have been much voluntary labour – even in the Middle Ages, Italians were too blasé for that – but every citizen with a cart was expected to bring two loads of marble from the quarries each year, earning him an indulgence from the bishop. One load must have been white and the other black for, under the influence of Pisa, the Sienese built themselves one thoroughly striped cathedral – stripes darker and bolder than Pisa's or even Pistoia's. The campanile, with its distinctive fenestration, narrowing in size down six levels, rises over the city like a giant ice-cream parfait. Most of the body of the church was finished by 1270; 14 years later, Giovanni Pisano was called in to create the sculpture for the lavish **façade**, with statues of biblical prophets and pagan philosophers. The upper half was not begun until the 1390s, and the glittering mosaics in the gables are, like Orvieto's, the work of Venetian artists of the late 19th century.

## The Cathedral Interior: the Marble Pavement

This is a virtual treasure box, fit to keep a serious sightseer busy for an entire day. Inside the main portal, the ferociously striped pilasters and Gothic vaulting, a blue firmament painted with golden stars, draw the eye upwards. The most spectacular feature, though, is at your feet – the marble pavement, where the first peculiar figure smiling up at you is **Hermes Trismegistus** (*see* p.344), legendary Egyptian father of alchemy, depicted in elegant *sgraffito* work of white and coloured marble. In fact, the entire floor of the cathedral is covered with almost 12,000 square metres of virtuoso *sgraffito* in 56 scenes, including portraits, mystical allegories and Old Testament scenes. Like the Biccherna covers in the Palazzo Piccolomini, they were a tradition carried on over centuries. Many of Siena's best artists worked on them, from 1369 into the 1600s; Vasari claimed that Duccio di Buoninsegna himself first worked in this medium, though he has none among the pictures here.

Even in a building with so many marvels – the Piccolomini Library, Nicola Pisano's pulpit, Duccio's stained glass, works by Donatello, Della Quercia, Pinturicchio, Michelangelo, Bernini and many others – this pavement takes pride of place. The greatest limitation of

Piazza San Giovanni

**Siena Cathedral**

Via Monna Agnese

Piazza
Jacopo della Quercia

Piazza
del Duomo

1 Pisano's Pulpit
2 Chapel of San Giovanni Battista
3 Tomb of Cardinal Pecci (Donatello)
4 Tomb of Cardinal Petroni (Tino da Camaino)
5 Stained glass of Duccio
6 High altar
7 Piccolomini altar (Della Quercia, Michelangelo)
8 Campanile
9 Sacristy
10 *Cantorie*
11 Choir
12 Piccolomini Library
13 *To cathedral museum*
14 Cathedral extension
15 Baptistry (lower level)

A *Hermes Trismegistus*
B *Allegory of Virtue*
C *Wheel of Fortune*
D *Massacre of the Innocents*
E *Judith Liberating Bethulia*
F *Seven Ages of Man*
G *Allegories of Faith, Hope and Charity*
H *Story of Absalom*
I *Emperor Sigismund on his Throne*
J *Sacrifice of Elias, Execution of the False Prophets*
K *Samson and the Philistines*
L *David the Psalmist*
M *Sacrifice of Abraham*
N *Moses Receives the Commandments*
O *Story of Jephta*

## Hermes Trismegistus

Hermes Trismegistus is rarely seen in art, though he is a mysterious protagonist in a great undercurrent of Renaissance thought. 'Thrice-great Hermes', mythical author of a series of mystic philosophical dialogues from the 2nd century AD, had a profound influence on Greek and Arabic thought, gradually becoming associated (correctly or not) with the Egyptian god Thoth, inventor of writing and father of a deep mystical tradition that continues up to this day.

The Hermetic writings were introduced in the West In the 1400s, thanks largely to Greek scholars fleeing the Ottoman conquest of Constantinople and Trebizond. These writings made quite a splash, prompting key figures to take action. So great was the impact that Marsilio Ficino, Florentine humanist and friend of Cosimo de' Medici, completed the first Latin translation of the Hermetic books in 1471 – Cosimo specifically asked him to put off translations of Plato to get this more important work finished!

To the men of the Renaissance, Hermes was a real person, an Egyptian prophet who lived in the time of Moses and may have been his teacher. They saw, revealed in the Hermetic books, an ancient, natural religion prefiguring Christianity and complementary to it – and much more fun than Christianity, for the magical elements in it were entirely to the taste of neo-Platonists such as Ficino. From a contemporary point of view, the recovery of Hermes Trismegistus was one of the intellectual events of the century, one that witnessed a tremendous revival of natural magic, alchemy and astrology.

The memorable Hermes in Siena is depicted surrounded by a bevy of 10 Sibyls: those of Cumae and Tivoli (the Italian contingent), Delphi, Libya, the Hellespont, Phrygia and others. These ladies, part of a pan-Mediterranean religious tradition even older than Hermes Trismegistus, are far more common in Tuscan religious iconography (as seen in the Baptistry and Santa Trinita in Florence, or most famously, on Michelangelo's Sistine Chapel ceiling), for the belief they all in some way foretold the birth of Christ.

Sienese art was always the conservatism of its patrons, accustomed to demanding the same old images in the same old styles. Commissions from the Office of Cathedral Works, controlled by the state, were usually more liberal, allowing the artists to create such unique and in some cases startling images, one of the greatest achievements of Renaissance Siena.

The *Hermes* on the cathedral pavement, by Giovanni di Stefano, was completed in the 1480s, a decade after Ficino's translation; he is shown with Moses, holding a book with the inscription 'Take up thy letters and laws, O Egyptians'. On either side, all 10 prophetic *Sibyls*, done by various artists at the same time, decorate the aisles. Nor are Hermes and the sibyls the only peculiar thing on this floor. Directly behind him begins a series of large scenes, including a *Wheel of Fortune*, with men hanging on it for dear life, another wheel of uncertain symbolism, and emblems of Siena and other Tuscan and Latin cities. Oddest of all is a work by Pinturicchio, variously titled the *Allegory of Virtue* or *Allegory of Fortune*; on a rocky island full of serpents, a party of well-dressed people has just landed, climbing to the summit, where a figure of 'Socrates' accepts a pen from a seated female figure, and another, 'Crates', empties a basket of gold and jewels into the sea. Below, a naked woman with a gonfalon has one foot in a boat, the other on land.

Many of the best scenes, under the crossing and transepts, are covered to protect them. The visionary works of Alessandro Franchi – the *Triumph of Elias* and other events in that prophet's life – and Domenico Beccafumi's *Sacrifice of Elias* and the *Execution of the*

*False Prophets of Baal*, are usually uncovered for a couple of months in late summer (*September and October; call the tourist office for confirmation*). Works uncovered all year include *The Seven Ages of Man* by Antonio Federighi, *Scenes From the Life of Moses* by Beccafumi, Matteo di Giovanni's *Massacre of the Innocents* (a favourite subject in Sienese art), and, best of all, the beautifully drawn *Judith Liberating the City of Bethulia*, a collaboration of Federighi, Matteo di Giovanni and Urbano da Cortona.

## Elsewhere in the Cathedral

Perhaps the greatest attraction above floor level is the great 1280s Carrara marble **pulpit** by Nicola Pisano. He started it directly after finishing the one in Pisa; one of the assistants he brought to help with the work was the young Arnolfo di Cambio. The typical Pisano conception is held up by allegorical figures of the seven liberal arts – more sibyls, prophets, Christian virtues and saints tucked in odd corners, and vigorous, crowded relief panels from the Passion as good as the ones in Pisa. Nearby, in the left transept, the **chapel of San Giovanni Battista** has frescoes by Pinturicchio and a bronze statue of *St John the Baptist* by Donatello, who also contributed the **tomb of Giovanni Pecci**, a 1400s Sienese bishop.

The **crypt** was rediscovered in 2000, a 13th-century space with walls painted with frescoes from between 1270 and 1280, now restored to their original glory.

Some of the **stained glass** in the cathedral is excellent, especially the earliest windows, in the apse, designed by Duccio, and the rose window with its cornucopia. Over the high altar is a bronze **baldachin** by Vecchietta, and in the north aisle the **Piccolomini altar** includes four early statues of saints by Michelangelo, and one by Torrigiano, the fellow who broke Michelangelo's nose and ended up in exile, working in Westminster Abbey. There is also a *Madonna* by Jacopo della Quercia.

Be sure to keep an eye out for details, such as the tiny, exquisite heads of the popes that decorate the clerestory wall. The Office of Works never settled for anything less than the best, and even such trifles as the holy water fonts, choir stalls, iron grilles and candlesticks are works of genuine artistic merit.

**Libreria
Piccolomini**
*t 0577 283048;
entrance off left aisle,
near Piccolomini altar;
open Mar–May Mon–
Sat 10.30–7.30, Sun
1.30–5.30; June–Aug
Mon–Sat 10.30–8, Sun
1.30–6.30; Sept and Oct
Mon–Sat 10.30–7.30,
Sun 1.30–7.30; Nov–Feb
Mon–Sat 10.30–6.30,
Sun 1.30–5.30; adm*

## Piccolomini Library

The **Libreria Piccolomini** is the room with the famous frescoes by Pinturicchio, built to hold the library of Aeneas Silvius, the greatest member of Siena's greatest noble family, who eventually became Pope Pius II. The very definition of a Renaissance man, he was probably the greatest geographer of his age – his works were studied closely by Columbus – plus a poet, diplomat and historian, founder of Pienza and important patron of artists and humanist scholars. During his busy clerical-political career, he worked fitfully to reform the Church of Rome and the constitution of his native city.

In 1495, 31 years after his death, Cardinal Francesco Piccolomini, who became Pope Pius III, decided his celebrated uncle's life would make a fine subject for a series of frescoes. He gave the job to Pinturicchio, his last major commission; among his assistants was the young, still impressionable Raphael, and anyone who knows his *Betrothal of the Virgin* will find these paintings eerily familiar. The 10 scenes include Aeneas Silvius' attendance at the court of James I in Scotland – a Scotland with a Tuscan fantasy landscape – where he served with an embassy. Later he is shown accepting a poet laureate's crown from his friend Emperor Frederick III and presiding over the meeting of Frederick and his bride-to-be, Eleanor of Aragon. Another fresco has him canonizing St Catherine of Siena. The last, poignant one portrays a view of Ancona, and its cathedral up on Monte Guasco, where Pius II went in 1464, planning a crusade against the Turks. While waiting for the help promised by the European powers, help that never came, he fell ill and died.

Art historians and critics, following the sniping biography of the artist by Giorgio Vasari, are not always kind to Pinturicchio. As with Gozzoli's frescoes for the Medici Palace in Florence, the consensus seems to be that this is a less challenging sort of art or perhaps just a very elevated approach to interior decoration. Certainly Pinturicchio seems extremely concerned with the latest styles in court dress and coiffure. However, the incandescent colour, fairytale backgrounds and beautifully drawn figures are irresistible. These are among the brightest, best-preserved of quattrocento frescoes; the total effect is that of a serenely confident art, concerned above all with beauty for beauty's sake, even when chronicling the life of a pope.

Aeneas Silvius' books have been carted away, but one of his favourite things remains: a marble statue of the *Three Graces*, a copy of the work by Praxiteles much studied by artists of the 1400s.

Around the side of the cathedral, off the right transept, Piazza Jacopo della Quercia is the name the Sienese have given to the doomed nave of their 1330s **cathedral extension**. All around this square, heroic pilasters and arches rise, some incorporated into the walls of later buildings.

## Museo dell'Opera Metropolitana

**Museo dell'Opera Metropolitana**
*t 0577 83048; open Mar–May, Sept and Oct daily 9.30–7; June–Aug daily 9.30–8; Nov–Feb daily 10–5; adm*

This museum, built into what would have been one of the cathedral transepts, is the place to inspect the cathedral façade at close range. Most of the statues on it are modern copies, replacing works of great sculptors such as Nicola Pisano, Urbano da Cortona and Jacopo della Quercia. The originals have been moved into the museum for better preservation, and there you can look the cathedral's remarkable marble saints in the eye. There are also architectural fragments and leftover pinnacles, and bits of the marble pavement that had to be replaced. On the first floor, a collection of Sienese paintings includes Duccio di Buoninsegna's masterpiece, the *Maestà* that hung behind the cathedral's high altar from 1311 to 1505. It's painted on both sides, with the main composition a Sienese favourite: the enthroned Virgin flanked by neat rows of adoring saints – with expressive faces and fancy clothes against a glittering gold background. Among the other paintings and sculptures are works by Pietro and Ambrogio Lorenzetti, Simone Martini, Beccafumi and Vecchietta.

On the top floor is the *Madonna dagli Occhi Grossi* ('of the Big Eyes') by an anonymous 1210s artist, a landmark in Sienese painting, and the original cathedral altarpiece. A hoard of golden croziers, reliquaries and crucifixes from the cathedral treasure includes another lovely golden rose from the Vatican – probably a gift from Aeneas Silvius. A stairway leads to the top of the **Facciatone**, the 'big façade' of the unfinished nave, with a view over the city.

## Baptistry

**Battistero**
*open Mar–May, Sept and Oct daily 9.30–7.30; June–Aug daily 9.30–8; Nov–Feb daily 10–5; adm*

Outside the unfinished cathedral nave, a long, steep set of stairs leads down around the back of the church to Piazza San Giovanni. In this lower but prominent setting, the Office of Works architects squeezed in a baptistry, perhaps the only one in Italy directly under a cathedral apse. Behind its unfinished 1390s Gothic façade, this contains yet another impressive hoard of art. It's hard to see anything in this gloomy cellar, though; bring plenty of coins for the lighting machines. Frescoes by Vecchietta, restored to death in the 19th century, decorate much of the interior. The crown jewel is the king-sized **baptismal font** with some of the finest sculpture of the quattrocento. Of the gilded reliefs around the sides, *Herod's Feast* is by Donatello, the *Baptism of Christ* and *St John in Prison* by Ghiberti. The first relief, with the *Annunciation of the Baptist's Birth*, is the work of Jacopo della Quercia, who also added the five statues of prophets above. Two of the statues at the corners of the font, representing the virtues Hope and Charity, are also by Donatello.

**🟊 Ospedale di Santa Maria della Scala**
*Piazza Duomo 2, t 0577 224811; open Mar–Nov daily 10.30–6.30; adm; joint 2-day adm available with Musei Comunali, see p.339, and Palazzo delle Papesse, see p.341*

## Ospedale di Santa Maria della Scala

Opposite the old cathedral façade, one entire side of the piazza is occupied by the Ospedale di Santa Maria della Scala. Believed to have been founded in the 9th century and for centuries one of the largest, finest hospitals in the world, it is now an exciting museum.

According to legend, the hospital had its beginnings with a pious cobbler, Sorore, who opened a hostel and infirmary for pilgrims on their way to Rome. Sorore's mother, it is said, later had a vision here of babies ascending a ladder (*la scala*) into heaven and being received into the arms of the Virgin Mary; consequently, a foundling hospital was soon added. Meticulous attention to the health of its citizens was always one of the most praiseworthy features of Siena; even in the decadence of the 1700s, advances in such things as inoculation were made here. In the 14th century, it insisted on such revolutionary practices as the washing of hands by doctors and nurses, meals adapted to each patient's illness, and the use of iron beds (to prevent the spread of bed bugs). To encourage donations, laws were passed allowing wealthy Sienese to deduct gifts from their taxes (remember, this was the 14th century) and not a few left huge sums in their wills; after the plague of 1348, the hospital was up to its ears in gold.

The Sienese say that their new museum, which is dedicated to all the arts and the city's history, will end up as one of the largest in the world, but don't ask when it will be finished; the point of this innovative exercise is that it will never be finished. The complex is conceived as a *cantiere didattico*, a kind of 'educational construction site', where the process of museum-building itself is part of the attraction. That said, many of the permanent exhibits should be in place in the next few years, along with shops, temporary exhibits and restoration workshops.

For now, it's worth the price of admission just to see the big frescoes in the **Sala dei Pellegrini**, the hospital's main reception hall. Another pioneering fresco cycle devoted to a secular subject, like those in the Palazzo Pubblico, this is a tribute to old Siena's advanced, humanistic outlook; all the scenes are devoted to the history of the hospital, including the vision of Sorore's mother and everyday views of the hospital's activities. In the best, Domenico di Bartolo shows how Sienese art was still keeping up with the Florentines in 1441 with his *Reception, Education and Marriage of a Daughter of the Hospital*; care of abandoned children, the *getatelli* ('little ones thrown away'), was one of the hospital's important functions. Other frescoes, by different Sienese artists, portray in loving detail the caring for the sick, the distribution of alms to the poor, and the paying of the wetnurses. They provide an insight into a side of old Siena you might not have thought existed.

There's also a collection of precious golden reliquaries and other church paraphernalia, some from medieval Constantinople, in refurbished chambers cheerfully marked *isolamento dei contagiosi*. Other original features include the **Cappella del Sacro Chiodo**, with damaged frescoes by Vecchietta, the elaborate **Cappella SS. Annunziata**, and the spooky **Cappella di Santa Caterina**, beginning with a leering skull and ending with an altarpiece by Taddeo di Bartolo. Old views and relics of the hospital are displayed in many of the long hallways; in some of the oldest, you see how the façade was covered with frescoes, by Pietro and Ambrogio Lorenzetti.

**Museo Archeologico**
*open summer daily 10–6; winter daily 10.30–4.30; joint adm with Santa Maria della Scala*

Another part of the complex houses the **Museo Archeologico**, with an Etruscan and Roman collection.

## The Piazza della Selva and Around

The ancient quarter of steep, narrow streets to the north of the cathedral is the *contrada* of the *Selva* (forest) – Rhinoceros country. At its heart, Piazza della Selva, one of the most charming of the new *contrada* fountains has a bronze statue of the neighbourhood's rhino symbol. Leaving the cathedral in the opposite direction, south down Via del Capitano, leads you into the haunts of the Dolphin and Turtle (*Onda* and *Tartaruga*).

**✪ Pinacoteca Nazionale**
*t 0577 281161; open Mon 8.30–1.30, Tues–Sat 8.15–7.15, Sun and hols 8.15–1.15; adm*

Where the street meets Via di Città, it changes its name to Via San Pietro, passing the 14th-century **Palazzo Buonsignori**, one of the most harmonious of the city's noble palaces, now home to the **Pinacoteca Nazionale**, the temple of Sienese art, with a representative sampling of this inimitable city's style. The collection is arranged roughly chronologically, beginning on the top floor with Guido da Siena and his school in the mid-13th century (Room 2) and continuing through an entire room of delicate, melancholy Virgins by Duccio and his followers, before reaching a climax with Duccio's luminous if damaged *Madonna dei Francescani* in Room 4. Madonnas and saints fill room after room, including important works by Siena's greatest 14th-century artists. One of the most famous is Simone Martini's *Madonna and Child*; the story goes that this *Madonna* was a great Palio fan. When everyone had gathered in the Campo for the event, she would wander out in the empty streets and tiptoe over for a look. One day, she lingered too long and had to run home, losing her veil in her haste. She has yet to find it, and according to the Sienese, weeps sweetly during the Palio, probably because she can't get through the Pinacoteca's security system.

Other Madonnas that stand out are those of Pietro and Ambrogio Lorenzetti (*Madonna Enthroned* and the *Annunciation*; Room 7) and Taddeo di Bartolo (*Triptych*; Room 11), with their rosy blooming faces and brilliant colour – a remarkable counterpoint to the relative austerity of contemporary painting in Florence. Evident in many of these paintings is Sienese civic pride; the artists take obvious delight in including the city's skyline and landmarks in the background of their works – even in Nativities.

Sienese Renaissance painters are well represented, often betraying the essential conservatism of their art and resisting the new approaches of Florence: Domenico di Bartolo's 1433 *Madonna* in Room 9; Nerocchio and Matteo di Giovanni of the 1470s (Room 14); Sano di Pietro, leading painter of the 1440s (Rooms 16–17). The first floor displays some of Il Sodoma's most important works, especially the great *Scourging of Christ* in Room

31 (1514); in Room 37 the *Descent into Hell* is one of the finest works by Siena's greatest Mannerist, Beccafumi.

### Around the Terzo di Città

Next to the Pinacoteca, **San Pietro alle Scale** contains *The Flight into Egypt*, an altarpiece by Rutilio Manetti, the only significant Sienese painter of the Baroque era, a follower of Caravaggio. **San Giuseppe**, off the end of Via San Pietro, marks Siena's uneasy compromise with the new world of the 1600s. One of the city's first Baroque churches, it was nevertheless built not in Baroque marble or travertine but good Siena brown brick. This is the church of the *Onda* (Dolphin) district; the *contrada*'s fountain is in front.

Around the corner, gloomy **Sant'Agostino** conceals a happier rococo interior of the 1740s by Vanvitelli, the Dutchman (born Van Wittel) who was chief architect for the kings of Naples. Most of the building dates back to the 13th century, however, and there are surviving bits of trecento frescoes and altarpieces all around.

Further west, the *contrada* of the Chiocciola (Snail) centres on **Santa Maria del Carmine**, a 14th-century church remodelled by Baldassare Peruzzi in 1517; inside is a painting of *St Michael* by Beccafumi and a rather grimly Caravaggiesque *Last Judgement* by an anonymous 16th-century artist.

## Terzo di San Martino

Beginning again at the Croce del Travaglio and Palazzo Piccolomini (*see* p.341), Banchi di Sotto leads into the quiet eastern third of the city, passing the **Logge del Papa**, a Renaissance ornament given to Siena by Aeneas Silvius Piccolomini in 1462. The most intriguing parts of this neighbourhood are on the hillside behind Piazza del Mercato: old streets on slopes and stairs in the *contrada* of the *Torre* (Elephant). Although they haven't won a Palio in decades, they have a fine fountain with their elephant-and-tower emblem on pretty Piazzetta Franchi. One of the most typical streets in this part of town is **Via dell'Oro**, an alley of overhanging medieval houses much like the ones in the Palazzo Pubblico's frescoes of Good and Bad Government (*see* p.340). **Via Porta Giustizia** leads you on a country ramble within the city's walls, along the valley that separates the Terzo San Martino from the Terzo di Città.

Among noteworthy churches in this *terzo* are **Santo Spirito** on Via dei Pispini, with further frescoes by Il Sodoma in the first chapel on the right; and **Santa Maria dei Servi**, south on Via dei Servi in the *contrada* of *Valdimontone* (Ram). Here, in the north transept, is one of the earliest, finest Sienese nativities, the altarpiece in the second north chapel, by Taddeo di Bartolo. Good paintings include a *Madonna* by Coppo di Marcovaldo and the *Madonna del Popolo* by

Lippo Memmi. An interesting comparison can be made between two versions of that favourite Sienese subject, the *Massacre of the Innocents*: one from the early trecento by Pietro Lorenzetti, another from 1491 by Matteo di Giovanni.

**Società Esecutori Pie Disposizioni**
*Via Roma 7, t 0577 284300; open Mon and Fri 9–1, Tues and Thurs 3–5.30, but call ahead*

Nearby, the **Società Esecutori Pie Disposizioni** has an **oratory** and a small but good collection of Sienese art. This *terzo* also has two of the best surviving city gates, the **Porta Romana** at the end of Via Roma, and the elegant **Porta Pispini** on the road to Perugia, with traces of a *Nativity* by Sodoma.

## Terzo di Camollia

Leading north from the Campo, the **Via Banchi di Sopra**, lined with the palaces of the medieval Sienese élite, forms the spine of this largest and most populous of the *terzi*. The first important palace is also one of the oldest: that of the Tolomei family, a clan of noble bankers who liked to trace their ancestry back to the Greek Ptolemies of Hellenistic-era Egypt. The **Palazzo Tolomei**, begun in 1208, is the soul of Sienese Gothic; it gave its name to Piazza Tolomei in front, the space used by the republic for its assembly meetings before the construction of the Palazzo Pubblico.

A few blocks down Banchi di Sopra, **Palazzo Salimbeni** on Piazza Salimbeni was the compound of the Tolomeis' mortal enemies; their centuries-long vendetta dragged Sienese politics into chaos on more than a few occasions. With the two adjacent palaces on the square, the Salimbeni is home to the **Monte dei Paschi di Siena**, founded by the city as a pawnshop in 1472, now a remarkable savings bank with a medieval air that has a tremendous influence over everything that happens in southern Tuscany, and branches as far away as Australia – they also have a good art collection, sometimes open to the public along with special exhibitions.

East of these palaces, in the neighbourhood of the *Giraffa* (Giraffe), is one of the last important churches built in Siena, the proto-Baroque **Santa Maria di Provenzano** (1594), at the end of Via del Moro. This particular Virgin Mary, a terracotta image said to have been left by St Catherine (*see* p.352), has had one of the most popular devotional cults in Siena since the 1590s; the annual Palio is in her honour.

The quiet streets behind the church, Siena's red-light district in Renaissance times, lead to **San Francesco**, begun in 1326, one of the city's largest churches. After a big fire in the 17th century, this great Franciscan barn was used as a warehouse and barracks. Restoration began in the 1880s and the 'medieval' brick façade was completed only in 1913. The interior is still one of the most impressive in Siena, a monolithic rectangle with vivid stained glass and good transept chapels in the Florentine manner. A little artwork has survived, including traces of frescoes by both Lorenzettis (north transept).

**Oratorio di San Bernardino**
*open mid-Mar–Oct daily 10.30–1.30 and 3–5.30; adm*

Next to San Francesco is the equally simple **Oratorio di San Bernardino**, begun in the late 1400s in honour of Siena's famous preacher and graced with his heart. Its upper chapel, a monument of the Sienese Renaissance, has frescoes by Beccafumi, Il Sodoma and the almost-forgotten High Renaissance master Girolamo del Pacchia.

The areas west of San Francesco, traditionally working class, make up the *contrada* of the *Bruco* (Caterpillar); their fountain is by the steps on Via dei Rossi. On the wall of the house opposite is an odd marble relief of a woman peering at a pomegranate from behind half-closed curtains. Caterpillars are everywhere. *Bruco*'s name recalls the Compagnia del Bruco, the trade union that initiated the revolt of 1371, temporarily reforming Siena's faction-ridden government. The workers paid a terrible price; while the revolution was underway, some young noble provocateurs started a fire that consumed almost the entire *contrada*. Today it is the unluckiest of the 'unlucky' neighbourhoods; it hasn't won a Palio since 1955.

## St Catherine, St Dominic and the Goose

Unlike the poor caterpillar, the equally proletarian *Oca* (Goose) seems the best organized and most successful *contrada*. On occasion during the Napoleonic Wars, with Tuscan and city governments in disarray, the *Oca*'s men took charge of the city.

**Santuario e Casa di Santa Caterina**
*Vicolo di Tiratoio; open daily 9–12.30 and 3–6*

The *contrada* stretches down steeply from Banchi di Sopra to the western city walls. At its centre, the **Santuario e Casa di Santa Caterina** includes the home of Caterina Benincasa (*see* box below) and her father's wool-dyeing workshop; each room is converted into a chapel, many with 15th- and 16th-century frescoes by Sienese artists. The adjacent oratory is now the *Oca*'s *contrada* chapel (note the goose in the detail of the façade).

### The Goose's Most Famous Daughter

Caterina Benincasa was the last but one of 25 children born to a wool-dyer, in 1347. At an early age the visions started; by her teens, she had turned her room into a cell, and, while she never became a nun, she lived like a hermit, a solitary ascetic in her own house, sleeping with a stone for a pillow. After she received the stigmata, like St Francis, her reputation as a holy woman spread across Tuscany; popes and kings corresponded with her, and towns sent for her to settle their disputes. In 1378 Florence was under a papal interdict, and the city asked Catherine to plead its case at the papal court at Avignon. She went, but with an agenda of her own – convincing Pope Gregory XI to move the papacy back to Rome where it belonged. As a woman, and a holy woman to boot, she was able to tell the pope to his face what a corrupt and worldly Church he was running, without ending up dangling from the top of a palace wall.

Talking the pope (a French pope, mind you) into leaving the civilized life in Provence for turbulent, barbaric 14th-century Rome is only one of the miracles with which Catherine was credited. Political expediency probably helped more than divine intervention – much of Italy, including anathemized Florence, was in revolt against the absentee popes. She followed them back and died in Rome in 1380, aged only 33. Canonization came in 1460, and in the 19th century she was declared co-patron of Italy (along with St Francis) and one of the Doctors of the Church. She and St Teresa of Avila are the only women to hold this honour – given in acknowledgement of their inspired devotional writings and their practical, incisive letters encouraging church reform.

Via Santa Caterina, the main street, slopes down towards the city walls and **Fontebranda**, a simple pointed-arched fountain of the 13th century that was an important part of Siena's advanced system of fountains and aqueducts. **San Domenico**, on the hill above Fontebranda, fails to impress close up from the bus depot on Piazza San Domenico, but from Fontebranda the bold Gothic lines of its apse and transepts give a great insight into the straightforward, strangely modern character of much Sienese religious architecture. Inside, the church is as big and empty as San Francesco; among the relatively few works of art is the only existing portrait of St Catherine, on the west wall, painted by her friend Andrea Vanni. In this church, scene of so many incidents from the saint's life, you can see her head in a golden reliquary. But the real attraction is the wonderfully hysterical set of murals by Il Sodoma in the **Cappella Santa Caterina**, representing the girl in various states of serious exaltation.

The open, relatively modern quarter around San Domenico offers a welcome change from the dark and treeless streets of this brick city, in a shady park, **La Lizza**, and the green spaces around the **Fortezza Medicea**. Though the site is the same, this is not the hated fortress Charles V compelled the Sienese to build in 1552; as soon as the Sienese chased the imperial troops out, they razed it to the ground. Cosimo I forced its rebuilding after annexing Siena, but to make the bitter pill easier to swallow, he employed a Sienese architect, Baldassare Lanci, and let him create what must be the most elegant and civilized, least threatening fortress in Italy. The Fortezza, a long, low rectangle of Siena brick profusely decorated with Medici balls, seems more like a setting for garden parties or summer opera than anything that was designed to intimidate a sullen populace.

The Sienese weren't completely won over; right after Italian reunification, they renamed the central space of the fortress **Piazza della Libertà**. The grounds are now a city park, and the vaults of the munition cellars the **Enoteca Nazionale**, the 'Permanent Exhibition of Italian Wines'. Almost every variety of wine Italy produces can be bought here, by the glass or bottle, and there's an annual *Settimana dei Vini* of regional wines (first half of June).

⭐ **Enoteca Nazionale**
*open Mon noon–8pm, Tues–Sat noon–1am; adm*

To the east of the fortress, beyond the Lizza and city stadium, lie the twin centres of modern Siena, **Piazza Gramsci**, the terminus for most city bus lines, and **Piazza Matteotti**.

Continuing north towards the Camollia Gate, you pass the little Renaissance church of **Fonte Giusta**, just off Via di Camollia on Vicolo Fontegiusta. Designed in 1482 by Urbano da Cortona, it has a fresco by Peruzzi (another sibyl) and a magnificent tabernacle over the main altar; there is also a whalebone, left, according to local legend, by Christopher Columbus.

**Porta Camollia**, in the northernmost corner of Siena, underwent the Baroque treatment in the 1600s. Here is the famous inscription 'Wider than her gates Siena opens her heart to you'. Old Siena was never that sentimental. The whole thing was added in 1604 – undoubtedly under the orders of the Florentine governor – to mark the visit of Grand Duke Francesco I, who wasn't really welcome at all.

# Peripheral Attractions

From Porta Camollia, Viale Vittorio Emanuele leads through some of the modern quarters outside the walls. Beyond the gate it passes a column commemorating the meeting of Emperor Frederick III and his bride-to-be Eleanor of Aragon in 1451 – the event captured in one of the Pinturicchio frescoes in the Piccolomini Library (*see* p.346). Next looms a great defence tower, the **Antiporto**, erected just before the Siege of Siena and rebuilt in 1675. Further down, the **Palazzo dei Diavoli** (1460) was the headquarters of the Marquis of Marignano during the siege.

There isn't much on the outskirts of the city – thanks largely to Marignano, who laid waste lovely and productive lands for kilometres around. Some 2km east (take Via Simone Martini from the Porta Ovile), in the hills above the train station, the **basilica and monastery of L'Osservanza** has been restored after serious damage in the last war. Begun in 1422, a foundation of San Bernardino, it retains much of its collection of 13th- and 14th-century Sienese art.

West of the city, the road to Massa Marittima passes through the hills of the Montagnola Sienese, an important centre of monasticism in the Middle Ages (*see* San Galgano, p.379). Near **Montecchio** (6km), the hermitage of **Lecceto**, one of the oldest in Tuscany, has been much changed but retains some Renaissance frescoes in the church and a 12th-century cloister. Close by, the **hermitage of San Leonardo al Lago** is mostly in ruins but the 14th-century church survives, with masterly frescoes (*c.* 1360) by Pietro Lorenzetti's star pupil, Lippo Vanni. Just outside the village of **Sovicille** 13km away is a 12th-century Romanesque church, the **Pieve di Ponte alla Spina**.

The village of **Rosia** (17km) has another Romanesque church. Just south is the Vallombrosan **abbey of Torri**, with much from its 1200s foundation, and a rare three-storey cloister with three types of column.

**Abbazia di Torri**
*open Mon–Fri 3.30–6*

ⓘ **Siena** >

*Piazza del Campo 56,*
*t 0577 280551, www.*
*siena.turismo.toscana.it,*
*www.terresiena.it,*
*www.benvenutein*
*toscana.it*

## Tourist Information in Siena

The tourist office sells 7-day **joint tickets** to the many of Siena's attractions (winter, €13; summer, €16).
**Post office**: Piazza Matteotti 37, t 0577 214295 (*closed Sun*).

## Shopping in Siena

Siena is blissfully short of designer boutiques and tourist trinkets. The back streets have lots of unpretentious artisan workshops, almost all so unconcerned with the tourist industry they don't bother hanging out a sign.

Antica Drogheria Manganelli,
Via di Città 71–73, **t** 0577 280002.
A gourmet treasure trove with its
original wooden shelving, crammed
with regional foods and wines.

⭐ **Relais La Suvera >>**

**Ceramics**, Via di Città 94. A wealth of
interesting pieces.

**La Fattoria Toscano**, Via di Città 51.
Gastronomic goodies.

**Libreria Senese**, Via di Città 62–64.
Siena's best bookshop.

**Morbidi**, Via Banchi di Sopra 73/75.
Picnic treats: cheeses, hams, salamis,
prepared dishes, wines and breads.

**Vetrate Artistiche Toscane**, Via Galluzza
5, off Piazza Indipendenza. Stained-
glass creations (mostly portable) in a
distinctive modern style. The artist
gives informal talks about his work.

## Market Days

There are markets round the Fortezza
and Via XXV Aprile on Wednesdays.

# Where to Stay

## Siena ✉ 53100

Much of Siena's best accommodation
is outside the walls or in the country
and needs to be booked well in
advance. If you come without a
reservation, head to the **Hotel
Information Centre**, Via Madre Teresa
di Calcutta 5, **t** 0577 288084,
*www.hotelsiena.com* (*closed Sun*).

⭐ **Palazzo Ravizza >>**

### Luxury (€€€€€€)

****La Certosa di Maggiano**, Strada
di Certosa 82, 1km southeast of city,
near Porta Romana, **t** 0577 288180,
*www.certosadimaggiano.it*. One of the
most remarkable establishments in
Italy, in a restored 14th-century
Carthusian monastery, with a pool,
tennis courts, beauty treatments, an
excellent restaurant serving local
cuisine (*see* p.356; half- and full-board
available by request), a library to make
antiquarians dream, a quiet chapel
and cloister, and a *salon* with
backgammon and chess.

*****Grand Hotel Continental**, Via
Banchi di Sopra 85, **t** 0577 56011, *www.
royaldemeure.com*. Rooms with fine
fabrics and antiques, public rooms
with original frescoes, a covered
courtyard with a winter garden, and a
sumptuous restaurant and wine bar.

***Park Hotel**, Via Marciano 18, **t** 0577
44803. A 16th-century building by
Peruzzi, on the hill that dominates
Siena, with pool, a tennis court, a
beauty centre, and Sienese cuisine.

*****Relais La Suvera**, Pievescola,
just north of city, **t** 0577 960300,
*www.lasuvera.it*. A medieval fort in
the Chianti hills, converted into a villa
for Pope Julius II, now a luscious
country hotel. Rooms are packed with
heirlooms; there's a pool, wellness
centre, restaurant and bar-terrace.

### Luxury–Very Expensive (€€€€€–€€€€)

****Villa Scacciapensieri**, Strada
Scacciapensieri 10, 3km north of city,
**t** 0577 41441, *www.villascacciapensieri.it*.
A quiet country house with spacious
rooms, glorious sunset views over
Siena, a pool and a good restaurant.

****Hotel Garden**, Via Custoza 2,
about 1km from city, **t** 0577 47056,
*www.gardenhotel.it*. A renovated 1700s
villa in a big garden, with antiques and
original frescoes, plus three annexes.
There is a pool, a good restaurant, an
American bar and a reading room.

### Very Expensive (€€€€)

***Duomo**, Via Stalloreggi 38,
**t** 0577 289088, *www.hotelduomo.it*.
A friendly, comfortably old-fashioned
place with some rooms overlooking
the Duomo and the Sienese hills.

***Palazzo Ravizza**, Pian dei Mantellini
34, near Porta Laterina just inside walls,
**t** 0577 280462, *www.palazzoravizza.it*.
An elegant 19th-century *palazzo* with
a lovely rear garden and a restaurant.

### Expensive (€€€€)

***Antica Torre**, Via di Fieravecchia 7,
**t** 0577 222255, *www.anticatorresiena.it*.
Siena's most popular small hotel, in a
restored 16th-century tower, with
marble floors, antiques and beams.

***Villa Liberty**, Viale V. Veneto 11,
**t** 0577 44966, *www.villaliberty.it*. An
elegant 'Liberty-style' villa near San
Domenico, in a peaceful garden, with
free Internet access in rooms, two of
which have private terraces. Breakfast
is included.

### Moderate (€€)

Many of Siena's 2- and 3-star hotels
are round the entrances to the city, but
there are some closer to the centre.

**Canon d'Oro**, Via Montanini 28, t 0577 44321, www.cannondoro.com. A hotel near the bus station, friendly and good value (breakfast is included).

****Il Giardino**, Via Baldassare Peruzzi 33, near Porta Pispini, t 0577 285290, www.hotelilgiardino.it. Highly recommended by readers, with good views and a pool. Breakfast included.

****Piccolo Hotel Etruria**, Via delle Donzelle 3, t 0577 288088, www.hoteletruria.com. A friendly, clean spot with rooms in the annexe opposite and two flats, plus a restaurant.

****Piccolo Hotel Il Palio**, Piazza del Sale 18, t 0577 281131, www.piccolohotelilpalio.it. Simple but comfy rooms in a quiet location a little way from the centre.

(star) Osteria
Le Logge >>

# Eating Out in Siena

Siena's eateries tend to serve simple dishes, washed down with something from three of Italy's greatest wine-producing areas (Chianti, Brunello of Montalcino, and Vino Nobile of Montepulciano), between which the city sits. The favourite pasta dish is *pici* – thick south Tuscan spaghetti served with a sauce of ground pork, pancetta, sausages, chicken breasts and tomatoes cooked with Brunello wine. As a university town, Siena is also a good place for snacks and fast food; try *ciaccino*, a variation on pizza.

The real speciality is sweets; visitors often find they have no room for a meal after repeated slices of *panforte*, a heavy but indecently tasty cake laced with fruits, nuts, orange peel and secret Sienese ingredients; or of *panpepato*, containing pepper.

Gastronomic tastings focusing on various regions of Italy are held at the Enoteca Nazionale (*see* p.353).

### Very Expensive (€€€€)
**Il Canto**, La Certosa di Maggiano, Strada di Certosa 82, t 0577 288180. Part of a luxury hotel (*see* p.355), offering modern *haute cuisine* served with some pomp – try gnocchi with lemon and cumin. *Closed Tues, Wed lunch, 1wk Dec, and 9 Jan–9 Feb.*

(star) Osteria
La Chiacchiera >>

### Expensive (€€€)
**Antica Trattoria Botteganova**, Strada Chiantigiana 29, few km northeast of Siena on SS408 to Montevarchi, t 0577

284230. Earthy meat dishes or more delicate fish options: try *tagliolini* with lemon and squid. *Closed Sun.*

**Compagnia dei Vinattieri**, Via delle Terme, t 0577 236568. A basement restaurant/*enoteca* with a vast choice of wines stored in a 14th-century cellar. There are snacks or excellent main dishes such as *tagliolini* with Tuscan herbs. *Closed Tues in winter.*

**Da Enzo**, Via Camollia 49, t 0577 281277. A traditional restaurant with a long, varied menu. *Closed Sun.*

**Osteria Le Logge**, Via del Porrione 33, t 0577 48013. One of the city's most pleasant places to eat; try spinach and ricotta ravioli with salmon, and chocolate *millefoglie*. *Closed Sun.*

**Osteria di Castelvecchio**, Via Castelvecchio 65, t 0577 49586. The old stables of one of Siena's oldest *palazzi*, with modern decor. It's a good place for veggie dishes. *Closed Tues.*

### Expensive–Moderate (€€€–€€)
**Guido**, Vicolo Pier Pettinaio 7, t 0577 280042. A traditional restaurant with a medieval feel. Booking is advised.

**Al Marsili**, Via del Castoro 3, t 0577 47154. Great Sienese fare, including green gnocchi with duck sauce and tomatoes. Book ahead. *Closed Mon.*

### Moderate (€€)
**Osteria di Ficomezzo**, Via dei Termini 71, t 0577 222384. Siena's oldest *osteria*, serving simple lunches and more inventive dishes for dinner. *Closed Tues.*

**La Torre**, Via Salicotto 17, t 0577 287548. A fun, lively place popular among students, offering good home-made *pici*, *ossobuco* and Florentine steak. *Closed Thurs.*

### Inexpensive (€€€€)
**Il Grattacielo**, Via dei Pontani 8, t 0577 289326. A popular student hangout serving simple cold meals and good wines. *Closed Sun.*

**Osteria La Chiacchiera**, Via Costa di Sant'Antonio 4, t 0577 280631. A tiny, friendly, trattoria serving excellent local dishes, including *tegamata* (pork casserole). There are outdoor tables for summer dining. Book ahead.

**Pizzeria Carlo e Franca**, Via Pantaneto 138, t 0577 284385. *Antipasti*, pizzas and *panini* not far from the centre. *Closed Wed.*

# Hill Towns
# West of Siena

In the late Middle Ages, this dramatically diverse, often rugged countryside was a border region, both culturally and politically, its people alternately subject to the strong pull of Florence and Siena. Its towns do not have that much in common: Poggibonsi is almost all new; Volterra goes back to the Etruscans. San Gimignano has its famous skyline of medieval skyscrapers, while parts of the Metal Hills show outlandish silhouettes of cooling towers from the geothermal power plants.

San Gimignano and Volterra, both beautiful cities containing remarkable works of art, are the main attractions. Massa Marittima, often overlooked, has one of the finest cathedrals in Italy.

Beyond that there is a doll-sized walled city, bubbling sulphurous pits, alabaster souvenirs, a Roman theatre, lonely moors and a sword in a stone (not King Arthur's but someone else's).

# 13

## Don't miss

**1** Medieval skyscrapers
San Gimignano p.362

**2** Etruscan relics and alabaster
Volterra p.368

**3** Whistling and puffing geysers and steam vents
Metal Hills p.375

**4** A spectacular cathedral
Massa Marittima p.377

**5** The sword in the stone
San Galgano p.379

*See map overleaf*

# Hill Towns West of Siena

To Pisa

Livorno

Montenero

Castiglioncello

S439

Casciana Terme

Montaione

S. Vivaldo

Certaldo

To Florence

Barberino
Val d'Elsa

S. Donato
in Poggio

Castellina
in Chianti

TUSCANY

S. Gimignano

Poggibonsi

Ulignano

Staggia

S206

S1

Montecatini
Val di Cecina

Balze

Volterra

Colle di Val d'Elsa

Saline di Volterra

S568

S429

S2

Monteriggioni

Quercegrossa

S222

R. Arbia

S408

Montescudaio

R. Cecina

Guardistallo

Cecina

S439

Casole d'Elsa

S541

Mensano

Siena

Montagnola

Sovicille

Montecolmo

S73

S223

Pomarance

Bolgheri

Castagneto
Carducci

Lago
Boracifero

Colline

Castelnuovo
di Val di Cecina

S439

Larderello

Radicondoli

Rosia

Torri

Metallifere

Chiusdino

Palazzetto

Abba. di S. Galgano

Monticiano

S441

S1

Campiglia
Marittima

Suvereto

Monterotondo
Marittimo

Montieri

Bagni di Petriolo

Pari

S198

Golfo di
Baratti

Massa Marittima

S439

Roccastrada

Civitella
Marittima

Piombino

Follonica

S573

Paganico

S223

S222

Isola d'Elba

Vetulonia

Tomba di Pietrara

Braccagni

Roselle

Roselle

Grosseto

To Rome

N

10 km

5 miles

SLOVENIA

CROATIA

BOSNIA-
HERZ.

FRANCE

Corsica

ITALY

Sardinia

Sicily

p.202

p.278

p.382

## Don't miss

⭐ San Gimignano **p.348**

⭐ Volterra **p.355**

⭐ Metal Hills **p.362**

⭐ Massa Marittima **p.364**

⭐ San Galgano **p.366**

# Monteriggioni, Colle di Val d'Elsa and Poggibonsi

## Monteriggioni

The SS2 passes a genuine curiosity 11km north of Siena: the tiny fortified town of Monteriggioni. For much of Siena's history, this was its northernmost bastion, often in the frontlines in the wars with Florence after its construction in 1219. Now it sits like a crown on its roundish hill, a neat circle of walls with 14 towers, with just enough room inside for two oversized piazzas, a few houses and their gardens, and the inevitable bars and restaurants. In late July, the town hosts a medieval festival – a re-enactment of medieval life with food, drink, music and dancing – the highlight is the third weekend in July. Some 3km further towards Colle di Val d'Elsa, there is a turn-off to the left for the 12th-century Abbey of Santi Salvatore and Cirino, better known as the **Abbadia dell'Isola**. The Cistercians began it in 1101 on an 'island' among the marshes, hence the name. Inside this stark Romanesque building is a restored fresco by Taddeo di Bartolo and a Renaissance altarpiece.

## Colle di Val d'Elsa

**Colle di Val d'Elsa** (pop. 16,300), a striking, ancient town up on a steep hill, presents an impressive silhouette if you see it from the right angle – it's long enough but at most only three blocks wide. Though probably as old as the Etruscans, Colle first became prominent in the 12th century, a safe, fortified stronghold that attracted many migrants from the surrounding plains. In later centuries, it was known for the manufacture of wool, paper and ceramics; today, Colle is Italy's largest producer of fine glass and crystal, and there are lots of shops selling its wares. There is also a new museum, the **Museo del Cristallo**, in a 19th-century crystal factory in the 'new' town (down the hill).

**Museo del Cristallo**
*Via dei Fossi, t 0577 924135; open Tues–Fri 3.30–5.30, Sat and Sun 10.30–12.30 and 3.30–6.30; adm*

The Collegiani will never allow the world to forget that their town was the birthplace of Arnolfo di Cambio, the great architect who built Florence's Palazzo Vecchio and began its cathedral. Down on the plain below the citadel, the modern part of the town surrounds the arcaded **Piazza Arnolfo di Cambio**. Via Garibaldi or Via San Sebastiano will take you up to old Colle – but for a proper introduction you'll need to come on the road from Volterra, passing through a grim Renaissance bastion called the **Porta Nuova**, designed by Giuliano da Sangallo, and then across the medieval-Renaissance suburb known as the **Borgo**. Between the Borgo and the old town, called the **Castello**, there is a picturesque narrow

# Getting around Monteriggioni, Colle di Valle d'Elsa, Poggibonsi

The main routes between Florence and Siena – the Via Cassia (SS2) or the parallel Superstrada del Palio – have exits for Colle di Val d'Elsa (27km/35mins from Siena, 49km/1hr from Florence) and Poggibonsi, 7km further north on SS68.

Poggibonsi is a major **bus** junction in south Tuscany, with easy connections with Florence, Siena, San Gimignano, Volterra and Colle di Val d'Elsa (TRA-IN buses if you're coming from Siena, SITA from Florence). Poggibonsi is also on the Empoli–Siena **railway** line, with a branch or bus beyond to Colle in 15mins.

---

bridge and the **Palazzo di Campana** (1539, by Giovanni di Baccio d'Agnolo); the arch in its centre is the elegant gateway to the town.

Via del Castello runs straight up the centre, with narrow medieval alleys on both sides. Here you'll find the **cathedral**, built in 1603 (Colle only got its own bishop in 1592) with a Victorian-era façade, a few Renaissance palaces, and some museums. Beside the cathedral, in the **Palazzo Pretorio**, a small **Museo Archeologico** displays Etruscan objects; there is a small picture collection in the nearby **Museo Civico**. The best is the **Museo d'Arte Sacra** in the old episcopal palace, with a few Sienese and Florentine paintings and the frescoes commissioned by some jolly 14th-century bishop – scenes of the hunt and from the Crusades, believed to be the work of Ambrogio Lorenzetti.

**Museo Archeologico/ Museo Civico/Museo d'Arte Sacra**
*open Nov–Easter Tues–Fri 3–7, Sat, Sun and hols 10.30–12.30 and 3–7; Easter–Oct Tues–Sun 10.30–12.30 and 4–7.30; adm*

Near the end of Via del Castello, the Collegiani claim an old tower-fortress as the **house of Arnolfo di Cambio**. Arnolfo's father, a gentleman and an architect, probably came to Colle di Val d'Elsa from Lombardy in the 1230s, bringing the great tradition of the Lombard master masons into Tuscany. He may have received his initiation into the new (for Italy) Gothic style from studying works in Siena or the new Cistercian abbey at San Galgano. He worked for Nicola Pisano on the Siena cathedral pulpit, and for Giovanni Pisano on the Fonte Maggiore in Perugia, and probably moved to Florence in the 1270s.

## South of Colle

Many of the villages in the hills retain their simple Romanesque churches from the 11th and 12th centuries, beginning with the isolated **Badia a Coneo**, a Vallombrosan foundation of the 1120s (5km from Colle on an unpaved lane off the road to Casole). At **Casole d'Elsa** (15km south, local bus), a town that took hard knocks in the last war, there is an interesting **Collegiata** church begun in the 12th century, with Sienese frescoes, two fine, late 14th-century sepulchres by Gano da Siena, and terracottas by Giovanni della Robbia. Casole's Sienese **Rocca** held out into the 16th century, long after the rest of the Valdelsa flew the Florentine flag. South from Casole, the road winds through pleasant, green countryside leading up to the Colline Metallifere, the 'metal hills' (*see* p.375), and you can seek out more Romanesque churches in **Mensano** (7km) and **Radicondoli** (15km, the church of **San Simone**).

## Poggibonsi

If you spend enough time in Tuscany, sooner or later you are bound to pass through Poggibonsi (pop. 25,700), a major knot on the SS2, SS429 and Superstrada del Palio roads linking Siena to Florence and Pisa. These days, residents of the pretty tourist towns of central Tuscany are not above having a laugh at the expense of this homely, hard-working industrial centre. Poor Poggibonsi! Founded only in 1156, the original Poggiobonizzo grew rapidly. By 1220 it was probably one of the largest cities in Tuscany, with a population of some 15,000; in that year, Emperor Frederick II declared it a *Città Imperiale* with special rights and privileges. Ghibelline politics and its imperial favour, however, were to prove Poggiobonizzo's undoing. In 1270, San Gimignano and Colle di Val d'Elsa, along with the Florentines and the troops of Charles of Anjou, besieged and conquered the city, then razed it to the ground. Some of the poorer citizens stayed behind, refounding the town as a market village on the plain. Poggibonsi was thoroughly wrecked again during the battles of 1944, but it has grown tremendously since, to become the biggest town between Florence and Siena.

There isn't much to see; the 14th-century Palazzo Pretorio and the collegiate church on the main street recall something of the appearance of pre-war Poggibonsi. Close by, the **Castello della Magione** is a small complex from the 1100s; the Romanesque chapel and outbuildings form a little closed square, a fortified pilgrims' hospice said to have been built by the Templars. Above the town, an unfinished fortress begun by Lorenzo de' Medici covers much of the original city of Poggiobonizzo.

Just 2km south of town near the SS2 is the austerely Franciscan **Basilica of San Lucchese**; inside are some good frescoes, including works by Taddeo Gaddi and Bartolo di Fredi. Not surprisingly, this strategically important corner of Tuscany is scattered with castles, including the 13th-century **Castello della Rochetta**, once the home of the famous *condottiere* Sir John Hawkwood (*see* p.109), and the romantically ruined **Rocca di Staggia** (5km south of Poggibonsi on the SS2), built by the Florentines in the 1430s – a counterpart to Sienese Monteriggioni, just a few kilometres further on.

## Where to Stay and Eat in Monteriggioni, Colle di Val d'Elsa, Poggibonsi

(★) Il Pozzo >>

(i) Monteriggioni >
Piazza Roma, t 0577 304810, www.proloco monteriggioni.it

### Monteriggioni ✉ 53035

This little castle village is a good lunch stop if you're heading from Florence to Siena, or from Siena to the west.

****Hotel Monteriggioni**, Via 1 Maggio 4, t 0577 305009, *www. hotelmonteriggioni.net* (€€€€). A hotel occupying two old stone houses, with a garden and a tiny pool.

Il Pozzo, Piazza Roma 2, t 0577 304127 (€€€). Here they do some of the simpler dishes very well – bean soup, ravioli with truffles, roast meats such as stuffed pigeon – but their real forte is fancy desserts (they even serve *crêpes Suzette*). *Closed Sun eve, Mon and 7 Jan–Feb.*

ⓘ Colle di Val d'Elsa >
*Via Campana 43,*
*t 0577 920389*

## Colle di Val d'Elsa ✉ 53034

**★★★Arnolfo**, Via Campana 8, **t** 0577 922020, *www.hotelarnolfo.it* (€€). A simple and comfortable option, in the town itself.

**★★★Villa Belvedere**, Via Senese, Località Belvedere, **t** 0577 920966, *www.villabelvedere.com* (€€). Located 1km or so east of the town, near the Siena highway, this pretty villa has a good restaurant with a terrace overlooking San Gimignano, a big garden, swimming pool and 15 simple rooms, as well as a cookery school.

**Arnolfo**, Via XX Settembre 50, **t** 0577 920549 (€€€). This occupies a Renaissance palace, the perfect setting for what is widely considered one of the top restaurants in all Italy. Menus change with the seasons, but you can always choose from two *menu degustazioni* – one 'traditional', one 'creative'. *Closed Tues and Wed, mid Jan–Feb, and 2wks July and Aug.*

**Osteria di Sapia**, Via del Castello 4, **t** 0577 921453 (€€). The decor in this elegant *osteria* situated in the old town is a refreshingly far cry from typical Tuscan rustic. The food, too, is different. Creative variations include vegetarian lasagne and pork tenderloin cooked with peaches and *vin santo*. The two set menus are good value and there is a lovely terrace. *Closed Mon, lunch Nov–Feb.*

**Fattoria di Mugnano**, 7km along the Colle–Volterra road, **t** 0577 959023 (€). An old farm among olive groves in the nearby hamlet of Mugnano. The delightful restaurant offers local and Sicilian cuisine; they will be delighted to sell you some of the wine and olive oil. They also offer a few spartan rooms. *Closed Thurs.*

**L'Oste di Borgo**, Via Gracco del Secco 58, **t** 0577 922499 (€). A nice little *osteria* with a terrace and marble-topped tables. You can eat a light meal (choose from an interesting selection of pastas and salads), or snack on *bruschette*, local cheeses, hams and salamis. *Closed Wed.*

## Poggibonsi ✉ 53036

**★★★Alcide**, Via Marconi 67a, **t** 0577 937501, *www.hotelalcide.com* (€€). Rooms with air-conditioning, breakfast included; there's a minimum 3-day stay. Their restaurant (€€€), open since 1849, is renowned for seafood in this landlocked province, featuring dishes with a south Italian slant, like Apulian *orecchiette* in a sauce with cuttlefish and several varieties of maritime risotto. *Closed Sun eve, Mon.*

**La Galleria**, Vittorio Veneto 20, **t** 0577 982356 (€€). Plain enough surroundings for superb food and an excellent wine list. Try the *bresaolo* on braised radicchio topped with gorgonzola, followed by a sublime *bistecca*. The charming staff will help you choose the right wines to wash it all down with. *Closed Sun.*

# San Gimignano

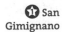 ⭐ San Gimignano

In the miniaturist landscape of this corner of Tuscany, San Gimignano, Italy's best-preserved medieval city, is an almost fantastic landmark. Seen from Poggibonsi or the Volterra road, its medieval towers, some of them over 160ft (50m) tall, loom over the surrounding hills. Once, almost every city in central Italy looked like this; more than just defensive strongholds in the incessant family feuds, these towers served as status symbols for the families and the cities themselves, a visible measure of a town's power and prosperity. By the 16th century, most of Italy's towers had succumbed to age, decay and the efforts of the urban *comuni*, which pruned and destroyed these symbols of truculent nobility at

# Getting to and around San Gimignano

The railway station is 11km away and is an infrequent stop on the Empoli–Siena line. Buses to the town *usually* coincide with the **trains**, but from either Siena or Florence you'll be better off taking the bus, which leaves you right at Porta San Giovanni, the main entrance to the town.

TRA-IN **buses** from Siena (38km/45mins – the same bus that goes to Colle di Val d'Elsa) are very frequent, though for most, you will need to change in Poggibonsi. Several daily SITA buses arrive from Florence (54km/1hr 15mins) and there are four buses a day to and from nearby Certaldo.

If you're **driving**, San Gimignano is 11km west of Poggibonsi, 13km south of Certaldo or 14km from Colle di Val d'Elsa, each route more scenic than the last. Within the walls, San Gimignano is usually closed to traffic; the main car park is outside Porta San Giovanni. Get a pass from the police to park at one of the hotels inside.

every opportunity. Oddly, this did not happen in San Gimignano, famous even in the 1300s as the *'città delle belle torri'*. Originally there were at least 70 towers (in a town one-eighth of a square mile in size). Only 15 remain, but in conjunction with the beautiful streets, churches and public buildings they are enough to give you the impression that the town has been hermetically sealed in a time-capsule since the Middle Ages – if you imagine away the gaggle of trinket shops.

## History

According to legend, the town was originally called Castel della Selva. When the Gothic army of Totila passed through in the 550s, the townsfolk for some reason chose to pray to an obscure saint named Gimignano, a martyred bishop of Modena, for their salvation from a near-guaranteed sacking. Gimignano came through in style, looming down from the clouds in golden armour to scare away the besiegers.

Although it must have been an important and prosperous place, San Gimignano does not cut much of a figure in the medieval chronicles. The city was an independent republic from the early 1100s until 1353, when it came under the rule of Florence. It certainly participated in the Guelph–Ghibelline strife, and in all the other troubles of the period, though today it is probably best remembered as the home town of the poet Folgore of San Gimignano (*c.*1250), famous for his lovely sonnets to the months of the year. San Gimignano has the air of a false start, a free *comune* that could build a wall and defend itself, yet lacked the will or the money to make itself into a Siena or a Florence. When it lost the wealth or the fierceness that briefly made it an important player on the Tuscan stage, the city crystallized into its medieval form, a perfect preparation for its role as a tourist town. Today San Gimignano has a population of some 7,700. On a good day in July or August, it may see several times that in day-trippers. Even during the Renaissance, the town was a resort for the Florentines: Dante, Machiavelli and Savonarola all spent time here, and artists like Ghirlandaio and Gozzoli were happy to come up for a small commission. Don't let the prospect of crowds keep you from visiting, though. San Gimignano handles them gracefully; its fine art, elegant medieval cityscapes and the verdant rolling countryside right outside its gates make this one of the smaller towns of Tuscany most worth seeing.

## Piazza del Duomo and the Palazzo del Popolo

From the southern gate, Porta San Giovanni, the street of the same name leads towards the town centre, passing the little churches of **San Giovanni**, built by the Knights Templar, and **San Francesco**, with a good Pisan-Romanesque façade, now deconsecrated and converted into a wine shop. Another ancient gate, the Arco dei Bacci, leads into the triangular **Piazza della Cisterna** and the adjacent **Piazza del Duomo** – a superbly beautiful example of asymmetrical medieval town design. Piazza della Cisterna contains the town's well and some of its towers.

On Piazza del Duomo, two stout, Gothic public buildings with Guelph crenellations and lofty towers compete with the Collegiata church for your attention. The **Palazzo del Podestà**, with its vaulted *loggia*, was begun in the 1230s by Emperor Frederick II at the height of imperial power. Above it stands the Torre della Rognosa, with a small cupola; at 167ft (51.4m) it once marked the height limit for private towers – the *podestà* didn't want anyone putting him in the shade. Later, when the *comune* was able to wrest effective self-government from the emperors, it built an even taller tower for the **Palazzo del Popolo** across the piazza; the 177ft (54.5m) Torre Grossa was completed about 1300 and the rest of the Palazzo about 20 years later.

Underneath this tower, an archway leads into the charming, thoroughly medieval **Cortile**, or courtyard, with bits of frescoes (one by Il Sodoma) and the painted coats of arms of Florentine governors from after 1353. A stairway leads up to the **Museo Civico**, with an excellent collection of art from both Florentine and Sienese masters. One of the oldest works is a remarkable painted crucifix by Coppo di Marcovaldo (*c.* 1270) that predates (and some might say surpasses) the similar, more famous crucifixes of Giotto. There are also two sweet Madonnas by Benozzo Gozzoli, a pair of *tondi* by Filippino Lippi portraying the *Annunciation*, and a big, colourful enthroned Virgin by Pinturicchio, famous for the Piccolomini chapel in Siena. Taddeo di Bartolo's paintings depict the story of San Gimignano; he is pictured calming the sea, exorcizing a devil who had been inhabiting the daughter of Emperor Jovian, and succumbing to

**Museo Civico**
*t 0577 990312; open Mar–Oct daily 9.30–7; Nov–Feb daily 10–5.30; adm*

the demands of the flesh while saying Mass (he has to pee, but on sneaking out of the church, a winged devil attacks him; fortunately, he has a crucifix to hand, and drives it away).

To the San Gimignanese, the biggest attraction of the museum is the Sala del Consiglio, or **Sala di Dante**, where the poet spoke in 1299 as an ambassador of Florence, seeking to convince the *comune* to join the Guelph League. The frescoes on its walls include more works by Gozzoli, a glittering company of angels and saints in the *Maestà* of the Sienese artist Lippo Memmi, and some trecento scenes of hunting and tournaments. After this, contemplate a climb up the **Torre Grosso** – several hundred steps, but the view is worth the effort.

**Torre Grosso**
*t 0577 990312;
same hours as Museo
Civico; adm*

## The Collegiata

The name Piazza del Duomo is misleading: San Gimignano no longer has a cathedral, but a collegiata, begun in the 12th century and enlarged in the 15th, which would make an impressive seat for any bishop. It turns a blank brick façade to the world, but the interior is a lavish imitation of Siena cathedral, with its tiger-striped arches and vaults painted with golden stars. Its walls, however, outshine the larger cathedral with first-class frescoes of the 14th and 15th centuries, mostly by artists from Siena, including Old Testament scenes done by Bartolo di Fredi in the 1360s. New Testament pictures by Barna da Siena (about 1380) cover the south wall; on the west wall, over the entrance, is a well-punctured *Saint Sebastian* by Gozzoli and the most perverse *Last Judgement* in Italy, by Taddeo di Bartolo – you may think you have seen the damned suffering interesting tortures and indignities before, but this is the first time delicacy forbids us to describe one. It's a little faded, unfortunately, but you'll find it near two wooden figures depicting an *Annunciation* by Jacopo della Quercia.

**Capella di
Santa Fina**
*t 0577 940348;
open April–Oct
11–5.30; Nov–6 Jan
11–5.30; 24 Dec 10–2; 25
and 31 Dec 10–5.30;
1 Jan 12.30–5.30; adm*

Off the south aisle, the **chapel of Santa Fina** offers a delightful introduction to one of the most irritating hagiographies in Christendom. Little Fina was going to the well for water, when she accepted an orange from a young swain. Upon returning home, her mother told her how wicked she was to take it, whereupon the poor girl became so mortified over her great sin that she lay down on the kitchen table and prayed for forgiveness without ceasing for the next five years. Finally, St Anthony came to call her soul up into heaven, and the kitchen table and all the towers of San Gimignano burst into bloom with violets. Domenico Ghirlandaio got the commission to paint all this; he did a splendid job (1475) in the brightest springtime colours. In the last scene, note San Gimignano's famous towers in the background.

## Around the Town

Just to the left of the Collegiata there is a lovely small courtyard where musicians sometimes play on summer weekends. Here, on the wall of the baptistry, you will see another fine fresco by Ghirlandaio, an *Annunciation* that has survived reasonably well for being outside for 500 years. The town's two other museums are housed here, in the same building as the **Museo Archeologico**: the **Museo Etrusco** has a small collection of local archaeological finds and the **Museo d'Arte Sacra** has some good painted wood statues from the late Middle Ages.

From Piazza del Duomo, it's not too difficult a climb up to the **Rocca**, a ruined fortress of the 1350s, offering one of the best views of this towered town. In the summer, it's the site of an outdoor cinema.

Along Via di Castello, at No.11, there is one of Italy's most important contemporary art galleries, **Galleria Continua**, occupying an old 1950s cinema. With new branches in Beijing and Paris, this hip space attracts some of the art world's finest to exhibit here. The garden has wonderful views over the valley. Further down Via di Castello, at the eastern end of town, the **oratory of San Lorenzo in Ponte**, now unused, has quattrocento Florentine frescoes and an exhibition of finds from the pharmacy of the Hospital of Santa Fina in the 16th to 18th centuries. The busiest and finest street of San Gimignano heads north from Piazza del Duomo: Via San Matteo, lined with shops and modest Renaissance palaces. It begins by passing the three truncated **Salvucci towers**, once the fortified compound of the Ghibelline Salvucci, one of the town's most powerful families (the towers of their enemies, the Guelph Ardinghelli, are the ones on the west side of Piazza della Cisterna).

In the quiet streets on the north side of town is the church of **Sant'Agostino**, famous for a merry series of frescoes by Gozzoli on the *Life of St Augustine*. Many of the frescoes are faded and damaged, but not the charming panel where the master of grammar drags sullen little Augustine off to school. Another well-preserved scene shows the saint in Rome, with most of the city's ancient landmarks visible in the background. Gozzoli also painted the *St Sebastian* on the left aisle. There is a haunting altarpiece (1483) by Piero Pollaiuolo, with an anticipatory touch of the El Greco to it, and some good trecento Sienese painting in a chapel off to the right. Across the piazza from Sant'Agostino, the little church of **San Pietro** has more trecento Sienese painting. Via Folgore di San Gimignano leads to the northeast corner of the town; **San Jacopo** stands under the town wall, another simple but interesting building left by the Templars.

Around much of San Gimignano, the countryside begins right outside the town's wall. Pleasant walks or picnics can be had in any

**Museo Archeologico/ Museo Etrusco and Museo d'Arte Sacra**
*t 0577 940348; open April–Oct 11–5.30; Nov–6 Jan 11–5.30; 24 Dec 10–5 and 31 Dec 10–5.30; 1 Jan 12.30–5.30; adm*

**Galleria Continua**
*t 0577 943134. www.galleriacontinua. com; open Tues–Sat 2–7 or else by appt*

## Local Wine

San Gimignano has its own wine, La Vernaccia di San Gimignano (makes one think of varnish), a dry, light yellow white, with a pungent bouquet and a slightly bitter aftertaste. It is generally drunk with fish dishes and as an *aperitivo*, but it's also good to try with typical San Gimignano dishes such as liver, tripe, rabbit and *panzanella*.

The wine is made only in the hills around San Gimignano and has been around since antiquity. It gets a mention in Dante's *Purgatory*: Pope Martin IV apparently drowned eels in Vernaccia before roasting them over a charcoal fire. It has recently been awarded the DOCG.

direction, with a few landmarks to visit along the way: the **Fonti**, arched, medieval well-houses much like Siena's, are just outside the Porta dei Fonti, south of San Jacopo. Further away, there is the **Pieve di Cellole,** a pretty 12th-century church in a pleasant, peaceful setting, 4km west of the Porta San Matteo; its harmonious serenity amid the cypresses inspired Puccini's opera *Suor Angelica*. There are a number of ruined castles and monasteries around the town, each offering a different view of San Gimignano's remarkable skyline.

## Tourist Information in San Gimignano

(i) San Gimignano >
Piazza del Duomo 1,
t 0577 940008,
www.san
gimignano.com

If you plan to visit all the key sights, it is worth buying the cheaper joint ticket (*biglietto cumulativo* €3.50) covers the four museums, the tower of Palazzo del Popolo and the Capella di Santa Fina, but not the Collegiata.

You can explore the surrounding countryside on horseback with **Il Vecchio Maneggio**, Sant'Andrea 22, Ulignano, t 0577 950232, *www. ilvecchiomaneggio.com*, 5km along the road to Certaldo. It is also an *agriturismo* offering rooms (€) and selling its own wine, saffron, olive oil and honey.

## Shopping in San Gimignano

There isn't any particular artisan tradition here, but so many tourists visit that enterprising shop owners have assembled a host of interesting things – the town hasn't quite turned into a great trinket bazaar, but it's getting there. **Ceramics** are everywhere; some of the local work is quite good and inexpensive.

**Linea Oro**, Via San Giovanni. Among the good buys are pretty things in alabaster from nearby Volterra.

**Via San Matteo 85**, north of Piazza del Duomo. One of the best shops for alabaster is here.

**La Stamperia**, Via San Matteo 88. Sells original prints including views of Tuscan towns and countryside.

Just within Porta San Giovanni is a 13th-century church now converted to a shop for local wine, olive oil and other farm products.

San Gimignano's other specialities are a formidable white wine called Vernaccia (*see* above) and a sweet called *mandorlato*, very like the *panforte* of Siena. Many local vineyards would be glad to sell you a bottle of Vernaccia. One such is **Cantine Baroncini**, Casale, t 0577 940600.

## Where to Stay in San Gimignano

San Gimignano ✉ 53037
In the summer, you may want a hand finding a place to sleep. The **Hotel Association** is just inside the gate on Via S. Giovanni, t 0577 940809.

***Le Renaie**, Loc Pancole, about 7km towards Certaldo, **t** 0577 955044, *www.hotellerenaie.it* (€€€€€–€€€€). If you prefer the tranquillity of the very lovely Tuscan countryside, head north of town to find this attractive modern building, with a garden, pool, fitness centre, free spa, bikes and tennis court.

★ Antico Pozzo >

***Antico Pozzo**, Via San Matteo 87, **t** 0577 942014, *www.anticopozzo.com* (€€€). Next to the main square, this is a stylish hotel with wonderful views from rooms at the top of the house. The building dates from the 1500s – several of the rooms even have delicately frescoed ceilings and there is Wi-fi Internet access.

***Leon Bianco**, Piazza della Cisterna, **t** 0577 941294, *www.leonbianco.com* (€€€). An excellent hotel with modern rooms.

***La Cisterna**, **t** 0577 940328, *www.hotelcisterna.it* (€€€). If the Leon Bianco is full, this is in the same square and also comes highly recommended.

To fill the vacuum of inexpensive accommodation, a score of San Gimignanesi rent out rooms. The tourist office can give you a list.

## Eating Out in San Gimignano

San Gimignano may entertain a good many visitors, but it makes a fine host.

**Dorando**, Vicolo del Oro 2, **t** 0577 941862 (€€€€). For the more adventurous. The chef attempts to recreate authentic Renaissance and medieval cuisine – *cibreo* (a chicken liver pâté so rich that Catherine de' Medici nearly died from a surfeit of it), boned guinea fowl with honey and black sesame seeds, *maccheroni* with duck and mushroom sauce and a truffle glaze, crème caramel flavoured with coriander, and things stranger still. Readers have praised it highly. *Closed Mon in winter*.

**Osteria delle Catene**, Via Mainardi 18, **t** 0577 941966 (€€). Good regional food such as guinea fowl with wine and juniper. *Closed Wed*.

**Le Terrazze**, in Hotel La Cisterna (*see left*), **t** 0577 940328 (€€). Popular for its panoramic views as well as the cuisine it has been dishing up since 1918. The *medaglione al vin santo* is a surprise treat, or else the *osso buco alla toscana* following old house specialities like *zuppa sangimignese* and *pappardelle alla lepre* (wide noodles with hare sauce). Booking is advised. *Closed Wed lunch, Tues*.

**Osteria del Carcere**, Via del Castello 13, **t** 0577 941905 (€€). A tiny restaurant that serves unusual cold cuts and terrines, a delicious saffron-flavoured goat's cheese mousse, soups, and lamb with pecorino cheese. *Closed Thurs lunch, Wed*.

**Enoteca Gustavo**, Via San Matteo 29, **t** 0577 940057 (€). A good choice for a glass of local Vernaccia and a snack, this wine bar serves all sorts of sandwiches and *crostoni* (a rustic toasted open sandwich), cheeses and meats. *Closed Tues*.

**Gelateria di Piazza**, Piazza della Cisterna, **t** 0577 942244 (€). Truly wonderful ice cream in a myriad flavours. *Closed Nov–Feb*.

# Volterra and Around

 Volterra

On a good day in spring or summer, the sunshine illuminates Volterra's elegant streets and *piazze* full of locals, and bouncing holidaymakers come to buy alabaster cups and lampshades. A cloudy, windy day may remind you of fate and of the Etruscans, who arrived here some 2,700 years ago. Like so many of their other cities, the Etruscans founded Volterra on top of a steep hill with a flat top; from afar, you see only a silhouette looming over an eerie, empty landscape. The soil around Volterra (pop. 12,796) is a thin

# Getting to and around Volterra

Volterra lies 81km/2½hrs southwest of Florence by way of Colle di Val d'Elsa and the winding SS68; it's 50km/1½hrs west from Siena; and 61km/2hrs southeast of Pisa by way of Cascina and the SS439. It isn't the easiest town to reach if you don't have a car.

The only **train** service gets as far as Saline di Volterra, 10km southwest of the city. This is an infrequent branch line that goes to Cecina, 30km to the west on the coast south of Livorno. Some trains continue on from Cecina to Pisa. (It wasn't like this in the old days: as late as the 1920s, a little steam train used to climb right up to the town.) Buses connect the Saline station with Volterra, but not always when you need them.

All **buses** leave from Piazza Martini della Libertà, which is just inside the walls. You can get information, timetables and buy tickets from the tourist office. There are plenty of buses which go direct to Pisa and Montecatini Terme, 4 a day to Florence and Siena via Colle Val d'Elsa, and a few to Poggibonsi and San Gimignano; 3 a day go to Livorno via Cecina; there are also 2 to Massa Marittima (usually with a change at Monterotondo).

**Cars** aren't allowed within Volterra's walls, but lots of parking space is provided all around the walls and at the gates. Strangely enough there are also some street parking spaces inside, and you can usually sneak your car into one that's near your hotel in the evening; it's best to check out the situation on foot beforehand.

---

clay, not much good for vines or olives. Few trees grow here. It makes good pasture land – not as barren as it looks, but disconcerting enough among the green woods and well-tended gardens of this part of Tuscany.

## History

Etruscan **Velathri**, one of the largest and most powerful cities of the Dodecapolis, grew up in the 9th or 8th century BC from an even earlier settlement of the Villanovan culture; it is undoubtedly one of Italy's oldest cities. The attraction that has kept this hill continuously occupied for so many centuries is easily explained – sulphur, alum, salt, alabaster, lead and tin; the town is at the centre of one of the richest mining regions in Italy. In Etruscan days, there was iron, too, and the people of Velathri did a thriving trade with the Greeks and Carthaginians.

Velathri reached the height of its prosperity in the 5th and 4th centuries BC, leaving as testament three great circuits of walls; the largest is over 8km in length, enclosing an area three times the size of the present city. The Romans captured it some time in the 3rd century and Velathri began to decline. Along with most of Etruria, the city chose the populist side in the Social Wars, and was punished with a siege and sacking by Sulla in about 80 BC. Yet Roman *Velaterrae* remained an important town. It was the home of St Linus, successor to St Peter and the second pope.

Even though many of the mines were giving out, Volterra managed to survive the Dark Ages intact. The Lombards favoured it, and for a time it served as their capital. Medieval Volterra was ruled by its bishops, who were increasingly finding themselves in conflict with the rising middle class. An independent *comune* was established late in the 12th century, a good Ghibelline town that participated in most of the factional wars of the period, before finally coming under the nominal control of Florence in 1361.

The Florentines were content with an annual tribute until the 'affair of the alum' in the 1470s, that wonderfully Italian ruckus that caused Pope Sixtus IV to plot the murder of Lorenzo de' Medici, excommunicate him and finally declare war on him. Lorenzo had taken over a syndicate to mine here for alum, a key material used in dyeing cloth, on which the popes had a monopoly from their mines at Tolfa. Besides alarming the pope, Lorenzo also caused the Volterrans to revolt when they realized that he wanted to keep production down and prices high without letting any profit trickle down to them (the Medici Bank, not surprisingly, also controlled the sale of the pope's alum). Lorenzo eluded the pope with some difficulty (*see* **Florence**, History, pp.92–4) and then hired the mercenary captain Federico da Montefeltro – none other than the famous broken-nosed Duke of Urbino, patron of artists and scholars – to subdue the Volterrans. This he did with a brutality quite unbecoming to the 'ideal Renaissance prince'. Lorenzo wept some crocodile tears over Volterra; after extinguishing the city's independence once and for all, he offered it the magnificent sum of 2,000 florins in damages.

Fortunately for the Volterrans, the mining business was picking up again. Between 1400 and 1800, many pits that had been abandoned since Roman times were reopened. In particular, Volterra became Europe's largest centre for the mining and working of alabaster, a craft tradition that is still the city's biggest business today.

## A Little Archaeology

Coming from Florence or Siena, the entrance to Volterra will be the eastern gate, the **Porta a Selci**, with a moving tribute to the *partigiani* of Volterra killed in 1944–5. Inside the gate, Via Don Minzoni leads towards Piazza XX Settembre, passing along the way at No.15 the **Museo Etrusco Guarnacci**, the repository for finds from the Velathri necropolises. Over 600 sculpted alabaster, travertine or terracotta cinerary urns make up the core of the collection. Exhibits are arranged in chronological order, except for the original Guarnacci collection which is grouped by subject matter. These tend to be conventional – an Etruscan family would ask the artist for a scene from Greek mythology, from the Trojan War perhaps, or something like the death of Actaeon, or a daemon conducting the souls of the dead down to the underworld. Perhaps the artist already had one in stock. One rule of Etruscan art, however, is its lack of rules. Expect anything: some of the

**Museo Etrusco Guarnacci**

*open mid-Mar–Oct daily 9–7; Nov–mid-Mar daily 9–2; adm exp, a joint ticket covers Volterra's other museums*

### Volterra's *Pietra Candida*

The craft of carving alabaster in this region, which dates back to at least 800 BC, has revived dramatically in the last 200 years, and Volterra is full of small workshops, and even a few large firms, that turn the stone into vases, figurines, ashtrays and everything else that's serviceable or collectable. Many alabaster-workers are genuine artists, turning out one-of-a-kind pieces at high prices; others produce vast numbers of attractive little baubles from €3 and up. Try:

**Artisans' Cooperative (Cooperative Artieri Alabastro),** Piazza dei Priori.

**Via Porta all'Arco 45.** Some of the most original creations in town.

**Via Porta all'Arco 26.** Unusual miniatures.

**Via di Sotto 2.** Simple, elegant vases and lamps.

**Via Antonio Gramsci 20 and 53.** Interesting shops.

**Via Guarnacci 26.** Splashy modern work in coloured alabaster.

For crafts of a different kind, head for **Via Don Minzoni 54** where Auro Bongini makes dolls'-house furniture from local olive wood in a 19th-century style; call in advance (**t** 0588 88040).

reclining figures of the dead atop the urns are brilliant portraiture, while others could be the first attempts of a third-grade craft class. All, holding the little cups or dishes they carry down into Hades, look as serene and happy as only a defunct Etruscan can.

As always, the Etruscans do their best to make you laugh. One terracotta, the *Urna degli Sposi*, portrays a hilariously caricatured couple who look as if they are about to start arguing over whose turn it is to do the dishes. Another Etruscan joke is the *Ombra della Sera* (evening shadow), quite a celebrity around Volterra, a small, carefully detailed bronze of a man with a quizzical expression and spidery, grotesquely elongated arms and legs. There are also prehistoric finds, Roman mosaics from the baths, artefacts discovered in the theatre, and some fine pieces of Etruscan jewellery.

The museum lies a stone's throw from Piazza XX Settembre; from here Via Gramsci leads towards the town centre. Climb any of the alleys to the south of the museum, however, and you'll reach Volterra's **Parco Archeologico** just inside the walls. There isn't much that's archaeological about it – some Etruscan foundations and a huge ancient cistern called the *Piscina Romana* – but the park is a marvel, a lush English garden of manicured lawns and shady groves unlike anything else in Tuscany. Above the park stretches an exceptionally long and elegant castle, the **Fortezza Medicea**, begun in 1343 and completed by Lorenzo de' Medici in 1472. You can't get in; it has been a prison almost from the day it was built, perhaps the fanciest in this nation of fancy calabooses.

**Parco Archeologico**
*open Nov–mid-Mar Sat, Sun and hols 10–4; summer daily 10.30–5.30; adm*

### Piazza dei Priori

This is a fine little republican piazza, surrounded by plain, erect *palazzi* that discreetly call your attention to the sober dignity of the *comune*. The **Palazzo dei Priori**, of 1208, is said to be the oldest such building in Tuscany, the model for Florence's Palazzo Vecchio and many others. Across the square, the simple **Palazzo Pretorio** is almost as old. Next to it, the rakishly leaning **Porcellino Tower** takes its name from the little pig sculpted in relief near the base, just barely visible after seven centuries.

## The Cathedral and the Etruscan Arch

Just to the right of the Palazzo dei Priori, a bit of green and white striped marble façade peeks out between the palaces. This is the back of the Archiepiscopal Palace, located around the corner in the **Piazza del Duomo**. Quiet and dowdy, the contrast of this square with the well-built Piazza dei Priori is striking, a lasting memory of the defeat of Volterra's medieval bishops by the *comune*. Its octagonal **baptistry**, begun in 1283, has its marble facing completed only on one side. Within, there is a fine baptismal font sculpted by Andrea Sansovino in the early 1500s, an altar by Mino da Fiesole, and a holy water dish carved out of an Etruscan boundary stone.

The plain **cathedral** façade has a good marble doorway. This forlorn mongrel of a building was begun in the Pisan-Romanesque style and continued fitfully for the next two centuries. The campanile went up in 1493, and the interior was entirely redone in the 1580s when the blatant Medici coat of arms was placed over the high altar. Do not pass this old Duomo by: the works of art inside are few in number, but of an exceptionally high quality. Fittingly, as this is Volterra, some of the windows are made of thin-sliced alabaster, a stone that was also used in the intricate, Renaissance **tabernacle** by Mino da Fiesole over the high altar.

The chapels on either side have excellent examples of Tuscan woodcarving: a 15th-century piece attributed to a local artist named Francesco di Domenico Valdambrino off to the left (the *Madonna dei Chierici*), and to the right, a polychromed *Deposition* with five separate, full-sized figures, certainly ranked among the best of 13th-century Pisan sculpture, shining immaculately after a recent restoration. Another chapel off to the right contains fragments of unusually good anonymous trecento frescoes of the *Passion of Christ*, very much ahead of their time in composition, in the figures and the folds of the draperies – even Giorgio Vasari might have liked them.

In the left aisle, the *pergamo* (**pulpit**) is one of the lesser-known works of the Pisani, less spectacular than the ones in Pisa, Siena and Pistoia, but still showing something of the vividness and electric immediacy seen in the best Pisan sculpture. Guglielmo Pisano did the fine relief of the *Last Supper* (note the faces of the Apostles and the sly metaphorical monster sneaking under the table). The pulpit's supporting columns rest on two lions, a bull and one unclassifiable beast, all by Bonamico Pisano. In the oratory, off the left aisle near the entrance, behind a 16th-century wooden statue group of the *Adoration of the Magi*, is a small fresco said to be by Benozzo Gozzoli, though perhaps because of its deterioration or its early date it lacks Gozzoli's usual charm.

**Museo d'Arte Sacra**
*open mid-Mar–Oct 9–1 and 3–6; Nov–mid Mar 9–1; adm*

Close by in the Archiepiscopal Palace, a small **Museo d'Arte Sacra** displays sculpture and architectural fragments, and a della Robbia terracotta of *St Linus*, Volterra's patron.

From the Duomo, if you retrace your steps back towards Piazza dei Priori and turn down Via Porta all'Arco, you'll find the quaintest old relic in Volterra, the **Arco Etrusco**. The Etruscans built the columns at least, though the arch above them was rebuilt in Roman times. Set into this arch are three primeval black basalt sculpted heads from the original gate, *c.* 600 BC, believed to represent the Etruscan gods Tinia (Jupiter), Uni (Juno) and Menvra (Minerva). Some of the features of Juno are barely traceable; 2,700 years of wind and rain have worn all three into great black knobs – carved out of the *voussoirs*, they resemble nothing so much as garden slugs.

## The Pinacoteca

**Pinacoteca**
*open mid-Mar–Oct daily 9–7, Nov–mid-Mar daily 9–2; adm, inc adm to other Volterra museums*

Just off Piazza dei Priori, the intersection of Via Roma and Via Buonparenti is one of the most picturesque corners of Volterra, with venerable stone arches and tower houses such as the 13th-century **Casa Buonparenti**. Via Buonparenti leads into Via dei Sarti; the elder Antonio da Sangallo's **Palazzo Solaini** (note the elegant arcaded courtyard) has been restored to hold Volterra's Pinacoteca, another small but choice collection. Trecento Sienese painting is well represented, including a glorious altarpiece of the *Madonna and Child* by Taddeo di Bartolo. To complement the remarkable 14th-century wood sculptures in the Duomo, the Pinacoteca has two figures portraying the *Annunciation* by Francesco di Valdambrino. Neri di Bicci was a quattrocento Florentine, but his *St Sebastian* here looks entirely Sienese – probably at the request of the customer. Among other Tuscan works, there is a shiny altarpiece by Ghirlandaio, and two by Luca Signorelli (or his workshop): a *Madonna and Saints* and an *Annunciation*. Only tantalizing fragments are left of another altarpiece by Giuliano Bugiardini (1475–1554), a little-known Florentine with a very distinctive style.

For all that, the prize of the collection is the Rosso Fiorentino *Deposition*, dated 1521 and perhaps his greatest work in all Italy. Even out in the boondocks of Volterra, it attracts considerable attention from the art scholars, being a seminal work and one of the thresholds from the Renaissance into Mannerism, with all the precision and clarity of the best quattrocento work, yet also possessing an intensity that few works had ever achieved. The *Descent from the Cross* is a starkly emotional subject; in Rosso's work it is terror and disarray, a greenish Christ and a small, nearly hysterical crowd dramatically illuminated against a darkening deep blue sky. You'll find little that this painting has in common with Rosso's contemporaries, not even with his fellow madman Pontormo (who did his own, quite different, *Deposition* in Florence's Santa Felicità) – but oddly enough, it could almost be mistaken for a work of Goya.

## San Francesco and the Roman Theatre

On the corner east of the Pinacoteca, the church of **San Michele** has a Pisan Romanesque façade. In the other direction, towards the Porta San Francesco on the western edge of town, you pass through back streets dusty with alabaster workshops, before finally arriving at the church of **San Francesco** on Via San Lino. Here the attraction is off to the right of the altar, the **chapel of the Holy Cross**, completely frescoed in 1410 by a Florentine artist whose name seems to be Cenni di Francesco di Ser Cenni – a rare soul, indeed, with a sophisticated, wonderfully reactionary, medieval sense of composition and his own ideas about Christian iconography, done in a bold style that in places almost seems like modern poster art. The *Legend of the Cross* frescoes generally follow those of Gaddi at Santa Croce in Florence (*see* p.157), and there are also scenes of *St Francis*, the *Passion*, and the *Massacre of the Innocents*, many with fantasy city backgrounds. Note the *Dream of Constantine* (or of Heraclius), in his tent adorned with the imperial eagle; naturally the artist had never seen a Roman eagle, but he painted a very nice medieval German one instead.

Back towards the centre, the vast façade of the 16th-century **Palazzo Incontri-Viti** is attributed to Bartolommeo Ammannati. It was built for Attilo Incontri, minister to the Grand Duke of Tuscany; recently the Vitis, wealthy alabaster merchants, started opening 12 of their lavish rooms to the public filled with heirlooms going back to the 15th century. in 1964 Visconti shot his film *Vague Stelle dell'Orso* here. Near the top of Via dei Sarti, the church of San Michele has a Pisan-Romanesque façade.

From here to Via Guarnacci leads down outside the walls to Viale Francesco Ferrucci, home to a lively outdoor **market** on Saturday mornings, and to ancient Velaterrae's large **Roman theatre**. Enough marble slabs and columns have survived for the archaeologists to reconstruct part of the stage building, an impressive testimony to the past importance of the city.

**Palazzo Incontri-Viti**
*Via dei Sarti 41, north of Palazzo Pretorio; t 0588 84047; open mid-Mar–Oct daily 9–1 and 2.30–6.30; rest of the year by appt; adm*

**Roman theatre**
*open mid-Mar–Oct daily 10.30–5.30; Nov–mid-Mar Sat, Sun and hols 10–4; adm*

## Outside Volterra: the *Balze*

Leaving Volterra from San Francesco Gate, you pass the Borgo San Giusto and its ruins of the 12th-century Pisan-Romanesque church of **Santo Stefano**. The road to Pisa exits through the outer **Etruscan walls**; though barely more than foundations, they are traceable for most of their length around the city and easily visible here.

Some 2km beyond, decorating the moors, are the *balze*: barren, clay-walled gullies that may have begun as Etruscan mining cuts. They've a life of their own; medieval chronicles report them gobbling up farms and churches around the city, and no one has yet found a way to stop their inexorable growth. In the 1700s they tried to atone for their appetite, revealing some of the most important Etruscan necropolises yet discovered, and contributing urns to the Guarnacci Museum. Now even the necropolises are all but gone, though on the edge of one cliff you can see the **Badia**, an 11th-century Camaldolensian abbey, now half-devoured.

## The Val di Cecina and the Metal Hills

There are few attractions in the romantic emptiness of the Volterran Hills. If you take the SS68 west from Volterra along the Cecina Valley to Guardistallo, you reach a rolling valley with pines and cypresses in just the right places – a suitable Tuscan backdrop for any Renaissance painting. **Montecatini Val di Cecina**, in the hills to the north, is quiet and medieval, with a 12th-century castle. Further west, a big wine area extends around **Montescudaio** (Montescudaio wine, red and white, is a distinguished though lesser-known dry variety with a DOC label).

🟠 **Colline Metallifere**

The most unusual road from Volterra, the SS439, leads south over the Metal Hills towards Massa Marittima and the coast. These 'metal hills', along with the iron mines of Elba, did much to finance the gilded existence of the Etruscans. Several mines operate today, though driving through the hills you may see little but oak forests and olive groves.

**Larderello**, self-proclaimed 'World Centre of Geothermal Energy', is the north boundary of volcanic Italy; the extinct volcano of Monte Amiata and the ancient crater lakes of Umbria and Lazio are not far away. This far north, the only manifestations of a subterranean nature are benign little geysers and gurgling pools of sulphurous mud. Larderello is a growing town; huge, ugly cooling towers of the type that signify a nuclear power plant anywhere else can be spotted wherever there is a geothermal source worth tapping. Near the centre, there is a strange, postmodernist church designed in the 1950s by Michelucci, the architect of Florence's rail

**Museo della Geotermia**

*t 0588 67724; open daily 8–12.30 and 1.30–5.30; closed Sat in winter; adm*

station, and the **Museo della Geotermia**, which may explain something of this overheated little town's career.

After Larderello, and almost as far as Monterotondo, the landscape is downright uncanny. It smells bad, too; geysers and steam vents (*soffioni*) whistle and puff by the roadside, while murky pits bubble up boric salts amidst yellow and grey slag piles. Follow the yellow signs of the '*itinerario dei soffioni'* to see the best of it.

Despite the sulphur and borax, the cooling towers and occasional rusting hulks of old mining equipment, the Metal Hills are quite winsome, especially south of Larderello (still on the SS439) around the medieval village of **Castelnuovo di Val di Cecina**, surrounded by chestnuts and the Ala dei Diavoli (Devils' Wing) pass at the crest of the hills. **Monterotondo Marittimo**, further south, has more than its fair share of subsurface curiosities; nearby **Lago Boracifero** is Italy's centre for borax mining. In some places, the ground is covered with strange webs of steam pipes, built since the *comune* discovered its unique resource could power almost everything in town for free.

## Where to Stay in Volterra

ⓘ **Volterra >**
*Piazza dei Priori 10, t 0588 86150, www.provolterra.it Palazzo dei Priori 19–20, t 0588 87257, www.volterratur.it*

**Volterra** ✉ 56048

Volterra does not see as many tourists as San Gimignano, but is nevertheless just as expensive – at least, inexpensive rooms are hard to find.

***Villa Nencini**, Borgo S. Stefano, t 0588 86386, *www.villanencini.it* (€€€€). A 16th-century house with beautiful views, located just north of the city centre.

****San Lino**, Via San Lino 26, near Porta San Francesco, t 0588 85250, *www.hotelsanlino.com* (€€). Upscale, with tastefully remodelled rooms in an old cloister, standing out only for being the only place with parking.

***Nazionale**, Via dei Marchesi 11, t 0588 86284, *www.hotelnazionale volterra.it* (€€). A pleasant old hotel, situated handily within the walls of the town.

**L'Etrusca**, Via Porta all'Arco 37, t 0588 84073 (€€). This has small apartments with kitchenettes just off Piazza del Popolo. Guests may use the pool at the sister hotel/restaurant **Sant'Elisa** (*see right*).

**Ostello della Gioventù**, Via Don Minzoni, t 0588 887257. Students aren't entirely out of luck: there's the youth hostel, providing an institutional atmosphere but at rock-bottom rates.

## Eating Out in Volterra

Many restaurants in Volterra specialize in roast boar and the like, medieval cuisine entirely in keeping with the spirit of the place.

**Del Duca**, Via di Castello 2, t 0588 81510 (€€€). Volterra is distinctly lacking in good restaurants, but this one stands out. The set *menu degustazione* is good value, or choose from the full menu: rabbit with black olives cooked in Vernaccia, duck breast or *foie gras*, and a delicious chocolate soufflé to finish. *Closed Tues.*

**Il Porcellino**, Vicolo delle Prigioni 16, t 0588 86392 (€€€). Lots of different set menus, combining seafood and familiar Tuscan favourites with local treats like roast pigeon and boar with olives. *Closed Oct–Mar.*

**Il Sacco Fiorentino** (the name refers to Lorenzo de' Medici's massacre of the citizens of Volterra in 1472), Piazza XX Settembre 18, t 0588 88537 (€€).

★ **La Vecchia Lira >>**

Combines a vast range of *crostini*, gnocchi with baby vegetables, penne with Tuscan cheeses, roast pork with black olives, rabbit cooked in garlic and *vin santo* and pigeon with red radicchio and *vin santo* – an imaginative menu that changes with the seasons. *Closed Wed*.

**Sant'Elisa**, about 3km away on the SS68, t 0588 80034 (€€). One of the restaurants most popular with the Volterrans. Superb simple, home-cooked food; it serves lots of game, such as *pappardelle* with wild boar or deer sauce, or wild boar stew with black olives. Also a 3-star hotel with pool. *Closed Tues*.

**La Vecchia Lira**, Via G. Matteotti 19, t 0588 86180 (€€). A jolly lunchtime self-service *tavola calda* with especially good mains – try the rabbit with artichokes or the duck stewed in chocolate and pine nuts – and a regular restaurant in the evenings. *Closed Wed*.

# Massa Marittima

This lovely, rugged area is part of the coastal Maremma district only in name; even in Roman times it was considered part of the 'maritime' province. And for just as long, Massa Marittima has been making its living from the mines, though today its 10,000 people are not enough to fill the space within its medieval walls. Albeit small, its brief prosperity left it beautiful, and well worth visiting: firstly, to see the second city of the Sienese Republic, a lesson in urban refinement within a small place; and secondly, to see its exquisite cathedral, one of Tuscany's great medieval monuments.

This town appeared as a free *comune*, the *Repubblica Massetana*, around 1225, just coinciding with a dizzying period of prosperity owing to its discovery of new silver and copper deposits nearby. Unfortunately, this wealth proved fatally attractive to Massa's bigger neighbours. Pisa and Siena fought over it for a century and it finally fell to the latter in 1337. Soon afterwards, the mines gave out, sending Massa spiralling into centuries of decline. Malaria was a problem from the 1500s, and not until the Lorraine dukes drained the wet places and re-opened some of the mines did things start looking up.

## The Duomo

✪ **Duomo di Massa Marittima**

This is quite a sight, rising incongruously on its pedestal, its effect heightened by its setting above and at an angle to Massa's **Piazza Garibaldi**, a true *tour de force* of medieval town design. Reconstruction of an earlier cathedral began around 1200 and finished in 1250, though some additions were made; note the contrast between the original Pisan-Romanesque style, with blind arches and lozenges, and the Sienese campanile, added about 1400. Its best features include Gothic windows, capitals and the carvings of animals protecting humans on the façade and the left side.

## Getting to Massa Marittima

Massa is only 22km off the coastal Via Aurelia at Follonica, and is absolutely worth the diversion if you are passing that way; direct from Siena it's a not particularly captivating 65km/1hr 20min **drive** on the SS73 (passing by San Galgano) and the SS441.

There are 3 or 4 **buses** a day from Volterra (change at Monterotondo), 5 to nearby Follonica, and frequent buses and **trains** from there to Grosseto (Massa is in Grosseto province); also 2 a day to Florence and Siena, and 1 direct to Grosseto. Information and tickets from *Agenzia Massa Veterensis* opposite the Duomo. Most buses stop on Via Corridoni, behind and a little downhill from the Duomo.

---

The interior, under massive columns with delicate capitals, each one different, has a few trecento and quattrocento frescoes, including one of St Julian tending the sick near the main entrance. On the left, there is a luminous *Madonna* by Duccio (1318) and unique reliefs from the original 11th-century church: staring priests and Apostles in vigorous, cartoon-like style. On the right hangs the *Nativity of Mary* by that most peculiar Sienese artist Rutilio Manetti (d. 1639): woebegone ladies and a jellicle cat attend a pug-nosed, thumb-sucking, very unbeatific baby Mary. Nearby is a fine font with reliefs by Giraldo da Como (*c.* 1250) and a Renaissance tabernacle added in 1447. A wooden crucifix by Giovanni Pisano hangs over the high altar; in the Gothic apse is the *Ark of San Cerbone* with more reliefs (1324) on the life of Massa's patron saint.

### Up and Down Massa

Next to the cathedral on Piazza Garibaldi, the 1230 **Palazzo del Podestà** holds Massa's **Museo Archeologico** (the Medici dukes carried the best finds to Florence) and the small **Pinacoteca**, in which the best work is a *Maestà* by Ambrogio Lorenzetti, aglow with rosy faces, flowers and golden trim. Note the angel with the distaff and spindle in the centre – a sure sign that the local wool guild paid for the painting. The museum also houses the offices of **La Coop Colline Metallifere**, which runs all Massa's museums.

Piazza Garibaldi is lively, often crowded with Teutons perching on the steps of the Duomo or swilling beer in the café-pizzerias. Via Libertà leads into the older quarter, a nest of arches and alleys barely changed over centuries. Like Siena, Massa is divided into three *terzi*; this is the *terzo* of Civitavecchia.

Via Moncini climbs to the **Città Nuova**, a 14th-century suburb behind unusual Sienese fortifications; the street ends at Piazza Matteotti, with the 1330 **Torre del Candaliere** (Torre dell'Orologio), linked to the fortifications by the **Sienese Arch**, a slender walkway; it's a beautiful ensemble, more for show than any military consideration. Up Corso Diaz, **Sant'Agostino** church (completed 1313) has works by Rutilio Manetti.

**Museo Archeologico/ Pinacoteca**
*Piazza Garibaldi,*
*t 0566 902289;*
*open April–Oct*
*Tues–Sun 10–12.30 and*
*3.30–7; Nov–Mar*
*Tues–Sun 10–12.30 and*
*3–5; adm*

**La Coop Colline Metallifere**
*t 0566 902289*

**Torre del Candaliere**
*open Nov–Mar Tues–*
*Sun 11–1 and 2.30–4.30;*
*April–Oct Tues–Sun 10–1*
*and 3–6; adm*

## Where to Stay in Massa Marittima

ⓘ **Massa** ›
*Via Parenti 22,
t 0566 902289,
www.coopcolline
metallifere.it*

### Massa Marittima ✉ 58024

Massa becomes ever more popular and its room capacity is often stretched to the limit.

**\*\*\*Duca del Mare**, Via D. Alighieri 1/2, **t** 0566 902284, *www.ducadelmare.it* (€€). One of the town's three hotels, just below the town centre on the Via Massetana, in a lovely setting with a garden and views over the country-side (Massa lies on a rather steep hill); it's set in a modern building and has a simple trattoria. Pool, too!

⭐ **Da Tronca** ››

**\*\*Girifalco**, Via Massentana, **t** 0566 902177, *www.ilgirifalco.com* (€€). Offers similar amenities (but no pool) and the same views as Duca del Mare, but cheaper, and there is an excellent restaurant using home-produced meat, veg and oils.

## Eating Out in Massa Marittima

Dining in Massa is uncomplicated.

**Da Bracoli**, Località Ghirlanda, **t** 0566 902318 (€€€€). Offers *haute cuisine* variations on local dishes and a formidable wine list in an elegant setting. *Closed Mon and Tues.*

**Taverna del Vecchio Borgo**, **t** 0566 903950 (€€€). This comes highly recommended, not only for its food – game dishes including pheasant, boar and venison – but for its long list of grappas. *Closed Sun eve and Mon.*

**Da Tronca**, Vicolo Porta 5, **t** 0566 901991 (€€). This rustic trattoria with its rough stone walls and arches has something of a medieval atmosphere. The food is local and delicious: *tortelli maremmani* (stuffed with chard and ricotta), anchovies in pesto, pasta with courgettes and ricotta, mushroom soup, wild boar, rabbit and tripe. *Closed Wed and lunch.*

*Museo di Arte e di
Storia della Miniera
Pza. Matteotti, t 0566
902289; open April–Oct
Tues–Sun 3–5.30;
Nov–Mar by appt; adm*

*Museo della Miniera
t 0566 902289; open
April–Oct 10–12.45 and
3.30–5.45; Nov–Mar 10–
12.45 and 3–4.30; adm*

Finally, no visit to Massa is complete without a trip to a mining museum (ask politely at the city library and they may show you the city's treasure, the 1310 *Codice Minerario Massetano*, modern Europe's first code of laws concerning mining rights). The **Museo di Arte e di Storia della Miniera** on Piazza Matteotti is very small, but there's another one, the **Museo della Miniera** on Via Corridoni. Here the entrance leads into nearly half a mile of tunnels, with exhibits to show how the job was done from medieval days to the present.

# San Galgano and the Sword in the Stone

*⭐ Abbey of
San Galgano
open daily
8am–11pm*

The SS73 east from Massa to Siena skirts the southern Colline Metallifere, through lands that saw a great medieval flowering of monasticism. The monks are mostly long gone, but they left one of the most unusual, least-visited sights in Tuscany – the ruined Cistercian **abbey of San Galgano**, some 2km north of Palazzetto. In some of the older paintings in Siena's Pinacoteca, you will see the oddly Arthurian figure of a man apparently drawing a sword from a stone. This is San Galgano and, in fact, he is putting the sword *in*.

Galgano Guidotti, from nearby Chiusdino, was a dissolute soldier who one day had a vision of St Michael on the slopes of Montesiepi, ordering him to change his ways. Thrusting his sword into a rock to symbolize his new life, Galgano became a holy hermit; an ensuing career of miracles ensured his rapid canonization in 1181.

Almost from the start, the community he founded here was associated with the Cistercian Order, attracting monks from France as well as from around Siena. For centuries they played a vital role in the community, draining swamps, building mills and starting up a small textile industry. The Republic of Siena found them indispensable as architects, administrators – and as accountants. Many of the *Biccherna* covers in the Siena archives show Cistercians puzzling over the books or handing out pay. With its immense wealth, and its French architects eager to initiate the backward Italians in the glories of the new Gothic style, the order began its great **abbey church** in 1218. The Cistercians were already in a bad way when the abbey was dissolved in 1600; soon after their departure the roof, the façade and the campanile collapsed, leaving the grandest French-Gothic building in Tuscany a ruin. Its beautiful travertine columns and pointed arches remain, with the sky as roof and green lawns as carpet. Parts of the monastery survive, now in the care of Olivetan nuns.

After Galgano's death, St Michael appeared again on a hill above the abbey to command his followers to build the **Cappella di Montesiepi** over the sword in the stone. The curious round chapel, one of very few in Italy, was begun in 1185. The sword is still there, protruding from its rock right in the centre. As with all the sites associated with St Michael, it is a reminder of a branch of medieval mysticism that, while not entirely lost, is hardly well understood. It's a very curious place – during a recent visit, a beautiful woman in black entered, carrying a gleaming silver sword, and went off to a side room with the caretaker (we didn't ask). Note the pair of human hands in a glass box, with a card explaining how they were bitten off by wolves. The altar has a cross of the type often seen on buildings of the Knights Templar, and the ceiling dome, patterned in 22 concentric stripes, may be a representation of the heavenly spheres of medieval cosmology.

# Southern Tuscany

*Not counting the coastal Maremma around Grosseto, the old territories of the Sienese Republic make a coherent landscape, of rolling hills mostly given over to farming and pastures. It isn't as garden-like as some other parts of Tuscany, though vineyards and avenues of cypresses are not lacking. Hill towns poke above the horizon – Montepulciano, Pienza and Castiglione d'Orcia. At times, it seems the whole region is laid out before you, bounded on one side by the hills around Siena, on the other by the cones of Monte Amiata and Radicofani. In the little tourist offices they remark that not many English or Americans pass through – missing beautiful countryside, some of the best food and wine in Tuscany, and delightful towns with reminders of the Renaissance and Middle Ages.*

# 14

## Don't miss

⭐ **An élite Renaissance monastery**
Monte Oliveto Maggiore p.384

⭐ **Pope Pius II's Renaissance city**
Pienza p.389

⭐ *Vino nobile* **and fine art**
Montepulciano p.391

⭐ **Underground mysteries**
Chiusi p.397

⭐ **Idyllic skiing and hiking**
Monte Amiata p.400

*See map overleaf*

# Southern Tuscany

## Don't miss

- **1** Monte Oliveto Maggiore **p.384**
- **2** Pienza **p.389**
- **3** Montepulciano **p.391**
- **4** Chiusi **p.397**
- **5** Monte Amiata **p.400**

# Asciano and the *Crete*

The SS326 from Siena heads east, its main purpose to get you to Cortona (*see* pp.428–32) then Umbria. Before leaving Siena province, it passes the village of **Monteaperti**, where the Sienese won their famous victory over Florence in 1260, and **Rapolano Terme** (27km), a small spa retaining some of its medieval walls. Besides the hot springs there is a surplus of natural gas in the area, some of it pumped from wells and some leaking out of the ground – take care not to drop a match!

**Asciano**, 10km south of Rapolano, has walls built by the Sienese in 1351 and a good collection of Sienese art. Its **Museo d'Arte Sacra** and the **Museo Etrusco** are in the same building, **Palazzo Corboli**. The house at **Via del Canto 11** has some Roman mosaics.

Southeast of Siena, the valleys of the Ombrone and the Asso enclose the country of the *crete*. Like the *balze* of Volterra (*see* p.375), the *crete* are uncanny monuments to the power of erosion. The countryside around Asciano is dotted with them, exposing chalk cliffs where the soil above has eroded; they often appear in the backgrounds of 14th- and 15th-century Sienese and Florentine paintings (similar eroded chalk hills are called *biancane*). This sheep country suffered a great deal after the Second World War, when many local men left to seek work in the cities. Today, immigrants from Sardinia make up a sizable minority of the population, born shepherds trying to get the business back on its feet.

Old **Sinalunga**, on its hill, is next (22km east); the main square is named after Garibaldi, to commemorate his arrest here in 1867 on the orders of King Vittorio Emanuele, afraid his volunteers were about to attack Rome. **Torrita di Siena**, an old Sienese border fortress 6km southwest of the junction with the A1 from Florence to Rome, owes its name to the tall towers of its walls (some remain).

**Museo d'Arte Sacra/ Museo Etrusco**
*Corso Matteotti 122, t 0577 719524, www.palazzocorboli.it; open April–Oct Tues–Sun 10–1 and 3–7; Nov–Feb Thurs–Sat 10–1 and 3–5.30, Sun 10–1 and 2.30–6; adm*

**Via del Canto 11**
*to visit, ask at pharmacy on Corso Matteotti*

# Monte Oliveto Maggiore and Around

South of Siena, the SS2 wends towards Rome, roughly following the Roman Via Cassia and medieval pilgrims' path to Rome, the Via Francigena. It passes **Lucignano d'Arbia** (16km), a charming, tiny village with a medieval church, and **Buonconvento** (27km), a gritty industrial town that hides a miniature walled medieval centre. The walls, no longer very proper or military, are peppered with windows of the houses built against them. There are two fine gates either end of the main street, and, in the middle, the 14th-century parish church with an altarpiece by Matteo di Giovanni.

In the broken, jumbled hills south of Asciano, austere green meadows alternate with ragged gullies and bare white cliffs. At the centre of these *crete*, in the bleakest and most barren part, is a

*14*

*Southern Tuscany | Asciano and the Crete*

⭐ **Monte Oliveto Maggiore**
*9km from Buonconvento on SS451; t 0577 718567; open daily 9.15–12 and 3.15–5 (until 6 in summer)*

grove of tall, black cypresses around the **monastery of Monte Oliveto Maggiore**. Gentlemen from Siena's merchant élite founded it, including Giovanni Tolomei and Ambrogio Piccolomini, jaded merchants and sincere Christians who retired here in 1313 to escape the fatal sophistication of the medieval city. Their Olivetan Order was approved by the pope only six years later. With such wealthy backers, the monastery became a sort of élite hermitage for central Tuscany. An ambitious building programme in the 1400s made it a marvel of Renaissance clarity and rationality, expressed in simple structures and good Siena brick.

The beautiful, asymmetrical **gatehouse**, which is decorated with a della Robbia terracotta, makes for a fitting introduction. Inside, the well-proportioned brick **abbey church** (which was finished in 1417) has an exceptional set of wooden intarsia **choirstalls** by the master of the genre, Fra Giovanni da Verona – it's among the best work of this kind in Italy. Note also the unusual dome with an octagon of interlocking arches, an Islamic Andalucian design that made its way here via Spanish Christian churches and the chapel of the Castel Nuovo in Naples.

The monastery's greatest treasure is the **great cloister**, with 36 frescoes of scenes from the *Life of St Benedict* (whose original rule Tolomei and the Olivetans were trying to restore). All 36 are currently being restored. The first nine are by Luca Signorelli, with formidable ladies and bulky, white-robed monks in his distinctive balloonish forms and sparing use of colour. The rest are by Il Sodoma (1505–8) – some of his best painting, ethereal scenes of Pre-Raphaelite ladies and mandarin monks, with blue and purple backgrounds of ideal landscapes and cities. Mr Sodomite himself appears in the scene '*Come Benedetto risaldò lo capistero che era rotta*' ('How Benedict repaired the broken sieve'); he's the dissipated fellow on the left, with the white gloves. He also painted in his pet badgers, of which he was very fond.

ℹ️ **Buonconvento**
>>
*Piazzale Garibaldi 2, t 0577 807181 (closed Mon)*

ℹ️ **Asciano** >
*Corso Matteotti 18, t 0577 719510*

## Where to Stay and Eat around Asciano and Monte Oliveto Maggiore

In this quiet corner, villages may only have one real hotel, or none. But there are plenty of *agriturismi*. Some private homes and restaurants, too, let rooms.

### Asciano ✉ 53041

**La Pievina**, Loc. La Pievina near Asciano on Laurentana road, t 0577 281711 *www.lapievina.it* (€€€). A very friendly place specializing in sea fish, fowl and veggie dishes. The owners also let a house in the centre. *Closed Mon, Tues, and lunch exc Sun.*

### Buonconvento ✉ 53022

**\*\*Albergo Ristorante Roma**, Via Soccini 14, t 0577 806021 (€). The closest rooms to Monte Oliveto Maggiore: simple and old-fashioned, with breakfast included. The very good restaurant serves traditional fare.

### Sinalunga ✉ 53048

**\*\*\*\*Locanda dell'Amorosa**, Loc. L'Amorosa, 2km south of Sinalunga, t 0577 677211, *www.amorosa.it* (€€€€€). A truly special place (book far ahead) – a medieval hamlet with a manor house, frescoed church, 16 beautiful rooms, an outdoor pool and a restaurant (€€€). *Closed Mon; restaurant Tues lunch.*

Unlike so many great Tuscan art shrines, Monte Oliveto, which is isolated in the Sienese hills, retains some of its original aloof dignity. Though Napoleon suppressed the monastery in 1810, a group of talented Brothers still works here, restoring old books. They're vowed to silence, but the monkish gift shop outside sells home-made wine and honey, as well as other products from the monasteries around Tuscany.

In the *crete* around Monte Oliveto, the village of **San Giovanni d'Asso** (8km southeast) is built around a Sienese fortress; the church of San Pietro in Villore is from the 12th century, with an ambitious, unusual façade. From here, unsignposted byroads lead east to **Montisi** (7km) and **Trequanda** (12km), two fine villages, seldom visited because they're hard to find; the latter has a 13th-century castle and Romanesque church. You might even find **Sant'Anna in Camprena**, between Montisi and Pienza, an ambitious medieval monastery complex that time forgot – until the location scouts from *The English Patient* arrived. The place is now being fitfully restored, and, if you liked Il Sodoma's work in Monte Oliveto, stop here to see another of his frescoes, portraying Christ with children, small dogs and fantasy Roman monuments.

# Montalcino and Around

On a lofty hill inhabited since Etruscan times, swathed in vineyards and olive groves, walled **Montalcino** (population 5,400) dominates the serene countryside 14km south of Buonconvento. Its major attraction is liquid – Brunello di Montalcino, a dark, pungent red proudly holding its own among Italy's finest wines.

Every year at the Palio in Siena, a procession of representatives from all the towns that once were part of the republic takes place. The honour of leading the parade belongs to Montalcino, for its loyalty and for the great service that it rendered in 1555 after the fall of Siena (*see* p.334). During the siege, diehard republicans escaped from Siena to the impregnable fortress of Montalcino, where they established the 'Republic of Siena at Montalcino', holding out against the Medici until 1559. Today, Montalcino is a friendly, resolutely sleepy town.

## Within the Walls

Piazza Cavour in home to the modest **archaeology museum**, set in a former hospital pharmacy, with detached frescoes by a student of Il Sodoma. Via Mazzini leads west to Piazza del Popolo and the attractive **Palazzo Comunale**, begun in the late 13th century, with a slender tower that apes the Torre di Mangia in Siena (*see* p.338). Nearby, **Sant'Agostino** is a simple Sienese church containing some original frescoes from the 1300s.

## Getting to Montalcino

There are regular **buses** from Siena (41km/1hr), a few involving a change at Buonconvento, near the SS2 crossroads for Montalcino. Buses stop at Piazza Cavour at the east end of town; you can get tickets at the bar on the piazza. There are no convenient buses to **Sant'Antimo**, around 10km south of town.

**Museo Civico e Diocesano d'Arte Sacra**
*t 0577 846014, wwwmuseisenesi.org; open Tues–Sun 10–1 and 2–5.40; adm*

The **diocesan and civic museum** round the corner has Sienese paintings and polychromed wood statues, including *Madonnas* by three great Sienese artists (Martini, Pietro Lorenzetti and Il Vecchietta), and some of the earliest successes of Sienese art, an illuminated Bible and painted crucifix, both from the 12th century. Besides some minor works of the 14th–15th-century Sienese masters, there's a collection of local majolica from the same period.

**Rocca**
*open summer daily 9–8; winter daily 9–6; adm to go up on walls*

Just down Via Ricasoli, at the east end of town, the impressive 14th-century **Rocca** was the centre of the fortifications that kept the Spaniards and Florentines at bay. This citadel was the last stronghold of the Sienese and a symbol of all the medieval freedoms of the Italian cities blotted out in the reactionary 1500s. Near the entrance is a plaque with a poem from the 'Piedmontese Volunteers of Liberty', extolling Montalcino's bravery in 'refusing the Medici thief'. Now a city park, the Rocca contains the last battle standard of the Sienese Republic and an ***enoteca***, where you can acquaint yourself with Montalcino's venerable Brunello and other local wines, such as Moscadello and Rosso di Montalcino.

Following the town walls on the north side, you pass through neighbourhoods largely made up of orchards and gardens. The **cathedral**, on Via Spagni, was mostly rebuilt in the 1700s. Follow that street past the Baroque church of the **Madonna del Soccorso**, and you come to the **city park**, the 'Balcony of Tuscany', with views over Siena and beyond.

## South of Montalcino: Sant'Antimo

**Sant'Antimo**
*about 10km south of Montalcino; open daily 6.45am–9pm (Mass sung Mon–Sat 9.15am and 7pm, Sun 11am and 6.30pm); adm*

One of the finest Romanesque churches in Tuscany, Sant'Antimo originally formed part of a 9th-century Benedictine monastery founded, according to legend, by Charlemagne. The present building, begun in 1118, incorporates parts of the Carolingian works, including the crypt. This half-ruined complex, reached by a long, winding avenue of cypresses, could easily serve as the set for *The Name of the Rose*. An important monastic community flourished here, and there are still some monks; they'll sell you a CD of their Gregorian chant, which you can hear them sing at Mass. The church is exquisite, with its elegant tower and rounded apse. Some of the stone inside, on the capitals and elsewhere, is luminous alabaster from Volterra. The sophistication of the architecture is impressive – in particular, the Byzantine-style women's gallery, and the ambulatory behind the apse with its radiating chapels.

## Shopping in and around Montalcino

A few of the **vineyards** that produce the famous Brunello di Montalcino are on the road south for Sant'Antimo. Two welcome visitors: the **Azienda Agricola Greppo** (t 0577 848087) and the **Cantine dei Barbi** (t 0577 841111, www.fattoriadeibarbi.it). Call ahead.

⭐ **Boccon Divino >>**

Besides wine, Montalcino is known for its honey, and in early September hosts the **national honey fair**.

## Where to Stay and Eat in Montalcino

ⓘ **Montalcino >**
*Costa del Municipio 8,*
*t 0577 849331*

**Montalcino** ✉ 53024

**★★★★La Vecchia Oliviera**, Porta Cerbaia, t 0577 846028, www.vecchiaoliviera. com (€€€€). A former olive press by the old gate into the town, with pretty, elegant rooms and a pool with a Jacuzzi, overlooking the hills.

**★★★Dei Capitani Dipendenza**, Via Lapini 6, t 0577 847227, www.deicapitani.it (€€€€). An old *palazzo* with rooms and little apartments furnished in the *Arte Povera* style; wonderful views, a small pool and (a rarity here) a car park.

**★★★Bellaria**, Via Osticcio 19, t 0577 849326 (€€). A farmhouse a short walk from town in a pine wood. Some of the simple but comfortable rooms, and the pool, have fabulous views.

**★★★Il Giglio**, Via Soccorso Saloni 5, t 0577 848167, www.gigliohotel.com (€€). Rustically styled rooms and apartments and a Tuscan restaurant. Rates include breakfast.

**Boccon Divino**, Loc. Colombaio Tozzi 201, t 0577 848233 (€€€). Some of the best food in the area, including a great onion soup and *scottiglia* (stew with hot peppers). Booking is advisable. *Closed Tues.*

**Osteria Osticcio**, Via Matteotti 23, t 0577 848271 (€€). A pleasant wine bar with magnificent views, serving meats, cheeses, *crostini* and salads. Try the fabulous Brunello wine. *Closed Sun.*

**Locanda Sant'Antimo**, Via Basso Mondo 6, Castelnuovo dell'Abate, t 0577 835615 (€). A good pizzeria plus rooms (€€). *Closed Tues.*

**Il Pozzo**, Piazza del Pozzo 2, Loc. S. Angelo in Colle, t 0577 844015 (€). Good-value traditional meals, including wild boar in Brunello wine sauce. *Closed Tues, and 2wks Aug.*

**14**

**Southern Tuscany | Val d'Orcia**

# Val d'Orcia

**San Quirico d'Orcia**, which is a humble agricultural centre where the SS146 from Pienza joins the SS2, still has some of its medieval walls. Once on the pilgrim route of the Via Francigena, it was endowed with hospices and hospitals to accommodate pilgrims en route to Rome. The magnificent **Collegiata**, rebuilt in the 12th century over an 8th-century church, has an exceptional façade of local travertine and three portals from the 1200s, sculpted with lions and telamons, the finest of their kind in the area. Just behind

**Palazzo Chigi**
*open by appt on*
*t 0577 898247*

it is the somewhat forbidding 17th-century **Palazzo Chigi** – a grand presence for such a tiny town. Since its restoration, the frescoed rooms are open to visitors.

There are a couple more attractive churches here: **Santa Maria di Vitaleta**, with a Gothic façade and an enamel *Annunciation* by Andrea della Robbia on the high altar, and the pretty little 11th-

**Horti Leonini**
*open daily*
*dawn–sunset*

century **Santa Maria Assunta**. There's also the **Horti Leonini**, a lovely garden designed in the late 15th century by Diomede Lioni, as a resting place for pilgrims.

There are a couple of points of interest nearby: **Ripa d'Orcia**, a hamlet with a stately castle (now a hotel), 7km south, and **Bagno Vignoni**, a small spa town just south off the SS2, where the piazza has a *vasca termale* built by Lorenzo de' Medici, who came for the waters. If you long for a bathe, you can get day tickets for the hot springs at the Hotel Posta Marcucci (*see* opposite).

Before the modern SS2 was built, the old Via Francigena traversed the valley of the Orcia, passing a patch of castles and fortified towns that began in the early Middle Ages. **Castiglione d'Orcia** (9km south of San Quirico) is as medieval-looking a town as you could ask for (though its cobbled piazza and fountain are from the 1600s), with two parish churches. The ruined fortress overlooking the town was built by the Aldobrandeschi family, who controlled much of southern Tuscany as late as the 1200s.

Just outside to the north, a pretty road winds up through olive groves to **Rocca d'Orcia**, another well-preserved medieval village clustered below its impressive castle, the **Rocca di Tentatenno**, which is used to host art exhibitions. Another 15km to the south of Castiglione lies **Vivo d'Orcia**, which began life as a Camaldolensian monastery in 1003; when the monastery withered the village grew, leaving only the attractive Romanesque **Cappella dell'Ermicciolo** in the woods above the town.

**Bagni San Filippo**, 8km east of Vivo, may be the world's smallest thermal spa, with its phone booth, handful of old houses and small hotel. It takes its name from San Filippo Benizi, a holy hermit of the Middle Ages who hid here when he heard there was a movement to elect him pope. Gouty old Lorenzo Il Magnifico came here, too, though he didn't leave any embellishments such as the piazza in Bagno Vignoni. You can swim in the natural terraced pools of the **Fosso Bianco**, a glistening limestone formation – a sort of stone waterfall – created by the flowing sulphurous waters.

## Radicofani

Some wonderfully rugged countryside lies in the valley of the Orcia, east of this chain of villages, especially along the roads approaching **Radicofani**, a landmark of southern Tuscany, with its surreal, muffin-shaped hill topped by a lofty tower. The ruined fortress around it, originally built by Pope Adrian IV (the Englishman Nicholas Breakspear), served in the 1300s as HQ for legendary bandit Ghino di Tacco, solid citizen of Dante's *Inferno* and subject of a story in the *Decameron* (Day 10, Number 2), about how he imprisoned the Abbot of Cluny in this tower.

The elegant loggias on the main road, just outside town, belong to the 17th-century Palazzo La Posta, once the only good hotel between Siena and Rome; most of the famous on the Grand Tour stopped on their way through.

## Festivals in the Val d'Orcia

**Incontri in Terra di Siena**, t 0578 69101, *www.lafoce.com*. A chamber music festival in late July, based at La Foce, home of writer Iris Origo, on the Monte Amiata road from Chianciano. **Festival del Val d'Orcia**. A month (late July–Aug) of music, theatre and dance.

## Where to Stay and Eat in the Val d'Orcia

### Bagno Vignoni ✉ 53027

**La Locanda del Loggiato**, Piazza del Moretto 30, t 0577 888925, *www. loggiato. it* (€€€). A B&B on the first floor of a lovely medieval house, with rustically elegant rooms; breakfast is included. A wine bar takes over the breakfast room in the evenings.

**\*\*\*Hotel Posta Marcucci**, Via Ara Urcea, t 0577 887112, *www.hotel postamarcucci.it* (€€). A hillside option with a thermal pool and terraces with

views over the Val d'Orcia, plus a tennis court. The restaurant is a bit dull but does have a veggie menu.

**Osteria del Leone**, Piazza del Moretto, t 0577 887300 (€€€–€€). Very good home-made *pici* with garlic, risotto with pear and *provola* chese, rabbit in orange sauce, and more. Book ahead. *Closed Mon, and 4wks Nov/Dec.*

### San Quirico d'Orcia ✉ 53027

**\*\*\*Hotel Palazzo del Capitano**, Via Poliziano 18, t 0577 899028, *www.palazzodelcapitano.com* (€€€). An elegant 15th-century *palazzo* in the medieval heart of town, with tasteful rooms (breakfast included), an outdoor pool and an excellent restaurant in the old bakery. *Restaurant closed Nov–Feb.*

### Radicofani ✉ 53040

**La Palazzina**, Loc. Le Vigne, t 0578 55771, *www.fattorialapalazzina.com* (€€€). A 200-year-old villa just outside the village, with a pool, and a minimum 3-night stay in high season. Superb home-made pasta is on the menu.

ⓘ **San Quirico** >>
*Piazza Chigi 2, t 0577 899724, www.comune sanquirico.it*

ⓘ **Radicofani** >>
*Via R. Magi 57, t 0578 55684*
★ **La Palazzina** >>

14

Southern Tuscany | Pienza

# Pienza

🏛 Pienza

Some 50km south of Siena on the SS2 is a perfect, tiny core of Renaissance order and urbanity, surrounded by a village of around 2,500 souls. Pienza is delightful, if touristy. Like Monte Oliveto Maggiore, it's a jewel among archetypal Tuscan landscapes.

During a period of political troubles, common in Renaissance Siena, the great family of the Piccolomini exiled itself temporarily in one of its possessions, the village of Corsignano. Aeneas Silvius Piccolomini (*see* p.345) was born there in 1405; later, as Pope Pius II, he determined to raise his birthplace into a city. No historian has discovered a compelling economic or military reason for a new town here. Bernardo Rossellino designed it, with help from Pius; the pennies of the faithful paid for it, and Pius named it after himself: Pienza. Perhaps fortunately, after the first wave of papal patronage, Pienza was nearly forgotten. The grid of streets that was to extend over the Tuscan hills never materialized, and only the central piazza with a new cathedral and a Piccolomini palace was completed.

## Pienza's Piazza Pio II

Piazza Pio II, heart of Rossellino's design scheme, is simple and decorous; it displays the chief buildings of the town without any of the monumental symmetry of the later Renaissance, relying on proportion to tie it all together. Such a square shows how, despite all its paintings of ideal buildings and streetscapes, the early Renaissance still followed the 'picturesque' urban design of the Middle Ages; Piazza Pio was made to be a stage set for daily life or the background of a painting.

Rossellino designed an elegant façade for the **cathedral** (1462), capturing the spirit of the times by omission – there is no hint it belongs to a Christian building, though the Piccolomini arms and papal keys are carved on the pediment. The interior, equally elegant, is tame Gothic – as if this bold Renaissance architect were a slightly embarrassed humanist who believed only Gothic suited a church. Rossellino also carved a marble altar and baptismal font in the lower church; there are also altarpieces by other leading Sienese artists. Nothing in this cathedral has been changed, or even moved, since it was completed; Pius's papal bull of 1462 forbade it. See it while it lasts: the cathedral, built on the edge of a slight cliff, has been subsiding almost since it was built, and occasionally sulphurous fumes seep from the floor. No one has discovered a way to shore it up permanently, and though restoration work has been done it could collapse, at least partially, at any time.

**Palazzo Piccolomini**

*open summer Tues–Sun 10–12.30 and 3–6; winter Tues–Sun 10–12.30 and 4–7; adm*

Next door, the columned **well**, a favourite sort of Renaissance urban decoration, is also by Rossellino. So is the restored **Palazzo Piccolomini**, a rehash of the more famous Palazzo Rucellai in Florence, the design of which follows Alberti. The best bit is the rear, where a three-storey loggia overlooks a 'hanging garden' on the cliff edge. The interior and the gardens are open to visitors.

**Museo Diocesano di Pienza**

*Corso Rossellino 30; open mid-Mar–Oct Wed–Mon 10–1 and 3–7; Nov–mid-Mar Sat and Sun 10–1 and 3–6; or by appt on t 0578 749905; adm*

Behind the Palazzo Piccolomini, the church of **San Francesco** predates the founding of Pienza; the 14th–15th-century frescoes inside include one attributed to Luca Signorelli. The **Museo Diocesano di Pienza**, in the sumptuously restored 15th-century Palazza Borgia, has objects from nearby churches, several paintings (some by Signorelli) and Flemish tapestries.

Few people visit the 11th-century **Pieve** of old Corsignano, 1km west of town. This unusual church, where Aeneas Silvius was baptized, has some even more peculiar carvings over its entrance. Mermaids, or sirens, turn up with some frequency in Romanesque *tympana* and capitals, in Tuscany and Apulia especially, as well as many other places in Italy and France. Here there are several – one spreading its forked tail to display the entrance to the womb, flanked by others, and a dancer and a musician, with dragons whispering in their ears. Such symbols are steeped in medieval mysticism but are not entirely inaccessible to the modern imagination. It has been claimed that they betray the existence of an ecstatic cult, based on music and dance and descended from the ancient Dionysian rituals.

Ask at the tourist office (*see* opposite) about **guided tours** of Pienza.

## Shopping in Pienza

Corso Rossellino, leading from the centre of the village to Porta Murello and the bus terminus, has trendy ceramics and leatherwork workshops, antiques shops, and health food stores selling the good local honey and preserves. Pienza's delicate variety of *pecorino*, maybe Italy's best sheep's cheese, is available in different strengths depending on how long it has been aged.

## Where to Stay and Eat in Pienza

### Pienza ✉ 53026

If you're on a budget, ask the tourist office for their list of private houses with **rooms to let**.

**La Saracina**, about 7km from Pienza on road to Montepulciano, **t** 0578 748022, *www.lasaracina.it* (€€€€€). Rooms, suites and an apartment in an old farmhouse with lovely gardens, a pool and a tennis court, in the countryside. Breakfast is included.

⭐ La Pergola >>

ⓘ Pienza >
*Piazza Dante Alighieri 18,*
*t 0578 749905,*
*www.comunedipienza.it*

**\*\*\*Il Chiostro**, Corso Il Rossellino 26, **t** 0578 748400, *www.relaisilchiostrodipienza.com* (€€€€). An old cloister in the centre. just off Piazza Pio II, with stylish, modernized rooms, beautiful gardens, a small pool, and a good restaurant. *Closed mid-Jan–mid-Mar.*

**\*\*\*Corsignano**, Via della Madonnina 9, **t** 0578 748501, *www.corsignano.it* (€€€). A comfy modern option with an Internet corner, restaurant and bar.

**La Pergola**, Via dell'Acero 2, just outside town on road to San Quirico, **t** 0578 748051 (€€€). An uninspiring building housing an excellent restaurant serving local cuisine, including an excellent *panforte*, in a garden in summer. *Closed Mon.*

**Latte di Luna**, Via S. Carlo 2/4, **t** 0578 748606 (€€). A place popular with locals for its roast pork and rabbit. Note that credit cards aren't accepted. *Closed Tues, and 3wks in July.*

**Sperone Nudo**, Piazza di Spagna 3/5, **t** 0578 748641 (€€). A great lunch stop; try *pici* with boar, tagliatelle with *porcini*, tripe, and nut cake. *Closed Mon.*

# Montepulciano

🅱 Montepulciano

Another graceful hill town lies south of Siena, also with a distinguished past and best known for wine. Montepulciano is larger (population 14,500) and livelier than Montalcino, with fine buildings and works of art. Old Montalcino was a home from home for the Sienese, while Montepulciano usually allied itself with Florence. Its Vino Nobile was praised by connoisseurs more than 200 years ago and can contend with Italy's best today.

Inhabitants of Montepulciano (Roman *Mons Politianus*) are called *Poliziani*, after its most famous son – Angelo Ambrogini, or Poliziano, one of the first Renaissance Greek scholars, and an accomplished poet and critic and scholar at the court of Lorenzo de' Medici and tutor to his children. Botticelli's mythological paintings may have been inspired by his *Stanze per la Giostra*. Today's Poliziani are a genteel, cultured lot still given to poetic extemporization and singing. The *Bruscello*, a partly improvised play on medieval and Renaissance themes in music and verse, acted by the townspeople in the Piazza Grande each August, is the town's biggest festival. A second August festival, the *Bravio delle Botti*, requires no poetry but plenty of sweat, as neighbourhood teams race up the steep main street pushing huge barrels.

# Getting to and around Montpulciano

Montepulciano is 12.5km/20mins east of Pienza on the SS146, 66km/90mins from Siena, and 16km/30mins west of the Chiusi exit on the A1.

The **train** station (Florence–Rome line), way out in the countryside, is irregularly served by buses to town, and only local trains tend to stop. It's better to use the station at **Chiusi-Chianciano**, which has bus links up to Chiusi town, to Chianciano Terme, Montepulciano and occasionally Pienza.

**Montepulciano bus station** is just outside the Porta al Prato, the main gate into the city. There are very regular buses to Chianciano Terme–Chiusi–Chiusi station; slightly fewer to Pienza; and one each in the morning and afternoon for Siena (via Pienza and San Quirico). There are also daily connections to Abbadia San Salvatore, Montalcino, Perugia and Arezzo. There is an LFI bus info booth (t 0575 39881, *www.lfi.it*) in the train station at Chiusi; outside, besides the buses mentioned above, there are rather infrequent LFI links to Cortona, Arezzo, Perugia, Orvieto and Città della Pieve.

If you aren't up to climbing up to the top of Montepulciano, the LFI runs a handy **minibus** service up the Corso to Piazza Grande.

## *Palazzi* and Pulcinella

Entering the city through the **Porta al Prato**, you encounter a stone column bearing the *Marzocco*, a symbol of Montepulciano's long attachment to Florence. Though nominally under Florentine control, the city was allowed a sort of independence up to the days of Cosimo I. The main street, called here Via di Gracciano nel Corso, winds in a circle up to the top of the city (if you follow it all the way, you'll walk twice as far as you need to, and think Montepulciano is a metropolis). This stretch is lined with noble palaces: No.91 and No.82 are the work of the late Renaissance architect Vignola, famous for the Farnese Palace in Caprarola, Lazio. Up at No.73, **Palazzo Bucelli** has the most unusual foundation in Italy, made almost entirely of Etruscan cinerary urns, filled with cement and stacked like bricks, many retaining their sculpted reliefs. Montepulciano was once Etruscan, though the urns probably came from Chiusi.

Piazza Michelozzo, where the street begins to ascend, is named after the Florentine architect of **Sant'Agostino** church, with an excellent, restrained Renaissance façade, similar to the cathedral in Pienza but more skilfully handled. Michelozzo also contributed the terracotta reliefs over the portal. Across the piazza, note the figure atop the old **Torre del Pulcinello**: to anyone familiar with Naples,

---

### Vino Nobile and Other Vinous Delights

Montepulciano and its environs are full of *cantine*, each full of people ready for long discussions on the virtues of this famous wine, which after two years carries the bouquet of unknown autumn blooms, a perfume that confounds melancholy; its colour is a mystery of faith.

A **wine tour of Montepulciano** begins with the Cantine Cantucci, on Piazza Grande, where they might show you the *salon* with frescoes by Baroque artist Andrea Pozzo. The Cantina Gattavecchia, next to Santa Maria at the south end of town, has a 1500s *cantina*; don't neglect the venerable cellar built into the embankment beneath Piazza Grande, next to the Teatro Poliziano.

Vino Nobile isn't the only variety of wine made in these parts. There is a version of Chianti – Chianti Colli Senesi – a creditable white Valdichiana and the sweet dessert *vin santo*. On evenings when quantity means more than quality, try any of the mass-produced Montepulciano reds; a more honourable plonk is hard to find.

this white *Commedia dell'Arte* clown banging the hours on the town bell will be an old friend. It is said a Neapolitan bishop was exiled here for indiscretions back home; when he returned, he left this bit of Parthenopean culture as a souvenir to thank the Poliziani. Along the main street, you pass a dozen or so more palaces, reminders of the city's aristocratic past. There is one florid Baroque interior, in the **Gesù** church by Andrea Pozzo. Further down, the street curves around the medieval *fortezza*, now partly residential, in the oldest part of town with its fascinating ancient alleys.

## Piazza Grande

These days, when even the stalwart citizens of hill towns are too spoiled to walk up hills, the old centres of towns sometimes become quiet and out-of-the-way. So it is in Montepulciano, where the **Piazza Grande** is city's highest point. On one side, Michelozzo added a rusticated stone front and tower to the 13th-century **Palazzo Comunale** to create a lesser copy of Florence's Palazzo Vecchio. Opposite is a Renaissance well in front of the **Palazzo Contucci**, built by the elder Antonio da Sangallo. On the west side, a tremendous pile of bricks, a sort of tenement for pigeons, proclaims the agonizing unfinishability of the preposterous **cathedral**, begun in 1592 and housing a single transcendent work of art: atop the marble Renaissance altar adorned with *putti* stands an *Assumption of the Virgin* by Taddeo di Bartolo, one of the greatest of 14th-century Sienese paintings. Set in glowing, discordant colours – pink, orange, purple and gold – this is a very spiritual Madonna, attended by a court of angel musicians. Don't miss the *predella* panels beneath, each a serious, inspired image from the Passion, including one panel of the *Resurrection* that can be compared to Piero della Francesca's more famous version in Sansepolcro.

**Museo Civico/ Pinacoteca Crociani**
*Via Ricci,* **t** *0578 717300; open April–Oct Tues–Sun 10–1 and 3–6 (until 8 in summer); Nov–Mar Sat and Sun 10–1 and 3–6; adm*

The **Museo Civico/Pinacoteca Crociani** unite several collections. On the first and second floors are some della Robbia terracottas from the dissolved convent that was downstairs, and the Crociani collection of paintings. The old collection, with a *Crucifixion* from Filippino Lippi's workshop, an *Assumption* by the Sienese Jacopo di Mino, an odd work by Girolamo di Benvenuto – baby Jesus as an *objet d'art* – and, even more peculiar, an inexplicable *Allegory of the Immaculate Conception* by one Giovanni Antonio Lappoli (d. 1552), has additions from other collections in Montepulciano. There's also an archaeological section at ground level, including the contents of five locally discovered Etruscan tombs previously housed in the Uffizi. Artefacts include Bucchero ware, ceramics and bronzes dating from the 5th to the 2nd century BC.

Continue down Via Ricci for the church of **Santa Lucia**, with a small *Madonna* by Luca Signorelli in a chapel to the right.

### Antonio da Sangallo's San Biagio

One of the set pieces of Renaissance architecture was the isolated temple – a chance to create an ideal building in an uncluttered setting, often on the edge of a city. Giuliano da Sangallo's Santa Maria delle Carceri in Prato was the first and worst, followed by Bramante's San Pietro in Montorio in Rome and the Tempio della Consolazione in Todi (Umbria). Montepulciano's example is south of the city (a long walk downhill and back), near the road junction for Chianciano. A stately avenue of cypresses, each over a small marker commemorating a local soldier who died in the First World War, leads to the masterpiece of Antonio da Sangallo, long in the shadow of his less talented brother Giuliano. **San Biagio**, a central, Greek cross church of creamy travertine, stands in a small park. As with so many other Renaissance churches, it has more architecture than Christianity in its design – a consciously classical composition with an adaptation of the 'Tuscan' order on the ground level, Ionic on the second and Corinthian on the upper storeys of the campanile, gracefully fitted into one of the corners of the Greek cross. The interior, finished in marble and other expensive stone, is equally symmetrical, rational and impressive. Over the handsome altar, a Latin inscription proclaims '*Hinc deus homo et home Deus. Immensum Concept – Aeternum Genuit*' (Hence God is Man, and for humanity, the created Eternity). The beautiful canon's house, with its double loggia, is also by Sangallo.

### Around Montepulciano

Among beautiful villages on the hills around Montepulciano, **Montefollonico** (8km northwest) has a frescoed church and Palazzo Comunale, both 13th-century. **Monticchiello**, 7km southwest on a back road towards Pienza, hangs languorously on its hilltop; it too has a 13th-century church, with a rose window, an altarpiece by Pietro Lorenzetti and Sienese frescoes (late 14th century).

## Shopping in Montepulciano

Besides Vino Nobile (*see* p.392), Montepulciano has jams, preserves, honey, *pecorino* cheese, ham or boar salami and other farm specialities to offer – the ideology of natural food has become as popular here as in the trendiest neighbourhoods of New York. You'll find them in almost any grocer's.

There are also some very good antique stores on the back streets, together with craft workshops, especially woodcarving.

## Where to Stay and Eat in Montepulciano and Around

Montepulciano ✉ 53045

There are lots of *agriturismos* in the surrounding countryside, and hundreds of rooms just south at Chianciano Terme (*see* p.396).

The best restaurants are outside town. Alternatively, any of the back roads off the SS146 will lead you at some point to an ideal spot for a picnic on those fine local products.

ⓘ Montepulciano
>>
*Via Gracciano nel Corso 59a, off Piazza Grande, **t** 0578 757341, www.proloco montepulciano.it*

***Borghetto**, Borgo Buio
**t** 0578 757535, *www.ilborghetto.it*
(€€€). Pleasant rooms, some with
great views over the edge of town,
plus Internet access.

⭐ Marzocco >

***Marzocco**, Via G. Savonarola 18,
**t** 0578 757262, *www.albergomarzocco.it*
(€€). An airy family-run establishment
next to the *Marzocco* itself, with
spacious rooms (breakfast included)
and large panoramic terraces.

***Il Riccio**, Via Talosa 21, **t** 0578
757713, *www.ilriccio.net* (€€). Tasteful
rooms (breakfast included) in a
renovated medieval *palazzo*, with a
pleasant rooftop terrace.

⭐ La Chiusa >

**La Chiusa**, Via Madonnina 88,
Montefollonico, **t** 0577 669668 (€€€€).
The best restaurant in southern
Tuscany, though its reputation has
wobbled in recent years, in an old
*frantoio* or olive press, with panoramic
views back towards Montepulciano.
Highlights are the tagliatelle with
truffles, lamb's liver with wine
sauce, duck with wild fennel, and
*pannacotta*. The wine list is short but
well chosen. Some suites and rooms
(€€€€€) are available. *Closed Tues.*

**La Grotta**, Loc.S Biagio 15, **t** 0578
757607 (€€€). A restaurant the
shadow of the dramatic San Biagio,
serving traditional Tuscan dishes with
a creative twist, such as squash tart

with aubergines in balsamic vinegar,
gnocchi in rabbit sauce, and boar with
spinach. *Closed Wed, Jan and Feb.*

**Osteria Borgo Buio**, Via di Borgo Buio
10, **t** 0578 717497 (€€). An excellent
*osteria* offering the likes of tagliatelle
with sardines, tomatoes and pine
nuts, ravioli filled with *pecorino*
cheese, pear and nuts, lamb with
herbs, potatoes and aubergines, and
grilled Fiorentina steak. *Closed Sun.*

**Caffè Poliziano**, Corso, **t** 0578 758615
(€). Montepulciano's old-fashioned
*gran caffè*.

## Monticchiello ✉ 53020

**L'Olmo**, just below Montichiello,
**t** 0578 755133, *www.olmopienza.it*
(€€€€). A beautifully restored stone
posthouse with gardens and a
swimming pool overlooking the Val
d'Orcia. Bedrooms are comfortable
and sophisticated; there are also
suites and apartments. Breakfast is
included, and dinner is available on
request. *Closed mid-Nov–April.*

**La Porta**, Via del Piano 3, **t** 0578 755163
(€€). An excellent *osteria/enoteca* with
wonderful views over Pienza and the
valley from its panoramic terrace.
Standout dishes are the *pici* with *cacio*
cheese and pepper, *ribollita*, *pappa al
pomodoro*, stuffed guinea fowl, and
cod. *Closed Thurs, and 10 Jan–5 Feb.*

# Chianciano Terme

'*Chianciano – Fegato Sano*' is the slogan you see everywhere in
Chianciano Terme (population 7,500): on the signs that welcome
you, on the municipal buildings, even on the garbage trucks:
'Chianciano, for a healthy liver'. And after rotting yours on too
much Montepulciano wine, how convenient it is to have a spa
close at hand to flush it out. The waters here were known to the
Etruscans but have only been exploited in a big way in the last
half-century or more. There is an old walled town, Chianciano
Vecchio, with a medieval clocktower and the **Museo d'Arte Sacra**;
at the gate is the bus station and info booth.

In a former granary situated just outside the old town you'll find
the **Museo Civico Archeologico delle Acque**. Here you can see a
collection of mainly Etruscan and Roman exhibits that have been
excavated in the environs since 1986. Reconstructed tombs built in
the hollows, which were originally carved out to hold wine barrels,

**Museo Civico
Archeologico
delle Acque**
*open April–Oct
Tues–Sun 10–1 and 4–7;
Nov–Mar Sat and Sun
10–1 and 4–7; or by appt
on **t** 0578 30471; adm*

# Getting to Chianciano Terme

For details of Chiusi–Chianciano **train** station and of local **buses**, *see* p.392.

contain finds from the excavation of the Tolle Necropoli at nearby La Foce (*see* below). These items are arranged more or less as they were discovered at the site.

Beyond, modern Chianciano stretches for kilometres down Viale della Libertà, passing hundreds of hotels, gardens with clipped lawns, and 1950s bathhouses in a clean, modern style. Besides liver repair, Chianciano has mineral mud packs for acne, hot aerosol douches and plenty of other treatments for every ailment, mistrusted by British visitors but medically respected.

## Around Chianciano: La Foce and Castelluccio

**La Foce**
*t 0578 69101,
www.lafoce.com;
gardens open Wed
3pm–dusk*

To the southwest of Chianciano lies **La Foce**, a large estate on the hills overlooking the Val d'Orcia. Its strategic position on the Via Francigena has long attracted settlers; excavations brought to light a burial place from the 7th century BC. The villa was built in the late 15th century as a hostel for pilgrims and merchants, and bought by Antonio and Iris Origo in 1924, when it was barren and poverty-ridden. They spent their lives regenerating the area; they set up a school, day clinic and nursery, and an orphanage during the war. English landscape architect Cecil Pinsent designed the delightful **gardens**. Iris Origo's autobiographical books *Images and Shadows* and *War in the Val d'Orcia* make fascinating reading.

Nearby, on the road to Montepulciano, the medieval **Castelluccio** is also part of the estate. As well as exhibitions, it holds concerts during the summer, as a venue for the **Incontri in Terra di Siena** music festival (*see* p.389).

---

## Where to Stay and Eat in Chianciano Terme

ⓘ **Chianciano Terme >**
*Piazza Italia 67,
t 0578 671122,
www.chianciano
termeinfo.it*

**Chianciano Terme** ✉ **53042**

Even if you aren't here for thermal torture, Chianciano can be useful in summer when hotels everywhere else are booked solid. The **Azienda Autonima di Cura**, Viale Roma 6, can help with accommodation.

**La Foce**, Strada della Vittoria 61, t 0578 69101, *www.lafoce.com* (€€€€€). Several farmhouses turned into upmarket self-catering apartments with plenty of antiques, sleeping 2–14. Each has use of a swimming pool and a private garden, and meals are available on request.

**La Rosa del Trinoro**, Castriglioncello del Trinoro, on road between La Foce and Sarteano, t 0578 265 529 (€€€€). A restaurant in a tiny, otherworldly hamlet with wonderful views. Come for risotti with *porcini* and prawns in balsamic vinegar, home-made *pici* in rabbit sauce, lamb with herbs, beans and pepper, and exquisite chocolate desserts. There are also some pleasant guest rooms (€€). *Closed Mon, and lunch Tues–Fri.*

**L'Oasi**, Loc. La Foce (just below La Foce on the road to Monte Amiata), t 0578 755 077 (€€). A useful, rustic, family-run bar/restaurant with a children's playground and a summer garden, serving home-made pizzas, pastas and more. *Closed Wed.*

# Chiusi and Around

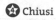 **Chiusi**

If anyone ever read you Macaulay's rouser *Horatio at the Bridge*, you'll remember the fateful Lars Porsena of Clusium, leading the Etruscan confederation and their Umbrian allies to attack Rome in brave days of old. Thanks to Horatio, Rome survived and made a name for itself; here you can see what happened to Clusium – or *Camars*, as the Etruscans called it. Most of its 9,500 citizens live in the new districts by the railway station, but the hill town on the site of Lars Porsena's capital still thrives.

## Archaeological Museum

**Museo Archeologico Nazionale di Chiusi**
*t 0578 20177;*
*open daily 9–8; adm*

From those brave days of old, Chiusi retains at least this excellent museum, beautifully laid out and well labelled. As with so many Etruscan collections, the main attraction is the large number of cinerary urns, and as usual, the Etruscans produced a bewildering variety of styles and themes. Large urns with thoughtful reclining figures are common, as well as mythological battle scenes with winged gods. Not all the tombs contained the well-known rectangular urns; some Etruscans chose to be buried in 'canopic' jars, surmounted by a terracotta bust of the deceased.

Camars was a wealthy town, and excavations at its necropolises unearthed a large amount of Greek pottery – note the urn with Achilles and Ajax playing at dice, and the Dionysian scenes with sexy maenads and leering satyrs. Many Etruscan imitation vases are on display; it's easy to believe local talent could have done as well as the Greeks, had they had thinner paintbrushes. Don't miss the glittering hoard of barbaric trinkets from 6th–7th-century Lombard tombs discovered on the Arusa hill just outside town.

## Etruscan Tombs and Tunnels

If you're interested in seeing some of the Etruscan tombs (5th–3rd century BC) in which various items in the archaeological music were found, ask the museum guards, who arrange tours (in fact, they'll probably ask you first). These are the only good painted tombs in Tuscany; the best, the **Tomba della Scimmia**, contains paintings of wrestlers and warriors, in addition to the monkey that gives the tomb its name. The **Tomba della Pellegrina** and **Tomba del Granduca** are also interesting, as is the **Tomba Bonci Casuccini**, in a different necropolis east of town.

## The Cathedral

**Cattedrale di San Secondiano**
*open daily 9–8, adm*

Across from the museum, Chiusi's cathedral is the oldest in Tuscany, though only parts – the recycled Roman columns in the nave – go back to the original 6th-century building. The rest was rebuilt in the 12th century and again in the 19th. At first glance, the

# Getting to Chiusi

For details of Chiusi-Chianciano **train** station and of local **buses,** *see* p.392.

mosaics that cover the walls inside seem astounding, an unknown chapter in Early Christian art. Then you notice they have a touch of Art Nouveau about them and realize they aren't mosaics at all, but skilfully sponged-on squares of paint, a crazy masterpiece of mimicry completed in 1915.

**Museo della Cattedrale/ Labirinto di Porsenna**
*t 0578 226490; open June–mid-Oct daily 10–12.45 and 4–6.30; mid-Oct–May Mon–Sat 10–12.45 and Sun 10–12.45 and 3.30–6; adm*

The small **cathedral museum** has Roman fragments and beautiful 15th-century illuminated choirbooks. You can also climb the campanile and descend into the mysterious network of **tunnels and galleries** underlying the town, bits of which go back to the Etruscans. Whatever their original purpose, some were converted into catacombs by Early Christian communities; there's also an underground cistern from Roman times.

## Around Chiusi: Lakes, Sarteano and More *Crete*

Just northeast of Chiusi, on the border between Tuscany and Umbria, pretty **Lago di Chiusi** and the **Lago di Montepulciano** are the smallest in the chain of lakes that begins with Lago Trasimeno. Lago di Chiusi is good for a picnic if you're headed from Florence to Rome or Orvieto on the *autostrada*.

**Sarteano** is a smaller resort spa, situated 9km to the south of Chianciano or Chiusi, attached to a fine old hill town with Renaissance palaces, a squarish medieval fortress, and the church of **San Martino in Foro**, with an *Annunciation* that is one of the best works of the Sienese Mannerist Beccafumi. A small, delightful Etruscan museum – the **Museo Civico Archeologico** – occupies the impressive Palazzo Gabrielli; note the wonderful funerary accoutrements and striking urns containing bones and other anthropomorphic paraphernalia.

**Museo Civico Archeologico di Sarteano**
*t 0578 269261 open Tues–Sun 10–noon and 4–7*

Another 6km south of Sarteano, off the ruggedly scenic SS321, you'll find **Cetona**, a small, untouristy gem with a growing population of discerning foreign residents who have rejected Chianti country and all it implies. The Palazzo Comunale is home to the **Museo Civico per la Preistoria del Monte Cetona**, documenting archaeological discoveries since the 1920s, including a massive bear some believe to be 50,000 years old.

**Museo Civico per la Preistoria del Monte Cetona**
*Via Roma 37, t 0578 237632; open June–Sept Tues–Sat 9–1 and 3–7, Sun and hols 9.30–12.30; Oct–May Tues–Sun 9.30–12.30*

Take the road to Sarteano, and after 6km or so you reach the **Parco Archeologico Naturalistico di Belvedere**, with remains from one of the most important Bronze Age sites in Italy. On the approach to Sarteano, visit the 14th-century ex-convent of Santa Maria a Belvedere, inhabited by the same community who run the upmarket La Frateria di Padre Egidio (*see* opposite), and housing frescoes attributed to Petruccioli and Andrea di Giovanni.

The SS478 from Sarteano towards Monte Amiata passes one of the loneliest, most barren regions of *crete* en route to the Val d'Orcia (*see* p.387). The road south from Cetona takes you on a beautiful, winding drive skirting Monte Cetona, punctuated by dramatic views as you pass through woods and olive groves towards **San Casciano dei Bagni**, a pretty spa town on the borders of Umbria and Lazio. There are a couple of ancient churches and a castle; the hot springs are just to the south. The resort's heyday was in the Renaissance, when Grand Duke Ferdinand built a villa here and developed the spa; the baths have been restored and the Medici villa transformed into a luxury hotel (*see* below).

## Where to Stay and Eat in and around Chiusi

(i) **Chiusi >**

*Pro Loco,
Piazza Duomo 1,
t 0578 227 667*

### Chiusi ✉ 53043

**Le Anfore**, Via Chiusi 30, just outside town on road to Sarteano, t 0578 265521, *www.balzarini.it* (€€€). A beautifully restored farmhouse with good-value family accommodation (breakfast included), a pool, a tennis court, horse-riding and a restaurant.

 **La Locanda di Anita >>**

**★★★La Fattoria**, Loc. Saccianese 48, Conciarese al Lago, t 0578 21407, *www.la-fattoria.it* (€€). An old farmhouse with lake views, a garden, good rooms and a great restaurant. *Closed Mon.*

**Ristorante Pesce d'Oro**, Loc Sbarcino 36, t 0578 21403 (€€). A pleasant place on the lake shores, specializing in fresh lake fish. *Closed Wed.*

**La Solita Zuppa**, Via Porsenna 21, t 0578 21006 (€€). A friendly *osteria* up in the old town, with four or five daily soups and home-made pasta. *Closed Tues, and mid-Jan–mid-Mar.*

 **Zaira >**

**Zaira**, Via Arunte 12, t 0578 20260 (€€). Speculative 'Etruscan cuisine', popular with Italians in the know. It's a harmless fancy; try rabbit in lemon sauce. *Closed Mon in winter.*

### Sarteano ✉ 53047

**Residenza Santa Chiara**, Piazza Santa Chiara, t 0578 265412, *www.conventosantachiara.it* (€€). A pleasant old building with a shady garden, simple rooms (plus a suite and an apartment) and a great restaurant.

**La Giara**, Viale Europa 2, t 0578 265511 (€€). Popular Tuscan fare and pizzas from a wood-burning oven. *Closed Mon.*

**Osteria Da Gagliano**, Via Roma 5, t 0578 268022 (€€). A simple *osteria*; try anchovies with pesto. *Closed Tues.*

### Cetona ✉ 53040

**★★★★La Frateria**, Convento di San Francesco, t 0578 238015, *www.lafrateria.it* (€€€€€). The most unusual hotel in the area, in a 13th-century monastery founded by St Francis, tranquil yet lavish. There's an excellent if overpriced restaurant (€€€€). *Closed Jan; restaurant closed Mon.*

**La Locanda di Anita**, Piazza Balestrieri 6, t 0578 237075, *www.lalocandadianita.it* (€€€). Beautiful rooms and a suite, and a pretty terrace for summer breakfasts (included). **L'Osteria Vecchia**, under the same management, serves good food.

### S. Casciano dei Bagni ✉ 53040

**★★★★Fonteverde**, Loc Terme 1, t 0578 57241, *www.fonteverdespa.com* (€€€€€). A spa hotel in and around a Medici villa, on the site of the restored thermal baths. Half-board is required. Packages including beauty treatments.

**★★★Sette Querce**, Viale Manciati 2, t 0578 58174, *www.settequerce.it* (€€€€). A delightful all-suite hotel (some have kitchenettes), with spa treatments and a beauty centre.

**La Fontanella**, Via Roma 6, t 0578 58300, *www.albergolafontanella.com* (€€€). Bright, comfy rooms and an excellent restaurant (€€–€). *Restaurant closed Tues.*

**Da Daniela**, Piazza Matteotti 7, t 0578 58041 (€€€). Interesting variations on local themes, including *tortelli* stuffed with pigeon meat. *Closed Wed in winter, and 10 Jan–10 Feb.*

# Monte Amiata and Around

 Monte Amiata

**Monte Amiata**, the rooftop of southern Tuscany, is an extinct volcanic massif with a central peak 5,659ft (1,722m) high. With no real competition close by, it has become a skiing and hiking centre – the closest to Rome, and as such, popular in summer and winter. The presence of Europe's second-largest mercury mine (a complex that has been putting dinner on the table for the Abbadia San Salvatore since the Middle Ages) does not detract from the area's natural beauty. The lower, uncultivated slopes are covered in chestnut and beech trees, while higher up are beautiful mature forests where the leaves catch the early frosts and change colour marvellously in the autumn.

## Abbadia San Salvatore

A thousand years ago you might have heard of this town, home of the most important monastic centre in Tuscany and a fair-sized city in its own right. History passed Abbadia San Salvatore by a long time ago; today it makes a modest living as a mountain resort, gateway to Monte Amiata.

Abbadia (population 7,900) appears modern at first, but just behind Viale Roma a narrow gateway leads into the grey, quiet streets of the small **medieval centre**, as complete and unchanged as any medieval quarter in Tuscany. Note the symbols carved into many doorways: coats of arms, odd religious symbols (a snake, for example) or signs such as a pair of scissors that declare the original owner was a tailor. The **abbey church** is a few blocks north in Via del Monastero; in the Middle Ages this must have been open countryside. According to legend – there's even a document telling the story, dated the Ides of March, 742 – the Lombard King Rachis was on his way to attack Perugia when a vision of the Saviour appeared to him. Rachis not only founded the monastery but retired to it as a monk. Historians consider the whole business a convenient fabrication, but by 1000 the abbey had achieved considerable wealth and influence, ruling over a large piece of territory and waging occasional wars with the bishop of Chiusi.

In 1036, the present church was begun; this excellent Romanesque work may seem plain to us, but it was undoubtedly one of the grandest sights in Tuscany when it was new. Behind the twin-steepled façade, it is surprisingly long; the eastern end has a raised chancel, which leads to a series of arches over the altar and choir. Here frescoes by Nasino, an early-1700s artist, tell the story of King Rachis. His **crypt**, located under the chancel, was the original 8th-century church. The proportions are thoroughly Byzantine, with some stone vaulting and oddly carved columns and capitals, no two of which are alike.

# Getting to and around Monte Amiata

There's a 'Monte Amiata' **train station** on an infrequent branch line from Siena, but it's some 40km on the northern side of the massif, near Castiglione d'Orcia. It's much easier to get a **bus** from Siena, Chiusi or Grosseto. Buses stop on Viale Roma in the centre of Abbadia San Salvatore (tickets/timetables available in the toyshop behind the information booth); a few go daily to Buonconvento and Siena (79km/2hrs 30mins), Montepulciano–Chiusi (48km/90mins); and 9 a day go from Abbadia to Arcidosso (25km/1hr) and Castel del Piano on the western side of Amiata.

Note that Arcidosso and the other towns on the west slope are in Grosseto province; almost all buses there go on to Grosseto. There are also at least 2 daily COTRAL (*www.cotralspa.it*) or SIRA buses (*www.sirabus.it*) through Castel del Piano, Arcidosso and Abbadia San Salvatore to Viterbo and on to Rome.

## Around Amiata

South of Abbadia San Salvatore, **Piancastagnaio** is a smaller mountain resort. It has a **castle** of the Aldobrandeschi (with a small museum), a 17th-century palace and, as its name implies, lots of chestnut trees. Chestnuts and chestnut flour were the staple food around Amiata; restaurants still sometimes offer chestnut polenta.

On the panoramic route around Amiata, **Seggiano**, 20km northwest of Abbadia, has an unusual 16th-century church with a square cupola, the Madonna della Carità. South another 7km is **Castel del Piano**, with an old centre, Belle Epoque parks and boulevards.

**Arcidosso**, 4km south, is the largest town (population 4,500) on the Grosseto side of Amiata, with a stately Aldobrandeschi fortress, and one church outside the town, the triple-apsed Santa Maria in Lamula, begun in the 900s and redone in the 12th century. It's best known for the strange career of David Lazzaretti, a millenarian prophet gunned down by the *carabinieri* during a disturbance in 1878. His movement combined reformed religion and plain rural socialism. Before his murder, his followers had started to create a sort of commune on **Monte Labbro**, 10km south. The tower, bits of buildings and remains of the church they built on Monte Labbro still stand, and the faithful occasionally hold 'Giurisdavidical' services there.

**Roccalbegna**, 20km south on the SS323, has an Aldobrandeschi castle, and some Sienese art in SS. Pietro e Paolo and nearby Oratorio del Crocifisso. Its landmark is one very conspicuous rock: a looming conical mass called simply 'La Pietra'. The Aldobrandeschi also built at **Santa Fiora**, a pleasant town 7.5km south of Arcidosso, with della Robbia terracottas in its three churches.

Just south of Arcidosso, on the northern slopes of Monte Labbro, is a nature reserve, the **Parco Faunistico del Monte Amiata**. Hiking trails offer a look at various kinds of deer, mountain goats and maybe even wolves – there is a project to reintroduce them.

Amiata's summit, decorated with an obligatory iron crucifix, lies about halfway between Abbadia and Arcidosso; roads reach almost to the top. The skiing area is here, too, at **Vetta Amiata**.

**Parco Faunistico del Monte Amiata**
*t 0564 966867,*
*www.parcodegli*
*etruschi.it;*
*open Tues–Sun*
*dawn–sunset*

ⓘ **Abbadia San Salvatore >>**
*Via Adua 25,*
*t 0577 775811,*
*www.amiataturismo.it*

ⓘ **Arcidosso >>**
*Piazza Castello 1,*
*t 0564 968010*

ⓘ **Castel del Piano >>**
*Via G. Marconi 2,*
*t 0564 951026*

⭐ **Albergo Ristorante Silene >>**

## Activities in and around Monte Amiata

One of the few good **skiing** areas close to Rome, Monte Amiata can get busy. Facilities include **ski schools** (t 0577 789740 and t 0564 959004). For snow news and info, call Abbadia San Salvatore tourist office.

It's also perfect for **cross-country** skiing and **hiking**, with a network of hiking trails marked as far as Castiglione d'Orcia. Ask tourist offices for the *Cartografia dei Sentieri* map.

## Where to Stay and Eat in and around Monte Amiata

### Monte Amiata ✉ 53021

***La Capannina**, Vette Amiata, t 0577 789713, *www.albergolacapannina.it* (€€). A cosy place near the summit, offering half- and full-board. Its restaurant is one of the best. *Closed Oct exc weekends, Nov–15 Dec, Easter–May.*

***Hotel Cantore**, 'Secondo Rifugio 10', along road from Abbadia, t 0577 789704, *www.ilcantore.it* (€€). Pleasant facilities near the summit, open all year (to cater for summer mountaineers too), and offering half-board accommodation.

### Abbadia San Salvatore ✉ 53021

This is popular for winter skiing but also as a cool summer retreat.

**Relais San Lorenzo**, Loc. San Lorenzo, t 0577 785003, *www.relaissanlorenzo.it* (€€€). An old building on the slopes, with ample grounds, an outdoor pool, comfy rooms and apartments with fridges, and an excellent restaurant. Half- and full-board are available.

****San Marco**, Via Matteotti 19, t 0577 778089 (€€–€). Clean, comfy rooms and a restaurant (€) serving a *menu fisso*. Half- and full-board are available.

### Arcidosso ✉ 58031

****Aiuole**, Loc. Aiuole, t 0564 967300 (€€€). Good-value rooms and a good restaurant serving the likes of *tortelli* with nettles, and pheasant with chestnuts (half/full-board available). *Closed Mon in winter, and Sun eve.*

### Castel del Piano ✉ 58033

****Contessa**, at Prato della Contessa, t 0564 959000, *www.hotelcontessa.it* (€€€). A hotel in a lovely setting on the slopes, organizing nature walks, cultural tours and more, and offering seasonal menus (full-board available).

**Albergo Ristorante Silene**, Loc. Pescina 8, t 0564 950805 (€€). A provider of beds and food (€€€) since 1830. Don't miss the boar with chocolate.

## The Lost Corner of Tuscany

The inland reaches of Grosseto province form the largest stretch of territory in Italy north of the Abruzzo without any well-known attractions. Part of the Etruscan heartland, these towns have been poor and usually misgoverned since – by the Romans, the noble Aldobrandeschi, the popes and the Tuscan dukes. Some don't even consider it part of Tuscany, and in many ways it has more in common with the haunted expanses of northern Lazio over the border.

### Sorano

This grim town clings tenaciously to its rock between two lovely wooded canyons. Bits of it have been crumbling into the valleys for centuries; many houses were destroyed in a landslide 85 years ago. It is still inhabited, but more houses have been abandoned as younger people move away for work. On the road to Sovana is a strange rock formation, the **Mano di Orlando** ('Hand of Roland').

## Sovana and the *Vie Cave*

**Sovana**, perched on a ridge 10km west, with a population of about 190, has almost perfectly preserved its 13th- or 14th-century look. An important Etruscan city, it thrived as the family HQ of the Aldobrandeschi in the 11th century. This clan, controlling much of southern Tuscany and northern Lazio, had a political role on a European level. The zenith of its influence came with the election to the papacy of one of its members in 1073, Gregory VII.

There is some interesting Early Christian and medieval sculpture in the 12th-century church of **Santa Maria** in the centre, including a remarkable 9th-century *ciborium* in bold barbaric arabesques and floral motifs, along with Renaissance frescoes. The **Duomo**, just outside the village, has an octagonal dome from the 900s, a crypt 200 years older, and sculptural work on the façade that may have been recycled from a pagan temple.

The *Vie Cave*, signposted all around this area, are sacred ways of the Etruscans, carved for part of their length out of the tufa, often lined with tombs. In many cases they follow modern roads, as with the pretty road from Sovana to Saturnia. Here you can stop to see the **Tomba della Sirena**, with a pediment carved with a much-eroded fork-tailed mermaid – possibly the original of the mermaids on the Pieve di Corsignano and elsewhere around Tuscany.

Not far away is the elaborate 3rd-century BC **Tomba Ildebranda**, which once had the façade of a Greek temple, though little of the colonnade survives. It resembles the rock-cut tombs of the same era common in Lycia, on the south coast of Turkey, built by people who may have been the Etruscans' cultural cousins.

## Pitigliano

Just 8km away is an ominous-looking place that could be Sorano's twin, perched along the edges of the cliffs; underneath are holes in the cliff faces, once Etruscan tombs, now stables or storehouses. Piazza della Repubblica has the 14th-century **Palazzo Orsini**, stronghold of the powerful Roman family that aced the Aldobrandeschi out of many holdings in south Tuscany. The castle has a small **museum of Etruscan finds**, and an analemmic sundial with a Latin inscription reminding us the hours are 'for work, not for play'.

Pitigliano has a picturesque medieval centre, and a 16th-century **aqueduct**. The alleys around Vicolo Manin, where parts of a **synagogue** still stand, once formed Pitigliano's **Jewish ghetto**; the centuries-old community was decimated in 1945. Other Jewish relics can be visited on the International Day of Jewish Culture, usually the first Sunday in September.

On the cliffs underneath the town, along the road for Sovana, is a Christian **cave chapel** (*c.* 400 AD). They claim it's the oldest in Italy.

**Remains of Jewish ghetto and synagogue**
*open Mar–May, Oct and Nov Sun–Fri 10–12.30 and 3–6; June–Sept Sun–Fri 10–12.30 and 3–6.30; Dec–mid-Jan Sun–Fri 10–12.30 and 3–5.30; adm*

14

Southern Tuscany | The Lost Corner of Tuscany

## Saturnia

Little Saturnia, 25km west of Sovana, sits all alone above the Val d'Albegna. One of Italy's most ancient centres, it claims to be the first city founded there – by the god Saturn, in the Golden Age. Fragments of pre-Etruscan walls can be seen, and aerial photos have discerned traces of an older city beneath the Roman level. There are hot springs, still used, and ruins everywhere, including an **Etruscan necropolis** (north) and **Poggio Buco** (road to Pitigliano).

West on SS323, the walled city of **Magliano in Toscana** has a Sienese-style Palazzo dei Priori, and the church of San Giovanni Battista, with a Renaissance façade. Its best-known attraction is the **Ulivo della Strega** ('witches' olive'), a gnarled tree more than 1,000 years old, said to be the site of ritual dances in pagan days, and still haunted. It's just outside the Porta San Giovanni, near the Romanesque **Annunziata** church with its Sienese frescoes.

# Where to Stay and Eat in and around Sovana

The region produces some good but little-known wines, notably Morellino di Scansano, a severe dry variety with a beautiful deep red colour, and also a delicious, crisp Bianco di Pitigliano.

(i) **Saturnia >>**
*Pro Loco, Piazzale Benvenuto di Giovanni, t 0564 601237, www. proloco-saturnia.it*

### Sovana ✉ 58010

***Hotel della Fortezza**, Piazza Cairoli 5, t 0564 632010, *www.hoteldella fortezza.com* (€€€€). Antiques-filled rooms (breakfast included) with fabulous views, set in the 11th-century Orsini fortress.

***Scilla**, Via del Duomo, t 0564 617030, *www.sovanahotel.it* (€€€). A good hotel offering half- and full-board in its restaurant (€€), serving Maremmana dishes. *Closed Tues.*

***Taverna Etrusca**, Piazza Pretorio, t 0564 616183, *www.sovanahotel.it* (€€€). Good rooms, breakfast included, above a restaurant (€€) serving the likes of nettle and ricotta soup.

(i) **Pitigliano >**
*Piazza Garibaldi 51, off main piazza, t 0564 617111*

### Pitigliano ✉ 58017

**Corano**, Loc. Corano, SS74 just outside town, t 0564 616112, *www.hotelcorano.it* (€€). Modern rooms, a pool and a restaurant (with half- and full-board).

**Guastini**, Piazza Petruccioli 4, t 0564 616065, *www.albergoguastini.it* (€€). A recently renovated, central option, with a restaurant offering the likes of *pappardelle* with boar.

**Il Tufo Allegro**, Vicolo della Costituzione, t 0564 616192 (€€€). A wonderful restaurant in a great setting carved out of tufa. Hearty dishes include lamb with artichoke sauce. *Closed Tues, mid-Jan–mid-Feb and 2wks July/Aug.*

**Hostaria del Ceccottino**, Piazza San Gregorio, t 0564 614273 (€€). A good place for boar *scottiglia* and *ribollita*. *Closed Thurs in winter.*

### Saturnia ✉ 58050

****Hotel Terme di Saturnia**, Strada Provinale della Follonato, t 0564 600111, *www.termedisaturnia.it* (€€€€€). The top spa resort in Tuscany, exploiting waters famous since Etruscan times, with airy rooms in a large park, four thermal pools, a re-created Roman bath, state-of-the-art health and beauty treatments, and an 18-hole golf course.

***Villa Clodia**, Via Italia 43, t 0564 601212, *www.hotelvillaclodia.com* (€€€). Good rooms, great views, a sauna, a fitness room, a pool and mountainbike loan.

**Locanda Laudomia**, Poderi di Montemerano, 7km south of Saturnia, t 0564 620013, *locandalaudomia@ tiscali.it* (€). Pretty rooms in the country, some ensuite, and a good restaurant.

### Montemerano ✉ 58050

**Da Caino**, Via Canonica 3, t 0564 602817 (€€€€). An elegant restaurant for such a small village; try ravioli with tomatoes and oil or cod carpaccio. There are some rustic rooms. *Closed Wed.*

# Arezzo and its Province

Between Florence and Umbria lies a lovely region of nature and art, most of which is included in the province of Arezzo. Watered by the newly born Arno and Tiber rivers, it occupies a keystone position in Italy, not only geographically but as amazingly fertile ground for 'key' Italians: Masaccio and Cosimo Il Vecchio's humanist Greek scholar and magician, Marsilio Ficino, were born in the Arno valley; Petrarch, Michelangelo, Piero della Francesca, Paolo Uccello, Luca Signorelli, Andrea Sansovino, Vasari, the satirist Aretino, Guido Monaco (inventor of the musical scale), Pietro da Cortona and the Futurist Gino Severini were born in Arezzo or its province. Its strategic location means battlefields and castles dot the countryside, yet here, too, is St Francis' holy mountain of La Verna.

# 15

## Don't miss

⭐ **Medieval mountain villages**
The Casentino p.410

⭐ **St Francis' rugged hermitage**
La Verna p.412

⭐ **Masterpiece frescoes**
San Francesco, Arezzo p.415

⭐ **A maze-like hilltown**
Lucignano p.426

⭐ **A surprising Renaissance art town**
Cortona p.428

See map overleaf

# Arezzo Province

p.202

p.382

## Don't miss

⭐ The Casentino **p.410**

⭐ La Verna **p.412**

⭐ San Francesco, Arezzo **p.415**

⭐ Lucignano **p.426**

⭐ Cortona **p.428**

There are two possible routes between Florence and Arezzo: the quick one, following the trains and Autostrada del Sole down the Valdarno, or the scenic route, through the Passo della Consuma or Vallombrosa, taking in the beautifully forested areas of Pratomagno and the Casentino.

# The Valdarno and Casentino

## Florence to Arezzo

If a Tuscan caveman ever yearned for the ideal Neolithic home, he would have wanted to live in what is now the Arno valley. In the Pliocene Age, the valley was a lake, a popular resort of ancient elephants, and farmers are not surprised when their ploughs collide with fossils. The typically Tuscan towns of the Valdarno, however, are hardly fossilized. On the contrary, it is a highly industrialized region: lignite and felt hats stand out in particular, but factories and power lines seem to go up all the time.

Besides the *autostrada*, the main valley routes are the old SS69 and the beautiful 'Strada dei Sette Ponti' following the old Etruscan road of 'Seven Bridges' from Saltino by Vallombrosa to Castiglion Fibocchi, along what was the upper shore of the ancient lake, between the Valdarno and the Pratomagno ridge. Along it are areas strikingly eroded into pyramids, around Pian di Scò and Castelfranco. By public transport the Valdarno's peripheral attractions are harder to reach; buses from Arezzo to Loro Ciuffenna and Castelfranco di Sopra stick to the Strada dei Sette Ponti.

The most scenic route from Florence to the Valdarno follows the A1 down to Incisa (23km), though it's worth turning off at Torre a Cona for **Rignano sull'Arno**, with sculptures by Mino da Fiesole and Bernardino Rossellino in the church of San Clemente, and for **Sanmezzano** (2km across the Arno). Here a medieval castle was converted into a Medici villa and in the 19th century purchased by the Ximenes d'Aragona family, who gave it a Spanish-Moorish fantasy facelift. Downriver, at **Incisa Valdarno**, Petrarch spent his childhood. There's an old bridge off which, the Italians claim, Lucrezia Borgia jumped in 1529, fleeing the Prince of Orange – despite the fact that she had died in childbirth 10 years earlier.

**Figline Valdarno** (population 15,000), 5km south, was the birthplace of Ficino in 1439. The historic centre has preserved the loggia of the old Serristori hospital, the Palazzo Pretorio, and the **Collegiata di Santa Maria**, containing among its works of art a beautiful painting of the *Madonna with Child and Angels* by the 14th-century 'Maestro di Figline' and a fresco by the school of Botticelli.

### San Giovanni Valdarno

San Giovanni (population 19,500), though one of the most industrial towns in the region, is also one of the most interesting. The Florentines fortified it in the 13th century against the warlike Aretini and sent Arnolfo di Cambio to lay out the streets and fortifications, and design the handsome arcaded **Palazzo Comunale**; its arches are echoed by the buildings opening on to the piazza and covered with escutcheons left by Florentine governors. The oft-restored **Basilica di Santa Maria delle Grazie** (1486) has a rich 17th-century interior, though most paintings have been removed to the adjacent **Museo della Basilica**: a *Madonna, Child and Four Saints* attributed to Masaccio (1401–28), an *Annunciation* by Jacopo di Sellaio, Baroque paintings by Giovanni di San Giovanni (born here; 1592–1636), and a fresco of a local miracle, in which a grandmother is able to give milk to her starving grandchild (14th century). Best is Fra Angelico's *Annunciation*, in deep, rich colours, seemingly a model for the *Annunciation* in Florence's San Marco, though here Adam and Eve are off to the left, fleeing the Garden of Eden. Earlier frescoes adorn the Gothic **church of San Lorenzo**.

Some 2.5km south of San Giovanni is the Renaissance **Convento di Montecarlo**. From here the road continues up to the Monti del Chianti by way of **Cavriglia**; the hills around are scarred with open lignite mines. Cavriglia is also a natural park, where modern deer and buffalo roam with other animals from around the world.

The Valdarno also offers a look at older species of animal, especially the *Elephas meridionalis*, in the **Museo Paleontologico** in **Montevarchi**, a major marketing centre of the region, famous for

**Museo della Basilica**

*open summer Mon, Tues and Thurs–Sat 10.30–12.30 and 4–7, Sun 4–7; winter Mon, Tues and Thurs–Sat 10.30–12.30 and 3.30–6.30, Sun 3.30–6.30; adm*

**Museo Paleontologico**

*open Wed–Sat 9–12.30 and 4–6, Sun 10–12; adm*

hats and chickens. In its ancient core, trace the oval medieval street plan. In the centre, the old **Collegiata di San Lorenzo** had a facelift in the 18th century. Within it is an unusual reliquary 'of the holy milk', brought from a cave in the Holy Land where the Holy Family is said to have rested and where a fountain of milky water flows; a small museum holds a quattrocento **Tempietto** covered inside and out with Andrea della Robbia's cherub friezes.

## Along the Road of Seven Bridges

East of the Arno, the panoramic Strada dei Sette Ponti passes several medieval towns en route to Arezzo. **Reggello** (8km east of Sanmezzano) stands amid its famous olive groves; some streets retain their medieval arcades, and the 12th-century parish church of **San Pietro a Cascia** has good, early Romanesque columns with carved capitals depicting lively scenes.

**Castelfranco di Sopra**, 12km south, was another Florentine military town laid out by Arnolfo di Cambio. Northeast, at **Pulicciano**, are pyramidical forms, or *balze*, like those at Volterra (*see* p.375). **Loro Ciuffenna** has picturesque medieval corners, a Romanesque bridge and tower, and a triptych by Lorenzo di Bicci in **Santa Maria Assunta**.

Best of all is the tiny 12th-century parish church of **Gropina** (from the Etruscan *Kropina*), 2km away, a fine example of rural Romanesque. Though it was referred to in the 8th century, the current church was built in the early 1200s. Dominated by its huge campanile, its façade is simplicity itself; the three naves and semicircular apse have never been altered. The columns are carved with primitive tigers, eagles and so on; the round marble **pulpit** is a bizarre relic of the Dark Ages, carved with archaic figures raising their arms over a marble knot; over them is a kind of totem pole, geometrical and floral decorations, and a siren with a snake whispering in her ear.

*15*

*Arezzo and its Province | Florence to Arezzo*

## Where to Stay and Eat from Florence to Arezzo

ⓘ **San Giovanni Valdarno >**
*Palazzo d'Arnolfo, Piazza Cavour 3, t 055 943748, www.prolocosan giovannivaldarno.it*

**San Giovanni Valdarno** ✉ 52027
***Hotel Masaccio**, Lungarno Don Minzoni 38, t 055 912 3402, *www.hotelmasaccio.com* (€€). Rooms with all comforts, a garden and a restaurant with Tuscan cuisine.
**Giovannino**, Piazza della Libertà 24, t 055 912 2726 (€€). A family-run place serving Tuscan fare. *Closed Wed.*
**La Lanterna**, Via Lavagnini 11, t 347 6742443 (€€). A simple restaurant offering the best local cuisine: try *tagliata* with *porcini* and truffles, and Chianina meat. *Closed Wed and Aug.*

**Montevarchi** ✉ 52025
***Delta**, Via Diaz 137, t 055 901213, *www.hoteldelta.it* (€€). A fair option, with parking and a restaurant. Breakfast is included.
**L'Osteria di Rendola**, Via di Rendola, Loc. Rendola 88, t 055 9707713 (€€€). Wonderful creative Tuscan dishes such as tuna in tartare sauce with baby vegetables, and gorgonzola cheese *tortelli* with peaches. *Closed Thurs lunch, Wed, and Nov–Feb.*

**Terranuova Bracciolini** ✉ 52028
**Il Canto del Maggio**, Loc. Penna Alta, near Loro Ciuffenna, t 055 970 5147 (€€€). A delightful restaurant in a stone house with a pretty garden, in a

**Hosteria Costachiara >>**

tiny hamlet. Meals are served under the olive trees in summer. Among standout dishes are Florentine-style *strozzapretti*, *pepose dei fornaciai*, and home-made chocolate cake. Adjacent buildings house a wine bar and apartments to let. *Closed Mon, Tues Oct–May, lunch exc. Sun, and Nov.*

**Hosteria Costachiara**, Viale Le Ville 129 (signed from Valdarno *autostrada* exit), **t** 055 944318 (€€€). A wonderful, family-run country restaurant where you can enjoy the likes of *pappardelle* with wild boar sauce and *pici* with pigeon. There are rooms in a nearby *locanda*. *Closed Mon eve and Tues.*

## The Pratomagno and Vallombrosa

The Strada dei Sette Ponti skirts the west of the **Pratomagno**, a wrinkled, forested mountain ridge. Its highest peak, Croce di Pratomagno (5,222ft/1,592m), is due north of **Loro Ciuffenna**; winding roads from Loro go through tiny mountain hamlets, while the Loro–Talla route crosses over into the Casentino.

Further north, the two routes from Florence into the Casentino take in fine, wooded scenery. The SS70 over the **Passo della Consuma** (3,362ft/1,025m) is a favourite Italian rest stop; the secondary route passes through **Vallombrosa**, famous for its abbey founded by San Giovanni Gualberto of Florence, and HQ of his Vallombrosan order. The abbey underwent remodellings in the 15th and 17th centuries and is mainly of interest for its splendid position.

**Saltino**, 1km away, is a small summer resort, an excellent base for a walk or a drive. One of the loveliest routes leads up to the Monte Secchieta (4,753ft/1,449m), with views over north-central Italy; in winter, skiing facilities spring up. For a longer outing, follow the **Panoramica del Pratomagno**, crossing nearly the entire Pratomagno to join the Strada dei Sette Ponti near Castiglion Fibocchi.

## The Casentino: North to South

 **Casentino**

The **Casentino**'s blue mountains, pastoral meadows and velvet valleys have long been Tuscany's spiritual refuge. Since the 18th century, travellers have trickled into the area, attracted initially by its famous monasteries, then charmed by one of the most beautiful and peaceful regions in Tuscany. The Arno, such a turgid, unmannerly creature in its lower reaches, is a fair, sparkling youth near its source at **Monte Falterona** (5,438ft/1,658m); a classic excursion is to take the trail up and spend the night, to witness the sunset over the Tyrrhenian Sea and dawn over the Adriatic.

**Stia** (population 3,000), the first town the Arno meets, is pretty and medieval, centred around large porticoed Piazza Tanucci and **Santa Maria Assunta**. The church's 17th-century façade hides a fine Romanesque interior, with some curious primitive capitals, a triptych by Lorenzo di Bicci and a *Madonna* by Andrea della Robbia. Wool – the thick, heavy, bright *lana del Casentino* – is the main

## Getting around the Casentino

A **car** is the only convenient way of seeing all the sights of the Casentino, but you might enjoy getting around on the LFI **narrow-gauge train** line (t 0575 28414, *www.lfi.it*) that goes through Stia, Poppi, Bibbiena and Subbieno on its way to Arezzo (about 17 trains daily).

**Castello di Porciano**
*open mid-May–mid-Oct Sun 10–12 and 4–7; rest of year by appt on t 055 400517; donations appreciated*

industry; in the old days, Stia was the market for the Guidi counts, whose ruined **Castello di Porciano** guarded the narrow Arno Valley from the 10th century.

Just north of Stia is the **sanctuary of Santa Maria delle Grazie**, a 14th-century church containing frescoes, works attributed to Luca della Robbia, and a painting by Lorenzo di Niccolò Gerini. This road continues into the Mugello (*see* p.215); the SS310 from Stia skirts Monte Falterona towards the **Passo la Calla** and Emilia-Romagna. Near the pass, the Alpine pasture **Burraia** (15km from Stia) is ideal for a cool summer picnic.

Down the Arno, **Pratovecchio** was the birthplace of Paolo Uccello in 1397; he would still recognize its narrow, porticoed lanes. Just 2km from the centre is the most beautiful Romanesque church of

**Pieve di Romena**
*open by appt with custodian, t 0575 583725*

the Casentino, **Pieve di Romena**, founded in 1152 and retaining its original lines in spite of several earthquakes and subsequent repairs. The façade is plain but the apse has two tiers of blind arcades, pierced by narrow windows. Inside, the capitals are decorated with a medieval menagerie. Among the works of art is a 1200s *Madonna* by the Maestro di Varlungo.

**Castello di Romena**
*open by appt on t 0575 58633; adm*

Nearby, the Guidis' **Castello di Romena** was one of the most powerful in the Casentino, with three sets of walls and 14 towers (reduced to three), and wide-ranging views. It houses a small **archaeological museum and armour collection**. Dante mentioned it in the *Inferno*. The writer knew this region well; at 24, he fought with the Guelphs against the Ghibellines of Arezzo and their allies at the **battle of Campaldino** (1289), just south of Pratovecchio. The victory made Florence the leading power in Tuscany; from there it went on to conquer Pisa and Arezzo. A column commemorating the battle was erected near the crossroads in 1921.

## Poppi and Camaldoli

**Castello**
*open mid-Mar–June daily 10–6; July–Oct daily 10–7; Nov–mid-Mar Thurs–Sun 10–5*

Between 1000 and 1440, the Casentino was ruled by the Guidi counts, whose headquarters were at **Poppi** (population 5,700). From many kilometres around, you can see their stalwart **Castello**, which was modelled on the Palazzo Vecchio in Florence. The best-preserved medieval castle in the region, it has a magnificent courtyard and stairs that zigzag with a touch of Piranesi. Ask the custodian to show you the grand hall with 1400s Florentine frescoes, the chapel with restored frescoes by Taddeo Gaddi, and the commanding views from the tower.

The centre of Poppi has ancient porticoed lanes winding around a small domed chapel; at the end of the main street is the Romanesque church of **San Fedele**, with a 13th-century *Madonna and Child*. Shops selling local copperware line the main street of lower Poppi, and there's the little **Zoo Fauna Europea** for kids.

A beautiful road runs northeast through the forest of Camaldoli, part of the **Parco Nazionale delle Foreste Casentinesi**, with wild deer and a huge variety of trees. It's ideal for walking. The road leads to the **hermitage and monastery of Camaldoli**, founded in 1012 by St Romualdo, a Benedictine monk. He was given this forest by Count Maldolo (hence 'Camaldoli') to found a community of hermits, similar to those of the Early Christians. A conflict arose, for the piety of the hermits soon attracted pilgrims and visitors who interfered with their solitary meditations. Romualdo ingeniously founded another monastery lower down, with a more relaxed rule, to entertain visitors and care for the forest domains. The Camaldolese are self-sufficient vegetarians whose rule orders them to plant at least 5,000 new trees every year. Little remains of the original foundation, save portions of the 11th-century cloister, the rich library and the 16th-century pharmacy, where the monks sell their herbal remedies and liqueurs. Part of the monastery is now a *foresteria* with simple accommodation and meals.

*Foresteria*
*t 0575 556013,*
*www.camaoldoli.it*

Some 3km further up, a beautiful hour's walk, is the **Eremo**, with 20 cottages set in an amphitheatre of pines, each with its own chapel and walled kitchen garden, where the hermits live in silence and solitude, meeting only on certain feast days and in the church, which was decorated inside by Vasari and has two marble tabernacles by Desiderio da Settignano. The church and St Romualdo's cell are open to visitors, but you may not go past the gate to the hermits' cottages.

**Badia Prataglia**, 10km from Camaldoli, is the region's most popular secular retreat – a summer resort spread out among the trees and hills, with beautiful walks along streams and waterfalls.

## Bibbiena and La Verna

As chief town of the modern Casentino, **Bibbiena** is enveloped in sprawl and lacks Poppi's quaint charm, though in its heart it retains its old Tuscan feel. Few buildings stand out – a good Renaissance palace, **Palazzo Dovizi**, and the church of **San Lorenzo**, with some excellent polychrome terracottas by Andrea della Robbia.

From Bibbiena, the S208 crosses east into a range of hills bravely called the **Alpe di Catenaia**, which divide the Arno from the Tiber valley, to the famous Franciscan monastery of **La Verna**, high on a bizarre rocky outcrop, which, according to one of St Francis's visions, had been rent and blasted into its wild shape at the moment of the Crucifixion. The land was given to Francis in 1213

🕎 La Verna

by another pious nobleman, Count Orlando, and the saint at once built some mud huts here for a select group of his followers. He found La Verna a perfect spot for meditation and came to his holy mountain on six occasions. During the last, on 14 September 1224, he became the first person ever to receive the stigmata – an event pictured in the frescoes of Assisi and elsewhere – after which he could only walk in extreme pain.

The churches, chapels and convent at La Verna are simple and rustic, though the main church, the chapel of Stigmata and St Francis's tiny church of **Santa Maria degli Angeli** are decorated by the most transcendently beautiful blue, green and white terracottas that Andrea della Robbia ever made, especially the *Annunciation*. You can also visit the **Sasso Spicco**, Francis's favourite retreat under a huge boulder, and **La Penna** (4,208ft/1,283m), on a sheer precipice, with views of the Arno and Tiber valleys.

# Where to Stay and Eat in the Casentino

ⓘ Stia ›
*Pro Loco,*
*Piazza Tanucci 65,*
*t 0575 504106*

★ La Foresta ›

## Stia ✉ 52017

**★★★Albergo Falterona**, Piazza Tanucci 85, t 0575 504569, *www.albergofalterona.it* (€€). Upmarket rustically styled rooms in the *centro storico* (23 has frescoes).

**★★La Foresta**, Via Roma 27, t 0575 504650, *laforestahotel@hotmail.com* (€€). Basic, comfy rooms, some ensuite.

**Ristorante Filetto**, Piazza Tanucci 28, t 0575 583631 (€€). *Pappardelle* with wild boar, excellent stewed game and other hearty fare. *Closed Sat in winter.*

## Poppi ✉ 52010

**★★★Casentino**, Piazza Repubblica, t 0575 529090, *www.albergocasentino.it* (€€). A good option opposite the castle, with rates including breakfast. The popular restaurant, set in the old castle stables, offers *tortellini*, ravioli, game, truffles and mushrooms.

**★★Campaldino**, Via Roma 95, t 0575 529008, *www.campaldino.it* (€€). An inn established in 1800, offering simple rooms (breakfast included). The restaurant uses lots of game, mushrooms, Florentine steak and grilled pork (half/full-board available). *Closed Wed, and 1st 3wks July.*

**★★★Il Rustichello**, Via del Corniolo 14, t 0575 556020 (€€). A small, modern resort hotel, great for families, with tennis, mini-golf and woodland walks.

The restaurant (€€€) serves great pasta dishes from Emilia-Romagna, grilled meats and Casentino cheeses. Half- and full-board are available.

**Poggio a Poppi**, Via Magrete 13, t 0575 529886, *www.poggioapoppi.it* (€€). A gorgeous *agriturismo* with sweeping views over the valley. There are rooms or apartments, a nice swimming pool and produce from the farm. Guests can help with harvesting fruit if they want to get back to nature.

## Pratovecchio ✉ 52015

**La Tana Degli Orsi**, Via Roma 1, t 0575 583377 (€€). One of the more interesting places to eat and drink in this remote area; it's a restaurant/ *enoteca* (the name translates as 'The Bears' Den'), so you can enjoy a bottle and a snack, or a full meal. Highlights are potato *tortelli* with prawns, pigeon with pan-fried radicchio, and deer in Chianti sauce. Note that you cannot pay by credit card. *Closed lunch, Tues, Wed, 10 days in early July, and Nov.*

## Passo della Consuma ✉ 52010

**★★★Miramonti**, t 055 830 6566, *www.hotelmiramonti-ar.it* (€€). A modern hotel with a spectacular setting at the top of the Passo della Consuma (3,480ft/1,058m). Bedrooms are functional but the grounds are lovely and there is a tennis court. The restaurant is a popular truck stop serving a cracking mushroom risotto.

# Arezzo

Strategically located on a hill at the convergence of the Valdarno, Casentino and the Valdichiana valleys, ancient Arezzo (population 92,000) was one of the richest cities of the Etruscan Dodecapolis. Nor is modern Arezzo a loser in the money game – it has one of the biggest jewellery industries in Europe, with hundreds of small firms stamping out gold chains and rings, and bank vaults full of ingots. Its second most notable industry, one that fills the shops around its main Piazza Grande, is furniture-making and marketing antiques; on the first weekend of each month, the entire square becomes an enormous curiosity shop.

Arezzo is a bit of a curiosity shop itself. It had only a brief, though remarkable, bask in the Renaissance sunshine, though in the Middle Ages it was a typical free *comune*, a Ghibelline rival to Florence and a city of great cultural distinction. Around the year 1000, it gave birth to Guido Monaco (or Guido d'Arezzo), inventor of musical notation and the musical scale; in the 13th century, it produced Margarito, or Margaritone, an important painter in the transition from the Byzantine to the Italian styles. In 1304 Petrarch, the 'first modern man', was born here into a banished Florentine

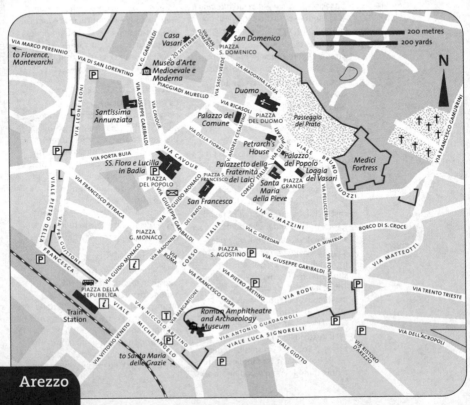

Arezzo

## Getting to Arezzo

The **train** is the easiest way to reach Arezzo from Florence (75km/90mins), Perugia (73km/90mins) and Cortona (32km/45mins). The **station** is at the southern end of town, where Via Guido Monaco meets the old city walls.

There are **buses** from Cortona and other towns in Arezzo province, as well as Siena (7 a day) and Florence (4 a day). The station is opposite the train station on Viale Piero della Francesca, t 0575 382647/382651.

Black Guelph family; his Arezzo contemporary was Spinello Aretino, one of Tuscany's trecento masters. Arezzo was at its most powerful in the early 1300s, when it was ruled by a remarkable series of warrior bishops. One died in the battle of Campaldino; another, the fierce Guido Tarlati, ruled the city from 1312 to 1327. He expanded its territory, built new walls, settled internal bickerings, renewed warfare with Florence and Siena, and was excommunicated. After Bishop Guido came the deluge – his brother sold the city for a brief period to Florence, family rivalries exploded, the plague carried away half the population and, to top it all, in 1384 French troops of Louis d'Anjou sacked the city and brought it to its knees, refusing to move on until Arezzo paid 40,000 florins. Florence came up with the ransom money, in effect purchasing Arezzo's independence. Henceforth an economic backwater, on the fringe of the Renaissance, it produced two leading personalities: Giorgio Vasari, and Pietro Aretino, the uninhibited writer and poet whose poison pen allowed him to make a fortune by not writing about contemporary princes and popes – the most genteel extortionist of all time.

If you arrive by train or bus, Via Guido Monaco leads up to the old centre by way of a stern statue of musical monk Guido, and passes on the left one of Italy's prettiest post offices, with an ornate ceiling, before ending in Piazza San Francesco, site of Arezzo's star attraction.

### San Francesco

**San Francesco**
t 0575 352757, www.
pierodellafrancesca.it;
open April–Oct Mon–Fri
9–6.30, Sat 9–5.30, Sun
1–5.30; Nov–Mar
Mon–Fri 9–5.30, Sat
9–5, Sun 1–5; booking
compulsory; adm

This dowdy barn of a Franciscan church contains Piero della Francesca's frescoes on the popular pseudo-classical/Christian subject of the *Legend of the True Cross* (*see* p.157), the most riveting cycle of frescoes of the 1400s and the gospel of Renaissance painting. Piero literally wrote the book on the new science of artificial perspective, yet, as strictly as these frescoes obey the dictates of the vanishing point, they make no concessions to realism; simplified and drawn with geometrical perfection, Piero's beings are purely spiritual creatures. It is intriguing that Piero and Uccello, the two artists most obsessed with perspective and space, created the most transcendent art; few compositions are as haunting as Piero's *Dream of Constantine*, a virtuoso demonstration of lighting, colouring and perspective, the angel swooping down from the upper left-front of the scene – and yet all is uncannily still: the soldiers stand guard, woodenly unaware; the

15

Arezzo and its Province | Arezzo

sleeping emperor's attendant gazes out with a bored expression. Note, too, the *Annunciation* in which Gabriel announces both the birth and death of her son to Mary.

That these frescoes exist at all is nothing short of a miracle. The walls have been damaged by an earthquake, struck by lightning, burned twice and shot at by Napoleon's troops, who scratched the eyes of the figures. To keep the church standing after so much abuse, the first restorers injected tons of cement into the walls, which, combined with humidity, nearly ruined the frescoes. Although they were cleaned in the 1960s, no attempt was made to protect them from further damage. Now, after nearly two decades of complex work, they are fully restored and, hopefully, saved. During restoration, it was discovered that the 'night' the art historians always referred to in Piero's *Dream of Constantine* is not night after all but a magnificent dawn hidden beneath layers of dirt. So much for the most famous night-time painting in the history of art.

## Piazza Grande

Few *piazze* in Italy have the eclectic charm of Arezzo's Piazza Grande, perfect backdrop for both the *Giostra del Saracino* in early September and the monthly antiques fair. For the former, the town sports from the four quarters of Arezzo don 13th-century costume to re-enact an event first documented in 1593, a celebration of the feats of arms against Saracen pirates who menaced the Tyrrhenian coast in the 16th century and penetrated inland as far as Arezzo. Revived in 1932, it begins with a parade of costumes and flag-tossing by the *sbandieratori*, followed by a test of individual prowess between eight knights, two representing each quarter, who tilt against a wooden figure, 'Buratto, King of the Indies', for the prize of a golden lance.

**Fiera Antiquaria**
*1st Sat and Sun of month but call tourist office (see p.420) to check if making a special trip*

The **Fiera Antiquaria** attracts hundreds of 'antiques' vendors from all over the country, selling everything from Renaissance ceramics to 1950s junk. The piazza and surrounding streets are also lined with antique shops. On one side of the piazza you'll find the **Loggia del Vasari**, a large building that Giorgio Vasari designed for his home town in 1573, with the idea of replicating a Greek *stoa*, with little shops, workshops, and expensive bars and restaurants under the portico.

Vasari also designed the clocktower of the **Palazzetto della Fraternità dei Laici**, an ornate building, half Gothic and half by Renaissance master Bernardo Rossellino. It looks like a town hall but is really the home of a lay brotherhood that was founded in the 1200s. The Palazzo del Popolo exists only in ruins, behind Vasari's loggia on Via dei Pileati. Like Pisa's, it was destroyed by the Florentines after they captured the city.

## Santa Maria della Pieve

Perhaps the most impressive building on Piazza Grande is the round, Romanesque arcaded apse of Arezzo's great 12th-century church, Santa Maria della Pieve; it turns its back on the piazza, directing its unusual Pisan-Lucchese façade towards narrow Via dei Pileati, where it's hard to see well. Each tier of arches is narrower than the previous one, in a unique rustic style with no two columns or capitals alike. The campanile 'of a hundred holes' has so many neat rows of double-mullioned windows that it resembles a primitive skyscraper. Under the arch of the front portal, note the restored early medieval *Reliefs of the Twelve Months*: April with her flowers, February with his pruning hook, and the pagan two-headed god Janus for January. The dim interior has an early Romanesque relief of the *Three Magi* on the entrance wall and decorated capitals in the nave. As in many early churches, the presbytery is raised above the low crypt, the most ancient part of the church, with primitive capitals – human faces mingling with rams, bulls and dragons. On the left wall is another primitive relief of the *Nativity* and *Christ's Baptism*; above in the choir is a beautiful polyptych by Pietro Lorenzetti (1320), featuring the *Madonna and Saints* modelling the latest Tuscan fashions and fabrics.

Below Santa Maria descends Corso Italia, Arezzo's main evening parade; above, Via dei Pileati continues into the oldest quarter of the city, passing by way of **Petrarch's house**, a replacement for the original bombed in the last war; it stands near the picturesque 14th-century **Palazzo del Pretorio**, decked with coats of arms of imperial and Florentine governors.

**Casa del Petrarca**
*www.accademia
petrarca.it; open
Mon–Fri 10–12 and
3–5; Sat 10–12;
booking required on
t 0575 24700*

## The Duomo

From Piazza Grande, narrow streets lead up to the **Passeggio del Prato**, an English-style park with lawns, trees, a café and a big white elephant of a Fascist monument to Petrarch. Arezzo slopes gradually upwards from the train station, ending abruptly here; the cliffs on the edge of the Prato have memorable view over the mountains towards Florence and Urbino. Overlooking the park is a half-ruined 16th-century Medici fortress.

At the other end is the back of the **Duomo**, with a lovely Gothic belltower from the 19th century. The cathedral itself, built in bits and pieces over two and a half centuries (1276–1510), has a nondescript façade but several great works of art in its dimly lit Gothic naves. Its stained-glass **windows**, created by the greatest 16th-century master, Frenchman Guillaume de Marcillat, seem almost like illuminated frescoes by Gozzoli or Luca Signorelli. The magnificent marble Gothic high altar is dedicated to San Donato, and there are some impressive tombs – the first of Pope Gregory X (1205–76) with a canopy and 4th-century sarcophagus, holding the mortal dust of the pope who holds the record for taking the longest to be elected; the enclave, in Viterbo, lasted from 1268 to 1271, and only ended when the Viterbans starved the cardinals into deciding. The second, even more impressive, is the 1327 **tomb of Bishop Guido Tarlati**, an early predecessor of the heroic sculptural tombs of the Renaissance, perhaps designed by Giotto. The tomb is divided into three sections, with a relief resembling a miniature theatre and a Ghibelline eagle on top; below lies the battling bishop's effigy; and below that, 16 fine relief panels tell the story of his life, battles and good works. Beside it is Piero della Francesca's fresco of the Magdalene holding a crystal pot of ointment.

**Museo del Duomo**
*t 0575 1822770,
www.oparezzo.it; open
Wed–Fri 10–1, Sat and
Sun 10–1 and 2–6; adm*

The **Museo del Duomo** contains detached frescoes by Spinello Aretino and his son Parri di Spinello, a terracotta depicting the *Annunciation* by Bernardo Rossellino and paintings by 13th-century master Margarito d'Arezzo, Signorelli and Vasari.

Diagonally opposite the cathedral is Arezzo's Ghibelline **Palazzo del Comune** with its distinctive tower; from here Via Ricasoli descends past the **birthplace of Guido Monaco** (with a plaque of Guido's do-re-mi) to the art museum.

## Museo d'Arte Medioevale e Moderna

**Museo d'Arte
Medioevale
e Moderna**
*t 0575 409050; open
Tues–Sun 8.30–7; adm*

Here you can get to know local medieval and Renaissance artists not often seen elsewhere. The collection – in a medieval palace remodelled in the Renaissance, perhaps by Bernardo Rossellino – is arranged chronologically. The courtyard has medieval columns and capitals, a fine sculpted horse's head and gargoyles. The two rooms on the **ground floor** contain sculptural details from the cathedral façade and a fine 10th-century *pluteo* carved with peacocks.

Among works on the **first floor** are a stylized Byzantine *St Francis* by Margarito d'Arezzo, painted just after the saint's death, and an *Enthroned Virgin* by Guido da Siena, studded with chunky, plasticky gems. Next come detached frescoes by Spinello Aretino, the city's greatest trecento artist, and his son Parri di Spinello (1387–1453), whose ghostly battle scene *Sconfitta di Massenzio* was found in the Badia after the war. Another native of Arezzo, Bartolomeo della Gatta, painted the plague saint Rocco praying to liberate the city from the Black Death. Also on the first floor is a fresco attributed to Signorelli; a huge busy canvas by Vasari of *Esther's Wedding Banquet*; a collection of small Renaissance bronzes; beautiful ceramics from Urbino, Deruta and Montelupo; and a plate by Master Giorgio of Gubbio with the ruby dye he kept secret.

On the **second floor** are a strange painting by Angelo Cacoselli (d. 1652), the *Maga*, of an enchantress with her animals, a few 18th-century Neapolitan *presepi* figurines, and some splashy Mannerist canvases by Vasari, Allori and the great Rosso Fiorentino.

## Vasari, Cimabue and More Vasari

**Casa del
Giorgio Vasari**
*Via XX Settembre 55,
t 0575 409040; open
Mon, Wed–Sat
8.30–7.30, Sun
8.30–1.30; adm*

Around the corner from the Museo d'Arte Medioevale e Moderna you'll find the **Casa del Giorgio Vasari**. Vasari was so fond of his own brand of spineless Mannerism, he wasn't about to leave it all for Duke Cosimo, and he decorated his own house with the same fluff. Mediocrity attracts mediocrity; besides the frescoes there are several rooms of nondescript paintings, of which three stand out: the most repugnant *St Sebastian* ever committed to canvas, a terracotta portrait of Galba, one of Rome's ugliest mugs, by Sansovino, and a painting by a follower of Santi di Tito, of *Christ and the Apostles* dining in the 17th-century equivalent of a greasy spoon.

From Vasari's house, Via San Domenico takes you to 13th-century **San Domenico**, with a simple asymmetrical exterior and a fine stone Gothic chapel (1360s) on the right wall. The main altar has a crucifix by Cimabue (*c.* 1265); the chapel to the left has a fine triptych of the *Archangel Michael* by the 'Maestro del Vescovado'.

Via Garibaldi from the art museum returns to the centre by way of **Santissima Annunziata**, Arezzo's late response to the Florentine Brunelleschi, begun by Bartolomeo della Gatta in the 1490s and completed by Antonio da Sangallo; the fourth altar has a painting by Pietro da Cortona and in the choir is a stained-glass window by Marcillat. Further up, off Via Porta Buia, is **Santissime Flora e Lucilla in Badia**, a 13th-century church with an unusual interior remodelled by Vasari. He also designed the two-sided altar, with reliefs from the Gospel of St Matthew on the front and St George slaying the dragon on the back. Over the presbytery the impressive cupola is a masterful fake by 17th-century *trompe-l'œil* master Andrea Pozzo. At the entrance is a good fresco of *St Lawrence* by della Gatta; the fine cloister is by Giuliano da Maiano, a student of Brunelleschi (entrance at Piazza della Badia 2).

On the southern edge of Arezzo, near the station on Via Margaritone, the remains of a small **Roman amphitheatre** have become a quiet city park. The restored Olivetan monastery, built on a curve over the amphitheatre's foundations, houses the **Museo Archeologico**. Not much has survived of the thriving Etruscan and Roman city of Arretium, but there are some mosaics and sarcophagi, Etruscan urns and Greek vases, examples of the Roman-era red *corallino* vases and an excellent portrait of a rather jaded-looking middle-aged Roman worked in gold.

**Museo
Archeologico**
*t 0575 20882;
open daily
8.30–7.30; adm*

## Santa Maria delle Grazie

It's 15-minute walk from Viale Mecenate through Arezzo's car-clogged southern suburbs to see the simple but exceptionally pretty Renaissance church of Santa Maria delle Grazie, finished in 1444, and given a jewel of a porch by Benedetto da Maiano in 1482. With its subdued, delicate decoration, and round arches braced with slender iron bars, this could be the archetypal creation of early Renaissance architecture – it calls to mind the backgrounds of any number of Tuscan paintings. The interior has an early Renaissance delight to match, a colourful terracotta altarpiece full of coloured fruit and *putti* by Andrea della Robbia, surrounding Parri di Spinello's *Madonna della Misericordia* (1430).

★ La Foresteria >>

ⓘ Arezzo >
*Piazza della Repubblica 28, in front of train station, t 0575 377678, www.apt.arezzo.it*

## Where to Stay in Arezzo

### Arezzo ✉ 52100

****Hotel Patio**, Via Cavour 23, t 0575 401962, *www.hotelpatio.it* (€€€€). An 18th-century palace with rooms in the style of countries visited by travel writer Bruce Chatwin – China, India, Africa, Morocco and so on. Breakfast is included, and there's an American-style bar/restaurant in the basement.

****Minerva**, Via Fiorentina 4, t 0575 370390, *www.hotel-minerva.it* (€€€€). Pleasant rooms west of the city walls in ugly modern suburbs, convenient if you're travelling by car (with parking). A buffet breakfast is included, and there's an excellent restaurant (€€) and a Turkish bath and fitness centre.

***Continentale**, Piazza Guido Monaco 7, t 0575 20251, *www.hotelcontinentale.com* (€€€). A fine, older hotel, with comfortable rooms (breakfast included) and a lovely roof terrace.

***Casa Volpi**, Via Simone Martini 29, a few km southeast of city, t 0575 354364, *www.casavolpi.it* (€€€). A pleasant old villa set above the road, with comfortable bedrooms with antiques, a large garden with panoramic terraces, and an excellent evening restaurant serving local dishes home-made from prime ingredients (half/full-board offered).

**Truciolini**, Via G. Ferraris 29, t 0575 380219, *www.truciolini.it* (€€). A good-value option with parking and its own restaurant, serving the likes of good ravioli filled with potatoes, grilled lamb, and chicken breast with lemon. Breakfast is included, and half- and full-board available.

*Toscana**, Via Perennio 56, near Porta San Lorentino, t 0575 21692, *info@ alberghotoscana.191.it* (€). Simple rooms outside the centre, most ensuite.

★ Antica Osteria L'Agania >>

**La Foresteria**, Via Bicchieraia 32, t 0575 370474, *www.foresteriaarezzo.com* (€). Simple but stylish rooms with shared facilities but beautiful frescoes (in most) in a former Benedictine convent approached via a lovely cloister. Meals are served in the refectory, and there's a TV room, Internet point and garden.

**B&B Petrarca**, Via Vittorio Veneto 101, t 0575 942196, *www.bebpetrarca.it* (€). Just south of the train station, this recently renovated B&B has wrought iron beds and the use of a kitchen.

## Eating Out in Arezzo

**Ristorante Logge Vasari**, Piazza Grande, t 0575 300333 (€€€). One of the city's top restaurants, serving Tuscan classics and creative cuisine. Two floors of romantic dining; if it's warm, try to bag a table outside to watch the floodlights slowly illumin?ate one of Italy's most beautiful squares.

**Bacco e Arianna**, Via Cesalpino 10, t 0575 299598 (€€). A restaurant in a 14th-century *palazzo*, offering the likes of meat with black cabbage and *crostone* with cannellini beans. The wines come from the *enoteca* round the corner. *Closed Mon, and Jan.*

**Buca di San Francesco**, Via S. Francesco 1, t 0575 23271 (€€). A tourist favourite with a medieval atmosphere and tasty Tuscan fare; try *tagliolini* in broth. *Closed Mon eve, Tues, and July.*

**Osteria La Capannaccia**, Loc. Campriano 51c, t 0575 361759 (€€). Specialities of the Aretine countryside, including great *minestra di pane*, plus Colli Aretini wines. *Closed Sun eve, Mon and Aug.*

**Antica Osteria L'Agania**, Via Mazzini 10, t 0575 295381 (€). A rustic option; excellent value. Try the Chianana meat.

**Torre di Gnicche**, Piaggia San Martino 8, near Piazza Grande, t 0575 352035 (€). A tiny wine bar with snacks. *Closed Wed, 3wks Jan, and 1wk July.*

# The Valtiberina and the Valdichiana

## The Valtiberina

The Valtiberina, or upper valley of the Tiber, birthplace of Michelangelo and Piero della Francesca, is a luminous patchwork filled with glowing pasturelands and pine and beech woodlands.

### Arezzo to Sansepolcro

While Michelangelo took fresh air and stone-flavoured milk from his native place, Piero della Francesca carried the light and luminous landscape along the Tuscan-Umbrian frontier with him through his career, and left more behind in his native haunts than Michelangelo.

From Arezzo, it's a pretty 41km drive to Sansepolcro, especially along the SS73, which ascends through the Foce di Scopetone (with panoramic views back towards the city) then continues 17km to the short turn-off for **Monterchi**. Dedicated to Hercules in Roman times, this town is a tiny medieval triangle; don't miss the curious underground passageway around the apse of the parish church, dating back to the Middle Ages but of uncertain purpose.

Monterchi is most famous for Piero della Francesca's extraordinary fresco, the *Madonna del Parto* (1445), perhaps the first (and last?) portrayal of the Virgin in the ninth month of pregnancy, a mystery revealed by twin angels who pull back the flaps of a tent empty but for Mary, weary and melancholy, one eyelid drooping, one hand on her hip, the other on her swollen belly, almost painful to see.

**Anghiari** (population 6,200), between Monterchi and Sansepolcro, is a fine old town on a balcony over the Valtiberina. Once a property of Camaldoli and later of the Tarlati family, it was the site of a 1440 victory of the Florentines over the Milanese – a decisive victory in corking up Visconti ambitions over Tuscany and the rest of Italy, and a nearly bloodless one, the epitome of Renaissance Italy's civilized chessboard wars: only one man died, and that was an accident. Leonardo da Vinci chose it as his subject matter in the Battle of the Frescoes in Florence's Palazzo Vecchio – one of the Renaissance's greatest unhappenings, though the cartoons left behind by the master were often copied and became one of the inspirations of Florentine Mannerism.

Anghiari's Renaissance Palazzo Taglieschi houses the **Museo delle Arti e Tradizioni Popolari dell'Alta Valle del Tevere**, with exhibits relating to traditional crafts of the Upper Tiber Valley.

*Madonna del Parto*
t 0575 70713; former schoolhouse, Via della Reglia (well signposted from all directions); open April–Oct Mon–Fri 9–1 and 2–7, Sat and Sun 9–7; Nov–Mar Mon–Fri 9–1 and 2–5; adm

Museo delle Arti e Tradizioni Popolari dell'Alta Valle del Tevere
Via Mameli 16; open Tues–Sat 8.30–7, Sun 9–1.30; adm

### Sansepolcro

Sansepolcro (population 15,500), the largest town of the Valtiberina, is famous for lace, pasta (the Buitoni spaghetti works are just outside the city) and Piero della Francesca. The painter was

# Getting around the Valtiberina and Valdichiana

CAT **buses** (t 800 223010, *www.catspa.it*) from Arezzo serve this area efficiently, if not especially frequently. Buses from Sansepolcro station (just outside the walls) go to Città di Castello, Caprese Michelangelo (26km/45mins), Arezzo (38km/1hr), Florence and Pieve Santo Stefano.

Sansepolcro is the terminus of Umbria's FCU **light rail line**, which slowly trundles you down to Città di Castello (16km/25mins), Umbertide, Perugia, Todi and Terni.

born here *c.* 1410–1420 and given his mother's name (his father died before his birth). Although he worked in the Marches, Arezzo and Rome, he spent most of his life in Sansepolcro, painting and writing books on geometry and perspective until he went blind at the age of 60. Piero may have had a chance to discuss his theories with a younger son of Sansepolcro, mathematician Luca Pacioli (born 1440), who wrote his *Divina Proporzione* with some help from Leonardo da Vinci (he also gets credit for the first book on accounting).

Sansepolcro was founded around the year 1000, and like Anghiari belonged to the monks of Camaldoli until the 13th century. The historic centre, with its crew-cut towers, has plenty of character. It is enclosed within well-preserved walls, built by the Tarlati and given a Renaissance facelift by Giuliano da Sangallo. **Piazza Torre di Berta** is the centre of town, where on the second Sunday of September crossbow-men from Gubbio challenge home archers in the *Palio della Balestra*, an ancient rivalry.

Strung out along Via Matteotti are many of the city's surviving 14th–16th-century palaces, notably the **Palazzo delle Laudi** and the 14th-century palace housing the **Museo Civico**. Here are Piero's masterpiece, the *Resurrection*, an intense, almost eerie depiction of the solemnly triumphant Christ stepping out of his tomb surrounded by sleeping soldiers and a land more autumnal than springlike, plus two of Piero's early works, the *Misericordia Polyptych*, a gold-ground altarpiece dominated by a serene, giant goddess of a Madonna, sheltering under her cloak members of the confraternity (note the black hood on one) who commissioned the picture, and a damaged fresco of San Giuliano. Other works are by his greatest pupil, Luca Signorelli, Pontormo, Santi di Tito, Mannerist Raffaellino del Colle, and the 16th-century Giovanni de' Vecchi, also of Sansepolcro, whose *Presentation of the Virgin* is interesting for its unusual vertical rhythms. You can see a 16th-century scene of Sansepolcro in the *Pilgrimage of the Company of the Crucifix of Loreto*, a relic of the days of the Black Death – as are the wooden panels of *Death* (one showing a fine strutting skeleton).

Near the museum is Gothic **San Francesco**, with a fine rose window and portal. The **Duomo**, on Via Matteotti, was built in the 11th century but has been much restored. Among the art is a fresco by Bartolomeo della Gatta and a polyptych by Matteo di Giovanni; note the huge rose window made of alabaster. Another church, **San Lorenzo**, has a *Deposizione* by Rosso Fiorentino.

**Museo Civico**
*t 0575 732218,*
*www.museocivico*
*sansepolcro.it;*
*open daily 9.30–1*
*and 2.30–6 (until 7.30*
*in summer); adm*

## Up the Tiber: Caprese Michelangelo

Signor Buonarroti, a minor noble of Florence, was *podestà* in tiny Caprese, 26km northwest of Sansepolcro, when his wife gave birth to little Michelangelo. As was the custom, the baby was sent into the countryside to be nursed by a mason's wife. 'If my brains are any good at all, it's because I was born in the pure air of your Arezzo countryside,' Michelangelo later told Vasari. 'Just as with my mother's milk, I sucked in the hammer and chisels I use for my statues.'

He only returned once to the Valtiberina, to select sturdy firs to float down the Tiber for the scaffolding in the Sistine Chapel, but Caprese does not let any chance slip by to remind us of its most famous son, even changing its name to Caprese Michelangelo. The artist's purported birthplace, the restored 14th-century **Casa del Podestà**, is a museum with photos and reproductions of his works.

From here it's not far into the Alpe di Catenaia and La Verna (*see* pp.412–13).

**Casa del Podestà**
*open April, May and Oct Mon–Fri 10.30–5.30, Sat and Sun 10.30–6.30; June, July and Sept Mon–Fri 9.30–6.30, Sat and Sun 9.30–7.30; Aug daily 9.30–7.30; Nov–Mar Mon–Fri 11–5, Sat and Sun 11–6; adm*

## Caprese to Sestino

East of Caprese the countryside is the biggest attraction; between **Pieve Santo Stefano** (Roman *Sulpitia*, mostly rebuilt after the Second World War) and **Badia Tedalda** (a small resort) lie the rolling Alpe della Luna, the 'Mountains of the Moon'.

**Sestino** (from the Roman woodland god Sextius), Tuscany's easternmost *comune* on the border of the Marches, was ruled by the Montefeltro dukes of Urbino until 1516. It has been the area's agricultural centre since antiquity and has many medieval buildings. Near its little Romanesque parish church, the **Antiquarium** has the headless *Venus of Sestino* and other local finds. The 8th-century church shows the influence of Ravenna, Byzantine capital of the west; its 13th-century altar sits on a Roman boundary stone.

Sestino is Tuscany's easternmost village; if you like this area, you cross the border into the Marches – specifically, the lovely upland region called the Montefeltro above the Renaissance city of Urbino.

**Antiquarium**
*open daily 9.30–12 and 3–6*

## Where to Stay and Eat in the Valtiberina

ⓘ Anghiari >
*Corso Matteotti 103, t 0575 749279*
★ Fiorentino >>

### Anghiari ✉ 52031

**Locanda al Castello di Sorci**, San Lorenzo, near Anghiari, t 0575 789066 (€). A country beanery in a former tobacco barn, in a beautiful setting. Guests eat an incredible-value set menu that includes wine, and the likes of *ribollita*, risotto with mushrooms, polenta, and *tagliolini* with mushrooms. *Closed Mon.*

ⓘ Sansepolcro >
*Via Matteotti 8, t 0575 740536*

### Sansepolcro ✉ 52037

★★★★**La Balestra**, Via del Montefeltro 29, t 0575 735151, *www.labalestra.it* (€€). Comfortable modern rooms and one apartment, parking and a good restaurant where you might enjoy pasta and chickpeas, *tortellini* with white truffles, and grilled lamb. Breakfast is included; half- or full-board are available.

★★★**Fiorentino**, Via L. Pacioli 56, near main gate, t 0575 740350, *www. albergofiorentino.com* (€€). The town inn since the 1820s, with basic rooms (buffet breakfast included), a garage, and Sansepolcro's best restaurant, serving great Italian onion soup and other local specialities, and a wide assortment of local cheese. *Closed Fri.*

**Il Convivio**, Via Traversari 1, t 0575 736543 (€€). A restaurant in a Renaissance *palazzo*, offering interesting dishes from the Valtiberina, including *tagliolini* with Fossa cheese. *Closed Tues and early Feb.*

**Locanda La Pergola**, Via Tiberina 17, Pieve Santo Stefano, 16km north of Sansepolcro on La Verna road, t 0575

797053 (€). An inn restored in a classy country style. A couple of the basic rooms share facilities. The restaurant serves superbly cooked country food, including ravioli freshly made daily with local ricotta. *Closed Wed*.

**\*\*Orfeo**, Viale Diaz 12, **t** 0575 742061 (€). Basic ensuite rooms.

**Enoteca Guidi**, Via Pacioli 44, **t** 0575 736587 (€€). A cosy wine bar with a rear dining room serving spaghetti with *speck*, *porcini* and rocket, risotto with asparagus and prawns, and Chianina meat with Parmesan and lemons. There are also a few rooms. *Closed Sun lunch, Wed and Sat*.

## Caprese Michelangelo
✉ **52033**

**\*\*\*Fonte della Galletta**, Alpe Faggeto above Caprese Michelangelo, **t** 0575 793925, *www.fontedellagalletta.it* (€). A pleasant little mountain hotel and restaurant set in a lovely forested landscape, with simple ensuite rooms (breakfast included). The restaurant (€€) uses the freshest local ingredients – chestnuts, wild mushrooms, truffles, game, mountain hams – to create tasty fare. Try the home-made pasta dishes, grilled meats and *semifreddo al croccante*. *Closed Mon and Tues*.

# South of Arezzo: the Valdichiana

The flat Valdichiana south of Arezzo is the largest, broadest valley in the Apennines, surrounded by hills and old towns. The Etruscans, headquartered at Cortona, were the first to drain its marshlands, making it their breadbasket – one so rich, it is said, that even after Hannibal's troops pillaged on their way to Lake Trasimeno, there was still more than enough to feed the army and its elephants. By the Middle Ages, however, the valley had reverted to a swamp, forcing the inhabitants back into the hills. And so it stayed, until the beginning of the 19th century, when the Lorraine grand dukes initiated a major land reclamation scheme. Now, once again, prosperous farms are the main feature of the Valdichiana. The equally prosperous-looking cattle are a prized breed called the Chianina, descendants of the primal herds whose fossils were discovered in the vicinity.

## Monte San Savino and Lucignano

But there is more to the Valdichiana than farms and *bistecca alla fiorentina* on the hoof. On both sides of the valley are some of the most beautiful villages in this part of Tuscany. Cortona is the most famous, but there are others, including **Monte San Savino** (21km from Arezzo, on the west side of the valley), birthplace of Andrea Contucci, better known as Andrea Sansovino (1460–1529), artistic emissary of Lorenzo de' Medici to Portugal and one of the heralds of the High Renaissance; his Florentine pupil Jacopo adopted his surname and became chief sculptor and architect in Venice in its Golden Age. Spread out on a low hill, this is an attractive town with a mélange of late medieval and fine Renaissance palaces. Andrea Sansovino left several works to his home town: an attractive portal on the church of **San Giovanni**, terracottas (with others by the della Robbias) in the little church of **Santa Chiara** in Piazza Jalta, and the

## Getting around the Valdichiana

LFI **trains** (t 0575 28414, *www.lfi.it*) head south from Arezzo for Monte San Savino and Lucignano, and Sinalunga (*see* p.383), with links to Chiusi and Siena.

lovely **cloister of Sant'Agostino** (13th-century, with a small rose window by Guillaume de Marcillat). Sansovino, or Antonio da Sangallo the Elder, designed the beautiful, harmonious **Loggia dei Mercanti** with its grey Corinthian capitals in the early 1500s; Antonio da Sangallo gets credit for the simple, partly rusticated **Palazzo Comunale**, originally the home of the Del Monte family, whose money paid for most of Monte San Savino's Renaissance ornaments. Foremost among the medieval monuments, the **Palazzo Pretorio** was built by the Perugians. The city walls are the work of the Sienese.

On a cypress-clad hill 2km east, **Santa Maria della Vertighe**, built in the 12th century and restored in the 16th, houses a rare 13th-century triptych by Margarito d'Arezzo and 14th-century works by Lorenzo Monaco. Some 7km west is pretty **Gargonza**, with its mighty tower dominating a tight cluster of houses on a wart of a hill, the whole of which is now a hotel (*see* opposite).

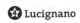 **Lucignano**

Cheerful little **Lucignano**, to the south of Monte San Savino, is unique among Italian hilltowns for its street plan – it is laid out in four concentric ellipses, like a kind of maze, with four picturesque little *piazze* in the centre. One piazza is dominated by the **Collegiata** with a theatrical circular stair, another by the 14th-century **Palazzo Comunale**, now the **Museo Civico**, with a good collection of 13th–15th-century Sienese works, a *Madonna* by Signorelli and, most famously, a 14th-century masterpiece of Aretine goldsmiths, the delicate reliquary *Albero di Lucignano*. There are more good Sienese paintings in the church of **San Francesco**. Outside the centre are a 16th-century Medici fortress and the **Madonna delle Querce**, a Renaissance temple sometimes attributed to Vasari, with a Doric interior.

**Museo Civico**
*t 0575 838001;
open summer Mon,
Thurs–Fri 10–5,
Sat–Sun 10–6*

**Marciano della Chiana**, 6km northeast, is another old fortified village with an impressive main gate that also does time as clock and belltower. **Foiano della Chiana**, just south, is encompassed by newer buildings, but in its **Collegiata** has a good *Coronation of the Virgin* by Signorelli and a terracotta by Andrea della Robbia. Between Marciano and Foiano is the curious octagonal church of **Santa Vittoria**, built by Ammannati for Cosimo I.

### Castiglion Fiorentino

East, on the last hill overlooking the Valdichiana plain, fortified **Castiglion Fiorentino** was Castiglion Aretino until the Florentines snatched it in 1384. Another old Etruscan settlement, with medieval streets, it nevertheless had more than a nodding acquaintance with the Renaissance. Like many a larger town, it has an ornamental geometric temple below the walls, the octagonal **Madonna della Consolazione**, untampered with since 1607. Then there's the 16th-century **Loggiato Vasariano**, overlooking the countryside from the old market square. The 1860 plebiscite that brought Tuscany into the kingdom of Italy made a big impression here: the **Palazzo Comunale** opposite has a marble plaque recording not only the precise vote but the exact day, hour and minute of the count.

Just behind and above the Palazzo Comunale, Castiglion's ancient heart, the Cassero (from the Roman *castrum*), has the **Palazzo Pretorio** and the church of **Sant'Angelo**, the latter home to the small **Pinacoteca Civica**. Its prizes are a French Renaissance gilded silver reliquary bust of Sant'Orsola, a pair of 13th-century crucifixes, the *Stigmata of St Francis* by Bartolomeo della Gatta, a *Portrait of St Francis* (1280) by the workshop of Margaritone di Arezzo, and the 15th-century *Probatica Piscina*, an uncommon subject (Jerusalem's sheep pond, with curative waters) by Jacopo de Sellaio. The **Collegiata**, rebuilt in the 19th century, has kept its art: *Enthroned Madonnas* by della Gatta, an *Adorazione* by Lorenzo di Credi, and, in the adjacent **Pieve Vecchia** Signorelli's fresco of the *Deposition*. The Gothic 13th-century church of **San Francesco** has a cloister, some frescoes and a wooden *Crucifixion* sculpted by Giambologna.

Dilapidated castles are all around Castiglion, most impressively at **Montecchio**, 4km south, with its tall honey-coloured tower and walls, visible all over the Valdichiana. In the 1400s it was the stronghold of *condottiere* Sir John Hawkwood (*see* p.109).

**Pinacoteca Civica**
*open Tues–Sun 10–12.30 and 4–6.30; adm*

# Where to Stay and Eat in the Valdichiana

① **Monte San Savino** ›
*Piazza Gamuzzini 3, t 0575 844891, www. prolocomonte sansavino.it*

## Monte San Savino ✉ 52048

**★★★Sangallo**, Piazza Vittorio Veneto 16, t 0575 810049, *www.sangallohotel.it* (€€€€). A fine hotel. Breakfast is included but there's no restaurant.

**★★★★Castello dei Gargonza**, 8km from Monte San Savino, just off SS73, t 0575 847021, *www.gargonza.it* (€€€). An entire walled village, medieval in atmosphere, with rooms, apartments/ houses and a pool, surrounded by forest. Local specialities are served at the popular restaurant (€€). *Closed Tues, Feb and Nov.*

① **Castiglion Fiorentino** ›
*Corso Italia 111, t 0575 658278, www.proloco castiglionfiorentino.it*

## Castiglion Fiorentino ✉ 52043

**Relais San Pietro in Polvano**, Loc. Polvano 3, t 0575 650100, *www. polvano.com* (€€€€). A family-run hotel in a peaceful setting, with a charming little pool. There are no TVs and small children are discouraged. Italian cuisine is served on a fabulous panoramic terrace, and breakfast is included in the rates.

**★★★Park**, Via Umbro-Casentinese 88, t 0575 680288, *www.parkhotelarezzo. com* (€€). A big, modern hotel with a pool, gym and restaurant for guests.

**Antica Trattoria la Foce**, Via della Foce 30, t 0575 658187 (€€). Authentic local food such as *agnolotti* with truffles and smoked swordfish with tomatoes, plus pizza. *Closed Mon, Tues–Fri lunch.*

## Lucignano ✉ 52046

**La Rocca**, Via Giacomo Matteotti 15, t 0575 836775 (€€). A place in the delightful *centro storico*, serving *pan di lepre* (with rabbit), roast duck and more since 1903. *Closed Tues and Jan.*

# Cortona

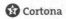 
High above the Valdichiana plain on terraced slopes of olives and vines, Cortona (pop. 27,000) is one of the crown jewels of Tuscan hilltowns. Some 2,000ft (600m) above sea level, sweeping down a spur of Monte Sant'Egidio, it has crooked, cobbled streets that climb precipitously to the Medici fortress – even halfway up, between the houses, you can see Lake Trasimeno in Umbria and mounts Amiata and Cetona near Siena. Three Cortonese became celebrated artists: Luca Signorelli (1441/50–1523); Baroque painter Pietro Berrettini (1596–1669), better known as Pietro da Cortona, master of the rooms in the Pitti Palace; and Futurist-Impressionist mosaicist Gino Severini (1883–1966); all left works in their home town.

According to Virgil and popular tradition, Cortona is nothing less than the 'Mother of Troy and Grandmother of Rome' – founded by Dardanus who, according to legend, was fighting a neighbouring tribe when he lost his helmet (*corythos*) on the hill, giving the name *Corito* to the city that grew up on the spot. He later went to Asia to found Troy and give his name to the Dardanelles. There may be a grain of truth in this myth. The Etruscans claimed to have come from Western Anatolia (around 900 BC), and inscriptions very similar to Etruscan have been found on the Greek island of Lemnos, near Troy; artefacts from the Iron Age found in Anatolia and Tuscany suggest cultural affinities. Cortona was an important Etruscan city, one of the Dodecapolis and one of the largest in the north; ragged Etruscan stonework is visible in the foundations of its walls. These stretch over 3km of the perimeter, but still cover only two-thirds of the area of the original Etruscan fortifications.

As a medieval *comune*, Cortona held its own against Perugia, Arezzo and Siena, while internally its Ghibellines and Guelphs battled until the Ghibellines won out. When that was settled, the ruling family, the Casali, spent the 14th century bumping each other off. This ended in 1409, when King Ladislas of Naples captured the city, selling it to Florence at a handsome profit.

Cortona's heart, **Piazza della Repubblica**, is a striking asymmetrical square. Dominant here is the **Palazzo Comunale** (13th century), with a tower from 1503 and monumental steps.

## Palazzo Casali: Museo dell'Accademia Etrusca

**Museo dell' Accademia Etrusca**
t 0575 630415,
www.cortonamaec.org;
open April–Oct daily
10–7; Nov–Mar
Tues–Sun 10–5; adm

Just behind the Palazzo Comunale is the 13th-century Palazzo Casali, impressive home of the city's murderous lordlings, now the seat of the Etruscan Academy, a cultural organization founded in the 17th century by the local nobility. Through the courtyard awaits the Museo dell'Accademia Etrusca, a fascinating collection begun by the Academy in 1727, encompassing bronzes (note the two-faced god Selvans); Greek vases, attesting to the city's wealth and trading

# Getting to Cortona

Cortona is just off the main Florence–Arezzo–Rome **train** line. The nearest station is Camucia, 5km west; if you're coming up from Umbria, the station is Terontola, 10km south. Both stations have frequent LFI **buses** (*www.lfi.it*) up to Cortona. There are also LFI train connections to Arezzo (34km/50mins), Castiglion Fiorentino, Foiano della Chiana and Castiglione del Lago on Lake Trasimeno (22km/30mins). Schedules for both buses and trains, and tickets for the former, are available in the office in Via Nazionale, near the bus terminus and car park in panoramic Piazzale Garibaldi, or call **t** 0575 398813.

contacts of long ago; Egyptian mummies and a doll-like Egyptian funeral barque; and Cortona's most famous relic, a 5th-century BC Etruscan bronze chandelier with 16 lamps, found in a nearby field. Each lamp is a grotesque squatting figure, uncircling a ring of stylized waves and dolphins, and in the centre an archaic gorgon.

There is a fine collection of paintings, the oldest being a Roman portrait of the *Muse Polyhymnia*. Others include works by Pietro da Cortona, *Two Saints* by Niccolò di Pietro Gerini, a 12th-century Tuscan mosaic of the Madonna, a fine polyptych by Bicci di Lorenzo, a *Madonna* by Pinturicchio, and another by Signorelli, who portrays her in the company of the saintly protectors of Cortona, with a nasty-looking devil squirming at their feet. One room is dedicated to Francesco Laperelli (1521–70) from Cortona, who built the walls of Valletta for the Knights of Malta; also ivories, globes of the earth and sky from 1714, costumes, the library founded by the Etruscan Academy in 1727, ceramics and a fine Roman alabaster *Hecate*, queen of the night. There's also a recreation of the inside of the Etruscan tumulus, the **Secondo Melone di Sodo**, excavated in 1991 (*see* p.43). Part of its unique platform altar, sculpted with a man stabbing a lion while it bites off his head, is displayed too.

Behind the civic museum signs point back to the **Duomo**, an 11th-century church unimaginatively rebuilt in 1560, probably by Giuliano da Sangallo; inside is a mosaic by Gino Severini.

## Museo Diocesano

**Museo Diocesano**
*t 0575 628300;*
*open April–Oct Tues–*
*Sun 10–7; Nov–Mar*
*Tues–Sun 10–5; adm*

Across from the Duomo in the deconsecrated Gesù church is the excellent diocese museum. It has two masterpieces: Luca Signorelli's *Deposition*, with scenes of the *Crucifixion* and *Resurrection* (the latter inspired by his master Piero della Francesca) with an excellent predella, and a beautiful, luminous *Annunciation* by Beato Angelico, who came to Cortona to paint this solemn angel gently whispering his tremendous message; it has another exceptional predella. Note how the frame echoes the Corinthian columns of the loggia. Other works include a 14th-century crucifix by Pietro Lorenzetti, a triptych by Il Sassetta, a fine Sienese *Madonna* by the school of Duccio di Buoninsegna, and a 2nd-century AD Roman sarcophagus with reliefs of the Battle of Lapiths and Centaurs that was closely studied by Donatello and Brunelleschi. Note the church's fine coffered wooden ceiling.

## Up and Down Cortona

Below Piazza del Duomo is one of Cortona's most picturesque lanes, medieval **Via Jannelli** (or del Gesù), where some houses have *porte del morto* ('doors of the dead'), more common in medieval Umbria than in Tuscany. Other picturesque streets to look out for are **Via Ghibellina**, **Via Guelfa** and **Via Maffei**, with its town palaces.

You'll need your climbing shoes if you want to see the other monuments, though **San Francesco** is only a short walk up from Piazza della Repubblica. St Francis's controversial lieutenant Brother Elias was a native of Cortona and founded this little church at an interesting angle in 1245; it retains its original façade and one side. Both Brother Elias and Luca Signorelli are buried here, and on the left wall is a fine fresco of the *Annunciation*, last work of Pietro da Cortona. On the high altar is a slice of the Holy Cross brought back from Constantinople by Brother Elias, housed in an ivory reliquary that Byzantine emperor Nicephoras Phocas carried into battle against the Saracens in the 960s, as described in the Greek inscription on the back.

From here, handsome Via Berrettini continues up to Piazza Pozzo and Piazza Pescaia and the medieval neighbourhood that surrounds **San Nicolò**. This handsome little Romanesque church, which was built by an anachronistic architect in the 1440s, was once the seat of San Bernardino da Siena's Company of St Nicholas, for whom Luca Signorelli painted a magnificent standard of the *Deposition* still hanging by the altar.

You can reach the loftiest church of them all, the pretty 19th-century neo-Romanesque **Santuario di Santa Margherita**, from San Nicolò; the views become increasingly magnificent. The original church was built by Santa Margherita (1247–97), a beautiful farmer's daughter and mistress of a young nobleman; upon his sudden death, she got religion, became a Franciscan tertiary and founded a convent and hospital where she cared for the sick. Her remains are in a silver urn on the altar; her fine but empty Gothic sarcophagus on the left wall is by Angelo and Francesco di Pietro. Right of the altar are standards and lanterns captured from the Turks in 18th-century sea battles, donated by a local commander.

Just above, the overgrown **Medici fortress** of 1556 occupies the site of the old Etruscan acropolis. Descend from Santa Margherita to the centre by way of Via Santa Margherita and the **Via Crucis**, which are made up of mosaic shrines by Gino Severini; they were commissioned in 1947 by the people of Cortona to thank their patron saint for sparing their city from the war.

As in many Etruscan and Roman towns, Cortona's gates are orientated to the four points of the compass. The northern **Porta Colonia** has an Etrusco-Roman arch and is near some well-preserved remains of the Etruscan walls; from here, it's a 15-minute walk to the late, tall Renaissance church of **Santa Maria Nuova**, partly by Vasari and one of the more serene works to come out of the Counter-Reformation, designed in a Greek cross and crowned by a dome. Outside the southern **Porta Berarda**, at the end of Via Nazionale, Gothic **San Domenico** has an elegant interior presided over by a grand triptych by Lorenzo di Niccolò Gerini (1402) given to the Dominicans by Lorenzo de' Medici; in the apse there's a *Madonna with Angels* by Signorelli.

Nearby you'll find a a good stretch of Etruscan wall and the beginning of the Passeggiata Pubblica through Cortona's shady public gardens, the **Parterre**, where you can enjoy more grandstand views over the Valdichiana.

## Around Cortona

In the Renaissance, it was fashionable in Tuscany and Umbria to decorate the outskirts of a town with a perfectly symmetrical church – exercises in geometry and divine order visible from all four sides. By the 16th century, this was impossible to do in the built-up town centres. Cortona has one of most graceful of these ornamental set pieces, **Santa Maria delle Grazie al Calcinaio**, 3km down the road to Camucia. Built in 1485–1513 by Sienese architect Francesco di Giorgio Martini, this Latin cross topped with an octagonal drum has a harmonious interior in Brunelleschian dark and light accents, luminous and airy and pure, with colour provided by fine stained glass by Guillaume de Marcillat.

*Santa Maria delle Grazie al Calcinaio*
*rarely open; ask at tourist office (see p.432)*

Ancient tombs pepper the plain. One of the most evocative of them, the Hellenistic **Tanella di Pitagora**, is signposted from the crossroads near Santa Maria delle Grazie. Named after Pythagoras – apparently the ancients confused Cortona with Croton in Calabria, where the philosopher lived – the 3rd-century BC hypogeum is surrounded by cypress trees and has an unusual vault over its rectangular funeral chamber.

*Tanella di Pitagora*
*open by appt on t 0575 630415*

Northwest of Cortona is the 7th-century BC **Melone di Camucia**, an Etruscan tumulus with two large chambers and corridors. Nearby, at **Il Sodo** ('the hard-boiled egg'), are two 6th-century BC tumuli with massive walls 650ft (200m) in perimeter, the **Meloni del Sodo**. You can visit the first; Tumulo II, with its five mortuary chambers, yielded the treasures and altar in Cortona's museum (*see* p.429) and is still being excavated.

*Meloni del Sodo*
*guided tours by appt one day in advance, t 0575 630415*

Beyond Santa Maria Nuova, the road continues 3.5km along the slopes of Monte Sant'Egidio to the **Convento delle Celle**, which was founded by St Francis in 1211 in a beautiful setting. Little has changed; its simple rustic buildings have preserved their Franciscan spirit better than many others – the humble founder's cell retains the saint's stone bed.

## Festivals and Events in Cortona

★ Locanda del Molino >>

**National antique furniture market,** Aug–Sept.

**Copperware show/market**: Show?case for a local handmade speciality, April.

**Umbria Jazz Festival**: Concerts throughout July in the public gardens.

*Sagra di Bistecca* (beefsteak festival): a huge outdoor grill, 15 Aug.

**Under the Tuscan Sun Festival**: Music festival with international performers, plus food and wine events, films, talks and seminars, Aug.

## Activities in Cortona

Just off the mountain road above Torreone, among the chestnut woods at Tornia, is the 'Priest's Hole', a quiet **swimming** pool (donations requested).

**Horses** can be hired from **Unione Popolare Sport Equestre**, Loc Ossaia, Montanino di Cortona, **t** 0575 67500.

## Where to Stay in Cortona

ⓘ Cortona >
*Via Nazionale 42,*
*t 0575 630352*

**Cortona** ✉ **52044**

Lodgings can be scarce: Cortona hosts a language school and a University of Georgia art programme (June–Oct).

**\*\*\*\*Il Falconiere**, San Martino a Bocena, 3km from town, **t** 0575 612679, *www.ilfalconiere.it* (€€€€€). Refined, frescoed rooms (breakfast included) with Jacuzzi, two pools and a first-class restaurant (€€€€) with a splendid terrace. Ask about cookery courses. *Closed Wed in winter.*

★ La Grotta >>

**\*\*\*Oasi**, Via Contesse 1, **t** 0575 630354, *www.hoteloasi.org* (€€€€). A restored monastery with a warm welcome, lovely gardens and a Tuscan Renaissance restaurant. *Closed Nov–Easter.*

**\*\*\*\*San Michele**, Via Guelfa 15, **t** 0575 604348, *www.hotelsanmichele.net* (€€€). An elegant Renaissance palace with painted friezes, ancient hearths and old waxed floors. Breakfast is included but the garage is €11/day.

**\*\*\*\*Residence Borgo San Pietro**, Loc. San Pietro a Cegliolo, 4km north of town, **t** 0575 604348, *www.borgosan pietro.com* (€€). Upmarket apartments sleeping 2–4 in a lovely 17th-century farmhouse and outbuildings, with pool,

gym and garage. Minimum 3-night stay Nov–Mar and 1wk the rest of the year. *Closed early Jan–early Mar.*

**\*\*\*San Luca**, Piazza Garibaldi 1, **t** 0575 630460, *www.sanlucacortona.com* (€€). Simple rooms, many with great views; breakfast is included.

**Locanda del Molino**, Loc. Montanare, **t** 0575 614016, *www.locandadelmolino. com* (€€). A converted stone mill house with an excellent restaurant.

**\*Athens**, Via S. Antonio 12, **t** 0575 630508 (€). Very basic lodgings high up in the old town; all but one room share facilities. *Closed Dec–mid-Mar.*

**Ostello San Marco**, Via Maffei 57, 3km up from Piazza Garibaldi, **t** 0575 601765, *www.cortonahostel.com* (€). One of Italy's best hostels, organizing Italian courses and archaeology tours. *Closed mid-Oct–mid-Mar.*

## Eating Out in Cortona

Local treats are *salumeria* and beef steaks from the Valdichiana, and local *bianchi vergini* ('white virgins') wines.

**Da Tonino**, Piazza Garibaldi, **t** 0575 630500 (€€€). Cortona's most elegant restaurant, serving wonderful *anti?pastissimo* (different *antipasti*). Book. *Closed Mon eve in winter, and Tues.*

**Osteria del Teatro**, Via Maffei 3, **t** 0575 630556 (€€). A 15th-century *palazzo* by the theatre; try duck breast with artichokes. *Closed Wed, and 2wks Nov.*

**La Grotta**, Piazzetta Baldelli 3, **t** 0575 630271 (€€). An intimate restaurant locals try to keep secret, with a pretty courtyard. Try grilled Chianina meat. *Closed Tues, 7 Jan–12 Feb, and 1wk July.*

**Miravalle**, Frazione Torreone 6, **t** 0575 62232 (€€). Simple cuisine, great views.

**Dardano**, Via Dardano 24, **t** 0575 601944 (€). A simple trattoria popular with locals; try *pici contadine* (with vegetables and mushrooms). *Closed Wed, and Jan and Feb.*

**La Saletta**, Via Nazionale 26/28, **t** 0575 603366 (€). A wine bar serving regional snacks, soups, lovely sandwiches and the odd pasta dish.

**La Bucaccia**, Via Ghibellina 17, **t** 0575 606039 (€€). This cosy place is located in a 13th-century cellar and run by a sweet couple who serve up wonderfully tasty seasonal fare.

# Glossary

**acroterion**: decorative protrusion on the rooftop of an Etruscan, Greek or Roman temple. At the corners of the roof they are called *antefixes*.

**ambones**: twin pulpits (singular: *ambo*), often elaborately decorated.

**ambulatory**: aisle around the apse of a church.

**atrium**: entrance court of a Roman house or early church.

**badia**: abbey or abbey church (also *abbazia*).

*baldacchino*: baldachin, a columned stone canopy above the altar of a church.

**basilica**: a rectangular building, usually divided into three aisles by rows of columns. In Rome this was the common form for law courts and other public buildings, and Roman Christians adapted it for their early churches.

*borgo*: from the Saxon *burh* of Santo Spirito in Rome: a suburb or village.

**bucchero ware**: black, delicately thin Etruscan ceramics, usually incised or painted.

**Calvary chapels**: a series of outdoor chapels, usually on a hillside, that commemorate the stages of the Passion of Christ.

**campanile**: a bell tower.

*campanilismo*: local patriotism; the Italians' own word for their historic tendency to be more faithful to their home towns than to the abstract idea of 'Italy'.

*campo santo*: a cemetery.

**cardo**: the transverse street of a Roman *castrum*-shaped city.

**carroccio**: a wagon carrying the banners of a medieval city and an altar; it served as the rallying point in battles.

**cartoon**: the preliminary sketch for a fresco or tapestry.

**caryatid**: supporting pillar or column carved into a standing female form; male versions are called *telamones*.

**castrum**: a Roman military camp, always neatly rectangular, with straight streets and gates at the cardinal points. Later the Romans founded or refounded cities in this form, hundreds of which survive today (Lucca, Aosta, Florence, Pavia, Como, Brescia, Ascoli Piceno, Ancona are clear examples).

**cavea**: the semicircle of seats in a classical theatre.

*cenacolo*: fresco of the *Last Supper*, often on the wall of a monastery refectory.

**chiaroscuro**: the arrangement or treatment of light and dark areas in a painting.

**ciborium**: a tabernacle; the word is often used for large, free-standing tabernacles, or in the sense of a *baldacchino* (q.v.).

*comune*: commune or commonwealth, referring to the governments of the free cities of the Middle Ages. Today it denotes any local government, from the Comune di Roma down to the smallest village.

*condottiere*: the leader of a band of mercenaries in late medieval and Renaissance times.

**confraternity**: a religious lay brotherhood, often serving as a neighbourhood mutual-aid and burial society, or following some specific charitable work (Michelangelo, for example, belonged to one that cared for condemned prisoners in Rome).

*contrapposto*: the dramatic, but rather unnatural twist in a statue, especially in a Mannerist or Baroque work, derived from Hellenistic and Roman art.

*convento*: a convent or monastery

**Cosmati work**: or *Cosmatesque*: referring to a distinctive style of inlaid marble or enamel chips used in architectural decoration (pavements, pulpits, paschal candlesticks, etc.) in medieval Italy. The Cosmati family of Rome were its greatest practitioners.

*crete*: found in the pasturelands of southern Tuscany, chalky cliffs caused by erosion. Similar phenomena are the *biancane*, small chalk outcrops, and *balze*, deep eroded ravines around Volterra.

**cupola**: a dome.

**decumanus**: street of a Roman *castrum*-shaped city parallel to the longer axis, the central, main avenue called the Decumanus Major.

**Dodecapolis**: the federation of the 12 largest and strongest Etruscan city states (*see* **History and Art**, p.8).

*duomo*: cathedral.

**ex voto**: an offering (a terracotta figurine, painting, medallion, silver bauble or whatever) made in thanksgiving to a god or Christian saint; the practice has always been present in Italy.

**forum**: the central square of a Roman town, with its most important temples and public buildings. The word means 'outside', as the original Roman Forum was outside the first city walls.

**fresco**: wall painting, the most important Italian medium of art since Etruscan times. It isn't easy; first the artist draws the *sinopia* (q.v.) on the wall. This is covered with plaster, but only a little at a time, as the paint must be on the plaster before it dries. Leonardo da Vinci's endless attempts to find clever short-cuts ensured that little of his work would survive.

**Ghibellines**: one of the two great medieval parties (*see Guelphs*), the supporters of the Holy Roman Emperors.

**gonfalon**: the banner of a medieval free city; the *gonfaloniere*, or flag-bearer, was often the most important public official.

**graffito**: originally, incised decoration on buildings, walls, etc.; only lately has it come to mean casually scribbled messages in public places.

**Greek cross**: in the floor plans of churches, a cross with equal arms. The more familiar plan, with one arm extended to form a nave, is called a *Latin Cross*.

**grisaille**: painting or fresco in monochrome.

**grotesques**: carved or painted faces used in Etruscan and later Roman decoration; Raphael and other artists rediscovered them in the 'grotto' of Nero's Golden House in Rome.

**Guelphs** (*see Ghibellines*): the other great political faction of medieval Italy, supporters of the Pope.

**intarsia**: decorative inlaid wood or marble.

**loggia**: an open-sided gallery or arcade.

**lozenge**: the diamond shape – this, along with stripes, is one of the trademarks of Pisan architecture.

**lunette**: semicircular space on a wall, above a door or under vaulting, either filled by a window or a mural painting.

**matroneum**: the elevated women's gallery around the nave of an early church, a custom adopted from the Byzantines in the 6th and 7th centuries.

**narthex**: the enclosed porch of a church.

**naumachia**: mock naval battles, like those staged in the Colosseum.

**opus reticulatum**: Roman masonry consisting of diamond-shaped blocks.

**palazzo**: not just a palace, but any large, important building (though the word comes from the Imperial *palatium* on Rome's Palatine Hill).

**Palio**: a banner, and the horse race in which city neighbourhoods contend for it in their annual festivals. The most famous is at Siena.

**Pantocrator**: Christ 'ruler of all', a common subject for apse paintings and mosaics in areas influenced by Byzantine art.

**pietra dura**: rich inlay decoration that uses semi-precious stones, perfected in post-Renaissance Florence.

*pieve*: a parish church.

**pluteo**: screen, usually of marble, between two columns, often highly decorated.

*podestà*: in medieval cities, an official sent by the Holy Roman Emperors to take charge; their power, or lack of it, depended on the strength of the *comune*.

**predella**: smaller paintings on panels below the main subject of a painted altarpiece.

**presepio**: a Christmas crib.

**putti**: flocks of plaster cherubs with rosy cheeks and bottoms that infested much of Italy in the Baroque era.

**quattrocento**: the 1400s – the Italian way of referring to centuries (*duecento, trecento, quattrocento, cinquecento*, etc.).

**sbandieratore**: flag-thrower in medieval costume at an Italian festival; sometimes called an *alfiere*.

**sinopia**: the layout of a fresco (q.v.), etched by the artist on the wall before the plaster is applied. Often these are works of art in their own right.

**stele**: a vertical funeral stone.

**stigmata**: a miraculous simulation of the bleeding wounds of Christ, appearing in holy men like St Francis in the 12th century, and Padre Pio of Puglia in our own time.

**telamone**: (*see caryatid*).

**thermae**: Roman baths.

**tondo**: round relief, painting or terracotta.

**transenna**: a marble screen separating the altar area from the rest of an early Christian church.

**travertine**: hard, light-coloured stone, sometimes flecked or pitted with black, sometimes perfect. The most widely used material in ancient and modern Rome.

**triptych**: a painting, especially an altarpiece, in three sections.

**trompe l'œil**: art that uses perspective effects to deceive the eye – for example, to create the illusion of depth on a flat surface, or to make columns and arches painted on a wall seem real.

**tympanum**: the semicircular space, often bearing a painting or relief, above the portal of a church.

**voussoir**: one of the stones of an arch.

# Language

The fathers of modern Italian were Dante, Manzoni and television. Each did their part in creating a national language from an infinity of regional and local dialects; the Florentine Dante, the first 'immortal' to write in the vernacular, did much to put the Tuscan dialect in the foreground of Italian literature. Manzoni's revolutionary novel, I Promessi Sposi (The Betrothed), heightened national consciousness by using an everyday language all could understand in the 19th century. Television in the last few decades is performing an even more spectacular linguistic unification; although the majority of Italians still speak a dialect at home, school and work, their TV idols insist on proper Italian.

Perhaps because they are so busy learning their own beautiful but grammatically complex language, Italians are not especially apt at learning others. English lessons, however, have been the rage for years, and at most hotels and restaurants there will be someone who speaks some English. In small towns and out-of-the-way places, finding an Anglophone may prove more difficult.

The words and phrases below should help you out in most situations, but the ideal way to come to Italy is with some Italian under your belt; your visit will be richer and you're much more likely to make some Italian friends.

## Pronunciation

Italian words are pronounced phonetically. Every vowel and consonant (except 'h') is sounded. Consonants are the same as in English, except the 'c' which, when followed by an 'e' or 'i', is pronounced like the English 'ch' (cinque thus becomes 'cheenquay'). Italian 'g' is also soft before 'i' or 'e' as in gira, pronounced 'jee-ra'. 'H' is never sounded; 'z' is pronounced like 'ts'. The consonants 'sc' before the vowels 'i' or 'e' become like the English 'sh' as in 'sci', pronounced 'shee'; 'ch' is pronouced like a 'k' as in Chianti, 'kee-an-tee'; 'gn' as 'ny' in English (bagno, pronounced 'ban-yo'; while 'gli' is pronounced like the middle of the word 'million' (Castiglione, pronounced 'Ca-steely-oh-nay').

Vowel pronunciation is: 'a' as in English 'father'; 'e' when unstressed is pronounced like 'a' in 'fate' as in mele, when stressed can be the same or like the 'e' in 'pet' (bello); 'i' is like the 'i' in 'machine'; 'o' like 'e', has two sounds, 'o' as in 'hope' when unstressed (tacchino), and usually 'o' as in 'rock' when stressed (morte); 'u' is pronounced like the 'u' in 'June'.

The accent usually (but not always) falls on the penultimate syllable. Also note that, in the big northern cities, the informal way of addressing someone as you, tu, is widely used; the more formal lei or voi is commonly used in provincial districts.

## Useful Words and Phrases

**yes/no/maybe** *sì/no/forse*
**I don't know** *Non lo so*
**I don't understand (Italian)** *Non capisco (l'italiano)*
**Does someone here speak English?**
 *C'è qualcuno qui che parla inglese?*
**Speak slowly** *Parla lentamente*
**Could you assist me?** *Potrebbe aiutarmi?*
**Help!** *Aiuto!*
**Please/Thank you (very much)** *Per favore/ (Molte) grazie*
**You're welcome** *Prego*
**It doesn't matter** *Non importa*
**All right** *Va bene*
**Excuse me** *permesso*
**I'm sorry** *Mi scusi, mi dispiace*
**Be careful!** *Attenzione!*
**Nothing** *Niente*
**It is urgent!** *È urgente!*
**How are you?** *Come sta/stai?*

Well, and you? *Bene, e Lei/e tu?*
What is your name? *Come si chiama?/ Come ti chiami*
Hello *Salve or ciao (both informal)*
Good morning *Buongiorno (formal hello)*
Good afternoon, evening *Buonasera (also formal hello)*
Good night *Buona notte*
Goodbye *Arrivederla (formal), Arrivederci/ Ciao (informal)*
What do you call this in Italian? *Come si chiama questo in italiano?*
What? *Che?*
Who? *Chi?*
Where? *Dove?*
Where is/are... *Dov'è/Dove sono...*
When? *Quando?*
Why? *Perché?*
How? *Come?*
How much (does it cost)? *Quanto (costa)?*
I am lost *Mi sono smarrito*
I am hungry/thirsty *Ho fame/sete*
I am sleepy/tired *Sono stanco/a*
I am sorry *Mi dispiace*
I feel unwell *Mi sento male*
Leave me alone *Lasciami in pace*
good/bad *buono bravo/male cattivo*
well/badly *bene/male*
hot/cold *caldo/freddo*
slow/fast *lento/rapido*
up/down *su/giù*
big/small *grande/piccolo*
here/there *qui/lì*

## Transport

airport *aeroporto*
bus stop *fermata*
bus *autobus*
coach *pullman*
railway station *stazione ferroviaria*
train *treno*
platform *binario*
port *porto*
port station *stazione marittima*
ship *nave*
car *macchina*
taxi *tassì, taxi*
ticket *biglietto*
customs *dogana*
seat (reserved) *posto (prenotato)*

## Travel Directions

One (two) ticket(s) to Florence, please *Un biglietto (due biglietti) per Firenze, per favore*

one way *semplice/andata*
return *andata e ritorno*
first/second class *Prima/seconda classe*
I want to go to... *Desidero andare a...*
How can I get to...? *Come posso andare a...?*
How do I get to the town centre? *Come posso raggiungere il centro città?*
Do you stop at...? *Si ferma a...?*
Where is...? *Dov'è...?*
How far is it to...? *Quanto siamo lontani da...?*
What is the name of this station? *Come si chiama questa stazione?*
When does the next ... leave? *Quando parte il prossimo...?*
From where does it leave? *Da dove parte?*
How long does the trip take...? *Quanto tempo dura il viaggio?*
How much is the fare? *Quant'è il biglietto?*
Have a good trip! *Buon viaggio!*

## Driving

near/far *vicino/lontano*
left/right *sinistra/destra*
straight ahead *sempre diritto*
forwards/backwards *avanti/indietro*
north/south *nord/sud*
east *est/oriente*
west *ovest/occidente*
round the corner *dietro l'angolo*
crossroads *bivio*
street/road *strada/via*
square *piazza*
car hire *autonoleggio*
motorbike/scooter/moped *motocicletta/ Vespa/motorino*
bicycle *bicicletta*
petrol/diesel *benzina/gasolio*
garage *garage*
This doesn't work *Questo non funziona*
mechanic *meccanico*
map/town plan *carta/pianta*
Where is the road to...? *Dov'è la strada per...?*
breakdown *guasto*
driving licence *patente di guida*
driver *guidatore*
speed *velocità*
danger *pericolo*
parking *parcheggio*
no parking *sosta vietata*
narrow *stretto*
bridge *ponte*
toll *pedaggio*
slow down *rallentare*

## Numbers

one *uno/una*
two/three/four *due/tre/quattro*
five/six/seven *cinque/sei/sette*
eight/nine/ten *otto/nove/dieci*
eleven/twelve *undici/dodici*
thirteen/fourteen *tredici/quattordici*
fifteen/sixteen *quindici/sedici*
seventeen/eighteen *diciassette/diciotto*
nineteen *diciannove*
twenty *venti*
twenty-one *ventuno*
twenty-two *ventidue*
thirty *trenta*
forty *quaranta*
fifty *cinquanta*
sixty *sessanta*
seventy *settanta*
eighty *ottanta*
ninety *novanta*
hundred *cento*
one hundred and one *centouno*
two hundred *duecento*
one thousand *mille*
two thousand *duemila*
million *milione*

## Days

Monday *lunedì*
Tuesday *martedì*
Wednesday *mercoledì*
Thursday *giovedì*
Friday *venerdì*
Saturday *sabato*
Sunday *domenica*
holidays *festivi*
weekdays *feriali*

## Time

What time is it? *Che ora è?/Che ore sono?*
day *giorno*
week *settimana*
month *mese*
morning/afternoon *mattina/pomeriggio*
evening *sera*
yesterday *ieri*
today *oggi*
tomorrow *domani*
soon *fra poco*
later *dopo/più tardi*
It is too early *È troppo presto*
It is too late *È troppo tardi*

## Shopping, Services, Sightseeing

I would like... *Vorrei...*
How much is it? *Quanto costa questo?*
Where is/are...? *Dov'è/Dove sono...?*
open/closed *aperto/chiuso*
cheap/expensive *a buon prezzo/caro*
bank *banca*
beach *spiaggia*
bed *letto*
church *chiesa*
entrance/exit *entrata/uscita*
hospital *ospedale*
money *soldi*
newspaper (foreign) *giornale (straniero)*
pharmacy *farmacia*
police station *commissariato*
policeman *poliziotto*
post office *ufficio postale*
sea *mare*
shop *negozio*
telephone *telefono*
tobacco shop *tabaccaio*
WC *toilette/bagno*
men *Signori/Uomini*
women *Signore/Donne*

## Useful Hotel Vocabulary

I'd like a single/twin/double room please
   *Vorrei una camera singola/doppia/
   matrimoniale, per favore*
with/without bath *con/senza bagno*
for two nights *per due notti*
We are leaving tomorrow morning *Partiamo
   domani mattina*
May I see the room/another room, please?
   *Vorrei vedere la camera/un'altra camera*
Is there a room with a balcony? *C'è una
   camera con balcone?*
There isn't (aren't) any hot water/soap/light/
   toilet paper/towels *Manca (Mancano)
   acqua calda/sapone/luce/carta igienica/
   asciugamani*
May I pay by credit card? *Vorrei pagare con
   carta di credito*
Fine, I'll take it *Bene, la prendo*
Is breakfast included? *È compresa la prima
   colazione?*
What time do you serve breakfast? *A che ora
   è la colazione?*
How do I get to the town centre? *Come
   raggiungo il centro città?*

For a list of vocabulary relating to Italian
food and drink, *see* **Food and Drink**, pp.53–6.

# Further Reading

De Blasi, Marlena, *A Thousand Days in Tuscany: A Bittersweet Adventure* (Algonquin, 2004). An American chef married to a Venetian recounts her experiences in rural Tuscany.

Dusi, Isabella, *Bel Vino: A Year of Sundrenched Pleasure among the Vines of Tuscany* (Pocket Books, 2004). A local ex-pat follows the making of Brunello di Montalcino.

Goethe, J.W., *Italian Journey* (Penguin Classics, 1982). An excellent example of a genius turned to mush by Italy; good insights, but big, big mistakes.

Hutton, Edward, *Florence; Assisi and Umbria Revisited*, in *Unknown Tuscany*, and *Siena and Southern Tuscany* (Hollis & Carter, 1995). Reprints of the travel classics.

Lasdun, James and Pia Davis, *Walking and Eating in Tuscany and Umbria* (Penguin 2005). An excellent guide to working up an appetite in the pretty countryside.

Mayes, Frances, *Under the Tuscan Sun* (Bantam, 2004). One of the better ex-pat-fixing-up-a-house-in-the-sun books that followed in the wake of Peter Mayle.

McCarthy, Mary, *The Stones of Florence* and *Venice Observed* (Penguin, 1986). Brilliant evocation of Italy's two great art cities, with an understanding that makes many other works on the subject seem sluggish and pedantic; don't visit Florence without it.

Romer, Elizabeth, *The Tuscan Year: Life and Food in an Italian Valley* (Orion, 1998). One of the best in recent years, with an emphasis on food, recipes and their cultural context.

Spender, Matthew, *Within Tuscany* (Viking, 1992). Poet Stephen Spender's son, on everything from porcupines to Pontormo's bowel movements.

## Art and Literature

Alberti, Leon Battista, *On Painting* (Penguin, 1991). Fine translation (by Cecil Grayson) of the little handbook (1435) on perspective and much much more that was a must-read for every Renaissance artist.

Ames-Lewis, Francis, *The Intellectual Life of the Early Renaissance Artist* (Yale University Press, 2002). Fascinating account of how artists struggled to get some respect.

Atalay, Bulent, *Math and the Mona Lisa: The Art and Science of Leonardo da Vinci* (Smithsonian, 2004). In search of the unity of art and science, and a paean to Leonardo.

Baxandall, Michael, *Painting and Experience in Fifteenth-Century Italy: A Primer in the Social History of Pictorial Style* (Oxford, 1988). Vividly puts Renaissance art in context with the painting trade, philosophy and social history of the period so you can 'see' paintings the way viewers did 500 years ago.

Boccaccio, Giovanni, *The Decameron* (Penguin, 2003). The ever-young classic by one of the fathers of Italian literature, full of refreshing irreverent worldliness.

Burckhardt, Jacob, *The Civilization of the Renaissance in Italy* (Penguin, 1990). The classic, published in 1860; the mark against which scholars still level their poison pens of revisionism.

Burke, Peter, *The Italian Renaissance: Culture and Society in Italy* (Polity Press, 1999). An excellent introduction to the period.

Castiglione, Baldassare, *The Book of the Courtier* (Wordsworth Editions Ltd, 2000). Essential reading for any Renaissance gent.

Cellini, B, *Autobiography of Benvenuto Cellini* (Penguin, translated by George Bull, 1999). Fun reading about the vicious competition of the Florentine art world by a swashbuckling braggart and world-class liar.

Chesterton, GK, *St Francis of Assisi* (Bantam Doubleday Dell, 1990). An enlightening biography by an author who converted to Catholicism because of St Francis.

**Clark, Kenneth and Kemp, Martin**, *Leonardo da Vinci* (Penguin, 1993). Classic account of the all-round genius.

**Dante**, *The Divine Comedy* (plenty of good translations). Few poems have ever had such a mythical significance for a nation. Anyone serious about understanding Tuscany or Italy and their world view will need more than a passing acquaintance with Dante.

**Ghibert and Linscott**, *Complete Poems and Selected Letters of Michelangelo* (Princeton Press, 1984).

**Hale, J.R.** (editor), *A Concise Encyclopaedia of the Italian Renaissance* (Thames and Hudson, 1981). An excellent reference guide, with many concise, well-written essays.

**Hall, James**, *Michelangelo: And the Reinvention of the Human Body* (Chatto and Windus, 2005). Fresh critical analysis of Michelangelo's obsession with the body, and how it influenced the way we see things, too.

**Hibbert, Christopher**, *The Rise and Fall of the House of Medici* (Penguin, 1965). One of the classics – compulsive reading. His *Florence: The Biography of a City* (1994) is also excellent.

**Hook, Judith**, *Siena* (Hamish Hamilton, 1979). A bit weak on art, but good on everything else.

**Kemp, Martin**, *Leonardo* (Oxford, 2004). Well written, with a light touch by an expert on the man of the moment.

**King, Catherine**, *Renaissance Women Patrons: Wives and Widows in Italy, c. 1300–c.1550* (University of Manchester, 2002). Readable  social history of women in the Renaissance.

**King, Ross**, *Brunelleschi's Dome: The Story of the Great Cathedral of Florence* (Pimlico, 2001). Just how Brunelleschi managed it.

**Leonardo da Vinci**, *Notebooks* (Oxford, 1980).

**Levey, Michael**, *Early Renaissance* and *High Renaissance* (both Penguin, 1991). Old-fashioned accounts of the period, with a breathless reverence for the 1500s – but still full of intriguing interpretations.

**Murray, Linda**, *The High Renaissance* and *The Late Renaissance and Mannerism* (Thames and Hudson, 1977). Excellent introductions to the periods; also Peter and Linda Murray, *The Art of the Renaissance* (1963).

**Norman, Diana**, *Siena and the Virgin: Art and Politics in a Late Medieval City State* (Yale, 1999). Lavishly illustrated study of Marian art and its meaning and politics in Siena.

**Origo, Iris**, *The Merchant of Prato* (Penguin, 1992). Everyday life in 14th-century Tuscany with the father of modern accounting, Francesco di Marco Datini. Also *Images and Shadows*; *War in Val d'Orcia*, about a Tuscan childhood, and life during the war.

**Petrarch, Francesco**, *Selections from the Canzoniere and Other Works* (translated by Mark Musa, Oxford, 2004). The most famous poems by the 'First Modern Man'.

**Procacci, Giuliano**, *History of the Italian People* (Penguin, 2004). An in-depth view from the year 1000 up to the present – also an introduction to the wit and subtlety of the best Italian scholarship.

**Richards, Charles**, *The New Italians* (Penguin, 1995). An observant and amusing study of life in Italy during and since the political upheaval and financial scandals of the early 1990s.

**Saunders, Frances Stonor**, *Hawkwood: Diabolical Englishman* (Faber and Faber, 2004). A cracker of a read – superbly evokes the man and the world he lived in.

**Strathern, Paul**, *The Medici: Godfathers of the Renaissance* (Jonathan Cape, 2003). Popular history, written to accompany the Channel 4 series.

**Symonds, John Addington**, *A Short History of Renaissance in Italy* (University Press of the Pacific, 2002). A condensed version of the authority of a hundred years ago, still fascinating today. The same publisher has reprinted all of his works, including many others on Italy.

**Vasari, Giorgio**, *Lives of the Painters, Sculptors and Architects* (Everyman, 1996). Readable, anecdotal accounts of the Renaissance greats by the father of modern art history.

**Waley, Daniel**, *The Italian City Republics* (Longman, 1988). Fine introduction to an exciting rough and tumble time in central Italy.

**White, John**, *Art and Architecture in Italy 1250–1400* (Yale University Press, 1993). The authority on all the early masters from the dawn of the Renaissance.

# Index

Main page references are in **bold**. Page references to maps are in *italics*.

## 5th edition published 2010

**Cadogan Guides** is an imprint of
New Holland Publishers (UK) Ltd
London • Cape Town • Sydney • Auckland

| | | | |
|---|---|---|---|
| New Holland Publishers (UK) Ltd | 80 McKenzie Street | Unit 1, 66 Gibbes Street | 218 Lake Road |
| Garfield House | Cape Town 8001 | Chatswood, NSW 2067 | Northcote |
| 86–88 Edgware Road | South Africa | Australia | Auckland |
| London W2 2EA | | | New Zealand |

*Cadogan@nhpub.co.uk*
**t** 44 (0)20 7724 7773

Cover photographs: © Jean-Pierre Lescourret/Corbis (front),© Guylain Doyle/Photolibrary (back).
Photo essay photographs: all photographers at www.istockphoto.com unless otherwise credited:
p.1 © Ingmar Wesemann; p.3 © Luis Pedrosa and © Carolina Garcia Aranda; p.4 © Steven Allan; p.6 © John
Woodworth, © miralex and © Stefano; p.8 © JTB Photo/photolibrary.com; p.9 © Tito Slack and © S. Greg
Panosian; p.10 © Kelly Borsheim and © Klaus Stammel; p.11 © sabrina dei nobili, © Peter Bates and © Rolf
Weschke; p.12 © Cuboimages/photolibrary.com; p.13 © Monkey Business IImages/iphotolibrary.com, © Tim
Hill/photolibrary.com, © Eddy Buttarelli/photolibrary.com; p.14 Raimund Kutter/photolibrary.com; p.15
© Gimmi Gimmi/photolibrary.com and © Jean-Pierre Lescourret/photolibrary.com; p16 © Gianluigi
Scarfiotti/ photolibrary.com, © Hedda Gjerpen, and © DEA/S.Vannini/photolibrary.com
Maps © Cadogan Guides, drawn by Maidenhead Cartographic Services Ltd
Cover design: Jason Hopper
Photo essay design: Sarah Gardner
Editor: Dominique Shead
Proofreading: Mary-Ann Gallagher
Indexing: Isobel McLean

Printed and bound in Italy by Legoprint
A catalogue record for this book is available from the British Library

ISBN: 978-1-86011-431-1

# Tuscany touring atlas

# here can only be one guide

*'A balance of infectious enthusiasm and solid practicality'*

Michael Palin

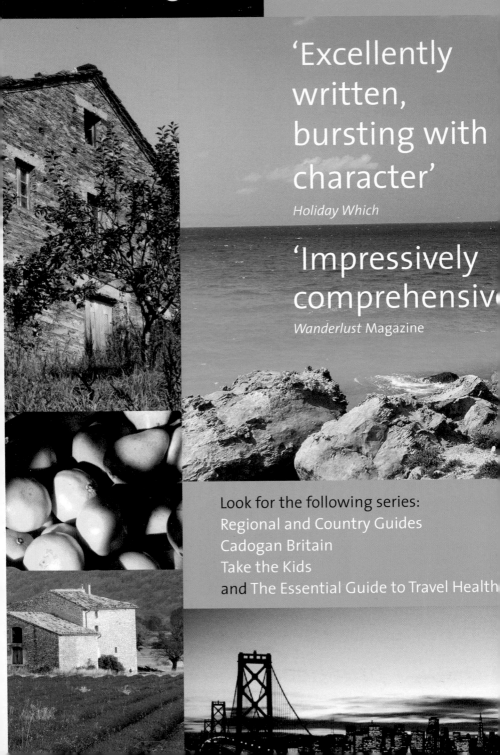

**CADOGAN**guides

'Excellently written, bursting with character'
*Holiday Which*

'Impressively comprehensiv
*Wanderlust* Magazine

Look for the following series:
Regional and Country Guides
Cadogan Britain
Take the Kids
and The Essential Guide to Travel Health